Malkeh and Her Children

For Iris and Dan,
    Welcome to California!
Hope you will enjoy this.
        Marjorie Edelson

Malkeh
and Her
Children

Marjorie Edelson

BALLANTINE BOOKS
NEW YORK

Copyright © 1992 by Marjorie Edelson

All rights reserved under International and Pan-American Copyright Conventions. Published in the United States by Ballantine Books, a division of Random House, Inc., New York, and simultaneously in Canada by Random House of Canada Limited, Toronto.

Library of Congress Catalog Card Number: 91-90650

ISBN: 0-345-37971-3

Cover design by James R. Harris
Cover art by Jeff Barson
Interior designed by Ann Gold

Manufactured in the United States of America

First Edition: November 1992

10 9 8 7 6 5 4 3 2

*For Eric, who embodies the goodness, gentleness,
and righteousness of a true tzaddik.*

Acknowledgments

I was raised on stories about the hardships of life for poor Jews in tsarist Russia and in the America they came to as immigrants. What impressed me about these stories was the commonthread of family solidarity which, no matter what the inner tension, presented an impregnable front to an indifferent or hostile world. That, in a nutshell, is the theme of *Malkeh and Her Children*. From family legend I have borrowed experiences which are reflected in the lives of the wholly fictional Mandelkerns; most events, however, were born within my imagination alone.

A valued source of information was my husband, Eric, whose firsthand memory of the civil disturbances following the Russian Revolution has remained vivid in his mind since his childhood in Vitebsk.

Many people, too numerous to name individually, have given me support and love during the long gestation period of this work. I want to specially mention Liz Johnson, who first encouraged me, Laurie Harper, who has been a most consistent mentor, and Peter S. Smith, who did a superb job of editing.

Who can find a virtuous woman?
for her price is far above rubies.
The heart of her husband doth safely
      trust in her
Strength and honor are her clothing.
In her tongue is the law of kindness.
She looketh well to the ways of her household
      and eateth not the bread of idleness.
Her children arise up, and call her blessed.
                              Proverbs 31

Part One

Malkeh
and Yoysef
1878–1892

Chapter 1

*T*he Jews of Dagda loved a wedding. What else was there to enliven the humdrum course of days and take their minds from hard work and lean times, taxes and conscription? Were things so wonderful for Jews this year that anyone should take a celebration for granted? When monotony could turn to danger in the flutter of a peasant's eyelash, it was the homely ceremonies of *bris*, bar mitzvah, betrothal, and wedding that punctuated the days and gave shape and meaning to Jewish lives.

Their everyday clothes discarded with the day's work, families made their way to the plain wooden shul, where Malkeh, the daughter of Mendel, the teacher of children, was to be married this day to the itinerant tailor, Yoysef Mandelkern.

It was only a short stroll, for Dagda was but one street of small wooden houses. Narrow dirt lanes led toward the fields held and worked by Russian farmers. The dozen or so Jewish families lived close together, clustered around the shul, their houses simple and unadorned, the unpainted walls made gray by time and weather. Each had its tiny vegetable garden and its chickens. Only the dairyman and the miller had cows and a dray horse or two. The Russian houses, indistinguishable from those of the Jews, were on the outer perimeter of the village, nearer to the fields.

Walking to the shul, the wedding guests agreed it would be a fine affair. True, the father of the bride was poor, sometimes scarcely able to provide a skinny chicken for the sabbath, but his brother Zalman, a rich man in Vitebsk it was said, was donating the dowry, and the mother's sister, Rivka, had married well and was providing the wedding supper. "May the rich ever be blessed!" thought many a guest.

It was a blessing that any husband at all had been found for the *melamed*'s only child. She was well past her prime—nineteen years old already!—and the family so poor that only Shmuel, the slow-witted son of the miller, had been offered before. It was said that Malkeh's mother had been tempted, for the miller was well off and would have been grateful to find a bride for his son, but the father, Mendel, had refused. There might not have been another match for Malkeh if the young tailor, passing through Dagda, had not happened to see her and fallen head over heels in love.

Today there would be fine food and drink. Thanks again to generous Uncle Zalman, there would even be a fiddler for dancing and entertainment.

*M*alkeh was angry. She had always expected to choose her own husband. Papa agreed with her that arranged marriages were old-fashioned, but he had gone back on his word.

The borrowed wedding dress was too heavy for summer, and she was hot and itchy. The stiff cloth chafed where the high collar rubbed against her throat, and Malkeh knew there would be ugly sweat stains under the arms.

She was hungry. Ritual demanded that the bridal pair fast on the day of the wedding, and it was already late afternoon. She was scared as well. The man who stood beside her under the wedding canopy was as big and dark as a cossack.

The rabbi, his mottled hands shaking, was lifting her veil so that Yoysef, the *khossen*, could inspect her. At this point the husband-to-be might change his mind and say the bride didn't suit him. Malkeh burned with resentment, for she had no similar choice. It was nothing more than a business transaction, Yoysef the buyer, she the merchandise. The groom scarcely glanced at her, but his nod was enough for the ceremony to proceed.

The rabbi was pushing the marriage contract toward the groom for him to sign. Now the bride. The families of both were pressing around them. Mammeh looked anxious, but she need not have worried. Malkeh had been told often enough that a girl with a small dowry doesn't have choices. With little grace she signed after the bridegroom, her signature rebelliously bold below the bridegroom's labored writing.

The groom turned to Malkeh, awkwardly pushing a thin gold band onto her unyielding finger. He spoke for the first time. His voice was pitched deep but very soft. "Behold, thou, Malkeh, art consecrated unto me, Yoysef, according to the law of Moses and Israel."

The wine was poured. The groom drank deeply and put the cup into the bride's hands.

"Man and woman created He them as He created all things. May the Lord God, Creator of heaven and earth, bless this union," the rabbi said.

Malkeh drank what wine remained in the goblet and passed it back to the rabbi, who wrapped it in cloth and placed it at the groom's feet, a reminder to the congregation that even in the midst of joy, they should remember grief for the destruction of the Temple in Jerusalem. The splintering glass under the groom's heel shattered the stillness of the sacred moment. Guests surged forward, joyously shouting *"Mazeltov! Mazeltov!"*

It was over. From father to husband, Malkeh the Teacher's was now Malkeh the Tailor's.

Yoysef was borne out of the tiny shul by a crowd of men. Malkeh herself was the center of a ring of excited women—Mammeh and the aunts were hugging her, and Mammeh was weeping from joy and from relief that it was over, her headstrong daughter now someone else's responsibility.

When a large woman bore down upon them, the circle grew quiet and parted to let Yoysef's mother pass. The older woman brushed dutiful lips to Malkeh's cheek and nodded coolly to Mammeh and the aunts. Her ponderous presence dampened their high spirits, and it was a relief when Yoysef's two sisters broke through the line of well-wishers, smiling and pressing Malkeh's lips warmly with their own. Encircled by their supporting arms, Malkeh was led into an outer room, where the veil was tenderly lifted from her head, releasing a cascade of brightly shining, golden hair.

Auntie Rivka grasped the soft curls at the nape of Malkeh's neck, and her mother gently wielded the scissors. Malkeh squeezed her eyes shut, flinching with every snip of the blades. Out of politeness Mammeh offered the scissors to the groom's mother. Malkeh experienced a sharp tugging and a pulling at her scalp. She jerked away from the rough hand but was restrained from flight by the other women. The tears came then in a bitter flood.

"Ah, cry, cry it out, my darling child!" Aunt Soreh whispered in her ear. "It will make your heart lighter."

The scissors passed to Yoysef's older sister, Yenta. In a few swift motions the ritual was finished. Malkeh's trembling hand went to her head, where now there was only stubble. "But why!"

"It has always been done this way!" Auntie Rivka snapped.

"It is commanded in the Bible," Yoysef's mother agreed.

Mammeh said calmly, "It is tradition for a married woman to cover her head with a wig or a scarf. It's just the way it is."

"I hate it!" Malkeh sobbed. "I look like a *babushka*!"

The voice of Yoysef's second sister, Golda, was soft and consoling. "You're still just as pretty. I wouldn't worry."

Malkeh's grief overwhelmed her. "I'll never be pretty again!" she wailed.

Yoysef's mother was firm. "You're a married woman. You're not supposed to be."

"Dry your eyes, child," Mammeh said, replacing the veil over the shorn head. "The guests are waiting for the bride."

It was summer, and tables for the wedding feast had been placed outside under an arbor. Malkeh was led to a seat at the center of the women's table. On the other side, Yoysef was seated among the men.

The guests were already beginning to help themselves to the roasted meats, chopped liver, pickled herrings, kugels, preserves, and rich cakes prepared by Mammeh and the aunts. The women heaped Malkeh's plate with food, giggling and nudging each other, and urging her to eat so she would be strong for the night ahead. The guests murmured among themselves, intent to hear what gifts had been presented to the newlyweds.

"A *tchervonitz* from Yaynkel the Horse Trader!"

"Aiee, such a present! Who else can afford to give a ten-ruble gold piece?"

"Two fat hens from Itzik the Butcher from Pskov!"

"May they never go hungry."

And so on through the set of hand-painted china from Aunt Soreh and Uncle Velvel, the embroidered Sabbath tablecloth from the groom's mother, the silver samovar from Uncle Zalman, and the practical household presents from the housewives of Dagda.

The bride's dowry was examined. Fine plump pillows and a quilt made by the bride from the down of geese she had tended herself. Hemstitched bedclothes and towels. Gleaming brass candlesticks that must have cost the bride's father the earnings of a half year at least!

Fine gifts! Food worthy of a rich man's feast! Toasts, and finally the fiddler to play for the dancing!

"Drink, my child." Mammeh pushed a glass of wine into Malkeh's sweaty hand. The sweet wine tasted of summer berries.

"A little wine makes the food taste better and strengthens the spirit," Aunt Soreh murmured gently, refilling the glass.

Malkeh drank in thirsty swallows as the women laughed and joked among themselves.

She ate the rich food and drank the fragrant red wine. The men drank *bromfen*, and someone had brought a bottle of the Russian spirit, vodka. A tiny glass of the colorless liquid was set at Malkeh's elbow. It burned her mouth but brought a glow to her cheeks and raised a line of dewy perspiration above her full upper lip.

Malkeh's spirits were reviving. All of her friends were there, their faces glowing and beautiful. The relatives, even mean-spirited Aunt Rivka, were smiling and happy. And not the least of it, for the first time in her life Malkeh herself was the center of attention! It was only when the bridegroom was called upon to make the wedding speech that she fully confronted the reality that this day she had been bound over to a stranger who on the morrow would take her to an unknown life far from home and family.

Yoysef began to speak the words an educated friend had written down for him to say. The text was obscure, and he faltered over unfamiliar words. The guests grew bored and restless, waiting for the speech to end so the dancing could begin. Even Yoysef's father stared fixedly at his fingernails when his son stumbled over words and finally lost his place completely.

Malkeh hiccuped and began to snicker. Auntie Rivka pinched her hard enough to raise a welt on her arm, and Mammeh threw her a black look.

He had heard her giggle. Over the heads of the guests, Yoysef's gaze met Malkeh's. His brows were drawn in a tight frown, and his dark eyes were flat and hard.

"Oh, I'm sorry," Malkeh whispered to no one in particular. "It is the wine."

Doggedly Yoysef continued to the very end of the prepared speech. The relieved crowd applauded and slapped him on the back. Yoysef, mopping his forehead with a silk handkerchief, sank back into his chair.

The fiddler was tuning up for the dance. Malkeh found that her glass had been refilled with the innocent sweet wine. She drank and was only a little light-headed when she was pulled to her feet and into the line of women waiting for the music to begin. She was aware that she was the focus of admiring glances, even from the men who were not supposed to notice tiny waists and high, round breasts. Unlike the others, Yoysef did not even pretend to look away, as was proper.

The fiddle was lively and Malkeh circled faster and faster, her feet stamping and hands clapping, the veil streaming out behind her. When the music stopped for a moment she drank more wine and fanned herself with her handkerchief, glancing across the grass to see if Yoysef was still staring at her. Each time she found that he was.

The men danced, too, lifting Yoysef on a chair among them. Women and men took turns, laughing whenever they accidentally merged. Malkeh danced every women's dance, and between the dances took sips of wine to cool herself.

It seemed to Malkeh that the party had scarcely begun when Mammeh and the aunts were suddenly surrounding her, casting meaningful looks in her direction. She saw Yoysef coming toward her, escorted by his parents and trailed by Papa. Surely it was much too soon! But Mammeh was lifting her from her chair, pushing her toward Yoysef. His hand reached out to support her when she stumbled. His grasp did not loosen when she regained her footing.

Where was Papa? Desperately Malkeh's eyes sought him out. His miserable eyes met hers and looked away. Perhaps they asked for her forgiveness, but it was hard to tell, for he had drunk a great deal and his gaze was clouded.

The gathering had grown still, the fiddle quiet, and only the nervous titters of the unmarried girls broke the silence. The community of Dagda waited solemnly for the bride and groom to be led by their parents to the prepared bedchamber.

The crowd parted before the slowly moving wedding party. Some of the men pressed supportive fingers into Yoysef's shoulder, some of the women mistily kissed Malkeh on the cheek as she passed.

A tide of comment rose from the guests. Such a beautiful bride, so small, so well-formed. Even with the small dowry, it was surprising a husband for her had taken so long to find.

Of course, they said, the courtship had been irregular. Not prearranged by a matchmaker in formal negotiation between the parents, but initiated by the groom himself! It was rumored that his parents were against the match, but Yoysef had been so bewitched that he would not listen. What a world it was when a young man decided for himself whom he would take to wife!

As was fitting, Aunt Rivka and Uncle Reuven had provided the bridal chamber. Not only were they relatives of the bride but also the leading family in the village. The bedroom had been made ready, the furniture rubbed with oil of lemons, the linens starched, the flowered carpet beaten and aired in the sun. Auntie Rivka triumphantly threw open the door, and the feebly resisting bride was borne inside by the groom.

Malkeh, mesmerized, could not take her eyes from the vast bedstead that dominated the room. It was dark, massive, and intricately carved, and hot though the night was, an eiderdown quilt billowed across it. An oil lamp with a hand-painted silk shade lit the room, its hanging colored beads stirring in the faint breeze and throwing wavering shadows on the walls. The unsteady light etched the cherub faces carved on the bedposts and gave them the expressions of drunkards and lechers.

*T*oo soon the parting embraces from the family were over, and the door closed behind them. For the first time in her life Malkeh was alone with a man, a stranger. She knew that something both terrible and exciting was supposed to happen, but wasn't exactly sure what. A trembling seized her, and she sat down abruptly on the bed, sinking helplessly into the eiderdown.

Pretending not to look at him, Malkeh watched Yoysef from beneath the lids of half-closed eyes. He had discarded his hat and long silk coat and was somehow less forbidding in his shirt-sleeves. He stood at the window, arranging the curtains to catch whatever breeze there was. His hands moved confidently, looping back the folds of the cloth. They were quite beautiful, really, large and square with silky black hairs growing on the backs, the fingers long with clean blunt nails. Malkeh's eyes moved up to examine his face, dark skin made ruddy by the sun, curly black beard well-cut below full red lips, a high-bridged nose, and eyes so brown they were almost black.

He turned from the window, looking at her directly for the first time since they had been left alone. "Well," he said. And clearing his throat, said "well" again. He seemed as much at a loss as she. Resolutely he moved toward her until he was standing over her, a tall, strong, and overwhelmingly masculine figure.

An unaccustomed feeling of warmth began to rise from Malkeh's lower limbs toward her belly.

Wetting her lips with her tongue, Malkeh said, "I—I have never been alone—with a—man before." She tried to remember how young women in the novels she loved handled this sort of thing and realized that they never did, that the romances she read ended either under the marriage canopy or at the grave, but never, never in the bedroom.

"I know."

"Have you—? I mean—" Malkeh flushed to the roots of her golden scalp.

"No," Yoysef answered, not completely truthful.

There was nothing else to say, and the silence between them grew.

Yoysef drew off his stiff collar and slowly began to unfasten the buttons of his shirt. Malkeh turned away in panic.

Yoysef's quiet voice compelled her to turn toward him. "I am a plain, uneducated man, Malkeh," he said slowly, "but I am a good tailor, and I work hard. I will make a living for you and be good to you. That I promise."

"I didn't mean to laugh at you," Malkeh said in a rush. "The speech, I mean. I'm not used to drinking much wine. It was—an interesting speech."

Yoysef seemed not to hear. "Whenever I came to Dagda," he said, "I could not take my eyes from your house. Do you remember the first time, when your father brought me home from shul for the Sabbath? You were wearing a blue dress that made your eyes bluer than the sky. After that first time I would see you often when I passed through Dagda, in the yard, feeding the chickens, or hanging clothes to dry. And your hair was so yellow, shining in the sun—"

The reminder of her hair lying thick and disembodied on the floor of the shul caused Malkeh a terrible wrenching pain, like a sudden blow to her chest. "Oh, my hair! My hair!" she cried, snatching off the veil and feeling only fuzz beneath her fingers.

Yoysef came to her side, his big hand touching his bride's head with a kind of reverence. "It's all right, Malkeh," he comforted her. "Someday I'll buy you the finest wig in Vitebsk!"

Wrapping her arms across her chest, Malkeh rocked back and forth, beginning to weep in earnest, her anguished cries echoing against the walls of the still room.

Yoysef knelt beside her. "What is it?"

"I don't want a wig!" she sobbed.

"You don't have to wear a wig if you don't want to," he offered, alarm growing as her shrieks escalated. "You can let your hair grow and hide it under a shawl. No one need know." His voice dropped. "I'd like that. I loved your hair. I always wanted to touch it."

Malkeh's wails subsided. "Really?" she asked, snuffling.

Yoysef stood to blow out the lamp that had been making crazy wavy lines on the quilt. As he turned to fold the coverlet back, his arms brushed against Malkeh's breast. She drew back as though burned.

The dark air was heavy. The greasy odor of lamp oil and the faint smell of sweat mingled with the captured heat of the day. Crickets chirruped outside the window, and a lone nightingale sang a few sad notes, then subsided. If she strained, Malkeh could hear the faint sounds of the fiddle.

Yoysef had moved to the other side of the bed. Something dropped to the floor. His boots, Malkeh guessed, one after the other. And then something more, a softer sound. What? His shirt? His breeches? A spot deep in her stomach began to burn, and it was difficult to breathe. The room began to turn even without the dizzying lamplight. To steady herself, Malkeh grasped the bedpost in both hands. What was *she* supposed to do? Her nightdress had been lying pristine and virginal upon the bed when they came into the room. She should find it, she supposed, and put it on in the darkness, yet she could not seem to move her limbs, suddenly grown terribly heavy.

In the breathless night of the bedchamber, Malkeh felt Yoysef's weight upon the bed. Hands were reaching toward her, touching her, gently exploring the shape of the body still hidden within her dress. There was no place to escape from those probing hands.

Still in silence, his fingers were unfastening the buttons of her bodice, reaching under the cloth to the soft, sweet mounds of her breasts. All was one long, slow movement of patiently tender hands. Malkeh shivered but did not move. Now the loosened dress was drawn over her head, the corset unhooked, releasing her flesh from its stiff bindings. She was naked in the room with the stranger. Malkeh groped frantically for her nightdress and couldn't find it. Rigid with fright, she pulled back from Yoysef's embrace. "Oh, God! Oh, Papa! Mammeh!" The bed had begun to slide and tilt beneath her. And then, wrenching herself from Yoysef's arms, Malkeh was sick, terribly sick, all over the carpet of Auntie Rivka's bedroom.

*I*n the morning Malkeh and Yoysef left Dagda, riding in the back of the wagon that Mischa, the farmer, was taking to Polotsk with a load of potatoes.

They were awake and dressed early for the journey. There had not been much left of the night when Malkeh had finally retched up the last of her stomach's contents and, exhausted, dozed off with her head still supported by Yoysef's arm.

Yoysef glanced quickly at Malkeh to see how the jolting of the wagon might be affecting her. She had been pale earlier, refusing anything but strong tea at the morning meal.

Parting from her parents had been painful. Malkeh's mother struggled to maintain her composure, but the father lost all control, and shameless tears rolled down his fat cheeks. Malkeh was dry-eyed and withdrawn. She scarcely murmured a few words of farewell and, in fact, closed her eyes to shut out the view of the little house where she had grown up, her parents still standing in the road, waving forlornly.

It was a long journey, a little more than a hundred versts from Dagda to Polotsk. It could take them the better part of four days to reach their destination. At the beginning, Mischa kept up a lively banter from his well-spring of coarse good humor. He got little response beyond a strained smile from the bridegroom. Mischa shrugged. "A Jew doesn't understand a joke" was a saying. No matter. Mischa didn't need an audience, and his repertoire of explicit sexual stories was enormous. When he turned on the wagon seat from time to time to see if the newlyweds were listening, he found them silent and distracted.

Strange people, these Hebrews, thought Mischa. Just wed, and yet look at the two of them, sitting as far apart as they can get, each with his eyes turned away from the other. *Boizamoi!* Crazy people!

The bride, now, she was a luscious berry, ripe for the plucking, yet she didn't look like a woman happy from a night of lovemaking. Mischa glanced at the groom. *He* looked to be able enough. Maybe their misery had something to do with some odd religious practice. Like cutting off the hair of a bride. Or like mutilating a boy's prick. Maybe Hebrews didn't screw like other people.

Mischa laughed inside himself, glad to be he. Whistling, he turned his eyes back to the road, flicking his whip over Zinka's back so that the surprised mare gave a sudden lunge forward, almost throwing the passengers out of the back of the wagon.

During the early part of the morning Malkeh huddled in her corner, half hidden among the potato sacks. She was feeling dispirited and heavy with the burden of shame. Oh, the utter humiliation of the night before! She wanted to die when she thought of how she had vomited time and again into the chamber pot Yoysef had held beneath her chin, he wiping her lips and forehead with a dampened cloth after each paroxysm. She was embarrassed to recall that when finally she had dozed off, his arms were still holding her, gently, like a parent might hold a child. Awake at dawn, Malkeh had found the sour smell in the room gone, the chamber pot emptied, and the carpet clean, if a little damp. Auntie Rivka need never know of her disgusting behavior. But Yoysef knew. Malkeh shrank into herself, silently contemplating her disgrace.

By midday they had traveled fourteen versts or so, and the countryside was beginning to change. They had left the hot flat fields of golden grain and the road ran now through thick birch forests. The change in scenery acted as a stimulant on Malkeh. She sat up straighter, her attention drawn to the shifting landscape.

They stopped to eat on a high piece of ground where a small clear stream ran through woodlands on its way to join the mighty River Dvina. The mare, released from the shafts, drank deeply from the stream and grazed among the trees. Mischa threw himself down on the mossy ground, rolling like a dog in the damp grass.

From a white cloth Malkeh unwrapped the meal Mammeh had prepared. As she busied herself laying out the food, curiosity overcame shyness, and Malkeh turned eagerly to Yoysef. "Is Polotsk like this, in the middle of a forest? Is it still far from here? Are the houses plain like ours in Dagda or do they have pretty carvings like those we passed this morning? Will we have a cow and chickens and a goat?"

Relieved that Malkeh seemed to have revived, Yoysef laughed at the tumble of questions. "Give some bread and meat to a hungry man, Wife, and I'll tell you all about Polotsk for your trouble."

Before accepting food for himself, Yoysef turned politely to Mischa. "Will you share our meal, brother?" he asked.

"*Spaseba, nyet.* I have my own." From beneath the wagon seat the farmer drew out a slab of black bread, some boiled potatoes, a whole onion, and a bottle of vodka.

The sight of the bottle renewed Malkeh's sense of shame. "How can you drink that in the middle of the day!" she cried.

Mischa was not offended. He roared with laughter. "Madam Jewess, if you drink, you die. If you don't drink, you die. So drink!" And he upended the bottle to his mouth.

While they rested, the sun rose high in the midday sky, but it was cool on the velvety ground beneath the birches, and the water they drank from the stream in their cupped hands was fresh and cold. Malkeh's stomach remembered it had been given nothing but tea, and she devoured the food. Yoysef helped himself to the roasted meat and the yellow *challah*, leftovers from the wedding feast, but he scarcely attended to his own hunger for the sheer pleasure of watching Malkeh eat.

Much refreshed by the meal and the opportunity to relieve themselves in the thick undergrowth, they were all cheerful when they clambered back into the wagon.

On their way once again, Yoysef continued to talk about his home, Malkeh's interest overpowering his usual reserve. He told about the River Dvina which ran along the eastern border of the city and about the grassy meadowlands on the perimeters. He told about Count Voronov's vast estate that covered many versts of forest, marsh, and farmland just outside Polotsk.

It was called Spokoinaya Zemlya, "Tranquil Land." He described the manor house, all pink-painted wood and rosy brick with a white-columned entrance and intricate gilt-edged balconies like lace trimmings on the facade.

Malkeh's eyes grew wide. She had heard of great landlords who ruled absolutely over areas so vast that they included whole villages populated by peasants still bound to the land even though serfdom had been abolished by the tsar years before, in 1861.

There was a vast cobbled courtyard before the house, where fine gilded carriages discharged guests who might arrive for a weekend and remain for weeks or months. Spokoinaya Zemlya, Yoysef told her, was like an independent state, growing its own staples and employing resident craftsmen, usually former serfs, as furniture restorers, carpenters, blacksmiths, horse trainers—whatever was needed. Inside the manor house there were servants in abundance to anticipate every need and wish of the count's.

"Count Voronov must have many children to have such a big house," Malkeh said.

"Not at all!" Mischa explained, turning backward on his seat. "It's plain to see, Madam, that you know nothing of the nobility."

Yoysef nodded. "The count is mostly there by himself. The countess is dead, may God rest her soul. There is one son who is in St. Petersburg at court. Even the count himself is not often in Polotsk, for he has another house in Moscow, grander still, they say."

"That is true?" Malkeh looked from one to the other to be sure that it was not a joke about someone having two houses!

"Yes, for I have been in Count Voronov's house myself and I hear what the servants talk about."

Malkeh's eyes were shiny with awe. "You have been inside the house!" she exclaimed.

Proudly Yoysef confided that a year earlier when no competent tailor was found on the estate to replace the elderly servant who had overseen the household liveries, Yoysef himself had received a commission to perform such services as were needed to alter or repair uniforms; they were always made in St. Petersburg, of course, where a special tailoring establishment specialized in the colors and crests of various noble families.

"Ah, then you have seen the count himself!" Malkeh said, her imagination soaring with images of a commanding figure in glistening uniform, medals flashing across his chest, and a sword swinging at his hip, by all appearances, a youngster.

"No, no," Yoysef admitted with reluctance. "I was hired by the steward."

"Oh." Malkeh was disappointed for a moment. Of course she should have known that a poor Jew would not be admitted into a noble presence. "But at least, Yoysef, you have seen the palace!"

Yoysef smiled to himself. He would not tell his bride that all he had seen of the interior of Spokoinaya Zemlya was the kitchen and the small office of the estate manager. Let her retain the illusion.

Yoysef and Mischa the Potato Farmer competed to tell Malkeh the most fantastic stories about the Voronovs. Their actual knowledge was limited, Mischa's based on marketplace hearsay and fantasy, Yoysef's on the gossip of the Voronov house servants. From these snippets Malkeh constructed a handsome, dashing aristocrat possessed of boundless power.

The versts flew under Zinka's hooves. Malkeh moved closer to Yoysef, the better to hear, and he coaxed her to lean against him. After a time Yoysef's talk drifted away from Spokoinaya Zemlya, his voice dropping to a near whisper as he told Malkeh of how Jews lived in a metropolis like Polotsk. Bored, Mischa's attention had turned back to the road. Yoysef told of neighbors and friends and what their lives were like. He described the marketplace where Jews and Russians had their stalls and where Yoysef's parents were in business to sell eggs and vegetables.

The wagon had descended to the river plain, and the sun was already beginning to throw long shadows when Malkeh at last asked what had been in the forefront of her mind. "And how will we live, Yoysef? You and I."

Yoysef fell silent, biting his lip as though he would cut short the words that must pass from his mouth.

"Yoysef?"

At last, sighing, Yoysef said, "Malkeh, you know I am a poor man. I carry my sewing machine and my goods on my back and go from village to village. Sometimes I am gone two or three weeks at a time."

"You are?" Malkeh said, surprised, wondering what would happen to her. Did he expect her to go with him?

"Now that I have a wife, I will try to come home for the sabbath. But a man must scratch out a living where he can." Yoysef shook his head, thinking of hard times which God knew were more frequent than not. "I dream of someday having a proper shop in Polotsk, a fine shop where people will come to be fitted for suits." A shadow passed over his face. "It is hard to put away enough money to get a start. The people I sew for are not rich."

Malkeh nodded. For all her life it had been no different.

After a few minutes Yoysef continued. "We will have to live in my parents' house, although I wish it were otherwise. If not, I will never have money for a shop of my own. Besides, if you are at home with Mammeh and Papa, I won't have to worry about leaving you."

Malkeh had always known that a poor bride could expect to live in the house of her mother-in-law. Still, her heart grew cold at the thought of Yoysef's mother.

Yoysef's arm tightened around her shoulders. "But my parents will not be home from the wedding for ten days! They are stopping at relatives' on the way. It will be like our own house," he said eagerly.

"For ten days," Malkeh murmured.

Mischa offered from the front seat, "You can find heaven in ten days, mistress!"

Yoysef said, "We have our own room. I built it behind the kitchen with my own hands. It will be warm there from the heat of the oven. There is a strong trunk for our clothes, and my grandfather, may he rest in peace, left a fine carved bed. And Malkeh! I have such a surprise for you! In the spring I traded a suit of clothes for a mirror so tall that you can see yourself all the way to the floor!" Yoysef's eyes were anxious. "It will be all right?"

Malkeh was not sure it would be all right. She said, "Yes."

The rest of that day's journey was quiet except for the clipclop of the horse's hooves. Even Mischa, a little tipsy from the vodka that had eased the tedium of the journey, was silent. Each was busy with his private thoughts.

Malkeh tried to imagine what her life would be like in the house of Mammeh Frumma and Papa Avrom. She had heard that Yoysef's parents had selected another girl, a Polotsker and rich, for Yoysef's bride. How, then, had the match with her been made? It was all very puzzling. She knew only that Yoysef had spoken to Papa, and afterward a cousin of Yoysef's father had come to Dagda and talked with the neighbors and the rabbi and finally with Papa, and had left shaking his head. She had heard the murmurings of Mammeh and Papa in the next room, catching some of what they said by pressing her ear against the wall.

Mammeh's voice was bitter. "They don't think she's good enough."

Papa's angry voice: "But he is not learned in Torah! A simple tailor, after all—"

"They have a bride in mind already."

"Maybe I can ask Zalman to add to her dowry."

"This match is not to be."

"He yearns for her."

"What difference does it make what *he* wants?"

Yet it *had* made a difference, for against all odds she had stood with Yoysef yesterday under the wedding canopy.

Malkeh looked curiously at the man beside her in the wagon. His earlier good humor had deserted him. Now he stared straight ahead, frowning into the oncoming dusk. She wondered where they would spend the night. They had passed an occasional inn, but Malkeh knew that rented lodgings came dear.

The sun was setting when Mischa pulled the wagon off the road and into a flat, grassy field. Yoysef helped Malkeh down from the wagon while Mischa gathered twigs for a fire. "We will have to spend the night in the open, I'm afraid," he apologized.

Malkeh looked around her uneasily.

Yoysef said, "I will make a place for you to sleep in the wagon, and Mischa and I will spread our quilts on the ground."

Malkeh nodded, relieved.

After a spartan meal of tea and bread, the three exhausted travelers bedded down for the night. They would start again before sunup; with luck, they might even complete the journey early.

Malkeh slept heavily, only peripherally aware that once or twice during the night a figure leaned into the wagon to pull the covers more snugly around her.

The next two days were much as the first had been. Yoysef told her funny stories about his customers, the rabbi so poor that his congregation had donated the money for a new suit after he had quite worn through the seat of his trousers, the peasant who had insisted on paying him with a piglet, the bride so stout that his supply of white sateen was too scant for her dress and had to be pieced with scraps of blue serge! Malkeh laughed a lot at that. She was interested in everything about the life they would soon lead together.

On the evening of the third day they reached the outskirts of Polotsk. "We are almost home!" Yoysef said happily.

Home! The word had a strange hollow ring for Malkeh.

When the wagon came into the streets of Polotsk, lamps were already shining from some windows. A few pedestrians hurried through the streets on their way home. Polotsk was a middle-sized provincial town, although to Malkeh it seemed a huge city. They passed large houses, a massive government building constructed of yellow bricks, and a large church, its blue and gold onion-shaped domes and its slender spire shining in the last light of the setting sun. The main street was wide and paved with cobblestones. Yoysef pointed to the roofs of the *gostinny dvor*, the bazaar where his family leased stall space. Malkeh strained her neck to see, but by then the wagon had turned away from the central district. They had entered an area where the houses grew progressively smaller and shabbier. Here the road was unpaved and narrow, reminding Malkeh of Dagda. She didn't know whether to be disappointed or comforted by the resemblance.

Malkeh and Yoysef alighted from Mischa's wagon in front of a house built of fat logs under a high-pitched roof. It sat directly on the street, had no front garden, and looked to be very small.

Yoysef lifted down Malkeh first and then their bundles from the wagon and carefully counted out the coins to pay Mischa.

"Is that all?" Mischa asked.

Yoysef sighed and felt in his pockets for additional kopecks.

Slyly Mischa quoted a peasant proverb: "If you don't oil the wheels, you get nowhere."

Yoysef smiled wryly as he handed over an additional sum, murmuring "But we are already there, brother" under his breath.

Mischa pocketed the coins. Satisfied, he bowed slightly to Yoysef and grinned at Malkeh. "God be with you!" Tossing the empty vodka bottle in the roadway, he clicked to Zinka and waved as the wagon lurched into motion. For a moment more in the twilight they saw his winking, leering face. His voice floated back to them: "The sun's gone down! It's time newlyweds were abed!"

Chapter 2

*E*ven after two months the Polotsk marketplace had not lost its fascination for Malkeh. Dagda had nothing to compare with it. There, the people bought from itinerant peddlers and traded with each other for necessities. Every week, unless there was no money in the house, Papa had walked or hitched a ride to the larger town of Zaytsevo to buy kosher meat and a carp. But here in Polotsk, there was a market with everything anyone could want, and occasionally Malkeh was permitted to go with her in-laws to help in the stall they kept.

With Yoysef away from home, Malkeh awakened early. It was different when Yoysef was beside her in the bed; then the snug little room behind the kitchen was a nest. Alone, Malkeh was painfully aware that the house was Mammeh Frumma's and Papa Avrom's, and she an uneasy guest.

Malkeh hurried to wash and dress herself and to finish the morning chores so that there would be no excuse for her mother-in-law to leave her behind when it was time to go to market. By the time Mammeh Frumma and Papa Avrom awoke, the water would be bubbling for the tea, the breakfast eggs steaming in the top of the samovar, and plates of dark bread and sweet butter would lie on the scrubbed tabletop.

Mammeh Frumma's eyes, sweeping the kitchen, could find no fault, and she had to content herself with a brusque reminder that the eggs needed to be collected for market.

"I've already done that," Malkeh said, pointing to the sideboard where the eggs, packed in a bed of straw, stood in their basket. "I'll bring your tea," she said brightly, reaching into the cupboard for the dish of lump sugar.

"Do that," Mammeh muttered, lowering her bulk into a chair. Sipping her tea, she remarked, "It is very strong. You must remember, Malkeh, that tea is very dear."

Malkeh lowered her eyes to conceal indignation. This was no time to start an argument. Yesterday Mammeh had complained that Malkeh had brewed the tea so thin it was tasteless. Malkeh bit her lower lip.

Taking the downcast look for meekness, Mammeh pressed her advantage. "I know that after your family, which is so poor, we must seem very well off to you. But we are just ordinary people who count every kopeck twice before it is spent. I want you to remember that, Malkeh."

"Yes, Mammeh Frumma," Malkeh murmured. Oh, how unfair it was! Just to be permitted to go to market, she had to keep quiet; she must not even defend her own dear parents! "I'll try to remember."

"Have you the cheese and bread ready for the midday meal?"

Malkeh nodded toward a packet wrapped in a clean linen cloth. "All ready," she said. "Golda will be at the market today?"

Golda's husband, Dovid, sold in the market, too, but Yenta's husband, the butcher, was more prosperous and owned a real shop. There was an infinite difference in status between doing business in a permanent structure and in a market stall.

Malkeh liked Yoysef's sisters. With Yoysef gone for the better part of each week, only the sisters made life in Polotsk tolerable. They were both good-natured young women. Yenta, the older, held herself a little aloof, appropriate for the wife of a shopkeeper and the mother of children, but as often as she could she tempered Mammeh Frumma's fierceness and shielded Malkeh from the worst of her scoldings. Nevertheless, it was Golda, only three years older than Malkeh and as yet unburdened by children, that Malkeh loved as a friend.

Avrom was pulling on high boots before going into the field behind the house to milk the cow. "Yes, Golda will be at the market today—and so shall you, little pigeon!" he said. As he passed from the room he patted Malkeh's cheek. "It will make the time go faster until Yoysef comes home."

Mammeh Frumma frowned but said nothing. Slurping the sweet tea, she watched Malkeh from under lids partly drawn over secret eyes. The girl was a puzzle, careless and impulsive, yet so eager to please. Look how gently she gathered the eggs, without disturbing the hens. Of course, she could also be reckless. Last week she mistook a row of onion seedlings for weeds and pulled them out. But she made up for it, getting new plants from Auntie Lifsa and mixing chicken droppings with the soil before tamping it around each slender root. And she seldom forgot to fetch water for the sunflowers or meal for the chickens. Tidy in the house, too, especially in the room that was hers and Yoysef's. The bedposts shone from polishing, and the clothes were hung neat and fine, each on its own peg, with packets of dried herbs pinned in their folds.

So what was it about Malkeh that bothered her so much, Mammeh pondered? Something in her attitude, faintly critical though not obvious enough to rebuke. Just the barest suggestion that her husband's family was inferior to her own. Indeed! When her father could barely earn enough to put bread on the table and her mother had been known to take care of other women's houses for money.

Avrom insisted she only imagined Malkeh's conceit; he saw none of it himself. And yet Mammeh was sure there was arrogance in the way she carried herself with a straight back, and the way she looked into your face with a clear, direct gaze. Yes, and in the way she pored over books by the lamp at night, books she had brought from home. What was that if not giving herself airs?

She had a hint of brazenness—nothing you could quite put your finger on, but something that attracted male attention to her person! Golda's Dovid was openly admiring and Avrom quite liked her. As for Yoysef, God Himself knew that he had been prepared to move heaven and earth just to make Malkeh his wife! What was it exactly? Mammeh remembered the fuss Malkeh had made at her hair-cutting after the wedding. On the other hand, her behavior was meticulous; she was a proper Jewish wife in every respect. She tied a *tichl* low on her forehead, wore her plain long-sleeved brown dress with fresh aprons, and kept her eyes lowered to avoid the gaze of any man. She was affectionate toward Avrom, and as respectful as any mother-in-law could expect. Friendly, too, with the neighbor women without being forward, listening to their advice and offering no opinions unless she was asked. Auntie Lifsa, Mammeh's confidante who lived next door, thought Malkeh a model daughter. But what did Lifsa know? She didn't have an only son who had thrown away the chance to marry a rich man's daughter because he had "fallen in love" with a poor village girl. Love yet! Who ever heard of love deciding anything!

Mammeh Frumma could scarcely bear to think of Yoysef and Malkeh together. Her face flushed red to think of the scandal of Yoysef's homecoming last week! Malkeh must have been watching for him, for as he turned into the street she had actually run to meet him! Bad enough, but worse still, she had thrown her arms around his neck, and he had lifted her off the ground, only acknowledging his parents afterward with the most sheepish of grins. Mammeh had scarcely been able to contain herself and had spoken sternly to Malkeh the next day.

"*Oy,*" Mammeh sighed, putting aside her glass of tea and rising heavily. Such a wife had Yoysef brought home to them. And he might instead have had Rochel, the dairyman's daughter. The dairyman might even have set Yoysef up in his own tailor shop.

Mammeh's heart was sore. She renewed the effort to put aside her unpleasant thoughts. What was done was done. Regret was like a worm in a bin of apples; you must ruthlessly cut it out before it spoiled the whole lot.

"Come, the sun is high in the sky already. Let us go to market," she called resolutely.

*T*he sun was in fact just emerging from the gray morning clouds when the three, Avrom, Frumma, and Malkeh, arrived at the *gostinny dvor,* the nerve center of every Russian community. Avrom carried the heavy basket of chicken and duck eggs. Malkeh bore the enamel pan of vegetables she had pulled from the garden that morning, the black loam left clinging to attest to the freshness of the carrots, cucumbers, and turnips.

All around, other Jewish families were setting up stalls, too, and noisy greetings passed back and forth. With the Russian farmers who were pulling their horse-drawn carts into the square, the greetings were friendly but more subdued.

Today there was even a black-eyed Gypsy tinker looking for a place to settle his colorful covered wagon. Malkeh stared at his dark, handsome profile and sweeping mustachios until Mammeh Frumma jerked her around.

By midmorning the hum of the bazaar had swelled to a good-natured roar, each merchant hawking his wares loudly in an attempt to drown out his neighbors. All was noise and a patterned confusion that Malkeh found exciting. Her voice rose as stridently as anyone's: "Buy our beautiful eggs, warm from the nest this morning!" she cried, holding up a perfect creamy oval for inspection. "Fresh eggs for sale! No cheaper price anywhere in the market! Come buy my eggs!" Her eyes sparkled and her cheeks were flushed.

"That's enough, Malkeh! You sound like a fishwife! It's vulgar!" Mammeh Frumma hissed.

"But everyone does it!" Malkeh said, resentment digging a furrow between her brows.

"That's enough! You're calling attention to yourself."

Hurt, Malkeh retreated to the back of the stall, where the tears which had sprung to her eyes would not be noticed. In time, the noise and bustling activity of the market helped her forget the reprimand. Customers were kind. They said things like "Frumma, Yoysef's wife is a beauty!" and "How lucky you are to have a daughter in the house again!"

The morning passed quickly; only a gnawing in the belly signaled the hour for the midday meal. Golda came to visit while they were eating. A somnolence settled over the bazaar as the late summer sun grew hot and other families, too, paused to eat and rest. This was the best time of the day, a time to relax, to exchange news and a bit of gossip. The life of the community was rich with events to savor, every day a new drama of love, infidelity, tragedy, unexpected twists of fate.

Mammeh Frumma, happily occupied with friends, agreed that Malkeh might walk about the bazaar with Golda. To tell the truth, it was a relief for Mammeh to have her out from underfoot.

Scarcely attending Mammeh's warnings to stay away from the Gypsies, who might steal from them (what was there to steal?) or kidnap them (with so many mouths to feed already, why would the Gypsies want any more?), the two young women set off arm in arm. They were a startling contrast, Golda brown-eyed and as red-cheeked as the apples she sold, and Malkeh all cream and gold, glowing both with youth and the joy of a perfect summer day.

There were all sorts of things for sale in the market: fat white chickens, their red combs sticking through the mesh of the cages; fish, silver against beds of green leaves; trays of red and yellow apples, small, firm citrons, and brown pears; little round watermelons split to reveal the sweet flesh inside; red potatoes no larger than a child's fist; creamy turnips and bright green cucumbers. There were baskets of lentils and split peas, and shiny pink and white beans.

The produce and food stalls were at the perimeter of the bazaar. As one went more deeply into the market, one found stands with combs for the hair and little lacquered pins and boxes, some with linens and sundry utensils for the house, and still others that displayed bright lengths of cloth for dresses. Malkeh stopped before one of these, holding against herself a length of blue cloth sprigged with pink and yellow flowers.

"Wouldn't this make a pretty dress, Golda?" she asked, wishing she could surprise Yoysef with it.

"Yes, for a shiksa," Golda replied in Yiddish.

Malkeh sighed. No bright dresses for Jewish women—too frivolous and seductive. Rebelliously she laid the colorful fabric aside. "I can't really see what harm there is in looking as pretty as you can," she grumbled. "Tell me, Golda, wouldn't it make Dovid happy to see you in—say, a red *sarafan* and an embroidered blouse? With your coloring, you would look like a picture!"

"Ah, Malkeh, you know it is not allowed—" Golda was wistful.

Malkeh mimicked Mammeh Frumma's unctuous tones perfectly: " 'For whom should a married woman want to look pretty?' " She added contemptuously, "As if the husband she goes to bed with each night does not count for anything!"

Golda looked around nervously. "Malkeh! What are you saying?" she whispered.

"Only that I love to have Yoysef look at me in that special way. I love for him to want me!" Malkeh turned a sharp gaze on her new sister. "Don't tell me that you don't feel the same about Dovid! I've seen how your face grows soft when you're with him."

"I—I am ashamed—"

"Of what?" Malkeh grasped Golda's hands. "That you love your husband and that he loves you?"

Golda whitened. "Sometimes I have thought that Dovid and I are selfish and that it is God's punishment that we have no child."

"You can't believe that!"

"Mammeh says—"

"I'm sick of what Mammeh says!" Malkeh declared bravely. Golda looked so stricken that Malkeh was immediately contrite. "It's just that older people don't remember what it's like to be young like us."

Golda linked arms with her sister-in-law. "Malkeh, you are such a free thinker!"

Malkeh smiled, wondering whether she should confide to Golda that beneath her *tichl*, her hair was growing. Already she loved the look and feel of its silky curls. Because it would worry Golda, she decided to say nothing.

They walked on, past the Gypsy wagon, where pans and basins of gleaming copper and tin were displayed, and the man with the flashing eyes asked if they had any pots to be mended. The young women ran past, holding fast to each other lest he snatch one of them for whatever dark purposes Gypsies might have.

Breathless and giggling, they stopped to catch their breaths when they were well beyond the tinker's reach. They were before a large velvet-draped stall that sold icons, brass crosses, religious amulets, and candles. A wisp of a man, so small and dry and old that it seemed as though the next breeze might take him, peered at them from eyes made rheumy either by disease or by the oily smoke of incense that wafted upward from a censer in the corner. Golda averted her eyes and tugged at Malkeh's arm, but Malkeh's gaze was riveted on the icons, painted on wood in strong, dark colors, pictures of the holy family and of martyred saints with elongated faces and rings of golden light circling their heads. Papa had told Malkeh that even the poorest of Russian homes had a "beautiful corner" for the family icons, but she had never seen any close up before. They were grand but forbidding! There was a dark, brooding sternness in the melancholy faces of the saints, and even more upsetting was the depiction of the death agonies of the Christ figure on his cross. For herself, she much preferred the Madonnas with fat-legged baby Jesuses in their laps, but in these, too, the eyes were filled with a pain past bearing. Malkeh wondered at this reverence for suffering. It was alien, disturbing, even frightening. She turned to comment to Golda, but Golda had walked on and was already at the next shop, pretending to study some sacks of dried fruits while she waited for Malkeh to join her. Noting Malkeh's interest in the icons, the ancient proprietor had tottered to the front of the stall. Now he thrust into her face a wooden crucifix for her kiss. Startled, she turned and fled.

"God be with thee, daughter!" The old man's cackle followed her.

Golda had the grace not to comment, and a chastened Malkeh held tight to her hand until her anxiety abated. To divert her attention from the encounter, Golda led her to her favorite place in all of the *gostinny dvor*— the bird-seller's corner. Here were nightingales, larks, and bullfinches in fancifully decorated wooden cages. Their songs floated, separately and together, on the soft summer air. With a flutter of wings a young nightingale clung to the side of its cage, its bright eyes seeming to peer directly at the girls.

"Oh, you sweet little thing!" Malkeh said, pressing her nose close. "How I would like to buy you!"

"What would you do with a bird?" Golda was curious.

"Why, I'd open the door, of course, and let him fly into the forest!"

Walking away, they laughed, Malkeh quite restored to liveliness.

At the stall that sold scarves and shawls, Malkeh draped a large black shawl, vibrant with red roses, around her hips. She made a low bow in Golda's direction. "It is the Sabbath queen herself!" she announced, prancing a few steps so that the shawl swirled about her slim body.

The fat Russian shopkeeper clapped her hands. "It suits the young lady very well."

"Oh, Malkeh," Golda laughed, "you are too terrible! Take it off before somebody sees you!"

Malkeh put the shawl back in its pile and dipped her knees toward the Russian woman. *"Spaseba bolshoi,"* she said. "It is a beautiful shawl."

The woman nodded.

They were almost at the end of the bazaar when they heard a murmur of excitement, and the ramshackle wagon of Eleazar, the book peddler, turned into the square. Before the horse was even hitched, girls and women had gathered around the cart, eager to see what new stories Eleazar had brought. The bookseller did not come often, and each appearance was an event, for his packs were full of romantic Yiddish novels for the women and spiritual texts for the men.

Golda and Malkeh crowded around Eleazar's wagon with all the others. Later there would be a more sober gathering of men in the courtyard of the synagogue, and for them Eleazar would produce leather-bound sacred writings, biblical texts, and the commentaries of the rabbis.

"Come, see what I have today!" the little man shouted. "Fine stories for all. I have a new storybook, more adventures of Prince Buvo. I have folktales from Galicia. Look at the pictures, ladies!" He held up an open book to appreciative "ahs."

"And here! A new romance from the pen of Shomer himself, all about the love of the rich man's daughter for the beggar who is really a prince atoning for a sin. Read it now. See how it turns out—maybe all for the best, maybe not!"

Women pressed forward, picking up the cheaply bound books. Here were volumes of instructive little homilies for Jewish wives to read on the Sabbath, and biblical stories written in Yiddish for women who couldn't read the original Hebrew. Although these were given respectful attention, enthusiasm was reserved for the novels that told about wives faithful against all odds, about self-sacrifice that was not recognized until "too late," about the thwarted love of scholars for poor orphan girls.

The luckier women, those with money in their apron pockets, carried books away with them. Baba Sima, acknowledged as the community's leading female intellectual, handed over a whole ruble for an armload of novels! Others, like Malkeh, with no money to spend, examined and discussed the merits of this book and that with as much enthusiasm as though they were making actual selections.

At last Malkeh, sighing wistfully, put down a collection of stories by her favorite writer, Isaac Mayer Dik, and motioned to Golda that they should leave. What must it be like to have coins to spend at will, she wondered. Maybe if Yoysef had had a good week, she would ask him for a little money of her own. But, no, even as she thought it, Malkeh knew she could not do that when every spare coin went into the little hoard hidden behind the bedroom wall, savings to buy a shop and home of their own. Resolutely Malkeh backed away from the enchanting book cart.

Eleazar the Book Peddler called after her. "Would you like to have that book you were looking at, little one?" he coaxed. "It is a fine storybook. It will keep you by the lamp all through the winter evenings to come. Take the book, my dear. It is only eight kopecks, cheap for a whole winter's joy."

"No," Malkeh said reluctantly, "thank you." She grasped Golda's arm more firmly and turned away.

"Wait!" the old man called. "Wait! Are you not—yes, you *are* the daughter of Mendel, the *melamed* from Dagda!"

Malkeh turned back, eyes glowing. "Oh, yes. Have you seen my father and my mother?" she cried.

"Yes, yes," Eleazar shrilled with the delight of recognition. "Less than two weeks back. I was in Dagda for the Sabbath, and your father, may God keep count of all the *mitzvoth* he performs, took me home from the shul for the Sabbath meal." His eyes became moist and distant remembering the luscious carrot tzimmes, glistening with the fat of brisket.

"Are they well?" Malkeh asked eagerly.

"Oh, fine. They are fine. They told me their daughter married a Polotsker tailor and is settled, praise be to God. And here you are!" He beamed at Malkeh, his face glowing with pleasure. "Let me see what I can tell you. The whole family is well. Your mother misses you. Your father too. He had a cold he got at the wedding. No, no," he added on, seeing Malkeh's look of alarm, "it is nothing, just a little cough that's probably quite gone by now. Nothing," he added hastily.

"But Papa has a weak chest!"

"Nothing," Eleazar repeated. "But why do you not want that fine book you were looking at?"

"I have no money," Malkeh said.

"Sha! Sha!" Golda cried, horrified. "You will make the family ashamed."

Malkeh shrugged. "It is no shame to be without money. It is a shame to pretend to have it when you don't."

"Ah, ah, I understand," Eleazar said, pulling at the wisps of his gray beard. "Well, Malkeh, daughter of Mendel, you shall have the book in any case." He thrust the thin blue-bound volume of Dik's stories into her hands. "It is a wedding present from your father's friend."

"Oh, I cannot take such a gift!" Malkeh exclaimed, all the while clutching the book to her breast.

"Yes! Yes!" Eleazar said. "It is but a small marriage gift. To refuse would be an insult."

Oh, an insult. Malkeh pursed her lips, considering. It was a sin to hurt another's feelings, was it not? Her qualms resolved, she beamed with pleasure. "Thank you, thank you."

Malkeh wanted to hug the old man for his kindness, but, of course, that was impossible. Instead, she invited him to visit if he was in Polotsk when Yoysef returned, and she gave him messages for her parents for when he next visited Dagda.

Malkeh hugged the book to her as she and Golda walked back to their places on the edges of the marketplace. Her heart was light as she thought about the lonely evenings when she would lose herself in the stories. She promised Golda that she could borrow the book.

"No, no," Golda said, pressing Malkeh's hand, "I am not a reader like you."

Golda seemed preoccupied. At last she said, "Forgive me, Malkeh, but I think maybe you should hide the book under your apron."

Malkeh was surprised. "Whatever for? Do you think the Gypsies will steal it?" She giggled at the thought.

Golda said slowly, "I don't think Mammeh will like your taking a present like that."

Malkeh was puzzled. "I don't understand. Eleazar the Bookseller has been to my parents' home. It is out of friendship that he gave me this book."

"Mammeh may think it is a charity. Or worse," she added darkly.

"Worse?"

"You know, a sinful gift from a man to a woman—"

Malkeh's eyebrows rose over flashing eyes. "I am grown-up and married. I can decide for myself whether it is right to accept a gift or not!"

Golda shook her head, troubled. The two young women were silent, the walk back shorter now that they had seen everything. The glow of the afternoon had diminished.

The crowd of shoppers was thinning by the time they came to the apple stall and Golda's husband. Dovid smiled shyly at Malkeh. "You are wonderful company for my Golda, but I'm glad you're back. Business was so good, praise God, that I was already looking for Golda to go home."

Malkeh smiled at her brother-in-law. She liked this gentle man for his friendship to her and for the way he followed Golda with his eyes though they were an old married couple of four years already.

It was late. Malkeh kissed Golda and waved good-bye to Dovid. She began to hurry. Many of the stallkeepers were packing to leave already, and she did not want to aggravate Yoysef's parents.

Mammeh Frumma saw the book in Malkeh's hand immediately "Where did you get it?"

Malkeh, still exhilarated by the afternoon's adventures, happily explained about the gift.

"A married woman does not accept gifts from a man. I will take it back to Eleazar the Book Peddler."

Avrom protested. "Frumma, it was a wedding present from a friend of Malkeh's family."

"It is not fitting," Mammeh declared, her lips tight with anger. "It is not fitting for Malkeh to accept a gift directly from a man's hand like that. Anyway," she added in spite, "Malkeh could better spend her evenings mending Yoysef's clothes or embroidering. What does a married woman have to do with books?"

"It is mine," Malkeh said, trying to keep her voice steady, "and I will keep it."

Mammeh Frumma's little eyes began to sparkle in anticipation of a quarrel. She would establish once and for all who was the head of the household. It would be a relief to get so many buried grievances out in the open at last!

"I am the mammeh," she said. "I say you will not have the book!"

Catching Malkeh unprepared, Mammeh Frumma wrested the blue book from her hands. Malkeh grabbed for the slim volume, but it was now held high in the triumphant grasp of Yoysef's mother. Frumma's eyes gleamed with a victory so easily won.

Mammeh Frumma did not intend for things to go as far as they did. Maybe it would not have happened if Papa Avrom had intervened or if Malkeh had not fought to get the book back. But as the two women struggled for possession, the cover gave way with a rending sound, the book's back splitting away from its pages.

Hot tears of fury sprang to Malkeh's eyes. "I will have it! I will!" she panted, throwing herself at her mother-in-law, a look of pure hatred contorting her face. Frumma was driven to new lengths by that look. Taller and stronger than Malkeh, she held the broken book high overhead and then deliberately tore out the pages, letting them flutter, one by one, like plucked goose feathers, to the ground at her feet.

"I am the mammeh," she said again. "You will obey me in my house."

Malkeh was stunned. In her father's house a book, damaged even by accident, was retrieved with reverence and pressed against the lips in contrition. Surely, at the very least, God would send down a lightning bolt to punish this desecration! The bile rising in her throat, she snatched the remnants of the book back from Mammeh's unresisting hand. She was pierced to the very heart. "Look what you've done to my book!" she screamed in anguish. "It is a *shandeh* and an *aveyreh*! A shame and a sin! I will never forgive you! Never! Never! Never!"

Mammeh Frumma was beginning to feel uneasy. Although neighboring stallkeepers were pretending not to notice the quarrel in the Mandelkern enclosure, she had no doubt that every detail was being committed to memory. The gleam of victory was fading fast as she realized the enormity of what had happened.

Papa Avrom knelt to gather the fallen pages. *"Sha!"* he said nervously. "Everyone hears. I will glue the book together, good as new."

Sullenly Mammeh said, "Such a scene, Malkeh, about a little accident!" Her eyes met Malkeh's. What she saw there was implacable contempt, Mammeh quailed. Perhaps things had gotten somewhat out of hand.

"You are a horrid, jealous woman," Malkeh said in a voice thick with angry tears. She turned and stumbled from the marketplace, searching for a place of asylum, she knew not where, from a world grown suddenly chilly and dark and infinitely terrible.

Chapter 3

As he strode along the dusty road, Yoysef hummed a happy tune of his own making, his off-key baritone breaking now and then into words:

> Going home, home, home,
> To my Malkeh—Queen, Life,
> Going home to her arms,
> Going home to my wife!

He was on the return journey to Polotsk after a week of walking from village to village, sewing machine strapped to his broad back, a pack with threads, scissors, and goods swinging from one shoulder. Now on the homeward leg, he carried a stout canvas sack as well. It had been a good week, and he was bringing home surprises. Several gold coins carefully wrapped in a handkerchief were hidden in the center of a bolt of black gabardine. He had a round of good white cheese, potatoes, some late summer pears, and a ten-*funt* measure of flour the miller had given for a pair of stout breeches. The miller, a husky man with thick forearms, had groaned upon feeling the weight of Yoysef's bundle. "You'll never get it home, *Chaver*!" he predicted.

Yoysef had laughed. "I can carry twice as much!" he boasted.

"When one is traveling home to a beautiful bride, no burden is too heavy! I can see that your feet have wings." The miller chuckled in high good humor, thumping Yoysef on the back hard enough to bring a lesser man to his knees.

Yoysef waved good-bye with his free hand and traveled briskly down the road, handling his burdens as lightly as though they contained only joys and laughter. The thought of his homecoming quickened his steps. He grinned, remembering the special present he was bringing for Malkeh. It had caught his eye in a shop window in Vitebsk—a scarf woven of thread so fine that the cloth was like tissue; its borders were a deep blue, its center patterned with azure and turquoise flowers. He had paid dearly for it, but the shadings reminded him of how Malkeh's eyes changed color with her mood: when she was serene, her eyes were the clear blue of early morning; in anger they resembled the translucent ice cut from the frozen river in winter; passion made them brilliant, hot, and dark. If it was a commandment that Malkeh's hair be hidden from the outside world, so be it, but nowhere was it written that the covering must be plain and dull!

How happy he was! How lucky! He had fallen in love with a girl worshiped from afar, a storybook heroine whose delicacy of form and face were the essence of femininity. At the beginning, Yoysef had scarcely dared lift his eyes to her lest his gaze in some way defile her purity. In his wildest dreams then he could never have imagined that his flesh-and-blood bride would tremble at his touch and match his body's eagerness with that of her own.

Yoysef had always supposed that women endured the marital act only for the sake of bearing children. Mammeh had, in fact, made veiled allusions to what women suffered at the hands of men. He had resolved on a course of tenderness and care, that he would never be the source of pain for the woman he loved. Yoysef grinned at his remembered innocence. Who would have dared to believe that women, after all, had the same hungers that dwell in men? Or perhaps his Malkeh was different, more passionately loving than others of her sex. Earlier experiences had not prepared him. He blushed now, remembering a clumsy attempt to kiss Rochel. She had turned her face to prevent his lips from touching hers. And there was that time in Pskov, the guilty gropings in a dark closet with Mindel, the full-bodied maidservant of the household! God alone knew how *that* would have ended if there had not been a step upon the stair!

Malkeh did not make him feel unclean because of his needs. Indeed, he and she were equals in love. She grasped him as tightly as he held her, heart against heart, thigh pressed to thigh. At the beginning Malkeh's lack of shyness had shocked him, but he had grown to delight in the open ways she expressed her pleasure in his body and her own.

Everything about Malkeh was forthright and direct—what she thought was what she said, usually in the same instant. She was trying hard to curb her tongue for his sake, but it was not an easy task.

God save him though, but what a problem he had between Malkeh and Mammeh, each claiming a part of him, each headstrong and quick to hurt and to anger. In time it would work itself out, Yoysef thought. Tonight both women would be happy. Mammeh would be pleased with the food he had brought, and Malkeh would dance around him when he teased her with the promise of the present in his pocket. And before they blew out the bedside candle, Malkeh and he would count again the little store of coins hidden in the wall, reveling in the week's rubles.

Yoysef the Tailor was a contented man as he trudged down the road on his way home. With any luck, he would be in Polotsk in time for *mincha*. With a twinge of guilt he realized that of late he had paid scant attention to his devotions. Surely, though, God would forgive. After all, God had led him to Malkeh, and He must understand how it is with a man and a woman, for He had made them both.

𝓜alkeh ran blindly from the marketplace, having no idea where she would go, only that it would be far from Mammeh Frumma and the scuffle that had torn her life apart no less than it had riven Eleazar's book. Frantic to put distance between herself and the scene of that humiliation, she fled blindly through narrow, unfamiliar streets, her scarf slipping sideways on her head and her face marked by the tracks of tears. Oblivious to the course of her flight, Malkeh did not notice the fat housewife whose cucumbers and radishes flew out of her basket and scattered on the cobblestones in her haste to make way, nor did she see the well-dressed man on the chestnut stallion who was forced to rein in sharply to keep from running her down. She did not hear the coarse Russian oath he directed at those who endanger honest citizens by permitting madwomen to run loose in the streets! Thoughts of cataclysmic destruction claimed her entire consciousness and drummed furiously in her head. Oh, just once to be allowed to pummel her mother-in-law's fat pudding face and spit in those piggish eyes! It was not only for the ruined book—although God knew *that* was abomination enough!—it was also for the days and weeks of mortification Malkeh had endured at Mammeh Frumma's hands. Malkeh would never give in to her! In a million years Mammeh could not bend her to her will.

Gradually the streets which had been full of shoppers near the *gostinny dvor* emptied. Malkeh hesitated, seeing that she was in an unknown neighborhood. Tall houses with windows heavily shuttered against the afternoon heat turned unfriendly faces to the street. She knew only that she was in a residential district where the families of rich merchants and professional people lived—where Mammeh Frumma had warned her never to go. Half of Polotsk's twenty thousand inhabitants might be Jews, but they were nevertheless barred from many parts of the city. Malkeh had begun to sweat, less from exertion than from fear, although in fact the air had become breathlessly close. She walked more timidly now, edging into the shadows of houses. She wondered if she might be arrested for being where she had no business, yet she could not find her way out of the maze of streets that seemed to curl one around another. If only there were some landmark, some familiar sign by which she could get her bearings. The buildings were larger now, the streets paved and broad enough to admit the occasional sleek carriage and *drozhki*, taking stylish women wearing hats and gloves to their afternoon's engagements. Today Malkeh had no interest in them. Today she wanted only to find a place of safety and refuge for herself.

In a small square Malkeh rested for a moment. Looking up through the leaves of the birch trees, she saw in the distance golden stars in a field of deep blue, a profusion of crosses, a tapering gilt spire. Surely the domes belonged to a great cathedral or a monastery—maybe to the very church Yoysef had pointed out when they first drove into Polotsk. If it were indeed the same church, she was close to the thoroughfare that ran laterally through Polotsk; following to its end she would reach the earthwork battlements that they called Napoleon's Wall. It formed one boundary of the city, the River Dvina the other. Beyond it was the road leading toward Dagda and home.

It was late afternoon, and thunderclouds were beginning to bunch in a dirty yellow sky. Though bruised in spirit and footsore, Malkeh felt more optimistic when she reached the wall. It was a little cooler on the periphery of the city. Yoysef had told her the story of that long-ago war with the French when the citizens of Polotsk had worked feverishly day and night to build up the earthworks that would keep the invaders from entering their city. Now grass and trees grew on its gentle hillside.

It was time to stop and seriously consider her situation. She would never go back to Mammeh Frumma's house! No more would she put up with that mean old woman's hostile forbearance, her cold, condemning eyes, her sharp tongue! Even if she was Yoysef's mother, Mammeh Frumma had lost her claim to respect. Thinking of the quarrel, tears welled in Malkeh's eyes, stinging and burning and making her nose run. Reaching into her apron pocket, she found that as usual she had forgotten a handkerchief.

Where could she go? She wanted to go home, where dear Papa would gather her into his lap and stroke her head and make everything all right.

But what of Yoysef if she fled to Dagda? A bride who returned to her parents' house was almost unheard of, a case for the rabbi! People would think that her husband had beaten her (scarcely a reason to leave a husband) or that he had subjected her to strange practices in the bedroom, or, worst of all, that he had been unable to consummate the marriage. She could never shame dear Yoysef like that! And what would she do if she ran home and Yoysef was so angry that he did not come after her? He might even divorce her, easy enough in a case of desertion! In time he might marry the dairyman's daughter. That would certainly please Mammeh Frumma, who used every opportunity to extoll Rochel's virtues! Cold fingers of apprehension clutched Malkeh's heart. Never to see Yoysef again? Never again to sleep with her head cradled in the hollow between his shoulder and his neck, never to come sweetly from sleep to feel his strong pulse against her cheek? Never again to lie with him in the act of love—plump Rochel in her place in Grandfather's bed?

If she could only talk to Yoysef, things would somehow get sorted out. But he had been away a week already and where would she find him? It was terrifying to consider what could happen to a woman on the road alone, traveling through strange villages. Suppose she were overtaken by the Gypsy caravan and spirited away by the dark people? And there was a practical consideration; she had no money in her pocket to buy food along the way.

Perhaps Eleazar the Book Peddler would take her with him on his wagon. He was a kindly man and he would understand better than most that she could no longer stay in Mammeh Frumma's house after the destruction of her book. Malkeh sighed, knowing it unlikely that Eleazar would be willing to get involved with a runaway bride. Besides, if she did persuade him to take her, could she be all that sure that they would meet Yoysef on the road Eleazar traveled? Why hadn't she listened more closely when Yoysef talked to her about his route?

Malkeh rose from the ground and brushed the grass from her skirt. She could not stay there on Napoleon's Wall, and she would not return to Yoysef's parents. She had to go someplace, though, that much was certain.

The first shadows had begun to fall when, walking briskly, she struck out in a direction chosen more or less at random. She would skirt the Russian villages and steal fruit and vegetables from the fields. Her path would surely cross Yoysef's. Her heart would be her compass, God would lead her. Papa had always assured her that every living person walked with his hand in God's palm. That heartening thought strengthened her resolve.

Back straight and arms swinging jauntily at her side, Malkeh marched along the broad main road, imagining Yoysef's surprise when she would come upon him. Maybe it would be tomorrow, although tonight would be better.

*D*arkness dropped suddenly like a heavy cloak around her. A growth of pine and birch obscured whatever light remained in the sky. There seemed to be no moon or stars. She paused for a moment, confused. Yoysef would have taken a road through the wheat fields of the river plain, for he had spoken of bringing home fresh-milled flour. Surely she could not have lost her way so soon; the plain was undoubtedly beyond this small wood.

The broad road forked once and then in a short distance forked again, each time narrowing and presenting her with choices. She tried to remember in which direction the sun had set, but she had been distracted by her thoughts and paid it little heed. The overhang of the trees, which were becoming more numerous, increased the difficulty of charting a course. Malkeh hoped it would not be much longer before the road began its descent out of the forest.

The deep growl of thunder, heard first as she rested on the embankment at the edge of the city, had begun to move in upon her. It would soon rain. She had best return to the main road to look for shelter. A place like this with so many trees was certainly not safe in a lightning storm. From the increasing thunder, she knew she did not have much time.

She seemed to have blundered deep into the forest preserve where Count Voronov hunted game. There were animals here too. Maybe the wild pigs that were so dangerous! She tried to remember what Yoysef had said about animals that lived in this region. Elk. Roe deer. Wolves? Already Malkeh imagined bright animal eyes peering at her from the underbrush. Her heart fluttered uneasily in her chest. Wild boars, it was said, were the most fearsome of all forest creatures. They could gore and trample a person to death in a matter of moments. She quickened the pace of her retreat. Back at the crossroads, Malkeh recognized the large boulder where she had leaned a moment to rest and get her bearings. At least she *thought* it was the place. Shadows gave the trees and rocks a certain sameness. Had she seen that stand of alders before?

A light rain had begun to fall, and thunder seemed to break directly above her. Lightning sent jagged spears into the forest floor. It was the kind of dirty night when God and angels stay at home and evil spirits choose to go abroad. The Polotsk road was surely just a little way ahead; it was merely a matter of putting one foot in front of the other. She would be there already if it were not for the prickly undergrowth that caught and held her skirts so that she had to stop every few minutes to free herself. Earlier the path hadn't seemed so obstructed by brambles!

Jagged flashes of lightning showed Malkeh that a relatively sparse growth of pine and birch had given way to thickly growing spruce, oak, and alder trees. There was a strong dank smell of fungi. A long wet rope coiled down from one of the trees and caught in Malkeh's hair. She panicked, shrieking and struggling to throw the thing off her, but it was only a piece of vine. Still, she could not stop shivering.

The rain had turned into a deluge. Malkeh's dress clung to her body. She had lost her *tichl*, and her short curls were plastered to her head. Her boots made a sloshing sound as they were sucked into the wet ground. The path seemed to have disappeared beneath a heavy carpet of fallen leaves, and for all she knew she might be following an animal trail leading nowhere. The leaves were slippery from the rain and Malkeh's feet slid out from under her, causing her to fall heavily. *Papa, Yoysef, help me!* But she was alone, flat on the ground with her face pressed against a layer of slime and rotting leaves, the smell of decay noxious and evil in her nostrils. After a few moments she eased herself to her knees, feeling herself with shaking hands to be sure her limbs were intact. With utmost care she regained her feet. Softly, softly, she counseled herself, sensing that she was on the edge of hysteria and struggling for control. No reason to be afraid. Just a question of retracing one's steps.

She had skinned her knee in the fall, and her left ankle was beginning to swell. Her teeth chattered from cold and fear. Where was God's hand now, the one that was supposed to lead her to Yoysef?

Malkeh knew it was hopeless to push ahead in the darkness, yet fear insistently drove her forward. Safety was surely beyond the next stand of trees, wasn't it?

Tears of self-pity now joined the rivulets of rainwater running off her cheeks and chin. The black evil of the place was insidious, pushing its way inside her very body. It was in wet dark woods like these that dybbuks dwelt. At any moment an evil one might appear to invade her mind, dispossess her soul, and leave her body to molder forever between the world of the living and the grave!

Ah, she knew about dybbuks. In Dagda when she was growing up, Papa had told her stories, and many a night under the covers with her best friend, Shprintze, she had shivered while exchanging tales. Legend told of young women who suddenly began speaking in the deep voices of men, saying unclean things and cursing God! Then it was known that they must be secret sinners and possessed of a dybbuk, for thus did the spirits of evil men barred from the Other World seek refuge in the bodies of vulnerable living persons!

With pounding heart Malkeh counted the sins of *her* commission:

The hot, unwifely feelings she had for Yoysef's body.

The way she tempted Yoysef to hurry through his morning prayers while she waited for him in the bed.

Her careless haste with the chores she hated, like cleaning the chicken coops.

Her contempt and disrespect for Yoysef's mother.

"Dear God," Malkeh said aloud, not praying exactly, but talking to Him like to Papa, "if through Your miracle I am rescued, I will be better, I promise it. I will not tempt Yoysef with my unclothed body. I will not let my hair grow in secret. I will not yearn after the embroidered blouses of the Russian women. And I'll put aside the reading of novels. Only save me, and I'll do Thy will in everything." Wiping her eyes with the edge of her sodden apron, she added reluctantly, "I promise I'll practice humility, like Mammeh says I should, even with Mammeh Frumma."

Malkeh took several deep breaths to calm herself. She had not the slightest idea which direction led to Polotsk. The Voronov forest preserve was generally east of the city, but she might have wandered in circles and could not be sure whether she was going toward or away from the main road. Woodlands in this part of Russia contained bogs that could suck one down into vile slime, fierce animals, poisonous plants, to say nothing of evil spirits. At least the trees were so thick that they formed a partial protection from the rain. Dropping to all fours, Malkeh began to creep like an animal, feeling for the faint trail with her hands in the dark. She tried not to think about what horrible things her fingers might encounter on the forest floor.

All of Malkeh's senses were alert to danger. Her eyes strained to pierce the darkness, her ears to catch hostile sounds. Once she sensed rather than saw a grass snake slither across her path and into the low-growing cranberry bushes. The smells of animal spoor, toadstools, and rotting leaves assailed her. She heard the patter of rain in treetops, the soughing of wind buffeting branches, the occasional scrabbling of a small animal in the vegetation. It took her a while to recognize that the dry, rasping sound that moved with her through the darkness was her own ragged breathing.

She had no way of gauging how long she had been in the forest. She inched forward, moving first one knee and one hand, then the other knee, the other hand. Her palms and knees were torn by sharp sticks and debris, her ankle throbbed, her back ached; still she moved forward. She felt she had been crawling for hours under a spell that doomed her to spend the rest of her life on her hands and knees. One knee and then the other, the left, the right, one, two, one—

She collapsed in the mud. She would die in the count's woods, or morning would finally come. She hardly cared which. Overcome by the trauma of the day's events, by fear and overwhelming exhaustion, her eyes fell shut. Far away amid the black silhouettes of birch trees, Yoysef appeared. She couldn't move. His face swam toward her, his arms straining to reach her. "Come, come!" His will moved her tired limbs in his direction.

"Wait, Yoysef, wait!" Shakily Malkeh crawled toward the apparition. And indeed the trees and brush seemed thinner. Using the trunk of a tree for support, Malkeh pulled herself up. As her mind cleared, she looked around her in disbelief. She was back at the Y in the path where she had taken the first wrong turning. It was unmistakable! She could almost see the main road just beyond the small clearing. She clung to the tree until she could force her cramped and trembling legs to take their first upright steps. The city could not be more than four or five versts from this place, not more than an hour's walk for a healthy person! Oh, to be home in the warm, lighted kitchen, even if it meant, as it surely must, a harsh scolding from the family.

Reaching the road, Malkeh's progress was distressingly slow although the way was broad and flat and the rain had moderated into a slow, steady downpour. With each step she took, pain shot up her leg from the twisted ankle. Raising her skirt, she could see flesh puffing over the top of her high-laced shoe. She stooped to loosen the ties. But now, without firm support, it was even more difficult to walk. This new discomfort quite took her mind off the lesser hurts of raw-scraped knees and deep scratches on face and arms.

Her perceptions heightened by pain, Malkeh heard the faint sounds of footfalls on the wet leaves of the woods she had left behind her. A sinister sound, hollow, unearthly. It came from the forest, and it rose and fell, rose and fell. Somewhere in the trees a spirit wailed eerily on a thin upwardly spiraling note that sent chills up and down Malkeh's spine. She stopped, listening to the sounds in the night. Something monstrously large was crashing through the trees at the side of the road. There was a snapping of branches as saplings gave way under a heavy weight, then a great turmoil of snarling and growling as though dybbuk wrestled dybbuk on the woodland floor! Was this to be her fate, then, saved from the forest only to lose her life in the very sight of home?

The noise of a thrashing fury came from the trees. The cacophony seemed one minute to be the neighing of horses, the next the squeal of a boar and the barking of dogs; once Malkeh even thought she heard the hoarse cry of a human. The incomprehensible babble of dybbuks, she feared, sounded like this. Gradually the demons withdrew farther into the trees. The snorting and pawing subsided and the baying of devils grew fainter. Malkeh dared to breathe again. Maybe it would still be all right. Cautiously she had begun to move once again when in a great whoosh, like a rush of wind, a huge creature emerged from the woods behind her. Its hot breath steamed from a dripping muzzle, and its eyes blazed fiery red! Malkeh knew that no person could outrun evil. Still, her instinct to save herself summoned up a last desperate strength, and disregarding her throbbing ankle, she began to run.

The thunder of feet was almost upon her. The creature had a cloven hoof; she could tell by the fall of it on the road. The Evil One had followed her from the forest!

"Blessed art Thou, Lord our God, King of the universe!" she panted. Then, as the sound threatened to engulf her, "Save me!" she screamed as she threw herself, fainting, upon the ground in front of the large black creature that was almost upon her.

*I*t was quite dark and the rain was falling steadily by the time Yoysef entered Polotsk and turned down the familiar street. He was later than he had planned, delayed by the fierce midsummer squall, and he thought with pleasure of the warm kitchen that at this hour would be fragrant with cooking food. He was soaked through, and while the meat finished roasting, it would be pleasant to sip hot tea through a chunk of hard sugar held between his cheek and his teeth and listen to whatever town gossip his father might have for him. Malkeh would be helping Mammeh with the meal, or perhaps would be reading a book, the lamplight making her plain brown dress golden.

Hurrying, Yoysef was soon standing under the slight overhang of his roof, shaking the rainwater from his coat. He called out greetings even before he reached for the latch.

The door flew open, but it was not Malkeh come to throw her arms around him. It was his sister Yenta, holding a baby on her hip, her face grave and drawn. Golda appeared as Yenta drew him inside.

"What is it? What is it?" Yoysef cried out in sudden alarm. "Why do you look like that?"

Mammeh burst into tears, hiding her crumpled face in the folds of her apron. Something was terribly wrong. The house was cold and the egg baskets stood on the floor, where they had been discarded on return from the market. Yenta's older child, Moisheleh, was sitting silently on the floor in a corner, his thumb in his mouth. Golda, white-faced, went to stand beside Mammeh's chair, but Malkeh was nowhere in sight.

"Malkeh! Where is Malkeh?" he asked, anxious. "What has happened?" Fearing suddenly for his wife, Yoysef strode across the room toward their room, his face tight and stiff.

"No, no." Yenta pulled at Yoysef's sleeve. "She is not here."

"Not here? Well, what—?" Yoysef began, staring in bewilderment from the face of one woman to the other, his throat constricting as his sense of disaster grew. "Mammeh! Golda! Anyone! For God's sake, tell me what has happened!"

Golda said faintly, "She had run away, Yoysef. Malkeh has run away." She began to sob.

"But—but—I don't understand—" Yoysef's face was blank with shock.

"Dovid and Yaynkel and Papa are out looking for her. They will find her," Yenta said with false confidence. "She couldn't have gone far on such a night."

Yoysef turned to Mammeh, silently rocking back and forth in her chair, her face hidden in her apron. "Mammeh! Tell me what has happened? Why should Malkeh run away?"

Everyone in the room seemed to have been struck mute.

"Mammeh?" Yoysef pleaded.

Mammeh Frumma continued to rock, the queer, detached noise of a low moan coming from behind her apron.

"For the sake of God, won't someone tell me?" Yoysef roared into the silence.

In a rush, Golda told her brother what she knew. "At the marketplace today, the book peddler gave Malkeh a gift, a book," she explained. "It was quite proper," she went on, glancing at her mother. "I was there and saw— only Mammeh did not think so."

A muffled sound came from behind Mammeh Frumma's apron.

"So? So?" Yoysef prodded. "I still don't understand."

"Mammeh told Malkeh to take the book back to Eleazar. I guess there was an argument and Malkeh got upset and ran out of the market square."

"Didn't someone go after her? A young girl alone and upset in a strange city!" Yoysef looked from one to the other of the women.

"I wasn't there, brother," Yenta said quickly.

"Nor was I," Golda echoed. "Dovid and I had already gone home."

"But that must have been hours ago!"

Yenta picked up the narrative. "At first Mammeh and Papa didn't think much about it. They expected to find Malkeh at home when they got back. But she was not in the house. Still, they didn't worry. They thought she might have gone into the field to see the new calf, or maybe next door to visit. But when it got late, Papa went to look for her. She wasn't at home or at Auntie Lifsa's, and she hadn't come to my house or Golda's either. By that time it was raining, and we all thought the storm would bring her home."

Golda began to weep.

"You mean no one saw her after she left the bazaar? What did people say when you asked them?"

Mammeh Frumma emerged from behind her apron. "Oh, Yoysef, you know we couldn't ask—people would have talked!"

Yoysef swore a huge oath in Russian. Mammeh did not rebuke him.

Golda said hopefully, "Papa borrowed a horse and wagon from Fyfka, and the three of them—Papa and Dovid and Yaynkel—have gone out on the roads in case Malkeh wandered farther than she thought and got lost. They haven't come back yet!"

Trembling with the effort to control himself, Yoysef stared at them. "I don't understand what has happened," he said, "but something terrible must have driven Malkeh from this house." He jammed his cap on his head and strode toward the door, his face set and grim. "May God help me, I will find Malkeh and bring her home. And if I have to knock on every door in Polotsk and let every person know that my wife has run away, I will do it to find her!"

"No! No, Yoysef!" Yenta cried.

"And if I have to go to the count," he said between clenched teeth, "to beg for the help of his men and his dogs, I will do that too. *I will find Malkeh!*"

Flinging open the door to the cold rain, Yoysef burst out into the darkness. Mammeh Frumma's keening followed him into the street.

Chapter 4

*M*alkeh regained consciousness in the strong grip of the dark figure. Its black wings billowed batlike in the wind while it raced forward with the rocking gait of a powerful animal. They were flying through the storm-black night, the dybbuk's hooves scarcely touching earth as it moved toward an unknown destination. Faint and weak though she might be, Malkeh nevertheless struggled, only to find herself held helpless, her arms pinned firmly to her sides. The creature lowered its shaggy head and uttered something close to her ear, but the wind carried away the sound, and all Malkeh heard was the roar of her own wildly pumping blood. Done! All was over and done! She was dead! Overcome with terror and despair, Malkeh fainted once more.

*S*ometime later Malkeh awoke suddenly, aware that the sickening jolting and the tearing of the wind had ceased. All was quietness and warmth. Had it then been nothing but a dream?

She thought she heard the homely ticking of a clock, the crackling of wood in a stove, the faint barking of dogs in the distance. Sounds of comfort and home, or a trick the dybbuk played? Malkeh risked opening her eyes the merest slit. Amazed, she lifted her head and her eyes fluttered wide open.

She was lying on soft cushions, draped with a silk-covered eiderdown. A tall, tiled stove in the corner radiated a delicious warmth and a golden light. The room was large, the ceiling high, its proportions princely. Carpets of rich Oriental reds and blues covered the softly gleaming wood of the floor. Velvet couches and marble-topped tables, fragile chairs and gilt-framed mirrors, furnished the room. From their places on the walls, paintings of gorgeously attired men and women looked down on her. The walls themselves were covered with a deep red silk cloth, the heavy-looped curtains, drawn over tall windows, of the same rich hue. It seemed a veritable palace, and she was quite alone amid its opulence.

Where could she be? The last thing she remembered was being carried off by a dark and terrible creature, half man, half beast. Malkeh shuddered, remembering its grip on her forearms. Apprehensive, she raised one arm from beneath the quilt; even in the faint light from the stove she could see the bluish imprint where strong claws had squeezed her flesh.

If this were not a dream, what was this place? Could it be that God, on whom she had called in that last moment, had been merciful? Hopefully she murmured her affirmation of faith: *Sh'ma Yisroel, Adonai Elohainu, Adonai Echod!* Hear, O Israel, the Lord is our God, the Lord is One! Reassured, she felt certain she had been spared by God's grace and had entered the World to Come.

Malkeh sank back on the soft pillows. Her mind drifted sleepily. She had imagined that heaven would be a garden, beautiful and vast to accommodate the souls of a multitude of generations. But why should God not live in a palace, after all?

It was all so very puzzling. She should be filled with joy, but instead was overcome with indescribable weariness and grief. She did not want to be dead. There was so much she had not yet experienced in life. She had never held a child of her own in her arms. She had not lived in a house of which she was mistress. She had never been to St. Petersburg nor owned a silk dress for the Sabbath. And Yoysef! He would marry again, of course, it being the responsibility of a Jew to marry and bring children into the world. She sighed, burying her head in the pillow to escape thinking of all she had lost.

It was also strange that she had not shed bodily sensations. Even now she was faintly aware of a need to urinate. And her hands, moving beneath the silk coverlet, felt the scab forming on her knee and the swelling of her ankle beneath a binding. Vaguely her body remembered cool unguents being applied to her hurts. There were deep scratches everywhere, and with her fingertips she could feel a gash on her cheek. She was stiff, sore, and her back ached. How odd! She had imagined that the whole physical side of life would disappear in death, but it had not at all!

The only part of her everyday self that she seemed to have shed was her clothing. What a sight she must have been at the Holy Gates in her wet and torn brown dress, her apron without even a handkerchief in the pocket, her shoes muddy, and her head uncovered! Giggling softly, she closed her eyes and slept once more.

*T*he light was still burning in the shul where the rabbi and several men had forgotten the time and were still studying Torah. Ordinarily Yoysef would have hesitated to disturb them.

"Excuse me, Rabbi, but I must ask your advice," he said from the doorway.

The elderly man at the center of the long table looked up. Carefully he closed his book, keeping a finger in it to mark the page. "My son?"

"Rabbi, my wife has not come home—"

"Ah, ah, ah," the rabbi said, rising with a sigh. "These problems with wives! All the time I hear about them! We will talk in private—"

"No, Rabbi, it's not like that," Yoysef said hastily. "She lost her way coming home from market. I don't know where to look for her, what to do!"

One of the younger men, Lippa Brozen, scratched his beard. "Maybe she was kidnapped, Yoysef. There were Gypsies in town today!"

"Kidnapped!" The blood drained from Yoysef's face.

"Remember," said Lippa helpfully, "when Zissel Gurevitch disappeared ten, twelve years ago? Later they found her body in the ravine outside of town."

The rabbi intervened. "Those were different times, Lippa, not the same at all."

"But what shall I do, Rabbi? Where shall I look?"

"Ask God's help, Yoysef, and wait until morning. No doubt she will come home."

*W*hen Malkeh awoke again, the room was light, and a large woman was setting down a tray on the table beside the sofa. Malkeh sat up, clutching the soft quilt to her body, her eyes round with awe at the appearance of this comfortable apparition.

Her voice squeaked. "*Zdrahstvoyteh!* Please, your honor, will you tell me—"

"*Nyet, malenkaya*, first you will have tea and food, and then you will ask questions."

The plump angel gave Malkeh a thin glass in a filigreed holder. The tea was hot and fragrant and a thin slice of lemon floated on top.

After a few swallows Malkeh tried again. "Why do you speak Russian in heaven?" she asked timidly.

The creature in the starched dress and apron threw back her head and laughed. "You are at Count Voronov's, child! I guess a village girl might think it heaven!"

"Oh," Malkeh said. Then after a while, thoughtfully, "I didn't think it could be heaven because there everyone would talk Hebrew like in the Holy Books."

The woman laughed so hard that her fat jowls shook. *"Ach da!"* she said finally, wiping her eyes on her apron. "You are *Ivrai*—Jew? Ha, ha, ha!" She began laughing again. "And is this what your heaven is like? You might well have reached it last night if the master had not found you on the road and brought you home."

She buttered a slice of fine white bread and spread it thickly with creamy white cheese before pushing it toward Malkeh.

Malkeh realized she was very hungry. The woman seemed to know it too, for she continued buttering slices of the good bread and refilling the glass with sugared tea.

While Malkeh ate, the woman told her that her name was Maria Feodorovna and that she was the count's housekeeper. The master had found Malkeh lying in a dead faint in the middle of the roadway, looking for all the world like a drowned cat. She might well have taken a fatal chill if she had been left to lie there in the cold rain. What was she doing in that remote place in the midst of a storm anyway?

Malkeh, embarrassed, said only that in traveling to Polotsk she had lost her way.

"But how did you hurt yourself?"

"An accident," Malkeh mumbled. "I twisted my ankle and must have fainted from the pain."

Maria Feodorovna shook her head in sympathy but asked no further questions, turning her attention instead to satisfying the girl's voracious appetite.

"But where are my clothes?" Malkeh asked when finally she pushed the plate from her. "I must go home! They'll be so worried about me!"

Maria Feodorovna assured her that the dress was in the kitchen, clean and pressed and with the rents mended as well as could be. She was afraid that the dress was quite ruined despite all their efforts. She herself had taken the wet clothes from Malkeh's unconscious body the night before, rubbing her skin dry with towels and wrapping her in a quilt before the master carried her into this little parlor.

Maria Feodorovna pulled the curtains aside for Malkeh to see that the sun was already high in the sky, the day clear and pleasant after the storm.

"But why should you—and the count—be so good to me? Why did he save me last night?"

"And what should he have done, left you lying in the road in the rain?" Maria Feodorovna asked, indignation making her voice loud. "You Hebrews! You think the rest of the world are devils." She put her arm around Malkeh to help her rise. "Since he didn't know who you were, there was nothing to be done but to bring you here and put you to bed on the couch. Now come. Wrap yourself in the quilt, and I'll show you where to wash and use the toilet. And then you shall have your clothes."

*A*t dawn, a haggard Yoysef presented himself to the duty officer at the police bureau. All night he had roamed the streets of Polotsk, peering into dark alleyways and staring up at the houses, stopping only where taverns were still open to ask if anyone had seen a small, fair woman who appeared to be lost.

"Please, sir, my wife did not come home yesterday. A small woman with white skin? I wondered if anyone like that had turned up here?"

The bored policeman yawned. It was almost the end of his shift. "We have had no reports of finding any lost persons."

"I see," Yoysef said. His shoulders sagged under the double burdens of fatigue and hopelessness.

"Do you want to leave your name?"

Yoysef shook his head. He could see there was no help for him here.

A few minutes later the duty officer's relief arrived. "Some crazy Jew in here just now misplaced his wife."

The second man winked. "You know how those Yids are, always sitting in church singing and praying. She probably went to the market for some good Russian sausage!"

The duty officer laughed.

*M*aria Feodorovna was right. The dress was utterly ruined, though someone had tried to sew up the worst of the tears. Malkeh was dismayed. It was the only everyday dress that she owned, and how could Yoysef afford to replace it? The family would be very angry with her. Not only had she worried and shamed them by running away, but she had ruined her dress and shoes besides! What would Yoysef say when he came home and heard the whole sorry story? She was sure it would be the first thing that Mammeh Frumma told him, even before she had a chance to present her side. If Malkeh had thought that living in that house had been uncomfortable before, this last incident would make it impossible!

When she was dressed in clothes still warm from the iron and had covered her head with a scarf borrowed from the housekeeper, Malkeh said her thanks nicely and prepared to undertake the long walk back to the city.

"Wait, little one," Maria Feodorovna said. "You can go home in the cart with Grisha, who is going to the sawmill in Polotsk today. But first the master would like to see you in his office."

Malkeh had hoped to escape the house without encountering the count. A mere village girl from Dagda, how would she talk to a lordship! Yet with the housekeeper already pushing her toward the door, she had no choice.

A broad-shouldered man, thick in build, was sitting at a desk entering numbers in a large book. He was younger than Malkeh had thought he would be, his hair and beard a rich chestnut color unstreaked by gray.

"*Gospodin*, my lord," Malkeh murmured tentatively from the doorway, bobbing her head to show respect.

The man looked up. "Ah, you have recovered this morning." The statement was partly question.

"Yes, sir," Malkeh said. "I thank you for saving my life."

He had clear light eyes, the color of Baltic amber. They narrowed a little. "Did I do that? And what exactly did I save you from?"

Malkeh was flustered by his cool, amused tone. She should have remained silent, but she felt compelled by the ironic gaze to explain herself. "Why, I was lost in the forest and couldn't find my way out, and then the dybbuk came for me, and I fell and hurt myself, and—if it hadn't been for your lordship, I would be gone now!"

"The what? What do you say was after you?"

"A dybbuk," she said. Did he not understand anything? "A ghost—a demon—a spirit that has lost its soul." Groping for explanatory words, she found that once more the enormity of last night's peril threatened to overcome her. In a paroxysm of gratitude, she moved toward the count, kneeling at his side and reaching for his hand to kiss.

Abruptly he withdrew his hand from hers, frowning.

Malkeh scrambled to her feet, fearing that she had committed an unpardonable indiscretion. She had meant it only as a courtesy, but perhaps it was forbidden for common folks to touch nobility? She flushed.

"You are babbling! Am I to understand that somehow you were trespassing in my woods and lost your way in last night's storm?"

Malkeh inclined her head.

"And you think a devil or something was chasing you?"

Malkeh nodded with certainty. "I know it was."

The man said flatly, "It was I in the forest, no spirit—whatever you called it! I was looking for one of the dogs that broke its chain when the thunder started. A good thing I went after him too! He'd cornered a boar. The count sets great store by his dogs," he added.

"But—but aren't you Count Voronov?" Malkeh asked in bewilderment.

"No." The man gave a somewhat sour smile. "I am his steward. My name is Fedotov, Yevgeny Sergeivitch Fedotov. The count is in Moscow for the season. I am manager of the estate."

"But the woman called you the master!" Malkeh stopped herself from saying more, afraid that she was being forward.

"Yes, I suppose she did." He did not smile. He did not explain. "Tell me your name and where you live, and I will arrange for you to be taken home by one of the servants."

"It is all right, *Gospodin*. I have been trouble enough, I think. I will walk."

"Don't argue! You have badly sprained your ankle and who knows what else you've hurt." The steward shook his head wearily. Dealing with these ignorant people exhausted him.

Malkeh said reluctantly, "My name is Malkeh. My husband is Yoysef Mandelkern, the tailor."

The man nodded curtly. "I know him."

Malkeh backed toward the door.

"A moment," the man said in a voice used to obedience. He rose and came from behind his desk. Gripping Malkeh by the shoulder, he was surprised to feel the fineness of her bones.

A shock had passed through Malkeh's body at Fedotov's touch. It was forbidden for a man other than her husband to put his hands on a Jewish woman. She felt defiled and excited at the same time. Involuntarily her breath had quickened and her eyes had taken on depth and a kind of brightness.

The steward was inexplicably stirred by her frailty. It was not fair to be angry with the girl, he thought. She was untutored. His voice was kind. "You were very strong and brave last night, considering that you believe in evil spirits." He held her so that she was forced to meet the steady gaze of his strange, transparent eyes. "But you see, there are no—dybbuks?—after all, and the noise you heard in the forest was only my horse and the dogs." His tone brooked no dissent. "There are no devils, no spirits." He dropped his hands and moved away from her. "I think there is not even God," he added.

Malkeh paled with alarm and instinctively raised her hands to cover her ears against blasphemy.

He laughed at her gesture. "Afraid I'll be stricken dead?"

Not daring to respond, Malkeh looked at the floor. Yoysef had warned her that it was necessary, insofar as possible, to be Russian in the world of Russians. Maybe this was the way Russians talked of the Holy One?

"The only certainty," the steward continued, "is in nature itself. In nature we can see and touch and smell the things of this earth. In nature there are laws that govern every living thing—"

"Laws made by God," Malkeh said bravely.

The count's manager, surprised at the contradiction, studied her narrowly for a moment. Finally he said, "Perhaps. I am not going to discuss God with a village girl! I am only trying to make a point about what happened last night so that you won't be so foolish another time."

Malkeh smarted under the reprimand. She longed to tell him that she might be a village girl, as he said, but wisdom wasn't confined to palaces, and God resided in humble people as well as in princes! Thinking of retorts she would like to make, she almost choked on her silence.

Yevgeny Sergeivitch was both annoyed and entertained. This skinny child in her torn dress was like the kitten he'd rescued once from a well, uncertainly swaying between desperate gratitude and hissing defiance. Look now at how she stood before him, teeth clenched, hands clasped tightly, her body stiff and wary as though afraid he might lift his hand to her! With the kitten it had taken long minutes of gentling with his hand stroking its fur before the tension left its body and it had relaxed its guard. What would it take to soothe this girl—and why should he want to try?

"Look," the steward explained, "if you could put your silly superstitious fears from you, you would find the world a safer place to live in. Take last night, for instance. It would have been sensible for you to have taken shelter from the storm and stayed put until daylight. As it was, you scratched yourself in the brambles, and you were so terrified when you heard my horse that you could have broken your neck running in the dark!"

Malkeh said stubbornly, "I know there was something evil in the forest. I felt it all around me."

"You were afraid of the dark," Fedotov said irritably. "Some primitive instinct makes even reasonable people uneasy when they're alone in the night. Do you know why the earth becomes dark?"

"Because God makes the sun go down," Malkeh said, indignant that he treated her like a child.

The steward laughed aloud. "And where does the sun go when, as you say, it goes 'down'?"

Malkeh stammered, "Well, I—somewhere in the west—it falls in the sea—"

"And comes up dripping the next morning? Listen, village girl, I'll give you a lesson to take home with you. The sun does not sink into the sea. It doesn't go anywhere. It is the earth that moves, revolving around the sun. The darkness is caused by the spinning of the earth as it follows its course around the sun. When our side of the planet is turned toward the sun, it is light, but when it is away from the sun, we say it is night."

Malkeh absorbed this, her nose wrinkling as she weighed the astonishing revelation. The sun constant and the earth moving around it! How could that be? Everyone knew the earth was unmovable and with his own eyes could see the sun sinking in the west!

Yevgeny Sergeivitch's tone was patient. "The falling of night and a summer storm, though they happen regularly, filled you with such fear that you conjured up devils. And because your terror was so unreasoning, you were running *away* from help and headlong into a danger of your own making! In the light of day, you must see how foolish that was!"

Unconvinced, Malkeh shook her head. *He* had not been there to sense what she had sensed and to feel what she had felt. There were things beyond what logic could fathom. "There were unclean spirits in the forest last night. I prayed to God and He had pity on me and sent you to rescue me."

The steward turned from Malkeh, and his voice, when he finally spoke, was angry. "Oh, the ignorance and stupidity of peasants! You will destroy Mother Russia with your superstitions."

Malkeh, stung, cried, "I am not a peasant, and I am not ignorant! And I am not Russian," she added.

The steward's eyes glinted with a certain sardonic amusement, but the full lips curled with sarcasm. "Ah, that's right," he purred, "you are one of the 'Chosen People,' are you not—different and, yes, better than us Russians?"

Malkeh was afraid now. She had blundered onto a ground more dangerous than the forest pathway of the night before. "I only meant, your honor, that I can read and write," she quavered. She edged toward the door. "I thank you for taking me into your house, *Gospodin*, but I need not trouble you any longer."

Behind her, Malkeh heard the steward snort, and his cold voice stabbed into her. "Your holy men—and ours too—tell fairy tales, but they will not be able to hold back forever the new ideas and the new ways that are coming to this land!"

Malkeh stared at him. Suddenly tired, his eyes fell away from hers, and he slumped back in his chair. "Do not deprive yourself of a little comfort because you don't like what I say. I will send you home in the cart as I promised. It is a long walk, and you are in no condition for it. Grisha will be ready with his load in a while. Sit down in that corner, village girl. Wait a little."

"Spaseba," Malkeh murmured, "but I'll wait in the kitchen."

"You'll be in the way there."

Meekly, Malkeh sat where he had indicated. The steward returned to his books. He worked for some time, not looking up from his ledger, having apparently dismissed her from his thoughts. Malkeh had plenty of time to study him, his concentration, the economy of his movements, the absent way he had of combing through his beard with his fingers. This was a man, she thought, without soft edges, a solitary man used to turning in upon himself. She resented his arrogance. She could read from Papa's books as well as any man! True, her reading had been limited to women's novels and Papa's collection of holy writings. Perhaps there were things written down in other books about where the sun went at night. She would ask Yoysef.

There was a knock at the door at the same moment that Maria Feodorovna pushed it open. *"Gospodin,"* she said, "there is a Jew from Polotsk at the gate. He wants the use of our dogs to look for"—she glanced at Malkeh—"his lost wife."

Chapter 5

 *M*alkeh's anxiety about her reception at home proved to be unfounded. Mammeh Frumma had little to say about her running away, and by tacit agreement the torn book was never again mentioned by either of them. The rest of the family was content to go along with the story that Malkeh had lost her way on leaving the *gostinny dvor* the day of the storm, although Yenta made an opportunity to assure Malkeh that if ever she was troubled, she should come to her; Mammeh, she said feelingly, could be very difficult. Golda had merely squeezed Malkeh's hand and stayed close at her side. Papa Avrom treated Malkeh with self-conscious consideration for a day or two, and then the happening faded from his mind. If Yoysef pursued the matter further with his mother, neither said anything about it. With Malkeh he was tender, cupping her face between his hands and swearing to her that the ties between them were the strongest in his life.

 Malkeh was able to mend her dress fairly well, although the skirt required several patches made from scraps in Yoysef's pack. The multicolored squares gave the dress a Gypsy flair, not unpleasing in effect, though Mammeh Frumma said that she could not permit Malkeh to leave the house wearing rags. Finally, Malkeh and Mammeh compromised by covering the dress with Mammeh Frumma's commodious aprons. Yoysef whispered in Malkeh's ear that she would have a new dress for *yontef*, the coming new year holiday, and even promised that it could be blue instead of the usual brown or gray.

 Like the dress itself, Malkeh's world gradually resumed a semblance of wholeness, at least when viewed from a distance. There were places where the fabric of her life had come apart beneath the appearance of normalcy. Her unquestioning trust in the goodness of others had faltered. She had become silent and unsmiling, and no longer begged to go to market. The experience in the forest had marked her as well. There were moments when she had spells of faintness or started at sudden noises, looking behind her in case the dybbuk she had cheated in the forest had come to claim her after all. The night spent in the Voronov manor house and the exchange with the estate manager receded from her mind, taking on the quality of a dream she'd had once.

 In time, a new excitement came into Malkeh's life and pushed the bad memories aside. Yoysef announced that he would soon be leaving on his *erev yontef* journey and planned to take Malkeh with him. Mammeh Frumma protested that it was not fitting for a young woman to be on the road, but her heart was clearly not in the argument, and Malkeh sensed her relief at the prospect of having her daughter-in-law out of the house. Perhaps time and distance would help heal the rift between them. After Mammeh extracted a promise from Yoysef that they would seek shelter each night in a Jewish household, her objections ceased.

For the week before they left, Malkeh was so exhilarated that she performed her household duties with the old joyful enthusiasm. She had not forgotten her bargain with God in the forest and she tried to please her mother-in-law, rising from the warm nest of her bed to perform the morning chores before Mammeh Frumma could remind her. If Mammeh noticed her diligence, she did not comment.

All would have been perfect if only Yoysef's planned route would take them to Dagda so that Malkeh could see her parents. But Yoysef had a commitment to make a suit of clothes for the shoemaker in Disna, in the opposite direction. Still, the anticipation of traveling to new places at Yoysef's side compensated for much. Malkeh prepared carefully for the journey, assembling their meager clothing and making ready the supply of cheese, dried herrings, and apples they would eat along the way. With Yoysef's concurrence, she expended some of their precious store of coins to replace her ruined shoes.

There was one thing more that Malkeh needed to do before the day of departure. Making sure that the weather promised to be bright with sunshine, Malkeh set off to walk to the estate of Count Voronov. She had anxiously memorized Yoysef's directions and knew that if she walked briskly, she could make the trip in under two hours. She carried a basket of eggs over her arm as a gift, Maria Feodorovna's laundered scarf covering them. On the way she stopped in a meadow to pick a pretty bouquet of late summer flowers, wild ginger and arnica, bluebells and cowslips. Briefly she considered whether she should also gather mushrooms from under the oak trees in the woods. But the memory of what had happened in that place was too potent and only served to quicken her pace toward Spokoinaya Zemlya.

When Malkeh arrived at the house, the count's dogs set up a clamor that almost drove her back into the road. The gateman remembered her from before, though, and restrained the animals, swinging open the gates for her to enter and pointing the way to the kitchen.

Malkeh felt ill at ease in the doorway of the huge bustling kitchen. Maria Feodorovna was supervising the preparation of plum preserves, the perspiration forming fat beads on her red face as she stood like a general before the tall double-tiered stove, skillfully placing birchwood in the firebox to ensure even heating under the pots, and simultaneously supervising the cooking. She stirred a bubbling caldron of fruit here, tasted a spoonful there, and shouted at the poor kitchen maid that she would earn a beating if the jam scorched. She did not see the visitor at first, and Malkeh stood uncertainly, looking around her.

The stove, tiled on the exterior and lined with earthen bricks, was by far the largest Malkeh had ever seen, and occupied the greater part of the room. It could accommodate numerous large pots on the grate of the *plita*, and had room in the oven to roast a whole sheep or to bake as many as ten loaves of bread at a time. In the coldest part of winter, the oven had the capacity to heat an entire wing of the house and sleep several people comfortably on its broad platform, although perhaps in a great house like this, the servants had beds elsewhere. Despite its size, the room was cozy with bright curtains and homely pieces of furniture. Along one wall stood a sturdy pine cupboard for dishes and utensils. The housekeeper's cushioned rocker was next to a small table holding a fat oil lamp, a shiny brass samovar, and Maria Feodorovna's rosary beads and missal. A deal worktable, on which there were now bowls of prepared fruit and jars of various sizes, occupied the center of the room. Several sturdy wooden chairs stood near it, although it hardly seemed likely that a taskmistress like Maria Feodorovna would allow her helpers to sit. To the right of the oven was the storeroom door through which Malkeh could just see shelves for jars and some casks and crocks on the floor. To the left was a door leading to the estate office where Malkeh had had the uncomfortable interview with the steward.

Malkeh wondered if she should not have come without permission, but Maria Feodorovna, noticing her at last, did not seem displeased to see her. Wiping her face with a corner of her apron, the housekeeper dropped thankfully into a chair, motioning for Malkeh to sit down beside her.

Maria Feodorovna made much over the gifts of wildflowers and the duck eggs, selected by Malkeh that very morning for their size and perfect shape. She coaxed Malkeh to stay awhile when, protesting that she did not want to interfere with the work, she would have left. Scarcely interrupting the cadence of her ferocious directives to the intimidated kitchen helper, Maria Feodorovna poured Malkeh a frothy glass of milk and broke off a large chunk of white bread, fine as cake, which she spread with hot sweet fruit from one of the copper kettles.

"Eat, *malenkaya*," she ordered. "You are far too thin. No man wants to bruise himself in bed on sharp bones!"

Malkeh thought she had never tasted anything more delicious. Her morning meal of tea and black bread had been very early, and the way from Polotsk was long.

Maria Feodorovna asked Malkeh questions about how things were in the city, listening with interest to the replies, disappointed only that Malkeh had so little gossip to share. In turn, she told Malkeh about the estate harvest and the many chores a housekeeper needed to supervise at this time of year—

the preserving of fruits for the winter, laying away root vegetables in the deep cool cellars, drying herbs. There were also preparations for the home-coming of Count Voronov from Moscow and of his son, young Captain Andrei Petrovitch, who would be bringing friends from St. Petersburg for the fall hunting.

Before Malkeh knew it, the sun was throwing long shadows, and she realized that in the comfort of a beginning intimacy with the older woman, she had overstayed her time. She rose hurriedly.

"I must go before it gets dark and I lose my way again."

"It has been *otchen priatno*," Maria Feodorovna said, "most pleasant."

"May I come again? After my journey perhaps."

"I would like that."

It had been a pleasing visit for Maria Feodorovna also, for, surrounded as she was either by lesser servants or by masters, she was often bored and lonely for someone from outside the household to talk to. On the night when Yevgeny Sergeivitch had come from the fury of the storm carrying the unconscious girl in his arms, a kind of excitement had been born in Maria Feodorovna, a feeling that only increased when she had examined the victim. Young she was, and her body was white and fine-boned. And like the Swan Queen of the ancient folktale, she had been found by Master Fe-dotov in most romantic circumstances, lying in a swoon in a forest the peasants thought enchanted.

The housekeeper had sent the steward away and stripped off the girl's wet and filthy clothes, gently bathing her wounds and dressing them with herbal ointments of her own making. Only the ankle was really bad—prob-ably not broken, thank the good God!—and that she had wrapped with firm strips torn from a linen towel. Once while Maria Feodorovna worked over her, the girl had started up, her eyes wild with fear, before she lapsed once more into unconsciousness. Poor child! Something had frightened her greatly to send her into a deep faint! The girl's vulnerability moved the older woman profoundly. Perhaps, she thought, a mother feels like this for a helpless child. Afterward she had helped the master settle the girl in a bed she had made up in the small family parlor, close enough to the kitchen for the house-keeper to observe the patient's progress through the night.

Now recalling their conversation of the next morning, Maria Feodo-rovna laughed quietly to herself. The girl had awakened, remembering nothing of being brought to Spokoinya Zemlya and thinking she had died and gone to the Hebrew heaven! The housekeeper had never before known one of the Hebrew people to converse with. She had long been curious about them, though, for had not the Lord Jesus Christ Himself been a Jew? Pro-foundly religious in her own way, she did not share the contempt in which her world held this peculiar people. Often and again, scolding the servants for their coarse taunts, she had quoted Matthew: "Inasmuch as ye have done it unto one of the least of these, my brethren, ye have done it unto me." A lot of good it did! As soon as her back was turned, they were at their Jew-baiting once more.

It was good that Malkeh Mandelkern had come today to say thank you. It was only proper and showed she had been well brought up.

Later Maria Feodorovna was to tell Master Fedotov of the visit, chuckling over Malkeh's innocent gift of eggs—the count's estate included large pens of chickens, ducks, geese, pheasants, and quail. Yevgeny Sergeivitch did not seem especially interested in her account. Maria Feodorovna hoped that Malkeh would come again as she had promised. She kept the little bouquet of flowers in a glass on the worktable until it faded.

It was the custom for itinerant craftsmen and peddlers to travel from one village to another, selling goods and services not available outside the cities. Visits by the tailor were very welcome in the shtetls. Yoysef not only provided a needed service but also could be prevailed upon to carry messages, letters, and packages from one place to another. Once he had led a cow for twenty versts between Usyaty and Zapadnaya Dvina to deliver her to a new owner. Another time it was a couple of squawking chickens, a present from some parents to their daughter who had just given birth half a day's walk away. It was not unusual for him to deliver cakes, jars of chicken fat, and fresh vegetables. Since Yoysef was so good-natured and accommodating, he was a popular visitor. Always there was a roof to shelter him, an evening meal to share, and a place to sleep on the broad shelf of a warm oven.

Yoysef thought that this, his busiest trip of the year, was not the most opportune time to take Malkeh with him, and yet he was reluctant to leave her at home with Mammeh when there was such an obvious strain between them. Still, he worried that Malkeh would be bored while he worked, and he wondered if she would be able to keep up the brisk pace that was necessary if he were to keep his commitments along the way. There was no time to loiter if they were to return home before Rosh Hashanah.

Yoysef might have had reservations, but it was with the lightest of hearts that Malkeh rose from their early morning meal on the appointed day to receive, with Yoysef, Avrom's blessing and Mammeh Frumma's final instructions. It was barely dawn when they left, Yoysef pushing a laden handcart before him. He had spent some of their cache of money for the little peddler's wagon. It permitted him to carry more goods than usual, rolls of fine cloth for caftans, bolts of heavy serges and gabardines for everyday trousers, silks and sateens for linings and dresses.

As the sun rose, sending shafts of pink and purple light across the heavens, Yoysef's spirits rose with it. The fragrance of dew-drenched fields drew him as always, and he took pleasure in the awakening villages, the sunflowers already turning their faces to the sun, and the women in flowered scarves and men in tunics and boots walking to their day's work on the land.

With Malkeh beside him, there was a special piquancy to everything. He wanted her to be part of every corner of his life. He wanted to take care of her. Her running away had shaken him more than he liked to admit. She had seemed quieter since that time and had a peaked look that frightened him. He longed to see her pale cheeks bloom under the warm sun. Already the excitement had brought a flush to her thin fair skin.

Horse-drawn wagons driven by peasants soon began to pass them on the road. Greetings were exchanged. "*Zdrahstvoyteh*, Jew. Where go you?"

"To the west."

"May God walk by your side."

"And may He smile on you also."

Men and women working in the fields waved or came to the side of the road to break the monotony of their work by exchanging news with the traveling strangers.

"A warm autumn, *nyet*?"

"But is the sunshine not good for growing your crop?"

"Yes, if we can gather it in before the storms. What are they getting for flour in the Vitebsk market these days?"

"I don't know, but in Polotsk flour is dear, a ruble a sack."

"Ah, well, the miller gets the cream and we get the leftover skim milk!"

"You don't trust the miller?"

"Ha! 'From honest toil, you don't build mansions.' "

"God willing, both you and the miller will make a living."

"If the miller's a good Russian! A safe journey, travelers!"

"And a good harvest to you."

Malkeh struggled to keep up with Yoysef. Despite his resolve to the contrary, Yoysef found himself shortening his stride and looking for a clump of trees near the roadside where they might stop for a midmorning rest. Yoysef himself could walk a whole day from sunup to sundown without slackening his pace, but he was acutely aware of the circles of fatigue already showing under Malkeh's eyes.

After a meager meal, Yoysef leaned his back against a tree trunk, stretching long legs before him, his cap pulled over his eyes against the sun. Malkeh searched in her pack and drew out a slim book.

"Shall I read to you while you rest, Yoysef?"

Yoysef nodded without opening his eyes.

Along with so much else, Malkeh had brought books into her husband's life. In the evenings she had begun reading aloud to him from the stories and poems that she liked best. Soon Yoysef asked her to read from a tattered history that he had found once lying in the road. Until he found the book, he had been largely ignorant of his country's troubled past, its bloody history of assassinations, uprisings, and peasant revolts that time and again had been brutally put down. How did those poor devils dare continue to challenge the power of landlord and tsar, Yoysef wondered. He had seen much that disturbed him on his journeys through the land, had felt the dark restlessness of the people and knew it would take little to fan it into cataclysmic conflagration. Pray God, it would not happen in his time.

Malkeh looked up from the book of Yiddish poems she was reading. "Yosseleh, are you listening?"

"I love the sound of your voice, and the way your face shines when you are happy."

"Oh, Yoysef," Malkeh said, "will we always be as happy as we are now?"

"Why do you question it?"

Malkeh put down the book and moved into the circle of Yoysef's arm. "Since the time I was lost in the woods I have been afraid that for every joy God sends, He eventually asks payment," she said bleakly.

Yoysef kissed the top of her head. "Malkeh, Malkeh, what foolishness you talk! Why would God make such a bad bargain with us? To pay back happiness with pain? It makes no sense!"

Malkeh sighed. "It sounds foolish, I know, but—"

Yoysef held Malkeh away from him so that he could look into her face. "You have not been yourself lately. What troubles you?"

"I don't know. Something comes over me all of a sudden, a coldness, here—" She pointed to her breast. "Maybe I think that I don't deserve to be so happy." Malkeh held tightly to Yoysef. "In the forest when I thought the dybbuk had come for me, I prayed, but didn't know why God would want to help such a sinful creature."

"Sinful!" Yoysef snorted. "You are an innocent!"

"I have had sinful thoughts, Yoysef. And I have been unkind and thoughtless."

"God forgives," he said, stroking her hair and smiling.

Malkeh was not to be comforted. "And I worry that someone seeing us so happy together will turn an evil eye upon us."

Yoysef laughed aloud then. "Oh, Malkeh, my little fool! You sound like an old shtetl grandmother!" He rose to his feet and pulled her up beside him. "I'll tell you what. We will quarrel and go about with sour looks so that all the world will feel sorry for Yoysef the Tailor and his miserable bride. And then no one will be envious and put a spell upon us!"

Malkeh smiled faintly. Yoysef pinched her cheek and with a chuckle picked up the shafts of the cart. "Come, my shrewish one. We will turn our unhappy footsteps toward Disna, where I have promised Zelig the Shoemaker a new coat for the holidays. Now, did I ever tell you about Zelig and the wrestling contest? It was a year past his bar mitzvah when—"

Yoysef's voice kept time with the footsteps they turned toward the west, and soon Malkeh had little room in her head for any thought but how her feet were aching in the new shoes.

*T*hey arrived in Disna in the late afternoon of the second day and were greeted warmly by the stocky young cobbler and his pretty wife and children. Zelig and Eshka were so amiable that Malkeh hardly felt shy at all.

As soon as they had tea to refresh themselves, Yoysef set to work measuring Zelig for his new coat, and before the evening meal was ready, he had cut the goods and was already pinning and basting.

They stayed with the cobbler's family for three days while Yoysef fitted and sewed and Malkeh visited with the wife and helped around the house. On the second day Malkeh timidly asked Yoysef whether it would not speed his work if she did some of the finishing by hand while he worked the sewing machine?

"You know how?" Yoysef asked, surprised.

"My mother did some sewing in the village—"

Ah, yes, Yoysef remembered now; it was said that Mendel's wife had had to turn her hand to many jobs to keep food on the table.

"Well," Yoysef said doubtfully, "you may try, but tailoring must be perfect or the suit won't fit."

Malkeh nodded and picked up Zelig's coat. The silk lining had already been cut and basted into place by Yoysef. Malkeh expertly threaded a needle with black thread, borrowed a thimble from Eshka, and began to stitch. Yoysef, seaming the trousers, lifted his eyes from the machine from time to time, watching Malkeh. After a while his shoulders relaxed, and smiling, he turned his full attention to his work. She could sew! Yet another surprising miracle about his beloved. Thank you, Lord!

Although Yoysef's masterpiece was the fine long coat with the velvet collar that he made for the cobbler, there was other work for him in Disna as well. He made a new suit of clothes for a bar mitzvah, repaired a split in the rabbi's coat, and altered clothing that had become too large or too small or had been handed down from one child to another.

Early on the fourth morning, Yoysef and Malkeh turned to the north, their destination Verkhnedvinsk. Zelig paid Yoysef in gold coins, having repaired Yoysef's boots besides. When the travelers went forth, it was with packets of food from the cobbler's wife and promises to keep in touch through letters and messages.

Before Verkhnedvinsk they made a detour to tiny Braslav. For years

Yoysef had visited Braslav before every Rosh Hashanah holiday to pay his respects to his grandfather's old friend, Menachem. Every year Yoysef was afraid that he would no longer find Reb Menachem alive, for, by anyone's standards, he was ancient.

As they reached the small house, Yoysef could not help but notice that the thatch on the roof was thin and ragged. When winter came in a month or two, the wind would find its way through the thatch, and the weight of snow would complete the disaster.

The old man shuffled out the front door. "Hah, Yoysef! I've been expecting you every day!"

"God be with you, Reb Menachem! How goes it with you?"

"How should it go for an old man? Thank God, I still have wheat to eat and teeth to eat it with! Come in, come in! This is your wife, then? I had heard you were married. You will share a meal with me."

"Many thanks."

They entered the dark house that was little more than a one-room hut, ruder even than many a peasant's *izba*. The old man was too frail to be living alone, but what was there to do? He had buried a wife and two sons, and the surviving third son had gone to America, never to be heard from again.

As they ate their meal, a few radishes from Reb Menachem's larder and the food that Eshka had sent with Yoysef and Malkeh, Yoysef was even more conscious of the poor state of the roof through which they could already see the sky.

"Now then, have you some work for me?" Yoysef asked while Malkeh was clearing away the remnants of their meal.

"Just a tear in my sleeve," the old man said, taking off his coat to show Yoysef.

"Yes, I see. The seam has come open. My wife, Malkeh," he said proudly, "is a fine seamstress. She will repair your coat while I fix your roof."

"But I can't ask you to do that, Yoysef!"

"You didn't ask me."

"I cannot pay you."

"I charge for sewing, not for roofs."

Malkeh made short work of the coat. Since Yoysef was still working atop the house, Malkeh set about cleaning and straightening Reb Menachem's one room; it did not take long. Then she went outside to sit under the oak tree. The old man was standing on the ground below Yoysef, vigorously directing the work. Yoysef took it in good stead. It was late before the work was finished.

Accepting ten kopecks from the old man for the coat, Yoysef and Malkeh continued on their way toward Verkhnedvinsk.

"If there are many days like that, you won't make what you expect from this trip, Yoysef," Malkeh commented.

"Oh well, God commands that we help each other."

Every stopping place was a little like and a little different from Disna and Braslav. The families they stayed with were hospitable and welcoming; the children universally searched Yoysef's pockets for sweets, and men and women alike were avid for news. There was much work for Yoysef, and Malkeh was a help, her stitches small, even, and fine. Scores of old friends dwelt along their route, and, apart from his tailoring, Yoysef did not hesitate to lend a strong arm when someone needed a ditch dug, a wall raised, a well cleaned. On the twelfth day of their journey, Yoysef and Malkeh were still some distance from their final goal, Dvinsk, and they knew that they must turn back to Polotsk if they were to arrive in time for the New Year.

The homeward journey went much faster. One day, too late to reach the next village before dark, Malkeh and Yoysef stayed with a Russian farm family. That night they spread their blankets in the fresh hay of the loft and fell asleep in each other's arms amid the warm animal smells and soft stirrings in the barn. Early in the morning they made love tenderly and with great sweetness, although Yoysef reflected that the Torah forbids a man and his wife to lie together in the presence of any other living thing.

"I don't believe you," Malkeh said. "You made that up."

"No, really."

Malkeh nuzzled his neck with warm lips, retorting, "Well, anyhow, we're hidden in the hay, and besides, horses and cows don't tell secrets!"

The trip was good for Malkeh. During the course of days spent in the sun and fresh air, her liveliness and the bloom of health returned. She and Yoysef had grown closer for the sharing of work and long days together. The weather was fine and crisp, and Malkeh was able now to walk farther without stopping to rest; of course, it helped that Zelig, the burly cobbler, had eased the leather in her new shoes. As they walked, they talked. Malkeh told her husband about her life as a girl in Dagda, about Papa, who had made their poor house a haven of warmth and love, and about Mammeh, who gave their days order. In turn, Yoysef told Malkeh what it was like growing up in Polotsk, swimming in the river with his friends, his bar mitzvah, about his *zeydeh*, the grandfather who had lived with them and taught Yoysef to carve wooden animals from chunks of firewood. And each day while they ate their midday meal, Malkeh read aloud to Yoysef in her clear, sweet voice.

The family at home was glad to see the travelers when finally, almost three weeks gone, they returned with time to spare before Rosh Hashanah. Mammeh Frumma even breached her usual habit of maintaining a cool distance and treated Malkeh to an unaccustomed solicitude. "You must be tired, Malkeh. Lie down and rest yourself."

They had reached Polotsk on the afternoon of *shabbes*, the Sabbath.

Golda and Yenta, with their husbands and the children, came to welcome them home. Although it was not a holiday, the whole family was together around the gleaming white-clothed table. Mammeh ladled up golden chicken soup, gefilte fish wrapped in its own silvery skin, and chicken that had simmered all afternoon on a bed of onions and paprika. A beautiful braided *challah* and a cake bursting with apples and almonds rested on the table. The *shabbes* candles threw a soft light over the table, and the kiddush wine was a rich dark red in its cup.

Yoysef told the family the news of distant villages where there were friends. Malkeh joined in, chattering almost as freely as she would have done at home in Dagda. Yenta was clearly envious of Malkeh's travels, and Golda hugged her and told her how much she had been missed. Yenta's Yaynkel asked about the price of beef in Disna and other towns and complained that the best and fattest beef cattle were to be had only farther to the west. Before Yaynkel could begin to brood about the unfairness of it all, Dovid, Golda's husband, began in his sweet tenor to sing *zmiros*, to mark the end of the meal.

By the time the table was cleared, Yenta's children were asleep and the adults were beginning to yawn. The talk faltered, and the Sabbath candles guttered in their holders. They hated to leave each other, but it was time to say good night.

After the others had gone, Yoysef and his father went outside to see that the animals and chickens were secured for the night. Malkeh and Mammeh Frumma were alone in the kitchen, finishing the final chores before bedtime.

"Malkeh," said Mammeh Frumma slowly, "you feel well?"

"Oh, yes," Malkeh answered, puzzled. "It was a fine trip, although I am a little tired, I think."

There was a brief silence, and Malkeh asked in alarm, "Is something wrong?"

"Wrong? No, I don't think so," Mammeh said. "It's only that Auntie Lifsa was here the other day, and she said something that made me think."

"Oh? What was that?"

"She said," Mammeh said, voice low and eyes on Malkeh's face, "that while you and Yoysef have been married now for over three months, you have not been to the *mikva* even once."

Quietly she added, "She congratulated me on being so soon a grandmother."

Chapter 6

alkeh looked upon her pregnancy as something outside herself, a curiosity in which her involvement was minimal. She had dreamed of giving Yoysef many sons. Someday. In her fantasy they were grave-faced, bearded rabbis and scholars, a line that stretched unbroken far into the future; she never envisaged them as other than grown men.

The possibility of an actual pregnancy had simply never occurred to her, and her emotions were bewildering. As a token of her oneness with Yoysef, the idea of a baby was gratifying; on the other hand, a flesh-and-blood child could not help but encroach upon the closeness that had grown between Yoysef and herself. It wasn't fair, she thought, that this had happened to her while the pleasure she and Yoysef took in each other was yet new and fresh! Could not God have waited awhile before thus blessing them?

Yoysef had no such mixed feelings. He wept with joy, unabashed, his head against Malkeh's swollen breasts, his tears dropping on her belly. He was awed and worshipful. In courtship he had discovered a romantic side to his nature; then marriage had revealed what was passionate and sensual in himself; now tenderness for the expected child completed him.

Mammeh Frumma declared Yoysef quite besotted. He whistled as he went about his work, grinning foolishly at nothing at all, and developed a passionate interest in infants. He indulged Malkeh, rising at dawn to feed the chickens and gather eggs before his own workday began. Malkeh protested only faintly while she luxuriated in having an extra hour beneath the warm quilt.

The pregnancy was scarcely visible when Yoysef began work on a cradle for the child. Mammeh Frumma shook her head and cautioned gravely that it was tempting fate to prepare for a child so far in advance. Malkeh heard her out with a little thrill of fear, but Yoysef only laughed and bent to his carving. On the head of the crib he was creating a Garden of Eden, fields of flowers and trees from among which peeped tiny animal faces.

In quiet ways the entire family showed its pleasure. Mammeh Frumma, while stating positively that pregnancy is not an illness and requires no special consideration, nevertheless nurtured Malkeh, relieving her of the heavier work and tempting her appetite with specially prepared dishes "to keep up your strength," as she said.

Golda's gladness was tempered with sadness because she herself seemed destined to remain childless. It was Yenta, an authority by now on childbearing, who was in her element as Malkeh's mentor.

A letter had been dispatched to Malkeh's parents via a passing peddler. Mammeh sent Malkeh jars of specially prepared unguents to rub on breasts and belly, and her usually terse letters were replaced with long advisories. Papa wrote that he was certain the child was a boy for whose *bris* they must prepare. Best of all, they promised to set out from Dagda as soon as word of the birth was received. Malkeh had not seen her parents since the wedding.

Despite Mammeh Frumma's forebodings about her daughter-in-law's delicacy, the pregnancy proceeded well. Malkeh's fragile appearance was deceptive. She possessed a wiry resilience and experienced few of the discomforts that afflict expectant mothers.

*I*n December Grisha brought a message from the steward, Fedotov, requesting that Yoysef come to Spokoinaya Zemlya to make repairs in the servants' livery so that they would look their best for the Christmas–New Year festivities. Ever fascinated by life at the manor house, tantalizingly glimpsed on occasional visits to Maria Feodorovna, Malkeh begged to go with Yoysef to help with the work. Yoysef teased that she was thinking more about treats from the great kitchen than about any assistance she could give him, but he was of a mind to indulge her.

One bright morning in the second week of December, Gospodin Fedotov sent a sleigh for the tailor. Yoysef and Malkeh clambered in and, wrapped snugly in fur laprobes, were borne across white fields and through stands of trees sparkling with icicles. The air was so cold and clear that the runners made a pleasant whispering on the surface of the snow, and the jingling of the harness bells rang with especial purity and joyfulness. By the time they arrived at the estate, Malkeh's nose and cheeks, where they peeked out from under her shawl, were rosy from the cold, and she was laughing aloud at the sheer pleasure of being outdoors on this perfect morning. As Yoysef helped her out of the sleigh, she thought she saw the steward watching from an upstairs window, but by the time she had freed a hand from her wrappings to wave, there was no one there.

There was only two days work for the tailor. Because of the freezing weather, Yoysef and Malkeh stayed overnight in one of the empty rooms in the servants' wing. The chamber was not so opulent as the beautiful little parlor where Malkeh had been put to bed the night of the thunderstorm, but it had a deep feather bed and was warmed deliciously by heat rising from the kitchen oven. Malkeh marveled that even the servants of Count Voronov lived like the richest of the rich!

Mammeh Frumma had packed a bundle of cold meats for Yoysef and Malkeh so that they would not be forced to eat nonkosher food at the estate house. But it was a great deal to ask of Malkeh that she forgo Maria Feodorovna's thick borschts, roasted fowls, and buttery pastries when her pregnancy had made her so constantly and ravenously hungry.

"Yoysef," she asked her husband innocently, "would it not be an insult to this house if we refused to eat their food?"

Pursing his lips and rubbing the bridge of his nose thoughtfully, Yoysef pretended to give Malkeh's question serious consideration. "The rabbis say that one should observe the laws of kashrut. On the other hand, they say that one should honor the hospitality of one's neighbor whether he be Jew or Gentile. So it is a matter of deciding which commandment takes precedence."

Malkeh wrinkled her nose, thinking this through. Finally she said, "I think we must consider the feelings of our dear friend, Maria Feodorovna."

Yoysef hugged her, laughing. "And so do I! But let's not tell Mammeh!"

In the end Malkeh fed Mammeh's boiled beef to the dogs, in itself a charitable act, as she told Yoysef, and she and he dined sumptuously at Maria Feodorovna's board.

On the second day the hospitable housekeeper found time to show Malkeh through the interior of Spokoinaya Zemlya. The house had been constructed after the style of the Alexander Palace at Tsarskoe Selo, Maria Feodorovna explained proudly, and indeed it was exquisitely graceful to the eye, the rooms large and high-ceilinged with sculpted cornices and soffits, the hardwood floors spread with carpets of rich Oriental design. So that Malkeh could appreciate the sumptuousness of the decorations, the housekeeper flung back the shutters, fastened now against the cold, and whisked dust covers off the furnishings. Maria Feodorovna was not disappointed in Malkeh's reaction. Her eyes grew enormous as one room opened to another, to another, and yet another, all equally elegant. Coming to the room where once she had spent the night, she was surprised to find it to be a family sitting room, a mere cupboard compared with the formal drawing room that occupied the whole front of the house. And still there was more. Next to the drawing room was a spacious dining room, all gold and white under sparkling crystal chandeliers, and beside that, a music room dominated by an intricately carved rosewood pianoforte. The ballroom occupied a separate wing, its mirrored walls reflecting the intricate geometric pattern of the inlaid wooden floor. One of the maidservants was performing a curious ritual there, skating back and forth across the expanse of floor, felt-wrapped bricks tied firmly to her feet. It made Malkeh laugh and clap her hands to see her antics on the slippery wood as it was buffed to a high shine.

Maria Feodorovna told Malkeh that while the countess had lived, there had been much entertaining in the house, with guests coming from as far away as Kiev for magnificent balls, splendid dinners, and, of course, the wild-boar hunts for which the region was noted. Why, even the young crown prince Nicholas had once been a guest for a fortnight!

Thinking about the glamour of the past made Maria Feodorovna sad, for it had been many years now since the ballroom had been used, and except for periodic cleaning, it was kept closed off from the rest of the house. "Maybe someday soon the count's son, Andrei Petrovitch, will marry and bring the house to life again!" Shrugging eloquently, she bent close to Malkeh and said in a low tone, so that the gliding maid would not hear, "It is too bad that young Andrei is more interested in wenching and gambling in St. Petersburg than in establishing a family and keeping the estate!" She shook her head. "He's a wild one, our Andrei! If only—" She broke off and did not complete the thought. "Still," she continued after a little while, "in time even spoiled young men settle down and become steady husbands and fathers! God knows, I could tell you a tale or two about Andrei's father, the old count, yet look at him now, a responsible landowner and the friend of princes!"

Quietly Maria Feodorovna closed the doors of the ballroom and led Malkeh back to the great hall. A staircase swept grandly from the reception area upward toward the sleeping rooms and servants' quarters. Malkeh followed Maria Feodorovna as the fat housekeeper mounted the stairs as lightly as a girl.

On the second floor were many bedchambers, each furnished with fine slim-legged furniture in the French fashion. The housekeeper pointed out the elegant silk wallpaper, made many years before in Rouen to the specifications of the countess. As was generally true in aristocratic families, the countess had always dressed herself in Paris fashions, had imported tutors from France for her son, and had insisted that only French be spoken in the family, except to the servants, of course, who she knew could not be expected to understand a civilized language.

The count's suite was very grand. There was a sitting room with an open fireplace instead of the usual tiled stove. Long French windows opened to a balcony overlooking a pond and the summerhouse. The bedchamber was simply furnished, but adjoining it there was a handsome wood-paneled dressing room and beyond that a room used only for bathing! On the opposite wall, a door gave into a library-study. Standing in the doorway of this room, Malkeh stared astonished at shelf after shelf of leather-bound books rising to the ceiling. She had never guessed at the existence of so many different books! A graceful desk dominated the room, beside it a globe of the world that could be turned on its carved wooden pedestal. Malkeh was reminded suddenly of what the steward had said about the earth revolving as it turned around the sun. She had quite forgotten about it until that moment. One of the books in this room would surely have an explanation for her, but of course she would never dare ask to see it. Bright winter sunlight flooded the room, setting the colors of the book bindings aglow— blues and reds and deep cordovans. Maria Feodorovna could hardly pull Malkeh away.

"The house is wonderful, is it not?" the housekeeper said with deep satisfaction as they emerged from the count's rooms.

"Oh, yes," Malkeh breathed, "it is, it is."

As they turned into a short corridor, they almost collided with the steward. He was so startled to see them there that he dropped the portfolio of papers that he was carrying.

He scowled at Malkeh from beneath beetling brows. "What are you doing here?" he demanded.

Malkeh flushed deeply. Because his odd golden eyes were staring at her, she felt embarrassed about her bulging belly and clasped her hands across her front. On being nudged by Maria Feodorovna, Malkeh made an awkward curtsy as she had observed the servants doing.

"I am showing the Jewess the house," the housekeeper explained as she stooped to retrieve his work.

Malkeh was indignant that Maria Feodorovna had spoken of her as though she did not have a proper name!

Yevgeny Sergeivitch was still looking only at Malkeh. "Since you are such an expert, have you found any devils or malevolent spirits here?" he asked her, thin-lipped and unsmiling.

"Not until just this minute!" Malkeh retorted, stung by his sarcasm. Immediately she could have bitten off her insolent tongue!

For a moment the stiff-backed girl and the furious estate manager stood glaring at each other, tension leaping between them.

Fedotov apparently did not choose to continue a demeaning exchange. "See that she does not keep you from your duties, Maria Feodorovna!" he said coldly before turning on his heel and clattering down the long stairs.

"Hoo, hoo! That is one angry man!" Maria Feodorovna did not know whether to laugh or to be angry. "And who can blame him? The little chick has a beak to peck with, does she not?"

"What will he do?" Malkeh asked fearfully.

"Do? Well, he won't set the dogs on you or run you off the estate, though I'm not sure that he shouldn't!"

"Maria Feodorovna," Malkeh asked, "why does your master dislike me so?"

The older woman drew her arm through Malkeh's as they moved toward the servants' back staircase. "To be sure, I thought that it was you who disliked him!"

"I think he has tried not to notice me these two days we've been in the house, and yet he was kind to me before."

"Ah, well, he's a moody man, difficult with people. Though I must say he runs the estate with a fair hand and guards the count's property as carefully as if he himself were the heir! If only he were!" Her voice sank to a whisper. "There are some who say that he has a right, for all that he was born on the wrong side of the quilt—"

Malkeh's eyes widened. She wanted to ask Maria Feodorovna more, but she sensed that the older woman had already said more than she had intended and wished to change the subject.

Malkeh found Yoysef in the kitchen with his sewing tools already put away, ready to wrap her shawl around her. Grisha was chafing to take them home.

After the encounter with the steward, the housekeeper seemed somewhat relieved to see Malkeh off; however, she kissed them both warmly on both cheeks and told them to return to receive New Year's greetings from the count. "There will be cakes and wine for the servants and the peasants who work our land," she said, "and the count will distribute gifts of coins to everyone who is here. It is a tradition!"

"Thank you," Yoysef said.

"Then I shall see you soon. At New Year's."

"No," Malkeh said stiffly, "we are not servants of the count's, nor peasants."

Maria Feodorovna frowned.

Yoysef said hastily, "We would not want to intrude on the *gospodin*'s party for his people."

Yoysef hustled Malkeh into the sleigh, and Grisha cracked his whip over the backs of the horses. Maria Feodorovna stood on the steps, waving and watching while the tracks the sled made in the new snow grew smaller with distance.

Yoysef pulled Malkeh deep under the robes so that Grisha could not hear their conversation. "Why must you be so rude with people, Malkeh?"

"Well," she said stubbornly, "we are not his serfs, and I don't want his gifts. If he'd pay the peasants their worth, he wouldn't have to give them coins for their holiday!"

"Hush!" Yoysef said angrily. "You don't know anything about this."

They rode a little while in silence. But neither could remain angry for long. Malkeh moved closer to Yoysef, fitting her body comfortably against his.

"Are you disappointed in me, Yoysef?"

"I love you. But why can't you learn to mind your tongue?"

"I always mean to. I'll try, really I will." Malkeh sought his hand under the furs and was relieved when she felt him return the pressure of her fingers.

They talked quietly of their visit. Yoysef told Malkeh he had intended to make a gift of his work as some measure of return for the steward's kindness in rescuing Malkeh that time. Yevgeny Sergeivitch would have none of it, though. "He's a difficult man, Fedotov, full of pride."

"He is that!" Malkeh agreed warmly.

Yoysef had not argued with the steward, just set his price ridiculously low. That the other man had not recognized the gift mattered only a little. "The rich simply do not understand the value of money!" he told Malkeh.

For her part, Malkeh told Yoysef about what she had seen of the house; he himself had never been invited beyond the kitchen and servants' wing. Spokoinaya Zemlya was, after all, the major point of interest around Polotsk. Finally she whispered in Yoysef's ear what Maria Feodorovna had implied about Yevgeny Sergeivitch's parentage. Yoysef knew the story and added to Malkeh's information. It was said, he told her, that the steward was the count's son by the wife of the carpenter, Fedotov, who, in order to keep his place, had accepted the count's bastard as his own child. It was one of those things that no one could prove or disprove. Certainly Yevgeny Sergeivitch had had unusual advantages for a carpenter's son. He had been given lessons alongside the heir, Andrei Petrovitch, and had traveled to St. Petersburg and Moscow, even to Europe, as a "companion" to the legitimate son. It was said that the two did not much like each other, which was perhaps understandable given the circumstances. After his mother, the carpenter's wife, died, Yevgeny Sergeivitch was given a bedroom in the family wing of the great house. Later Andrei had accepted a commission in the Semyonovsky Guards in St. Petersburg, a place he much preferred to the country, and Yevgeny was left behind to manage the estate.

Malkeh thought it a good story, more romantic even than her novels. From the beginning she had found Fedotov an object of fascination. Perhaps it was his arrogance, so different from the self-conscious diffidence of her own people. Or the wealth and scope of his knowledge that he took so completely for granted. It could also have been the ruthless strength of will that looked out at the world from his golden eyes. The exchange between them that morning had made her uneasy. Since Yoysef had already scolded her for her brashness with Maria Feodorovna, Malkeh did not tell him about it. Suppose she had so angered Fedotov that he found it necessary to punish her? She had never seen anyone so furious as he had been! "A Jew must whisper among gentiles," Yoysef always told her. "Fit in; whatever you do, do not call attention to yourself," he said. Why could she not remember that!

Malkeh slid further into the luxurious warmth of the fur robes. It seemed she was forever promising God that she would do better, while at the same time, she raced impulsively from one catastrophe to the next.

Chapter 7

February was bitterly cold. Midwinter boredom settled like a shroud over Spokoinaya Zemlya. The end-of-year merriment was long since past, Count Voronov and his guests returned to Moscow or the capital, and there was no special work until spring planting. The steward employed the slack period to make necessary repairs in the farm equipment, the stables and outbuildings, and the house itself. But by mid-February all that could be done in winter had been accomplished.

On a gray day, Fedotov sat in the kitchen with Maria Feodorovna, drinking tea to pass the time. He had spent the morning taking inventory of the wine cellars, had written to a firm in Germany inquiring about a new kind of machinery which was supposed to till soil mechanically, and after the midday meal had gone to his bedroom with a book he had long intended to read. He was unable to concentrate, however, and his restlessness had finally driven him to the cheerful kitchen where Maria Feodorovna sat knitting under the window.

"What are you making?" the steward asked idly.

"A shawl for the Jewess's baby," she said, holding up the woolly white rectangle so that he could see.

The annoying girl had come fleetingly to his mind from time to time since he had last seen her. She was not worth thinking about, of course, but still his mind had insisted on framing things he wished he'd said to her. "Has it come yet?"

"No. Soon, I think. I lit a candle in the church. She is very small to birth a child."

The man said, "That one will manage."

"May God will it."

The clock on the wall ticked loudly. A piece of wood sputtered in the oven. Maria Feodorovna's knitting needles made a steady clicking noise. Irritably, Yevgeny Sergeivitch pushed back his tea glass. "*Boizamoi!* I feel like I've been cooped up in this mausoleum for months!" He kicked back his chair as he rose.

The housekeeper looked up from her work.

He paced the kitchen from storeroom to window, oven to table.

"Please, Master Yevgeny, do not tread so heavily in here. I have a cake rising in the oven."

"I think I will ride into Polotsk. I've been meaning to have a word with the police captain."

Maria Feodorovna said slyly, "And maybe also a visit to a girl some-place on one of the back streets? And then a glass of vodka in the tavern?"

"You are very forward, woman!" the steward said, but he was grinning.

"Why should you be different from the rest? These dull days you'll have plenty of company from Spokoinaya Zemlya at the inn."

Taking his heavy sheepskin-lined coat from the peg near the door, Yevgeny Sergeivitch said, "I may not be home until tomorrow."

Maria Feodorovna nodded. "This place may be able to manage for one day without you."

On his way out, Fedotov lightly pinched the woman's plump cheek. "Just see you remember who's in charge here!"

When he'd gone, she sat smiling over her knitting. She wished Yevgeny Sergeivitch would marry, but if he would not, at least it was good that he took comfort somewhere.

*M*alkeh was in her eighth month, heavy and swollen, that bitterly cold February. Yoysef had been gone for two weeks already when at midday she put on her heavy shoes and wrapped a heavy shawl around her ungainly bulk. She could not bear to sit in the house alone when the others had gone to market.

In the winter months, the Polotsk bazaar sheltered under the arcade that surrounded the stone government building. Market days were Mondays and Thursdays only, for a few hours in the afternoon, and there were few stalls, for, of course, there were no fresh fruits or vegetables to be sold. People who had chickens, geese, dried fish, eggs, honey, preserves, or home-made articles still came, but business was generally slow.

The snow beneath Malkeh's feet was dirty and slushy, the wind sharp. Malkeh's pace was slow with the burden of the child she was carrying and very cautious lest she slip on a patch of ice, but it felt good to be out in the street.

Malkeh found Mammeh Frumma and Avrom at the very end of the arcade, where it opened into a street of small businesses and a poor inn frequented by peasants. Her in-laws must have arrived late to find such an inauspicious spot to set up business, Malkeh thought.

Mammeh was not pleased to see Malkeh. It was not proper for her daughter-in-law to be in public view at this stage of her pregnancy. Moreover, the girl could take a chill in this weather. Her first impulse was to order Malkeh home. On the other hand, Mammeh reflected, Malkeh could use a change. She was impatient and fidgety now that she was nearing her time, and she missed Yoysef. It was not right for him to be away now for so many days in a row. Men! They never thought! Visitors might have cheered Malkeh, but Golda was down with a croup and Yenta's baby was getting over chicken pox. It was too bad. Pray God that Yoysef would return tonight.

Mammeh said kindly, "Why don't you help us for an hour, Malkeh?"

"Really?" Malkeh asked eagerly. "Is it all right?"

"Yes, it's fine," sighed Mammeh Frumma, "as long as you promise to go home if you get cold or feel tired. Come, stand here, out of the wind."

"Oh, I love it so on market days!" Malkeh said, rearranging the jars of golden chicken fat on the counter.

There was very little traffic in the arcade, just a few housewives who came mainly to get out of their houses. Still, Malkeh took pleasure in being outside in the crisp cold air and was almost able to forget the dragging weight of her body and the ever-present ache in her back. The women who stopped at the stall were universally interested in Malkeh's condition and full of anecdotes and counsel. Malkeh thought to herself that if one were to believe the advice-givers, there had never yet been a normal childbirth in the history of Polotsk. Mammeh Frumma discouraged such female horror stories, even from some of her best customers. Malkeh only smiled, knowing she was strong and healthy and convinced that her baby would arrive sweetly and easily.

The first half hour passed pleasantly, and Malkeh assured Mammeh that she scarcely felt the cold at all. She was counting out a dozen duck eggs for a customer when Yenta's husband, Yaynkel, arrived, gasping for breath, and rudely shoved the woman at the counter aside.

"Yaynkel!" Malkeh began crossly, but stopped when she saw the look on his white face.

"Mammeh! Avrom!" he cried. "Come! Come quickly! Moisheleh fell from the top of the table, and he is hurt!"

Mammeh's face went gray, but she did not waste a moment. Quickly she pulled her shawl over her head and struck out after Yaynkel, her pace surprisingly brisk for such a large woman.

Moishe was Avrom's favorite, a bright, mischievous three-year-old, so curious that he was forever climbing on things to see better, and so quick that Yenta was at her wit's end to keep him from harm. Malkeh saw the stricken look on Avrom's face.

"Go with Mammeh and Yaynkel, please, Papa. Hurry!" Malkeh begged. "They may need you, and I will watch the stall quite well alone."

Avrom was torn, looking from Malkeh's bulging belly toward Mammeh's quickly disappearing back.

Malkeh pushed him gently. "What's to watching the stall? I can stand here quite as well as you can. Hurry now!"

His protests dying on his lips, Avrom bobbed his head. "Yes, yes, if you're sure—" He was halfway out from behind the plank counter.

"I'm sure. Go on, Papa, hurry."

"You're a good girl, Malkeh."

He ran to catch up with Mammeh and Yaynkel, and in a moment all three had turned the corner and vanished from view.

Malkeh said a prayer that Moisheleh was not badly hurt. But even as she hoped, she knew that it would take a major accident to drive Yaynkel from his butcher shop on a Thursday afternoon when housewives were buying their chickens and briskets for *shabbes* dinner. She wished she could have gone too. It was hard to sit there worrying and not knowing what was happening.

Malkeh settled down to wait, bored because business had dropped off to almost nothing. She was aware that the wind had risen and a few lonely snowflakes had begun to drift across the courtyard. She pulled her shawl tighter, but the cold seemed to find every opening in her clothing.

The Russian woman in the next stall called out, "It's time to go home, Missus! There'll be no more business today!"

Malkeh nodded. Many of the stallkeepers were packing up to leave. "I have to wait for my family to come back," she explained regretfully.

The kindly Russian eyed her. "I'll have my son Pavel carry your baskets home for you if you like."

"Thank you very much, but I think I should wait." Malkeh recalled that other time when she had fled the marketplace and frightened the family. Better to stay until Mammeh or Papa came for her.

The Russian shrugged and turned to the task of fitting her jars of honey snugly into her basket.

Surely, Malkeh thought, Papa Avrom would return now that it was beginning to snow. She hoped so because there was no way she could get home with the baskets of unsold eggs and jars of rendered fat, nor could she leave the merchandise behind. She wavered. Perhaps she should take up the offer of help from the Russian woman, though Mammeh did not like taking favors from gentiles. No. She would wait until someone came. If only it weren't so cold.

After a while the main sound in the arcade was the faint echo of men's laughter which drifted up the street from the nearby tavern. It would be warm *there* at least, Malkeh thought enviously.

Malkeh scarcely noticed a man leaving the inn and weaving toward the shelter of the arcade. He sang a Russian song in a hoarse voice, its words so coarse that Malkeh blushed to hear them. It had been the sound of his voice that had made her look up; at the same time that Malkeh noticed him, the man saw her. He grinned a silly, drunken, smirking grin. Uneasily Malkeh looked around her, but almost everyone had gone home. When the man reached her, he staggered against the stall front. His broad face was sweating, and his breath was foul and heavy with drink, raw onions, and rotting teeth.

Instinctively Malkeh shrank back, an involuntary expression of revulsion crossing her face. Her look had the effect of turning the man's alcoholic bonhomie to rage. Blood flooded his face and colored the whites of his eyes red. He stared at Malkeh, his mouth open and wet. In the moment that their faces stared across the counter at each other, she could see the black and broken teeth in his mouth and could feel the heat from his breath on her face.

"Bitch," he muttered, "I want to buy some eggs."

Malkeh looked at him blankly, unable for a moment to focus her attention; his rough country accent was almost incomprehensible besides.

"I want to buy some eggs, I said. You have eggs to sell, haven't you?" he shouted in fury.

"Yes, yes," Malkeh said, forcing a smile, placating. Her eyes searched the market for help, found none. She must stay calm. She would humor him and he would go away. "We have fine fresh eggs. How many do you want?"

"I want all of them! What! Do you think that I don't have money to buy eggs for my family?" The *mujik*'s little red eyes glared at her.

"They are two kopecks apiece for duck eggs, one for chicken eggs," Malkeh said, steadying her voice. "How many do you need?"

"I said *all!*" the peasant screamed, lurching across the stall toward the baskets of eggs. In the process a jar of chicken fat and several eggs rolled to the ground; the yolks made little yellow puddles in the snow.

In a state of near shock, Malkeh realized that she was virtually alone, the peasant drunk and possibly dangerous. Hastily she made a cone of paper, putting some eggs inside, careful so that her shaking hand should not drop any. Folding the paper over the top, she handed the package to the man.

"Ten kopecks, please, sir."

"You are cheating me," the man said, his voice rising. "You are charging me too much for your rotten, stinking eggs!"

"No, no, truly, I am not," Malkeh said, frantic. "There are a dozen eggs here, almost all I have left, and I won't charge you for those you broke."

"You are cheating! The Jewish bitch is cheating an honest Russian out of his money!" His voice was loud, and he leaned toward her aggressively.

Excited by the altercation, the few remaining shoppers began to gather around them. A thick stillness surrounded Malkeh and the drunken man. A dozen or so peasants, newly emerged from the inn and eager to join in the fun, pressed close. Sensing trouble, the few Jews still in the arcade huddled at a distance or unobtrusively edged out of sight altogether.

"The Yid is cheating me! Like all the Jews! She wants my money but won't give me an honest count. Thief! Whore!" he screamed, turning to the audience of his fellows and warming to their interest.

The crowd moved in closer. Some of the men had been laughing and singing in the tavern only moments before. Now their faces were closed and hostile.

Malkeh pressed back as far as she could, the rough stone of the building against her back. Thoroughly frightened now, staring at the blank-faced men ringing the stall, she held out the last basket. "Here, take the eggs, all you want," she offered in a shaking voice. Pogroms were made from incidents as slight as this.

Now that he had gained the advantage, the *mujik* swaggered. "Now! Now you see how it is, brothers!" he called to the watching men. "The Jew-whore admits that she cheated me and wants to make it up by *giving* me her eggs!" He spat on the ground at Malkeh's feet. "Well, Jew, honest Russians don't want the leavings of scum like you!" With a sudden movement he leaned across the plank counter and grabbed Malkeh by the ends of her shawl, pulling her roughly from the shelter of the flimsy stall. "But thieves and whores and bitches like this one need to be punished, don't they, friends?" He drew back a hamlike hand and struck Malkeh hard across the face. She reeled and fell to her knees on the wet stones of the courtyard.

Cheered on by three or four of the others, he advanced, his fist raised. Malkeh doubled over, her arms crossed over her abdomen to protect the child from the blows that now rained down upon her. She was silent, unable to bring herself to cry out, to beg the onlookers for help or her tormentor for mercy. Some of the men began to shuffle their feet uneasily, and a few drifted away. It was no fun when the woman was still like a stone. Besides, there was guilt for the child in her belly, Jew though it might be.

Enraged, the drunken peasant redoubled his attack. A kick aimed at Malkeh's head failed to connect, and a second glanced off her ribs.

"I'll teach you, you turd of a female dog!" he shouted.

Malkeh closed her eyes against what she knew was coming. God willing, the end would be mercifully swift. She heard rather than saw a horseman gallop into their midst. His horse, rearing and snorting in the small space, scattered the onlookers. Malkeh's attacker was too besotted with drink to move out of the horseman's path and would have been trampled if the rider hadn't reined in sharply. The horseman was shouting. He had a whip in his hand which he brought down hard across the back of the peasant. Once, twice, many times the whip rose and fell on the peasant's back and shoulders and head until Malkeh began to scream in panic at the sight of blood flowing everywhere. Surely the man on the horse meant to kill the *mujik* with his whip! Shrill screams rose higher and higher, filling Malkeh's head with noise. She did not realize that the sound came from her own mouth.

When the peasant was finally motionless, lying in a pool of blood and egg yolks, the horseman leapt to the ground and ran to Malkeh where she knelt in the snow. He took hold of her by the shoulders. Frantically she pulled away, protecting her body from him the best she could. Was he meaning to kill her too? Was the long-feared pogrom coming to pass?

"Please, please," she cried desperately, "my baby—"

Now the horseman was on his knees beside her in the filthy snow, his hand lifting the strands of loosened hair that had fallen across her face. "My God! What did he do to you?" he cried, seeing the bruises already darkening on the white skin. "I'll kill him! And the others, for letting it happen!" He gathered her close in his arms and then once more held her away so that he could gauge the extent of her injuries. "How badly are you hurt? Do you think you can stand?"

Without waiting for a reply, he lifted her gently to her feet. Malkeh swayed, gasping from the fiery burst of pain in her side. He caught her before she collapsed. "Lean against me," he said. "Let it pass a moment." His arm held her steady.

Malkeh slumped against the stranger, waiting for the pain and dizziness to subside. Whoever he was, he seemed to mean her no harm. Gradually her vision cleared. She looked up into the depths of amber eyes grown so dark with a mixture of rage and fear that it took her a moment to recognize to whom they belonged.

"*Gospodin* Fedotov!" she whispered. What was he doing here? Was this a dream? "He wanted to kill me." Her voice came in broken bursts. "No one helped—my baby—"

"It's all right now." His arms tightened around her. "Rest against me until you feel stronger."

Malkeh looked from him to the figure lying in the slush like a pile of dirty, blood-soaked rags. Her heart was hammering and bitter bile was gathering in her throat. "But how did you come here?—When—?"

In a few words Yevgeny Sergeivitch explained that he had heard a commotion as he left the office of the police chief and had come to investigate.

There was a roaring in Malkeh's ears. She was very tired. Everything seemed beyond her comprehension. All she knew was that he had been here to save her, again. He was talking to her. She made an effort to understand. He was asking her where she was hurt and whether she could walk.

"Yes, yes," Malkeh said, "but you have killed *him*!" She could scarcely bear to look at the inert creature at their feet.

"Hardly!" The steward spat on the ground. "He's so drunk he didn't even feel the whip. Tomorrow he won't know what happened to him."

He passed gentle fingertips over the raised marks on Malkeh's face. His voice was rough. "Anyway, he deserves to die!" After a few moments he asked, "Are you all right to leave now?"

"My baby—"

"Shall I take you to a doctor?"

Malkeh shook her head in renewed alarm. Doctors came only for the dying.

"Then I will take you home."

"Yes, please," Malkeh said, so exhausted that she was only too willing for someone else to take charge.

He began slowly to lead her toward his horse.

"Oh!" Malkeh said, remembering. "The eggs! The jars and jam—"

"Someone will bring them," Yevgeny Sergeivitch said.

Carefully, so as not to hurt her again, he lifted Malkeh in his arms and placed her in the saddle of his horse. His arm continued to support her as he slowly led the animal out of the courtyard and toward home.

Chapter 8

$\mathcal{A}$s the men filed silently into the rude peasant hut bearing the limp body of Ossip Ivanovitch, Serafina, the wife of the injured man, began to scream and beat her breast with her fists. Two little girls, babies yet who did not understand what was happening, joined their wails to their mother's, creating a din that filled the close, dark interior of the hut. The oldest child, a five-year-old boy, stood silently in the doorway, his flat dark eyes taking in the whole scene. In one glance he registered the inert, waxy arm dangling helplessly from his father's sleeve and the pulpy face streaming blood. More curious than moved by the sight, the boy moved closer to inspect the body that had now been eased onto a straw pallet. Its chest moved to the rhythm of shallow, rasping breaths. His father was hurt but not dead.

"Who did this?" he asked in an oddly adult voice.

"*Gospodin* Fedotov," one of the men replied. "It was awful to see. And all because of an argument with a Jewish whore at the *gostinny dvor*."

Impassively the child digested this information. He knew who Fedotov was. Every peasant family at Spokoinaya Zemlya knew. Even at five Vassily was well aware that whether they ate or not, whether they had a roof over their head, whether they lived or died, all depended on the will of Yevgeny Fedotov, the keeper of the count's estate.

"We will starve!" Serafina moaned. "He will turn us out now! Who will feed us, who will take care of us? Oh, my God, to have come to such an evil end!"

The men shrugged and shuffled their feet. Someone had to say something to the grieving wife. "Fedotov should be killed—and the Jew-bitch too!" muttered the first speaker darkly.

"Yes," another agreed. "He thinks he owns us, but someday he'll find out different. We'll get back at him and his sort!"

A giant of a man grimaced. "There are ways to fight back even now. The forest hides everything."

The boy, Vassily, took in what the men said; he was a careful listener.

"What shall I do now? How will I feed my children?" Frantically Serafina searched each face in turn for an answer.

The big man shook his head. "I don't know. It's hard, missus. Ask the priest."

"I spit on the priest!" Serafina fell on the floor beside the broken body of her husband. The little girls sobbed anew at seeing their mother prostrate.

First one, then another, of the men emptied his pockets, silently laying his remaining coins on the table. There was nothing besides this that any of them could do for Ossip or his children.

One by one, they backed out of the hut.

Chapter 9

*I*n his fall from the tabletop, Yenta's Moishe had broken a leg, a simple fracture. This occasioned a visit from the doctor, a spare, bearded man in frock coat and fur-lined cape, his astrakhan hat, which he kept firmly on his head during the visit, placed squarely above chilly eyes. The doctor's shiny ebony carriage was seen in the poorer streets of the city only on occasions of the most dire distress, when all other resources had failed. He accomplished the setting of the bone with a minimum of fuss for either himself or for the child, who was so frightened that he dared not even whimper with the pain. The time spent in arguing the pros and cons of sending for the doctor was longer than it took to snap the bone into proper alignment and immobilize the leg on a board.

The doctor's visit became a reference point in the family history: "two months after Moishe had to have the doctor" or "the year before the doctor came to us."

As children do, Moishe healed rapidly, and it was not long before he left off climbing on the furniture and began hoisting himself into the branches of trees or even onto the roof of the house. Yenta could be heard up and down the street, screeching at him to come down from wherever he had gotten to.

Malkeh's recovery was slower. Mammeh Frumma insisted that she stay in bed for a few days, and for a change Malkeh did not argue. Poor Mammeh, beset with anxiety, ran between Moisheleh's bedside and her daughter-in-law's. In that time, her fat cheeks became wasted and drained of their usual rosy color.

Malkeh's injuries were not serious, and with Mammeh's healing compresses, the pain was brought under control. For a time Malkeh's face remained discolored and swollen, her breasts and back marked by welts. It was not the punishment to her body that caused Mammeh Frumma to brew sedative drafts and to consider whether she should send Avrom in search of Yoysef; it was the injury to her spirit. Malkeh lay in bed like a pale, empty shell. Unless Mammeh or Golda sat near her bedside and urged every spoonful, she left her food untouched. And night after night in drug-induced sleep she moaned and tossed or screamed aloud in terror.

Malkeh was preoccupied with the fate of the peasant who had attacked her. To ease her anxiety, Papa Avrom made quiet inquiries and was able to establish that he lived, although he had lost an eye and the use of one arm. Malkeh could not believe he was not dead. She had seen him lying on the ground, the blood seeping from his body into the gray snow. So much blood, running, gushing, spurting, until she had dizzied with the sight. "Are you sure?" she asked Yoysef's father repeatedly. "Did you see him alive?"

"He lives. You must put him from your mind, daughter."

"Yes," Malkeh said, "I know."

But she could not. In repetitive dreams the drunken peasant came toward her again, his mouth loose and leering, a giant fist upraised to strike her while the milling crowd circled slowly, chanting, "Kill! Kill the Jew! Kill!" In the terror of the dream, Malkeh called on God to punish the *mujik*. But when her cry was heeded and a dark figure loomed out of nowhere to strike down her tormentor, she started up in a cold sweat, her heart pumping noisily in her chest and her body trembling violently. Before she could sleep again, she was compelled to seek out Papa Avrom to ask if he was really sure that the peasant lived.

A day after Yevgeny Fedotov had led Malkeh home on his horse, he came again to Polotsk. There had been such a heavy snowfall the night before, it was necessary to take the sleigh. With him Maria Feodorovna had sent a packet of medicines and balms prepared by her own hands. "These should set her right," she had said, frowning. The attack was especially bad luck so late in the pregnancy. She decided to light still another candle to the Virgin.

Fedotov was worried also. Suppose the girl had sustained internal injuries not immediately apparent? Perhaps he should ask Dr. Maslenkoff to stop by whether she wanted to see a doctor or not.

On entering Polotsk, he directed Grisha to stop at the confectioner's shop off Ekaterina Street. There he chose a selection of bonbons and directed the chocolatier to pack them in a lacquer box. While he waited impatiently for his package to be wrapped, his mind reviewed what had happened. He had gone through it a number of times already, not able to get the girl's stricken face out of his mind. There she had been, like the picture of a Christian martyr, kneeling on the stones of the courtyard, resigned to death for herself but not for her unborn child. Damn the peasants for the violence that seemed always to seethe just below the surface! And damn Yoysef Mandelkern, too, for allowing his pregnant wife to go alone into the marketplace!

"Here is your parcel, *Gospodin*. Will there be anything else?"

"No, thank you."

The sleigh went quickly and smoothly, riding on top of the snow. Grisha remembered the way to the tailor's house.

Fedotov recognized that he had been very shaken by yesterday's events. He told himself it would have been the same for him if it had been any other helpless creature he saw so abused. After all, hadn't he beaten the groom more than once for cinching the horses' bridles to an unconscionable tightness? And had he not forbidden the drowning of unwanted kittens and put a stop to starving the dogs to make them avid hunters?

This girl, skinny, ignorant waif though she was, there was something about her that interested him. He sensed an unawakened intelligence and a fierceness of spirit akin to his own. He felt challenged to set her free—should she survive long enough, that is! Two dangerous accidents had involved him with her already. Had she been his woman instead of the tailor's, he thought, he would not have been so careless with her safety!

Mammeh Frumma did not know what she would have done if the Voronov steward had wanted to see Malkeh where she lay in her bed. She had been alarmed to have someone so grand come to the door of her house, and how could she have said nay to anything he asked?

"Won't you come in, your lordship?" she had asked nervously.

"Thank you, no." He remained standing in the small, sheltered porch, hesitant to step even into the entrance room. "I was just passing by and wanted to see how your daughter fared."

"God be thanked, she is doing well."

"Perhaps she should have the doctor? Dr. Maslenkoff is very good."

"It does not seem necessary, but I thank you for your care."

"Since it was a peasant from Spokoinaya Zemlya who attacked her, I feel responsible. The count would insist on paying the doctor's fees."

"I will keep it in mind, *Gospodin*."

"Well, all right, then. My housekeeper has sent some herbs and ointments that are effective for bruises"—he thrust the packages into Mammeh Frumma's hands—"and the other is a small gift from me."

"It is very good of you both."

Later Mammeh Frumma told Malkeh how polite the steward had been. Important as he was, he seemed really to care how Malkeh was getting along.

Malkeh looked at the lovely little box of chocolates, and tears came to her eyes. How kind they were to concern themselves with her welfare. And she did not deserve it since it was for her sake that the drunkard had been beaten so savagely he might have died!

Yoysef arrived home a few days later. He had been gone more than three weeks and was tired and dispirited. Money was difficult to earn in the winter months, and his family had been forced to use some of its savings for living expenses. That was why the promise of an important commission in Dvinsk had lured him from home in midwinter. His punishment for his greed was arriving there only to find that the rich prospect had suffered business reverses and changed his mind. Disappointed and in a hurry to get home, he had traversed only a few versts when the heaviest snowfall of the winter caught him on the road. He barely fought his way through a blizzard to a farmer's house, where he was forced to stay for the better part of five days, cursing the skies that continued to loose the snows. When finally he was able to travel, the roads proved icy and treacherous, slowing his homeward journey. Almost a month on the road, and he had not a kopeck to show for it!

Home at last, Yoysef gathered Malkeh into his arms. Her face was puffy and she seemed to him to be generally unwell. His first thought was that her time must be very near. Malkeh clung to him, weeping as though her heart would break. "What is it, Malkeh? Mammeh—?"

"I'm so happy that you're home!" She clung to him. "Don't leave me again, Yoysef. I've been so afraid!"

"Afraid? Come, Malkeh, women have babies every day! It will be fine."

"You think I'm afraid about the baby?" The story came out in a half-choked, incoherent rush: "Moishe broke his leg and—and afterward one of the Voronov peasants wanted some eggs, but he was drunk—and then it was like a pogrom starting—the men from the inn wanted him to kill me and the baby—I couldn't believe it, what did they have against me—and he kept hitting me—only then *Gospodin* Fedotov came and he whipped the man and I think he hurt him bad or maybe killed him—he was lying in the snow, all bloody, and—and it is my fault!" Dissolving in tears, she pulled away from Yoysef and hid her face in her hands.

Although he had understood only part of what she said, Yoysef turned white as stone. Disbelieving, he repeated what he thought he had heard: "You were attacked in the market? One of the peasants from Spokoinaya Zemlya struck you? Is that what you're telling me? Dear God, I should never have left you! Only tell me where you are hurt. Malkeh, Malkeh, stop crying! I won't let anyone hurt you again, only stop crying!" Yoysef held her close, tenderly kissing the top of her head, her wet cheeks, her cold lips.

After a long while her sobs subsided into little hiccuping sighs and she lay still and exhausted in his arms. The crying had washed her mind clear. That night, secure, with Yoysef's body pressed around hers, Malkeh slept dreamlessly. In the morning she was able to get out of bed.

Malkeh's son, Boruch, was born a few days after Yoysef's return from Dvinsk. The baby was early. It was a hard labor that lasted many hours. Gittel, the midwife, arrived during the afternoon, and after examining Malkeh, settled down to tea in the kitchen. Gittel was a tiny, wiry woman of indeterminate age. She exuded an air of confidence, and Malkeh, who had been straining since early morning, relaxed under her confident hands and was even able to doze a little between pains.

Silently Mammeh Frumma placed a bowl of hot, soapy water and a linen towel near the bed and provided the midwife with a voluminous snowy apron that covered her dress, which was stained from food and other births. Gittel was the best they had—she was very good in even the most difficult deliveries—but her indifference to cleanliness offended Mammeh.

Until Gittel appeared, Yoysef had sat by the bed, stroking Malkeh's hand and rubbing her back. Relieved to be dismissed by the midwife, he had fled outside, where he busied himself raking the chicken yard and cleaning the coops. Babies, thank God, were women's work.

Malkeh's world was blurred with pain, an incredible, horrifying amount of pain. This was not the tender bringing forth of new life that she had so sweetly imagined. It was awful, it was terrifying, and it seemed that it would never end. Sunk in a black pit, Malkeh was alone with searing pain. She no longer heard Gittel's voice or felt Mammeh's damp cloth on her forehead, and she knew in her heart that she was surely in hell.

Yoysef sat in the kitchen, staring ahead and biting his lips in anguish. Never again, he thought. One child is enough. Nothing is worth the torment he heard from the other room. At each moan he winced and cringed back in his chair. No one had told him it would be like this, so long, so hard, so much pain. Avrom sat with him and from time to time the two men, father and son, self-consciously looked at each other and then away. When the screaming started, Yoysef ran from the room and paced around the outside of the house, welcoming the bite of the winter wind.

In the bedroom, the dark, wet top of the baby's head had crested, but at the next contraction it was apparent that all was not well. The babe was not coming in the normal position. Instead, it was emerging face up, the head thrown back on the stem of its frail neck. Gittel tried to bring the slippery head forward so that the child could move smoothly out. Her hands grasped the tiny shoulders, fearful that the infant might strangle before it was free.

Gittel was sweating herself now. "Try not to push, little one," she commanded Malkeh, striving to control the fear in her voice. "I need to turn the child just a little." She bent over Malkeh, her hands again seeking to bring the head down. Malkeh held back, breathing deeply and biting her lips. Gittel saw that the baby was going to come with its chin high in the air, but there was nothing to do since the head was well and truly in the birth canal now. Malkeh screamed as an enormous contraction gripped her in a vise. Gittel exclaimed, "Now! Push hard! The baby's almost here."

Panting and heaving, Malkeh bore down, straining to rid her body of its burden. Again. Yet again. The pain, the pain would tear her apart. She knew she did not have the energy to push once more, and yet she could not stop.

A prolonged animal-like scream burst from Malkeh's throat, and Gittel gently freed the head. The tiny body followed quickly on its own. The infant was born dead, the cord twisted around its neck.

At the last tearing second, Malkeh felt the child leave her body and knew that she did not have to do any more. She could let go now. But first, she must know. "What is it?" she whispered.

"A son."

Satisfied, Malkeh gave in and sank into blackness. For the next several hours she was conscious only intermittently, surfacing from time to time as from the bottom of a deep, swirling well and then falling back into the welcoming darkness.

When she finally awoke, the first streaks of daylight lay across the bed. The bloody sheets and wet nightgown had been changed, and the birth debris cleared away. Gittel was nowhere in sight. Yoysef was asleep in a chair in a corner of the room, snoring softly. Mammeh Frumma, awake, was sitting motionless by the side of the bed.

Mammeh smiled a little when she saw Malkeh's open eyes. "You are awake now, Malkeh," she said. "It is morning." She helped Malkeh to sit up and held a glass of water to her cracked lips.

Malkeh tried to speak, but she was so tired, so very tired. There was something she wanted to ask, but she could not quite remember what it was. She lay back on the pillows, closing her eyes, her mind straining to discover the thing she wanted to know.

Mammeh put a little package in Malkeh's hands. "See, I have a present for you, Malkeh. I bought it last month when the book peddler was here. He said you would like it." Mammeh stripped off the wrappings and held up a little book bound in soft red leather. "See. It is the same book that got torn that time. I want you to have it."

A book? Malkeh struggled to focus on the important thing she needed to remember. Why a gift? Oh, yes, of course. "The baby?" she asked faintly. "Where—?"

"The baby was a boy, a big man-child." Mammeh's voice was thick with tears.

"I want to see him."

Mammeh was choking. "He was born dead. God's will—no one's fault—"

She held Malkeh in her arms, her tears wetting her daughter-in-law's head as she rocked her gently back and forth.

Chapter 10

*I*n the face of death, the urgent physical need Yoysef and Malkeh felt for each other became for them an affirmation of life. Other children arrived in rapid succession. Chaya Leya was born within a year, in January of 1880, and then, as if God wished to compensate for snatching back their first child, He sent Yoysef and Malkeh twins, Channah and Yaakov.

The children were a delight to both parents. Chaya Leya was a cheerful, stolid little girl who gave little trouble. Surrounded by doting relatives, she indiscriminately held out her arms to any adult who happened to be nearby and was obligingly picked up. It was not unusual at day's end to find her leaning against Mammeh Frumma's ample bosom, her grandmother's voice lulling her into sleep.

> *Oyfn pripetchik brent a fayerl,*
> *Un in shtub iz heys.*
> *Un der rebe lernt kleyne kinderlekh*
> *Dem alef-beyz.*

"Mammeh, you spoil the child," Malkeh told her. "She doesn't have to be rocked to sleep every night."

"She's only a baby once," Mammeh Frumma said firmly. "God knows, since the twins, you have little enough time for her!"

Malkeh bristled. "I wish you would stop criticizing me! I'm doing the best I can. The twins take a lot of time, and Chaya Leya is almost fifteen months old!"

"Oh, yes," Mammeh said with sarcasm, "a real old lady already!" She turned back to the child in her lap, indicating to her daughter-in-law that the conversation was finished.

> A flame burns in the fireplace,
> The room is warm,
> As the teacher drills the little children,
> In their letters.

"Your mother gets more difficult every day," Malkeh told Yoysef that evening.

He sighed. It was an old story. "Truthfully the house is too small for four adults and three children. We are under one another's feet all the time."

Malkeh said sharply, "It's all right for you! You're not here for most of the week!"

"Ah, Malkeh. Just be patient. Another good year, and we will have enough money for a house of our own."

"I try, but as far as Mammeh's concerned, I never do anything right!"

Yoysef wearily passed a hand over his face. "Maybe it won't be a whole year until we have enough. I'll work harder."

In a rush of contrition, Malkeh flung her arms around Yoysef's neck. "Oh, Yoysef, I'm sorry to be so hateful. Mammeh and Papa give us a roof over our heads, and I know I couldn't manage three babies if Mammeh didn't help. It's only that she always has to be right! And she spoils Chaya Leya terribly!"

"It can't be easy for them either, Malkeh. In a little while we'll have our own house."

One thing that everyone could agree on was that Channah and Yaakov were enchanting children. From the moment of birth they had been unusually beautiful, fair of skin and fine-featured, with Malkeh's high cheekbones, delicate nose, and tilted dark blue eyes. Moreover, they were uncommonly responsive from an early age. Golda said they were like sunbeams, and so they were, bright and quick and mercurial.

Yoysef's business had grown steadily. He had replaced the pushcart with a little wagon pulled by a horse he had bought in the livestock market in Pskov. The farmer who sold the ancient mare to Yoysef went home laughing to think that a foolish Jew had spent good rubles for a beast intended for the slaughterer's mallet, but when Yoysef held the bridle in his hand, he felt like a lord. Never mind that the animal had spavined joints and a hollow in her back; she also had beautiful liquid eyes with long lashes. It was a case of love at first sight for man and beast.

The mare was put out to pasture, and her thin sides gradually plumped out. Yoysef's frequent currying turned a dull, patchy coat shiny, and affection eventually cured her skittishness. Katya, so named by Yoysef, tolerated Malkeh and the children, but she adored Yoysef and gave more than anyone could reasonably have expected.

Because he now owned a horse and wagon, Yoysef could cover many more versts and still be home in time for the Sabbath. The bag of rubles hidden in the chinks of the bedroom wall grew heavier.

*T*here were changes at Spokoinaya Zemlya as well. One evening at dinner at Prince Yakushkin's in Moscow, Count Voronov had stood to propose a toast when a sudden puzzled look crossed his face and he fell heavily to the floor. The Moscow doctor who examined him shook his head. There was no remedy for stroke; the count might live for months or years in a semi-vegetative state, or he might have additional strokes, any one of which could kill him. Since the count had often said that he wished that he might be buried at his estate in Byelorussia, arrangements were made for Fedotov to bring him home. For several weeks Maria Feodorovna nursed the sick man diligently and tenderly, and then one day, without further fuss, he died.

After the funeral, the heir, Andrei Petrovitch, relinquished his post in the Semyonovsky Guards and assumed his place in the capital as a titled landowner. For a time at Spokoinaya Zemlya the change was scarcely noticeable. More interested in the cosmopolitan life of St. Petersburg than in farming, the young count Andrei seldom visited. Yevgeny Fedotov, as before, was left to manage the holdings.

The steward, always a somber man, had grown more unsmiling and more tight-lipped over the years. It was said that he had occasional brief and loveless liaisons with women in Polotsk, but he showed no signs of wishing to marry. When Maria Feodorovna teased him that he was wed to Spokoi-naya Zemlya, he did not disagree. If he had one passion in his life, it was for the land; in pursuing it, he spent long hours poring over agricultural books and journals and corresponding with agronomists all over the world. Maria Feodorovna brooded about her friend. A woman of his own, children—these might have softened Yevgeny's sharp edges and permitted him to forget old wounds. But marriage seemed unlikely for him. He was thirty-five years old already and set in his ways.

The men who labored on the estate knew Fedotov as a hard and exacting master. They missed the old Count Voronov. Most had been serfs on the estate before the Great Emancipation of 1861; they were still bound to the land since none could move off it without special permission. Although for years the old count had been remote from the management of Spokoi-naya Zemlya, the peasants spoke with affection of the times that he had ridden through their villages, stopping to talk to the men, to admire the children and give compliments to the women. They remembered how he had received them in the manor house every New Year, distributing coins and sweetmeats to all who came. "A prince of a man" they called the old count, "a good friend to the farmer." Dead, his reputation grew.

The villagers agreed that the young count was a different sort from his father, proud and self-centered with little interest in either the people or the land. They had heard that he might soon take a bride. With new family responsibilities, perhaps Count Andrei Petrovitch would come home and

take charge of things. It would be an improvement over the steward, Fedotov! God knew it was difficult to get along with *him*!

Death had come not only to Spokoinaya Zemlya. It arrived that same
winter of 1881 for Tsar Alexander II, assassinated on a street in St. Petersburg. The sad event was announced by the mournful tolling of bells in
the churches of Polotsk. The monks at the monastery on the outskirts of
the city kept vigil through many days and nights of fasting and prayer. The
devout crowded into the churches or knelt in the snow before the monastery. Great bunches of hothouse flowers, yellow, the symbol of mourning,
appeared at the foot of monuments, in windows, and before the icons of
church and home.

The Jews of Polotsk lived in fear each day that passed with the names
of the conspirators still unknown. If a Jewish name were to be among them,
no Jew in all of Russia would be safe from reprisals. It was with a peculiar
joy that they read the names of those arrested, none of which was obviously
Jewish. The pogrom would not come after all.

In his solitary, silent way, the boy Vassily, son of the unfortunate
peasant Ossip Ivanovich, turned over in his mind what he had heard about
the plot to kill the tsar. To the mind of a child, one tyrant was the same as
another, Alexander no more nor less a monster than Fedotov. Nevertheless,
he was fascinated by the tsar's killers, the five who were hanged. If he had
been one of them, he would have been clever enough to escape! When he
was grown and the time came for him to kill Fedotov, no one was going to
drag him to the scaffold! Peasants learned early there were ways to hide
crimes so no one would ever know. For now Vassily watched and listened,
tended his anger and prepared himself for what he must eventually do.

Fedotov, who rode proudly through the fields like a king on his stallion, was the enemy who had hurt his father and might at any time turn
Ossip's family from their home. Jews were at the bottom of the whole thing;
therefore, they, too, were the enemy. Vassily had nothing but contempt
for that poor, weak creature, his father. So different were they from each other
that sometimes he even doubted Ossip's paternity. Still he knew that Ossip
had suffered a grievous wrong that had gone unpunished. Vassily must set
that right. He might have to wait for years, but he would use that time to
plot his revenge. It would be worthy of the steward's crime even if it should
mean destroying Spokoinaya Zemlya itself.

In time Ossip had made a recovery of sorts, although one eye had no
vision and his left arm continued to hang lifeless at his side. It was enough
so that he never worked again. He spent his days lying on his cot, swilling
vodka whenever he could beg or stealing a few coins from wife or friends.
Otherwise, he roused himself only to curse the children and beat his wife.

Despite Serafina's fears that Yevgeny Fedotov would put them off the
land, this did not happen; in fact, the steward seemed to have forgotten the

incident. That it had destroyed a whole family meant so little to him that he could quite put it from his mind, Serafina thought bitterly. Nothing had changed for the family except that now it was Serafina who went every morning to work in the fields with the men, leaving the children at the mercy of their drunken, loutish father. There was no help for it. Her labor was exchanged for their food, shelter, and a bit of cash. By the time he was seven years old, Vassily was toiling beside his mother. He hated it, but hated dodging his father's blows at home even more. Hard work and heavy responsibilities dried up the woman Serafina had once been, and she was old before she was thirty. Vassily saw all. It was forever burned into his brain.

Ossip Ivanovich never understood what had happened to him that day at the market, but he was careful to keep himself beyond the vision of the steward who, he was convinced, had meant to kill him, for what reason he didn't know. Ossip was never a clever man, and after a while he dismissed Fedotov's attack as yet another of the steward's eccentricities. Why, every person at Spokoinaya Zemlya knew about Fedotov's bizarre ideas! Had he not forced them to leave fallow, sometimes for years at a time, fields that had produced barley and rye for generations? A waste of good land! And had he not ordered latrines dug—latrines! when squatting in the fields had always been good enough!—and at such an inconvenient distance from the wells where they took their midday meal. And one more thing that irked— his insistence that mothers no longer use poppy juice to put their babes to sleep while they worked the fields! How could a woman weed a row with a howling baby on her back! In the context of the steward's overall strangeness, his savage protection of the Jew-bitch was just another example. It was only too bad that Ossip Ivanovich had stood that day in the path of his insanity.

*T*he twins were infants and Chaya Leya a mere toddler still lurching on unsteady legs when Golda came one day to make an unusual request.

Embarrassed, she began, "Malkeh, you know it will soon be Rosh Hashanah!"

"What are you talking about?" Malkeh laughed. "The New Year is months away!"

"Not so long if you want to do something special to prepare."

"Like what?" Malkeh was mystified.

Golda sighed. "Like learning to read."

"Learning to read! I don't understand? I have lent you books for years!"

Golda colored. "I took them so you wouldn't know how ignorant I am." She looked down at the floor. "Oh, Malkeh, I so want to read the papers in shul this New Year's!"

Malkeh grew increasingly perplexed. "You always say the prayers."

"*Say* them, yes! I learned them by rote when I was little."

"I've never heard of such a thing!"

"Oh, Malkeh, don't be so silly! Most of the women you know learned the blessings from their mothers or grandmothers!" She clutched Malkeh's hand. "Please, Malkeh, will you teach me to read in time for Rosh Hashanah?"

Malkeh hugged Golda. "Gladly."

So it came to pass that three times a week, when the children had been put down for afternoon naps, Golda and Malkeh sat together at the kitchen table, heads bent over the text of the prayer book. Malkeh was glad to return a favor to dear Golda, but she had not been prepared for the surge of excitement and joy she herself experienced from the teaching itself.

Golda was not a quick student, but Malkeh was patient and thorough, and Golda's pride was enormous when on Rosh Hashanah she opened the siddur and followed for herself the words the men were reading aloud in the sanctuary. Seeing Golda reading, other women wanted to know how this had come about. Soon Shivka and Chaska, Zissel and Etka were clamoring to learn too. Almost without volition, Malkeh slipped into the role of women's teacher.

The Jews of Polotsk were more or less trilingual. The men read the Hebrew of the synagogue, taught them from the time they entered *cheyder*, the religious school, at age three. Daughters learned the few prayers that a woman must say by listening to their mothers; rarely could either of them decipher the Hebrew letters. At home and among themselves, Jews spoke Yiddish, a medieval Germanic language written in Hebrew letters. In commerce, Jews spoke Russian. Some had at least a rudimentary ability to read and write in the Cyrillic alphabet, though few Jews were admitted to government schools, where they might study Russian grammar and usage and be exposed to the beauty of the literature.

If Jewish men were deficient in the refinements of secular language, women tended to be completely ignorant. Malkeh was an exception, being literate in all three tongues. Her father was that oddity, a Jew who had been to Russian schools. With his exceptional education, he should have been a rich and successful man but was not. The best he had been able to manage was to follow that humblest of shtetl occupations, the teaching of small children. He was not even a gifted teacher since he could neither inspire nor control the boys who were his pupils. But to Malkeh, his only child, he had passed along a curiosity about the world and a fascination for its languages.

There were women in Polotsk hungry for knowledge. As word passed among them that Malkeh could teach them, they came eagerly for lessons. One of these, Sorkeh, had a husband who three years past had gone to

America to see if he could make a better life. Sorkeh had had to depend on the letter-writer to keep in touch with her husband, Nissel, in New York, and to read Nissel's letters to her in return. It was an unsatisfactory arrangement, the letters stilted and careful lest the letter-writer use their words to gossip about their affairs. Sorkeh, an enthusiastic woman with a lively intelligence, learned to read and write Yiddish in a matter of weeks.

Many husbands besides Sorkeh's Nissel had fled to America, either to avoid conscription or because they could not make a living at home. Their wives, too, yearned to talk to their men firsthand through letters.

Women brought Malkeh many different sorts of language needs. Some who kept stalls at the *gostinny dvor* wanted practice in adding figures, writing simple receipts in Russian, and generally understanding the language of business. Some, like Golda, cared only to be able to read the Hebrew prayers directly from the page regardless of whether the meaning of the words was understood. In exchange for lessons, the women brought produce from their gardens, took Malkeh's laundry and mending to do with their own, and helped her with chores. Month by month her students grew in number.

Mammeh Frumma felt put upon and was not hesitant to share her resentment. Partly it was a matter of territorial rights. Now there seemed always to be strange women underfoot, interrupting the normal flow of housework and interfering with the cooking. More often than not, these "students" forgot to whisper when the children were sleeping so that Chaya Leya, Channah, and Yaakov awakened still cranky from their naps. Not, Mammeh complained, that Malkeh was bothered; she simply handed over the children to their grandmother—a wonderful example, if Mammeh did say so, for all those young women.

What's more, Mammeh did not like the idea of strangers bringing food to her house and taking Malkeh's laundry home with them. It wasn't seemly. Foolish Yoysef! she thought. His pride in Malkeh was both boundless and blind. Yoysef did not hear the jeers of other men who said that the tailor's wife was the man of the family.

Chapter 11

*C*aptain Andrei Petrovitch, lately of the Semyonovsky Guards, now Count Voronov, was handsome and elegant, a man of considerable, if somewhat brittle, charm. He had been brought up by his mother, the late countess, to regard the finer things of life as his due. His uniforms had always been tailored in Savile Row, London, his conveyances drawn by the black Orlovs that horsemen called the finest carriage horses in the world, and his bachelor quarters decorated by the Italian Branchetti. The parties he gave were legendary for their wit and extravagance.

Andrei and his father had never been close; he was completely his mother's son. As long as Andrei could remember, he had hated the slow pace of life at Spokoinaya Zemlya, the isolation from neighbors of their own station, and the sameness of the days. He loathed the landscape with its endless flat fields punctuated by forest and bog. There was no escape from the monotony. The nearest city, Polotsk, was as boring as Spokoinaya Zemlya; it had no racing track, no opera house, and no parlors for games of chance, only all those infernal churches, the bells tolling at all hours of the day and night! Let Yevgeny Fedotov enjoy the bucolic charms; he was born and bred to them! Andrei could do without them, and without Yevgeny, for that matter.

Andrei could forgive his deceased father much. Even the old count's meanness with money had not been an insurmountable problem, Andrei at an early age having developed considerable skill at cards and baccarat. The one thing for which he could not forgive the old man was Fedotov. Let the count take his pleasure with a pretty housemaid—everyone did that! Let him even provide for the bastard if he had enjoyed the mother. But that he had brought a peasant's spawn into the house, insisting, against all of *Maman*'s protests, that the bastard eat at the same table, be dressed by the same tailor, and tutored by the same masters was inexcusable. There had been many hot words exchanged over this caprice. Andrei's face flamed, remembering. Whatever Papa had believed, it was not true that Andrei's hatred for Yevgeny was based on jealousy over the other's brilliance. What else had the peasant to do besides learn Greek and Latin! Papa might have treated the bastard like a true son of the family, but the rest of society kept him firmly in his place—with the house servants.

Andrei had been only too happy to be commissioned in the Guards, enabling him to leave Spokoinaya Zemlya for good. Life at court in St. Petersburg suited him very well, and ridding himself of the enforced companionship of Fedotov was a bonus. The stewardship of the estate was a job made to order for Yevgeny, neither so low as to insult the father nor so high that anyone could mistake him for anything but a servant to the family. Andrei supposed that Fedotov had done well enough at it. The Voronovs had not been plagued by economic troubles, nor had there been signs of rebellion among their people. His father had trusted Fedotov completely; there seemed no reason for Andrei to do otherwise.

Now his father was dead. As the new Count Voronov, Andrei needed a proper house. He would have to make an accommodation with Fedotov about access to funds. There would be a row, but maybe it was as well to get that over with immediately and establish once and for all who was the master of Spokoinaya Zemlya. In the meantime, though, he would have his bills sent directly to the estate. It took money to attract money, and at the time of his father's death Andrei Petrovitch, Count Voronov, was very much interested in attracting the money of one Natalya Ivashev, a distant cousin to the royal family and, in her own right, heiress to a large fortune.

*B*y the fall of 1883, there were savings enough for the Mandelkerns to have a place of their own. Yoysef might have delayed if it had not been for the constant squabbling between his mother and his wife which brought matters to a head. That summer Malkeh had seven pupils, enough to establish an actual class. Sorkeh Feldman had volunteered as assistant teacher, and while she conducted the rote drills which were then the principal teaching device, Malkeh began to develop a basic course of study. As long as the weather was good, the women, carrying their copybooks, pens, and foolscap, met under the trees by the pond behind the house. Mammeh Frumma had given her ultimatum: Malkeh's students were not welcome in her house.

"But it will be cold soon! We cannot sit outside in the snow!"

"That is no business of mine," Mammeh had said primly. "It would be far better if you spent as much time taking care of your husband and children as worrying about these silly women! Where in Torah does it say that a woman should read?"

"Where does it say that she should not?" Malkeh retorted furiously.

It was like that between them every day. Yoysef could not tolerate such strife in his family.

The house that Yoysef found was not large, but it was built solidly of heavy round logs carefully fitted together and chinked with moss so that the winter winds would not blow through. It had one story, but its floor was raised far enough above the ground to accommodate a space beneath for storing root vegetables. To prevent cold air from circulating under the living space, earth and sod had been mounded to floor level around the exterior base of the house. The roof was pitched high for the snow to slide off, and the windows were double-hung with shutters that could be snugly fastened.

Yoysef proudly led Malkeh around the outside of the house, pointing to how skillfully the logs had been fitted together, how tight the windows and solid the roof.

"It seems small, Yoysef, for a family as large as ours," Malkeh said doubtfully.

"We have to start someplace."

Behind the main structure there was a barn where Katya could be stabled and chickens could roost. "And look, Malkeh, there is space enough and to spare! You can grow all the vegetables we'll need for the table."

"Flowers too," Malkeh said, thinking of the dahlias she could plant in the dooryard (Mammeh Frumma's idea of a flower bed had been a few rangy sunflower stalks!). Already Malkeh could visualize how the lilac bushes, growing wild all around the house, would release a delicate fragrance in the spring, and the soft white flowers of the "bird cherry" trees would lie like warm snow upon the ground. In the summer the fruit would hang thick on apple, pear, and plum trees. She would ask Maria Feodorovna for her recipes and fill the kitchen shelves with preserves as elegant as those at Spokoinaya Zemlya.

Rounding the house, Yoysef pointed to the carved rooster that flapped its wings on the edge of the roof's ridge beam. "Just look, Malkeh! Have you ever seen anything like that!"

Malkeh stepped back, shading her eyes with one hand. It was a cockerel right out of a fairy tale! The same whimsical woodcarver who had decorated the shutters with a fanciful pattern of leaves and vines must also have put the fierce cock on the roof. Malkeh succumbed on the spot. "Whatever it costs, we must have this house!"

Yoysef laughed. "But you haven't even looked inside yet!"

"I don't care about the inside!"

When, however, they walked through the door, Malkeh found that her first impression had been accurate; the interior was cramped and dark. The family living space would be confined to a kitchen with an adjoining store-room, and one sleeping room. Of necessity, the largest and brightest room, the one that faced the street, would be reserved for Yoysef's tailor shop. The kitchen would have to serve all of the family's communal needs and be Malkeh's schoolroom besides. She sighed deeply.

Yoysef took her hand in his. "There is plenty of room to build another bedroom and a front room. We'll do it as soon as we have a little money."

"Oh, Yoysef, I wasn't thinking about bedrooms or front rooms! I want a proper school with desks and chairs and slates to write on! I want books so we can read about the world outside Polotsk. The other day Zissel asked me where is Chicago—her husband is there—and I didn't know for sure."

Yoysef drew Malkeh to him. His arms were comforting. "Do you remember when I first brought you to Polotsk, and I promised you that we would only live with Mammeh and Papa for a little while? Ah, Malkeh, it has been five years since I made you that promise. The house may not be everything you want, but it will be your very own."

Malkeh felt the tears sting. Yes, Yoysef would take care of her; with him, everything would eventually come right.

Yoysef asked, "Shall we take the house, then?"

Thinking of the rooster and the lilacs, and of fruit preserves on the shelves, Malkeh said, "I love it already!" Her face was radiant, and her eyes shiny with gladness.

With the move into the new house, Malkeh at last became mistress of her own domain. She was happy, and happiness made her beautiful. With some women, the bearing of children adds a pleasing roundness to the body; this was true for Malkeh. The hollows of her face filled out, and the haunted look that had sometimes shadowed her eyes had disappeared. Her skin glowed from working outdoors, and her arms were brown and firm. Her golden hair, left uncovered now except on the street or in the company of men not part of the family, was long and thick, worn twisted into a knot at the nape of her neck.

These days Malkeh smiled a good deal. And why not? Freed from Mammeh Frumma's carping supervision, she could be her own complete self. The whirring of Yoysef's sewing machine in the next room was a constant reassurance that he was near. A new baby slept quietly in his cradle near the oven while the three older children toddled back and forth between the kitchen and the shop, delighting in and being delighted by the attention of first one parent and then the other.

God had granted them much, Malkeh thought. And if the babies had come more quickly than she would have chosen, still they were beautiful and healthy, and she adored them, every one.

From time to time Malkeh saw the count's steward as he rode his fine chestnut stallion through the streets of Polotsk on some business or other. She found it hard sometimes to recognize in this stern, distant man her rescuer with the anxious eyes. When he noticed her at all, he offered a cool smile and a nod.

Malkeh and Yoysef were not strangers to the manor house. Indeed, after Yoysef's shop was fully established, all of the estate livery, following the pattern of the original St. Petersburg tailor, was made there. This necessitated many trips to Spokoinaya Zemlya to measure and fit the garments. Occasionally Malkeh went along with Yoysef. She enjoyed her afternoons in the kitchen with Maria Feodorovna, who fed her pastries and gossip, admired the babies, and sent her home with presents of honey and preserves.

During one of these visits Maria Feodorovna told Malkeh of the attempt Yevgeny Fedotov was making to establish a school on the estate. "It has become a madness with him," she said, "that the *mujiks* must learn to read and write." The village priest, Father George, and a seminary student newly arrived from St. Petersburg, had been unwillingly pressed into service as teachers, and Yevgeny Sergeivitch had ordered every male between the ages of eight and thirty to attend class for two hours a day.

Maria Feodorovna's face creased with worry. "There is anger in the village over his high-handed ways. The men have little enough free time, and I can tell you that none of them want to spend it sitting on hard benches in the church vestry when they could be drinking kvass and playing at dice!"

Malkeh was puzzled. "But how can he force them if they don't want to go?"

"Ha! When owners absent themselves, the steward is master of the estate, and the peasants are his to do with as he pleases! If they cross him, he can put them out of their huts or let their families go hungry by refusing them work! Not that *Gospodin* Fedotov would do that!" the housekeeper added hastily. "But every peasant knows he lives at his master's whim." Maria Feodorovna pushed a plate of sugared cookies toward Malkeh. "Here, my dear. I made them this morning." Malkeh shook her head, and the older woman went on, concern wrinkling her forehead. "As far as I can see, it is enough that the priests are educated. What is the point of teaching a peasant to read and write? If you ask me, Master Fedotov has forgotten the carpenter's hut where he was born!"

This topic interested Malkeh even more than the news about the village school. "Did you know *Gospodin* Fedotov's mother?"

Maria Feodorovna laughed. "Know her! Of course I knew her! Didn't I take her out of a hovel in the village when she was thirteen years old? There was something about her, you know, and I thought to give her a better life in the manor house." She sighed with remembered remorse. "A pretty little thing she was, Elena—as it turned out, too pretty for her own good. It was no wonder that she caught the count's eye!"

"Was *Gospodin* Fedotov very young when she died?"

"Ah," Maria sighed, "not too young to have felt the carpenter's boots in his ribs! It was after a terrible beating that the count brought him into the house to live. In time the carpenter Fedotov would have killed him."

Maria Feodorovna and Malkeh reflected on this bit of history in silence.

"Maybe it's because he knows what it's like that he wants to help the villagers have a better life."

"They don't see it that way." Maria Feodorovna shook her head sadly. "Sometimes I think he has lost his mind altogether!"

"Do you indeed?" the steward asked mildly, coming into the warm kitchen. He turned to Malkeh abruptly. "I have heard that you have a school in town where you teach women. Do you really think that females need book learning?"

Malkeh stiffened. "Are women so different from men? They have no need to add numbers, write letters, or read a newspaper?"

"They have men to take care of them," Fedotov said flatly.

"Sometimes," Malkeh agreed. "But how does that change anything? Or maybe you think that if women are educated, they won't need men at all?" she suggested sweetly.

"Oh, they'll need them all right," he said with a crude laugh.

Color flooded Malkeh's cheeks, and a response deserted her. How she hated this arrogant side of him!

"I should have been disappointed if I hadn't managed to upset you!" he said, pleased and relaxed.

The steward poured himself a glass of tea and sat down at the table between Malkeh and Maria Feodorovna. Sipping, he said, "My dear friend Maria Feodorovna thinks I am obsessed, if not completely insane, to try to establish a school here. But, you see, I have no choice. I am a man pursued." He bit into a cookie. "My dream is to see the motherland thrive. More than any other country in the world, Russia has land, it has natural resources, and it has manpower. Why, then, have we failed to take our place among the great nations of the world?"

Helplessly, Malkeh shook her head.

"Because we are a nation at war with itself. The gap between rich and poor is too wide, and there are too few opportunities for people to better themselves. The hopelessness of the poor infects the whole country." Fedotov tapped his forefinger on the table to add emphasis to his words. "Apathy, born of hopelessness, is the sickness that feeds like a cancer on Russia's innards!"

"Pardon me, *Gospodin*," Malkeh said nervously, "but are you not afraid to talk like that?"

Fedotov's eyes flashed. "Fear is another product of the lower-class mind!"

A white line showed around Malkeh's mouth. Noticing, the steward grimaced. "I forgot how sensitive you are! I was not referring to you." He brushed the cookie crumbs off his coat before he completed his thought. "There are no informers here, and I am no revolutionary. It should be obvious to anyone that the key to solving our country's problems is education, not revolution."

"But," Maria Feodorovna objected, "the peasants don't want your school! Can't you understand that?"

"They have no choice!" Contempt made Yevgeny's voice thick and harsh. "What do you think, schoolteacher?"

Malkeh cleared her throat, unsure that she should say more.

Yevgeny did not wait for a reply. "Do you know that there are countries in the world where government schools are open to everyone? In America a farmer's son can become a landlord or an artisan, even a doctor or a lawyer!"

Malkeh looked up from her tea. "In America!" Many of her friends had husbands in America. "That is true?"

"Yes, and in England and Germany and Scandinavia—"

Fedotov thrust his tea glass from him. His voice registered disgust. "But we are a backward country. Do you know," he raged, "there are some

so-called intellectuals who have made a cult of worshiping the Russian peasant! Yes, the peasant—the Russian in his most primitive state—is to be regarded as the repository of all the virtues: selflessness, spirituality, devotion
to family and community! Education, they say, will contaminate that pristine peasant self and expose it to the perniciousness of the rest of society! I
read *that* in the writings of his excellency, Count Lev Tolstoy, a landowner
who should know better!" He slapped the table in anger. "And the villages,
the dirty, stinking villages, with their corrupt little village councils, do you
know what these 'intellectuals' write about them? Why, *they* are supposedly
early forms of pure socialism. That should make the tsar take notice!"

"Calm yourself, Yevgeny Sergeivitch," the housekeeper said.

Malkeh said carefully, "Maybe this Count Tolstoy is saying that even
poor people have some good in them."

Fedotov ignored her. "Well, I'll tell you something. Those men who
would call the common man holy have either forgotten or have never known
their precious peasants drunk, raping their daughters and beating their wives,
and, by God, destroying their little pieces of land through sloth! *That* is the
Russian peasant that I know. The fact is that generations of submission have
corrupted and shriveled his soul. He stinks of decay. Believe me, the peasant,
left to his own devices, will destroy the motherland!"

Yevgeny Sergeivitch sank back in his chair, and Maria Feodorovna, bored
with the talk, rose to stir the fire and bring him a fresh glass of tea. But Malkeh's
eyes never left him. This was a Fedotov she did not know. She was familiar
with the tough-minded, sometimes cruel Fedotov who was said to rule Spokoinaya Zemlya with an iron fist. Once she had experienced the man of tenderness
and compassion who was also Fedotov. But just now another window into
Fedotov's usually impenetrable soul had opened briefly, and for those few moments Malkeh had glimpsed a man in love—in love with the very peasants who
outraged him by wanting so little for themselves.

"You have a school, Mistress Teacher. What do you hope to accomplish?"

Malkeh said slowly, "Only what my women want—to read a prayer
or write to a husband or add up a bill in the *gostinny dvor.*"

"My peasants want nothing. They are illiterate, dirty, and diseased,
and there are forty-eight million of them in this country! Shall we wait until
they perceive a need?"

Malkeh helplessly shook her head, not knowing the answer.

The glow had died from the steward's eyes, and his face fell into its
accustomed lines of bitterness and fatigue. "It may be that most of the men
and boys in my school will never learn to read and write, not because they
are stupid but because reading and writing mean nothing to them. Maybe
out of a hundred, four or five will go on to become teachers or priests or
shopkeepers. Will it be worth the struggle, do you think, for those few?"

Malkeh felt herself drawn into the steward's deep sadness. She longed to put a consoling arm about him, to pull his head close to her breast, for the sake of friendship. He was a man of strong beliefs, she thought, a good man destined always to be misunderstood and mistrusted by those he most wanted to help. She longed to say something that would comfort him, but she could not share his vision. For her, Russia was the shtetl in which she had grown up and the Jewish quarter of a provincial city where she lived with her husband and children. His country was not her country, his people were not her people, and whatever reforms eventually came about because of men like Fedotov, would likely have little effect on the Jews who were present in, but not part of, Russia.

Slowly she answered his question. "We say that to save one life is to save the world."

Yevgeny stared hard at her. "Yes? Jews say that? It is a good saying for all that in my opinion it is not true!"

Malkeh stood. "Yoysef will be waiting for me," she said. At the door she lingered uncertainly.

Fedotov looked up, his thick eyebrows raised in a question mark.

Malkeh turned. "Nothing," she mumbled.

"You wanted something. Spit it out!" he said irritably.

In a rush Malkeh asked, "*Gospodin*, I need to know. Were you teasing or does the earth truly revolve around the sun?"

Fedotov threw back his head and roared with laughter. Humiliated, Malkeh fled the kitchen. He caught her before she reached the gate. "It does," he said, wiping his eyes with his handkerchief.

A few days after this encounter, Malkeh was surprised to find the servant Grisha on her doorstep, holding out a package to her. "The master bade me put this into your hands, mistress!" he said.

The parcel contained a Russian dictionary and a proper grammar, a geography atlas, and a basic science text. And there were three Russian novels: *The Idiot*, *Fathers and Sons*, and *Anna Karenina*. Malkeh was unfamiliar with the authors. She repeated the names—Dostoyevsky, Turgenev, and that selfsame Count Lev Tolstoy who had been chastised the other afternoon for his view of the peasant society.

She knew by the gift that Fedotov acknowledged her.

Chapter 12

*M*alkeh and Yoysef doted on their children. In seven years of marriage they had produced five (not counting the infant who had died at birth): Chaya Leya, the twins Channah and Yaakov, Chaim, and the baby, Dvoreh. Mammeh Frumma worried that the parents' devotion was excessive. Not that they weren't children anyone would be proud to have, but it was reckless to tempt the evil eye to fall upon them.

At age eight, Chaya Leya was a cheerful, responsible little girl. She was already a help to her mother, frequently pressed into service to tend the two youngest. Women who came to the house marveled at how competently Chaya Leya cared for the babies, both still under three. "Like a little mother!" they said. Chaya Leya looked to see if her mother heard and was proud.

Chaya Leya loved to visit her grandparents, where *Zeydeh* Avrom allowed her to feed the ducks and gather the eggs. And, if she was very, very careful, she could clean the eggs and place them in the market basket. *Bobbeh* Frumma told her stories, taught her to crochet, and allowed her to knead the *challah* dough for *shabbes* dinner. Chaya Leya was not exactly a pretty child, but the openness of her round, freckled face and the warmth of her large brown eyes were appealing. Both grandparents adored her.

The twins, Channah and Yaakov, a year or so younger than Chaya Leya, had always been exceptionally beautiful. Although they looked alike because of their fair coloring, high cheekbones, and deeply set eyes, Channah was delicately made, utterly feminine, while Yaakov was taller with a broader face and heavier bone structure. The twins were inseparable, in the way of twins, and perhaps it was this that set them apart from the rest of the family. They whispered endlessly in a secret language unshared by anyone else, disappeared into the woods for whole afternoons at a time, and invented imaginative games with rules only they understood.

At the age of three Yaakov had been sent to *cheyder*. Neither twin had been able to comprehend the separation. Every time the *melamed*'s back was turned to the class, Yaakov had run home to Channah until, exasperated, the teacher had thrashed him soundly and forced him to sit at the front of the room. In time, Yaakov found playmates among the other boys and began to look forward to school. On the whole, the adjustment proved easier for Yaakov than for Channah. For two or three weeks she had followed Yaakov to shul. When turned back by the stern teacher, she had stood on tiptoe, her face pressed against the window. This so unnerved the *melamed* that he had begged Malkeh to keep her home, which proved difficult until Malkeh hit upon the idea of allowing the child to sit beside her while she conducted classes with the women. Channah was not yet six when Malkeh realized that she had advanced beyond the level of most of the adult students.

In Malkeh's secret heart she knew that Channah and Yaakov were spiritually her very own. Their way of moving in and out of fantasy was Malkeh's. Their fearless adventuring mirrored the flight of her own heart. They were tuned to the same high pitch as she, responsive to the same stimuli, made joyful or unhappy by the same things. Surely, Malkeh thought, Yaakov would grow up to sit at the feet of a famous rabbi and Channah would wed a promising yeshiva student. And through their accomplishments, Malkeh also would be complete.

After the twins, whose birth had been hard, it had been two years before there was another child. Chaim, born shortly before the family moved into their own house, was a large, lusty boy, physically strong and stoical even in the cradle. Where Chaya Leya was the child of her grandparents' hearts, and Channah and Yaakov of Malkeh's, Chaim was Yoysef's child. From the time he could crawl, it was impossible to keep him away from the sewing machine. He liked to sit on the floor beneath the machine, working the treadle. Malkeh often joked that he was a born tailor. To Yoysef it was no laughing matter. He would nod solemnly and hand Chaim an empty thread spool to play with.

Dvoreh, the baby, arrived when Chaim was scarcely out of swaddling clothes. A pretty little thing with Yoysef's dark hair and her mother's blue eyes, she was strong-willed and stubborn, given to defiance and temper tantrums but also capable of great sweetness. Her disposition was unlike that of any of the others; perhaps it was because she, of all the children, had not found a special place for herself in anyone's heart. It was said that Dvoreh resembled Malkeh's mother, and perhaps she did, but they saw each other seldom, no more than once or twice during a year's time.

In his shop, Yoysef had added a large stationary sewing machine to the portable he had once strapped to his back, and, just as momentous, he had taken an apprentice. Herschel Rosen was slight, underfed, and possessed of an earnest myopic gaze. Malkeh had objected to him. "He is so thin and small, it will cost us more to feed him than he will be worth," she told Yoysef.

"*Oy*, Malkeh!" Yoysef exclaimed, kissing her on the tip of her nose. "You are so learned in Torah that you are the wonder of the town, and yet you don't even know that it is a mitzvah to educate the orphan to support himself!"

"There are other orphans, bigger and stronger than Herschel."

"But I like the boy. He doesn't mind watching out for Chaim or running after Channah and Yaakov. And Katya takes sugar from his fingers as if from mine."

"But can he sew a seam, Yoysef?"

"He will learn. And he won't cost so much. He will sleep in the barn loft, and he will share whatever we have on the table."

So it was settled, and the shy, pale boy became a member of the growing household. At the beginning he skulked in corners like a shadow, and at table took on his plate only the smallest helping of food. "Here, boy," Yoysef would say, adding a ladle of soup or a chicken leg to the boy's portion. "You need food if you're to grow."

Around Malkeh, Herschel was silent, but gradually he learned to trust Yoysef. The tailor was a rare master, both kindly and sensitive to what it was to be an adolescent. It was probable that no one had taken Herschel seriously before Yoysef. Cholera had claimed both his parents when he was still a small child.

In time Herschel did learn to sew a straight seam. He grew, too, although not quite as tall as Yoysef, and remained slender and pale. After a while, when he had become proficient, Yoysef was able to send him out on the road behind Katya, the portable sewing machine in the wagon ready to mend a pair of trousers or make a simple garment.

*A*s promised, Yoysef had added two more rooms to the house. Malkeh and Yoysef now had the new, the smallest, bedroom for themselves; Chaya Leya, Chaim, and Dvoreh had the original sleeping room, and the twins slept on the shelf of the oven. The kitchen was as small and dark as ever, but Malkeh had persuaded Yoysef to expand the storeroom into a classroom. This, of course, meant that the jars of fruit, sacks of lentils and grains, cones of sugar, the salted fish, and other sundries were ranged on shelves in the kitchen proper, making it more cramped than ever. Sorkeh Feldman had at last departed to join her husband in America, so Malkeh no longer had help with the classes. After Dvoreh's birth, Malkeh had been so overwhelmed by her household duties that she had been tempted to forgo her school entirely.

It was Yevgeny Fedotov who encouraged Malkeh to persist with her teaching.

The steward might tease Malkeh about her women, but since the day they had talked about his dream of a basic education open to all, Fedotov had supplied Malkeh with texts and supplies for her classes. They always arrived by Grisha with the laconic statement that the master had ordered him to deliver them into her hands.

For Malkeh's own personal education, he sent novels, books of essays, poetry. Everything that came to her from Spokoinaya Zemlya, Malkeh read hungrily, as she used to read the Yiddish "women's novels" that now seemed so flat and trite. Fedotov, prompted by the freshness of her outlook and knowing that her comments would both pique and entertain him, introduced her to a wide range of writings. For Malkeh the books were a window on a world outside the narrow community where she lived. Many times she was bewildered by things that her experience had not prepared her to understand. She puzzled over the concept of spiritual love and ecstatic renunciation in Tolstoy's writings. In Malkeh's world, happiness and unhappiness were related to concrete things—having enough money or not having enough, good husbands or bad, mean mothers-in-law or kindly ones. And love between man and woman was physical, spiritual love reserved for God alone. Sacrifice she understood. Yiddish novels were filled with it, though the price was anguish, not ecstasy. Malkeh puzzled over the disparities between Tolstoy's world and her own. She asked Fedotov once what made these differences.

The steward had pondered the question. "Class, I think. Education. Money. Sensibilities of Tolstoy's sort are a luxury accessible to those with the leisure to enjoy subtlety."

Shortly thereafter, the steward introduced Gogol to Malkeh's growing library, and she felt more at home. Ignorance, oppression, and poverty she understood very well.

Malkeh's reaching out to the Russian world made her an anomaly in her neighborhood. Jews lived on an island of Jewishness, surrounded by indifferent or hostile Christians who owned the land they both shared. Since Jews who had lived in Russia for generations still regarded themselves as transients on their way to Jerusalem, what the Russians thought, experienced, or felt was irrelevant to them.

Yoysef was uneasy. One evening he had picked up the book Malkeh had been reading before the evening meal. He was able to decipher the title, *Dead Souls.* "You know, Malkeh, how I have always been proud of your work. To teach someone to pray, even a woman, is a mitzvah. But lately people have been saying that you are getting more Russian than the Russians."

"You mean your mother has been saying that!" Malkeh snorted.

"Not my mother!" Yoysef said irritably. "I hear it in the square and at the bazaar and even at shul. Jews have no business becoming involved in Russian affairs. It does no one any good."

"Oh, Yoysef, you are being old-fashioned! We live in Russia, surrounded by Russian culture, Russian language, Russian customs! We need to understand Russians if we are to survive."

Yoysef said heavily, "It seems to me we have already survived a long time *because* we have kept to our own ways and been true to ourselves."

"I have to do what I have to do!" Malkeh said coldly.

Carefully Yoysef laid the book he was holding on the table. Maybe the men who whispered that he had let Malkeh go too far were right. He turned away.

*A*ndrei, Count Voronov, was not always pleased that he had succeeded in his pursuit of the heiress Natalya Ivashev. She was a
colorless, rather nondescript woman some years his senior. Unlike some
plain women, she had neither wit nor vitality to compensate for her looks;
she was, in a word, dull. What she did have were impeccable connections at
court, a very large patrimony, and no brothers or close relatives to protect
her interests. Andrei had to admit that Natalya's money made up for much
that was lacking. With it he had enjoyed an extensive trip to Italy, purchased
a more elaborate residence, and been able to pay off his gaming debts. When,
a year after their marriage, Natalya gave birth to an heir, Andrei considered
his marital duties fully discharged. He removed himself permanently from
his wife's bed, and in large part from her life.

If Countess Natalya was discontented with her marriage, she had no
one with whom to share her misery. She had been raised an only child on
an isolated estate near Rostov, her mother dead when she was three, her
father remarried to a cold, indifferent second wife; he, too, was dead now.
Not knowing what to do with herself and in a last effort to stave off spin-
sterhood, Natalya had come to a cousin in St. Petersburg to spend the season.
She had been about to return south when, at a ball during the final week of
her stay, she had met the dashing ex-guardsman, Andrei Voronov. He had
quite swept her off her feet. That first night he had completely filled her
dance card, the next morning had had delivered a huge bouquet of hothouse
flowers, and had called that very afternoon. He continued to lavish attention
on her all the succeeding days of her visit.

Thus began a whirlwind courtship that culminated a scarce two months
later in a brilliant St. Petersburg wedding. If Natalya had been less of an innocent, or if she had had an older, more worldly woman to advise her, she would
have recognized that Andrei loved not her but her inheritance. Now it was too
late. But at least she had the child Pyotr, whom she called "Petya."

Having lost her husband, if indeed she had ever had him, Countess
Voronova became increasingly reclusive, her life defined by the dual poles
of church and child. Mornings found her kneeling in prayer at the great St.
Isaac's Cathedral. She preferred the first mass because it was unlikely that at
that early hour she would meet acquaintances who might subject her to
titters and knowing glances. At home, several times a day she prostrated
herself before the icons in her bedroom. She could lose herself in the image
of Christ on her wall; there were times, she believed, when she experienced
the True Mystery, when her whole self was drawn into and consumed by
Him. Natalya longed for the peace of the convent and a spiritual marriage
to replace her earthly one. But when she looked at her infant son, she knew
that she could not leave him, even to become the bride of Christ Himself.

Andrei's life remained virtually untouched by family responsibility. As
before, he conducted his affairs with ballerinas and flirtations with ladies of

the court, bet on horses, dice, and cards, outcaroused his guardsmen friends, and spent, spent, spent!

Timidly, as Andrei devoured her dowry and began to sell off pieces of her estate, Natalya questioned her husband's extravagant life-style.

"You are becoming a terrible bore with your stinginess, Natalya," Andrei would always reply. "It is no wonder that I prefer the company of my friends to you!"

For a time Natalya, intimated, subsided, but as she saw everything that had been hers slipping away, her reproaches grew increasingly shrill. The final straw came when Andrei mentioned that he had accepted an offer for what remained of her ancestral properties.

White-faced, she said, "You cannot mean that, Andrei! The estate has been in the Ivashev family for generations! I had thought that someday it would belong to our son!"

Carelessly Andrei said, "It is so remote from anyplace, I was lucky to find anyone who wanted to buy it! What do we need it for? We never go there. Certainly I would never for a moment consider living in such a god-forsaken hole!"

Natalya was cruelly stung. "All I hear is what *you* want, what *you* would consider, what *you* need!" she cried. "Do you never give a thought to me or to Petya?"

"Certainly I do. And lately, Natalya, I have been thinking that you and the boy would be far more comfortable away from St. Petersburg. You are much too involved with the church here! All that religion confuses you."

"What do you mean, Andrei? Away—where?"

"I thought that a little respite in the country at Spokoinaya Zemlya would suit you and the child very well."

"What you mean," Natalya said bitterly, "is that a little respite from us would suit you very well."

Andrei smiled. "That too."

Countess Natalya would have been well enough content living at Spokoinaya Zemlya if she could have put thoughts of Andrei's betrayal away from her. She had no doubt that he was spending her inheritance as fast as he could convert her property into cash. Natalya's infatuation with Andrei had long since faded, but she found his liaisons with other women a humiliation and his excesses soul-sickening. Only her son could mitigate her suffering.

Petya at two had his father's good looks but otherwise, fortunately, inherited little of either his father's nature or his mother's intellect. The boy loved the wide open fields of Spokoinaya Zemlya and thrived on the attentions of Maria Feodorovna and the other servants. Not in the least did he miss the father who had had so little to do with him. Appearances suggested he had selected a new father for himself. To the best of his limited physical capabilities, he dogged the footsteps of Yevgeny Fedotov, his fat legs running to keep up with the man's wide stride, and his china-blue eyes watching the steward for a sign that he was noticed.

*Y*evgeny Sergeivitch's school had been a failure, although most of the men were proud to be able now to write their names. Fedotov thought privately that it might have been more of a success if Father George had shared in his own vision of an educated peasantry. But Father George believed that God had deliberately placed the peasant where he was in the scheme of things, and it was wicked to interfere with God's will.

Perhaps after all, Fedotov mused, the men were still too close to serfdom to benefit significantly from schooling. Maybe the next generation, or the one after, would be ready. In the meantime, he could point to two successes: the young man who had gone to be a monk at the monastery at Vladimir, and fourteen-year-old Vassily Ossipovitch. Father George had found little to endear the latter to him. The boy was sullen and hostile, contemptuous of the other students and barely civil to the priests. Still, even Father George had to admit that the youngster was intellectually beyond any of the others. How that could be, he did not know. The family was one of the worst on the estate—a father who was a common drunk, a mother who worked in the fields like a man, and a daughter who would go to bed with anyone for a handful of change. He resigned himself to the mystery of God's intent.

In the two years that the school was in existence, Vassily had learned to read and to write in complete, mostly grammatical sentences. It was never Father George's ambition to teach the peasants to read more than a few simple words, and here was this youngster reading whole books—books, incidentally, that he had stolen ("borrowed," he had insisted) from the priest's own bookshelf! Vassily received a proper beating for that crime and would have been dismissed from the school if Fedotov had not intervened.

When the school closed, what to do with Vassily was a dilemma. As Father George smugly pointed out to the steward, all that learning had made the boy unfit for his place in life. "I told you how it would be, *Gospodin*," the priest had said. "Education spoils them for the fields. And it makes them restless and discontented."

"Is that how you interpret the doctrines of St. Thomas Aquinas?" the steward asked mildly.

Father George flushed. "I am as versed in Christian-Rationalist tradition as the next man!"

"So it would seem." Fedotov smiled coldly.

"But the fact of the matter is, the boy no longer wants to do farm work, and, with his irreligious bent, we will never make a monk or a priest of him. That is all there is for him!"

"Not quite all. I will give him a job and further his training myself. Call him in, and we'll ask him."

When it was explained to Vassily what the steward had in mind, the boy looked warily from one to the other of the two men. "Why?" was all he asked.

Fedotov was amused. "Why what? Why should you continue your education, or why would I want to do it, or why you and not someone else?"

Vassily's face was a thundercloud. "What will you get out of it?"

"Ah, I see. You think I want to exploit you."

"I must have wages."

"Of course."

"As much as I would have working in the fields." The boy was bargaining now, his eyes dark and hard like flint.

"Well, I don't know about that. I will be teaching you arithmetic, penmanship, bookkeeping—and manners! Is that not worth something to you?"

"My family needs my wages."

"In time you will earn more than any of them."

Vassily turned toward the door. "I am not interested. My father can't work, and my mother earns too little to take care of us all. I will go back to work in the fields."

In consternation, Fedotov stopped him. "Wait, Vassily. It seems you already have a head for business! All right, I will pay you the same wages you would earn outside."

"Agreed," said the boy with a slight smile.

Despite initial misgivings, the arrangement had worked surprisingly well. Father George's warnings about the boy's surliness were perhaps overstated, or maybe at the moment it suited Vassily to be outwardly civil. He made himself useful to the steward, no task too menial for him, from running errands to brewing tea or shining boots. He carefully attended the steward's instruction and practiced his lessons diligently. He never forgot anything he had been told once. He was, in fact, a model student, molding himself exactly to the paradigm that existed in Fedotov's mind. The steward liked to boast that Vassily was being trained to work anywhere, in time to be followed by many other Vassilys, all moving from the darkness of ignorance into the sunlight of a new middle class.

"But what do you really know about him?" Malkeh asked one day as they sat over tea.

"Know about him? He can keep ledgers, and he has an acceptable hand for copying letters."

"You talk about him as though he were a piece of furniture or a zero on a page."

"Nonsense!" Yevgeny was testy. The woman could be incredibly irritating at times.

Malkeh persisted. "Do you ever just talk to him? Do you ask him about what is happening in his life, his worries—his hopes?"

"Just like a woman to bring up irrelevancies!" Fedotov grumbled. "No, I do not sit around discussing his problems with him. It should be enough that I have given him an opportunity to better himself. He is my example of what you can teach a peasant to do."

"*Gospodin* Fedotov's a gifted animal trainer," Maria Feodorovna said acidly.

"I think you should ask him what *he* wants," Malkeh insisted.

"You'll probably find out he wants to murder us all in our beds," Maria Feodorovna said. She did not like Vassily.

An uncomfortable silence grew among them. Malkeh realized that she did not much like Vassily either. There was something about those flat, opaque eyes that tugged at a memory she could not quite place.

Chapter 13

*D*amn the woman, Fedotov thought. What business was it of hers how he treated the boy Vassily? But since the day he had first met her, Malkeh Mandelkern had had opinions on everything, and never had she kept her thoughts to herself! What was this anyhow? Was she his self-appointed mentor and his conscience? What a mistake it had been to get involved with her in the first place! It gave her pretensions and made her unpleasingly forward. Of course, he could cut off the relationship at any time he chose. He could stop supporting her so-called school, not wait to hear what she would say about books he loaned her, avoid the kitchen when she came to see Maria Feodorovna. Before he met her, he had managed quite well without a critical voice in the background.

Ah, God! He was fooling himself if he thought it was not too late to turn back. He had but to see her little cart draw up in the yard or hear her light voice in the kitchen to be compelled into her presence. What a joke! A bastard to find himself in love with a Jewess!

The boy Vassily was another matter. Did Malkeh and Maria Feodorovna really think that he did not understand what it meant to a poor boy to make the transition from peasant's hut to a grand house like Spokoinaya Zemlya? Indeed, who knew better than he!

*Y*evgeny had been scarcely seven when he was taken out of the carpenter's hut to live in the manor house. His memory of what led up to the move was blessedly vague; the facts he knew only from Maria Feodorovna. She had told him that his stepfather, the carpenter Fedotov, always a drinker, had stayed drunk for a long time after Yevgeny's mother died. Self-control dissolved by vodka, his hatred of his wife's bastard had exploded into violent rage, and he had come after the boy with a heavy dowel. He would have succeeded in murdering him if Maria Feodorovna had not come that day on an errand of mercy, to deliver a pot of *ukha* to the bereaved pair. She had grabbed the stick from Fedotov's hand and pushed him off the unconscious child.

"I'll kill him! Just wait! I'll kill the snotty little bastard!" The carpenter's little red-rimmed eyes were venomous. "You can't be here to watch him all the time, Maria Feodorovna. I'll get him, be sure of it!"

Her screams brought others running. The coachman Grisha lifted the bloodied body of the boy in his arms and carried him into the big house. Maria followed, praying to all the saints, to God, to the Blessed Virgin that the child was not too damaged to live. "The master must be told! The count must know at once what has happened!" she muttered.

After Grisha had laid the boy on the housekeeper's bed, he had asked anxiously, "You will not really tell on Fedotov, will you?" The code among the servants to protect their own was clear.

"I must. He wants the boy's life."

On hearing of the matter, the count had come to view for himself the damage inflicted on Yevgeny. The boy had sustained a severe concussion, a badly lacerated face, a broken arm, and there was scarcely a place on his small body that was without hurt.

The face the child turned up to the master was so swollen that his eyes were mere slits in a doughy mass.

"What did you do that your father beat you like this?" the count asked.

"I was born," the child said, his voice faint but clear. "And he is not my father, *Gospodin*."

The count nodded. The boy's eyes were amber, like hers, like the girl Elena's. He went away then.

Yevgeny stayed in Maria Feodorovna's bed until he had recovered. He was still there when the carpenter Fedotov was removed to the estate of a landowner in the next district; the count had hated to lose such a skilled worker, but, after all, he was only a serf, and lately he had been drinking too much and had become a danger to have around.

There being no place for him to go, the child settled down for a time with Maria Feodorovna in the kitchen. In retrospect it was the most tranquil period of his life; it had not lasted long. As soon as he acquired basic manners, was taught some personal hygiene, and learned to eat with a knife and fork, Count Voronov pronounced him suitable for the role of playmate to his heir. In the count's view, Andrei had lived too long without youthful companionship, and it had made him selfish and arrogant. How fortunate it was, then, that Elena's child had dropped into their lives almost as if heaven had sent him! For Yevgeny Fedotov, moving into the main house was less a gift from heaven than a scourge from hell.

*V*assily's situation was not as Fedotov's had been. Vassily had a mother, a father, sisters. He still had a home where he had always lived, simple though it was. At Spokoinaya Zemlya he had a defined place with a role to play and a job to do. It was not the same at all. Still, remembering that other child, the man experienced a twinge of guilt. Maybe he could have been more sensitive to how Vassily might feel. Awkward and self-conscious, Fedotov made a halfhearted attempt to draw him out.

"Well, Vassily, and how is your family these days?"

"Why do you ask?"

"I am interested."

"They are as well as they can be."

Vassily had erected impenetrable barriers between them. It would, the steward thought, require enormous effort to breech them, and then it might never happen. Everyone has his own way of protecting himself, he thought. He would try a little longer, and then, if there was no sign from the boy, he would give it up.

"Tell me, Vassily, have you thought about what your goal in life might be?"

"Goal, *Gospodin?*"

"Yes, what would you like to be when you are, say, my age?"

The peculiar lightless black eyes did not blink. "Master of Spokoinaya Zemlya."

Fedotov laughed. Later, with a shudder, he remembered Maria Feodorovna's half-joking comment that day about what Vassily might really want.

*S*ome of Fedotov's innovations at Spokoinaya Zemlya were producing excellent results. The *mujiks'* fear that they would be displaced by tractors gradually disappeared when they found that the farm machinery cleared more land to be worked and created the possibility of earning additional wages. Four days a week the peasants tilled the count's fields, two days they could work their own individual strips of ground, and on Sundays they rested. But no matter how hard they worked, the income was seldom enough. Many a peasant rued the day the Emancipation Edict had replaced serfdom with the yoke of taxes and redemption payments due to the government, and rents for their huts and allotted land due to the landowners. Many at Spokoinaya Zemlya had never understood all this completely until it was explained to them by Igor Karpovitch of the *zemstvo.*

"The Emancipation Edict," Karpovitch told them, "allowed the landlords to keep two-thirds of the land on their estates."

"Yeah, all the best pasture and forest land!" someone in the crowd shouted. "We got the rocks and the bogs!"

Karpovitch allowed the bitter laughter to die down before he proceeded. "The rest of the land—as you say, the rocks and the bogs—was distributed to the serfs. So the landowners wouldn't suffer any"—he paused to let the irony sink in—"the government paid them eighty percent of the price of the land they gave up to you. But it wasn't a gift, like some of you thought. *You* have to pay the government back for what they paid the landowners. That means that you will have 'redemption payments' to make for the next forty-nine years."

"Forty-nine years! But that means my grandchildren will still be paying for that lousy little bit of ground they gave me!"

"Not 'gave' you, friend," Karpovitch corrected one of the peasants. "Your redemption payments are buying it. But that's not the whole of it. You still have to pay the remaining twenty percent of the price of the land directly to the landlord."

"That's right," said a thin, dour-faced man, "and to pay the government and the landlord, I have to borrow money! The usurer in the village charges a fortune! Every year I get in deeper. I was better off before I was freed!"

"You don't have to borrow in the village," someone offered. "Count Voronov will lend you money at less."

Karpovitch summed it up: "Since emancipation, many of you owe every kopeck you earn for rents and loan payments. What's more, for most of you, the land the government allocated to you is not enough to support your families. If you have six sons, will that thin little strip of ground feed them? And suppose those six sons each marry and have six sons of their own, are you all going to have to starve together? Or will your children be forced off the land to try to find work in a factory?"

"Not fair! They've buggered us again!"

"Emancipation was a hoax, my friends," Karpovitch said calmly. "We will have to think of ways to make things more equal."

*I*t was at about the time that the Countess Natalya and her little boy came to live on the estate that Fedotov received a letter from Andrei, directing him to increase the quarterly rents. He raged over Andrei's arrogance for a day or two and then put the letter away in his desk drawer and forgot about it. A second, stronger letter followed two months later, for Andrei Petrovitch needed a great deal of money to maintain himself in style. This time the steward prepared a careful reply that pointed out that if the peasants were forced to the wall, the estate could lose the labor needed to harvest the Voronov crops.

The receipt of this letter prompted a visit from Count Voronov himself. Maria Feodorovna told Malkeh about what had happened one afternoon as they sat together by the kitchen fire.

The count had arrived unannounced just after the midday meal. His carriage was new, his sleek horses had finely worked bridles set with semiprecious stones, and the count himself was resplendent in a cloak cut to the latest Paris fashion. Yet Andrei Petrovitch looked distraught, his long fair hair unkempt and his blue eyes bloodshot. Not pausing either to greet his countess or to ask after his son, the count stormed into the estate office. For an hour or more Andrei and Fedotov were closeted together. Maria Feodorovna could hear the boom and thunder of Andrei's enraged voice and occasionally the sound of an angry retort from the steward, but, try as she might, she had been unable to catch the words spoken. She knew, of course, that they were arguing over the rents. Finally, face flushed, the young count came out of the office, slamming the door so hard it rattled in its frame, and went directly to his bedroom, ordering Grisha to bring a bottle of cognac. When Yevgeny emerged a little later, his expression was equally black. He had poured himself a tumbler of vodka and tossed it down in one draught, glaring at Maria Feodorovna, his look daring her to say anything about it. Then he stomped out into the night with a parting sneer about leaving the count and countess alone to their tender reunion.

After the count's return to St. Petersburg, Fedotov issued the order that increased payments to the estate. Maria Feodorovna suspected that the raise was less than the count had demanded, but nonetheless it added significantly to the burdens borne by the peasants. The *zemstvo* sent a delegation of five to protest, led by Igor Karpovitch.

Fedotov welcomed the group politely into his office but continued to sit behind his desk while the peasant group stood. Vassily found a vantage point for himself in a shadowy corner; he did not want the steward to order him out.

Karpovitch was a short, thick, barrel-chested man. He had a broad, flat face with a pugnacious nose and a chin that thrust forward, giving him the aggressive look of a wild boar. On this day he wore the traditional peasant costume of a collarless homespun shirt over pants belted with woven hemp. Greasy black hair stuck out from beneath his cap. Incongruous to the rest of his attire were his fine leather boots. Fedotov's initial glance told him everything he needed to know about the man.

Fedotov had seen Karpovitch around the village, but no words had been exchanged between them. He had arrived a year or two past and had promptly been elected to the local council. No one seemed to know where he had come from. He had neither land to till nor any visible occupation, and yet he appeared to have some measure of education and enough money to live rather more comfortably than the other villagers. Fedotov suspected that he had been sent to Spokoinaya Zemlya from one of the revolutionary groups in the capital. Since he had caused no trouble, there had been no reason for the steward to confront him thus far.

"*Gospodin* Fedotov," the spokesman, Karpovitch, began without pre-amble. "About this demand you have made for increased quarterly pay-ments—"

"The rent increase, yes."

Karpovitch said sharply, "Let us be accurate; rent is only a small part."

"That is true," Fedotov conceded. "Also included are loan repayments and so forth. For the sake of convenience, we call it all rent. It is under-stood."

"A way to flimflam the people, is it not?"

"No." The steward's tone was controlled.

One of the others of the men ranged around Karpovitch asked, "What is the purpose? Times are hard!"

"It is the landlord's perogative."

There was a chorus of angry protests. "Our families will starve!" "I can't feed four children on a plot big enough for one!" "Why should you get rich on our backs?" "Bloodsucker!"

A truculent Karpovitch demanded to know why Fedotov had not cleared the "rent" increase with the *zemstvo*.

"That is not within the purpose of the councils."

A burly peasant who towered over the rest rumbled, "Well, I'm not going to work anymore—and I'll knock the block off anyone who says they will! Your crops can rot on the ground for all I care!"

Karpovitch backed him up. "You heard him. What do you say to that, Master Steward?"

"You are making a threat, are you?" Fedotov asked carefully. "I think you need to reconsider." He looked each of the five men in the face. "If you don't work, there will be no wages and no food on your tables. And if you try to block other men from working, you can be certain that I will call in the police."

The men huddled around Karpovitch, whispering. Dark looks were directed at Fedotov, and the big man shook his fist.

The steward stood up to indicate that he had heard them out and considered the meeting at an end. "Let me tell you something. Most of you have lived at Spokoinaya Zemlya since you were born, and your fathers before you. If you don't like it here, if you feel mistreated by the Voronovs, feel free to find a place to live and work where you will be happier. Be assured I will give my written permission for any of you to leave. Now, I have nothing further to say to you except good afternoon!"

"I think you'll be sorry for this," Karpovitch said darkly as the delegation filed out.

When they were gone, Fedotov sighed. I already am, he thought.

He caught sight of Vassily. "So what did you learn from that, Vassily?" he asked.

"That the rich can do anything they want to the poor."

The steward grimaced. It was a lesson no one had to teach Andrei.

The winter of 1888 was a mild one. By November there had still been no snow, and people felt uneasy about the unseasonable warmth. Malkeh could not remember another such late winter, although some of the older generation agreed that there had been other strange years—1857, when it had not snowed until almost December, and 1862, when spring arrived almost as soon as winter was well under way. When the apple trees began to put out their pale blooms in October, everyone agreed that it was a bad sign.

There was a rash of colds, coughs, and sore throats in November. Parents wished for the coming of the snow, which would clear away the miasma.

Over the years Malkeh's children had had their share of childhood illnesses but, God be thanked, they were quite strong and healthy, and so far that year none had suffered so much as a sniffle. Chaya Leya and the youngest, Dvoreh, wore little cloves of garlic on strings around their necks, hung there by Mammeh Frumma to ward off infection; the other children discarded theirs as soon as their grandmother was out of sight. Their cousin Moishe, now a big boy of eleven, joked that Mammeh Frumma's grandchildren might not all *look* alike but they certainly *smelled* the same!

Malkeh didn't put much credence in her mother-in-law's preventatives, but it seemed reasonable to her that the children would be less likely to catch cold if they stayed away from others who might be infected. When some of the boys in the *cheyder* began to cough, Malkeh kept Yaakov and Chaim at home, although Yoysef thought that the boys should not be encouraged to miss school.

Channah was delighted to have her brothers home. Malkeh set the children to work at lessons, but Yaakov did not readily accept his mother's authority and either squabbled with Chaim, or, together with Channah, devised tricks to play on their older sister, who finally retreated to the barn in tears.

Malkeh cut herself a switch from the willow tree with which she threatened the twins, but they were seldom intimidated by their mother. By the third day of enforced isolation, Malkeh felt her resolution weakening and decided she would send the boys back to school the next morning. She was worn out from being up all night with Dvoreh, who had an earache, and her patience with the twins' mischief was at low ebb.

When Golda dropped by to visit, Yaakov threw his arms about his aunt and appealed to her to talk Mammeh into letting them go outdoors to play. The other children joined in the clamor.

"Malkeh?" Golda pleaded. "Before they destroy the furniture and take away your sanity?"

Malkeh laughed, relenting.

With her admonishments to stay away from children who were sick largely unheard, the four older children hastily dispersed before Malkeh could change her mind. Chaim disappeared into his father's workshop, and Chaya Leya hurried off to her grandparents'. The twins were gone in a moment, to where, no one knew.

With Dvoreh finally napping, Malkeh sank into her rocking chair near the warm oven and allowed Golda to bring her tea. She sighed. Three days housebound with a flock of noisy, restless children and a sick toddler had made her irritable. It was good to have Golda to talk to. Chairs drawn close, the women settled themselves for a peaceful afternoon.

While Golda demonstrated a new crochet stitch she was working into a shawl, she told Malkeh the news from the outside. Reb Avraham's young wife, who had run off with a peddler, had returned in disgrace, with child, it was said. Malkeh clucked sympathetically, Reb Avraham being fat, bald, and toothless. Poor girl!

Golda also brought news of the soon-to-be wedding between the pale, thin daughter of the rabbi, and one of her father's most gifted pupils, Mordechai, beardless and not yet fourteen. It was an arrangement, of course, but what kind of marriage could it be for a shy little boy and a listless bride? Malkeh agreed that marriage between children was wrong, and Golda said that she felt fortunate to have fallen in love with Dovid the first time she saw him, on their wedding day.

Golda had heard that there was anger among the peasants about the raise in rents at Spokoinaya Zemlya. With a lurch of her heart Malkeh listened as Golda related what she had overheard a *mujik* say in the bazaar. He had made sly mention of a heavy tree limb's having crashed close to the count's steward as he rode through the forest. It had barely missed him and had frightened his horse into bolting. Fedotov was a master horseman, and he had brought his mount under control with no harm done either of them. But there was talk that it was not an accident, that the limb had deliberately been sawed through.

Malkeh turned white, and her hand trembled on the tea glass.

"But that's terrible!" Malkeh said. "Do you know more?"

Golda shook her head. "Only that the Voronov peasants feel that the steward deserves whatever he gets. The *mujik* told Dovid that something bad would surely happen now. Feelings are running high. This Fedotov must be a real devil. Imagine, raising the rents in winter so that a lot of families will surely go cold and hungry!"

Malkeh said hotly, "You don't know anything about it, Golda! If *Gospodin* Fedotov raised the rents, there must have been a reason. He's a good man, and I know he cares about his people!"

Golda stared at Malkeh. What was she getting so excited about? Ah, well, Malkeh spent a lot of time at Spokoinaya Zemlya, and maybe she saw things differently because of that. Tactfully, she changed the subject.

Chaya Leya came home from her grandparents' house with a chicken wrapped in newspaper. It would make good strong soup, Mammeh Frumma said, for the little one with the earache. Dvoreh was awake now, being rocked gently on the lap of her aunt. Chaim's squeals of delight could be heard from the shop, and Malkeh knew that Yoysef was again letting the boy work the powerful sewing machine. She wished he wouldn't do it, it frightened her so. There was not yet any sign of the twins, and Malkeh had gone to the window several times to see if they were coming.

"Malkeh, you worry too much," Golda said. "They have probably stopped to play at Yenta's, or maybe they are outside somewhere with their other friends."

Malkeh fretted, "I don't want them to go near anyone who has a cough or a sore throat. There's so much sickness in the city!"

"A cold is only a cold," Golda said, "and you can't keep children wrapped in swaddling clothes. What is there to worry about? A little cold? After all, they haven't been near Chaika's Menkeh, God forbid."

"What is it with Chaika's Menkeh?" Malkeh asked with a rising sense of alarm.

"Why, the choking sickness. Hadn't you heard?" Golda asked in surprise. "Oh, Menkeh isn't bad, thank God. He had trouble breathing and swallowing for a day or two, but he's better now, almost well, in fact. Gittel came and wrapped his throat and chest with red flannel smeared with goose grease, and day and night she poured scalding tea down his throat to keep it from closing over. He will be fine, they say."

Malkeh shivered at the thought of the sickness that came once every several years, forming a membrane over throat passages and suffocating little children. Menkeh was in Yaakov's class at the *cheyder*. Yaakov had been to his house to play, when? A few days ago?

"Maybe it wasn't that at all," Golda said, seeing the fear on Malkeh's face. "He recovered so fast, it was probably just a cold. You know how Chaika exaggerates." She placed Dvoreh into Malkeh's arms. It was time for her to go home to fix the evening meal for Dovid. As she prepared to leave,

Channah and Yaakov clattered into the kitchen, their excited chatter filling the house with noise.

"See, the children are home and lively as sparrows," Golda said as she hugged the two children. "Don't worry your mother so," she admonished them, kissing their rosy cheeks. "How bright your eyes are! And how toasty warm you feel!" she said, unwinding the scarf from around Yaakov's neck. Turning to Malkeh, she added, "And you worried about their catching a chill!"

Chapter 14

*Y*aakov woke Malkeh. "Mammeh, it's too hot in the kitchen," he complained. "Can I sleep in your bed?"

Sleepily Malkeh rolled over toward Yoysef, making room for her small son beside her. "Go to sleep now, Yaakov."

The boy crept into his parents' bed and obediently closed his eyes, but he was fretful and his twisting and turning woke his mother a second time an hour or so later. He was muttering in his sleep. Apparently a bad dream, Malkeh thought, reaching an arm around the child to calm him. His skin was hot to the touch, very hot. Alarmed, Malkeh sat up in the bed.

"Yaakov, Yaakov," she said, shaking him a little. "Wake up, Yaakov."

His head continued to roll from side to side, but he did not open his eyes. Malkeh leaned over him to hear what he said in his dream, but she could make out only an occasional word—"beast," he said, "dark," "black."

Urgently Malkeh touched Yoysef's shoulder. "There is something wrong with Yaakov!"

Yoysef was instantly awake. He lit the oil lamp. "Probably caught cold," he said, but one look at the child's flushed face was enough to make icy fingers of fear close around his heart. He dressed hastily. "We must try to bring down the fever. A wet sheet, I've heard. We'll wrap him in a wet sheet."

While Yoysef went to prepare the sheet, Malkeh continued to try to rouse the boy. "Yaakov, wake up! Wake up, Yaakov!" She lifted him from the bedcovers, holding him in her arms and alternately shaking him and pressing urgent lips to his burning forehead. Although he sighed and murmured, moving restlessly in her embrace, he did not wake.

Yoysef and Malkeh stripped the boy and wrapped the wet sheet around him, pinning it securely so that he could not throw it off in his delirium. The heat of his body dried the sheet in a short time. Again and again Yoysef remoistened the bedclothes with cool water, and toward dawn Yaakov seemed quieter.

"Thank God," Malkeh said, touching his cheek with her fingertips, "the fever has broken. He'll be all right now."

"A bad cold," Yoysef nodded, "only a bad cold."

They spoke to each other with more confidence than either of them felt.

In an hour it was light. Channah came padding into the bedroom. "What's the matter with Yaakov?" she asked, frightened.

"He is not feeling well." Malkeh took the little girl by the hand. "Come, I'll tuck you into your quilts. It's much too early to get up."

"He looks funny, Mammeh. Yaakov looks very funny."

Malkeh turned to look at him. Channah was right. The deep flush of the night had been replaced by a blue-tinged pallor.

"Get up, Yaakov!" Channah called sharply to her brother. "Get up!"

They could almost see Yaakov's spirit struggling to respond. Malkeh and Yoysef held their breaths, but Channah did not question that Yaakov would open his eyes. "Come on now, Yaakov! I want you!" Channah said in a cross voice. The boy's eyelids fluttered, he fought the darkness that held him, and then his eyes opened, seeking Channah.

"I—can't—breathe," Yaakov whispered. "Help—me."

"Oh, my God!" Malkeh clutched at Yoysef for support.

All that day and into the evening Malkeh and Yoysef did whatever they could think of, whatever it was they had ever heard mentioned as a remedy for the choking sickness. Gittel was sent for and Mammeh Frumma, and late in the day Yoysef tried, without success, to reach the doctor. By that time Yaakov had again lapsed into unconsciousness. By midafternoon they had an additional worry; Channah had begun to complain of a sore throat, headache, difficulty in swallowing.

Yaakov died during the second night of his illness. Channah, though she was herself very ill, seemed to know it. As always, she was in a hurry to join Yaakov. Within a few hours she had.

They were buried next to each other in one grave. The funeral had been a hasty one with none in attendance besides Mammeh Frumma, Papa Avrom, Golda, and Dovid, for there was great fear in Polotsk, and each locked his doors against his neighbors lest there be contamination. Yenta had sent a heartfelt message of sympathy but was terrified for the lives of her own children. From Spokoinaya Zemlya a week or so later came a great bunch of yellow roses; Maria Feodorovna and Yevgeny Fedotov had only just heard of the deaths.

Chaya Leya, who had been in and out of the sickroom carrying basins of hot water and heated flannel cloths, was the next to fall ill, complaining of headache on the very day of the funeral. The diphtheria that had swept the city and the nearby villages was virulent, moving rapidly from house to house, felling children and adults alike, killing even strong men in just a day or two. It seemed likely that Chaya Leya would follow her brother and sister in death. Fiercely, her grandmother, who had come to take care of her, would not permit her to die.

Malkeh appeared unaware of Chaya Leya's illness. For days following the funeral, Malkeh had gone about the house as in a dream, picking up Yaakov's books where they had been dropped and Channah's doll from under the oven. Talking aloud in a strange, flat voice, she said she must surely chide the children severely when they came home because of their untidiness and for being gone so long without permission.

Yoysef said to her gently, "Malkeh, let the things be. Chaya Leya is feverish and her throat is sore. She needs you."

"Yes, yes," Malkeh replied from a distance. "That bad child! She has caught a cold from Drayzl Bashinka when I told her to stay away from other children."

Yoysef shook his head and went away. Malkeh sat stiffly in a chair near the window, looking out between the curtains and watching for Yaakov and Channah to come home. She had been there all night and part of the day, waiting, always waiting. In the meantime, her eldest child lay gasping for breath in the next room. A grim Mammeh Frumma, sleeves rolled to the elbow, fought the angel of death for her grandchild's life, Yoysef beside her and the pale, tense apprentice boy, Herschel Rosen, doing as he was told to help.

Golda had taken Chaim and Dvoreh to stay in her house. Malkeh seemed unaware of that too. She had no more interest in Chaim and Dvoreh than in Chaya Leya. On the second night after the burial of the twins, she allowed Yoysef to take off her dress and lead her to bed, where she fell into a heavy sleep that provided no rest.

The next day Chaya Leya, struggling to get even a trickle of air through the tiny passage in her throat not yet covered over by the membrane of sickness, began to show the characteristic blue color of impending death. A desperate Mammeh Frumma sent Herschel for the doctor, though she knew it was a miracle and not a doctor that was needed.

The frantic boy ran here and there through the streets. The doctor? Yes, he had been at the Chernyakovs to see the mother of the family. One street away only. "If you hurry, you might catch him there—"

But when Herschel reached the Chernyakovs, the doctor's buggy was gone. He had gone to the blacksmith's, just the other side of town in the shadow of Napoleon's Wall. And at the blacksmith's there were only the sounds of wailing from within, and no one answered Herschel's knock.

A neighbor child called out that the doctor had gone to Pleshkov the Baker. Herschel sped through the streets to the bake shop, but the doctor had already left. The baker's wife told him that the doctor had gone to the count's estate to attend the gardener's child.

Despairing over all the time he had wasted, Herschel ran home to the stable and threw himself on the back of a surprised Katya. Though the old mare was not accustomed to being ridden, she seemed to sense Herschel's urgency and did her best to take him where he wanted to go.

Panting, Herschel stood in the open doorway of the gardener's hut, telling the weary doctor how sick Chaya Leya was and begging him to come at once. The doctor only shook his head. "No, no, I cannot come. I am only one, and there are so many sick. So many—I can't get to them all, and there isn't much to be done when I get there anyway."

"But Doctor, she's turning blue. She's dying!" The boy did not seem to know he was weeping, the tears rolling unheeded down his cheeks and dropping off the end of his chin.

"They are all dying," the tired doctor said sadly.

"But—but what are we to do, then?" the boy demanded, furiously clutching at the doctor's coat.

"Do? Do?" the doctor said, angry because he was helpless. "How do I know what to do!" Then, getting hold of himself, he said with a semblance of his usual measured tones, "Keep the child warm and quiet so that she won't waste whatever's left of her strength. You must get some nourishment inside her, a drop at a time if necessary, so that she still has energy to fight the disease. If all else fails and if the membrane completely closes her windpipe, you must carefully cut a little hole to let the air pass through. And then she might die anyway, either because you've cut in the wrong place or because it's too late and she's too weak to go on!" The elegant doctor, disheveled as no one had ever seen him, paused to wipe his perspiring face with a square of silk. When he looked up, the boy had gone, the clatter of hooves already in the road.

The doctor shook his head. He doubted whether the old horse the boy was riding could go at that pace all the way to Polotsk without dropping dead. And what in the name of Christ had he told the boy anyway? To perform a tracheotomy, untrained, on a weakened child who was already near death anyway? He must have been out of his head. And yet, he thought, the weariness flooding over him in a great wave, what difference would it make, for the child would die in any case, and putting a knife to her throat might at least spare her the agony of slow strangulation.

When Herschel arrived home, Chaya Leya had reached crisis stage, her brown eyes fairly bugging out from her head, her tongue swollen and half out of her mouth. Mammeh Frumma was bent over her, her mouth against the child's, hoping against all odds that some air might still force itself into the air-starved lungs.

Breathing heavily, Herschel reported what the doctor had said. Yoysef, white with shock, shook his head and ran from the room. A man could stand only so much!

Mammeh Frumma said grimly, "Herschel, go into the kitchen and find the sharpest knife in the drawer, the one used to cut up the *shabbes* chicken. The oven is hot. Put the knife on the coals until it turns white. Then go to the marsh behind Elef's house and cut some fat green reeds. They must be clean, do you understand, not from where animals do their business. Bring the things here with the bottle of schnapps. Be quick now!"

The boy flew to do the old woman's bidding, relieved to be away from the terrible sound of Chaya Leya's gasping breath. While he was gone, Mammeh Frumma made her preparations, tearing a clean linen cloth into strips which she placed in readiness on the table next to the bed. Then she laid the child flat, head back, a rolled towel under the neck for support. By this time Chaya Leya was only semiconscious. All the time she was preparing, Mammeh Frumma was praying under her breath, asking God to keep her from killing her grandchild and exhorting Him to prevent further tragedy from destroying this broken household.

Yoysef did not come back into the room, but stood, weeping, his head pressed against the wall near the door. Malkeh, alone with her uncomprehending suffering, did not seem to know what was taking place elsewhere in the house.

When Herschel returned with the things he had been sent for, the grandmother told him to hold the child's head firmly lest she suddenly open her eyes and jerk forward at the sight of the knife. Herschel knelt by the side of the bed, his hands on either side of the small brown head. He dared not look at the knife that Mammeh Frumma held in her hands.

Carefully the grandmother felt for the windpipe where it made a small bump under the white skin. Shuddering as she thought of the times she had watched the *shokhet* cut quickly through the jugular vein of a chicken, she bathed the child's throat with schnapps, picked up the sharp knife still warm from the oven, and ever so carefully made a thin vertical incision, pressing the blade gently through several tracheal rings and then using the knife handle to spread the edges of the opening. Chaya Leya scarcely stirred. The cut was clean and sure, and with God's hand on hers, it had been made in the right place. Almost at once Mammeh Frumma and Herschel could hear the bubbling intake of air into the lungs, and the blue color began to fade from Chaya Leya's face. Mammeh Frumma washed the largest of the hollow reeds with brandy and inserted it into the hole she had made, finishing by bandaging it in place with clean linen strips.

Exhausted, the child drifted from unconsciousness into sleep while Mammeh cleaned up the blood and then sat down next to the bed to watch and wait, eyes closed, lips moving in prayer. She had to be ready if the reed should become clogged with mucus.

Chaya Leya lived.

When Yoysef went into the bedroom later to tell Malkeh that it seemed that their eldest would recover, she seemed confused. Vaguely she said, "I'm glad her cold is better—"

Yoysef stared at his wife.

"But where are Channah and Yaakov? It's getting dark and they're not home yet!" she fretted, picking at the coverlet.

Yoysef took her by the shoulders and shook her roughly. "They are not coming home, Malkeh!" he shouted. "Yaakov and Channah are not coming home! They are buried in the ground—" His voice broke, and the tears streamed down his cheeks. "They are dead. Do you hear me, Malkeh? *They are dead!*"

Malkeh looked at him, her eyes dark with recognition of something she did not want to acknowledge. "No—oh, no—" she whispered.

"God has spared our other children. We have much to thank Him for. Chaim and Dvoreh have no signs of the sickness. And Chaya Leya will live!" Yoysef wrapped his arms around his wife, lifting her from her pillow, his tears in her hair. "Malkeh, we must thank God that our other children have been spared. They need you to look after them."

"The twins are—they are—dead—?" she asked, the dreadful word a whisper on her tongue. "They are not coming home?"

"No," Yoysef answered wearily. "You know that, Malkeh. You saw them placed in the earth. You yourself threw the handful of earth into the grave. They are dead."

Malkeh's crazed scream reverberated through the little house, rousing Mammeh Frumma where she dozed by Chaya Leya's bedside and bringing Papa Avrom and Herschel running. But there was nothing to be done, for Malkeh had fainted.

Cared for by her grandmother, Chaya Leya gradually improved. It was a long, slow process. Malkeh could not bring herself to take much interest in Chaya Leya's convalescence. When she looked at her waxy freckled face and too-big eyes, she had to turn away lest the child read in her face the question she was ashamed to admit was in her mind. Why had this child lived while the bright golden lives of Yaakov and Channah were snuffed out?

Unable to find peace, Malkeh paced the house like a caged spirit. Why, oh, why had she allowed Channah and Yaakov to leave the house that day? Just because they had sulked and begged and she had been tired! If they had not gone, they would not have caught the sickness. If she had been a better mother—oh, God, why hadn't she died with her little ones?

She was angry, too, and the anger, expressed in sharp cruel outbursts, was difficult for the family to bear. Golda, Malkeh said, should not have urged her to let the children outdoors to play when she knew there was sickness in the city. She should have told Malkeh right away that Menkeh was sick. It was hatefulness on Golda's part. Just because she had no children of her own, she had turned the evil eye on Malkeh's babies! To hear this drove Golda sobbing from the house.

Malkeh was furious with the dead children too. They had been willful and disobeyed their mother, needlessly allowing themselves to be exposed. And then they had gone from her, without a word, and now she was alone, bereft, with a life that had lost its meaning. Malkeh's thoughts pounded in her head, allowing her no peace. She could not sleep. She could not rest. She could not swallow the sustaining food prepared by Mammeh Frumma.

The snow came finally, blowing away the last of the illness. The little community began to gather itself up and to count its dead. In the Jewish district alone, fifty-four children and almost as many adults had been stricken, and seventy-eight had died. Almost every Russian family had its dead as well. It had been the worst epidemic in the history of Polotsk.

Malkeh, always delicate in appearance, had become skeletal, her wide eyes staring dully from a diminished face, her skull bones prominent beneath transparent skin. She had no interest in things around her. She no longer taught the women or read her books. She threw her prayer book in a corner, blaspheming that God did not exist. She took no interest in the household and was frequently in bed, even during the daylight hours, losing herself in long periods of unconsciousness.

More and more, Chaya Leya stayed with her grandparents, and Chaim and Dvoreh with their aunt Golda and uncle Dovid. Malkeh scarcely noticed they were gone. For Malkeh the days dragged on, empty of meaning, and the nights brought dreams that did not heal and brought no surcease from the thoughts that made her waking life a hell. She envied the twins, for they were past all suffering. One day she found herself standing on the banks of the ice-filled river with little knowledge of how she had come there. She so wanted to die that it frightened her, and she ran home in a panic.

Yoysef tried to understand, but while he shared Malkeh's pain—after all, they were his children too—he was determined to put his anguish behind him for the sake of the others. During the short, dark days after winter had finally clamped down upon them, Yoysef did little work. He sat beside Chaya Leya, encouraging her to swallow the healing broths and custards that Mammeh Frumma made and helping Chaim build a train of empty spools. Holding three-year-old Dvoreh on his lap, he gathered Chaim and Chaya Leya to him in the shop while he spun comforting tales about the life Channah and Yaakov were enjoying in *Olam Habo.*

"And do they have *marozhenoye* every day?" Dvoreh asked, sucking a thumb.

"Oh, yes," Yoysef nodded confidently. "All they want."

"I'll bet there are lions and tigers!" Chaim said, rolling his train up the side of the counter.

"Yes, of course, but they have no reason to be fierce there."

"And angels to take care of the children without mothers," Chaya Leya added. This broke Yoysef's heart.

Malkeh moved through the days with unseeing eyes, turning a face of indifference to Chaya Leya, Chaim, and Dvoreh. Their pain hurt Yoysef more than Malkeh's anger toward him. Ever since the day he had forced her to acknowledge the death of the twins, Malkeh had turned a cold back to him when he lay in bed beside her. How long could it go on like that? One night he gently put his hand on her, turning her so that she must face him. His hand trembling a little, he stroked her hair, feeling how dry and lifeless it had become in just a few weeks. He nuzzled her neck, his lips finding the soft, sensitive place near her ear. She was unmoving, a piece of wood. Tentatively he reached down to rub her thin thigh, his hand moving up in long, slow motions to touch her where it had given her pleasure in the past. Angrily she pushed him away and pressed her forehead to the cold wall.

Yoysef's hands were insistent when he forced Malkeh back toward him. "Malkeh," he said quietly, "you have spent time enough in mourning. Yaakov and Channah are happy in God's house. Let them go in peace. All your tears will not return them to us. Perhaps God will be good and send us another child to make up for what we have lost."

Malkeh sat upright in the bed, her tortured eyes gleaming in the lamplight. She swung her arm back and struck Yoysef full across the face, her nails leaving a trace of blood on his cheek. She pummeled his chest with her fists, panting and crying out in inarticulate rage. She was like a convulsed animal, mad with grief. Yoysef threw her down, pinning her flailing arms to her side and heaving his body across hers. The contact of their bodies after such a long time roused him, but his mouth on Malkeh's was hard and bitter, and the penis he pushed into her was an instrument of anger.

Malkeh struggled and freed herself, crying, "I hate you! Don't ever touch me again!"

Yoysef's passion evaporated in hopelessness. Wordlessly he swung himself from the bed and padded out to the shop to spend what remained of the night. Thereafter he made a bed for himself in the workshop. Silence grew between them.

In February, though the roads were deep in snow, Yoysef, in worried conference with the family, decided that Malkeh must be taken from the memory-laden house if she was ever to recover. He told Malkeh that arrangements had been made for her and the children to go for a visit to her parents in Dadga. Malkeh had little will to resist, and she allowed Golda and Mammeh Frumma to pack a trunk with clothing and otherwise prepare for the journey. She cared little what happened to her. Dagda or Polotsk, it made no difference.

In mid-month, Yoysef set off with his wife and children for the home of his wife's parents. Katya heaved and strained to pull the sleigh over roads heavily drifted with snow.

As the sleigh moved past the place where the road to the count's estate branched off, the appearance of a solitary horse and rider caused Yoysef to slow Katya to a near halt. The count's steward, Fedotov, drew alongside the sleigh. "I will ride with you a ways," he said curtly.

Yoysef nodded silently and flicked the reins.

Fedotov dropped back, peering into the little nest of blankets and shawls that protected Malkeh and the children. His eyes, when they met Malkeh's, were unexpectedly dark with pain and soft in compassion. His look penetrated Malkeh's numbness as little else had in the past weeks. She closed her eyes against the unwelcome intrusion.

After a half hour or so, Fedotov reined in. As the sleigh continued past him, he raised his hand in parting. Malkeh turned to look back, and she saw him, still there, dark and motionless against the snow, his image shrinking gradually as the distance between them widened.

Chapter 15

When they arrived, Malkeh was surprised to see how small and shabby was the childhood home she had left eleven years earlier. Moments after the sleigh drew up before the house, Malkeh's welcoming parents were in the roadway. Papa, stuttering in his excitement, lifted the shy children one by one from the sleigh, and Mammeh herded everyone before her into the warm kitchen.

Mammeh looked the same as always, tall, thin, and straight-backed, the lines of her face as severe and deep as Malkeh always remembered them. Her voice, as always, was firm and positive, but there was an anxious question in her eyes when she scolded Malkeh for how thin she had become, scrawny like an old lady! "Is that any way for a woman scarce thirty to look?"

Papa, his fringe of hair quite white now and his spectacles thicker than ever, hugged Malkeh to him. He frowned at his wife. "*Sha, sha,* already, woman! We will see the roses blooming in Malkeh's cheeks again! All she needs is some rest and some of your good soup." His eyes bright and impish behind his lenses, Papa beamed at Malkeh. "Your mammeh has made your favorite dish for supper, a *lokshen kugel,* and it's not even *shabbes* yet!"

How like Papa to think the world would come right just because Mammeh had baked a noodle pudding, Malkeh thought.

Yoysef, blowing on his freezing hands, came in from stabling the horse. Pretending to a heartiness he did not feel, he said, "No one makes *lokshen kugel* like your mother, eh, Malkeh?" He put a tentative arm around her waist.

Malkeh pulled away, and Yoysef's arm dropped to his side. He turned brightly to the children. "Just wait till you taste *Bobbeh*'s delicious cooking!"

Chaim and Chaya Leya were silent, standing awkwardly near the bundles brought from home. Dvoreh began to cry. "Where will I sleep, Papa?"

Yoysef picked her up. "Why, I believe there's a big feather bed just for you! Shall I show you?"

Malkeh's father led his son-in-law and Dvoreh into the small room that would be Malkeh's and the children's during their stay. Chaim and Chaya Leya followed. In the kitchen Malkeh had sunk into a chair and closed her eyes. Exhaustion had etched deep circles under her eyes, and her skin looked blue. Her mother looked at her, and her mouth set in a grim, worried line. It was worse than she had ever imagined.

Yoysef left for home the next morning. Saying good-bye, he smiled reassuringly at the children and talked about the wonderful time they would have with *Zeydeh* and *Bobbeh*. "*Zeydeh* knows wonderful stories that he will tell you," Yoysef assured a tearful Dvoreh, hugging her to his chest. "And Chaim," he said, turning to the long-faced little boy, "when the snow melts, you can go visit Uncle Zalman in Vitebsk. Would you like that?"

Chaim nodded to please his father, but there was no break in the gloom.

Yoysef knelt beside a silent Chaya Leya. She was still so thin and pale, it wrenched his heart. "You must ask *Bobbeh* to teach you to make that *kugel* we all like so much! Then when you come home, you shall make it every *shabbes*, especially for me!"

Turning away from the children, Yoysef's shoulders sagged and his eyes glistened. The tears streamed unrestrained down Dvoreh's face until her grandfather picked her up and she hid her face in his shoulder. Chaya Leya clung to her father's hand as though she meant never to let go. Even Chaim, struggling to be a man, had to look away to hide his panic. "I know you will be good children," Yoysef said in a choked voice, "and not give your mother or your grandparents any trouble."

"Papa, Papa, must you go?" Chaya Leya asked.

"I don't want to, but I have a business to tend to. And who would keep an eye out for young Herschel?"

Only Malkeh seemed indifferent to his leaving, the face she turned for Yoysef's good-bye kiss cold and closed.

"Write to me, Malkeh," he begged in a low voice. "Some peddler will bring it."

She shrugged. He knew she would not write.

"If not before, I will come at Passover."

"Good-bye, Yoysef," she said politely, as if he were a stranger.

He drove away, looking back over his shoulder until Malkeh had gone into the house and he could no longer glimpse the waving children.

$\mathcal{M}$alkeh and her offspring settled into a life in which they were all children together. There was a sameness to the days, a routinized structure that was comfortable because of its very predictability. Malkeh's mother was not unsympathetic, but she was matter-of-fact. Malkeh was not allowed to stay in bed mornings, as there were chores to be done and the little ones to supervise. Chaim was taken to *cheyder*, and Chaya Leya was set to lessons by her grandfather. Dvoreh was enrolled in a class for the littlest children.

Considering that she was a meticulous housekeeper, Mammeh had a surprising number of household chores that needed catching up. The walls, soiled by a winter grime apparent only to Mammeh, needed to be washed down and whitewashed at once. That very first morning, Mammeh tied a scarf over Malkeh's hair, an apron around her middle, and set her to work with pail and brush. Malkeh, who tired quickly these days, wanted to lie down before the first hour had passed, but Mammeh shook her head. There was a need to make everything immaculate before Passover. She kept Malkeh at the work another hour before allowing her to lie down to rest on the bed.

"But Mammeh, *Pesach* is still two months off!" Malkeh protested when her mother roused her to finish scrubbing the front room.

"We can't wait until the last minute."

It had never been useful to argue with Mammeh, and it was not now. Malkeh worked the afternoon away under Mammeh's critical eye, scouring invisible dirt until her hands were red and chapped and she thought she would drop from weariness.

"That's all right," Mammeh assured her when she complained, "you'll sleep well tonight."

At the end of the afternoon the walls of the room were ready for the whitewash. Although Malkeh's back and legs trembled with fatigue, she felt a small flush of satisfaction as she scanned the spotless walls.

Mammeh said, "That's a good job."

One day followed another. At first light, Malkeh awakened to remembered sounds. Her eyes closed, pretending she was still a child in a time of her life that had been simple, Malkeh absorbed all the different timbres of sound that came to her through the thin partition—the high singsong of her father's voice chanting the morning prayer, the clanging of the oven door as her mother added wood to the fire, the splash of water into the samovar, the rooster's call. Soon Mammeh would be at the door, whispering, "A good day, Malkeh! Hurry and get dressed."

She would slip into her icy clothes in the cold darkness, waiting to put on her shoes and stockings in the kitchen, where it was warm. She would have liked to linger near the stove, but Mammeh was already handing her a shawl and a basket for collecting the eggs. "If we are lucky, there may be eggs for our meal."

Outside, it was so cold that the air seemed to freeze Malkeh's breath, and each shallow intake stabbed her chest. She had to clench her teeth to keep them from chattering against one another. She brought the shawl up to cover more of her face against the frigid bite of the wind. Yet there was a peacefulness in being about in the thin morning light, and a blessed stillness before the day's activities began.

Returning with the eggs, Malkeh's cheeks would be red, and her eyes watery from the cold. Mammeh would have warmed the children's clothing on the oven before rousing them, and they would be almost dressed by the time Malkeh came into the house.

"Chaim! Stop shoving me! You made me drop my stocking!"

"Chaya Leya, can you help me with my buttons?"

"Ow! Stop pinching me. I'll tell *Zeydeh*!"

After the meal, Chaim would pick up his books and hurry into the road to join the other boys on their way to *cheyder*. Chaya Leya would help her grandmother with morning chores and then settle at the table to laboriously trace letters in her exercise book while Dvoreh sat at her favorite place, on the oven, swinging her fat legs and practicing the *aleph bet*. "I can read almost as good as you, Chaya Leya!"

"Cannot!"

"Can too!"

Each day Malkeh worked under her mother's watchful eye, readying the house for the Passover. All the walls washed down, all the walls whitewashed, the kitchen floor freshly sanded, the curtains boiled in a large copper kettle and hung outside, where they froze as soon as they touched the line, the bedding aired and beaten, the Passover pots and pans scoured with sand to a shine in which she could see her face. And nothing pleased Mammeh short of perfection. Malkeh stopped begging her mother to let her rest. It was useless, because Mammeh had some kind of schedule in mind that would not be denied. "First let us finish this batch of washing, and then we will sit a little," she would say, or "Just two more pots and we will be all finished. Let's do that before we rest."

Malkeh went to bed at night bone-weary, but she began to drop into the dreamless sleep of physical exhaustion, which was better than nightmares, or the heavy unconsciousness which did nothing to refresh her mind or body.

Malkeh refused to see old friends and resisted the visits of the aunts and uncles. Mammeh merely shrugged and did not press her. How she held them off, Malkeh never knew.

When, during the day, they sat at the kitchen table for a glass of tea, Mammeh talked and did not seem concerned that Malkeh remained silent and preoccupied. The lack of expectation was a relief to Malkeh. Sometimes Mammeh's conversation was desultory, small bits of village gossip, plans for *Pesach*, household things. Gradually Mammeh began to talk about the family, its history, her parents and grandparents, and Papa's, as far back as anyone remembered. Sometimes the stories were old and familiar, sometimes new to Malkeh. Listening to Mammeh talk of the past, Malkeh had a sense of being linked with forebears who had been strong or been frail but who, in either case, had survived hardship and had lived their lives creditably.

One afternoon Mammeh talked about her life with Papa. Mammeh had always been a reticent woman, and Malkeh's interest was piqued by surprise.

"Ours was a marriage arranged between my parents and Papa's," Mammeh began, like a proper Yiddish story, "but from the first I liked him, and he respected me." She shrugged. "The only thing was Papa never made much money. But I managed. Why not? I could have had a man who was unfaithful or who beat me." She added ruefully, "Believe me, Malkeh, rich is not always better if you're someone's wife." Mammeh's eyes turned inward to the past. "Somehow Papa and I got along. I think we were even happy together, though in my time, who talked about happiness or unhappiness in a marriage? There was only one thing wrong—in ten years I never quickened with child. Papa's family said it was long enough, he must divorce me and take another wife. They were quite right, of course. A man has a duty to 'leave a name after himself' and someone to say the kaddish prayer when, God forbid, he dies."

Malkeh shivered.

"I was desperate to have a baby. It shamed me as a woman to be barren. But worse, I was afraid that Papa would have no choice but to put me aside."

"Papa would never have done that!"

Mammeh smiled slightly. "Papa's a man like any other. Your aunt Rivka and uncle Zalman had their eye on a widow for him. She had three children to prove her fruitfulness, and Papa had talked with the rabbi already. I know it for a fact, though Papa will deny it."

"How awful!"

"Yes. Awful. Aside from the disgrace, what do you think is the future for a woman set aside by her husband?"

"Why, I don't know," Malkeh said slowly.

"Only one thing—to go as a servant to a rich man's house." In the telling, an old pain made deep creases in Mammeh's face. To hide it, she rose to pour more boiling water into the tea glasses.

Malkeh shivered. If Yoysef should divorce her—? A wife who refused to lie with him? Not possible—was it?

Sitting down again in her chair, Mammeh stirred sugar into her tea and resumed her story. "There was an old Russian *babushka* who lived in a hut in the forest. People said she had powers beyond those of heaven or earth. I had already prayed to God, swallowed all kinds of herbal concoctions, lain with Papa only in the light of the full moon, and nothing, *nothing* had given me the child I wished for. What did I have to lose, then? In secret I went into the forest to find the old woman."

"Mammeh, you didn't!" Malkeh exclaimed. Surely her sensible, matter-of-fact mother was the last person on earth to subscribe to magical cures!

"You try anything when things are desperate enough," Mammeh said calmly. "I found the old woman's *izba* hidden away in the woods, almost covered over with brambles. I was very afraid, and I almost turned back. When I pushed through the bushes, a dog or a wolf, I do not know which, began to growl deep in its throat. I would have run if the *babushka* had not come just then to the door. I saw that she was very, very old, dark and wrinkled like a walnut, and she walked bent over, holding on to a gnarled stick. She calmed the animal with a look, and I saw that her eyes were like bright black beads. When I saw how the ferocious animal lay down at her feet, I knew this was the witch."

Malkeh leaned forward, listening intently.

"She motioned me to take a seat on the mound built up around her *izba*, and she sat on a stump nearby. I told her how it was with me, that unless I could have a child, my husband would divorce me. I remember she spit on the ground in disgust."

"And then what happened?"

"Oh, then she asked me many embarrassing questions about the private times between me and Papa, and how regular were my monthly fluxes, things like that. After I had told her everything I could think of, she sat a long time with her eyes closed. I thought for sure she had fallen asleep, but I guess she was thinking about what I had said. Finally she looked up at me with those black-bead eyes. 'It is sometimes the seed of the husband that is too weak to find its way home to the womb,' she said. I was amazed! Surely, I thought, it is always the woman's fault! The rabbis say so and even grant the husbands of such women divorces! But can it be that there are also barren men? I asked the old woman what she thought."

"What did she say?"

Mammeh smiled. "She said '*Nu da!*' Of course!"

"Do you think that is true?" Malkeh asked.

Her mother shook her head. "I don't know."

"But then, what was to be done?"

"Ah, the *babushka* had a suggestion." There was a wicked look in Mammeh's eyes. "She said that if I lay with some other man, then I would know for sure whether the barrenness was mine or Papa's."

"Mammeh! You couldn't!"

"Of course, I told the witch that. She said that was too bad, because it was the surest way. But if not that, she would have to think of something else."

Mammeh sat back in her chair, enjoying some private recollection.

Malkeh asked impatiently, "What happened?"

Mammeh laughed. "Well, Malkeh, you are here, aren't you?"

Now that the painful part of her story was over, Mammeh spoke more quickly. "The old woman went into her hut and was gone a long time. I was afraid that the dog—or the wolf—might harm me, but she had made it some sign, and it didn't move. When she came out, she gave me a packet and a little jar. In the packet was a powder—she said it was an herb to cause the male juices to flow more hotly. She told me to bake it in my bread. She promised it would not harm Papa, and I believed her."

"And the jar? What was that?"

"Oh, that was a good-smelling ointment I was to rub on my body before I went to Papa. There was more. I was not to lie with him for a whole month so that his seed would grow strong, she said. After that, we were to be together only during a certain few days that she told me how to calculate."

"And was that all you were to do?" Malkeh was curious.

"No, she said I should have faith and pray to God. And she told me not to worry if it did not work the first month. I was to try again a month later, but only on those special magic days."

"And did it happen right away?" Malkeh asked.

"When I got home, I lied to Papa. I told him that I had a message from my sister in Vitebsk, asking me to come to her because she was sick. And, of course, he said I should go right away. I went and stayed with your aunt Eshka in Vitebsk until I was sure it was the right time for getting a child. And you know, I felt better than I had in years, not worried because, you see, I believed in the old woman. When I came home from Vitebsk, Papa had missed me a great deal. Maybe it was the powder I had mixed in the bread dough or the fragrant herbs I rubbed onto my breasts and thighs. Anyway, the spell worked the one time. God made us a gift of a child. One precious child."

Mammeh stared into her tea glass. Softly she said, "God gives us what He thinks we need. Papa and I, so afraid that we would have no child at all, thank Him every day of our lives that He blessed us with you, Malkeh. And now we have a fine son-in-law and grandchildren besides. It is much to be grateful for."

Malkeh's face flushed and she stood so suddenly that her tea glass clattered to the floor. "You are telling me that I should thank God that I have three left out of the six babies I bore!" Malkeh flared. "Well, I don't think that is such a bargain, Mammeh!" Bursting into tears, she fled.

Mammeh sat on, rocking in her chair. Malkeh always was a greedy, ungrateful child she thought.

*A*lthough it did not happen immediately or even at any steady pace, in time a degree of quietness came over Malkeh. There were still bad times when she lashed out in unreasoning anger, and there were nights when she woke bathed in sweat from nightmares and paced the house until dawn, but gradually those spells grew less frequent. There came a time when for whole hours, and later whole days, her mind was free of thoughts of Channah and Yaakov.

The children, who had been so silent, became livelier, and their laughter made a welcome noise in the house. Chaya Leya lost the white line around her mouth, and her eyes no longer seemed too large for her face. Dvoreh stopped wetting the bed, and Chaim became less watchful. Their grandfather pretended displeasure at their bickering, but it was a secret joy for him to observe them behaving like children instead of sad adults.

Mammeh's good cooking, as Papa had predicted, worked its own magic. Malkeh's appetite was the last to return. At first she ate out of sheer necessity because her body demanded replenishment after its physical labor; then she ate out of enjoyment. She had forgotten the good taste of food. Mammeh was a wonder in the kitchen, producing thick broths of barley or lentils, boiled chicken and beef, fish that flaked off the fork, puddings of carrots, potatoes, or egg noodles, and compotes of fruits that had been dried the previous autumn. Malkeh and Chaya Leya gained weight and both Chaim and Dvoreh shot up in height.

Suddenly spring arrived, it was April, and the preparations for the Passover were under way in earnest. Yoysef had promised to come in time for the first seder. For a week before, the children were gripped with excitement.

For the first time in weeks Malkeh found herself unable to sleep. She was confused by her feelings. She was frightened that Yoysef would be a potent reminder of the deaths that had all but destroyed her. She could not risk sinking into that terror again! Nor was she prepared to acknowledge the deep pool of anger she harbored toward him. Had he not summarily deposited her with her parents as soon as there was trouble?

But there was also a sparkle of excitement, somewhat akin to the children's, but different. For the first time in months Malkeh looked at herself, standing for a long time before the little mirror that hung near the front door. Mammeh was right. She looked like an old woman! Experimentally, Malkeh pinched her cheeks to put color in them. She was surprised at the mirror by Mammeh coming in behind her.

"A little fresh air will help more than rubbing your face in front of the glass," Mammeh said mildly.

"I don't care how I look!" Malkeh exclaimed petulantly, turning away.

But when Mammeh would spare her the time, Malkeh began to walk out to the end of the village street and into the woods and fields beyond. She came back with little bunches of violets which she stuck in a glass on the table.

Now the pre-holiday pace quickened, and room by room all the furniture was carried out into the yard and scrubbed down, every cupboard and drawer emptied and cleaned, and the special china and cutlery kept only for Passover were unpacked and made gleaming clean.

On the day before the holiday, Yoysef had still not arrived. In the afternoon the children had walked along the road, watching in vain for their father. They returned crestfallen. *Zeydeh* restored their spirits by organizing a hunt through the house for *chometz*.

"*Bobbeh* and Mammeh have cleaned everything so much, we'll never find any!" Dvoreh complained.

"Oh, even your grandmother can miss a few things," *Zeydeh* assured her.

As if to prove the point, a gleeful Chaim discovered some crumbs on a window ledge, and Chaya Leya a crust behind a door.

"There won't be anything left for me!" Dvoreh cried, her little face puckering.

"Silly!" Chaim said. "*Bobbeh* hid bread for all of us to find! Look on the kitchen dresser, why don't you?"

Dvoreh had to stand on a chair to see. Disappointed, she shook her head. "I told you I wouldn't find any!"

"You haven't looked behind the plates," Chaya Leya prompted her.

"It's here! It's here!" Dvoreh shouted, making a fist around a small bit of cake so that she would not drop it.

Carefully, with a feather, *Zeydeh* swept the three bits of *chometz* into the bowl of a wooden spoon, then emptied the contents of the spoon on a piece of cloth to be tied and burned, thus ridding the house of all impurities before the Passover began. Following the ritual, the grandmother gave tea sweetened with generous dollops of raspberry preserves to everyone, and *Zeydeh* told the familiar Passover story of the foolish son and the wise son, and even Malkeh joined in a rehearsal of the song, "One Only Kid."

The next day Yoysef had still not come, though it was almost time for the holiday feast to begin. The house shone with cleanliness, the table laid with a dazzling white cloth, the special Passover dishes looked fresher and prettier than those used every day, and the goblets for wine were set to cast circles of reflected candlelight at each place, even that of the littlest child. Delicious smells emanated from the kitchen.

It was late afternoon before Yoysef arrived, walking beside the wagon that a tired Katya pulled. The horse had thrown a shoe on the way, and it had taken a day to have it replaced, as the blacksmith had gone to the next village for a wedding. Then, too, Katya was not able to go as she used to, and Yoysef had been forced to stop frequently to rest her, finally walking the rest of the distance beside the little wagon so that she would have less weight to pull.

The children hardly knew what to do first. Each had to pat Katya's flanks and rub her soft nose, but mostly they clamored around their father. He embraced and kissed each one in turn and then gathered all together in a giant bear hug. How tall Chaim had become in two months, Yoysef exclaimed. And how pretty Chaya Leya was now that she had some color in her cheeks and the shine had returned to her long brown plaits! But where was his little Dvoreh? Surely, this *big* girl could not be baby Dvoreh? Dvoreh, giggling, hid her face against her father's thigh until he lifted her high in the air, bringing her small face level with his own. Yes, he laughed, this great girl *was* Dvoreh, he could see the resemblance now! For her there was an extra kiss because she was the youngest.

Malkeh felt shy and stood back. Yoysef was also uneasy, and after one long, questioning glance, he looked away from Malkeh, busying himself with distributing gifts of new clothing to the children. Hastened by their grandmother, they ran off to change into the new garments before the seder. Tactfully Malkeh's parents also withdrew, ostensibly to put the finishing touches on the holiday meal before sundown was upon them.

After the excitement of his arrival, it was quiet in the street where Yoysef and Malkeh remained alone beside the wagon.

Yoysef cleared his throat. "You look pretty, Malkeh," he said at last.

She shook her head. "I'm too thin," she protested, though she had looked into the mirror when she heard Yoysef's wagon and knew that she was prettier than she had been in a long while. Too thin, yes, but even that only accentuated her fine bone structure.

"Come, walk with me to the barn so that I can feed Katya and let her have her rest. I have gifts for you too. But first this poor old lady must have her holiday feast!" Lovingly he stroked Katya's neck.

Watching him, Malkeh could almost feel the imprint of his big warm hand upon her breast. She trembled, and her knees grew weak.

It took an unnecessarily long time to rub down the mare, settle her in a stall, and feed her the oats that Yoysef had brought with him in a sack. Both Malkeh and Yoysef were eager to protract the chores if only to postpone the moment when they would be forced to turn to each other.

Malkeh watched Yoysef as he moved about his tasks. How tired he looks, Malkeh thought. He has grown much older in the months since Channah and Yaakov died. There is even some gray showing in his beard. A wave of pity for him swept over her, and her throat became tight with swallowed-back tears. He has suffered, too, she thought in surprise. And he has suffered alone. Filled with shame, she thought how he had lost children *and* wife when the two of them might have comforted and strengthened each other.

"Yoysef—" Malkeh said, her voice uncertain.

He looked up.

"I have been so wrong, so foolish!" She held out her arms to him. He did not move for what seemed to Malkeh an eternity. Despairing, she thought that perhaps he no longer wanted her.

And then he came to her, folding her to him, kissing her cheeks and her lips, her eyes and her throat, each in turn and with wonder, as though he could not believe she was truly there.

"I have missed you so terribly," Yoysef said at last. "If you only knew how I have needed you."

"I thought you were so strong. I thought you didn't need anyone."

"Oh, Malkeh, how could you make such a mistake!" He began to cry, the hot tears falling like rain on Malkeh's head. He had not cried like that even at the side of the grave.

They held tightly to each other. The memory of the past months ebbed, and the hurt that had been between them eased a little.

Yoysef asked humbly, "Will you come home with me, Malkeh?"

"Where else would I go?" she answered, crying and laughing at the same time.

Yoysef bent down his head, his mouth seeking Malkeh's. Their kiss tasted of salt tears but for all that was sweet with reconciliation.

They could not seem to let go of each other. Katya nickered softly, and the light through the slats of the barn grew dim. Finally stirring in his arms, Malkeh remembered with a start what day it was. "See, the sun is almost set. And we stand here in the barn. Mammeh and Papa will be upset that we aren't in time for the seder."

Laughing a little like naughty children, Malkeh helped Yoysef take the packages from the wagon. Yoysef insisted that however late it was, she must open them now. There were honeyed Passover candies from Mammeh Frumma, their gingery fragrance making Malkeh's mouth water, and a large basket of eggs from Avrom for the holiday baking. There was an embroidered handkerchief in Golda's ragged stitches, and a tall Passover cake from Yenta. Maria Feodorovna had sent a bright red and yellow scarf, so much gayer than those worn by Jewish women. Yoysef laughed when he told how hard it had been to persuade the housekeeper that they would be unable during Passover to eat the Easter cake she wanted to send as well. There was a book from Yevgeny Fedotov. A note in his brusque hand explained: "This is by a new writer, Anton Chekhov, whom some say will be great. I think it myself. A happy holiday to you."

Malkeh's heart ached. These were the signs of love she had been unable to recognize when she needed them most. Despite everything, she was still in the hearts of Mammeh Frumma and Papa Avrom, Golda and Yenta, Maria Feodorovna and dear, dear Yevgeny Fedotov. She wanted to embrace them all. She wanted to go home to Polotsk.

Quickly Yoysef undid the wrappings on the last parcel and shook out a dress made of shining blue silk.

"But Yoysef," Malkeh murmured, "it must have been so dear!"

"Wait!" Yoysef said in excitement. "That is not all!" From his pocket he drew a smaller package and unwrapped it with trembling fingers. There lay a short string of perfect round and gleaming pearls, something that Malkeh had never thought to own for herself.

"You like them?" Yoysef asked anxiously.

Malkeh nodded, though her eyes were too misted to see them. It was hard to imagine that she had turned so completely from Yoysef when in fact they were two parts of a whole, each so much less when apart and so much more than the sum of each part when they were together.

It was dark when Yoysef and Malkeh came from the barn.

Chaim was aggrieved. "Look! The sun is down and we haven't even lit the *yontef* candles yet!"

"Yes, that's a sin, isn't it, *Zeydeh?*" Dvoreh piped.

Their grandmother was not annoyed by the delay. She only said, "God understands all things, children." She rocked contentedly in her chair while Malkeh changed into her new dress with the pearls, and Yoysef washed himself and put on his best clothes.

It was long past the appointed time when they sat down together at the holiday table. Malkeh's mother lit the candles and said the blessings that begin every Jewish holiday at sundown. As in years past, Malkeh and Yoysef searched each other out through the candle flames that separated them.

And then their attention turned to the holiday ritual, for Chaim's shrill boy's voice was demanding in Yiddish and then in Hebrew the answer to a timeless question: *Papa, ich vill dir fregen die fier kashes. Ma nishtana halailah haze mikol haleilot?* Why is this night different from all other nights?

It *was* different, Malkeh's mother thought, a time for family, a gathering in.

It was not Rosh Hashanah, the beginning of the cycle of the seasons. Yet even the children had a sense that a fresh new year had just begun.

Chapter 16

$\mathscr{B}$y the time the tailor's family made the return journey to Polotsk and home, Malkeh knew in her heart that once more a new life stirred within her womb. God's eternal promise to quicken winter-barren soil had come to pass yet again.

In their time away from home, the children had grown and were again rosy with good health. Their mother had attained a measure of peace, but had changed; she was now a woman in whom a deep sadness and stillness lay just below the surface.

In Polotsk the tall dahlias, so beloved by Malkeh, had been nurtured by Yoysef, and they bloomed in great profusion through that summer and into the fall. The hens laid perfect eggs like special gifts for the returned family. There was even a particular sweetness in the taste of vegetables and fruit from the garden that year.

The business thrived as never before. Since there was more than Yoysef and Herschel could handle, Yoysef made Herschel an assistant and took another apprentice, the boy Zelig, the son of a distant, ne'er-do-well cousin.

Malkeh was quite well throughout her pregnancy, and in December Gittel delivered a healthy bawling nine-pound boy. They named him Simcha, a name which signified "joy" and "celebration." There was rejoicing in the family, but the *bris*, the ritual circumcision, was celebrated quietly lest the evil eye fall upon the child.

$\mathscr{I}$f things were well with the tailor and his family, trouble was no stranger to the people who lived and worked the land. Rents, which had been raised before, were raised again. Fedotov had gone to each of the tenants and given him the bad news. It was received with sulky looks to the steward's face and with insults as soon as his back was turned. *Oobloudok!* they called him. Bastard! Droppings of a whore! If he heard, he gave no sign.

The steward knew better than most the lot of the *mujik*. Young though he had been when he was taken from his stepfather's hut, he had but to close his eyes for a moment and his mind was awash with soul-searing images. His stomach even now remembered the gripping emptiness of a belly whose only meal for a day was a crust of black bread, grudgingly given. Once, when his mother was already sick and unable to care for him, the boy Yevgeny had fought the carpenter Fedotov like an animal, savagely kicking, biting, and scratching, all for a couple of handfuls of *grechnevaya kasha*.

Virtually starving, he counted the beating that followed a small price for having something in his belly. Of his mother's last illness, the steward hardly dared think even from the perspective of adulthood. He knew now that hopelessness, not consumption, had killed his mother. He had always known that the carpenter Fedotov's drinking and brutality were but signs of the sickness of despair.

In the old count's time, the rents at least had been nominal. A man with strong sons to work beside him in the fields could earn enough to feed and clothe his family and occasionally to put a ruble or two aside for hard times. Now he worked long hours just to pay for his house and the bit of land that he scarcely had time to cultivate. The strongest and youngest of the peasants were beginning to leave to seek new masters or menial jobs in the cities.

Misfortune occasionally overtook a peasant family so that it could no longer meet its obligations. Then the family lived in an agony of anticipation, waiting for the visit from the steward that would put them off the land. Miraculously the steward might miss a family for months, but eventually, if the rent was not paid, the family was evicted. Then there was nothing for them but to join other homeless families on the roads. Maria Feodorovna was generous with handouts to those who were hungry enough to brave the dogs at the gates. But in the winter, sometimes, people froze to death on the roads.

Wherever they congregated—in the fields, the taverns, on benches in front of their huts—the peasants muttered darkly against the masters who held their lives and those of their children in a strangehold. Every year times grew crueler, and the hold tighter.

Although the *zemstvo* was almost without power of any kind, Igor Karpovitch was an active force at Spokoinaya Zemlya, making the most of the peasants' discontent. He sat often with the men, drinking and dicing at the village inn. "Brothers," he told them, "Fedotov wants to drive you off the land. Listen to him when he speaks. How many times does he say '*my* land, *my* fields, *my* peasants'—as if he owns everything already! The raise in rents is a plot to put you so far behind that he can throw you off your land."

He circulated among the tables, picking out the grumblers, talking quietly to this one, to that one. They knew him well, since he often stood them a kvass or a vodka.

"My taxes are higher than ever!" a fellow in a ragged coat complained.

"Well, Anton, you know where the blame lies!" he said with a nod of his head in the direction of the manor house.

Moving on to Timofey, he asked, "And how goes it with you, my friend?"

"Every year I borrow more, and when I can't pay back, I borrow again! When will it end?"

"When do you think?" he asked, his face twisted in a look full of meaning.

A peasant with a potbelly said to Karpovich, "Tell us what to do, Master Council Member! Now Fedotov has raised the rents again. And we must pay the tax just at the time of year when grain prices are lowest! I hardly got anything for my harvest!"

Karpovitch shrugged. "It's hard."

Potbelly grimaced. "All our lives we have served the Voronovs, and now they squeeze the lifeblood from our veins!"

"Not the Voronovs—Fedotov, the Voronov steward!" Timofey called from across the room.

Igor Karpovitch sat down and sipped his kvass, a slight smile playing about his lips.

A quiet voice murmured, "Fedotov is but a servant. The count, not the steward, raises the rents."

With a frown, Karpovitch looked around to see who had spoken. A slender, dark-eyed boy was looking at him impassively from across the table. Karpovitch glared at him.

"And it is the tsar's new minister of finance who increased taxes." The voice was barely audible, meant for Karpovitch alone.

"Who are you? Haven't I seen you someplace before?"

"My name is Vassily Ossipovitch."

"Why are you defending Fedotov?"

"I'm the last person in the world to defend Fedotov. I only wondered what *you* are up to."

Igor Karpovitch rose. "Let us go outside to talk," he said.

Vassily followed him out the door.

*A*n air of desperation hung like a curtain over the miserable hut where the drunken peasant, Ossip, lived with his wife, Serafina, his daughters, Olga and Lyuba, and his only son, Vassily. When taxes fell due that year, there was only one steady wage earner, sixteen-year-old Vassily. Serafina had collapsed one day, vomiting a black stream into the ground she cultivated, the familiar stomach pains so sharp that she could not straighten up but had to creep from the field on all fours like an animal. Try as she might, she had been unable to rise from her bed again. Ten-year-old Lyuba was a sickly child who was useless in the fields. At twelve, Olga had already started selling her body to men at the inn, but her earnings together with Vassily's wage were not enough.

Vassily sat at the deal table, again counting the money, as if that would magically make it more. "It is short," he said finally. "There's no way—"

Olga glanced spitefully at Ossip, who was nursing a glass of vodka. "If you'd hidden the money better, brother, that one couldn't have stolen any for his bottle!"

Ossip's hand shook so that some of the liquid dribbled out of the glass. "I need it! It's medicine for my pain! You don't know how my arm aches all the time—" He began to cry. "Why did Fedotov take his whip to me that day? He ruined my life!" It was an old cry. No one answered.

On her pallet Serafina moaned with pain. It was more than Vassily could bear. He grabbed the front of his father's tunic and pulled him up. "You bastard!" he hissed. "*Drink* ruined your life! Does it make you proud to see Mother dying there in a corner? Or Olga a whore on the streets? Or Lyuba—oh, what's the use!" He let the old man fall back in his chair.

"It was the steward—Fedotov," Ossip whimpered.

"Yes, all right," Vassily said, overcome with sudden weariness, "whatever you say."

"What will we do, Vassily?" Lyuba asked, clutching his arm and looking into his face with wide, frightened eyes.

He passed a hand over his face. "I'll get money. Don't worry."

So it had come to this, Vassily thought as he walked toward the Voronov house. Another faggot for the fire of his hatred. He did not mind the thievery—after all, the money should belong to all of them who worked for it—except that he put himself in peril of a long penal sentence in Siberia. Maybe it was time to join with Igor and Timofey and the others who had plans for the steward Fedotov.

*A*ndrei Petrovitch, Count Voronov, was seldom at his estate to observe the misery of the peasants. It was said he wished to avoid that unhappy lady, Natalya, his wife; certainly his interest in his son was not great enough to draw him to Spokoinaya Zemlya. Months passed sometimes with no letters or messages from St. Petersburg. Then a messenger would arrive with the count's greetings—usually a request for gold.

In the fall of that year, the Countess Natalya was especially stung by her husband's financial demands because now all the countryside talked openly of Andrei's scandalous goings-on with the young wife of Prince Alexander Popov. Instead of sending rubles, the countess dressed herself in her most splendid gown and jewels and rode to St. Petersburg to confront her husband.

She returned home silent and red-eyed. Retiring to her bed, she stayed with her face to the wall for the better part of a week. Her personal maid told Maria Feodorovna that the beautiful diamond and emerald necklace that the count had given Natalya as a wedding present was missing when she returned from St. Petersburg.

The countess called the steward to her suite of rooms.

"All is lost!" Natalya told him, weeping. "He needs money to buy an even finer house, on the Nevsky Prospekt. He says to send money even if we must raise the rents again."

"We'll see about that!" Yevgeny Sergeivitch said, glowering. "There's a limit."

The countess mopped her wet eyes with a sodden handkerchief. "Andrei knows no limits. You should know that by now."

The next morning Yevgeny set off for the capital. Andrei was a damn fool! With the new methods of farming, the land was becoming more productive every year. By exercising a little restraint, the flax would be sold at a profit, and in a year or two Andrei could have his new house in St. Petersburg, maybe even another in Moscow.

It was early evening when Fedotov arrived at the elegant house on Ulitza Illinskaya. So full was he of the urgency of his business that he had gone there directly upon entering the city. He had been ushered into the library by a house servant and left cooling his heels. Tired and dusty though he was, he had not been offered refreshment.

The steward seethed. How like Andrei! Restlessly he paced the room. On his third turn he noticed decanter and glasses on a table. To hell with Andrei! He poured some cognac and sat down with it.

Andrei, he thought, never missed an opportunity to let him know who was master and who servant, who the count and who the bastard. Closing his eyes against his fatigue, he reflected on a long history of cruelties, both large and small, that Andrei had visited upon him since the time he became the involuntary "companion" of Andrei's boyhood.

In sharp detail he remembered a summer when relatives of the countess's arrived from Odessa for an extended visit. Andrei was twelve that year, and Yevgeny not quite ten and still small for his age. Among the visitors was a boy a year or so older than Andrei, named Maxim. Bored eventually with swimming in the pond, collecting grass snakes to loose on the screaming housemaids, and destroying the beaver dams in the stream, there was not much else that Spokoinaya Zemlya had to offer the pair. Yevgeny then earned a role as the natural target for any prank their fiendish imaginations could conjure.

On the grounds of the estate, at some distance from the house, was a piggery where the count kept a stud boar, a thoroughly undomesticated animal of vicious temperament but prized for the number of stoats he had sired. On a hot August afternoon, Andrei and Cousin Maxim set out to see a two-headed piglet that had been born a few days earlier. As an apparent afterthought, Andrei asked Yevgeny if he wanted to come along. He should have been alerted by Andrei's friendliness, but what boy that age could forgo a chance to see a two-headed pig?

The swineherd was dozing under the trees when the boys arrived. Awakened by the voices of his visitors, he sprang to his feet and saluted the young masters with a bow of his head. "Is there something I can do for you, young masters?"

Andrei was at his most charming. "Ah, don't bother yourself with anything. We just want to look at the freak pig."

"God be praised, the animal died this morning. Would the young sirs like to see it?"

The peasant led the way inside the piggery. It was hot and close there, and the odor of pig, trapped by the wooden walls, was overpowering. The dead piglet was disappointing, too, as it did not really have two heads, more like one normal one with a little knoblike protuberance emerging from the same brain stem. They did not stay long.

Emerging from the building, Maxim scoffed, "Is that all? It was hardly worth the walk from the house!"

Andrei eyed Yevgeny. "Maybe we'll have some fun yet," he said slyly. Turning to the peasant, he suggested, "It is much too hot to work this afternoon. Why don't you go home and rest yourself?"

"Oh, no, sir," the swineherd said nervously, "I couldn't do that, sir."

"You could if I ordered you to," Andrei said with a hint of threat, then added kindly, "Take an hour or so off during the heat of the day. Look, man, the pigs are all asleep, and even the boar is in its shelter. You don't have to stay here and watch them sleep."

The swineherd shifted his weight from foot to foot, uncertain what to do. "I guess it would be all right—"

"We caught you asleep when we came anyhow; you might as well go home and be comfortable."

"Yes, young master, if you say so."

Even before the swineherd disappeared, Yevgeny knew for a certainty that he was to be the butt of some trick. He weighed the possibility of outrunning the older boys but recognized that the chase would only whet their appetites. It would be hopeless, anyway, because Andrei, bigger and faster, always beat him in contests of physical strength. Yevgeny clenched his teeth in anticipation of whatever might come next and resolved not to give Andrei and Maxim the satisfaction of seeing him cringe, no matter what.

But Andrei was ignoring Yevgeny and talking to Maxim. "Do you know that peasants eat pig food?"

"No? Really?"

"Yes, indeed! They eat groats and they eat cabbage and all sorts of disgusting stuff. Don't you, Yevgeny?"

The child looked from one to the other of the bigger boys.

"Don't you? Tell Maxim, Yevgeny!"

He said in a small voice, "I eat kasha and cabbage—"

"And all sorts of disgusting stuff! Say it, Yevgeny!"

"No."

Andrei grabbed him by the arm and gave it a vicious twist. "And all sorts of disgusting stuff," Yevgeny repeated shrilly.

"That is truly interesting," Maxim said thoughtfully. "I'd like to see you do that, Yevgeny!" In one swift motion, Maxim had picked up the smaller boy and thrown him across the fence into the trough of pigslop in the boar's enclosure.

Yevgeny had not anticipated that. The slop was viscous and smelled bad. He tried to extricate himself from the mess, but every time he began to scramble out, Maxim or Andrei, standing on the fence rail, pushed him back into the trough.

"Aren't you enjoying your meal?" Andrei snickered. "Eat up nice and hearty now!"

Maxim grabbed a handful of mash and shoved it into Yevgeny's mouth. Yevgeny choked and gagged.

The noise at the end of the enclosure woke the boar. Its disposition was not improved by having its nap interrupted. With a grunt that sounded to Yevgeny like the roar of a train, it tore out of its shelter to charge the intruder. Fear almost paralyzed the boy. He sank back into the feeding trough, submerging himself in the slop the best he could. The boar was puzzled. His snout poked at the unfamiliar object in his mash. He backed off, snorting and pawing the ground, and then returned to the trough, worrying at Yevgeny. The boy felt the heat of the boar's breath upon him, and sharp tusks tore a long rip in Yevgeny's trousers. By a miracle only the surface of the boy's skin was scratched.

His heart thudding with terror, Yevgeny waited for Andrei and Maxim to save him by distracting the animal. It took him a few moments to realize that they had run off. Maybe, he thought hopefully, they had gone for help, but even as he thought it, he knew that he had been left to his fate. He was suffocating in the trough and afraid to raise his head lest it become a target. The boar poked at Yevgeny another couple of times with his snout and his tusks, but he could not fathom the situation. Finally, bored and hot, the animal ambled back to its shelter, where the swineherd had prepared a nice mud bath for him. By the time he had rolled himself in the cooling mud, he had forgotten the strange object in the pig trough. The flies made a somnolent whirr-whirr around the boar's head, and after a while the buzzing sound and the heat put him soundly to sleep.

Ever so carefully, Yevgeny climbed out of the trough and over the fence. Stopping only to submerge himself, clothes and all, in the pond, he trudged home, but not until he had controlled his sobs.

When Maria Feodorovna saw him, she exclaimed over his torn and muddied clothes. "Have you no sense, boy?" she scolded.

He gave her such a look that she subsided at once.

Andrei and Maxim were somewhat subdued at the dinner table that evening. But Andrei could not resist twitting the younger boy. Seated next to him, he whispered "Oink oink, Piggy!" in his ear. It was too much for Yevgeny. He picked up his water goblet and turned it upside down over Andrei's surprised head.

When the bedlam at table had subsided, Yevgeny was sent to bed without an evening meal and banished to the kitchen for meals during the remainder of the summer.

Yevgeny never once spoke about that afternoon to anyone. As he enjoyed *shchi* and *chornyi khleb* at the kitchen table with Maria Feodorovna, he counted himself lucky.

*I*t was almost the whole of an hour before Andrei appeared in the library. The count was bathed and perfumed, dressed in evening clothes with the ribbon of the Semyonovsky Guards in his lapel.

Andrei frowned at his visitor's rough clothes and wrinkled his nose at the smell of sweat and horse. "People who want to see me usually ask for an appointment and arrive a little more presentable."

"My apologies, Andrei." Yevgeny Sergeivitch realized that his impulsiveness had led him into error.

"I see you have helped yourself to a drink," Andrei said with distaste.

"I knew it was an oversight that your servant forgot to offer it."

"And what brings you here?" the count asked coldly, flicking an imaginary bit of lint from his waistcoat. "I grant you that the country is deadly, but that hardly warrants my having to put up with one delegation after another from Spokoinaya Zemlya. And who will you send next? The fat housekeeper? Oh, I beg you, keep her home and send the little parlor maid with the delicious ass instead."

"You know why I've come," Yevgeny said, determined not to be goaded. It was an old game with Andrei, played since they were children, a game in which Andrei coolly tormented Yevgeny until he exploded with temper and was then punished for his intemperance and lack of control.

"I daresay I do know why you're here." Andrei smiled. "I believe my dear wife came about the same matter. Some drivel about how hard the poor, unhappy peasants have to work to support my vices. If you keep putting such things into the countess's head, Yevgeny Sergeivitch, I shall have to forbid you to talk with her at all."

"Things are very bad for the people. She sees it. She can't help but see it. There are hungry children at our gates."

"They overbreed. Besides, peasants always snivel. My dear Yevgeny, you have spoiled them, and my father before you. They were born to work for us and to be grateful."

"Serfdom is dead," the steward said. "The *mujiks* are free men who work for wages and pay for their cottages and their land with money they earn. The high rents on top of high taxes are too much for them."

"Then let them work harder," Andrei said carelessly. "Really, Fedotov, you are beginning to bore me."

The steward's light eyes narrowed, but he took care that his voice held no edge. He would not play Andrei Petrovitch's game tonight. He said quietly, "I don't ask you to think about what's happening to the people, only to consider the possible gains and losses for yourself. There will be some ready cash for you in higher rents, but I point out to you that the gain is limited. Our crop yield was good this year and will be even better next if we can keep the better workers on the land. Squeeze them with high rents and they will leave us. In the end we—*you*, Andrei Petrovitch, will be the loser."

"Quite a speech," the count drawled, lighting a cigar without offering one to Fedotov.

"Think, Andrei," Yevgeny said, looking steadily into the other man's languid eyes, "think of what has come to you through your father and his father before him. As far back as anyone remembers, there were Voronovs in Polotsk province, and each Voronov has improved the land and added to it. I know you don't like the country. All right. You don't have to live there, but it is the land that gives you the money to live like this." His gesture encompassed the paneled room. "It is the land that will support your son. Be good to the land, and it will take care of you. Strip it, and there will be nothing for anyone."

The count took a silk handkerchief from his sleeve and blew his nose daintily. His eyes drooped with feigned weariness. "Really, my friend, you are terribly tiresome." His voice purred with malice. "All this talk of the old family manor and the ancestors. You'd almost think that *you* were the son of the family instead of the—bastard."

"An accident of birth," Yevgeny Sergeivitch said, "but how do you account for yourself?"

There was a split second that trembled on the brink of a deadly encounter, when Andrei fingered the heavy glass paperweight on the desk and Yevgeny's hand reached for the knife in his boot. The moment passed, the hands came back to their sides, and the two men stood looking at each other, each seeing his own hatred reflected in the other's eyes. Then the count tapped the ash off the end of his cigar. It landed on the steward's boot. His voice dismissing Yevgeny was the same as he might have used to his valet.

"Your journey was for nothing. You have my orders. I suggest you get back to your work."

"Yes, my lord," the steward said with fine sarcasm, bowing silently. "But you will remember that I have warned you. God help us, I think we will all pay in the end."

*J*n the fierce winter that followed, Fedotov was often abroad on the land, examining the outbuildings for signs of vandalism, for there had been an outbreak of thievery, some mischief with the farm machinery, and even some small fires. More often than not, the steward was accompanied on his rounds by his constant shadow, the count's son, Pyotr, striving to sit his horse with the same insolent mastery as that of his model. It was perhaps an irony of fate that the ten-year-old boy was more son to Yevgeny Sergeivitch than to his little-known father in St. Petersburg. Strangers thought that the steward and the boy were indeed father and son, for there was the same look of scowling intensity in each face, the same quick intelligence, and the same swaggering carriage. Only the boy was fair with his father's china-blue eyes, and Yevgeny Sergeivitch had thick red-brown hair and amber eyes that seemed too light for his dark skin.

As they rode across the frozen fields and through the winter-heavy forest, Yevgeny Sergeivitch mused unhappily about the state of his world. A little pilfering had always gone on. After all, the disappearance of a little grain from the warehouses was expected and tolerable. But lately there had been theft on a wholesale scale, so widespread that it was well nigh impossible to assign blame. When he asked questions, the peasants protected and shielded one another. If allowed to continue unchecked, there would be anarchy on his land. To stop it, he needed to identify a culprit, make an example. In time someone would be caught, no doubt of it, and he promised himself that person would lose his home and his livelihood, and would be publicly whipped in the bargain.

Yet, Yevgeny thought, he himself would probably steal in the same circumstances, out of spite if not out of hunger.

The steward and young Pyotr were riding down a rutted road that led though a heavy stand of trees. The air was cold and so clear that the sound of their horses' hooves could be heard for a quarter of a verst. Breaking through to a little clearing, the boy, who was slightly ahead, reined in so suddenly that Yevgeny's horse almost ran him down.

"What is it? Why do you stop here?" the steward asked irritably.

The boy was pointing toward the trampled earth, evidence that many feet had been there not long before. "Yevgeny Sergeivitch! Look!" he said quietly.

The steward held his horse still, cursing himself for letting his own thoughts so possess him that he had not noticed what was now abundantly clear to both him and the boy. In the moment of realization he saw that it was already too late. The horses were surrounded by men, seven or eight of them, who had run out of the trees with hatred in their eyes and clubs in their hands.

"Run! Go!" Yevgeny shouted to Petya, striking the flank of the boy's pony with his whip as the peasants closed around him. "They don't want you! Go!"

The men were heavily swaddled in long sheepskin-lined coats, scarves pulled around the lower halves of their faces partly to prevent recognition and partly as a shield against the bitter cold. Shouting and cursing, they laid hands on the steward's legs and pulled him from his mount. He fell to the ground and was instantly surrounded by flailing men with sticks. But Fedotov was of a powerful build and in superb physical condition. He scrambled to his feet, fighting off his assailants with his whip and his feet. He kicked out at the nearest man, finding his most tender part so that the man fell screaming to the earth, clutching himself in agony. Another who clung to his back he seized by the arms, and in one smooth movement flipped him over his shoulders so that he crashed to the ground. He dropped his whip and used his thumbs to gouge eyes, he punched and kicked, twisting and turning so that his assailants could not bring him to ground. In the melee it was difficult to see exactly what was happening, but it was clear that the steward had eventually to fall because of the sheer advantage of his opponents' numbers. Already he had been forced back against a tree trunk, and two crouching men waited their turns at him.

Yevgeny Sergeivitch, his vision misted from perspiration and blood, was only peripherally aware that a small form was hurtling toward him through the massed bodies of the angry men. Suddenly Petya was there, a diminutive figure of defiance standing in front of the steward, feet apart and arms held wide to shield his uncle. Before Fedotov could put the boy behind him, Petya became the target of one of the clubs. The blow glanced off the boy's head, and he sank to the ground spurting blood.

The men had no quarrel with the count's son. He was just a boy, and the grandson of their beloved old master. It was the steward that they'd plotted to punish, maybe to kill. Appalled now that blood had been drawn from the count's family, they drew back and, frightened, melted into the trees.

Yevgeny Sergeivitch knelt beside the bleeding, unconscious boy, pressing his neckcloth to the scalp wound to stop the bleeding. It was the amount of blood that was so terrifying, for actually the wound was superficial, and the boy had fainted as much from terror as from injury. The steward pressed the cloth tightly against the cut, packing a handful of snow around it to numb the pain. By the time he caught the frightened horses and led them back to the clearing, the boy had opened his eyes and sat up, dazed.

"Why did you not go when I ordered you to?" Yevgeny Sergeivitch asked severely.

"I thought they would kill you," the boy said, his voice catching and his blue eyes filling with tears.

The man lifted the boy to his feet, his eyes checking him anxiously for injuries. "Are you still faint or can you ride?" he asked.

The boy swallowed hard. "I can ride."

The steward helped Petya onto his own horse and mounted behind him. Holding the rein of the pony slack in his hand so that it could trot behind them, he walked his horse toward the house.

"Thank you, Pyotr Andreivitch," he said gravely to the boy he held in the saddle before him. "I owe you my life today." His arms tightened around the child. "We are joined now forever by ties of blood."

Chapter 17

The assault in the forest during which Petya was injured, coming as it did on the heels of the humiliating confrontation with Andrei in St. Petersburg, filled Fedotov with a sense of angry impotence. His black moods were well known at Spokoinaya Zemlya, but usually they burned out in short order. This was different, darker and more savage, and it showed no sign of remitting. Meals were pushed aside, and he talked to no one unless it was to bark an order or to strike out in rage. He slept little at night, and he spent his days sitting in his room, staring out the window. To Vassily alone was left the task of estate paperwork, and to his credit, he seemed always these days to be in the office, poring over the ledgers.

Maria Feodorovna, reading her missal through the dark hours of her own sleeplessness, heard Yevgeny's footsteps dragging back and forth, back and forth, all the night through. She was frightened for him. He had never seemed more alone. To the world he had always shown a shell of stoic indifference; perhaps Maria Feodorovna was the only one who knew how soft and vulnerable was his inner core. Wiping her eyes with a corner of her shawl, she thought about Agrappina, Yevgeny's first love. Maria Feodorovna had thought that he would go mad with grief when the girl hanged herself from a rafter in the old barn. "Why? Why did she do such a thing?" he asked over and over though surely he knew, as *everyone* did, that she had been savagely brutalized and raped. Some said Andrei's valet had done it, others thought Andrei himself—they were two of a kind. At the time only Maria Feodorovna heard the muffled nighttime weeping of a heartsick sixteen-year-old; only she knew that the steward Fedotov still kept a certain isolated grave weeded and put flowers there on a particular saint's day.

Ai, the old count Voronov, she thought, not for the first time, had done Yevgeny no favor by taking him into the house and educating him. It had resulted in his belonging nowhere. Neither gentry nor peasant, accepted by neither, he was condemned to live out his days without friends, without wife, and without child. Maria Feodorovna reproached herself anew. How much better for them both if, when Elena died, she had listened to the stirrings of her heart and taken the boy to bring up as her own! But younger then, uncertain of herself and with no husband, she had hung back, afraid she lacked the maternal instinct to raise a child. Better a spinster housekeeper, though, than an indifferent aristocrat; unfortunately, by the time she came to that realization, it was too late—just as it was too late now to give the man the boy had become any comfort. And so she sat helplessly by in her kitchen, seeking solace from her missal and hearing the creaking floorboards overhead.

Petya was beside himself with guilt, his child's mind concluding that his uncle's anger was because he had disobeyed and got himself hurt. It cut him to the very soul for Fedotov to look at him without seeing him, as though he had ceased being a person that day in the forest. Petya moped about the house, getting under the feet of the servants and forcing his tutor to cane him for inattention.

Malkeh, too, bringing the baby to visit, could not understand what had happened to so change her friend. When she tried to engage him in conversation about plans for the school, soon to reopen, he was not merely disinterested but cruel, like in the old days. "What does it matter what Jews or women learn—it's like teaching a dog tricks!"

When Malkeh started to answer him back, Maria Feodorovna silently shook her head, and Malkeh fell silent. In a little while, troubled, she left to return to Polotsk.

Countess Natalya wanted to send to St. Petersburg for a specialist but was dissuaded by Maria Feodorovna. It would not do to give the count an excuse to relieve Yevgeny Fedotov of his post.

Weeks passed in this way, a month. Then one night before the dawn had grayed the shadows in his room, Fedotov awoke from a troubled sleep and sat bolt upright in his bed. It was as though a compelling hand had raised him, and in that moment he felt the darkness lift from his spirit. In one blinding instant of revelation he knew with certainty that he had been given life for one purpose alone, to protect Spokoinaya Zemlya for young Pyotr and the generations to come. No effort was too much, no cost too high in pursuit of that purpose. Now the estate was in serious peril. One decisive act, awesome though it might be, was all it would take to free Spokoinaya Zemlya from its danger. Andrei, Count Voronov, must die. When a weevil is eating the wheat, you destroy the weevil and save the wheat. It is a central fact of farming.

Fedotov was nothing if not honest and self-aware. He recognized that the resolve to kill his half brother had long lain dormant in his mind and in his heart. We are like Cain and Abel, he thought, one beloved by the father, the other the despised tiller of the ground. So be it, then, he thought, that I am Cain to Andrei's Abel, and he will die by my hand.

It was the land that counted. For Yevgeny Sergeivitch all the frustrated and pent-up passion that smoldered within his breast found release in one place alone, the land. Land was the predictable mistress that responded to love with an outpouring of riches, and never rejected a man because he happened to be the careless spawn of an aristocrat. Land must be preserved at all costs. He knew that it was but a step along Andrei's path to begin to sell off the estate, parcel by parcel, as he had sold off his countess's land in Rostov.

Seeing now a clear path of action, Yevgeny felt a great weight lifting from him. The weeks of indecisive rage and depression were like a bad dream from which he had awakened. Briskly, he set about bathing himself in the cold water from his pitcher. It was scarcely light when, shaved and freshly dressed, he strode into the kitchen. The kitchen maid, who was struggling to light the fire in the oven, was so startled, she shrieked and dropped the kindling with a clatter loud enough to waken the housekeeper.

"Hurry it up, girl!" Fedotov said not unkindly. "I have a lot of work to do today, and I need my tea. I'll be in the office when it's ready."

He was already busy with his papers when Maria Feodorovna herself brought his glass of tea. "Masha told me you were in here working, but I had to see for myself," she said. "You seem to feel better this morning—?"

He looked up. "Yes, fine. I've fallen behind a little."

Maria Feodorovna's broad face was troubled. She did not put credence in overnight cures; maybe this was just another aspect of his illness. "May I ask you to explain?"

He looked her straight in the face, and she thought she saw the shadow of one of his rare boyhood smiles. "Just the revelations of night."

He seemed unwilling to say more, and Maria Feodorovna left to prepare him a proper meal. There was little else she could do for him, she thought.

No one was happier than Petya over Fedotov's recovery. The past month had been like the darkest days of midwinter, except that the sun did not shine even for one weak moment. With his uncle's renewed interest in him, the boy lost his pinched pallor. The only tension that remained between them was over Fedotov's forbidding Petya to ride with him on his daily inspections of the estate.

"There is unrest now, Petya," Fedotov explained. "There may be more unpleasantness, and I don't want you to be hurt again."

"I understand that, but aren't two together safer than one?"

"I want no arguments, Pyotr Andreivitch. I forbid you to ride by my side!"

"Very well, Uncle."

But like all the Voronovs, Petya was strong-willed. The steward would not have him at his side? Very well, he would canter along behind. No amount of scolding deterred him. "Who knows?" the boy said reasonably. "I saved your life once, and I might again."

At a loss, Yevgeny Sergeivich conceded that it was safer for Petya to ride at his side than to trail behind.

*M*aking the decision to kill the count was infinitely easier than performing the act. It would be tricky in St. Petersburg. A duel would be the best way, the honorable way, to settle a matter so crucial, but, of course, it was out of the question for a bastard, no matter how well brought up, to fight a duel. If the gentleman's route was closed to him, the steward would have to rely on the peasant's way of guile and trickery. After all, Yevgeny thought wryly, it is my heritage. It would be easy enough to accomplish the desired end when Andrei next came to Spokoinaya Zemlya. "Accidents" frequently happen in the country away from the eyes of others. Fedotov had only to wait for Andrei to come. And there was no doubt that he would come. Natalya's connections at court were too important to neglect the appearance of a marriage. When he came, his assassin would be ready.

It was shortly before Easter when Andrei sent a message that he would arrive for the holiday with high-ranking guests from the capital. In a cold note he instructed the steward to see that the house was prepared for a great Easter celebration and for a week of hunting. The countess, by separate letter, was ordered to invite the neighboring nobility to a banquet and ball.

His heart cheerful, Yevgeny saw that the count's instructions were followed to the letter. The guest bedrooms were cleaned and aired and the grand parlor, dining room, and ballroom made ready. Yoysef the Tailor and his assistant came from Polotsk to refurbish the servants' wardrobes. Grisha, resplendent in a livery seldom worn, was sent into the countryside to deliver invitations to the banquet and ball, while Maria Feodorovna supervised the routine baking and cooking.

They came on a fine day in April, the men astride fine sleek horses, the women swaying in the carriage. Elderly Prince Alexander Popov rode in the carriage with his wife, Catherine, and two other ladies, the Baroness Anna Propotkina and the much-touted Moscow actress, Madame Irina Sappanova. Beside their host rode Gregory Propotkin, husband of the baroness and Andrei's companion in numerous escapades, the Count Maximilian Orlofsky, and Captain Yuri Kuznetsov of the tsar's Horse Guards. It was a handsome, colorful group in holiday mood who dismounted, laughing and joking, in front of the manor house.

On the steps to greet the guests were Countess Natalya, young Pyotr, and Yevgeny Fedotov. For once the count was not displeased with Natalya's appearance—her gown was presentable, and the color high in her usually sallow complexion. Petya, scrubbed and pressed for the occasion, hung back from his father's embrace and scowled at the complimentary remarks from the men and friendly squeezes of the perfumed ladies. With annoyance Andrei thought that the boy was too much under the influence of his uncle; they had the same sullen look about them. Still, today, Yevgeny Sergeivitch, standing a little behind the countess and the boy, as was proper, was smiling and cordial.

The company, except for Prince Popov, who begged off to rest before the fire, hunted the next day and brought home a brace of pheasants and several grouse. Although it was a Lenten fast day, Maria Feodorovna was ordered to prepare the game for dinner that very night. Grumbling only a little, she roasted the birds to a crackling doneness and served them to the guests napped in a fine Madeira sauce.

Although Yevgeny Sergeivitch ordinarily dined with the family, he had sent word that urgent estate business claimed his attention. Andrei was both irritated and relieved. Judging from Fedotov's uncharacteristic cheerfulness, he obviously bore watching, damn him!

On Saturday, after another sumptuous evening meal, the family and their guests rode off in the carriages to the cathedral in Polotsk for the midnight service that would usher in Easter. The house servants, dressed in holiday finery, followed on foot or rode in open summer carts. On the main Polotsk road, they joined the colorful stream of peasants walking or riding into the city, their way lit with lamps or torches. Countess Natalya graciously exchanged greetings with this one and that, and even Andrei inclined his head. It was sometimes difficult to recognize his own villagers usually seen in aprons and head scarves, breeches and homespun shirts, in these gorgeously attired strangers. For this most important of all holidays, the women, resplendent in elaborate headdresses called *kokoshniki*, wore embroidered white linen blouses with billowing sleeves under long flowing blue or red *sarafan*s, trimmed at the bottom with ribbons or bands of silk; for the occasion, the men wore caftans with copper or silver buttons and embroidered felt boots.

Stepping down from the carriages at the cathedral, the little group from the manor house of Spokoinaya Zemlya entered the church. When the priests arrived just before midnight to read Mass, a wave of excitement swept the great crowd of people who had squeezed into the interior of the cathedral and stood now, holding unlit candles before them. At a signal from the patriarch precisely at midnight, all the candles were lit simultaneously, flooding the interior of the dark church with a burst of sudden light. The golden doors of the iconostasis, the screen which concealed the sanctuary, were thrown open before the priests led a solemn procession of candle-holding congregants out of the church, their ranks swelled by those who had been unable to find room inside. Singing hymns, the worshipers circled the cathedral three times, symbolically searching for the risen Christ. After the third time, the patriarch solemnly announced, *Kristos voskrese!* "Christ has risen" to which the people responded with a resounding *Voistinu voskrese!* "Truly He is risen!" The great bells of the church tolled joyously. In the distance similar bells from smaller churches and from the monastery joined in the clamor. All was sound, flickering light, and the heady odor of incense. Even Andrei and his pleasure-loving friends felt the prickle of religious awe.

Once more the plea of "urgent business" had kept the steward from the Mass, but no one was surprised at this. It was well known that Fedotov scoffed at religious customs. He was waiting when the party returned from the church, however, and received the solemn kiss and Easter greeting from Natalya and then from Andrei.

"*Kristos voskrese!*" the count and countess said, each in turn.

"*Voistinu voskrese!*" the steward responded, his manner detached. His eyes followed Andrei.

His look softened when he exchanged the Easter embrace with young Pyotr. Petya's lips were warm on Yevgeny's cheeks, and his eyes, when they met the steward's, were wistful with longing.

On Easter Sunday the landowning aristocracy from miles about came to Spokoinaya Zemlya for the grand ball. For days before the event the French chef, brought from St. Petersburg for the affair, had taken over Maria Feodorovna's kitchen. She had retired in high dudgeon, emerging from her room from time to time to glare balefully about her invaded domain.

Finding her peering into the kitchen from the doorway the night of the banquet, Yevgeny Sergeivitch, looking quite unfamiliar in evening dress, squeezed her around the middle and whispered in her ear that soon the outsiders would be gone and they could all enjoy her superior cooking once more.

"Ah, my dearest Yevgeny Sergeivitch," Maria Feodorovna sighed, "you should be master here."

"No, young Pyotr should. And so he shall be."

Maria Feodorovna patted his cheek. "Too late to help you, I fear," she whispered. "You know Andrei hates you."

Fedotov smiled but did not answer.

At supper, course after course of richly sauced foods were served, each accompanied by fine wines from France. A small orchestra from the provincial conservatory had been engaged to play softly in an alcove during dinner and later in the ballroom for dancing. At each place at the banquet table there was the favor of an intricately ornamented Easter egg executed in vermeil. It was fabulous! Never had there been such a party in Byelorussia! Surely, the guests whispered to each other, the rumors that the Voronov estate was in financial difficulties must be wrong!

No one who was there for the ball that night missed the fact that after the obligatory opening dance, Countess Natalya was quite ignored by her husband.

"Of course," said the Baroness Propotkina with malice, "she is a pale moth to Catherine's butterfly!"

"More like a caterpillar!" her husband giggled, gesturing toward Natalya's green satin gown. The color was unfortunate, drawing what color there was from the countess's cheeks and washing the blue from her rather pretty eyes.

For most of the evening Natalya sat beside drowsy Prince Popov, conversing with as much animation as she could contrive. After the courtesy dances with the gentlemen guests, the countess had been largely abandoned, except for the attentions of Yevgeny Fedotov, who brought her champagne, leaned over to remark on the dancers, and escorted her to the dance floor for the waltz and the mazurka. Many of the guests remarked on what a cheeky fellow Fedotov was. He was rumored to be a poor relation of the family but nevertheless a kind of servant. Still, in his evening clothes, he cut quite a handsome, distinguished figure, and he seemed quite attentive to the countess. Maybe with the count playing at cat and mouse in St. Petersburg, the colorless little countess was similarly engaged at home? It was enough to titillate the imagination!

*I*t was two days before spring rain showers cleared sufficiently for Andrei and his guests to go out to shoot again. Princess Popova pleaded a headache, and some of the others offered to stay at home to keep her company. Andrei was torn between jealousy at leaving Catherine Popova with the lusty Orlofsky and his love of the hunt. He was still vacillating about whether or not to join the hunters when Fedotov observed that it would be a shame to miss the chase that day since the weather was exceptionally fine and he knew for a fact that a peasant cutting back brush in the far south field had flushed several coveys of fine, fat birds. Still, the steward shrugged, the peasants could always set traps for the last birds of the season—

"Traps indeed!" Andrei snorted. "I will hunt, after all, and anyone else who cares to join me!"

In the end, Gregor Propotkin, Captain Kuznetsov, Madame Sappanova, Prince Popov, and Baroness Propotkina rode off with Andrei, accompanied by Yevgeny Fedotov and several field laborers recruited as beaters. Petya might have been invited by his father to join the hunting party, but he had not appeared for breakfast, and the steward said that he had sent him with his clerk Vassily on an errand to the other end of the estate.

There were a great many people milling about in the woods, some on horses, and the beaters, who had gone before to flush out the birds, on foot. The steward had been accurate in his report. There was a great deal of game to be had for the shooting, and the pheasants and the woodcocks, the grouse and the quail, were the biggest and fattest of the year. The excitement of the kill infected hunters and mounts alike, and soon the party had scattered, each pursuing his own birds into the underbrush. The shouts of the beaters and the echoing reports from the rifles came from every direction.

In the midst of the sport, Count Voronov inexplicably slid from his horse and lay facedown in the dirt. The rider closest to him, Gregory Propotkin, was surprised that Andrei, a skilled horseman, had somehow lost his seat. A laughing jibe died on Gregor's lips, however, when Andrei did not immediately scramble to his feet. With growing horror Propotkin realized that something was very wrong. Jumping from his saddle, he knelt by the body of his friend where it lay unnaturally sprawled. Gingerly he turned the body and saw the blood that was already soaking through Andrei's coat. A stray shot must have felled him. Anxious now, Gregor felt in the neck for a pulse and found none. It had indeed been an unlucky mischance for Andrei, for the bullet had passed through his heart as cleanly as though it had been aimed. He must have died instantly. Gregor crossed himself, feeling a chill pass through him.

It was some time before Propotkin could attract the attention of the others. Yevgeny Fedotov was the first on the scene. Briefly he examined the body, sadly shaking his head before rounding up the party for the funeral procession to the house, the body drooping across the saddle of Andrei's gelding.

*T*here were some malicious few in the neighborhood who said later that it might not have been an accident at all. But the official inquest into the death did not concern itself with naughty gossip. Heaven only knows how many hunters get careless with their weapons in the heat and excitement of the chase!

Still, the count's demise did settle problems for some. Countess Natalya, for instance. It was no secret that Andrei had been a cold, indifferent husband, a philanderer and a spendthrift. As mother of the heir and a widow, she would probably make a better second marriage than the first.

Prince Popov, the cuckold husband of Andrei's mistress, could not have been anything but glad that his host was dead. It was no great thing in St. Petersburg society for a wife to take a lover. After all, had not the late tsar taken Princess Dolgorusky as mistress, even installing her under the same roof as the tsaritsa? On the other hand, a husband had a right to expect a certain amount of discretion and good taste in these matters, and Andrei had made the prince the laughingstock of the capital.

Fedotov benefited from the count's death as much as anyone. There had been bad blood between him and Andrei, and it was known that the count had threatened to dismiss him. Now his position was more than secure for he enjoyed the countess's trust and her son's love.

The peasants who lived on the estate hoped they would be better off with a new heir in the manor house. Certainly things for them could not be worse than they had been in recent years.

As it always does, in time interest in the event diminished and normalcy prevailed on the estate. Nothing changed very much. Of course, young Pyotr Andreivitch inherited the lands and the title, but he was still a boy of eleven, and everyday affairs remained the domain of the steward. If Petya had imagined for a moment that being elevated to the title of count would allow him privilege, he was quickly disabused of that idea. Yevgeny Sergei-vitch drove him harder than ever. "You must learn well everything there is to know about managing an estate!" he said to Pyotr time and again, and would not let the boy beg off from his lessons. "There is no time to lose!"

Two important events occurred shortly after Count Andrei was laid to rest in the family crypt. Pyotr Voronov through his steward made it known that the estate would advance cash at low interest to small landhold-ers to pay taxes so that they would not be forced to sell their crops at a loss. Second, the rents were sharply reduced.

The peasants said it was a good omen of the kind of master the new count would be. Blood would tell, after all, and wasn't young Pyotr just like his sainted grandfather?

Chapter 18

The year 1891 was a drought year. In Polotsk, vegetables shriveled in the baked clay of household gardens, and the dooryard flowers drooped on frail stems. In the fields outside the city, the grain, which had been so full and green in the spring, withered and died.

On the Voronov estate, Yevgeny Fedotov watched the hot white sky for signs of rain and considered what to do. After the feeder streams from the River Dvina dried up, turning irrigation ditches into dusty troughs, the steward knew that the estate's principal cash crop, its flax, must be aban-doned. What little water was available was needed for barley, wheat, and rye, for without these there would be no bread.

The hopelessness of the Russian peasant enraged the steward. The little self-farmed parcels of land were the first to turn to dust. The men shrugged and stopped going into the fields. That no grain grew was the will of the Lord God, they said. One must accept what happens. *Vsyo proidyot*, every-thing will pass, they said. Staring toward the fields with apathetic eyes, they sat smoking home-rolled *papirosi* on the stoops of their houses or at the inn, where they drank vodka and cursed the rainless heavens.

The women lit candles and prayed on their knees before bland-faced Virgins and Jesuses who looked back at them with mournful eyes from icons in the dim churches. Suffering was part of the Christian life, Father George told them, and they must endure and love Christ.

And the sun still shone in a cloudless sky.

Day after day Fedotov and the young count rode about the fields, eyes moving from the sun to the dying fields and back again to the skies, searching for a break in the unremitting sunshine.

"It will surely rain," Petya said brightly. "It always rains. It's just a little late this year."

"If it doesn't, people will go hungry this winter," Yevgeny Sergeivitch muttered. His eyes, looking at the parching fields, were hard and his mouth grim.

When April turned into May, May into June, with only a trace of rain, the steward recognized the true desperation of the situation. He selected a certain few fields and marked these with red rags fastened to poles at the corners. "These fields," he told Petya, "have good drainage and are easily reached from the road. We will water these by hand. The rest will die."

Word was passed to the peasants to come to the stables behind the great house the next day at dawn—everyone, men, women, and children. They were to bring with them buckets and pails. In preparation, the steward worked all that day with a picked crew of strong men, reinforcing the flat-bottomed farm wagons to take the weight of the great metal-bound casks that were normally used for fermenting barley for kvass. By afternoon the reinforced wagons were rolling many versts to the River Dvina, where the casks were filled with the muddy water that remained in the riverbed, hauled back to the estate, and emptied into smaller barrels, troughs, and crocks. Back and forth the teams of horses plodded in the heat, pulling the wagons with their loads, light on the way to the river and so very heavy on the way back. The trips continued until there was not a single receptacle left to fill. Fedotov, surveying the lot, was not satisfied. It was not enough. He sent his clerk, Vassily, to Polotsk with Grisha to buy up all the barrels the cooper had. Still, it was not enough. At dusk he had the casks of wine dragged up from the cellars. Countess Natalya, who had stood helplessly on the sidelines, objected to the spilling of the wine, for the French and German vintages were choice, and even the lesser wines, made on the premises from their own small crop of grapes, were treasured throughout the province.

"*Mamushka*," Petya said impatiently, "right now water is more precious than wine."

"But—" the countess began thinly.

"We shall decant the oldest and the best, dearest Mama." Petya knew how to charm his mother. "For a special occasion, eh? For when you marry Prince Trubetskoy?"

"Oh, Petya!" The countess's cheeks flushed at mention of her recent courtship by an old family friend. "How wicked you are!" But she said no more about the wine.

The barrels were emptied, the best saved for the household as Petya had promised, the rest available to anyone who came with bottle, flask, or basin. What remained was spilled into the ground. Soon the whole compound reeked with a sour grape smell.

It was past midnight before Fedotov wearily accepted the fact that there was not one additional container to hold water. God knew, it wasn't enough!

The steward's plan was simple. The full barrels would be deposited at the selected fields. The peasants would fill their smaller receptacles from the barrels and water each row of grain by hand, bucketful by bucketful. As the large kvass casks, now filled with water, were emptied into the smaller barrels, they would be replaced with filled ones and the empties taken back to the river for more water. The process would be repeated for each of the red-flagged fields. When all of the marked fields were watered, the process would be repeated. Since God—or nature, or fate—saw fit to deny them rain, they would make their own from the waters of the Dvina insofar as was humanly possible.

As instructed, the peasant families, carrying their pails and buckets, gathered as soon as light began to streak the sky. Bearded men, already burned dark by the summer sun, were dressed for work in loose shirts and trousers, their legs and feet wrapped in strips of cloth and their feet in the bast slippers called *lapti*. The women were equally plain in their work dresses with squares of cloth tied around their heads; many had infants in cloth slings on their backs, and almost all had two or more small children clinging to their skirts. The summons from the steward had introduced a kind of excitement into the sameness of days without work, and there was chattering and laughter in the stableyard. Fedotov looked around, counting heads. Some little boys were playing tag, weaving in and out of the groups of adults, a small girl was rocking a rag doll in her arms, a mother was sitting on a wagon wheel nursing her child. The steward, with Petya nearby, climbed atop a wooden box to explain what the irrigation process would be. A few grumbled that this was a new madness of the steward's and hopeless, but others, accustomed to doing the bidding of the Voronov masters, picked up their buckets and headed for the closest flagged fields. Even as they looked at the skinny stalks of grain poking bravely through the cracked earth, some felt a surge of hope that there might be something they could do, after all, to stop the grain from blowing away in the hot winds of summer.

The first day was spent in a holiday mood. Maria Feodorovna directed the women who were too old or too pregnant for field labor, in preparing food for the workers. At midday there were huge kettles of borscht, slabs of black bread, and pitchers of kvass to feast on in the shade of the birch grove. No one was in a hurry to return to work. It was hotter now, and the monotony of the work was beginning to pall. Fedotov allowed the children and the women with infants to leave but managed to herd the others back to the fields.

"Pyotr Andreivitch," he said to the boy, "I have sent the children home."

Petya glared at his uncle. "I am not a child. I am Count Voronov, and I will be here among my people!"

Fedotov nodded. When Petya turned his back to pick up his pail, he allowed himself a proud smile.

Relaxed after the meal, there was a great deal of laughing confusion, people bumping into each other, the same lines of grain watered more than once, an uncertain milling about. Fedotov scowled and shouted but was largely ignored. He seemed to be the only one who regarded the project as other than a picnic or a game.

By the second morning the steward had sorted the people into work crews, put each in the charge of an appointed leader, and established a steady working pace. The routine was backbreaking. Fill the pail. Down the row. Water the roots of each stalk of grain. Back to the barrel. Refill the pail. Down the next row. Water the roots. Empty the pail. Start again. New barrels of water appeared as soon as the old ones were emptied. People began to grumble. Why should they kill themselves working to save the count's fields? What was it to them if the estate lost money this year?

Yevgeny Sergeivitch, everywhere among the people, his face gray with dust and fatigue, heard the mutterings. "Fools! Ignoramuses!" he berated them. "You work for yourselves and your families, not us! Don't you know that without grain *no one* will eat?"

The sun rose high overhead and the peasants moved from one field to another, kept at their work by the leaders, the steward moving among them, cajoling and cursing in turn. When the workers rested, Fedotov did not. The system depended on every part functioning so that there was a continuous supply of water to the fields where it was needed. He seemed to be everywhere at once. The first day's laughter had been replaced by sullen looks. There were outbursts of quarreling when someone was jostled. It was hot. The work was hard and discouraging. The water vanished beneath the dry surface of the ground, and the plants seemed as thirsty as ever.

Fedotov ordered an ox and a sheep slaughtered and roasted so that the people might be strong and motivated for the work yet to come. It helped for that one day.

By sundown of that second day, all of the marked fields had been watered at least once, and Yevgeny sent the tired families home early, keeping back only a small group of men to take the wagons once more to the river to fill the casks for the next day. The steward himself did not pull off his boots and sit down to bread and tea until he had made a final tour of the fields. Exhausted though he was, Pyotr accompanied him.

"You will save the crop," he said.

For reply Fedotov tousled the boy's yellow hair, now white with dust. "How is it you neglected your washing today, Pyotr Andreivitch?" he joked.

"And you!" the boy retorted, looking at the steward's filthy boots. "Have you been to Baden-Baden for the mud baths?"

A surge of tenderness pierced Yevgeny's numbing weariness. This was a Voronov worthy of the land. His arm circled the thin boy's shoulders, and Petya glowed with the pride of shared work and shared responsibility. He hugged the older man fiercely about the waist.

Day followed day, each a repetition of the one before. The grain stalks in the watered fields began to stand up and to green. It was late in the growing season, the water was sparse, and damage had already been done; the sheaves were not full, but neither were the tended fields dead. There would be a harvest of sorts.

As the grain ripened, the people grudgingly acknowledged that Fedotov's scheme had worked. For their help they had been promised a full share of whatever was reaped. They were better off than others in the province. Most of the landowners had done little to save any part of their crop.

In the fall, when the granary was filled, Petya was pleased, but Yevgeny Sergeivitch was grim. "There will be famine next year," he predicted.

"Oh, Uncle! How you worry! There's plenty of grain for our people!"

"Ours is not the only estate, and ours are not the only people who need bread to live."

"Well, of course, if other people didn't plan ahead— But anyway, there's wheat in the Ukraine. There'll be enough."

"No," the steward said. "The newspapers from St. Petersburg say that there has been a general crop failure."

"But not here," the boy said, gesturing toward the warehouse.

"And will you eat while others starve, Pyotr Andreivitch?" the steward asked shortly. "And if you will, are you prepared to defend your grain from the hungry with guns?"

"You are always a pessimist. It will never come to that!"

The Jews did not own fields or grow grain. Still, they watched the hot, rainless skies that spring and summer of 1891 with as much dread as anyone. If the crops failed, the farmers would have no money to buy goods from Jewish merchants, could not afford to have Yoysef make their clothes or Itzaak mend their shoes, could not buy chickens and eggs from Mammeh Frumma and Avrom. If the Jews were without business, there would be no money in their pockets and no food on their tables. Drought would have the same inevitable result for them as for those who farmed.

Observing the relentless dryness that spring, Malkeh and Yoysef talked as they lay in their bed at night.

"We must prepare," Malkeh said over and over again. "Unless it rains, it will be a time of hunger."

"I cannot bear to think of hoarding food," Yoysef said. "Also prices are very dear already. We would have to spend the gold we've put by for an emergency."

"What do you think this will be if not an emergency!" Malkeh scoffed, her face dark. Her hand caught hold of Yoysef's arm. "We have four children to feed."

Yoysef sighed. "Yes, yes, I know it well. Let us think on it a little longer."

But quietly that summer Malkeh used gold to buy flour, sugar, groats, and beans at prices already inflated, and Yoysef was able to purchase a catch of herring which Malkeh salted and dried in the hot sun. The stores in the root cellar beneath the kitchen seemed sorely inadequate for their needs.

As the cloudless days passed in monotonous succession, Malkeh and the children hauled water from the river, even as Yevgeny Sergeivitch had done, to sustain their vegetable garden. The flowers had long since died. When Chaim whined and complained about carrying the heavy buckets from the river, Malkeh cuffed him so hard that, big as he was, he had to clench his teeth to keep from crying. Chaya Leya and Dvoreh dared not risk their mother's wrath even when Chaya Leya developed a blister on the back of her neck from the wooden yoke Papa had devised to carry two pails at once, or when Dvoreh stumbled and lay on the ground too tired to get up. Despite their efforts, the yield from the garden was disappointing. Malkeh pickled in great crocks what cabbage there was, and there were some undersized potatoes and carrots, rutabagas and apples to store loose, covered with sand, in the cool space beneath the house.

On the farms and estates around Polotsk, nothing grew. The men in the shul talked in whispers of the bad times yet to come.

"Not to worry," Reb Kagan told the others. "The imperial storehouses are filled with grain. The tsar won't let the people go hungry."

Some few raised their eyebrows and exchanged doubtful looks but said nothing.

By winter Yoysef had little work to occupy him. Malkeh suggested that he let his assistant, Herschel, and young Zelig, the apprentice, go.

Yoysef shook his head. "No, I can't do that," he said. "Zelig's family is poor. They will have enough trouble feeding all the mouths at home. And Herschel has no one but us."

"And you, Yoysef?" Malkeh retorted sharply. "You will have no trouble with four children to feed and our parents as well?"

"Herschel is like a son to me, and Zelig is a relative. What we have, they will have," Yoysef answered mildly.

Malkeh's face contorted with anger, but when she began to speak, Yoysef cut her off. "Enough already!" he said sharply. "I have said how it will be."

Malkeh began to ration food. They made do with a thin crust of unbuttered black bread and weak tea in the morning, and boiled potatoes and cabbage at night. There was no midday meal.

After the stifling summer, the winter had come on hard with gusting winds, the snow driving across the empty fields and piling up in great drifts against the houses and barns. The icy wind made it an agony to go outside, even to clear a path to the barn or to the street. The bitter cold seared throat and chest with each breath. Great icicles hung from the eaves, and the snow was packed solid against the double-hung windows so that the houses were like night inside even during the few hours when a pale sun shone.

The house seemed very small with eight people crowded into several rooms waiting for the weather to break. It did not improve Malkeh's disposition, already sharp-edged with worry. Children died of starvation, did they not? The baby, Simcha, looked small and scrawny already and was not walking at an age when the others had.

It was no use brooding, Malkeh thought. "Come, it is no holiday," she admonished her older children. "You have lessons to do. Bring me your book, Dvoreh, and show me how you can read."

"I don't want to read," Dvoreh wailed. "I'm hungry!"

"It will take your mind off food." Malkeh opened the primer. "Do you remember the poem I taught you yesterday, Dvoreh?"

"No. My stomach is making noises. Can I have a piece of bread?"

Chaim snickered.

Malkeh turned on him. "Are you waiting for the Messiah or something? Why aren't you studying your Torah portion for this week?"

"Do I have to do it now?" Chaim grumbled. "I was just getting ready to play a game with Zelig."

"Oh, yes, fine!" Malkeh said, throwing down Dvoreh's primer in a temper. "Then you can both grow up to be ignoramuses!"

"Mammeh," Chaya Leya said softly, "it *is* very hard to think when you're hungry. Maybe Chaim can study after supper, and I'll help Dvoreh with her poem then too."

"If you have so much time, Chaya Leya, how is it that you didn't finish the sums I gave you yesterday?"

"Don't you remember, Mammeh, you asked me to help you with the washing?"

Malkeh glared at each of the three in turn. "Excuses! All of you have excuses, don't you? You don't want to do lessons? All right, don't! Do I care? Go play games, Chaim! Boys who don't study grow up to be beggars or thieves! Go on! Go sit in the shop and play games with Zelig!" She rounded on the girls. "And you two, the way you whine and carry on, you deserve to marry paupers! You are stupid, wicked children, all of you!"

Dvoreh began to cry.

"Please, Mammeh," Chaya Leya begged, "you are frightening Dvoreh."

"Be quiet, Chaya Leya! Sometimes you sound more like your grandmother than your grandmother!"

Malkeh flung out of the room, slamming the door behind her. Leaning her forehead against the wall of her bedroom, helpless tears rolled down her cheeks.

Malkeh's outburst left Chaya Leya shaken and Dvoreh tearful.

Yoysef, coming from the shop into the kitchen, scooped up the weeping child. "Now, now, Dvorehleh," he said, "why should a big girl like you cry?"

"Mammeh is mad at us again!" Chaim said, sullenly kicking the toe of his boot against the oven.

"Chaim didn't want to study his lesson, and Dvoreh said she was too hungry to remember her poem." Chaya Leya looked at the floor, her lip trembling. "And Mammeh's *always* mad at me."

Yoysef put his free arm about her, sighing to see the children unhappy. "Ah, well, children, you have to understand that Mammeh seems angry only because she loves you and she worries about whether you are getting enough to eat! She doesn't mean anything by it."

"Are we going to starve, Papa?" Chaim asked with sudden interest.

Yoysef laughed. "Certainly not!"

The face of Yoysef's worry was never turned to the children. Unlike Mammeh, he seemed to them as cheerful as ever, and this eased their minds. He spent afternoons with Dvoreh gathered into his lap, played finger games with the toddler Simcha, and showed Chaim and Zelig how to carve little farmyard animals from a block of soft wood. It was Herschel who came to Chaya Leya's side when her mother's scolding reduced her to despair. The silent pressure of his hand on hers comforted her, and sometimes he could even coax a smile to her lips.

Malkeh was worried also about her parents in Dagda, but there was little that she could do for them. Her mother wrote that they should not be concerned because the rich uncle in Vitebsk was sending them enough food to get by. Of course, Malkeh thought, Mammeh would say that whether it was true or not.

As often as he could get through the icy, snow-blocked streets, Yoysef went to see how his parents fared. Often he took Herschel and Zelig with him, and they cut and stacked wood and tended the animals to spare Avrom, who had developed a worrisome cough that winter. Whenever the sun shone and warmed the air a little, Malkeh and the children ventured out of the dark prison of the house.

Outside, the children worked off their tensions in snow fights and sled races, shrieking and screaming with delight at being out of doors. Malkeh remembered how it was to be a child in winter. She taught Chaim to aim a snowball so that it flew straight as an arrow, and she made angels in the snow with Dvoreh and Chaya Leya. After such an afternoon, they all came in with rosy cheeks and sparkling eyes, laughing and hugging each other like in the days before the famine.

As the winter lifted, they were able to venture farther from the house. Looking back on that time, the children remembered afternoons when they visited Aunt Golda and Uncle Dovid, who always seemed to have a little sugar for an impromptu tea party, and excursions to Aunt Yenta's, where there were cousins to play with, or trips to the grandparents' house, good-smelling even though the baking Sabbath loaf was now coarse, dark, and puny.

It was not until the spring of 1892 that the full effect of the crop failure was felt. Then it was that less prudent families began to come to the tailor's to "borrow" flour or herring, sugar, potatoes, or carrots. Malkeh would have turned them away, angry that they had wasted while Yoysef and she had been prudent, but while there was food in the cellar, Yoysef would let no one leave without something from their storeroom.

In the spring, destitute Russian families began to appear on the streets, more often than not trailing a string of empty-bellied children whose beseeching eyes stared out from thin faces. Yoysef gave of their meager supplies to any who came to their door until Malkeh, past the stage of anger, wept and entreated her husband to think of his own hungry brood.

"God will provide," Yoysef said. "Rabbi Eleazer has said that if you look through a clear glass, you see the world. But if you cover one side with silver, it becomes a mirror from which only yourself is reflected."

"You made that up!" Malkeh accused him.

"Yes," Yoysef said, smiling, "but it is true nevertheless. We will not let our concern for ourselves separate us from the rest of the world."

Many people died of hunger. Thanks to Fedotov's prudence, the peasants of Spokoinaya Zemlya, with the exception of those already weakened by age or illness, were spared. Ossip Ivanovich, unable to cadge more vodka, died in an alcoholic delirium. His wife, Serafina, had been taken by her illness months earlier, and their little girl Lyuba, alone now except for her brother, was too frail to survive the harsh, hungry winter. Olga had long since departed for St. Petersburg in the company of a soldier, and who knew what had become of her? Vassily Ossipovich buried his family, one by one, in the frozen earth, and then gave up the hut and the strip of land they had called their own, moving into the servants' quarters at the big house. He was quite alone now, and his bitter thoughts turned increasingly to his enemies. The steward and the Jewess, the Jewess and the steward—thoughts of them clamored incessantly in his mind. The steward and the Jewess were responsible for killing his family. It was twelve years past, but the time for revenge was coming.

Passover came, and then a week later the Russian Easter. At the tailor's, there was little enough for the Passover table. Mammeh Frumma contributed a tough, skinny hen from which they had soup and boiled chicken, and Malkeh used the last of the carrots and rutabagas to make a tzimmes of sorts. Each of them had a small square of matzo, only enough for the blessing. The sweet Passover wine was the last bottle from the year before and had already turned sour. There were stewed apples to finish the meal, but no Passover sweetmeats or cakes. Still, after the long, hungry winter, the family declared it the best seder meal they had ever had.

The cathedral on the other side of the city was as crowded as ever that Easter. The people wore their best clothing, gay with ribbons and sprigs of lilac, but the mood of the worshipers was sullen. The winter had been hard. It would be months before the ground produced a harvest, and if it was another drought year—well, better not to think of that.

Now that Andrei was dead, Yevgeny Fedotov felt responsible for accompanying Natalya and Pyotr to the Easter service. It was, he thought, his obligation to prepare Petya to take his place in respectable provincial society. It had been a long while since he himself had had any use for churches, but it was a different story for the titular head of the Voronov family. Fedotov had forgotten how hypnotic the service was, the moving shadows made by black-robed clerics swaying in the light of hundreds of candles, the swinging censers, the monotonous cadences of the chanted Mass, the cloying odor of incense. Father George of the village church and its failed school, was now Bishop George of the Polotsk Cathedral. Yevgeny noticed that he had grown fat and prosperous in the city. He closed his eyes, hearing the old Russian cadences, only half listening when the priest began his Easter sermon.

"My children," began Father George in his deep baritone, "you ask why the Messiah has come and still the promised paradise on earth is not ours. Instead of paradise, there is famine in the land. Our people die. Our children go abroad with swollen bellies. You ask, is that the way our Lord God, Jesus Christ, keeps His promise to us? Do not revile Him! I tell you, my children, it is not God who denies us paradise on earth. It is God's murderers who yet mock His death! He suffers still on His cross, yes, even as we celebrate His resurrection, He is nailed to His cross! Let us not forget on this, His day of glory, that the Jews, who betrayed Him, go unpunished. They betray you as well as Him. In this time of suffering in our land, who profits from Christian misfortune? The Jews! Who loans money at high interest to good men in desperate straits? The Jews! Who bought up grain so that they could raise the prices that honest people must pay for bread? The Jews! That is the agony of Jesus Christ, our Lord God, and it is your agony as well. As a reminder of what He suffered on the cross, you have been sent this travail. What will you do to avenge Him, my children?"

Yevgeny Fedotov frowned. He would have to talk to the priest about this clerical practice of inciting hostility. It was not only stupid but destructive. If Father George dragged out that old story about the Jews and ritual murder, the steward would walk out of the cathedral and take the Voronov family with him. That would tell the people what to think of such rubbish!

But Father George had finished what he wanted to say about Jews. The service was drawing to a close. What, Fedotov wondered, had all that been about? Father George was not a stupid man nor an intemperate one. Yevgeny would have expected better of him. Unless— His forehead wrinkled as he pondered. Unless the government had decided to take the peasants' minds off the famine by scapegoating the Jews again. The steward was thoughtful, chewing at his underlip. He had once had high hopes that the underground revolt of the past decade would do away with superstition and prejudice. But its leaders had turned out to be a cynical lot who, as a matter of political expediency, encouraged the peasants to rise up against Jewish "oppressors" to create momentum for an even wider revolt. And they called themselves idealists and true revolutionaries! In Fedotov's book they were all fools and charlatans!

On the way home to Spokoinaya Zemlya, Petya asked, "Why are you so quiet, Uncle? Was it not a beautiful service?"

"Was it?"

"Oh, the part about the Jews, of course—but the people like to hear that. It doesn't mean anything. They say something like that every year."

"I know. But every year is not a famine year," the steward said with a heavy heart. "I would not want to be a Jew this year."

Chapter 19

On a day early in May, Yoysef and Herschel went to Spokoinaya Zemlya, leaving young Zelig to watch the shop. Not that there was much to watch with business not yet recovered after the famine year. Yoysef was grateful that Countess Natalya had ordered new draperies to be made for the formal parlor while she and Pyotr were away for the season in Moscow. Malkeh said that the countess might be getting married in the summer, possibly the impetus for the new curtains. Whatever the reason, the project was a gift from heaven. The earnings should tide them over until the crop was in and, pray God, life returned to normal.

After the morning meal, Malkeh made the short, pleasant walk to Mammeh Frumma's house. This was the day appointed for the women to make soap. Malkeh left Chaya Leya, a big girl of twelve, in charge of the younger children, with instructions that Chaim and Dvoreh were to do their lessons and Simcha to have his nap.

Chaya Leya wished that she could have gone to her grandparents', too. Aunt Golda would be there, and Aunt Yenta, and there would be family gossip and laughter. *Bobbeh* would make tea with teaspoons of rich raspberry preserves in the bottom of each glass, and there might even be fresh-baked bread to eat with it—even if the slices might not be as thick and luscious as before the drought. It wasn't fair that she always had to be stuck at home watching her brothers and sister!

Chaya Leya lifted the baby Simcha in her arms and carried him to his bed. He was already sleepy, his thumb in his mouth. Chaya Leya bent to kiss his cheek. Sighing with contentment, Simcha closed his eyes. The long, thick lashes lay like shadows on his pink skin. Chaya Leya stood a moment by the cradle, admiring the little boy. Someday she would have a baby of her own. The thought made her feel warm and happy.

"A peaceful sleep, little one," Chaya Leya whispered.

In the kitchen she settled at the table with six-year-old Dvoreh at her elbow. She was making a dress for Dvoreh's doll, and Dvoreh was sorting buttons from Mammeh's sewing box. For a change, Chaim was outside working on some project of his own involving sticks of firewood, a hammer, and nails.

So absorbed were the children in their various projects that they paid scant attention to the summer cart that stopped in the dusty street before the house. Vassily, the clerk from the Voronov estate, had to rap loudly at the door to get Chaya Leya's attention.

*I*t was a fine, warm day without wind, just right for making soap out of doors. By the time Malkeh reached the house, Papa Avrom had built a good steady fire and constructed a sturdy tripod to hold the kettle of fat and lye. Golda, Yenta, and Mammeh were already busy at work, cutting the fat supplied by Yenta's husband into chunks. Malkeh rolled up her sleeves and fell to helping them.

By midmorning the women, taking turns at the kettle, were cooking their second batch of soap. Malkeh stood over the fire, stirring the contents of the large pot with a long stick. Her face was red and wet with perspiration, and she had discarded the *tichl* that she normally wore on her head while visiting Mammeh Frumma. Her long hair, which had worked its way out of its knot, curled damply over her ears. The fat and the lye bubbled merrily in the pot, and from time to time Malkeh asked her mother-in-law if she thought the mixture was ready. Mammeh Frumma would peer into the kettle, inhale, test the viscosity with a big spoon, and shake her head. Not ready. In the meanwhile Yenta and Golda prepared the wooden trays where the soap would cool before being cut into fat brown squares. When they finished, there would be enough soap for the three families for a year.

While they worked, the women talked companionably. Inevitably they spoke about the famine. Sometimes it seemed to Malkeh that they never talked about anything else. This year's rains in March and April had soaked into the soil, and the new growth appearing in fields and gardens was promising. Also the government had finally sent wheat from the imperial granaries to help until the crop was in even though what arrived was never enough. Officials with full bellies never understand people with no bread.

Mammeh Frumma's forehead creased with worry. "A funny thing happened this week," she said.

"Funny? What?"

"Zoya didn't come when she usually does, and so I—"

"Who is Zoya?" Malkeh interrupted.

"The Russian washwoman I got to help me after Papa couldn't lift the kettles from the stove anymore. You remember, it was two or three years ago she first came."

"Ah, *that* Zoya. I don't think I knew her name before."

"So what happened?" Yenta asked, taking the stick from Malkeh's hand for her turn stirring the soap.

"I went to her house to see if maybe she was sick or something. But no, she looked like always."

"She's a great big woman," Golda said, "strong like an ox."

"I asked her why she had not come, and do you know what she said?" Mammeh looked fearfully from one to the other. "She said she did not work for Jews anymore."

The young women stared at Mammeh Frumma, dumbfounded.

"So I said to her, 'But, Zoyinka, you have helped with the washing for years! And you need the money for food.' And she said, 'I don't need it that much.' What do you think of that?"

Malkeh sighed. Hunger had put a terrible strain on relationships. Just a week since, she herself had been walking on the road to the forest to see if there were mushrooms, when a cart driven by Marina, a farm wife she knew well, passed her by. Malkeh waved, but there was no return greeting. Vaguely troubled, she had dismissed it. It was always possible that Marina had not seen her, but now she was not so sure. She decided not to mention it. Mammeh Frumma was worried enough.

Soon, soon there would be grain for bread, there would be vegetables and fruits in the gardens and for sale at the *gostinny dvor*. Malkeh's mouth watered thinking about how it would be to bite into a juicy apple just picked from a tree. The apples were almost ready. A few days earlier Chaim had eaten some that were too green and had been sick all night with stomachache. But in a little while now, the apples would be ripe, and other things would return to normal.

Shyly Golda told Mammeh and Malkeh that after the summer harvest, Dovid planned to visit the great Kotzker Rebbe to ask for advice about making their marriage fruitful. There might be additional prayers to offer.

Malkeh remembered her own dear Mammeh's old woman in the woods. "Have faith, Golda," she said. "Everything is possible."

The sun had passed its zenith and begun its slow, steady decline when the women were distracted by a commotion in the street before the house. Mammeh Frumma went to investigate. She came back in a few moments with a puzzled look on her face and beckoned Malkeh. In the roadway stood an open summer cart. Chaya Leya and Chaim were looking abashed and Simcha was screaming in Dvoreh's lap. A tall boy, whom Malkeh recognized as Yevgeny Fedotov's assistant in the office at Spokoinaya Zemlya, stood by the horse's head, waiting to speak with her.

"Now, what is this?" Malkeh asked, astonished.

"My master, the steward Fedotov, sent me to bring you and the children to the estate. We are to make haste."

"Why?" Malkeh asked. She was perturbed and not a little irritated. She had not seen or heard from Fedotov all during the winter and spring of the drought, when she'd thought he would have shown some concern for them. And now all of a sudden he was giving orders? Who did he think he was? Were they his *mujiks* to be ordered about in this fashion?

"Madam," Vassily said, an edge of rudeness in his voice, "get in the cart. The master said you were to come at once."

Malkeh glared at him. She did not like his tone of voice nor his insolent flat black eyes. "I happen to be busy here," she said, "and I don't understand why we should go to Spokoinaya Zemlya."

Chaya Leya said in a small voice, "Please, Mammeh, get in." She was near tears.

Vassily shrugged. "Personally I don't care, but Fedotov said to bring you to your husband."

"Has something happened to my husband, then?"

"No." He shrugged. "Get in or not as you wish, but I have to get back to the estate."

Mammeh Frumma said uneasily, "Maybe you'd better go with him, Malkeh."

There was no comprehending this. Malkeh was racked with indecision. She had been given no reason for Fedotov's request. Besides, the soap wasn't ready yet, and Yenta had gone home to nurse her newest baby. If Malkeh should leave now, Mammeh was not strong enough to lift the kettle, and Golda would probably let the fat scorch and ruin the last batch of soap. What's more, she did not like to be ordered about, and she especially disliked the arrogant young fellow whom Yevgeny Sergeivitch had sent to fetch them.

Vassily said into the silence, "If you do not wish to come, that is your business. I shall tell the *gospodin*. He will be very angry."

Malkeh sighed. "I'll tell you what—Vassily, is it? Take the children to their father, if you must, but I have things to finish here."

"Please, Mammeh," Chaim pleaded. The children were uneasy with Vassily.

Her decision made, Malkeh became brusque. "You'd better hurry, Vassily. *Gospodin* Fedotov will just have to be satisfied that you've carried out part of your orders anyway. Take the children, but I don't wish to go."

Vassily stared at Malkeh for a moment. There was distaste in his look, something even more than distaste, Malkeh thought. As usual, she found herself disquieted by him. Fedotov had allowed him too much authority, and he had taken on unbecoming airs. Still, looking into those hard, dark eyes, she felt, not for the first time, a twinge of recognition.

With a glance at the descending sun, Vassily nodded and flicked his whip over the back of the horse.

"Be good children now," Malkeh called after them.

Turning back to the house and the soap kettle, she thought she could already smell the mixture beginning to burn.

*V*assily, guiding the horses along the road to Spokoinaya Zemlya, was filled with rage. Through long afternoons of daydreaming over the ledgers, he had envisioned how it would be, his enemies together in the kitchen of the big house, Fedotov forced to watch while the Jews died one by one then the house torched with the steward inside, bound so that he could not escape the flames. Now the Jew-bitch had spoiled his dream! She would have to be killed in Polotsk—that could not be helped, but at least the rest could come off as planned. He would like watching Fedotov beg for mercy. Only then, when his revenge was complete, would he be free to leave Spokoinaya Zemlya forever.

*M*alkeh lifted the kettle from the fire and, careful not to burn herself, poured the contents into the cooling tray. She was momentarily blinded by vapors that rose from the hot mixture. A vision projected itself on the white cloud of steam, something she had not consciously thought about in years, and suddenly she knew why Vassily had always seemed familiar to her. Stunned, she set the kettle on the ground.

"Malkeh?" Golda asked at her elbow. "What is it, Malkeh?"

She closed her eyes, and she could see herself as though in a dream, standing on the stoop of a rude *izba* on the very edge of the village. In response to her knock, a tall, haggard woman of about her own age swung open the door, standing in such a way as to block her view of the dark interior.

"I—I—I have come to see how Ossip Ivanovitch might be," she stammered.

Silently the woman stood aside to allow her to enter.

"No, I just want to know that he is—all right. I have been worried."

"Come see for yourself," the woman said, putting a hand on Malkeh's arm.

Trembling so that she could scarcely walk, Malkeh entered the small hut. It took her a moment to adjust her eyes to the dim light that filtered through the filthy window.

"There he is!" The woman pointed to a straw pallet on the floor, where a still figure lay.

"Oh, my God!" Malkeh said. "He *is* dead, then, like I thought!"

"Dead drunk!" the woman said with contempt.

Malkeh was afraid she would faint. She was still weak from Boruch's birth and the shock of his death. Helplessly she sank down on a bench near the door. When her head cleared she could see that indeed the man breathed. She could see, too, that there were children in the room. A little girl shyly touched her skirt, and Malkeh involuntarily pulled away from the child's dirty fingers. There was a smaller child lying listlessly on a quilt on the floor. And then there was a boy of five or six. He stared at her with eyes like shards of flint, ancient eyes in which no light shone, eyes that were filled with hatred so strong and so implacable that it took her breath away.

Into the woman's hands Malkeh pressed a few rubles, robbed from the cache in the bedroom wall. "I'm sorry!" she mumbled and fled from the hut.

To this day not even Yoysef knew that she had gone to find the peasant whom she thought had been murdered on her account.

"Malkeh?" Golda said again, her hand on her shoulder.

It could not be, Malkeh thought, that all these many years later, the steward's prize pupil, Vassily, was that same boy. That family must long since have left the estate. Memory is a tricky thing, she understood that. It was only that eyes so black are not common in Byelorussia.

"Malkeh! Are you ill?"

She shook off the chill that had come over her. "No, of course not. I just thought of something. It's not important. Let's finish the last batch of soap, Golda."

The children dismounted near the kitchen door and were hustled inside by the fat housekeeper. Yoysef took the weeping Simcha into his arms. The toddler's head drooped at once against his father's comforting shoulder, and he stopped crying and fell asleep. Maria Feodorovna bustled about, fixing a simple meal of bread and milk for the older children. No one seemed to know why they had been sent for. Orders from Fedotov, the clerk Vassily had said, shrugging.

When the steward strode in from the fields an hour or so later, dusk had already fallen. Seeing the four children, he nodded in satisfaction. Good.

While he poured himself a glass of tea, Yevgeny said, "I'm glad their mother didn't put up an argument as usual. Where is she?"

Yoysef said, "Malkeh's at home. Only the children came."

"*What!*" the steward roared, banging down his tea.

Vassily was sent for. The kitchen boy who went to look for him came back after a time, saying that no one had seen Vassily since he'd come back from Polotsk.

"I told him to bring them all, *all!*" Yevgeny shouted at the hapless boy as though he were responsible for Vassily's shortcomings.

Her voice trembling, Chaya Leya offered, "He tried. Mammeh would not come."

Yoysef smiled at the steward. "No one orders Malkeh," he said.

"You fools!" Yevgeny Sergeivitch said savagely, slamming out of the kitchen.

*W*hen Malkeh had cut the last of the cooled and hardened soap into cakes and packed it in straw, she bid Mammeh and Papa Avrom a good night and walked home. She was tired. Months of short rations had taken their toll, and she looked forward to spending an evening resting. She had given over puzzling over Fedotov's summons, being well acquainted with his erratic behavior. Maybe he had suddenly bethought himself of their plight and decided to give them the gift of a good meal for a change. The children would appreciate that, she thought, and return home with their father and Herschel, full and content, their arms filled with goodies from Maria Feodorovna's kitchen. She smiled, imagining their delight.

At home, Malkeh trimmed the wick and lit the lamp on the kitchen table. It glowed golden in the dusk, and, too tired to prepare food for herself, she sank into a chair and leaned back, closing her eyes. Yevgeny Sergeivitch was a strange fellow, she mused. He had the irritating habit of treating them like upper-caste servants, expecting Yoysef to drop everything to come immediately when summoned. She had often told Yoysef not to go, not that he listened.

She fell asleep in her chair. It was quite dark when a banging on the kitchen door awakened her.

"Yes—yes, what is it?" she called, starting up in terror.

Expecting Yoysef's return at any moment, she had neglected to bar the door, and now it burst open, crashing against the wall and making the lamp flicker. She leapt from her chair, a scream dying in her throat as she recognized the figure who had broken his way into her house.

"Yevgeny Sergeivitch!"

The steward, curiously pale and disheveled, was striding toward her, relief and fury fighting for dominion in his face.

He took her roughly by the shoulders. "You stupid, willful female! What do you want to do? Get us both killed!"

Malkeh shrugged his hands off. What did he mean, talking to her like that! "What are you saying? How dare you—"

"I dare, I dare!" he shouted.

He loomed over her, and she was suddenly afraid. She put up her hands in a defensive gesture, but his anger was strong. He shook her so hard her hair fell loose and her shawl dropped to the floor. Her rage flared, matching his. She pounded at him with her fists. In an instant he had caught her hands and twisted her arms behind her back.

"Let me go, you—you—"

"Keep quiet for a change!" he snapped.

For a long moment they stood, glaring at each other. His eyes were almost yellow in the lamplight, the irises flecked with black, the pupils contracted. They pulled her strongly. They always had. Malkeh began to shake. Fedotov pulled her to him in a rough embrace. His body was hard from days in the fields, and his mouth was hot and sweet. Where his hand touched her breast, her flesh burned.

Malkeh's senses quickened. She felt the warmth rising from his skin and smelled his sweat and the odor of his horse. Her ears filled with murmuring sounds, and for a moment she was not sure whether the love words were his or hers. What was happening to her? God forgive her, a weakness possessed her body. Shamelessly she pressed against him, her fingers trembling in his beard, touching his cheeks, his lips, the place where the pulse beat in his throat. For years he had been in her dreams and in her imagination. She knew how his naked body would look, how the broad chest would taper into narrow hips and muscular legs, how the reddish hair would curl on his chest and in his groin. She knew the slippery feel of his body entering hers and the harsh sound of his breath before the cry of release. She had not the strength to resist him. She wanted him. She had *always* wanted him, from the first time they spoke at Spokoinaya Zemlya, when she had been yet a bride, may God and Yoysef pardon her for what she could not help!

The thought of Yoysef shamed her. Was it possible she could love Yoysef and desire Yevgeny? Desperately she pulled back from Fedotov's embrace. His face above hers was dark and strained; a vein pulsed in his forehead.

She pleaded, "Let me go—"

He released her so suddenly she fell back against the table.

"Damn you, Malkeh! Why can't you do as you're told? Why didn't you come when I sent for you? Don't you know you're in danger here? Do you know what a pogrom is?"

The desire that had possessed her a moment before died in the instant she heard the word. "Pogrom," she said faintly. "Tonight?"

He nodded. "Pick up your shawl. There may still be time."

"My children—"

"Safe."

Malkeh blew out the lamp, and they stood a moment in the darkness. She put her hand on Yevgeny's sleeve. "Why do you risk yourself for us—for me?"

He laughed harshly. "Always you have to talk, have to have answers! Even when your life is in danger."

"Why, Yevgeny?"

He grabbed her by the arm and dragged her toward the door. "Didn't what just happened tell you anything? You need the words? All right. You have put a spell on me. I burn to possess you. God knows, if there'd been time enough tonight— Let's get out of here!"

Outside, he hoisted her into his saddle and then mounted behind her in one swift motion, gesturing for her to be silent.

"Wait!" she whispered. "My family, my friends—they must be told!"

With a grunt, Fedotov kicked his heels into the stallion's sides, and the beast took off at a gallop. Malkeh continued to protest and found a hand clamped against her mouth. "Be still!" he said in her ear. "I don't want to hurt you!"

They flew along the ground as they had done once long ago. Hearing a pack of men riding hard on the road behind them, he pulled off into a clump of trees and waited for the riders to pass. Malkeh was so frightened that she was sure the horsemen heard the hammer strokes of her heart. She leaned back against Fedotov, absorbing his strength. His steady arm quieted her. She could not see the roadway, but from the sound of the hoofbeats she knew it was a large party. Where had so many men come from? There weren't that many peasants with horses in the whole province! Had they come from the outside? How could this be?

Resolutely Malkeh closed her mind to the possibility that the horse might whinny and betray them. With an effort of will she concentrated on her children. Yoysef. She listened intently to the rise and fall of her own breath and to that of the man who held her. Even in this moment of gravest danger she was supremely aware of him, remembering without wanting to the moment of flaring passion in the house. She knew she must fight against her weakness. He could shatter her life as surely as the mounted hoodlums.

When the sounds on the road grew distant, Fedotov did not immediately spur his horse onward. He sat, waiting and listening. Finally the only noise to be heard was the occasional snorting of the horse and their own fast, shallow breaths.

Malkeh spoke into the silence, her voice louder than she had intended. "It must not ever happen again. Don't ever touch me again—*Gospodin*."

"Is that all you have to worry about?" Fedotov laughed mirthlessly, his eyes in the moonlight hard and cynical.

Malkeh flushed. Their kiss was nothing to him if he could laugh about it. *She* was nothing, an ignorant woman. Well, good, this was the end of it. That was what she wanted—was it not?

When he was sure that all the horsemen had passed, Fedotov urged his stallion homeward. They went swiftly but with care. Every once in a while, he stopped to listen, his eyes frowning with concentration.

At the manor house, the children were upstairs in Maria Feodorovna's room, bedded down for the night. The stalwart housekeeper sat beside the bed like a fierce sentinel; no one would get past her to harm a hair on one innocent head. Yoysef sat uneasily at the kitchen table with Herschel. He rose as Malkeh came in from the darkness with Fedotov, but was unprepared for the fury of her emotions as she flung herself upon him, clinging to him and sobbing with relief. So disjointed were her words that he could not immediately understand what she was telling him.

Fedotov stood with his back to the door. "Enough, Malkeh!" he said with curt authority.

She was surprised into drawing a shuddering breath.

"There is a pogrom in the city," Yevgeny said to Yoysef, "but you are safe here."

Yoysef was momentarily stunned.

Herschel raised anguished eyes to the steward. "Why do you people want to kill us? My God, what have we ever done to you?"

"Done?" The steward laughed bitterly. "Done? Why, the bishop says you killed Jesus Christ! And according to the tsar, you've bought up all the grain while Russians are starving in the streets! Isn't that enough?"

Yoysef started up, his eyes glazing with the horror of realization. "My parents, my sisters—Yenta's children— I must go back to the city!"

Fedotov barred Yoysef's way. Yoysef was strong, but the other man was stronger.

"You don't understand. I must bring them to a safe place!" Yoysef's eyes accused the steward. "Why did you wait so long to tell me? Come, help me! We can still save them!"

Yevgeny's face twitched. He struggled unsuccessfully to bring himself under control. "You people!" he raged. "First Malkeh and now you, tailor! I save your lives and you want me to save the whole city. Who do you think I am? What power do you think I have? I'm not responsible for the world!"

A furious Malkeh grabbed his arm. "*Not* responsible? You know the Jews didn't make the famine or hoard grain! You know the Jews didn't kill your God."

He swung around to face Malkeh, his face pale and his eyes like two holes burned in his skull. "Leave me be! I am one man. I don't have the power to turn back the flood! I've done my best. I can do no more! They would kill me, too, without a thought. Is that what you want?' He sank down in his chair, shoulders hunched as if under a weight. "What makes you Jews think you have a special right to be saved?"

"Because we don't deserve to be killed!" Malkeh said coldly.

Yoysef shrugged into his coat and wrapped his scarf around his head and neck against the cold of the spring night. "I must go," he said again, moving toward the door. "You won't stop me."

The steward sprang forward. "You will not leave this house! Your people in Polotsk may escape, but you will surely die if you are on the road this night."

"He's right, Yoysef," Malkeh said dully. "It is too late. The men passed us on the road, more men than you can imagine."

Yoysef stood against the door, head bent.

"The children," Malkeh said into the stillness. "You must save yourself for our children."

Herschel rose from the table. "Let me take the horse and go. I will spread the word. If I am killed, I have no family."

Malkeh's voice was sharp. "Sit down! *We* are your family. No one will go. It's too late."

Yoysef looked at the steward with despairing eyes. It hadn't yet been too late when he had sent Vassily for the children.

They sat at the table, three men and a woman. The night was long, the very stillness hostile. Yevgeny had closed the shutters over the windows and barred the doors. The lamp had been turned low so that there was but a dim glow in the room. Anyone passing by outside would think that the kitchen fires had been banked and that the household was abed for the night. Toward dawn the sleepless group heard the sound of riders returning home, the hoofbeats loud in the cold air, the voices drunk and excited.

Yoysef, agitated, ran to the door and threw it open, but Fedotov was behind him in a moment, forcing the door shut and roughly pushing him back into the room.

"Don't be a fool!" he said. "They will be spent by morning and will pass the day sleeping off the vodka. Then I will ride into Polotsk and see what damage has been done."

To the steward's surprise, the horsemen turned in at the estate gate. Unaccountably it was open, as it should not have been. Where the hell was the gateman! Horses clattered into the courtyard. The group in the kitchen could hear the jingle of bridles and the murmur of men's voices.

A voice, apparently not as drunk as the rest, called into the silence. "Send out the Jews, Fedotov, and we'll leave the house alone."

They could hear some kind of explosive exchange outside but could not make out the words. A falling out among thieves? What now!

Herschel and Yoysef sprang to their feet. The steward shook his head and motioned for them to be silent.

"We know you've got them in there! Give them to us or we'll set fire to the house!" shouted the same voice.

Now that they had been discovered and the worst was upon them, Yoysef, Herschel, and Malkeh were as still as stone. None of them had noticed before the shotgun leaning against the wall. The steward picked it up, checked the shells, released the catch. Still, he did not respond to the challenge from outside. He was trying to recognize the voice, trying to figure out how they had known there were Jews in the house.

"This is your last warning, Fedotov! Open the door willingly, or we'll come in and get them!"

Ah! He knew. It was Karpovitch from the village *zemstvo*. He had challenged the authority of the Voronovs before. Yevgeny seemed to remember that his clerk, Vassily, had some kind of relationship with the man. He had heard him address him respectfully as "Uncle" when he came on business one day. Was perhaps the missing Vassily riding at his side tonight?

"I count three! One—two—"

The steward waved the occupants of the kitchen into the passageway that connected the main house with the office. At the same moment that he threw open the kitchen door, he loosed a shotgun blast over the heads of the riders. The peasants were tired from the night's rampage in Polotsk, and drunk besides. They had not expected resistance at Spokoinaya Zemlya. Karpovitch had assured them there would be no fight. Besides, ex-serfs never completely lost their fear of the steward. Seeing him with the gun, they turned and fled. Only the leader and one other, who remained in the shadows, were left to face Fedotov.

The steward took careful aim this time and fired directly at Karpovitch, but at the moment of discharge the agitator's horse unexpectedly shied and the shell went wide of the mark. While Fedotov reloaded, Igor Karpovitch, realizing that he had lost his men, wheeled his horse about and galloped toward the gate. Successive shotgun blasts hurried him along his way. The second man had by this time melted into the darkness.

It was almost morning. Malkeh leaned against her husband, weeping quietly. Yoysef bit his lips till the blood came. Herschel slumped against the wall, his eyes staring into the distance. The steward paced.

The Jews had been brought to the Voronovs secretly. Only Fedotov himself, Maria Feodorovna, a few incurious household servants, and Vassily Ossipovitch knew they were here. Yet Igor Karpovitch and his gang had known. How? Later he would ask questions, find out who had left the house that evening. The gate had been left open for the mob, the dogs had been silent. That meant that someone had expected them. The gateman? Surely not. He had been with the count's family for more years than Fedotov could count. It had to be someone who hated either the steward or the Jews, or both, which, he thought bitterly, narrowed the field to almost anyone!

*W*hen the sun rose in the morning sky, Malkeh and Yoysef insisted on accompanying Fedotov into Polotsk. The fury of the peasants had burned itself out and they had skulked home to their beds. Most would awaken later to shame. The outsiders who had come with weapons were undoubtedly gone by this time, not willing to be identified in the bright light of day.

As the three approached the Jewish quarter, Fedotov dismounted and Malkeh and Yoysef stepped down from the open cart; because the streets were clogged with broken furniture and discarded goods, it was easier to continue on foot. A drifting pall of smoke from buildings that smoldered somewhere in the center of the district stung the eyes and made it difficult to catch a clear breath. They had the feeling of entering a doomed city. Pictures etched themselves sharply in Malkeh's mind. In the dust of the road lay one tall brass candlestick and near it a body curled up as for sleep. Feathers from a torn quilt fluttered prettily in the morning breeze and settled on the stiffened body like so many white butterflies. Yoysef bent over the corpse and stood quickly, his face white with shock. Placing himself between Malkeh and it, he gestured for Fedotov to look. Malkeh broke away from Yoysef's restraining arm and knelt in the dust. The body's penis had been hacked off and was stuffed obscenely in its mouth; between the legs was only a gaping hole where the blood had already dried. Fedotov and Yoysef together raised Malkeh to her feet. Dizzy and covered with a sheen of cold, sick sweat, Malkeh leaned against a tree and vomited. Fedotov covered the corpse with his coat. They moved on cautiously, like people who had stumbled into a nightmare.

"My family—" Yoysef muttered, quickening his pace. His skin was ashen and he was bent over like an old man.

Thinking about Mammeh Frumma and Papa Avrom, Golda and Dovid, Yenta and Yaynkel with their children, Malkeh began to run but Yoysef caught her arm.

As a grisly joke, someone had loosed several pigs in the streets, and they nosed the debris and trotted in and out of houses whose doors hung crazily on torn hinges. Through the opening to one such house they could see that the walls had been smeared with what looked to be blood. The mutilated body of a dog, perhaps a household pet, was dangling from a ceiling beam and someone who could write had scrawled *sabachee dom,* house of a dog, on the doorposts. God only knew where the human inhabitants were.

Fedotov's jaw had tightened and his eyes were hard as stone. *"Boiza- moi!* Where were the police!"

A few people were cautiously emerging from hiding places to assess the damage, tend the injured, and lay out the dead. The eyes of friends and acquaintances slid past Malkeh and Yoysef, answering their anxious questions with hostile shrugs. It puzzled Malkeh until she recognized that it was because they were with Fedotov, who was Russian and therefore Enemy.

"What happened? When did it start? Have you seen my people?" Yoysef asked again and again.

Itzaak the Shoemaker looked away and did not answer.

Yoysef grabbed an elderly man by the arm. "Reb Kagan, my family—?" A tear rolled down a wrinkled cheek before the old man resolutely turned his back on them.

Fedotov suggested that they go their separate ways. He had seen enough. He had something he wanted to say to Yuri Marozov, the chief of the police bureau.

Frightened of what they might find when they reached there, Yoysef and Malkeh turned toward the quiet street where Yoysef's parents lived. Passing the synagogue, they saw that the building had been gutted by fire, and the Torah scrolls were torn and lying in the street. Someone had defecated on the holy words. My God, Yoysef thought, what kind of animals are they?

Overwhelmed by so much horror, a kind of protective numbness set in. Neither Malkeh nor Yoysef was aware that tears were streaming unheeded down their cheeks. Suffering and death were everywhere. The dying and the dead lay side by side in the dust. The sweetish smell of decay had already set in, mixing with the acrid odor of smoke. The gutters ran with blood and filth. No deed was too terrible for the imagination of last night's mob.

A mother had been cut down, her infant still at her breast. The ax stroke had cut both cleanly in half. Through the clotted blood Malkeh could distinguish one long-lashed blue eye and a softly rounded cheek; the mother had been very young.

An old man wrapped in an ancient prayer shawl had been eviscerated; shiny white coils of intestine spilled out into the dirt of the road. His mottled hands were clasped. Was he beseeching his tormentors or praying?

The father of a family, still in his nightshirt, had been nailed to a crude cross in the dooryard of his home. He was barely alive. Malkeh was afraid and drew back, but Yoysef ran to lower the crucifix to the ground.

"Kill me, kill me now," the victim begged in a whisper. Blood and spittle ran out the corners of his mouth.

Yoysef withdrew his pocket knife, stood looking at it.

"No!" Malkeh screamed. "God, no!" She clung fiercely to Yoysef's arm.

Yoysef shook her off. "Let me, alone! I will try to pry out the nails."

Malkeh sank, sobbing, to the earth, her eyes closed against the torment in the man's face. When she opened them again, Yoysef was covering the face with his handkerchief. She stared at her husband. Yoysef would not have—no, of course he would not—?

Yoysef lifted her to her feet. "I could not save him. Come."

It was not until they came to the children, three from a family they knew well, lying one on top of the other, their throats slit and flies already collecting in their pool of sticky blood, that Malkeh collapsed. Yoysef picked her up in his arms and carried her the short distance to the house of Mammeh Frumma and Papa Avrom.

God was selectively merciful; Yoysef's parents were all right. They had hidden themselves in the straw in the barn. It was their good fortune that looters had been too busy with the schnapps they'd found in the house to bother searching the outbuildings. When Yoysef and Malkeh arrived, Mammeh Frumma was standing, her hands on her hips, surveying the destruction of her home. She blanched when she saw Malkeh's limp body.

"She fainted. She's all right, Mammeh. We were at Spokoinaya Zemlya last night. The children and Herschel are safe. The house—I don't know yet."

Everything that was breakable had been smashed. Mammeh Frumma was impassive. The only flicker of emotion was a twitch in the thin skin under an eye when she saw that the family pictures had been maliciously cut from their frames and shredded.

When she had somewhat recovered, Malkeh cried out at what she saw. In the midst of a horror for the dead and dying, too huge for a mind to encompass, the shards of Mammeh Frumma's beloved cut-glass bowl, handed down through generations of Mandelkern women, threatened to break Malkeh's heart.

Mammeh's lips tightened. "It is only a thing, Malkeh, and things are not worth tears. *People* we cry for. Golda, Yenta—I am so afraid."

"I will go see," Papa Avrom said. He had become a frail shell since his heart attack two or three years before. The events of the night had drained him, and his hands shook more than usual.

"No," Yoysef said. "I will go."

"And I," Malkeh said firmly. "I won't faint again."

Golda and Dovid had been caught without warning, asleep in their bed. Gentle Dovid lay dead at the door of his house, where he had been dragged by the intruders. A kitchen knife was buried to its haft in his chest, and his eyes were frozen forever in a look of disbelief. Golda, dazed, sat beside the body, her dress torn and bloodied, her eyes vacant. She seemed incapable of speech and looked up at them with blank eyes when they talked to her. Gently Malkeh lifted her away from the body and gathered her close in her arms. There would be no pilgrimage to the Kotzker Rebbe for Dovid. Hope was dead with Dovid. Yoysef tenderly closed Dovid's eyes and kissed his cheek. The men of the *chevrah kaddisha* waited to take the body until together they recited the words of the kaddish prayer, *Yitgadal veyitkadash shemei raba*— When Yoysef was finished, he wiped his eyes on his sleeve. Dovid, Dovid! How could Yoysef come to terms with losing him!

While Yoysef ran on to see what had happened at Yenta's, Malkeh led a stumbling and uncomprehending Golda to her parents.

Yenta and Yaynkel with their children had been passed by entirely, probably because their house stood on the very edge of the Jewish district. Yaynkel's butcher shop on the market square had been burned to the ground, but what was there to grieve over when the children were safe? Reassured on their account, Yoysef hurried back to his parents' to collect Malkeh. They did not tarry since they had no idea what had happened to their own home and whether young Zelig was safe. When they left, Papa Avrom was doing his ineffectual best to restore order in the house while Mammeh Frumma sat in the darkened bedroom beside Golda, who had been given a dose of laudanum. It was almost noon, and most of the dead had been removed from the streets. A profound silence hung like a heavy curtain over the district, pierced occasionally by the thin wail of a frightened child.

"I wonder if anyone has checked Auntie Lifsa." Malkeh had noticed that there was no sign of life in the little house next door. Auntie had been a warm friend in the turbulent years when the growing family had lived with Yoysef's parents.

"Wait here, I'll go in," Yoysef said.

But Malkeh followed him through the unlocked door. They had seen so much death on this day that they should not have been surprised to come upon yet another corpse; yet they were stunned. Auntie Lifsa sprawled in the backyard where she had fallen in her headlong flight from her pursuers. The old woman's skirt was half ripped off, and her modest drawers were around her ankles, exposing her withered trunk to the sky. She had been brutally raped—from the condition of her body it would seem many times. There were quantities of blood and semen on her thighs, in the thin gray hair of her pubic mound, and on her belly. Malkeh mechanically drew down the old woman's tattered skirt and tucked her own heavy shawl about the body, but she could not hide the rictus of the old woman's mouth that made it seem that she screamed even now in outrage and loathing.

Yoysef said gently, "We will arrange for her to be buried."

It was impossible to grasp the scope and depth of the mob's rage, impossible to come to terms with a God who let it happen, impossible even to mourn yet. That would come later. For now the same blank, dazed look was on every face they passed on their way home.

Yoysef and Malkeh's house was still intact but much of the furniture had been carried away. What hurt was the mindless destruction that made nothing of something that had once had value. What was served by slashing clothes, breaking dishes, gutting feather beds! Yoysef stood in the doorway of his shop. His fine large sewing machine, for which he had saved half a lifetime, had been mutilated by the blows of an ax. He sank down on the doorstep, rocking back and forth. How could anyone have imagined so much hate?

Malkeh stared around the workroom. A gleam of red fabric beneath the edge of the broken sewing machine caught her eye. Without conscious will she moved toward it, kneeling to see what it might be. Her hand touched flesh. She began to scream. When Yoysef ran in, she was struggling to lift the heavy machine.

"What is it?" Yoysef said. "What is it?" And then he saw what Malkeh had seen.

Together they heaved and pulled at the heavy machine. When they had toppled it on its side, they saw that it had crushed Zelig's thin chest. His new red Passover shirt was dark now with his blood.

Malkeh's mind was whirling and spinning with all she had seen. It might be Yoysef who lay in the road, his body violated, or a knife through his heart. It might be her children dead in a heap or crushed to death like Zelig. It might be herself raped and left to bleed out her life in the dooryard.

What kind of a country did they live in? They had buried their dead for generations beyond number in this hostile soil. Was it not enough that Jews were not permitted to live outside the Pale of Settlement? Or that they were considered foreigners despite their years in the land? Was it not enough that they were already bound by laws that limited the occupations they could follow, the possessions they could accumulate, the place they could occupy in society?

Jews are a remarkably patient people, Malkeh thought bitterly, always willing to placate their neighbors. A fatal flaw in a people who want to live. And is this what they had gained from turning away from their own righteous anger? This obscenity in the streets of Polotsk?

Her papa used to tell her, "Forgive them. It is the poor people, the uneducated ones who hate Jews. They see us only as shopkeepers they have to buy their goods from, or moneylenders they must ask for succor. They don't understand that we have not been permitted any other way of life. They are ignorant. Forgive them."

But Papa was wrong. It was not only the common people, the poor, the uneducated who hated them. Pogroms were tolerated—no, encouraged!— by the highest officials of the land, by the tsar himself. Hatred of Jews was a bond among people at all levels of Russian society. Had not Yevgeny Sergeivitch himself, their "friend," had not he known in advance that there would be slaughter in the streets of the Jewish quarter? And where had the police, sworn to keep the order, where had they been when the mob had rampaged through the city?

Malkeh stood beside Yoysef, her hand gripping his arm. Her face and voice were without expression but her words were iron. "We will leave this accursed place. We will leave Russia. We will go to another land, where we can live in peace. I swear it."

Part Two

Straws
in the Wind
1892–1906

Chapter 20

*D*awn broke in a sky spectacularly streaked with shades of rose that turned pink and then lilac before fading in the light of the rising sun. The day would be clear and warm. Eighteen-year-old Vassily clattered out of Polotsk on a stolen chestnut mare. Few were about that early to witness his departure. His employer would have been astonished to see him wearing a suit of fine dark broadcloth with a shirt and cravat stolen from his own wardrobe. He would have been more surprised if he had opened the mare's saddlebags to find several fine pieces of Countess Natalya's jewels concealed within articles of clothing. But on the morning after the pogrom, Yevgeny Fedotov's mind was on things other than his missing clerk.

Still fresh in Fedotov's mind was the image of a bloody corpse swallowing its own mutilated genitals. Like a firestorm that had swept him, disgust and loathing had devastated him. *Boizamoi!* It might have been Malkeh lying dead in the road, or Yoysef so unspeakably savaged! *His* people, simple Christian folk, had perpetrated these atrocities; perhaps it was the swineherd from Spokoinaya Zemlya who had hacked off a man's private parts with a rusty blade, or Yuri, the baker, or old Kolya, from whom he bought chocolates in the city. It was impossible to know what ignorant people would do when inflamed by rhetoric and vodka. Damn Father— *Bishop* George—for his Easter sermon, and damn the tsar and his cynical wolfish ministers!

The Jews, always the Jews, Fedotov thought wearily. They brought out the worst in men. Maybe the country *would* be better off without them. Their clannishness offended those whose ties were less, and their everlasting piety was an affront to everyone who considered himself Christian. If he looked closely enough within himself, he would have to acknowledge that he was not immune to irritation over the aura of moral superiority that clung to the least among them! And yet, in all fairness, what had these people actually done to deserve punishment like *this*?

Malkeh had accused him of being part of the pogrom, but there was no way for him to have stopped it. It was true that for some time acquaintances in the local government had dropped hints about plans for the Jews, but there was no certainty, was there? And when hours before the rioting started, a friendly policeman had whispered that the time was upon them, was it not already too late? What did Malkeh expect him to do, ride through the Jewish neighborhoods spreading a general alarm? How long would he have survived such a mad action?

Fedotov ineffectually dabbed his handkerchief at the perspiration on his forehead; the linen came away from his skin black with soot from the still-smoldering fires. It seemed like half of Polotsk was burning. His head ached, and he could not force his mind to leave off its disturbing meanderings; yet he told himself that the band of pain, like a vise twisting ever tighter around his head, was caused by inhaling the smoke. To acknowledge that he cared so little for the Jews that he had not stood against his own people for the sake of justice was to accept that he was no better than those who had committed the crimes. But was that fair? Had he not sheltered Malkeh and her family under his own roof even at the risk of his life? No one could have done more! Yet his heart remained heavy with a feeling of failure.

After leaving Malkeh and Yoysef, Fedotov had gone directly to police headquarters. He was well acquainted with the director of police, Yuri Marozov. When the steward was in the city, they sometimes shared a meal or took a glass of vodka together. He found Marozov sitting idly behind his desk, a glass of tea on an embroidered napkin before him.

Coming in from the heat of the morning, Yevgeny found the building pleasantly dim and cool, its thick stone walls almost impervious to the smell of smoke and death that hung over the city. Marozov waved his visitor to a deep leather armchair at the side of the desk. The oversized room was rich with Turkish carpets glowing on polished wooden floors and good pieces of furniture comfortably arranged. A fan in the high ceiling made a slow, soothing whirring sound. Considering the terrible events that had occurred just outside these walls, the serenity struck Fedotov as not only incongruous but obscene.

"I'm surprised to see you relaxing here when a whole section of the city has been destroyed by vandals!" Fedotov said sharply, quite neglecting to greet his acquaintance.

Marozov did not answer immediately. He sipped his tea and frowned, shouting for an assistant to bring him another lump of sugar. "They don't know how to serve tea, these peasants! Since the *zemstvo* insisted we hire locals, it's been hell around here!"

"What about the pogrom?" Fedotov persisted.

"Not my business," the policeman said.

Fedotov's brows arched upward. "Whose, then?"

"There were 'suggestions' from St. Petersburg. The *Okhrana* arranges these things for the government. You know that." He nodded his head in the direction of the portrait hanging on the opposite wall. Tsar Alexander III, serious yet benign, looked down upon them with tranquil eyes. It was not for nothing that the populace called him "Little Father."

"I saw some of the mob last night. They were not all local people. Who were the others?"

Marozov blew on his tea. "I don't ask questions about some things. Would you like a glass of tea, Yevgeny Sergeivitch? You look tired."

Fedotov was not to be deflected. "How did they know there were Jews hidden at Spokoinaya Zemlya?"

"Don't be naive! There are spies on your estate. Someone in your own household, I would guess. I don't know who, and I wouldn't tell you if I did. Come now, Yevgeny Sergeivitch! It's not the end of the world. The Jews have been taught a lesson. The peasants are satisfied. And no one is blaming the government for the famine. In a month no one will remember what happened, not even the Jews. My advice to you is to go home and forget about it."

Fedotov stared at Marozov for a moment. "Do we not live in a wonderful country, Yuri Ivanovitch, where there is a scapegoat handy for all occasions?"

The policeman looked up at the other man, his eyes mocking. "Yes, don't we? But I would not say it too loudly. Spokoinaya Zemlya is not the only place where there are spies."

*I*n St. Petersburg it was a simple enough matter to dispose of jewels, and with the rubles from the sale plus an additional amount skimmed from the household accounts over a period of years, Vassily had the wherewithal to invent a new identity. He knew that it was only a matter of time until Fedotov came looking for him, but Fedotov would be searching for a humble clerk, not for Vassily Yulevitch Chernov, a relative of the Minsk Chernov clan, come to St. Petersburg to complete his gentleman's education.

Vassily had the chameleon's talent for assuming another skin. He took uncommon joy in giving his imagination free rein to create even the smallest details of his new life. Where would a young man of the merchant classes, raised in Minsk, live when he came to the capital, what would he do with his days, how would he dress, eat, with whom would he socialize? Fedotov would expect the peasant Vassily to be greedy, spending his stolen wealth on luxuries, but Vassily Chernov from Minsk, who had never wanted for anything, chose to live modestly in a furnished flat in a tall, narrow house facing one of the city's lesser canals. The district was good but not too good, a neighborhood where a well-brought-up young man of means, but not substantial wealth, could live comfortably.

Between Polotsk and St. Petersburg Vassily had worked out the new persona. He must have a family, he decided, which could not be expected to visit nor be visited; therefore, his invented parents must, alas, be dead, a sister also dead in the '88 cholera epidemic. Quite alone in the world with the exception of distant and uninterested relatives, Vassily Chernov would have been left an adequate living, at least until he decided what to do with his future. At loose ends, he would have come to the capital to read and attend lectures at the university. Well-spoken, good-mannered, and as educated as most of the middle classes, who could doubt that the young man was who he said he was? Fedotov had taught Vassily well, and if there should be an occasional misstep, it would undoubtedly escape detection.

At the university Vassily was careful to call no special attention to himself. When attending lectures he carried a leather satchel filled with books and papers and dressed conservatively in jacket and stiff collars; at home, where he occasionally entertained acquaintances, he was casual in narrow breeches and a loose linen overshirt belted at the waist. His thick black hair was cut to lay close against his head but had been left long on the sides to conceal an earlobe that had been chewed in infancy by one of the count's dogs. He had made the focus of his face a pair of thick-lensed spectacles, unneeded for vision but useful for concealing his distinctive eyes. With these minor modifications in appearance, Vassily was satisfied that nothing identified him with Spokoinaya Zemlya nor set him apart from other students. It was simplicity itself to find a group in which to lose himself. Generous with those who had overspent allowances, he was gladly included within a circle of young men of somewhat frivolous bent. Vassily Chernov from Minsk now owned a complete life.

It had never been part of Vassily's plan to become a student in fact; however, one day out of boredom he attended a lecture in the mathematics faculty and was surprised to find in himself a genuine interest. Almost despite himself, he found himself returning again and again to the classes of Professor Dmitri Lichtenthal and even toyed fleetingly with the notion of pursuing a genuine career. But no, that would only deflect him from the driving force in his life, and this he could not have. He had clung too long and too tenaciously to the dream of destroying his enemy Fedotov and the Jewish whore. Hate had given him the strength to withstand a childhood of abuse and degradation. Fantasies of revenge had protected him from acknowledging unbearable pain and despair. Without these, his life would have no center, his days no focus or purpose.

How close he had been to realizing his dream, only to be thwarted by Fedotov and the cowardice of Karpovitch's peasants! Even now he had but to close his eyes to imagine the Jewess's screams, to smell the sweat of fear on her Jew-bastard husband, and witness the helplessness of Fedotov, forced to watch what happened to the others. Afterward, Fedotov would have died, too, ever so slowly. The dream vivid before him, Vassily licked his lips and felt the blood course hot and strong through his male organ. Revenge had been almost within his grasp! And when it was done, he would have been free!

*A*t a restaurant frequented by students for its generous portions and low prices, Vassily was finishing a bowl of a most satisfying borscht. His two companions were already done and were leaning over a pastry table in a corner of the room. Even disguised as a Chernov from Minsk, Vassily could not regard eating as casually as the others did. His head was bent to his food, and so intent was he on soaking up the last bit of broth and cabbage with his bread that he did not notice when Pavel Rysakov paused beside him.

"Ho, Vassily Yulevitch! You handle that food like a man who's known hunger!" the newcomer cried.

Vassily's spoon clattered as it hit the plate. The look he turned on the speaker was both wary and venomous. "What do you mean?"

"Nothing, nothing," the other said hastily. "It's only that I've been standing here for ages waiting to get your attention!"

"I'm sorry, Pavel." Vassily had recovered himself. "I was thinking about something. Sit down. Razin and Ogarev are here with me."

"Good! I wanted to ask you to join me at a meeting at Professor Samarin's house tonight."

"What kind of meeting?"

"It's a Marxist discussion group. Quite a few people you know will be there."

The young men had returned with their pastries in time to hear the last remark.

"That might be fun," Sasha Razin remarked as he slid into his chair. "There are always girls at those meetings."

"An excellent point," Mischa Ogarev agreed, "though I didn't know your tastes ran to women with hairy arms and mustaches!"

"What are you complaining about? At least they're female. I'll bet you haven't talked to a girl since you got to St. Petersburg. How about it, Vassily? Want to go?"

"I don't know anything about Marxism," Vassily said slowly. This was not true. His friend Karpovitch had lent him Karl Marx's *Das Kapital*. He had had to steal a dictionary from Fedotov's library in order to read it, and even so there were things he did not wholly understand. But none of this was part of Vassily Chernov's imagined past. "I never even heard of Marx until I came to the university," he lied.

"So?" Mischa shrugged. "People go to meetings to make new friends—

and eat cake and drink wine. You don't have to say anything. It is just *called* a study group."

"But isn't it against the law to criticize the government?" Vassily asked, his demeanor ingenuous.

"The meeting's at the Samarins', so you know it has to be all right."

"Well—" Vassily considered, "there's nothing else to do tonight. I guess I'm for it."

Pavel's directions to the professor's house had been so vague that the young men blundered, and it was nearing ten o'clock when they finally arrived. The dozen or so students and faculty were adjourning for tea and cakes by then. They did not mind. Sasha and Mischa had come to find girls, and only Vassily had a passing interest in Marxism.

He edged up to a group surrounding Professor Samarin of the history faculty from where he could listen to what was said without participating.

"The really great reforms of the century were those made under Alexander the Second," the professor was saying, "the emancipation of the serfs, the distribution of land, and the development of the *zemstvo*—"

Ha, thought Vassily, some reforms! In the distribution after the emancipation of '61, his father's father had drawn lots for a poor strip of land for which he had to pay redemption dues to the count and taxes to the government. When *he* died, that unproductive bit of soil was divided among his four sons—with Vassily's father, the youngest, ending up with nothing but rocks and clay! As for the *zemstvo*, what was so great about them? The landowners held the voting majority, and the provincial government made the rules! Samarin didn't know his ass from a hole in the ground!

A thin, pale boy with a scraggly beard asked his host, "How do you account, Professor, for the fact that the peasants today are worse off than when they were serfs?"

The professor's face turned red. "Worse! Well, that's your opinion, young man!"

Looking down at some scribbled notes, the boy persisted. "In his *Communist Manifesto*, Marx wrote 'The proletarians have nothing to lose but their chains. And they have a world to win.' When the peasants and the factory workers realize that, won't there be revolution? All it would take is a little pulling together, some organization—"

These fools, Vassily thought in disgust, will never understand the poor. They don't see that poverty makes people suspicious, divides them, and isolates them. Unite and organize the peasants? It was enough to make one laugh!

Professor Samarin was saved from answering by a fat, pimply girl who interrupted. "What do you think of this man Ulyanov, Professor?"

"Ah, yes, the new messiah who calls himself Lenin—"

"Is he really the one to lead Russia into the twentieth century?" the student asked eagerly.

The older man shrugged. "A fly-by-night! Like so many of our revolutionaries, he'll create some noise for a little while and then fade from the scene! We've seen it before."

Vassily turned away, looking around for Ogarev and Razin.

Pavel hailed him. "Come on, Vassily! I want you to meet Samarin's daughter Katya." Taking him by the arm, Pavel pulled Vassily toward the crowd of young people in the corner.

The Mandelkerns buried Dovid and the apprentice, Zelig, with the other dead in the Jewish cemetery on the edge of the city. Golda, without the linchpin that had anchored her life, swung helplessly to and fro. One day she talked extravagantly about expanding her stall at the bazaar, the next she forgot to eat and to bathe. The family was in agreement that Golda should move home with Mammeh and Papa. When the idea was broached to her, so relieved was she not to have any further decisions to make that she agreed more promptly than anyone expected.

Mammeh Frumma was glad to have Golda at home to help her. Avrom's heart had not been strong for a long time, and now his health had taken a sharp downward turn. Even the slight effort to rise from his bed left him weak and gasping for breath. Golda was tender and strong with her father and company for her mother. Slowly, within the shelter of her parents' home, Golda rebuilt a sort of life for herself, slight and shadowy though it was. Yenta nagged that Golda should marry again—God knew there were many widowers since the pogrom—but Golda would not risk herself again. In time they let her be.

Physical things could be repaired or rebuilt. Yaynkel established another butcher shop on the main market square, and Yenta became pregnant with her fifth child. Yoysef and Herschel cleared away the debris in the tailor shop, and after they had painted the large room (Yoysef had insisted although it had already been scoured clean of Zelig's blood), they reopened for business. Yet Yoysef's natural optimism was slow to rebound.

"We are beginning to have a backlog of orders, Yoysef," Herschel remarked one day. "When will you take another apprentice?" Yoysef was staring into the street and seemed not to hear. Herschel prodded, "Yoysef?"

The gaze that Yoysef turned on his young assistant was full of sadness. "Perhaps we won't take an apprentice again."

Herschel put a comforting hand on Yoysef's sleeve. "You are grieving still."

"I always shall. If I hadn't left Zelig to watch the shop while we went

to Spokoinaya Zemlya— If I had never persuaded my cousins to let me take
him into the shop—"

"Yoysef, I have heard you say many times that God alone decides when
to take a soul," Herschel reminded him.

"Yes."

Herschel nodded. "I, too, feel like somehow it is my fault because I
am alive when so many have died."

The rebuilding of the shul had commenced almost before the embers
of the old building had cooled. Families contributed what they could in
memory of loved ones and in gratitude for their own lives. A handful of
sheepish Russian donors pressed rubles for the building into the hands of
Jews they knew. Shuls in Vitebsk and Dvinsk and from communities even
farther away sent money and ritual objects. Men who had seldom labored
with their hands now carried bricks and lifted and nailed heavy timber sup-
ports. Women worked in one another's kitchens to fashion Torah covers
and embroidered curtains for the Ark. The torn and desecrated Torah scrolls
were tenderly cleansed and given a sacred burial, new ones commissioned
from a yeshiva in Jerusalem. Almost every Jew in Polotsk could point to
some way that he had participated in restoring the center of Jewish life to
the community. Yoysef Mandelkern and young Herschel Rosen were among
the first of the volunteers.

There were murmurings against the Mandelkerns among their neighbors. Many had seen Malkeh and Yoysef ride into town with Fedotov on
the morning after the pogrom and had understood that they had been singled
out for protection. Even before, of course, there had been talk about the
relationship that Yoysef and his woman, Malkeh, had with the gentiles at
Spokoinaya Zemlya. Sometimes Grisha, the count's man, had been noticed
delivering packages to the Mandelkern house. It was well known that supplies for the women's school came from the estate and that Malkeh had a
close friendship with the fat housekeeper as well as with the steward. It was
a *shandeh* they said, that Yoysef had abandoned his poor parents and sisters
to the mob while he, his wife, and his children hid snug and safe in the
manor house! How, they asked, could the pair of them live with themselves
after what had happened to Dovid and the poor little apprentice?

Some among the men had been against allowing Yoysef to help with
the shul, but the foreman had gauged the strength of the tailor's arm and
spirit, and he had been adamant in Yoysef's behalf.

"Let us ask the rabbi!" insisted Nissim, who was in charge of laying
the foundation.

The rabbi did not need time to reflect. "The great Hillel said 'Judge
not thy associate until thou comest to his place,' " he admonished Nissim.

"But Rabbi, Yoysef saved himself and his family without thought for anyone else!" Nissim's mouth set in a stubborn line. "Does it not say someplace that one should shun a wicked neighbor?"

Rabbi Nachman sat for a moment with his head in his hands, eyes closed, and the upper part of his body rocking as he marshaled his thoughts. "Ah, Nissim, Nissim," he said finally. "Do you know for a fact that Yoysef Mandelkern is wicked? Simeon the Just wrote that the world stands upon three things: 'upon Torah, upon worship, and upon the showing of kindness.' Of those, I think the third is most important. Times are troubled enough. Let us not divide ourselves one from the other."

Reluctantly Nissim withdrew his objection.

If Yoysef knew of the discussion with the rabbi, he said and did nothing to reflect hurt or anger, and his dedication to the rebuilding never flagged. In the end, even the men who had been most outspoken against him had to acknowledge that Yoysef was a powerful asset, cheerful and tireless, and willing to assume the most difficult tasks.

Early in the construction, a large farm wagon laden with lengths of lumber pulled into the street and stopped beside the men who were applying mortar to the foundation bricks. A big man whom Yoysef recognized as the carpenter from Spokoinaya Zemlya jumped down from the seat.

"*Zdrahstvoyteh*, Gregor Feodorovitch," Yoysef said, walking over to the wagon, "what brings you here?"

"Ah, Yoysef! *Gospodin* Fedotov thought you could use this wood here for your church."

"We thank you kindly. It looks to be very fine lumber."

"The best cedar we have on the estate! He said to tell whoever is in charge that we can loan you men skilled in building."

"I will let the others know of the offer. Please thank the *gospodin*."

Later, when Yoysef told Malkeh of Fedotov's generosity, she nodded without commenting. To herself she thought that the steward's conscience had been stirred and this gave her great satisfaction.

The pogrom had the unexpected result of renewing interest in Malkeh's school. During the famine years, attendance had dropped drastically. Most were too busy grubbing for food or too enervated to make the effort to study. Many times during those dark days Malkeh had thought to abandon the school, but a sense of pride, not completely divorced from a need to show Yevgeny Fedotov what women could achieve, had been reason enough to hold on.

The pogrom had frightened the Jews, and many were thinking about the skills they would need if they were to leave Russia. Women were again knocking on Malkeh's kitchen door. "Please, help me, Malkeh! My man is in New York, and I want to go there soon with my children. I need to know how to read and write Yiddish, how to figure sums—"

A new phenomenon was the women who came with their daughters in tow. "My husband was killed in the pogrom. My sons learn in *cheyder*, and I don't want my girls to be ignorant lest they have to care for themselves as I do now. Can you teach them?"

Once more she emptied the small storeroom off her kitchen. She taught the little girls for two hours in the mornings, the adults for three hours in the afternoons. Evenings were for private lessons. Progress was slowed by Malkeh's need to divide her attention among so many. And still they came to her kitchen door. "Will you see that my child learns her letters? Will you teach me to read the Yiddish newspaper? Will you help me to speak proper Russian? Do sums? Understand where the Mississippi River is?"

Exhausted at the end of every long day, Malkeh desperately needed another teacher. Since Sorkeh Feldman had left for America to join her husband, there had been no one. Two insurmountable obstacles were the unavailability of anyone capable of teaching, and the lack of adequate space to hold concurrent classes.

On nights when Malkeh did not drop immediately into exhausted sleep, she lay awake, endlessly reviewing the problems that beset the school. She longed for a place where girls and women might study literature, languages, and science—she still blushed to remember how she had quarreled with Fedotov over whether or not the earth revolved around the sun!—as well as the practical necessities involved in making one's way in the world.

Gathering tomatoes from the garden at the end of summer, Malkeh began another of her recurrent discussions with her husband. "Yoysef," she said, "what shall I do? Every day more of them come to the door, asking, begging me even." They had been over the same ground during meals, in bed at night, when Yoysef helped with the household chores.

Yoysef shook his head. "I don't know. You can't go on this way. You have children to care for; Simcha is still a baby."

"They are so eager to learn, and I give them so little! There's not enough time, and the need is so great!"

Not meeting her eyes, Yoysef said slowly, "Even without a women's school in Polotsk, people managed to live."

Malkeh scrambled to her feet, her cheeks flushed with anger. "So that's what you think, Yoysef? We don't need the school? You're just like the others! Women are good for just two things—keeping the house and—"

"And?" Yoysef said mildly. "There has not been much 'and' lately." He stood, unfolding his long legs, and brushing the damp soil from the knees of his trousers. His arms circled his wife's waist.

Malkeh leaned against him. "Yoysef, what am I to do?"

"Finish picking the tomatoes—and then let's hide from the children in the hayloft."

"Yes, but that doesn't answer the problem."

Yoysef kissed her dirt-smudged cheek.

"Well," Malkeh said, "I guess the tomatoes can wait until tomorrow."

Malkeh would have liked to know what advice Yevgeny Fedotov would give her, but she was uncomfortable in talking with him now. She told herself it was because he had done too little to save the Jews.

At the beginning of autumn, as though God Himself had taken a hand, the Finkelstein family, about to depart for America and unable to sell their house, was persuaded to donate it to Malkeh's school; Raizel Finkelstein, after all, had been one of Malkeh's early pupils. It was a sturdy house with two large, airy rooms beside the kitchen. Malkeh could not have been more delighted and immediately set some of her pupils the task of whitewashing the interior and arranging chairs and tables. One of the enthusiastic helpers in this endeavor was the *rebbetsen*, who confided in Malkeh that her daughter Hodl had fallen in love with a married man in Vitebsk—God help them!— and was returning home to Polotsk. And God's second miracle as far as Malkeh was concerned, was that Hodl Nachman was a teacher! Of course Malkeh was sorry for Hodl, whom she remembered as a pleasant, compliant sort of girl, but it was difficult to weigh one woman's despair against the need of so many others!

*Y*evgeny Fedotov raised no public alarms over the disappearance of his protégé, Vassily Ossipovitch, even when he discovered that he had been systematically plundering the estate accounts over a period of years. The thefts had taken place so gradually and were so cunningly hidden that Fedotov was never able to determine the exact amount. It was also months before Countess Natalya returned from her travels to find that several valuable necklaces and a tiara had disappeared. When the crimes were reported to Director of Police Marozov, he promised to post circulars throughout the province, but the trail by then was cold.

In any case, Fedotov preferred to search out the culprit himself. For his own sake he needed to confront him. Why would a boy steal from those who had befriended him, why spy against them? And what could the boy possibly hold against a Jewish tailor whom he barely knew? It puzzled Fedotov that Vassily would behave so badly when the Voronovs had been good to him. With his native intelligence he might in time have learned enough to become a steward in his own right, perhaps on some small nearby estate.

The only clue to Vassily's whereabouts was the disappearance of a horse from the stable at the inn on the night of the pogrom, leaving one very unhappy traveler stranded in Polotsk. It told Fedotov that his clerk had intended to travel some distance. A logical destination was St. Petersburg, where a man could lose himself and where Vassily's only living relative, the prostitute sister, had gone before him. Now, what was the sister's name? Fedotov searched his mind. Had there not been a couple of sisters? It was said that one of them had followed a soldier to the capital. The steward was notoriously poor at listening to gossip, but Maria Feodorovna kept track of all the village people. She would surely know the details, and then he would have a place to start his search.

Riding toward St. Petersburg later, Fedotov wondered what he should do with Vassily when he finally found him. He could have him arrested, of course. That would mean a long term for him in Siberia. But what a waste of an education that would be! It would be better to mete out an appropriate punishment himself—but what should it be? On general principles, Fedotov hated the floggings practiced by many of the landowners. At best, a beating left the malefactor humiliated, at worst, maimed; in either case, the peasant's value to the estate was lost. Fedotov administered beatings only for the gravest of crimes—gross thievery, pederasty, arson—and then with a measured detachment so that the culprit would understand that it was not a personal matter between them.

Only once had he regretted a necessary punishment. Years ago on a wintry afternoon, he had ridden his horse into a courtyard in Polotsk to find a drunken peasant assaulting a heavily pregnant woman with his fists and his boots. The woman had been doubled over to protect the unborn child and Fedotov did not at first recognize her. Then Malkeh lifted her head and his simple revulsion for a cruel act turned to uncontrollable rage. His head had exploded with the violence of his feelings. Hot blood surged and roared in his ears and obscured his vision with a film of red. For a time, he was aware of little except the woman's screams and the rise and fall of his arm as the whip came down on the peasant's back. He had almost killed the fellow. His regret was not for that. The peasant deserved whatever he got. No, the regret was that he had lost control over himself completely, irrationally, violently. He tried never to think about that day, and yet there had been a softer side to it, for from the moment that he had knelt beside the woman in the snow he had recognized what he felt for her.

His thoughts lingered on Malkeh, the pale oval of her face, the eyes that were luminous and somehow mysterious, the full lips that promised much. Beneath the drab dress, the breasts were deep and soft, begging for his mouth, and the waist narrow above the gentle swell of her hips. Fedotov's breath raced when he remembered how he had found her sitting so calmly in her kitchen on the night of the pogrom, unaware of the disaster about to overtake her. Relief and fury had inexplicably merged as desire. That night he might have taken her there, in her husband's house, if the urgency of their situation had not prevailed. In the whole of his life, he had never wanted a woman as he had wanted her. And she? Although later she had been stern and forbidding, he knew the yielding he had felt in her body when he held her in his arms. Fedotov smiled to himself. This train of thought made a much more pleasant accompaniment to his journey than thinking about that rogue Vassily.

*H*alf the soldiers who had been stationed in Polotsk seemed to have been a little too well acquainted with local girls; several of the women had followed lovers to St. Petersburg. One of these was Olga Ossipova. Fedotov was able to trace her movements. She had lived for a while with one of the men, but when his wife came from the south, he had put her out the door.

When questioned by Fedotov, the man said, "You understand how it was, *Gospodin*—I couldn't keep them both. And I gave her some money, after all—"

"How much?" Fedotov asked, his eyes cold. "How much did you give her when you threw her out?"

"Well—maybe ten or fifteen rubles— She probably went into a brothel."

"Is that all she was worth to you?" The steward's memory flashed on the child who used to stand before her mean home, holding out her hand for coins when he rode by.

*A*lthough her youth might be in her favor—she could not be more than thirteen or fourteen even now—Fedotov surmised that Olga would certainly not have been taken into the employ of a high-class establishment. He would most probably find her in a place that catered to the scum who prey on little girls. The steward set out to canvass whorehouses that serviced the army camp. By luck he found Olga at the fifth house.

He had a hard time recognizing her for the child who had begged in the road. She was thin to the point of emaciation, wearing a dirty shift, and as they talked, she coughed.

"Olga, do you know who I am?" he asked.

"Yes, *Gospodin*," she said, bobbing her head.

"Do you know that your brother, Vassily, has disappeared?"

"No, *Gospodin*."

"Do you know where he is, Olga?"

"No, *Gospodin*."

The steward sighed. "A pity. There'll be a reward for information."

He glanced at Olga and saw her consider this, change colors, begin to cough again. Ill at ease under his scrutiny, she tugged the hem of her chemise over bony knees. Fedotov had not remembered her being so thin. Did she earn so little that she could not buy a decent meal? "A lot of money, Olga. Fifty rubles. Maybe a hundred if I find him."

Hopelessly she shook her head.

Hating himself for what he was doing, the steward threatened her. "Your brother is wanted by the police, Olga Ossipova. If you know where he is and don't tell, you'll be arrested too. Do you want to go to prison?"

When the girl stopped coughing, she gave him a wan smile. "I wouldn't mind having a rest from—this." She tossed her head toward the bed with its rumpled gray sheets.

He sighed. "I will write down where you can reach me. Let me know if you hear from Vassily. It's important."

She looked so ill, Fedotov gave her the fifty rubles anyway.

*V*assily found Olga a short time later. He gathered her into his arms, weeping and raging against those responsible. "Fedotov," he whispered, his black eyes like obsidian.

"Don't!" Olga said, laying a frail finger against his lips. "You are too hard."

"I will kill him someday."

"Don't—" she said again, her eyes filling with tears.

"First Father, then Mother and Lyuba, now—"

"Vassily, he was here—Fedotov—looking for you," she whispered. "He gave me money."

"Will you—?"

She shook her head. "How could you think I would betray you?"

"Don't worry. He does not think to look for Ossip's son at the university. He will not find me."

"That is good, then," Olga said with a soft sigh. She closed her eyes and turned her head on the pillow.

But when the time is right, Vassily thought grimly, I will find him.

Although Vassily had moved Olga to a clean room with a woman to look after her, within a week she had sunk into a deep sleep from which he could not rouse her. He sat by her bedside for the days it took her to die, holding her hand while tears of love and hate mingled and ran down his cheeks.

Chapter 21

*A*lthough Fedotov had made sporadic forays into nearby cities, he had had no luck in locating his thieving clerk. Perhaps Vassily had settled in some rural townlet after all, and yet Fedotov could not quite abandon the certainty that if only he knew where to look in St. Petersburg, he would find him there. Never had it crossed his mind that Vassily might have gone to cover at the university. Gradually, Fedotov gave up the search.

For the most part, he thought, people eventually bring down upon themselves the punishments they deserve. Fate would deal with Vassily sooner or later.

For his part, with the passage of time Vassily had gradually stopped expecting Fedotov. In fact, at times he quite forgot that he was not actually a Chernov from Minsk. Like others at the university, Vassily had grown increasingly frustrated with the regression of the young tsar's autocratic ways. By a natural progression he had moved from the Marxist study group at Professor Samarin's house to membership in a splinter radical group that supported the fiery lawyer, Vladimir Ilyitch Lenin. In part also, the fact of Olga's death had had a profound effect on him, increasing his sense of root-lessness and alienation. Despite his "friends" and the good life he enjoyed in St. Petersburg, he craved something more, some ties to claim his loyalty.

From the time Vassily first heard Lenin speak, he felt a kinship with the man on the podium, as though Lenin were looking only at him, talking only to him. Wearing a shabby suit and the cap of a simple worker, Lenin told his audience that he understood what it was to be poor and powerless and preyed upon. Vassily believed him even though it was patently untrue. He became like a man with a fever. He deserted the lecture halls of the university and began to follow Lenin from one meeting to another; wherever he spoke, Vassily was in the audience. Eventually he was noticed and given small tasks to perform, at first as slight as distributing leaflets at the door, then gradually more important errands, like carrying confidential messages. Once when he handed Lenin a package, the leader favored him with one of his wintry smiles before turning away. For the moment it was enough for Vassily.

The shaky start to the reign of Nicholas II gave the revolutionary movement its greatest momentum thus far. Radical violence was matched by police brutality. A wave of general strikes virtually shut down St. Petersburg, and the government took swift action against the leaders.

Pavel Rysakov, meeting Vassily on the street one afternoon, was surprised to see how pale and gaunt his friend had become. "I haven't seen you at the Samarins' for months now. Where have you been? Have you been sick?"

Vassily shook his head.

"Well, then, have you heard the news? That whole bunch—Lenin and Martov and heaven knows how many others—have been sentenced to exile in Siberia! The police are still looking for anyone else involved in the strikes."

Stricken, Vassily tottered back on his heels. Pavel took hold of his arm. "What is the matter with you, Chernov?"

"I have to go now," Vassily said, shaking off the other man and beginning to run down the street.

Pavel shrugged. Chernov had always been a strange one.

Hurrying toward home, Vassily's mind churned. Lenin in exile! The police dragnets sweeping up the rank and file! Within twenty-four hours he had slipped over the border into Poland.

*P*olotsk was more or less a backwater, uninvolved in the troubles that racked the major cities. In the six years since the pogrom, the Mandelkerns had recouped, indeed had flourished. The tailor shop had been restored, even to a new power machine imported from Germany, and the women's school now boasted two teachers beside Malkeh, and a two-year academic curriculum developed by Hodl Nachman.

Yoysef worried that the school had become too much the central focus of Malkeh's life. From the time she was herself a child, Chaya Leya had picked up the slack in the family. Initially perhaps it had been to gain her mother's approval, but gradually she became trapped in expectations she had herself fostered. Now Chaya Leya was eighteen and still keeping the house while Malkeh was busy elsewhere. Instead of Malkeh, it was Chaya Leya who listened to Chaim's confidences, mediated the constant petty disputes between the younger children, and bandaged Simcha's hurts. Yoysef feared that in doing so she had missed her own childhood, but when he brought it up to Malkeh, she shrugged and said that Chaya Leya enjoyed being the little mother. Yoysef was not so sure. He had caught flashes of quickly swallowed anger in Chaya Leya's eyes, even if Malkeh did not.

More and more often these days, Yoysef's troubled gaze rested on his older daughter. She was a rather plain young woman, but with her soft brown eyes and the sprinkle of freckles across her nose and round cheeks, she retained the appealing appearance of a winsome child. He was not the only one who thought so. He had observed the glances that passed between his daughter and young Herschel, the way their hands touched as though by accident, the soft conversations that suddenly broke off when he approached. Marriage would save Chaya Leya, he thought, and Yoysef promised himself that when she and Herschel were ready to take that step, he would help them to establish a home of their own, separate from the family. Malkeh would not like it, but that was too bad. When the day came, Dvoreh would inherit household responsibilities that had been Chaya Leya's, but Dvoreh was not Chaya Leya by either temperament or inclination. Matters would come to a head, and Malkeh might then be forced to cut back her hours at the school. Until it was finally resolved, though, Simcha would suffer at Dvoreh's hands. At eight, Simcha was shamelessly spoiled by everyone, and doted upon by his mother, so it was little wonder that Dvoreh felt an unremitting jealousy of him. Raising a family, Yoysef thought, shaking his head in perplexity, is not a job for weak resolve and a faint heart—nor for a largely absent mother either!

Chaim was almost fifteen that year, tall for his age and strongly built like Yoysef, whom he closely resembled. Another black Cossack, as Malkeh described him. After Chaim's bar mitzvah, he had gone into the tailor shop as an apprentice. He had grown up in the shop, and he had a talent for the trade. Chaim felt sorry for friends who had been sent to drudge under mean-spirited masters. For him and for Berel, the second apprentice, the tailor shop was home, family, and school combined. Herschel taught the boys basic tailoring skills, how to measure for a coat, turn a hem, sew a straight seam. Over Malkeh's objections, Yoysef had made Herschel his partner.

"I thought that someday you would take Chaim into the business, Yoysef. What are you thinking of to give away his inheritance like this? You would think that Herschel is a blood relative!"

Yoysef's answer was mild. "How much closer can Herschel be? Did he not save our daughter's life, survive famine and pogrom with us, and rebuild the business at my side? To say nothing of the fact that someday he might become a son in fact. There will be room enough for Chaim."

"But—"

"No more discussion. I have decided. Do I interfere in the school? Please pay me back in the same coin."

Unlike many other apprentice situations, neither Herschel nor Yoysef made fun of the boys for mistakes or raised a hand to chastise them. While they worked at assigned tasks, Yoysef talked quietly, recounting stories of his travels beyond the Pale of Settlement and instructing the boys in Talmud and history.

Neither Herschel, Berel, nor Chaim had been farther from Polotsk than Dvinsk to the west or Dagda to the south, and they liked to hear Yoysef tell how, as a wild youth, he had run away from home for one whole summer and traveled on foot through the countryside, earning his way as he went. He had traveled due east and then south as far almost as the shores of the Caspian Sea. A wide and beautiful world existed beyond Polotsk, he told them, a world that they were not likely ever to know since tsarist edicts had evicted Jews from their homes and forced them to move to towns within the Pale.

Berel asked, "But why can't we live wherever we want, Reb Yoysef?"

"Ah, I am afraid that is not so easy to explain." Yoysef reached out and stroked Berel's flyaway sandy-colored hair with his big hand. "I'm afraid we Jews are an irritating presence, like dust in the eyes of the Russians. They tolerate us only as long as they can control us."

"I will go to America someday!" Berel said stoutly.

"Yes," Yoysef sighed.

Orphaned early in life, as Herschel had been, Berel had come to them a year or so after Zelig died. Before Herschel had chosen him for apprenticeship, there had been a series of places—not homes, for they had not been homes to Berel—where he had stayed until the fostering family grew tired of him or decided it was time to move him on to the next place. There is nothing colder than charity, Yoysef thought, remembering that there is no word for it in Hebrew, the holy language.

Herschel had picked well. Although often unsure of himself, and always afraid he would make a mistake, there was an inner sweetness and constancy in Berel's character that it was good for Chaim to be exposed to. Lately, it had seemed to Yoysef, Chaim had become cocky and much too full of himself. Yoysef had discussed his concerns with Herschel.

"Why don't you talk to him about it?" Herschel asked.

"Maybe it's a stage he's passing through. Anyway, boys don't like to be talked to."

"I know, Yoysef. I remember the Rabbi Hillel stories."

Yoysef smiled.

When he was a couple of years younger, Chaim had led Berel in a rebellion against the weekly bath. After all, the only free time they had was from noon on Friday until the sun set on the Sabbath. What boy would voluntarily spend an afternoon at the bathhouse when he could be swimming in the river or looking for treasures in the woods!

Yoysef said to the pair one Friday morning, "I have a Rabbi Hillel story to tell you."

Yoysef often talked about his favorite sage, and they settled back to listen.

Yoysef put down the trousers he was seaming, and closed his eyes, the better to imagine the scene. "One afternoon," he began, "when Rabbi Hillel left the study house, some of his students walked along beside him, asking where he was going. He answered that he was on his way to perform a meritorious deed. The students were excited, and each one tried to guess what deed might be worthy of such a great and holy teacher. One suggested that he was surely going to feed the lepers. Another said, no, he was going to the widow's house to cut wood for her fire. Still another insisted that anyone could feed lepers or cut wood, but only a man as wise as the rabbi could dispute Talmud in the temple. Finally one of the students, being as polite as he knew how to be, dared to ask, 'What is that deed, Rabbi?' Rabbi Hillel did not break his stride while he answered them matter-of-factly. 'Why, to take a bath, of course.' You can believe that the students were astonished at this answer! 'And is *that* your meritorious deed?' they asked. He answered, 'It is. Let me explain. If the marble statues erected to kings in the Forum are washed and scrubbed regularly by those in charge of them, is it not then even more incumbent upon those created in God's likeness to take care of bodies which are a monument to the Lord? For as it is written: In the image of God made He man.' "

"Oh, Papa!" Chaim laughed. "If you wanted us to take a bath, why didn't you just say so!"

"I just did."

Chaim's education was not limited to the tailor shop. A few months earlier, Chaim had discovered sex, in the barn behind the house, with the aid of the neighbor girl, Sheyna, a voluptuous black-haired beauty three years his senior. To Chaim's regret, the very next day Sheyna went with her trunks and bundles to Dvinsk, where she was to work in a shop. Still, Chaim was changed forever. Sitting cross-legged over his basting, his thoughts strayed often, reliving the moments in the barn. Sometimes he thought he would like to talk about it to Berel, but he never did.

Try as he might to put sexual thoughts from him, Chaim was shamed to find that many a morning there was evidence on the bedclothes of his lustful dreams. One morning he saw his mother's thoughtful eyes fixed upon his bedding, and he flushed scarlet and fled to the shop without his morning tea.

It was shortly after this when Chaim, awake in the bed he shared with his brother Simcha, heard his parents talking in the kitchen.

"Yoysef, Chaim is growing up," Malkeh said.

"Yes, he is big for his age."

There was a pause. "Yoysef, Chaim is almost a man."

"Of course he is!" Yoysef sounded surprised. "He was bar mitzvah over two years ago."

"He spends a lot of time—well, thinking about girls."

There was another silence while Yoysef absorbed this. "Oh." After a moment, "Malkeh, Chaim scarcely has a beard yet!"

"But he's tall and strong, and some think him handsome. I've seen girls looking at him. Zussel's Tziporeh, and the shoemaker's Bashka, and heaven only knows how many others! When he went to Mammeh Frumma's last week with *challah* to make the *shabbes*, Chava, the blacksmith's girl, came out of her house and walked down the street with him, laughing and holding on to his arm."

"So? They've played together since they were children."

"Yes, but they are not children now, Yoysef! Don't you see?"

After a time, he said, "Malkeh, I know you didn't bring up this subject out of nothing, so let us be clear. What exactly is it that you are thinking?"

"It is time that we arranged a betrothal for Chaim."

Chaim slipped out of bed and laid his head against the door, the better to hear the outcome of this extraordinary conversation. Straining in the dark, Chaim could hear his father laughing. "Oh, Malkeh, Malkeh! What is in your head! The boy is only just fifteen!"

"So they can be betrothed for a year or two."

"What's the rush? There will still be plenty of girls to choose from a year from now."

"Some boys settle down better when they have—well, something to look forward to," Malkeh said.

Chaim could not make out what was said next, and he prayed that Mammeh was not telling his father the secret revealed by his mattress. He would die of shame if Yoysef knew. Of course, he could always pretend that Simcha had wet the bed a little. After all, Simcha was still a little boy and no one would care.

After a while the whispered conversation in the kitchen stopped, and Chaim could hear his father's voice plainly. "Well, well, we'll see about it. We don't have to decide tonight."

A few weeks later, Pinchas the *shadken*, who arranged marriages for the whole region, was called to meet with the family about Chaim's future. It being such a serious matter, Malkeh had taken a whole day off from the school, and the whole house had been polished until it shone. The special schnapps had been brought from the cupboard, and Mammeh Frumma had baked her special honey cake for the occasion. When Pinchas presented himself early in the evening, they were all there to meet with him, Malkeh and Yoysef, Mammeh Frumma, Aunt Yenta and Uncle Yaynkel, Aunt Golda, Chaya Leya, and Chaim himself, he the least involved among the whole family. Dvoreh and Simcha were relegated to a corner and cautioned not to interrupt the adults. In the conference, the amount of dowry acceptable to the family was weighed against Chaim's potential worth. To Chaim, hovering on the edge of the family group, it felt uncomfortably like marketplace barter.

At the conclusion of the meeting, Pinchas shook hands all around and departed with a promise to look around and return within the month with a list of eligible young women.

There was a feeling of unreality about the whole process. Chaim discussed it with Berel as they sat one evening on the riverbank. "If it were you, what kind of wife would you want," he asked seriously, "one that could cook or one that was smart—"

Berel laughed and pulled Chaim to his feet. "Neither one! I'd like to have Nadja, the new maid at the inn! Come on, Chaim, let's go down to the square and have a glass of kvass! Nadezdha Ivanovna, now, that's a girl I'd like to have!"

"Fat chance! They say even the landlord can't get into her bed!"

"I tell you, Chaim, she's just waiting for us!"

Over the next several weeks the Mandelkerns came together often to review the prospects presented them by Pinchas. It was a serious matter, not to be rushed. This girl and that one were discussed with the intensity of statesmen arranging a royal match and sometimes with the earthy practicality of Gypsy traders at a horse fair.

"This Yochka from Disna sounds to be a good, strong girl who will work hard and have many sons," Mammeh Frumma offered.

"No, no!" Yenta objected. "The family is coarse, and you know what they say, the apple doesn't fall far from the tree."

All nodded agreement, and silence ensued while tea was sipped and further thought given to the names Pinchas had submitted.

Yaynkel, grown portly with the success of his new butcher shop, belched behind his hand before making a weighty pronouncement. "A good wife is important to a man." Yaynkel was blessed with an understanding of the obvious.

" 'For her price is far above rubies,' " Malkeh quoted from the psalm. Smiling, she passed a plate of cookies to her brother-in-law.

Chaya Leya's voice was timid because she was the youngest admitted to full participation in the family council. "Why do we have to look in other places? I like Bluma. Always a smile on her face."

"Yes, for every man in sight!" Mammeh Frumma scoffed.

"Well now," Yoysef said thoughtfully, "Chaim seems to like Chava."

"Like? Like!" Mammeh Frumma exploded. "What has like to do with marriage?"

Malkeh smiled at Yoysef across the table. "I've known cases where it had a lot to do with it."

Yenta suggested a distant cousin in Vitebsk, and the new prospect was given due consideration in a silence broken only by the indrawn sup-sup-sup of the tea.

Finally, her voice tinged with regret, Malkeh said, "The family is rich. They can buy the girl the most promising yeshiva student! Maybe even a rabbi—"

Mammeh Frumma sighed. "Maybe Chaya Leya is right. If we pick someone from Polotsk, we will at least know firsthand about her."

The little group nodded their agreement.

Pinchas was summoned once more. Yoysef presented him with the family's choices—four local girls. Two were eliminated at once, one because negotiations were already under way for her marriage, and the second because she had a fault hitherto unknown to the Mandelkerns. Pinchas whispered that she was said to have fits in which she fell upon the ground. Very sad, and a girl from a good family, too, and pretty. Her dowry would come high because of this one little weakness. It was an opportunity they would be foolish to overlook.

Malkeh shook her head, no.

Pinchas coaxed, "Maybe you should talk it over."

Yaynkel was tempted. "How high a dowry?"

Yoysef said, "We have already decided on the other two, Reb Pinchas."

"So be it." Briskly the matchmaker shook hands all around, swallowed another little glass of schnapps, and departed with the promise to feel out the parents of the two candidates. He would return soon with full information. With a sinking sensation, Chaim felt the marriage yoke inexorably dropping over his head. It no longer seemed such an adventure.

True to his word, Pinchas was back in a few days to say that Chaim was acceptable to either family. Dowries, as they all knew, were negotiable between the parties, but it appeared that the financial advantages of one match were fairly equal with those of the other. What needed to be considered then, were the attributes, the character, and the learning in the family background and, of course, the disposition, talents, and physical health of the girl herself. As family members took sides and backed their favorites, a battle raged back and forth into the evening, the *shadken* as involved and vocal as anyone. The stalemate was broken by Yenta, who remembered hearing from Rochka's aunt's sister that the girl had bad teeth. Ahh! The family breathed a sigh of relief that the deadlock could so readily be resolved. If Rochka had bad teeth at such a young age, and if she then lost a tooth with every child, she would be a toothless crone at thirty! The decision now clearly went to Chava.

Betrothal negotiations could now proceed with Reb Efrem, the blacksmith and horse doctor. Chaim had known Chava always. Like him, she was fifteen, a toothy, strong-boned girl who looked, Chaim thought with a measure of disappointment, a little like one of the horses her father shod. He knew that what he felt was largely irrelevant. Marriages might be made in heaven but they were arranged by families. Besides the crucial financial settlements, Chaim's mother, grandmother, and his two aunts would meet with Chava, her mother, and the other women of her family. Samples of the bride's handwork would be examined, and she herself quizzed to determine the extent of her domestic capabilities and poise. If all proceeded on schedule, it would still be many months before the wedding. For the time being Chaim could relax.

here was a very good reason that Chaim did not want to remember his wedding. It had to do with the new maid at the inn. Nadja was indeed all that Berel had said. She was young and lushly developed, her bosom billowing softly over the top of her embroidered blouse, her bottom twitching under full skirts. Her legs, when she gathered up her hem to climb the stairs, were long and slender. Her hair was like none Chaim had ever seen. It was red and thick, and it curled in little wisps and tendrils around her face when she perspired in the heat of the crowded room.

Nadja treated all the customers the same. She was a jolly girl who laughed and joked with the men and did not seem to mind if one of them patted her buttocks or cupped a hand under her breasts. Nonetheless, she was adept at maintaining a certain safe distance. Chaim thought that she was the most enchanting girl he had ever seen, and he wished that he had the courage to reach out his hand to the softness under her blouse or to nuzzle the soft white nape of her neck beneath its cluster of curls. But when Nadja came to the table for his order, Chaim studiously examined the floor. He had to clear his throat several times to find a voice to ask for kvass.

Late on one such afternoon, before the inn became the noisy, bustling place it would become later, Nadja came to Chaim's table, carrying two glasses of kvass. She sank down beside him, stretching her legs before her and sighing with fatigue.

"You've been here almost every day for a week," Nadja noted.

"I—I—l-l-like kvass," Chaim stammered.

Nadja laughed her merry laugh, and Chaim was sure that she knew what he really liked at the inn. He colored and in his agitation overturned his full glass so that it dribbled into his lap.

"Oh, dear," Nadja said, jumping up and coming around to him. "You've soaked yourself! Here, let me dry you off!" In a moment she was kneeling in front of him, rubbing at the front of his damp trousers with the cloth she used to mop the tables.

With horror, Chaim realized that under Nadja's touch, his penis was hardening, becoming monstrously obvious. "Please—" he said, trying to push the girl's hand away. "Please—"

Nadja's green eyes sparkled with mischief. She made a final deliberate pass between his legs with her cloth before she backed away. She was breathing deeply. "So," she said, and she sat down again across from him.

Chaim was too humiliated to stand, helpless to control his male organ, which had taken on a life of its own.

Nadja leaned across the table and took Chaim's hand. She pressed it against her blouse, and he could feel her nipples grow hard against his palm, just like in his daydreams. Her voice was soft and breathy. "I like you," she whispered. "I've noticed you. You're different from them—from the others."

Chaim lost himself in the pools of her devastating green eyes, unable to look away. Finally, hoarsely, he said, "I'm a Jew," and stood to leave.

Nadja pulled him down. "The landlord told me," she said, smiling, "or else I'd never have known. They say that sex with one of you is different. Better because of the way they trim your thing when you're born. Do you think that's so, that it's better?"

Chaim did not trust himself to speak. He shook his head helplessly.

Nadja patted his hand. "It's all right," she said. "I've had sex only a few times myself. It's nice, makes you feel good, like being warm all over. But I've never had one like you, my own age, you know, and strong and big." She stroked his arm with one slim finger.

Chaim was spared the need to answer, for just then the door swung open, and a group of roughly dressed men came into the room. Elizabeth, the innkeeper's fat wife, shouted for Nadja to get off her behind and serve them.

"I have to go now," Nadezdha Ivanovna whispered, "but next week on Tuesday I will have an afternoon off. Will you meet me?"

Chaim nodded, still mute.

"The old shack where they used to store the dried herring, near the river. Do you know the place? It's not used for anything now."

Chaim nodded again.

"At midday," she said, and was gone.

*F*or the rest of his life Chaim was to associate the pungent smell of dried salt herring with sex. Later he was to know women in many different ways, but with Nadja Ivanovna sex was sweet and sensual, uncomplicated and undemanding, and it was perfumed for him by the odors in a musty shed on the banks of the River Dvina, where he fell in love for the first time.

On that first fateful Tuesday, Chaim pleaded a headache in order to leave the shop early.

Yoysef frowned, concerned. "A headache? Are you getting sick, my son?"

"No, no, Papa. It's the close work on this coat. My eyes burn—"

"Go into the house and lie down until you feel better. Some tea maybe?"

"No. I think I'll go to the woods, where it's cool. If I go to the house, you know how Mammeh is—she'll just worry, and I'm not sick, really. I just need to rest my eyes a little."

Yoysef was doubtful. "In the woods? Well, I don't know if that's really best. A dark room maybe, a cloth on the eyes—"

"But Mammeh will worry," Chaim argued desperately.

"Yes, I guess so. Well, all right, go rest where you will. We wouldn't want to upset your mammeh."

As soon as he was out of Yoysef's sight, Chaim broke into a run. It had been so easy to deceive Papa that he was both relieved and guilty at once.

Chaim had no trouble finding the abandoned drying shed, for he had sometimes played there as a child. It was a little distance outside the city and around a bend in the river quite out of sight of occasional fishermen on the banks. He had to admit that Nadja had chosen well. Since the building had not been used in many years, most people had forgotten its existence. By now it was mostly obscured by tall grass, but approached more closely, it could be seen that the weathered walls were warped, slanting crazily, as though they had been surprised in their intention to lie down.

Inside, the shed was dim and close with the heat of the day, although a gaping hole in the roof let in air and provided a shaft of sunlight through which the dust motes played.

Nadja was not there when Chaim arrived, and he thought with disappointment that she had changed her mind about meeting him. She's had second thoughts about being with a Jew, he thought. He should never have become involved with her!

But she had told him that she liked him, and she had looked at him with eyes that were hot and moist and full of wanting. Maybe she would come after all.

There was a pile of sacks in a corner of the hard-packed dirt floor, and Chaim sat down on these to wait. It seemed to him a long time that he waited, but it was actually not even a half hour before Nadja was at the door of the shed. She slid inside and quickly swung the wooden door shut, blinking in the sudden dimness.

For a moment before Nadja's eyes adjusted to the darkness, Chaim could see her better than she saw him, and the full glory of that softly rounded body fairly spilling from her dress made his breath catch in his throat.

"I'm here," he said hoarsely. He scrambled to his feet.

She came to him then, smiling her bright smile and taking his hands in hers in an easy comradeship. "I knew you would be," she said.

Nadja put down the bundle she was carrying, glancing around the shed with housewifely concern. "It's sort of dusty, but we'll make it nice in a little bit. What's your name?" she asked suddenly. "Chaim? That's a funny name! Well, Chaim, let's make a comfortable place to sit on these sacks, and then I've brought some bread and butter and kvass for us."

Nadja selected the cleanest of the sacks, wrinkling her nose at the smell of must and herring. She smoothed the burlap and laid other sacks beneath the first to make a sort of couch, which she covered with the bright flowered shawl in which the food had been tied. She tried out the makeshift bed, sitting on it and bouncing a little, then frowning while she added more padding and adjusted the shawl before pronouncing it comfortable. She motioned Chaim to sit beside her.

"This is an adventure!" Nadja exclaimed, breaking off a piece of bread and using her finger to spread it with butter from a little pot. "I'm starved! I'm always hungry," she confessed. "Let's eat first. We've lots of time!"

Chaim could scarcely swallow the thick bread Nadja handed him. His throat felt too parched to allow the passage of food, and his stomach twisted with anxiety. Mostly he just watched the girl wolfing down the simple meal. Nadja's appetites were simple and direct, and she took a child's uncomplicated pleasure in their satisfaction. That day, and for as long as he knew her, Chaim was to feel a heightening of tension and excitement just watching Nadja's way with food—her eyes shiny with enjoyment, her little pink tongue licking the glistening fat from lips and fingers, and the sharp white fox teeth purposefully bearing down on the bread.

"You're not eating," the girl noticed. "Wait!" She drew a small jar of colorless fluid from the pocket of her skirt. "Vodka," she said needlessly. "It's just what you need for appetite!" She giggled and shoved the jar into Chaim's hands. "Go on. Just this once. It won't hurt you."

Chaim swallowed and gagged, and Nadja laughed, her laughter filling the dusty shed with liquid sound. And then they were both laughing, Chaim a little hysterically, to be sure. Chaim drank again, and this time the fiery liquid went down more smoothly. Nadja gulped from the same jar, and then Chaim finished what was left. The vodka helped. The tightness in his chest and the churning in his gut lessened. His hunger not for food, Chaim leaned back against the wall, content to watch Nadja eat what she had brought. When all the food was gone, Nadja wiped her fingers on a sack.

"Oh, but that was good!" she sighed.

Chaim was uneasy, uncertain how to begin. He need not have worried; Nadja was clearly in charge. She rose from the sacks and stretched luxuriously so that her swelling breasts almost burst from her bodice. Chaim watched, pop-eyed, while Nadja unhurriedly stripped off her dress. There was nothing beneath.

"Is this your first time?" she asked companionably.

Chaim, unable to summon his voice, shook his head. But this was different from that other time with Rivka. Then it had been a hurried, furtive coupling in the darkness of the barn, and both had been fearful lest someone come unexpectedly upon them. Chaim had fumbled for Rivka beneath her clothes, and in the dark had seen no part of her body. In fact, he had never before seen the body of a woman completely revealed. Now his mouth gaped at the radiant sight before him. Nadja's naked skin glowed with a faint luminosity in the shadowy shed. Appearing almost unaware of Chaim, the girl grasped her breasts in her hands, fondling them and using her fingertips to make the nipples rise, plump brown berries in a paler aureole. Proudly the breasts thrust forward, large and firm, white except for the faint blue lines of veins beneath the skin. Slowly her hands moved downward on her body, stroking the curving flanks lovingly, moving to the gentle rise of the belly and at last using her fingers to part the tangle of curly red hair where her thighs met.

"Take your clothes off," Nadja commanded, her breath coming in quick little pants.

Chaim in his nervousness tore a button from his fly and threw his clothes on the earthen floor without a thought for them. In a moment he was upon Nadja, using his strength to pin her down on the makeshift bed.

Nadja was laughing in his ear. "Slowly, *lubezhni*, slowly, beloved—taste, taste before you swallow me whole!" And she showed him how, taking gentle mouse nibbles at his ear until he felt he would die from the pleasure. And then, holding his head between her palms, she put her mouth to his, her pointed little tongue forcing his lips apart, exploring, reaching, darting—

When Chaim could bear no more and sought to possess her, Nadja held him off, her throaty voice murmuring endearments, her silken body teasing him and bringing him to still a higher plateau of desire.

"Oh, God! Oh, God!" Chaim groaned. "Let me—"

Still she held him off. Overwhelmed, he could hold back no longer. His penis enormous, he used it to force his way into her body. Not that force was necessary. Nadja was wet and warm and open to him. He came immediately in an explosive climax that left a sticky residue over Nadja's thighs.

The release was ecstasy mingled with shame. Dimly Chaim realized that something more had been required of him. He sought to roll off her body, but Nadja held him tightly. "Wait, *galuptchik*," she whispered. "You must help me now." She took his limp penis in her hands, rubbing it against her body, against her soft belly and in the wet pubic hair, crooning softly, and slowly beginning to thrust her hips rhythmically upward.

Chaim stared into her face. She seemed not to see him. Her eyes were rolled back in her head, her mouth slightly open. Beads of sweat stood out on her forehead and her breath came hoarsely. For a moment he was afraid that he had somehow hurt her and she might die there in his arms.

After a while she climaxed in a long, shuddering jolt. Grasping Chaim's hand, she held it against her vaginal cleft. He felt the tremors there, the waves gradually subsiding.

She sighed, closing her eyes. "Next time we will not hurry so, little Jew. And it will be so good!"

Then they rested in each other's arms. Chaim slept and perhaps Nadja also. After a time they awoke and made love again, and as Nadja had commanded, this time it was slower, good, and satisfying.

Much later, with shadows already falling on the river, they started together through the woods to the city. Nadja stooped to pluck stalks of wild fennel weed. "Here, chew!" she ordered, showing him by putting a stem into her own mouth.

Reluctantly he followed her example, grimacing at the strong taste. "Why are we doing this?"

"It will cover up the smell of vodka." Her nose wrinkled. "And maybe you'd better have a wash before you get home. I don't know what smells more—the old herring or the juices from our loving."

*A*s often as it was possible after that first Tuesday, even several times, God forgive them, on the Sabbath, Chaim and Nadja met in the herring shed. Their meetings had a pattern. Together they made a bed of the sacking, and Nadja always had her clean shawl to cover it. When it grew cold in the fall, the ever-resourceful girl secreted a heavy quilt from the clothesline at the inn; a Gypsy band was accused of the theft. Chaim learned to build a fire of twigs and sticks, so small that it would not send smoke signals through the countryside. Always they ate a little, enjoying feeding each other from their fingers as a prelude to other satisfactions. They ate scraps from the inn tables and stolen delicacies from Malkeh's larder. And they drank a little vodka, at first to ease Chaim's guilt and anxiety, later for warmth. Chaim learned to swallow the liquor more easily, though he never learned to relish it the way Nadja did.

Afterward there was the lovemaking, earthy, sweet, passionate. Nadja taught Chaim how to prolong the pleasure by bringing her slowly to that fevered state that gripped him almost as soon as he held her naked body in his arms. The Russian girl loved her body and its sensations and was marvelously inventive in exploring all the possibilities for giving and taking pleasure. Chaim was a willing and apt pupil.

The deceptions that made it possible for Chaim to get away from the shop and from home became more practiced and easier for him to carry off. His need for Nadja was so overwhelming that even though he tossed through nights of guilt and remorse, he was unable to stay away from the delights of the herring shed. The focus of his week was whatever day Nadja was free from the inn. The rest of the time seemed meaningless and wasted. He was often preoccupied in the shop and shamefully neglected Berel. At first he went often to the inn just to look upon his love, but he was so tormented by jealousy that Nadja herself finally forbade his coming. So the months passed in a dreamlike rush and it was the summer of Chaim's sixteenth year.

The arrangements for Chaim's marriage to Reb Isaac's daughter Chava were proceeding, the date set for just after Simchas Torah. Chaim would be just seventeen, Chava a month or so younger. Since the engagement, Chava had been busy preparing for marriage. She had spent weeks gathering soft goose down to make pillows and a soft quilt to cover their bed. She had embroidered linen pillow covers, crocheted edges on dresser and table scarves, and had almost completed a fine white *shabbes* tablecloth. For herself she had made two high-necked, long-sleeved lawn nightdresses and two flannel ones, two petticoats, four aprons, and dresses—two for everyday, a black sateen for *shabbes* and the holidays, and a white dress with lace for her wedding.

Now that the wedding was almost upon them, Chaim was expected to increase the frequency of his Sabbath visits to the blacksmith's house. Stilted and awkward with each other when the parents left them alone in their little parlor, Chaim tried to ease Chava's embarrassment by recalling the common childhood. Once, he reminded Chava, he had enticed her to climb the wall into the rabbi's garden to steal apples.

"I remember," said Chava shyly. She was still making her way down from the tree, her apron full of fruit, when the rabbi had come outside to take the air.

"You were so scared, you missed your footing and fell out of the branches right at the rabbi's feet!" Chaim remembered the rest of it, too, how she had never said a word about his part in the escapade even when her father whipped her. That's the kind of girl Chava was, never mind her horsey looks!

Their betrothal seemed scarcely to alter Chava in Chaim's sight. She was—well, just the Chava he had always known. If occasionally he saw her eyes fill with a different kind of awareness, he put it down to a trick of the lamplight.

*M*alkeh was somehow uneasy about Chaim. She spoke one night to Yoysef about her feeling that Chaim was changed.

"Of course," Yoysef laughed. "He's become a man."

"It's not just that," Malkeh said slowly.

"What then?"

"Something—"

"Oh, Malkeh, what kind of answer is that—'something'!"

"Where does he go afternoons when you're not busy in the shop? Sometimes I notice you looking for him even when you are busy!"

"Malkeh, the boy is in love. I read it in his eyes, and he goes to the woods, I imagine, to think about his bride. Maybe we shouldn't wait so long for the wedding?"

Malkeh's forehead puckered with worry. "I could believe what you say, Yoysef, except that he acts toward Chava like a brother or a friend. There is something here I don't understand."

Yoysef put his arms around Malkeh and held her close. "My Malkeh," he said, stroking her hair. "You have such an imagination. Where would a boy go in the spring if not to walk through the woods or fish in the river?"

"He used to go with Berel, but now he runs off alone," Malkeh said slowly.

"Well," Yoysef said, "I'm sure it's only because he wants to be alone to think about Chava. To marry is a big step. Now, enough of your worries! Let's not invent troubles when things are so good for us."

But Malkeh's disquietude had communicated itself to Yoysef, and he began to notice things, like how often Chaim made excuses to leave the tailor shop and how eager he was to be sent on errands, how slow to return from them. He noticed, too, that Berel, loyal, faithful Berel, was left behind and had grown silent and sad as he looked after his friend's departing back.

Chapter 22

It was summer. They were lying naked on the couch of gunny sacks in the hot, dark shed. Their loving was good. Chaim's hands caressed Nadja as she had taught him, and she moaned and writhed under him. Limbs twined about each other, mouths locked, Chaim felt himself rising to a place that was as close to heaven as he was ever likely to get.

It was at this moment that the wooden door swung open on its rusted hinges to reveal Papa, dark against the daylight outside. Chaim's father loomed above their naked bodies, his size gigantic, his demeanor fearsome. Chaim scrambled to his feet, grabbing at his trousers but unable to get them on because of the trembling in his limbs.

Yoysef's voice when it came was hoarse and unnaturally loud. *"Oisvarf! Dreck!* Offal and scum! What have you done to disgrace me!"

"Papa, please—I didn't mean—" Chaim could scarcely control his voice. When it emerged, it sounded thin and childish even to his ears.

Yoysef strode forward and struck Chaim across the face with the palm of his large hand. Standing over the naked pair, he was an Old Testament prophet with burning eyes and mighty arm uplifted to chastise sinners. Chaim put his arms about Nadja, surrounding and protecting her with his own body, but he knew how puny and weak he was compared with Papa, and he was both frightened and ashamed of his weakness. Like a baby, the tears burst forth, coursing down his cheeks as he wept.

"You want to lie with the gentile whore? All right, then, for us you are dead! Mammeh will turn the mirrors to the wall, and we will sit on the floor and beat our breasts in sorrow and mourning. *Do not come home!* My son is dead!"

Papa spat into the corner of the shed before turning on his heel. Naked as he was, Chaim ran after his father, tugging at his sleeve, sobbing, pleading. "Papa! Papa!" But Yoysef merely walked faster. "Papa! Don't leave me! Papa! I'm sorry!" sobbed Chaim. *"Papa!"*

But he was gone, and Chaim's voice drifted back on the empty wind.

When Chaim forced his eyes open, he was shaking and clammy with the sweat of fear. Simcha, in the bed beside him, was drowsily telling him to keep still and let him sleep. Chaim stumbled outside to the outhouse. His bowels were like water, and he sat there in the dark for a long time.

It was, he reflected, just a dream, a warning that they had grown careless. He would talk to Nadja about taking a roundabout way to the river. Maybe they should find a different place to meet. Nadja was smart, resourceful. They would work it out.

The fear drained away, the cramps in his gut subsided. He went back to bed and fell into a restless sleep. Over the next weeks the dream recurred several more times. It was usually Papa who found them in the herring shed, though once it was Mammeh, who came upon them rutting on the carpet in the front room of their house.

Chaim found the dreams so disquieting that he tried to keep himself from falling asleep. Most mornings his eyes were red-rimmed from lack of sleep, his complexion unnaturally sallow. Every morning he determined that he must break off with Nadja, but the resolve did not last through the day. He had but to reflect a moment on remembered pleasures for his decision of the night to fail him.

The longer Chaim knew the red-haired girl, the more bewitched he was. Someday, he knew, Nadja would find the husband she was waiting for. Or she would grow restless and move on to another city, another inn. But in the end, it was she who would have to leave him, for Chaim knew that married or not, he would never have the will to leave her.

Malkeh determined to make an opportunity to talk with Chaim. With all her heart she wanted to believe Yoysef's assurance that the only thing wrong with their son was normal anxiety about the approaching marriage. If Chaim could convince her of that, she would gladly drop the matter from her mind and get on with other concerns.

Early mornings were crowded with activity in the Mandelkern household. On a normal day Malkeh drew the water for tea, sliced bread, put eggs to boil before the others rose from their beds. On Fridays she arose well before dawn to prepare the Sabbath *challah* and a week's supply of everyday loaves; often there were special treats, like *babka* studded with nuts and raisins and redolent with cinnamon and sugar. On mornings when the smell of warm yeast dough, fresh from the oven, wafted through the house, there was never a problem in rousing the family.

Among the multiplicity of domestic tasks performed by housewives, only this one gave Malkeh a sense of profound personal fulfillment. The weekly baking of bread affirmed a link with her own mother and through her to a barely remembered *bobbeh* and so on, reaching backward to all the generations of women in her line. More immediately, there was simple tactile pleasure in the kneading and shaping of the dough; it had the satiny smoothness of a baby's skin, a lover's back. The making of the bread was a jealously guarded task, one that Malkeh did not willingly turn over to Chaya Leya.

Yoysef, having washed himself under the pump, returned to the bedroom to bind tefillin on his arms and forehead before reciting the morning prayer. Sometimes Chaim joined him. By that time, Chaya Leya was usually in the kitchen or helping Simcha dress for *cheyder*. Dvoreh, at thirteen, liked to lay abed feigning sleep as long as possible. Except for Dvoreh, Herschel and Berel, having completed their own morning prayers, were usually the last to appear for the morning meal.

On this particular day, Chaim had not come to the table with the others. Simcha complained that his brother had kept him awake with his groans and thrashing all the night through. Malkeh and Yoysef exchanged glances but did not comment. After a while Yoysef disappeared into the shop with Herschel and Berel; Simcha had already run off to school. Malkeh poured another glass of tea while Chaya Leya carried the plates and glasses to the sink to wash.

"Today will be a good day to air the quilts outside, Chaya Leya," Malkeh suggested, peering through the window at blues skies.

When there was no answer, Malkeh turned her head to discover that her daughter had disappeared. Probably whispering in some corner with Herschel, Malkeh thought with a frown. One day soon Herschel would ask for Chaya Leya in marriage and there would be no gainsaying him. Resigned though she was to the inevitable, Malkeh could not help but feel that Chaya Leya could do better than a man who had no family background!

Malkeh was pondering this when Chaim emerged from the bedroom, shamefaced and hurriedly tucking his shirt into his trousers.

"I overslept," he said unnecessarily. "I'll just take my tea into the shop—"

"No, wait, Chaim," Malkeh said. "Sit down beside me and have something to eat. We hardly have time to talk anymore."

"About what?" Chaim asked, his eyes wary.

Malkeh shrugged. "Maybe you'll tell me, my son. All I know is that you are not looking well these days, and to me you seem troubled."

Chaim did not say anything. His spoon scraped the sides of the glass as he stirred his tea around and around.

After a while Malkeh asked, "Does it have something to do with Chava?"

Chaim shook his head.

"The marriage—you are worried perhaps about the responsibilities of marriage? The wedding can always be put off for a while—"

"No, Mammeh, it's not that.'

The burden of guilt weighed heavily on Chaim. Perhaps the awful nightmares would stop if he could just confess, throw himself on the mercy of his mother. Many were the times when she had heard out his troubles, soothed his fears, and helped him set his feet on the right path. But those had been small problems, little sins; how could he tell his mother about Nadja? His face flamed at the thought.

Malkeh saw and was silent, waiting for Chaim to speak out.

Finally in a rush Chaim said, "Mammeh, can I talk to you about—love? Is it true that you and Papa already loved each other when you married?"

"So that's it," Malkeh nodded. "You worry about whether you will be able to love Chava."

Chaim sighed. No, not that. He wanted to know whether his mother could possibly understand the depth of his passion for the Russian girl.

"Well," Malkeh went on, "the answer is yes and no. Papa loved me, but when I stood beside him under the wedding canopy, I wasn't even sure that I liked him. That came later. When you are close with someone, eating your bread with him and sleeping in the same bed, well—"

"Yes?" Chaim stared intently into her face, waiting for a revelation.

But at that moment Hodl Nachman burst through the kitchen door without knocking. Tall and so thin that one got the impression she never took time to eat, she wore a constantly tense and worried expression on her face.

"Malkeh! Thank God you're here! A man from the government is at the school, looking through all the books! I can't imagine what he's after. You've got to come!"

Malkeh's heart seemed to turn over in her chest. "Oh, Hodl, how terrible!" Hastily she rose from the table and reached for her shawl.

"I left Gittel to keep an eye on him and ran all the way here to get you. Oh, Malkeh," she wailed, "what are we to do?"

"*Sha! Shtill!*" Malkeh said sternly. "Be quiet now! It will be all right." At the door she remembered Chaim. Turning, she gave him a faint smile of encouragement. "We'll talk some more tonight," she promised.

Chaim continued sitting at the table after she had gone, his spoon making its endless circles, always coming back to the same place. He was still sitting there when Chaya Leya came through the door from the tailor shop.

Seeing Chaim's face, she asked, "What's wrong?"

"Nothing, I guess. I was just going to talk to Mammeh about something really important, and Hodl came in, and Mammeh—"

"And Mammeh left," Chaya Leya finished, laying a comforting hand on her brother's shoulder. "I saw them going down the street with their heads together."

"The school's pretty important to her."

"More important than us," Chaya Leya said bitterly.

*T*he events of the day drove all thoughts of Chaim's problem from Malkeh's mind. First, of course, the man from the *Ohkrana*, the government's secret police, had to be dealt with. By the time Malkeh and Hodl reached the premises, the man had emptied the cupboards on the floor and had even torn pages from some of the texts. The newest teacher, Gittel, was in tears, which seemed to please the hard-eyed government man.

"Can I help you find something, *Gospodin*?" Malkeh asked politely.

He looked up to see a small, straight-backed figure standing in the doorway. Her face was set in grim lines, and his practiced eye immediately gauged her as not so easily intimidated as the other two women. "I don't need your help!" he snarled.

"All right, then I'll just watch you," she said, sliding into a seat. She turned to the other women. "Go, please, and let the students know that there will be no classes today."

Relieved to be dismissed, Gittel scurried out the door. Hodl lingered uncertainly, afraid to stay but unwilling to desert Malkeh.

Smiling ever so slightly and speaking quietly to reassure Hodl, Malkeh ordered, "Help Gittel with the students."

Alone with the policeman, her lips pressed tightly together, Malkeh watched silently while he flung papers every which way and used the knife from his boot to slash the wall map to ribbons. She had retreated into a state of passive detachment, the only way she could keep from throwing herself upon him in her outrage. In this removed frame of mind, she was able to reason. The agent's destructiveness was so random, she concluded that his purpose must be harassment and not a serious search for subversive materials. Eventually he must tire of the game, and then he would leave. Malkeh mentally toted up the cost of the wasted books, the paper, chalk, and other supplies. It would be difficult to find money to replace everything, she thought. Inkwells had been emptied onto the clean plank floors or smashed against the whitewashed walls. Windows had been broken, desks overturned, legs broken off chairs. In her head she revised class schedules to accommodate the cleanup.

"All right, Jew," he said finally. "I didn't find anything this time. But remember that we have our eye on you. We know how you Jews operate, spreading sedition from your schools and churches. Next time we'll burn the place to the ground!"

Malkeh bowed her head slightly to indicate she understood him. There was just the slightest edge of mockery in the gesture.

The man from the *Okhrana* flushed but said nothing more. It was enough that a message had been given and received.

*I*t was already late when Malkeh told the two other women to go home for the day. Wearily she washed her stained hands and face at the outside pump and pinned the loose strands of fair hair into the bun at her nape. She had badly wanted to run home to the comfort of Yoysef's arms as soon as the pig of a government man had left, but she had not gone. Still operating on a plane of protective detachment, she had gauged it crucial to immediately reinstate confidence within the frightened teachers and students.

Tonight she would talk things over with Yoysef. The men at the synagogue would undoubtedly discuss the ramifications of the assault. It was not clear whether this was a random incident or the beginning of a new wave of anti-Semitism; she thought the former. They would all watch and wait. And tomorrow morning, after she set the students to their tasks, she would go to Spokoinaya Zemlya to ask Yevgeny Fedotov for help in replacing the lost books.

As desperately tired as Malkeh was, she decided not to alarm Mammeh Frumma and Golda by omitting her daily visit to them. Papa Avrom had long since ceased to recognize comings and goings, but the women looked forward to these respites in the daily routine. Malkeh had made it a daily habit to stop on her way home from the school. Today, because she needed time to put the trauma of the day behind her before entering the house of sickness, she took a longer and more circuitous route to the house of her in-laws.

As she approached the familiar house, Malkeh heard a low keening sound that pierced her like a knife in the breast. Pushing open the kitchen door, she saw Yoysef and Chaim carrying chairs from the house (for mourners sit on the floor or on boxes) and Yenta turning the mirrors to the wall. Mammeh Frumma, supported by pillows, lay prostrate on the floor. Chaya Leya and Golda knelt on either side of her, Chaya Leya pressing a wet cloth to her grandmother's forehead, Golda, looking dazed, tightly clasping her mother's hands. Dvoreh and Simcha, pale and big-eyed, sat on the floor, uncharacteristically close to each other. Already two neighbor women moved quietly about the kitchen, preparing food for the mourners.

"Why didn't you send for me!" Malkeh cried.

Yoysef put his arms around her. "It just happened," he said quietly. "Chaim looked for you at the school and on the street—"

"Oh, my God!" Malkeh moaned. "I didn't even have a chance to say anything to him at the end."

From the floor Mammeh Frumma said, "Don't blame yourself. You have been the best of daughters. He would not have known anyway."

Chaya Leya made room, and Malkeh sank to the floor beside the old woman. She began to cry, laying her head against Mammeh Frumma's bosom.

She thought of how Papa Avrom had been when she first came to this house twenty-one years ago. Mammeh had been distrustful of her, but Papa Avrom had been unfailingly kind. She remembered the times he had covered her mistakes before Mammeh could find out, thought about how he had chosen the choicest pieces of fruit for her during her pregnancies, and how he had suffered for her as well as for himself when the twins died. Even in the last few years with his health failing, he had been staunch to support her when her "modern" ways caused others to criticize. "So? My daughter Malkeh doesn't cover her head on the street, that doesn't make her a bad woman!" he would say. And "Maybe if all of us were like Malkeh and made friends with the gentiles, there would be no pogroms." He was inordinately proud of the school, too, no matter that most of the other older people shook their heads and predicted that only trouble would come of it.

If Malkeh would miss him so sorely, how much more would Yoysef, who was like him in so many ways. Malkeh stumbled to her feet and went to find her husband. He was sitting alone in the darkness of the front room. She sank down beside him. They sat a long time, their hands touching for comfort. After a while the pain of the day overcame Malkeh and she shut it out in sleep.

*W*hen the day of discovery actually came, it was not like Chaim's dream at all. It had been unusually warm and pleasant for late summer, and Chaim and Nadja had spent the afternoon swimming in the cold river, talking, and making love. When they emerged from the shed in the late afternoon, they were making jokes, as lovers do, and Chaim's arm rested lightly about Nadja's shoulders. Almost at the same moment each realized that they were not alone. Chaim thrust Nadja behind him.

Slouching carelessly before the hut was a dirty, pimply youth, ragged and barefoot. He grinned and made a mocking half bow in their direction. Chaim recognized him at once. In the town, Mottel was considered simple, a ne'er-do-well child of a sluttish mother and a father who shoveled manure for the dairyman. He made a living of sorts by gathering twigs and branches to sell in the city for kindling.

They looked at each other. An unhealthy prurient expression was on Mottel's sallow face. That look told Chaim that Mottel knew what he and Nadja had been doing in the shed. While they made love, he might even have been peering at them through a chink in the wall. The thought made Chaim feel sick and dirty.

"Well, Mottel," Chaim said with a heartiness he did not feel, "you are far from the city today! Your business must be good to bring you such a long way to find wood."

Mottel did not answer, just stood staring at them, his eyes cunning, his lower lip thrusting forward. Mottel might not be quite all there, but Chaim could not discount his shrewdness.

Chaim tried again. "Look, Mottel, I'll buy what you have there. You see"—his voice dropped to a confidential level—"I've hired Nadezhda Ivanovna here to help me. I'll need a lot of wood, all you've got there, in fact. Only I don't want you to tell anyone about my new business until I have some smoked fish ready to sell in the city." Chaim found some coins in his pocket and held them out toward the boy.

Mottel ignored Chaim's outstretched hand. Spittle trickled from the corner of his slack mouth and his dull face flushed with excitement. "I know what you've been doing with her!" He pointed a finger at Nadja where she cowered behind Chaim. "And I'm going to tell everyone that the tailor's fine son puts his thing in a *goyisheh* whore!" He turned and ran in the direction of the road.

"Catch him! Do something!" Nadja screamed, pushing at Chaim. He did not move.

"How can I keep him quiet?" Chaim asked hopelessly. "The whole of Polotsk will know before we get back to town. It's all over for us." Chaim felt tears prickling behind his eyes. "I always knew it would happen, that someone would find us together. I had a sign. I dreamed many times that my father found us. In a way, it's better it happened this way."

Sadly the lovers walked back to the city. When they came to the soft, grassy mound that had been Napoleon's Wall, Chaim pulled Nadja close and kissed her, not caring if anyone saw them. "You'd better run home before the innkeeper's wife sends someone to look for you!" he said, slapping her gently on the rump to start her on her way.

"I could have loved you, Chaim," the red-haired girl said softly.

"Go home now," he told her again.

She turned to wave once, a shaky little gesture, a mere flutter of her hand.

The pain of losing her was scarcely bearable to Chaim, and yet it was secondary to the realization that now his crimes would be revealed in all their enormity to his parents. How could he ever explain to them? He had shamed them and himself! His faithlessness toward Chava would be the talk of the Jewish quarter for months to come, never forgotten, never forgiven.

Chaim shuddered. It was not unknown for the male relatives of a betrayed maiden to take vengeance on the family. From pumping the anvils in his forge, Reb Isaac the Blacksmith had a burly physique and enormous biceps. Yoysef might be strong but was certainly no match for Reb Isaac. Chaim hoped that Chava's father would take out his anger only on him, who so richly deserved the punishment of iron fists. With a certain morbidity tinged with pleasure, Chaim imagined himself lying broken on the ground.

He remembered his nightmares and wondered whether Papa would order him from the house while Mammeh declared him dead to the family. Somewhat late, he thought about what it would mean for Chava. There would be gossip, and she would be humiliated. People would wonder if there was something lacking in her that she could not keep a bridegroom. He was sorry for that; she was a nice girl who had never done him harm. It was unthinkable that he could now remain in Polotsk. By leaving, his family and Chava might be spared at least some of their pain and embarrassment.

Anguished, Chaim thought about the loss of home. Never again to sit in the cozy tailor shop and listen to his father's stories. Never to sip the Sabbath wine and sing *zmiros* with the family gathered together around the table. Never to be awakened before sunup by his mother to taste the fresh-baked bread as it came from the oven. Nevermore to lose at chess to Simcha, nor to tease Dvoreh about her interest in the *cheyder* boys. He would even miss Chaya Leya's nagging at him to pick up his clothes and improve his manners.

Chaim sat on the grassy knoll until the light began to fade and a chill came up off the river. He tried to wish that he had never known Nadezhda Ivanovna, but as soon as he thought it, he knew that it was not true. He had never known, perhaps would never know again, a woman so open and honest and direct, so giving in her loving. Nor could he regret that she had taught him what joy was possible between a man and a woman. No, whatever he had lost because of her, he would never renounce Nadja nor belittle what they had experienced together.

With dragging feet Chaim started toward home. While halfheartedly considering plans to run away, he hoped against all odds that Mottel would have pity on him. It was a thin hope considering Mottel's satisfied sneer at the moment of discovery. Chaim had been one of the boys who had mercilessly poked fun at Mottel when they were together at *cheyder*. It was Mottel's turn now, and he would revel in evening the score.

Near the house, Chaim found his friend Berel striding along the road toward him.

"Your mammeh sent me to look for you, Chaim! Everyone has eaten already, and she is very angry that you weren't home." Berel smacked his lips remembering the goodness he had left at the table. Berel was never full. "There's pot roast with tzimmes."

Chaim took Berel's arm urgently. "Listen, Berel, I'm sorry it's late, but I have to talk to you!"

Pulling Berel into a little copse off the road, Chaim, beginning to weep, told his story, sparing himself nothing in the confession, not his lust nor his disloyalty nor his deceit, only leaving out how deeply he felt for the red-haired girl.

Berel said little during the recital, and it was too dark for Chaim to read his friend's face. When Chaim told about the afternoons of lovemaking in the shed, he could hear Berel's breath quicken but Berel did not interrupt. And when he told of his terrifying dreams, Berel's hand reached out and clutched his arm in sympathy. Finally Chaim's voice faltered to a halt, and Berel heaved a sigh.

"Mottel has not been at the house yet, though God only knows how many he has already told. Any way you look at it, I'm afraid it's all over for you, Chaim. You will have to go away. It's the only thing you can do."

On hearing this confirmation of his own opinion, Chaim could not suppress a cry of pain.

"Yes, my friend," Berel continued gently, "there is no way out. You have disgraced your parents and insulted Chava. Her father will surely come for you with a whip in his hand!"

"But where will I go?" groaned Chaim. "I've hardly been ten versts outside Polotsk ever, and I have neither money nor a horse. Nothing! How will I manage? I don't even know which direction to take!" Chaim sank down on the ground and put his head in his hands.

Berel said into the ensuing silence, "I will go with you. I have some money from the wages your father paid me—I haven't had anyplace to spend it. And anyway, Chaim, we are not exactly beggars. We are tailors, after all. We can earn our way!"

At this astonishing suggestion a wave of relief flooded through Chaim. "You—you would come with me!" he exclaimed. "You would give up your place with my father to come with me? But why? Why would you do that? I haven't even been much of a friend to you all these months, and yet you are willing to give up everything to come with me!"

Berel was offhand. Looking away from Chaim, he spoke words that Chaim heard but which made no sense. He said he was restless and longed for adventure. Now that he was almost seventeen it was time for him to make his own way in the world. Since he was without ties, if not now, when? He said he had been thinking for a long time about going to America.

In the midst of Berel's brave show, Chaim grasped his hand. "No, Berel, none of that's true. You want to come with me because you are my friend."

There was a little silence. Berel said in an embarrassed voice, "Yes, it's because of that."

The boys stayed a long time in the little grove of trees, making plans. They decided they would head south toward the Ukraine, plotting their journey to stop where Jews along the way would give them shelter and a chance to earn a little money. Since Mottel's story would be common knowledge by morning, there was not much time to prepare. They should leave no later than daybreak. It would take them the rest of the time left to gather things for the journey, clothing and whatever food they could carry with them, and each would have to decide which special things to take, which to leave.

"That's not hard," Berel said wryly. "I don't own anything I can't leave behind."

Chaim was silent. He was thinking of the little wooden farm animals carved by his father during long winter evenings near the fire. He could carry only one, he decided, and thought it should be the wobbly-legged calf Papa had fashioned the winter of the famine. After some thought, Berel said he would take with him the siddur, the prayer book, that the congregation had given him on his bar mitzvah.

After much discussion, they decided that it would be all right for Chaim to take cash from his father's money box because Yoysef would have paid Chaim an apprentice wage if he were not related. If Chaim left a note explaining, it would not be the same as stealing. They would take some of their trade tools as well, needles and thread, scissors and tape measures, things like that.

By the time they left the sheltering trees and started toward the house, Chaim was surprised to feel the tingle of not unpleasant excitement.

The details of those final hours at home imprinted themselves permanently on Chaim's mind. It was an ordinary evening and yet special because it was the last. Life seemed to flow around him in slow motion, and he captured it all: Mammeh correcting exercise papers under the lamp while Papa looked up from his newspaper from time to time to comment on what was happening in the world, Dvoreh sewing lace on the collar of a dress, and Simcha pressing the last wildflowers of summer between the pages of a book. If he craned his neck, he could just make out Chaya Leya leaning against the trunk of the birch tree in the yard, Herschel sitting beside her. His family. There was enfolding warmth, peace, and love within these four walls. His breath caught and for a moment he thought he would be unable to go.

His mother noticed his melancholy. "Is something the matter?"

"No." Impulsively Chaim came to her and hugged her, saying his good-bye in the silence of his heart.

"Do you feel all right?" Malkeh asked, frowning.

"I'm fine, just tired. I think I'll go to bed soon."

Chaim and Berel had planned to leave so early in the morning that Berel was even now assembling their supplies in the stable. Before Chaim went to bed, he quietly rolled his extra clothes into a bundle, putting the carved calf carefully in the middle of the pack. He was exhausted, but once in bed could not sleep. He put his arm around Simcha's thin boy's body, but his brother sighed in his sleep and turned over.

It was eleven o'clock, or perhaps later, when there came a furious knocking at the door and then a rumble of voices in the kitchen. Chaim recognized the threatening boom of the blacksmith, then his mother's anxious shrill, and his father speaking in tones whose incredulity carried through the wall even if the words did not. Chaim cringed in bed, wondering what he should do, and doing nothing. After what seemed a long time, the voices stopped and the door slammed shut.

Heavy footsteps approached the bedroom. Yoysef in his nightshirt, his face in shadow behind the candle flame, stood at the door.

"Chaim," he said, "get up and come into the kitchen."

Chaim, heart thudding relentlessly, padded on bare feet behind his father into the other room, where his mother was sitting, rocking gently back and forth in her chair. Her face had a peculiarly blank look that Chaim could not read; he saw that her hands were nervously plucking at threads in the shawl that she had thrown over her nightdress when the knock on the door came.

Papa looked tired, the skin around his eyes puckered. He said only, "Is it true, Chaim?"

Chaim nodded. He could not look into his father's face and stared instead at the floor.

"She is pretty, this girl?" Mammeh's voice was so soft that it was like a breath, and Chaim wasn't exactly sure that he had heard the surprising question.

Chaim looked up. He said urgently, passionately, "Not just pretty, Mammeh! She is—she is *good*!"

Almost imperceptibly his mother sighed. "I'm glad for that."

Yoysef said only, "Go to bed, Chaim. We will talk in the morning about what's to be done."

Only Chaim would not be there in the morning.

As soon as the house was still, Chaim slipped from his bed, took up his bundle, and went to the stable to awaken Berel. All was ready, and the moon was still riding high in the sky when the two boys trudged out of Polotsk on the long road toward the great city of Kiev.

Chapter 23

*C*haim and Berel set off on their journey in high spirits. There was a sense of adventure waiting to happen, of challenges to meet and obstacles to overcome. Probably Yoysef, at that age, had run off on his journey of exploration stirred by the same heady feelings. Chaim and Berel each carried a clean feed sack containing clothes, tools, and food.

As leader, Chaim set a rapid pace. In the predawn chill, brisk movement kept sluggish blood circulating comfortably. In a whispered conference they had decided on a general direction, following the Zapodnaya Dvina River as it veered southwest toward Vitebsk. They had decided to avoid the main road, where they might be apprehended, in favor of the towpath along the riverbank. The river route would lengthen their journey considerably because, of course, the river did not run in a straight line but twisted and turned back upon itself as it ran its course. They dared not risk cutting across open country, where they might blunder into one of the treacherous swamps that crisscrossed Byelorussia and had sucked many a man to his death. The towpaths, made for the boatmen who hauled traffic up and down the river, would be firm underfoot even if slow. And there were plenty of places to conceal themselves if pursued.

By midmorning Polotsk and its familiar environs had long vanished from sight. They were famished, Chaim acutely aware that he had barely touched the cold supper his mother had set before him the previous evening. Finding a grassy slope in sight of the slow-moving river, they dropped their packs in the shade of some alder trees and sprawled to rest. They ate heartily of the meat, bread, and plums they carried and drank water from the bottles they had had the foresight to bring with them. Afterward they dozed a little in the warm, drowsy air.

By the time they resumed the journey, the sun had climbed higher in the sky. Berel was hobbling slightly from a blister on his heel, and both were sweating from the close humidity. Swarms of gnats rose in clouds from the reeds in the shallows. At a place where the riverbed dropped steeply, creating a pool of clear, clean water, they stopped to strip off their clothes and plunge into the river. For an hour they dove and swam and splashed cool water over each other. But when they started off again, their bundles seemed to have become heavier and implements like scissors had tended to work their way loose to poke into legs, hips, or shoulders, depending on where the sack was slung. Chaim finally suggested that they see what might be discarded.

"This blanket, now, what do I need it for?" Chaim asked rhetorically, putting it to a side. "The nights are hot. Besides, it weighs like a flatiron!"

Berel was somewhat dubious. "But if it *does* get cold before we get to Kiev—?"

"You know that it never gets cold until after Yom Kippur! I'm leaving my blanket here."

"All right," Berel said, "then I'll leave mine too."

"And this old coat of mine! By the time I need it, we will be earning money, and I will buy a better one." Chaim laid the coat on the blanket.

Berel did not follow suit, having experienced deprivation too many times to discard anything wearable.

"And look at all this food we're carrying! You'd think there'd be no place to buy anything on the way! Between us we have lots of money!"

"Well, I don't know," Berel said uncertainly.

"Look, Berel, we have five loaves of bread and all this cheese. And the apples are as heavy as can be."

"I think we should keep the food."

"Then you carry it," Chaim said peevishly.

In the end, they agreed to leave the apples and two of their five loaves. Chaim discarded some underclothes, a second pair of everyday trousers, and a pair of shoes. At the last minute Berel, who had few extras, decided to take Chaim's shoes for himself.

"But look, you idiot! They're much too big for you!"

"I can stuff paper in the toes," Berel said. "My boots are killing me."

"Well, all right, then."

They repacked the bundles, redistributing some of the weight. It was easier to walk after that, a good thing because the path climbed and dipped, twisting tortuously between woods on one side and the river on the other. As the day lengthened into afternoon, the boys stopped talking to save breath for the upward-climbing path.

They met no one until late in the day, when they heard the faint chant of boatmen coming toward them from downstream. To avoid being trampled, they scrambled off to the side of the towpath. Very soon they saw them, eight men, fastened to each other in a tight line, their rope harnesses passing over their shoulders and across their chests. Knees and backs bent against the weight of a lumber barge headed toward Polotsk, they heaved together in a steady cadence set by the leader. *One-two-three. Breathe. One-two-three. Breathe.* Of course there was no pausing to acknowledge passersby, and they overtook Chaim and Berel without so much as a glance.

"My God!" breathed Chaim. "What a way to earn a living!"

"If you're hungry enough, you'll do anything," Berel responded. Chaim did not ask him how he knew.

When Chaim judged that they had traveled about twenty versts, he signaled that they should stop for the night, but it took them another hour or so to find a level clearing. They ate some more of their bread and meat and drank the last of the water from their bottles. Tomorrow they would need to replenish their supply of water from one of the little freshets that tumbled over rocks on its way to join the river. After eating, they gathered leaves to make their beds and lay down to sleep, their packs serving as pillows.

It was only then that Chaim let his thoughts stray toward home. At this time of day, Mammeh and Chaya Leya would be putting supper on the table, most likely a dairy meal, since there had been meat the night before, maybe blintzes or a pirog made with cheese and onions. Dvoreh would be teasing Papa to take her after supper to see the new calf, and Simcha would be complaining about how he hated *cheyder* and why did he have to go when he didn't want to be bar mitzvah anyway? As usual, Herschel would be silent as a ghost, only his eyes speaking, and then solely to Chaya Leya.

But, of course, it would not be like that today, because today was the day that the whole town would know that he had deserted Chava for a Russian girl and then fled from home.

S imcha was the first to discover that Chaim was missing. Stirring in his sleep, he sensed rather than knew that his brother was not beside him in the bed. Opening his eyes in the dark, he lay there for a while, trying to remember what had awakened him. Tentatively he reached out a hand but felt nothing except the empty pillow. He sat up. Chaim was not there. Maybe he was at the outhouse. Simcha lay down again and closed his eyes, waiting for Chaim to come back to bed. A long time passed and still Chaim did not come. Simcha rose and pattered into the kitchen to see if his brother had gotten up to get something to eat. He was not in the kitchen, but the door to the yard was unlatched. It was all very strange. Simcha went into his parents' bedroom and shook his mother. "Chaim's not here."

"What do you mean? Go back to bed, *zuneleh*," Malkeh said drowsily.

"He's gone away!" Simcha's voice rose insistently.

"Nonsense! He has gone to use the outhouse," Malkeh said, sitting up in bed. "Yoysef, will you go see?"

In a few moments Yoysef returned, ashen-faced. He was shaking his head.

Malkeh dressed hurriedly and went outside as though she really believed that she would find Chaim returning from a predawn stroll.

Yoysef came out to where she stood, straining her eyes to see down the road. "His good jacket and extra pants are missing," he said quietly, putting a hand on Malkeh's arm. "I wish he had waited. There are always ways to work things out."

"Are you sure he's gone, Yoysef?"

He nodded. "I'm sure."

Simcha had dressed himself and was sitting, huddled into himself, at the kitchen table.

Automatically Malkeh moved to the pump to draw water for tea. When she opened the larder for bread, she said, "All the loaves are missing." Her voice was toneless.

Simcha began to cry, and even though he was a big boy of nine already, Yoysef picked him up and held him against his shoulder.

The noise in the kitchen had brought Chaya Leya and Dvoreh, still in their cotton nightgowns, to the door of their bedroom. "What is it? Has something happened?"

"Chaim has run away," Malkeh said, beginning to weep.

"Not just Chaim," said Herschel, entering the house. "Berel's bed has not been slept in."

*T*he first night on the river was not too bad. Sometime toward morning Berel took his worn jacket from his pack and snuggled under it the best he could. Glancing toward Chaim, he saw that his friend was curled up in a tight ball against the chill. He shook his head. Chaim should not have discarded his coat, and neither of them should have left their blankets by the side of the path. They had much to learn about running away from home, he thought grimly.

During the morning they settled to a steady gait that was neither as fast as when they had started from Polotsk nor as lazy as when they had ended their first day. They did not know exactly how far it was to Vitebsk, but they hoped to be there in a day or two. Chaim remembered that he had a great-uncle, whom he had never met, in Vitebsk; perhaps they could stay with Great-uncle Zalman for a day or two before proceeding on.

"But won't your father find us there?"

"Oh, by the time a letter reached Polotsk, we'd be gone again."

With that prospect urging them forward, the boys were less wasteful of time on this second day, resting only as often as they really needed and not dawdling over their food. From yesterday's experience they knew they would make their best time in the early morning before it grew too hot, so they pressed on despite the fact that Berel was limping badly now. Chaim's shoes were no improvement over his boots, but loath to part with them, he had tied them together and slung them around his neck, where they swung heavily as he walked. In any case, walking barefoot was an improvement.

They did not meet anyone on the path until afternoon. An elderly peasant was fishing from the riverbank.

"Any luck, Grandfather?" Chaim asked politely.

The old man shook his head. "No bait. I just like to sit here and watch the river."

The boys nodded.

After a while Berel asked, "How far might it be to Vitebsk, sir?"

"I'm not a sir, you fool! Are you going to Vitebsk?"

"Yes."

"Then you should know how far you have to go yet."

Exasperated, Berel turned away, but Chaim just laughed.

As they moved on, the old man shouted at their departing backs. "Ninety versts to Vitebsk!"

Ignoring what surely must be an exaggeration, they continued on their way, determined to walk at least until dusk. The golden adventure was fast tarnishing. As they went, they talked in desultory fashion about what they would eat in Vitebsk. Berel spoke dreamily of Malkeh's tzimmes, exquisite in its blending of carrots, potatoes, onions, and prunes. Their reality was that they had devoured all the meat and the plums they had brought with them, and the bread had gone stale.

That night, when they prepared to sleep, Berel took the jacket from his pack and stood staring at it for a long time. Finally he said, "Chaim, suppose you wear the coat for half the night, and then give it to me for the other half."

"I shouldn't have left mine by the river."

"But you did, and we both left our blankets. We still have one jacket. Half and half?"

"It's not fair to you."

"Let's not argue. Take the coat."

As they lay on the damp ground, waiting for sleep to overtake them, Chaim said, "You don't suppose the old man was right—about how far it is to Vitebsk?"

"If he is, we will run out of food."

"There must be settlements on the river, don't you think?"

"I hope so. Good night, Chaim. I'll wake you later."

*Y*oysef and Herschel had set off at once to follow the boys. The problem was that they did not know where to look. The wanderers might have gone north toward St. Petersburg or west to Riga, east to Vitebsk, or due south to Minsk. Main roads connected all of those cities with Polotsk, and surely they had the sense not to risk the marshlands by straying off the roads. It was decided that Herschel would take the western road and

Yoysef the eastern, and if there was no sign of them in those directions, Herschel would travel north and Yoysef south. Someone would have seen two boys traveling on foot.

Polotsk was agog. Reb Isaac was tramping through the city threatening to catch young Mandelkern and geld him. Chava and her mother had packed and fled town for an extended visit to relatives in Bialystock. And the simpleton Mottel was telling his story all over town; the more he repeated it, the more lurid it became. To cap it all, rumor had it that Chaim and the apprentice, Berel Levy, had stolen the tailor's cash box and gone to Moscow on a spree! There had not been such scandalous goings-on since a former *rebbetsen* had run off with a peddler!

Malkeh grieved for her lost son, grieved also for the girl Chava and perhaps a little also for the Russian girl. She wondered if there might have been something she could have done to have prevented this from happening. If only she hadn't been so preoccupied with the affairs of the school, she might have seen it coming! Every animal in nature knows to guard its young, but she had been blind and deaf to hers.

*T*hey did not reach Vitebsk until the evening of the sixth day, by which time they were filthy, footsore, and hungry. Berel, who had a weak chest, had caught cold from sleeping on the damp ground, and Chaim was worried that he had fever. Neither of the boys had expected Vitebsk to be such a large city. They were of two minds about what to do next, find a place to purchase food, or go directly to Great-uncle Zalman's. When Berel had another fit of coughing, Chaim made the decision for them.

It was easier than he had imagined. When they stopped a man on the street and asked if he knew a Zalman Siegel, he shrugged—who didn't know Zalman Siegel? Good, Chaim thought. Did he know where Zalman Siegel lived? Another expressive lift of the shoulders. What a question! Well, then, might he direct them to the house? Yes, he would lead them there himself.

Mammeh had always told the family that her father's younger brother was rich, but Chaim would never have dreamed how rich! The kindly stranger had deposited them before a tall house that rose two whole stories from the ground and had small-paned windows on each floor! Not exactly Spokoinaya Zemlya, perhaps, but much more than what the Mandelkerns of Polotsk were used to. And, it turned out, Uncle Zalman lived there all by himself except for a servant to cook for him and another to clean his house!

Great-uncle Zalman was not the ancient that Chaim had expected. Although his hair and beard were white, his back was straight and his complexion ruddy with health and good nature. He welcomed Malkeh's son and his friend to his house with no more fuss than Mammeh would have made had a relative dropped in unannounced. If he was surprised at how dirty and haggard his visitors looked, as a good host, he did not remark on it.

He was concerned for Berel. "Perhaps we should call a doctor?"

"No, no, I'm all right," Berel said hoarsely.

"Well, we'll just get you fed and to bed. That may be enough to turn you around."

One of the plump, middle-aged servants was summoned to lead them upstairs. When they had dropped their packs on the floor of an unused bedroom, she threw open the door to another room that was empty except for a high-footed porcelain tub. Chattering all the while, she turned the spigots and hot water spurted into the bath. Indoor plumbing—a miracle! She brought soft towels and clean nightclothes from Uncle Zalman's cupboard and showed them an adjoining closet where there was a toilet. In the house! Uncle must be rich indeed!

"Supper's long past, but I'll bring a tray up to you. Master Zalman said you would talk in the morning after you've rested."

By morning Berel's fever had somewhat abated, and Chaim, quite restored, was eager to set out to see the sights of Vitebsk. But first there was the interview with Great-uncle Zalman to be gotten through.

Sitting across from each other in the dining room—another marvel, this separate room in which to do nothing but eat!—Chaim was prompted to start at the beginning and tell Uncle Zalman everything that had led him and his friend on such a long journey. Once he was fairly started, Chaim found it easy to talk, and the story tumbled out of his mouth, only the part about Nadja proving difficult to talk about. Uncle Zalman was not a quiet listener. Throughout the recital he moved about in his chair, combing his white beard with his fingers, pinching the bridge of his nose, sighing, nodding, occasionally acquiescing with a melancholy "aie-aie-aie."

When Chaim had finished speaking, the old man pushed his chair back from the table and stood, stretching to the utmost of his very short stature. He scratched his beard, he bit his cuticles, he paced. When he turned toward Chaim, it was to point an accusing forefinger at him. "I don't suppose you ever thought how you might hurt and worry your parents?" he demanded.

"I—we—I—I wanted to save everyone from embarrassment!"

"And running away is going to do that? I can just hear what the gossips must be saying—'That boy must be guilty of more than we know to leave home in the night!' "

Chaim was silent.

"And what about your friend? For the first time he had a place in a good home and was learning a trade with a kind master. Now what will happen to him?"

"He wanted to come with me!" Chaim exclaimed, stung.

"I hope you sufficiently value his friendship."

"Are you going to send for my parents?" Chaim asked.

Uncle Zalman nodded. "I owe them that."

"We planned on pushing on to Kiev—"

Sighing, his uncle said, "Do not think that I do not remember what it is to be young. I will tell you what I have decided, Chaim. I will send to your parents to let them know that you are safe and what your plans are. But because I remember what it is to yearn for adventure, I will tell them you have already left my house. Go then to Kiev, if you must. Get the restlessness out of your system. And then, for the sake of God and your parents, go home!"

"All right," Chaim said meekly. "Thank you."

To give Berel time to recover from his cold, the boys stayed four days with Great-uncle Zalman in Vitebsk. Berel spent his time lying in bed, enjoying the ministrations of the two motherly women servants. The housekeeper made hot mustard plasters for his chest and carried up various steaming lemon and herb concoctions; the cook saw to it that he had plenty of nourishing chicken soup and egg-rich custards.

While Berel was thus occupied, Chaim walked the city streets, marveling at all he saw. Vitebsk was twice the size of Polotsk, its population having virtually doubled in size after '91 as a result of an influx of Jews exiled by governmental edict from Moscow. In the crowded narrow streets of the Jewish quarter there walked not only "modern" Moscow-born businessmen in ordinary business suits and laborers dressed like Russian *mujik*s in high-necked blouses and boots, but also Hasidim wearing long black caftans and flat hats trimmed with fur beneath which straggled the earlocks known as *payos*. Vitebsk was not only a city for business but was also a center for traditional Orthodox Judaism and a haven for the growing Hasidic movement. It supported two yeshivas and many synagogues, both traditional and Hasidic.

Its shops held wonderful luxuries like silver samovars, embroidered linens, ornately decorated candlesticks, and lengths of brocade for draperies.

At a produce market Chaim found pineapples from Egypt, blood oranges from the Holy Land, and plums and grapes brought from the Caucasus; he parted with some of his precious coins to purchase two oranges to carry back to Berel. Turning a corner, he found clothing stores, the most impressive a shop that specialized in winter overcoats lined with otter, fox, and sable.

Continuing his wandering, Chaim came back to the river that he and Berel had left on entering the city. In the light of day he could see that there was a bustling port here, the terminus of much of the Dvina River traffic. He stood for a while, watching several men unload a grain barge. Above the port, dwellings became sparse, and the landscape reverted to forest, birch, and spruce, and cedar struggling for supremacy.

Returning to the city streets, in the Russian section now, Chaim found wide new boulevards backing on twisted alleys that dated back to the sixteenth century. A huge white and gold cathedral with multiple domes dominated the center of the city. As he stood peering up at it, a procession of black-clad monks came through the ornate doors and into the street, bearing crosses and an icon held high above the heads of the throng that followed. A priest held out his crucifix and someone in the crowd pushed Chaim to his knees. Almost fainting with terror, as soon as they had passed by, Chaim struggled to his feet and pushed through the crowd, retreating toward the familiar safety of the Jewish quarter.

*W*hen Berel and Chaim left Vitebsk on the morning of the fifth day, they were equipped with a map and a compass, tightly rolled blankets, warm clothing, and packets of food, gifts from Great-uncle Zalman.

"Go in peace and good health, and return in peace and good health," he said, kissing each on both cheeks. "And remember, Chaim, that you have promised me to write your parents a letter as soon as you reach Kiev."

*G*reat-uncle Zalman's message reached Polotsk shortly after Yoysef and Herschel had returned discouraged from their respective searches.

"Imagine!" Malkeh said wonderingly. "Chaim and Berel found my uncle Zalman without any trouble!" She added wistfully, "And I have never been to Vitebsk."

"The young fools, following the river paths! They might have been attacked by bandits! Why didn't they keep to the road?"

"They knew you would be looking for them. Would you have brought them home, Yoysef?"

"Of course. Chaim has to learn that you can't outrun trouble. Anyway, in bad times, where else should you be but at home? It's too bad that your uncle didn't keep the boys until I could get there."

Malkeh smiled slightly. "This might be their only chance to see the world."

*M*any miles away, to the west, another fugitive from home slipped into Poland and from there made the easy journey by train to the heart of Germany.

Staying in a nondescript boardinghouse near the main Berlin train station and calling himself by the surname Golovine, Vassily settled in to await the triumphant return from exile of his mentor, Lenin. While it seemed unlikely that the *Okhrana* would be sufficiently interested in Vassily Chernov to follow him to Germany, he had nevertheless made the effort to change his appearance again, letting his neat dark hair grow shaggy and discarding his thick spectacles. He had sold his better clothing at a suburban street market, keeping only the oldest and shabbiest garments. Now, he thought, he looked like any ordinary laborer you might pass on the street. Just on the outside chance that anyone should ask about him, he had given the landlady a cock-and-bull story about traveling from Russia to live with an uncle who, unfortunately, had died while he was en route.

The cheap boardinghouse suited Vassily. The money stolen from Spokoinaya Zemlya had all but disappeared, and it was impossible for a Russian national without papers to find regular work in Berlin. There was nothing to do with his time. In the mornings he walked the streets, expending a few coins to ride a tram to the end of the line when rain made walking impractical. There seemed to be a great deal of construction going on in Germany, and occasionally he was able to earn a few marks at day labor. To save money, he ate no midday meal but went instead to a museum or public library, where he could rest his feet and read for an hour or two. The high point of his day was late afternoon, when he indulged in the luxury of a cup of coffee in a cheap café and pored over a discarded newspaper for news of the revolution.

There were, of course, other exiles in Berlin, men and women who had fled Russia to escape arrest. They formed a loose group. Many had covert lines of communication to the political underground in Russia and were always eager to share gossip. One of these was a young woman calling herself Marta Pirumova, the Pirumova probably not her real name any more than Golovine was Vassily's. She was darkly beautiful, both sensuous in her movements and primly elegant in her speech and dress. Like many of the others, she had discovered her revolutionary zeal in the university, in her case Kazan University, which had also been Lenin's. While her family might deplore her politics, they continued to support her in style even now, when she was a fugitive in Berlin.

After Vassily had been introduced to Marta, he seemed to run into her with increasing frequency. Eventually he decided that this could not be accidental, and he worried that she might be a police agent. He had not yet decided what to do about it when, sitting in his usual shabby coffee bar, he looked up from his paper to see her peering through the window at him and realized that it was the second time that week he had seen her. His stomach contracted with fear and anger, and he half rose from his chair. Taking this as an invitation to join him, she hurried through the door. It had been raining heavily, and her cloak dripped water all over the dirty tile floor.

Roughly Vassily grabbed her arm. "Are you following me?" he demanded.

"Wha-what?" She seemed shaken.

His face darkening, he shook her. "You're a police spy, aren't you, Marta Whatever-your-name-is? The *Okhrana* sent you!"

She began to laugh, her merriment bubbling out of her in little gasps. Vassily was disconcerted.

"Let go of me, and let me sit down, Vassily Yulevitch!" she said. "You must have assassinated somebody to believe the secret police would send someone all the way to Germany to trap you!"

Feeling foolish, he let go of her arm, but he was not done with his suspicions yet. It was not lost on him that she had not answered his question.

She slid into a chair across from him. "Go get me some coffee, will you, Vassily?" she ordered, sliding her wet wrap off her shoulders. "I'm soaking wet! I'll never get back to my pension on foot!"

"You didn't answer me," he said stonily, not moving from his chair.

"What? Oh. Of course I'm not from the police! What a thing to say to me!"

Vassily was not satisfied. "Everywhere I go, I see you. On the Kurfürstendamm. At the library. At the newspaper office. And now here. No one knows I come here. It's no accident. You're following me, aren't you?"

She dimpled beguilingly. "Of course it is no accident. I've been throwing myself in your path."

"But why?' he asked, astonished.

"Don't look at me like I'm a traitor! I am attracted to you. I want to know you better."

Vassily sat back in his chair, conscious that his left eyelid was twitching violently. She was leaning across the table toward him, her face so close to his that he could feel her breath on his cheek. He didn't know what to make of her. He had had little experience with women.

"Don't be tiresome, Vassily," she said. "I want some coffee, and then, if it's still raining, I'll go home with you. I know where you live, and it's a lot closer than my place."

*B*erel and Chaim set their course for Orsha on the Dnieper River. Uncle Zalman had marked on their map the cities where he knew there were Jews. He was full of advice. They should plan to stay, he told them, in shtetls along the route. Where there were Jews, they would be welcome. If, however, they found themselves between towns at nightfall they should sleep in the open fields rather than approach a Russian. Only a few months ago, a Jewish peddler had been beaten to death by Russian *mujiks* near the city of Gomel. Also, he warned, they should plan to skirt Mogilev, where there had been some recent anti-Semitic activity. They had promised to heed his counsel and he had let them go after a final embrace.

It was good to be on the open road again, where sunshine and fresh air could put the color back in Berel's face. Chaim had to admit that Berel had given him a scare. Glancing sideways at him, he thought that his friend seemed thinner and more rangy than ever, his nearsighted blue eyes a bit rheumy still, and his skin doughy and unhealthy-looking. His thin, sand-colored hair hung limply around his ears and across his forehead.

"Do you feel all right, Berel?"

"Fine. The cold's almost gone."

*J*t took them the better part of another month to reach Kiev. By the time they arrived, the two youngsters who had left Polotsk had become travel-hardened veterans of the road. They had walked a total of six hundred fifty versts. They had earned their keep mostly by their nimble fingers, but on more than one occasion had had to labor for their food alongside the peasants in the fields. Despite what Uncle Zalman had said, the Russians along the way treated them with fairness and courtesy. On the other hand, one night while they slept in a Jewish barn, their pockets had been rifled. Being without money after that disaster, they were totally dependent on the kindness of strangers; once they were forced to steal food, near Chernigov, at which point Chaim discovered that Berel had developed some interesting skills in the course of his difficult childhood.

One night early in October they lay down to sleep on the banks of the Desna River. With luck and good weather they might reach Kiev the next day, for sure the day after. They lay close to each other for warmth, wrapped in Uncle Zalman's blankets. A huge harvest moon hung like a giant yellow pumpkin in the night sky.

"Uncle Zalman thinks we should see Kiev and then go home to Polotsk," Chaim said thoughtfully.

Berel was cautious. "What do you think, Chaim?"

"I think that now that we're on our way, we should go ahead and see all we can of the world."

Berel nodded as though that had been his thought all along. "That's what I think too."

Chapter 24

C haya Leya was shelling peas for supper, sitting silently with the bowl in her lap. In the weeks since Chaim and Berel's disappearance, each member of the family had lived with a pain of which no one spoke. Any signs of grief were indirect. Dvoreh and Simcha's quarrels were more frequent than ever; today nothing Chaya Leya could do distracted either of them. Separating them helped only for as long as it took them to get back in the same room together. Threats of punishment enraged Dvoreh and amused Simcha. Promises of rewards were equally futile. Simcha teased. Dvoreh whined. Simcha's grimy fingers soiled Dvoreh's shirtwaist. She tumbled his chess pieces to the floor in retaliation. Taunts and insults were hurled, tears were shed.

The jangle of shrill voices and petty recriminations escalated until Chaya Leya snapped. As her scream tore through the room, the heavy crockery bowl flew from her hands as though of its own volition, narrowly missing Dvoreh. It smashed against the opposite kitchen wall.

There was a shocked silence as Simcha's and Dvoreh's eyes traveled in tandem from the pieces of broken crockery and peas on the floor to Chaya Leya's white face which had become alarmingly mottled. As bad as it had been to have Chaim disappear into the night, to witness the disintegration of Chaya Leya was worse still. Their pillar of strength and calm had dissolved and was now sobbing in great wrenching gasps. The culprits, rigid with panic, looked uncertainly at each other and then back at Chaya Leya.

"I'm sorry, I'm sorry," Dvoreh murmured over and over, beginning to cry herself.

Yoysef in the shop heard the commotion and came to investigate. In a glance he took in the situation, dispatched the chastened younger children to separate rooms, and drew Chaya Leya down beside him at the kitchen table.

Yoysef put a comforting arm around her heaving shoulders. "Everyone is having such a hard time," he said. "You, too, *feigeleh!*"

Chaya Leya buried her head against her father's chest, sobbing as though her heart were shattered. When the storm had subsided somewhat, she said, "Why can't Mammeh stay home and take care of us!"

Yoysef said soberly, "I don't know."

Chaya Leya lifted a ravaged face to his. "It's not fair! With Mammeh it's always 'Remember to iron the clothes today, Chaya Leya,' 'Be sure to scour the pots with sand' and—" She began to cry again. "I don't even have my own home yet, and already I'm tired of cleaning and cooking and taking care of children!"

There was nothing for Yoysef to say. It was too true. He held Chaya Leya close to him until she had emptied herself of tears. Poor child, he thought, she has been angry for such a long time now. "Go, *feigel*, wash your face and lie down for a little bit. I'll take Dvoreh and Simcha into the shop with me."

After Chaya Leya had gone into the bedroom and closed the door, he continued to sit at the table with his head in his hands. Although the family had been superficially reassured by Uncle Zalman's letter, there remained an underlying sense of loss and a devastating certainty that wholeness and well-being had disappeared along with Chaim and Berel. It was not just the hole their absence had left in the family but also an awareness that this was but the first crack in its integrity. Even when—if—the pair returned, innocence and a belief in invulnerability would be gone forever.

From the outside it looked as though all was normal with the Man-delkerns, when in fact Yoysef and Malkeh had merely turned to accustomed routines for solace. Thus, Yoysef and Herschel toiled from dawn to dusk in the tailor shop—a somber place without lively boys!—and at the school Mal-keh buried herself in minute details that had been previously left to Hodl.

It was not only the parents who were affected. Chaim's absence left a void in Chaya Leya's life. Perhaps she had never before fully grasped the depth of their relationship. Thinking about it now, Yoysef realized that their bond had been forged out of terrible need in the days when Malkeh hadn't seemed to care what happened to them and they had turned to each other for reassurance.

Yoysef sighed and shook his head. He resolved to make Malkeh listen to him before they lost this child too.

*I*t was because of Yoysef's insistence that she relieve Chaya Leya that Malkeh had decided to take Simcha with her when she drove to Spokoinaya Zemlya to consult with Yevgeny Fedotov about plans for the new school year. Since Chaim's disappearance, she had been preoccupied with a wish to begin teaching English and American history to those who were planning to emigrate. The younger pupils should be exposed to the classics of world literature, composition, science. She was driving Hodl mad with her grandiose plans, staying late at the school every night, drawing up lists of books, sample curricula, study guides, plans for recruiting teachers. Yevgeny Sergeivitch would help her get started.

As the little summer cart rolled through the changing autumn land-scape, Malkeh thought proudly of what she had so far accomplished. The school had grown from its humble beginning of teaching Golda to read to a student body of forty-five adults and children. In the next year they might double that number. Why not? Polotsk had a population of twelve thousand Jews, at least half of them women.

Simcha was excited. He loved snuggling close to Mammeh's side while she drove. She always smelled deliciously of the lavender that she hung in her cupboard, and her face, when he touched it with his fingertips, was soft and smooth, warm.

"I'm going to stay with you always!" he declared.

Malkeh turned to smile at him. "You'll change your mind," she said. "When you get older, you'll want to go away to study with a great rabbi."

"No, I won't! I want to grow up to be like Petya Voronov and go to St. Petersburg University and wear a hussar's uniform!"

Malkeh laughed. "Wherever do you get such ideas? Those things are not for Jewish boys!"

"Why not?"

"You'll understand when you're older." She patted Simcha's hand, smiling inside herself at how much gladness Simcha brought to her heart. How dear he was! Not only the handsomest of her children, he was the smartest as well! She remembered that when he was scarcely more than a baby, he had begun bringing leaves and insects inside for her to identify, and once told forever knew their names. He made out words in books before he could yet speak clearly, and at age ten he had read all the books in the house. In the bazaar, he beat the shopkeepers at adding the bill and figuring change. A remarkable child. The *cheyder* did not challenge him. Every morning there was a struggle to get him out the door.

Simcha said, "I like going to Spokoinaya Zemlya, Mammeh."

"Oh, yes, I know! You like the good things Maria Feodorovna gives you to eat!"

"Yes, and I like it when *Gospodin* Petya is home and lets me play with the dogs."

"They all spoil you."

"And I like to listen to *Gospodin* Fedotov talk."

Malkeh was surprised. The steward never made a special effort with children, and the others found him rather formidable. "Why is that, Simcha?"

"Oh, I don't know! He sounds different from Papa."

"Because he speaks Russian and Papa speaks to you in Yiddish?"

"Because he talks about interesting things to me just as if I were grown up."

"I see."

Simcha had been a very young child when Fedotov first noticed him. Eternally irritated that Malkeh had such a large brood, it was nevertheless impossible to ignore the youngest of them. For one thing, the boy looked startlingly Slavic, his cheekbones high and broad, his blue eyes with a Tatar slant, his hair the color of wheat. Fedotov had also noticed how intently he listened and how he seemed to take in everything at a single glance. The other children, the two girls and the older boy, whose names he could never remember, were wholesome and well-behaved enough, but this one was different.

Today, leaving the boy to Maria Feodorovna's indulgent attention, Fedotov led Malkeh to his office, where they reviewed the plans Malkeh had drawn up for the school.

Fedotov leaned back in his chair and thoughtfully pinched the bridge of his nose. At last, aware of how he must disappoint her, he said, "Pretty ambitious, isn't it?"

"I think we're ready," she said carefully. "I've proved that women can learn just as well as men."

"Let's not argue that! My reservations are about timing. Look, Malkeh, so far your school has concentrated on very basic skills. You started where your students were. That was good."

"We've added subjects every year," Malkeh said defensively.

"Yes, I know," Fedotov agreed. "Still, what you have is elementary. Suddenly you propose to make a huge leap upward toward higher education. To what end? Are your girls going to go to the university?"

"Why not?"

"You know why not! Let's not go over that!"

"My women have a right to choose to learn something beyond reading and writing."

The steward nodded. "I will agree to that if you can show me that your students, not just you, want it."

"And if I can prove it to you?"

"I'll still advise you to take your time. It is too soon. Your students have to walk before they run," he added dryly.

Malkeh sighed. There was common sense in what he said. "Maybe you're right. My women will walk for now." Her mouth turned up in a mischievous smile. "But believe me, they'll walk very fast."

Later, enjoying tea and cakes around the big kitchen table, the conversation turned to recent events. Simcha sat on the warm shelf of the big oven, his mouth crammed with sweetmeats, listening to the grown-ups talk.

"I can't see where it will all end," Fedotov said, "or maybe I don't want to see."

Maria Feodorovna said, "Taxes are bleeding the peasants white." Her kind face was worried.

"Yes," Fedotov agreed, "if they stay on the estates, they face starvation; if they go to the cities, they starve even faster. Desperate people commit desperate acts. Last week at an estate over by Dusiata, the peasants tied the landowner and his family—six children, mind!—to chairs and set the house on fire."

Simcha put down his cake. "They burned—children? Why did they do that?"

Maria Feodorovna was cross. "You are frightening the little one, Yevgeny Sergeivitch! Let it be!"

Malkeh said, "You don't have to worry about it, Simcha. It has nothing to do with us."

"Nonsense!" Fedotov snapped. "It has everything to do with us! Do you think you can sit out a revolution?"

"Do they always burn children?" Simcha persisted.

Fedotov lifted the boy down from the oven. "It will be our business, young man, to see that they don't." He smiled into Simcha's troubled face. "We will insist on a peaceable revolution or none at all!"

Malkeh rose to her feet. "I think we should go now."

"I'll ask Grisha to bring your cart around."

When he had left the room, Maria Feodorovna whispered, "He worries a lot. That man Karpovitch from the *zemstvo* was here the other day, calling Fedotov and young Master Petya bad names and demanding this, demanding that. As if it's *their* fault about the taxes!"

After a short time the steward came back to accompany the visitors to the side yard, where the cart was waiting. As he handed Malkeh up to the seat, he remarked casually, "Isn't it time that this youngster got some education?"

"He goes to classes at the synagogue, like all Jewish boys," Malkeh said stiffly.

"I see."

Simcha said, "All we do is memorize Hebrew."

Fedotov looked questioningly at Malkeh.

"It is our tradition."

"Yes, I see," he said again.

"Besides, government schools don't take Jewish children," Malkeh said angrily.

"You're not missing anything by that!" After a pause, Fedotov, his tone self-consciously offhand, suggested, "Suppose he comes to me for lessons a couple of times a week?" It was a surprising offer. Perhaps, he thought, this was his way of making it up to Malkeh that he had not supported her aspirations for the school. Or maybe it was because there was something about the boy that intrigued him. More likely the plan had lain unacknowledged at the back of his mind for some time now.

Malkeh's eyes fastened searchingly on him.

Fedotov shrugged slightly.

Malkeh said, "I will have to talk it over with his father."

"Yes," he agreed, handing her the reins.

Restless after they had left, the steward went to the stable for his horse. He would ride to the eastern quarter, to the place where a fast-flowing stream came crashing through the forest on its way to the river. This was the location he had chosen to build a sawmill. He had drawn the blueprints himself, following the plans outlined in a Swedish lumbering journal. Having his own sawmill instead of barging the logs down the Dvina to Polotsk would permit Spokoinaya Zemlya to sell its timber as board lumber at a substantially higher profit. He was worried that the project would not be completed before winter set in. If the building was not enclosed before the snows came, the raw interior might deteriorate and the new machinery rust. Despite having offered the men bonus pay to complete the work before November, he had noticed that whenever he was not there to watch, they slacked off. It would not surprise him to find the workers sitting on the ground, puffing their eternal handmade cigarettes and playing at dice. When he had last spoken to the lead carpenter about the need to push to the completion date, the man had touched his cap with a semblance of respect and said, "Master, what is well done is slowly done."

Indeed! Fedotov had thought, holding his tongue, but not if it is slowly done because no one is working!

On the way to the building site, Fedotov detoured to the north section, where fields of wheat were ripe for harvesting. Yesterday he had told his foreman, Kuibashev, not to delay longer in getting in the wheat, but when he rode up, the fields were empty. A costly McCormick reaping machine, lately imported from America, had been abandoned where it stood in the middle of the field. Now, what the devil—? he thought. Where was Kuibashev? Where were the men? It was only three o'clock in the afternoon!

Perturbed, he veered east to the sawmill. Hammers, kegs of nails, and saws lay scattered on the ground. There was not a human soul anywhere in sight.

Fedotov nodded to himself, his suspicions confirmed. So that was it! A week ago Karpovitch had hinted that work would be "more efficient" if he let the outsider Kuibashev go and permitted the village council to appoint its own foreman to oversee the men. This, then, was the result of his refusal—a stoppage of work plus the probability that Kuibashev had been run off; his training in an agricultural institute would not have prepared him to deal with threats of violence.

He wanted to thrash Karpovitch within an inch of his life! There was a time when he could easily have done just that, but not in these times. Mindful of Dusiata, he knew he must tread carefully. Still, he'd be damned if he would cave in to Karpovitch even if he had to harvest the wheat and finish the sawmill by himself!

Furious, Fedotov turned away from the sight of the half-finished mill and urged his horse to a gallop. In time the physical sensation of speed and controlled power soothed his troubled spirit. Slowing his lathered mount to a moderate pace, he turned its head toward home. He wished Petya were there so he could talk to him about the Karpovitch problem. But Petya was off doing his officer's training in the Hussars, and when he finished in two months' time, he was to go to Moscow for a long visit with his mother. At least Natalya was well out of the troubles. A year ago she had made a successful second marriage and had left Spokoinaya Zemlya for good.

By the time Fedotov had rubbed down his horse and had seen the stable boy lead him away, he was resigned to the inevitable. The village could name a titular foreman, but if he could find Kuibashev or someone like him to actually oversee the work, the situation might still be manageable. Fedotov had not felt so depressed since his half brother, Andrei, had been alive.

*I*n Moscow, Colonel Leonid Nicolaevitch Brusnowsky of the Third Infantry Regiment had been summoned to the quarters of his major-general for an important conference. The fact that General Burychkin had received Colonel Brusnowsky in his bedroom, where he was being dressed by his valet, did not reflect the seriousness of the subject at hand.

"Sit down, sit down!" the general ordered Brusnowsky, waving to a nearby chaise. He tried on a uniform jacket and peevishly discarded it for some flaw that was invisible to his subordinate. The valet presented a second, holding it so that the general could slip his arms into the sleeves. Peering intently into his mirror while he turned first one way and then another, he nodded; this one would do.

"We are going to have to speed up the conscription process, Leonid Nicolaevitch. I have just had word from St. Petersburg—direct from the office of the Minister of the Interior." The major general had now seated himself on the edge of the bed and motioned his man to bring his boots.

"Yes?" Colonel Brusnowsky said, noncommittal.

"This is confidential, Colonel," his commander said. "Minister Plehve instructs us to bypass the usual procedure of letting the military districts select men by lot to meet their quotas. We are to move quietly to round up additional recruits ourselves."

"But why, General?"

"Not that it is any of your business, Brusnowsky, but the army is to be deployed to support the police in putting down the damned Marxist troublemakers." The general carefully inspected the boots presented by his valet, rubbing a minuscule speck of dust from the toe of one with his handkerchief. He nodded that the man could proceed to put the boots on his feet. "Some of the new recruits," he continued, "will go to outposts near the Manchurian border to deal with the Boxers. We can't have those bandits pulling up the tracks of the Trans-Siberian as soon as they're laid!"

"I see," the colonel said. "But why the secrecy? Certainly if the tsar ordered a general mobilization—?"

"Are you crazy?" General Burychkin scowled. "There'd be an outcry all the way from here to Vladivostock!"

"But, General, as soon as we begin rounding up men, the country will know—"

Burychkin sighed. "Did you learn nothing at Officers' School? What about the element of surprise? What about the efficacy of a fait accompli? Besides, Leonid Nicolaevitch, if you concentrate on Jews and peasants, who will complain?"

The general took one final look at himself in the pier glass and, satisfied, motioned for Brusnowsky to follow him into his office. "Come, we will go over some plans I have drawn up. You will be in charge of our push in Byelorussia!"

*M*alkeh was sure that Yoysef must agree that Fedotov had offered Simcha a wonderful opportunity. As soon as the children had gone to bed, she knelt beside Yoysef's chair and put her arms about his knees.

"What's this? What's this?" he asked, stroking her hair and smiling.

"I have something to tell you, Yoysef, a piece of good news!"

"So tell me."

Her eyes shining with excitement, Malkeh repeated the conversation she had had with the steward that afternoon. "I know he sees the same thing that we do in Simcha, that he is truly special! Yevgeny Sergeivitch will be able to help him become something—maybe even go to the university, where he can learn to be a lawyer or a doctor or a professor!"

"Dreams!" Yoysef exclaimed, abruptly getting up from his chair. "What did you say to him?"

"Why, I said that I would talk it over with you."

"And what did you promise Simcha? I saw how excited he was during supper, he could scarcely swallow his food! You did tell him, didn't you, Malkeh, that he could study with *Gospodin* Fedotov?"

Only slightly abashed, Malkeh admitted it. "Well—I guess—there was no reason not to say it, Yoysef, when I knew you would feel as I do!"

Yoysef frowned. "When will he study his Hebrew? When will he do his chores? How will Dvoreh feel? It is not fair to the others."

"Oh, don't you see, Yoysef, God has given our son a gift. It must be

His intention that Yevgeny Fedotov teach him. I'll see that Simcha doesn't neglect the other things, I promise. As for Dvoreh, I'll give her more of my time. As a matter of fact, I've been thinking she should be enrolled in the school."

Yoysef's forehead wrinkled. "Simcha is not only your son, he is also mine," he said slowly. "You had no right to make such an important decision for him without talking to me."

"I thought you would be proud and glad! Like I am!"

"You're not thinking of the consequences," Yoysef insisted, his mouth set in a stubborn line, "but I am."

"Consequences! What consequences! You're jealous!" Malkeh raged. "Is that what this is all about, Yoysef? Jealousy?"

"I hope I have no reason to be jealous." Yoysef's gaze rested for a long moment on his wife's flushed face. "I am against this because it seems to me a bad thing to make a child different from his family and his people."

Malkeh was angry. "You are envious for the other children, for Dvoreh and Chaya Leya, but they are not Simcha, and he is not them! If they can only crawl, must he crawl also! Let him fly, Yoysef! Let him fly!"

In the following days, Simcha begged, importuned, and pleaded with his father, and Malkeh marshaled all her arguments. Yoysef remained obdurate. Then came the sullen looks, the weeping, and the quarrels at the table. Dvoreh entered the fray, telling her father it would be a relief to get Simcha out of the house a couple of days a week. Still, Yoysef resisted. Chaya Leya watched all that went on and thought that the whole house had gone crazy. Finally came the nights in bed when Malkeh turned a cold back to her husband.

In the end Yoysef capitulated.

Chapter 25

*M*y dearest *Mammeh* and *Papa*, Chaim wrote laboriously in his awkward hand, *can you believe that Berel and I have come finally to Kiev?*

Chaim sat staring at the words he had just written on the paper. It was his first letter home, actually the first letter he had ever written in his life. If only he had the words for it, there was so much he wanted Mammeh and Papa to know. About the long, arduous journey. About people who were kind to them on the way, and the Jew who stole their money. About thunderstorms when there was no place to shelter, and cold nights spent in open fields, Berel and him sleeping spoon fashion for warmth under Great-uncle

Zalman's blankets. About fine meals when they were lucky enough to find a shtetl on the Sabbath and about times when they went hungry except for wild apples picked along the roadside.

It was a long trip, and Berel and I had many . . . Uncertain how to spell "adventures," he crossed it out and continued: *Many things happened to us along the way.* Chaim bit his lower lip in concentration as his pen made scratching noises on the paper. *But don't worry, Mammeh, because we always found a Jewish home to stay in*—a blatant lie—*and we went to shul on* shabbes, *just as if we were at home. Rosh Hashanah we were with a* melamed's *family at Orsha, and we were in a place called Gomel for Yom Kippur.*

That was half true—the part about Rosh Hashanah. Having arrived in Orsha the night before the holiday, on the morning of the New Year they had accompanied the family of the teacher Bernstein to shul. Chaim still remembered how overwhelmed he had been with painful longings; he had never before spent a holiday away from home and family. When he closed his eyes, he could imagine the rustle of silk from Papa's *tallis*, the dry sound of pages being turned in prayer books; instead it was Berel standing on one side of him and Reb Bernstein on the other. At the conclusion of the long service, he had the fantasy that the blowing of the shofar had summoned God Himself to the sanctuary. He had shivered at the thought that God's scrutiny was upon him, and His judgment would decree the future. Berel had pressed his hand reassuringly, a friend, Chaim thought, worth having.

The feast that the *melamed*'s wife had prepared was the best food they had eaten since leaving home, but it was not Mammeh's, and Chaim had been unable to throw off his depression. Mammeh would have distributed pieces of sweet *challah*, cut from a round loaf symbolizing the continuity of life, and Papa would have filled the glasses with wine made from their own luscious purple grapes. Already stuffed with fish and chicken and a rich pudding made of egg noodles, they would somehow have found room to conclude the meal with strudel, rugelach, and apple slices dipped in honey to auger a sweet year to come. Chaim sighed. When would he ever taste Mammeh's cooking again?

If Rosh Hashanah was melancholy, Yom Kippur, the Day of Atonement that followed ten days later, was worse by far. This holiest day of the Jewish year had found them lying in a hollow in an open field some thirty versts outside of Gomel. Some of the food they had carried with them from Orsha had gone bad, and both Berel and he had been sick, Berel violently so. When the community of Israel in Gomel was standing in fear and repentance while the cantor sang the ancient prayer of Kol Nidre, they were huddled in the open, sick, weak, and utterly miserable under leaden skies that promised rain before the night was over. When he should have been beating his breast for the grievous wrongs he had done Chava and his parents, Chaim was staggering under Berel's weight as he led him into a thicket to relieve his cramps. Ah, well, Chaim thought, chewing the end of his pen, it was best not to remember; somehow they had survived all that.

Chaim scratched his head. What else to say to Papa and Mammeh? He read aloud to Berel what he had written so far. Berel was sprawled on his back on a cot in the narrow attic room they shared in the house of Reb Shloyma Pinsker of Kiev. Frau Pinsker had apologized for the meanness of the room, but, in fact, it was not so bad. Tiny as it was, just big enough for the two beds, it boasted a dormer window from which a patch of sky could be seen, and that was worth a lot in a crowded city like Kiev. Since there were no other furnishings in the room, they had no choice but to sit or lie on the cots when they were home. In any case, neither Chaim, who was admittedly tall, nor Berel, who was only a little less so, could stand upright because of the steep pitch of the roof.

"What else should I say?" Chaim asked.

"Tell them you're sorry you ran away," Berel suggested.

"Yes, I guess I should." But Chaim did not have the vocabulary to express how every day of his life he wished that he were home in Polotsk working with Papa and Herschel in the pleasant, sunny tailor shop. He should never have gone near the inn on the market square! But no, he thought, he could not wish away Nadezhda Ivanovna! She would always be the one love of his life, worth everything he suffered.

I think about you all the time. I wish I were working with Papa. But it was better that I go away so that everyone can forget what happened.

Chava would not forget, of this he was certain. He had hurt her as no human being should ever hurt another. Fervently he hoped that Pinchas the Matchmaker would find a good marriage for her. She was a fine girl, Chava, and she deserved better than she'd got.

I had to run away because if I had stayed to say good-bye, I wouldn't have been brave enough to go at all. I left because I love you. And Berel came with me because he didn't want me to be alone. I hope you can find it in your hearts to forgive us.

"I guess that's enough for a first letter," Chaim said, frowning at the page. "At least Mammeh will know that we're safe and well."

Berel sat up on his bed, in the process cracking his head on the sloping ceiling. "You haven't said anything yet about the Pinskers, Chaim, or where you work or about Kiev! Here, let me—" He reached for the pen.

Chaim snatched the letter closer. "I guess you write a better hand than I do, Berel, but my mother and father want to have a letter from me!"

Berel shrank back on the bed. As though, he thought, Chaim had to remind him again that Malkeh and Yoysef were *his* parents!

Chaim, pondering what to say, did not notice. *We have been in Kiev since just after the High Holy Days*, Chaim wrote, remembering how astonished they had been when they first came through the great gates of the city. Nothing had prepared them for Kiev's broad boulevards and the crowds jostling one another on the sidewalks. What a diversity of peoples there was in Kiev! Besides the staid urban Russians in their western European suits and dresses, there were Ukrainian peasants in colorful tunics and leather boots, Tatars, whose flat Mongol faces and impassive eyes looked out from beneath embroidered skullcaps, casually attired university students identifiable by the satchels they carried, Hasidic Jews in caftans, and Arab and Chinese traders in the dress of their countries.

Berel had pointed out the many policemen in high-collared uniforms, standing on street corners or strolling the boulevard, watching the surge of traffic with cynical eyes. Maybe because it was too hot that day for the policemen to bother, no one stopped the boys to ask for papers.

You would not believe what a large city Kiev is, almost a half million people. Most of the Jews, though, live outside the city, Chaim wrote.

If one were a Jew, one had to have a special permit to live in Kiev, and the police conducted sporadic *oblavy,* roundups of Jews who had no proof of legal residence.

During his first naive month in Kiev, Chaim had been caught in a Jew hunt. It was a terrifying experience for a seventeen-year-old from a provincial town. There was the claustrophobic sensation of being confined in a small space after being corraled by club-swinging policemen who barked guttural commands in Ukrainian, a language Chaim understood so imperfectly that he did not move fast enough and was promptly clubbed to his knees. Scrambling to his feet, he followed the officer's pointing finger and queued up behind the others in a line where no one spoke and no one looked at one another. Trembling, he had fished in his pockets for the residence permit and identity card that had been issued him with his job. They were the difference between life and jail. His fingers closed around them.

If he lived to be a hundred, he would never forget the old woman standing with her heavy market basket near the head of the line. She had been unable to produce the required documents either because she was too frightened to understand what was wanted or because she was in fact illegal. She had begun to plead with the policeman, clutching at his sleeve. The fact that she had actually put her hand upon him seemed to infuriate the officer beyond all reason. In one swift movement he had lifted her off the ground by grasping her shawl in one strong hand while with the other he struck her across the face. When he let go, she fell to the street, her nose gushing blood, her spectacles shattered on the cobbles. No one moved to help her. One or two, waiting in the queue, coughed in embarrassment, and there was a nervous titter from well back in the line; most turned their heads away. Chaim, rooted to the spot, stared at the old woman, seeing *Bobbeh* Frumma mistreated and hustled to the waiting police conveyance. He thought he should at least pick up the old woman's basket, but, no braver than the rest, he did nothing. Thinking about it still, weeks later, Chaim's hands began to shake.

He gritted his teeth, forcing himself to take up his pen once more.

We are staying with a family in the Jewish section of the city they call the Podol. You would like the Pinskers. Reb Pinsker is a tailor like Papa.

Chaim reflected on how things always seemed to work out, one way or another. Arriving in the city late and directed by a passerby who wore the *payos* of an observant Jew, they made their way to the Podol in the ancient heart of the city. Confused here by the profusion of streets that seemed to know no order, Chaim entered a store to ask for the shul, always their first stop in a new place.

The shopkeeper came with them to the door of his shop, pointing to a simple wooden structure, unmarked in any way. "That's it," he said. "That's the only shul still standing." He spat on the cobbles. "They burned down the synagogues, they burned the yeshiva and all the other Jewish schools, and they set fire to the Podol itself! Only those who escaped to the countryside lived. That was nineteen years ago. May God curse them with all the plagues of the Bible!"

He seemed to want to talk, but Berel and Chaim hurried on because it was growing late and they needed a place to stay for the night. Mounting a flight of steps, they pushed open the heavy door to the synagogue. A few men were still sitting, studying Talmud at a table in the dim interior. The arrival of the boys sparked a little interest in a day that had been dull.

"Who are you?" an old man asked, peering through the darkness. "Do we know you?"

"No, sir," Chaim answered. "We have just arrived in the city."

"From where?"

"From Polotsk—in Byelorussia."

"A long way." There was a murmuring among the men at the table.

A thin fellow who wore his black hat pushed to the back of his head walked over to them. "Do you know," he asked, poking a finger in Chaim's chest, "that you'll be arrested unless you have residence permits?"

"What's that?" Berel was frightened.

"They don't let Jews live in this city unless you've got papers."

"Well, how do you get papers?" Chaim asked.

"You've got to have a job here. They have to have a use for you."

A man with a heavy paunch poking against his white shirtfront said, "They're big, strong boys. They could probably find jobs in Brodsky's beet factory!"

"But we are tailors!" protested Berel. "Why should we go to work in a factory!"

"Tailors! Ha!" said the old man who had spoken first, slapping his leg with a wrinkled hand. "If the way you are dressed is a sample of your work, as tailors you will make good beet sorters!"

Thinking back on it, Chaim had to smile. They *had* looked pretty disreputable by the time they arrived in Kiev!

A quiet, middle-aged man who had sat listening in the shadows spoke up. "My name is Shloyma Pinsker," he had said softly. "I am also a tailor. You will come to my house, and we will eat and decide what is to be done with you."

Reb Pinsker had led the two young men through the confusing streets to a building that seemed to have been squeezed into its tall, narrow shape by the houses crowding it on either side. They saw that on the street level was a small, dark room crowded with bolts of cloth and dominated by a power sewing machine and a tailor's dummy. A steep flight of well-worn wooden steps led to the living quarters above. Chaim, raised near open fields and woods, felt oppressed; there was no space between the run-down buildings that pressed one against another. Since they'd entered the Podol, the air had seemed to bear down on him, heavy and stale. He tugged at Berel's coat and whispered that they should plan to go south in the morning.

The tailor introduced Chaim and Berel to his fat, sour-faced wife and to a daughter who looked to be in her twenties, Zipporeh, quiet, colorless, self-effacing. It was not immediately clear how welcome the travelers were to Frau Pinsker, but she accepted the responsibility of feeding them. She immediately bid them to sit down at a table already laid in a dining room separate from the kitchen and the front room. There followed such a procession of food that the boys wondered whether they had forgotten a festival or a feast day. But it turned out that Klara Pinsker loved to eat and was a genius in the kitchen; her sour look was purely the result of chronic heartburn, not temperament. The three males sat at table while Zipporeh and her mother served fragant dishes, one after another, each more delectable than the last. Where or when the women ate was not clear.

When the edge was off their hunger, they talked.

"So how is it that you boys are traveling?" Shloyma Pinsker asked.

"To see something of the world," Chaim replied, feeling expansive after a second helping of *kugel*.

"You are not in trouble with the law, then?" Reb Pinsker asked delicately.

"Not at all!" Berel answered, indignant at the suggestion.

"We may even go to America!" Chaim boasted. "My older cousin Moishe is leaving for New York any day now."

"Well, then, tell me something of your work. How many years were you apprentices?"

"Three," Berel said promptly. "And to a master tailor!"

"My father is the best tailor in Polotsk! He does all the work for Count Voronov's household!"

Reb Pinsker seemed impressed. "Indeed?" he said, motioning to Zipporeh for more bread.

Chaim did not hesitate to exaggerate Yoysef's reputation. "Oh, yes, and none of the Russians go to St. Petersburg to be fitted anymore!"

"Hmn-hmn. Then your father must be a very rich man."

"Not exactly," Berel conceded.

Reb Pinsker cleaned his teeth with a toothpick.

While Zipporeh deftly cleared the table, the older tailor asked technical questions about what kinds of garments they had experience with, the kind of sewing machines they were accustomed to using, how they measured a client, faced a lapel, turned a hem. At one point he rose from his chair and came around the table to examine Berel's jacket, pursing his lips and pointing out how the collar would have lain better if notched in a certain way.

Chaim bristled at the implied criticism but had to admit that Shloyma Pinsker was probably right. "My father would like to know how that's done—"

"I wish I could speak to him. He must be a fine man and a fine tailor."

By the time the tailor's wife and daughter had brought in the steaming glasses of tea, Reb Shloyma was asking about the boys' immediate plans.

"I don't know," Chaim said, thinking of the crowded city.

"Well," the older man told them, "as you heard at the shul this afternoon, if you plan to stay, you must have jobs and apply to the office of the governor general for residence papers."

"Well," Chaim said thoughtfully, "we had thought about staying for a while, but it does seem very hard for Jews here."

"*Oy,*" sighed Shloyma Pinsker, blowing on his tea to cool it, "for Jews where isn't it hard?"

Berel helped himself to another piece of strudel. "What a fine cook your wife is!" he said with deep feeling.

"Yes," Reb Shloyma said absently, apparently turning something over in his mind. After a while he said, "Well, then, why don't you plan to stay with us? I can use a little help in the shop. Unfortunately mine is a small business and I can hire only one of you."

"And what about the other?"

Their host shook his head. "Well, there's always the sugar mill!"

"Yes, there's that," Chaim said thoughtfully.

Before the meal was over, it had been agreed that for the time being, the boys would remain in Kiev. Since their skills were about equal, Reb Pinsker did not care which he hired. What finally decided the matter was that Chaim, being the bigger and stronger of the pair, had the better chance of tolerating the rigors of mill work.

Chaim went on with his letter. *Berel went to work for Reb Pinsker, but there wasn't enough work in the shop for both of us. I found a job in a sugar factory. Would you believe that a big factory is owned by a Jew? His name is Ephraim Brodsky, and he has almost three hundred people, all Jews, working for him! I started as a sweeper in the factory and then I learned to sort the beets. Now I am working one of the machines they use to crush the beets. It is very hard work, and we work fourteen hours every day except* shabbes *for three rubles a week. Still, it is a living.*

The world of a sugar-refining plant was something that Chaim had not the courage to describe to his family. Nor would they have understood it. The factory was a cluster of large open-sided buildings of flimsy construction. In autumn when Chaim went to work for the Jewish sugar magnate Brodsky, the sheds were incredibly hot, most of the men working bare-chested. But as soon as the weather turned, the wind swept through the structure with a vengeance. Chaim could not decide whether it was better to burn or to freeze. By the time the first snow came, he preferred the heat, for he developed severe chilblains and hands so chapped that they cracked open and bled. Snow blew into the sheds, and someone was constantly having to chop ice from the tops of the water tanks. Many times that winter Chaim thought that he would never be warm again, that his very bones must have turned to splinters of ice. His teeth chattered constantly, and his breath emerged in blue clouds even while he was inside the plant.

Beside the cold, it was the noise that bothered Chaim the most. The machinery made a roaring, stamping noise like an army of giants marching in lockstep. Workers shouted to one another over the clatter of machinery, and by the end of each day Chaim had been so deafened by the noise that his voice was still abnormally loud when he reached home, his ears unable to accommodate to normal speech.

The day started at six, and the workers did not leave until eight at night, except on Friday, when they were permitted to go home at four to prepare for the Sabbath. On Saturdays the plant was shut down. After he started working at Brodsky's, Chaim looked forward to *shabbes* as never before. As soon as the factory whistle blew on Friday afternoon, Chaim flew home, running for much of the way. Snatching up the bundle of clean clothes that Frau Pinsker left on his cot each week, he dashed on to the bathhouse to join Berel and Reb Pinsker.

Paying his kopecks at the entrance, Chaim stripped off his filthy clothes in a cubicle before entering the long low room of the *banya*, where the steam was so thick that he could scarcely make out the other figures sitting or lying naked on three tiers of shelves that ran along the sides of the room. Luxuriating in the hot water and the steam, Chaim washed himself, rinsing off with running water from a faucet. Sometimes he had to soap and rinse himself several times before he felt cleansed of the stench and dirt of the mill. When satisfied, he filled a dipper with cold water and splattered it over the bed of heated rocks to make the steam hiss and swirl up around him with delicious warmth.

Berel had saved him a place on one of the high shelves, where the heat was greatest. Chaim let the steam work its way into his pores before he picked up the bundle of birch twigs given him at the door. He thrashed himself over chest and shoulders to bring the blood to the surface and then turned to allow Berel to do the same to his back. Lying prone on the slatted wooden bench, he felt himself relax, the aches gradually easing out of his arms and legs and back. Afterward there would be the comfort of clean clothes and a Sabbath meal to linger over.

Goltz, Chaim's friend at the sugar plant, watched Chaim's *erev shabbes* activity with tolerance. "And what will you do with yourself tomorrow?" he asked.

"Why, I will go to shul. What else?" Chaim was surprised.

Goltz seemed amused.

"Why do you look at me like that, Goltz?" Chaim asked him.

"I'm taking the measure of your Jewish piety, is all. I give it not more than another month."

"You're crazy."

Before the bitterest days of winter had come, Chaim had ceased to keep the Sabbath, his spiritual needs secondary to the comforts of a warm bed in a noiseless room. Nothing, not even Frau Pinsker's good cooking could tempt him to rise on the Sabbath morning to go to shul.

Berel reproved him gently. "Chaim, you are losing your *Yiddishkeit* in Kiev."

Chaim flew at him in a rage. "You nebbish, you! You sit in a warm room and stitch seams all day! It's no trouble for you to be pious on the Sabbath! But I am in hell itself the whole of the week! God sees how it is to work in Brodsky's mill, and He won't judge me. Don't you!"

Berel might not understand how it was that a body could be so abused that replenishment and rest were the only commandments that counted, but Chaim had seen what could happen in the factory to a worker so tired that he dozed at the machinery.

Despite his hard life, being young and vigorous, Chaim needed more than the sugar mill and subsistence at the Pinskers'. He was in one of the most glamorous of cities, and even his chronic fatigue did not dampen his curiosity. Feeling rested by Sabbath afternoon, Chaim could usually persuade Berel to stroll around the city, staring at the exotic foreigners and the gorgeous displays in the shop windows.

Kiev, at the confluence of two great rivers, the Desna and the Dnieper, was a great commercial city where traders from all over Russia did business with the Orient. It was a city of handsome palaces and public structures, manicured parks, and a university that attracted students from abroad as well as from far parts of Russia. Sometimes after sundown brought the Sabbath to a close, Berel and Chaim would venture into one of the cafés. There for the price of a glass of tea and a Turkish pastry, they could sit all evening, watching the crowds and ogling the girls of Kiev, the prettiest, it was said, in all Russia. Occasionally the swing of a woman's hip or the toss of a bright head would remind Chaim so strongly of Nadja that he could almost persuade himself that he smelled the perfume of her skin!

Thoughtfully Chaim put his pen to paper once more. *I am making friends in Kiev*, he wrote, but then paused, uncertain what more to say. Hastily he appended, *They are good men, Jews, who work with me in the factory. My partner at the crushing machine went one year to the university.*

It was pleasant for an evening or a Saturday to sit with friends, smoking hand-rolled *papirosi* and talking. The Brodsky men tended to gather at one particular café near the Great Gates, and Chaim began slipping away from Berel to meet Elihu Goltz. Goltz was old already, probably twenty-five, a man of burning eyes and dark moods. He had undertaken to show Chaim the ropes at the factory and had saved him from a dressing down by the foreman more than once. Sometimes, though, he said outrageous things that made Chaim uneasy. He talked a lot about exploitation of workers by their bosses. Goltz said often and feelingly that Brodsky was a pig.

Chaim was confused. Brodsky a pig? Wasn't he a Jew who owned a huge business that anyone would be proud of? Chaim envied Brodsky but dared not say this to Goltz. He was happy to have been accepted as one of Goltz's inner circle, and he certainly did not want to endanger his relationship by a show of ignorance. He did not discuss with Berel the things he heard the others say in the café. If Chaim had told him, he would only have worried. For all the change it made in his life, Berel, sewing in Reb Pinsker's shop, might still have been in Polotsk.

It was getting late, and Chaim, never a writer, was grateful to bring his letter to a close: *Well, I'll write again to let you know how we are. I really miss you both, and Dvoreh and Simcha and Chaya Leya. I hope the work isn't too hard for Papa and Herschel. Or did you get some new helpers? I don't like to think of anyone sitting in my place in the shop, but I know it is all my fault that I had to go away, and I hope you can find it in your hearts to forgive me. Be well. Berel sends his love. Your son, Chaim Mandelkern.*

Chapter 26

"What is the matter, Yoysef?" Herschel asked, looking into his partner's strained face.

"The matter?"

"You've been sitting there for at least ten minutes, rubbing your forehead and frowning at Reb Kagan's coat."

Yoysef picked up his needle and the spool of basting thread. "Yes, yes, you're right to scold me, Herschel. Reb Kagan wants this coat for his daughter's wedding next week."

"What were you thinking about?" Herschel lowered his voice. "Are you worried about Motka and Mordecai? I know Motka is flighty and lazy, but—" He looked toward the two apprentices who were bent together over the cutting table.

"No, they are fine, both of them. I have no complaints."

Six months had passed before Yoysef had resigned himself to the idea that Chaim and Berel would not soon return. Herschel had been reluctant to again raise the subject of new apprentices, but finally one morning Yoysef himself came to the decision that they had waited long enough. That was over a year ago. Young Mordecai had proved a good choice; he was a serious and conscientious boy who was happiest when he was working in the shop. With Motka it was something else again. He had come several months later and still showed no sign of settling down.

Yoysef added, "You have to expect boys to act like boys and not men."

"You were thinking about Chaim and Berel, I think?"

Yoysef shook his head. He realized with some surprise that in fact he had not thought about his elder son or about Berel for some time. No, the matter that had caused him to neglect his work was not Chaim and not the apprentices, but Simcha.

After the Sabbath morning service the previous week, Rabbi Nachman had pulled Yoysef aside, whispering, "We need to talk, Yoysef." Without his saying more, Yoysef had steeled himself for a complaint about Simcha's inattention to his Jewish education.

"I don't know how Simcha can sit through nine years of *cheyder* without learning anything! He doesn't seem to care that in a year's time, when he is bar mitzvah, he will have to take his place in the congregation as an adult Jew! I tell you, Yoysef, the boy's head is someplace else! And lately it is worse than ever."

"I'll talk to him," Yoysef promised.

He had had this conversation with the rabbi before, more than once. As before, he would go home and speak sternly to Simcha, and Simcha would look at him appraisingly out of those cool blue eyes and promise that he would do better. And nothing would change.

Yoysef basted a sleeve into the garment, but his mind was not on his work, and, dissatisfied, he had to rip it out and begin again.

He did not understand the boy. It was as though Malkeh and he had brought a stranger into their Jewish home. Though undeniably theirs, Simcha always had one foot in the gentile world. Recently he had tried to persuade the family to address him as "Semyon," the Russian name by which the steward called him. Yoysef's mouth tightened. It was a father's duty to raise his sons to love Torah. The enormity of his mistake in allowing Simcha to go to Spokoinaya Zemlya to study with Fedotov came sharply home to him. Since that day, all had been disaster.

It had been no surprise to Yoysef when he found Malkeh, not Simcha, currying the horse. He had learned since that it was also she who dug the garden, carried the water, and cleaned the hen house. Malkeh had been only slightly abashed that she had been caught. "Yevgeny Sergeivitch gives him so much work to bring home," she explained.

"We agreed, though, that he would not slight his responsibilities."

"Well, I know, but, after all, Yoysef, he is still a child, and—"

"So is Dvoreh still a child. And in a sense, Chaya Leya also."

"Please. I don't want that argument again."

On the morning when he had heard out Rabbi Nachman's most recent grievance, Yoysef had returned home with a heavy heart. Simcha had not come with him to the shul that morning, having somehow disappeared before his parents were awake.

Reaching the house, Yoysef found Malkeh reading by the kitchen table. Curtly, he asked her, "Where's the boy?"

"Why, I don't know," she said, looking up from her book. "Didn't he go to shul?"

"He did not."

Dvoreh flounced into the kitchen. "I hate *shabbes*!" she announced. "Never anything to do! And Chaya Leya's always gone the whole day, holding hands with Herschel down by the river!"

"Have you seen Simcha?" Yoysef asked.

"Not since early this morning. He was going off toward the woods with some boards and a hammer. Boys get away with anything!"

Yoysef removed his Sabbath coat, hanging it from a hook near the door. Grimly he sat down in the rocking chair to wait.

At midday Simcha having still not appeared, the family silently sat down to pick at their portions of *cholent*. In order not to profane the day of rest, it had been cooking in the last heat of the untended oven since before sundown of the previous day.

Nervously Malkeh suggested, "Maybe you should go look for him, Yoysef. Maybe something happened to him."

"No," he said shortly. "We'll wait."

It was near three o'clock before Simcha, muddy but happy, came into the house.

"What were you building by the stream?" Yoysef asked sternly.

"A bridge, Papa. Yevgeny Sergeivitch explained to me about fulcrums and counterbalances, and I was trying it out, building a cantilevered span. It really works, Papa! It works!"

"Do you know what day it is, Simcha?"

"Saturday. I have no *cheyder* today—" The boy's voice faltered and stopped. He looked shamefaced at his father. "It is *shabbes*. I forgot. I'm sorry, Papa."

Yoysef wondered what punishment might make an impression on the boy. He had never raised a hand to the children, and he doubted the effectiveness of beating Simcha now. Finally he said, "You will not go back to Spokoinaya Zemlya until you have memorized next week's Torah portion, Simcha."

It was a task before which grown men would have quailed. Simcha had it letter perfect in two days.

All of these worries had been on Yoysef's mind when Herschel had asked him what was so preoccupying him that he neglected Reb Kagan's coat. Now, as though they had been speaking of Simcha all along, he said to Herschel, "I need to spend more time with the boy."

"What?"

"Next month when I go to Dvinsk to buy woolen goods, I think I'll take him with me."

Colonel Leonid Nicolaevitch Brusnowsky was not feeling his best. He and his hand-picked party of veteran soldiers had been on the road for two months now, and both his digestion and his piles were bothering him fiercely. Their route had taken them due west from Moscow through Smolensk and Vitebsk, hitting all the smaller cities and townlets en route. They were now in Gorodok on their laborious progress through Byelorussia. The process of conscription had grown increasingly simple, becoming both more efficient and, coincidentally, more brutal. Using an established army encampment as their base of operations, they would fan out in a series of day or preferably night raids on the surrounding communities. Any male who was not obviously impaired was conscripted without further ado. At the beginning, Colonel Brusnowsky had been rather more selective, taking only men over the age of twenty and respecting certain traditional exemptions for reasons of health, family hardship, or occupation. Peasants on the estates of certain powerful landowners had also been passed over. By the time they reached Vitebsk, though, the colonel had realized that such fastidiousness would not yield the numbers that General Burychkin required, and he had consequently revised the procedure. The commanding officers of the local military districts were not pleased.

Lieutenant Colonel Pavlov of Gorodok District complained, "No one told me you were coming, Colonel. And I have received no official documentation in regard to an augmented conscription."

"Surely an oversight," Brusnowsky said mildly.

"It is very irregular, sir. Our district has already sent its quota of men to Moscow."

"Really," the colonel said ironically.

"Besides, what you plan is outside the law. There are rules about who is eligible to be conscripted, you know, and even from that group we are supposed to choose by lot!"

"Lieutenant Colonel Pavlov," Brusnowsky said in a dangerously quiet voice, "what authority would it take to convince you? The tsar's?"

"Well—not exactly the tsar's—" Pavlov said, becoming nervous at this turn in the discussion.

"How about the interior minister?"

"Well, yes, I guess—"

Brusnowsky took his time unfolding the orders signed by Minister Plehve. "Here you are," he said, handing the document to Pavlov. "Are you satisfied it is authentic? See, it has the imperial eagle over the signature."

"In that case—"

"Please read it, Lieutenant Colonel. It says that failure to cooperate with the bearer, *who is on a special mission for the tsar*, will result in immediate arrest and imprisonment."

Pavlov paled. "I didn't understand, Colonel. If you had said at once— believe me, I want to do everything in my power—"

"Then I can expect no further disagreement?"

"Of course, of course. Anything I can do for you—"

"Well, there is one small thing more. I will need an escort of soldiers from your command to march the conscripts back to Moscow."

"What! But that is outrageous!"

Brusnowsky waved the imperial order under Pavlov's nose.

"Of course, Colonel," Pavlov conceded, bowing slightly, "whatever you say."

$\mathcal{M}$oishe, the eldest of Yenta and Yaynkel's five children, was as mischievous and adventuresome at twenty-four as he had been as a tree-climbing toddler. His career in the world had thus far shown little promise. In *cheyder* he had been an indifferent scholar, more interested in playing pranks than in studying Torah. In the butcher shop, where he had worked with his father, he was bored and careless, slipping away whenever Yaynkel turned his back. He resisted attempts by Pinchas the Matchmaker to find him a wife, saying he would find his own, though none of the eligible girls ever suited him. He was a young man of exceedingly good humor and meant no harm to any living creature. Moreover, he possessed an insouciant boyishness that could not fail but charm. Dvoreh, for instance, even as a sullen adolescent, continued to adore him.

When long ago Moishe began talking about going to America, everyone had said, "Yes, yes. Isn't that just like Moishe, always talking big plans! Don't worry, he'll settle down in the butcher shop!"

But Moishe Fleischman had a will of his own, and he had made up his mind to seek his fortune in the United States. Neither his mother's tears nor his father's warnings had moved him a fraction. Finally, worn down by his single-minded determination, his parents had capitulated and financed a ticket in steerage to New York City. Yaynkel decided to accompany his son as far as Königsberg in Germany, where he was to board the steamship. Moishe was the first of the family to strike out for new lands across the sea.

On the pre-departure evening the family gathered for a bittersweet farewell. Malkeh hugged Yenta to her and whispered that Moishe was a man now, well able to care for himself. Someday, she would see, he would make them all proud.

"Oy, Malkeh, it is so far away! When will I ever see him again? At least you know that Chaim is on the same side of the ocean that you are!"

Yes, thought Malkeh, though it was almost two years since she'd seen him, and his letters never mentioned coming home.

Golda came across the room to Malkeh. "How pretty Dvoreh looks tonight! You'll be looking for a bridegroom for her soon!"

Malkeh laughed. "Come now, Golda, she's only sixteen!"

Golda said pensively, "I was sixteen when I married Dovid."

Malkeh glanced toward Dvoreh, who was standing beside Moishe, her hand on his arm. As usual, Moishe was teasing her, and her eyes were bright, the color in her cheeks high. Malkeh had never thought much about Dvoreh's looks, but Golda was right, she *was* pretty; all that wealth of curly black hair, so like Yoysef's, and against it the eyes, as blue as Malkeh's own, were striking! Maybe they should begin thinking of a match for her, only— to be honest, she could not get used to the idea of having grown-up children.

At least one was still a baby. Her eyes swept the room to find Simcha. He was playing some game with Yenta's Lippe, who was about the same age. Lippe might be the taller of the two, but Simcha was altogether made from a finer mold. It gave Malkeh pleasure just to feast her eyes on him! She made a mental note to talk with Yevgeny Sergeivitch about giving Simcha fewer assignments in the next few months so that he would have time to prepare for his bar mitzvah. Yevgeny would not be pleased about that! He fought anything that interfered with Simcha's studies. She had to laugh, thinking how it irritated Fedotov that Yoysef was taking Simcha to Dvinsk with him tomorrow. Such a fuss over nothing, as though it might destroy Simcha's entire future! Yoysef would be gone only four days, five at the most. Sometimes it felt to her like the two men were engaged in a struggle for the boy. She hurriedly turned away from that unpleasant thought.

Mammeh Frumma was sitting alone against the wall, her eyes partly closed. Malkeh carried a glass of tea to her, making sure it was not filled full because lately Mammeh's hands had begun to shake quite badly. Tonight she looked tired, and her color wasn't good.

"We shall all miss Moishe," Malkeh said, sitting down beside her mother-in-law.

Mammeh Frumma's sigh came from deep inside. "Yes, but I will never see him again," she said quietly. A tear crept out from under one drooping eyelid and trickled slowly down her wrinkled cheek.

Malkeh nodded. A sadness came upon her. Chaim. Moishe. Where would it end?

With the first alarm in the night, Malkeh sprang from her bed. Not finding Yoysef beside her, she was disoriented at first; then she remembered that he and Simcha had left for Dvinsk at dawn. Although she had not witnessed a forcible conscription since she was a child in Dagda, she knew immediately what was happening. She woke Chaya Leya and Dvoreh and ran barefoot to the barn, where Herschel and the two apprentices, Motka and Mordecai, slept in the loft. Chaya Leya was at her heels.

"Run! Run!" Chaya Leya screamed, banging open the doors.

But Herschel had also heard the commotion in the streets and was already dressed and hurrying the boys into their boots.

Malkeh grabbed Herschel by the arm. "Go to Spokoinaya Zemlya. Yevgeny Fedotov will know what to do! For God's sake, hurry!"

The three dashed from the barn, keeping clear of the road and making their way across the empty fields. If they could reach the forest, they could lose themselves among the trees and eventually make their way to the manor house.

After they had faded from sight, Malkeh led a white-faced Chaya Leya back to the house. "If you cry, I shall slap you!" she hissed.

Dvoreh was standing at the kitchen door, looking out. "Get into your clothes at once," Malkeh said brusquely to her daughters. "If the soldiers come to the house, stay in your room out of sight. I will talk to them myself."

"Mammeh, Mammeh," Chaya Leya whispered, clutching Malkeh's arm, "will they be all right?"

"It is in God's hands," she said, pushing Chaya Leya toward the bedroom.

Luckily the night was without moon or stars. Avoiding habitations, Herschel led Motka and Mordecai across open fields. Reapers had already done their work, and mounds of hay dotted the flat expanse. The stubble left by the scythes was uncomfortable to run through, and they soon found it was capable of piercing clothing and drawing blood.

Plump Mordecai was soon winded, and Herschel drew the boys down behind a hillock of hay.

"Will they catch us, Herschel?" Mordecai was pale and sweating, and his breath came in gasps.

Herschel shook his head. "I think not. It is only a little farther now to the forest. We should be able to hide there."

From some distance away they heard the chatter of gunfire. There must be resistance in Polotsk.

"It sounds like they're killing people!" Motka exclaimed. If Mordecai was terrified, Motka was delirious with excitement.

Mordecai said, "I think I'm going to vomit."

Herschel gripped his arm. "Don't!" With a reproving look at Motka, he said, "They are probably firing their rifles in the air to frighten people. It wouldn't make sense to shoot men they plan to take to the army!" Crouching behind the haystack, Herschel strained to see into the darkness. Were any of the raiders nearby? Peering and listening, he heard no rustlings in the field. They should move to the cover of the forest at once. He motioned the boys to follow, hoping that he was still going in a northwesterly direction. Without stars for guidance, it was difficult to be sure.

In ten minutes the broad road was in sight, the thick growth of trees stretching away on the other side of it, Spokoinaya Zemlya not far beyond. Herschel breathed a sigh of relief. "We've made it," he whispered. "Keep your heads down crossing the road in case anyone's coming, and then make for where the trees and brush are thickest." He pointed. "Keep to the west— there are paths."

Colonel Brusnowsky's aide-de-camp, Lieutenant Khromov, carried tea and a bowl of *grechnevaya kasha* to his commander long before dawn. The colonel pushed the porridge away but swallowed some hot tea.

"Have the men left?" he asked.

"Yes, sir, shortly after midnight. They should be in Polotsk by now."

Brusnowsky stretched and swung his legs to the floor. *Boizamoi!* Camp food, military cots, and full days in the saddle were wearing him down! "Let's just get this finished!" he growled, referring to the whole Byelorussian operation.

"Yes, sir," the lieutenant said. "Shall I have your horse brought around?"

"What time is it?"

"Shortly after three o'clock."

"Yes. Wait five minutes while I dress," he said pulling on his breeches.

They rode in a small tight group, Colonel Brusnowsky at the fore with his aide at his side, twenty veteran cavalrymen bringing up the rear. They were on their way to join the bulk of their forces in Polotsk. The colonel was thinking about his career. This Byelorussian operation could make or break him. If he were able to send ten thousand men back to Moscow, maybe his next posting would be more desirable—St. Petersburg perhaps; in time he might even attain the rank of major general! His wife would be pleased about that! God knows, they had earned a better life, living in one miserable army camp after another!

He considered the logistics of the action at hand. There had been pockets of resistance here and there. Near Vitebsk, peasants, armed, he suspected, by landowners protecting their labor force, had had to be harshly dealt with. And not just there! Some of the Jews on the other side of Gorodok had put up a fight. Jews! Of course, the appearance of a large force of armed men had inflamed the populace. There should have been some preparation for their coming, a campaign of propaganda, a statement from the tsar, something! He had nagging doubts himself about the highhandedness of this maneuver. Probably illegal. He, at least, was in the clear. He was following orders.

The first streaks of light were showing in the eastern sky when they came around a bend in the road and surprised three shadowy figures just emerging from a field.

"Halt! Halt!" the colonel shouted, pulling at his reins.

Two of the figures, ignoring his command, sprinted across the road practically under the hooves of the horses. The third slowly straightened himself and walked forward with raised hands.

"Get the other two!" the colonel screamed at his men. Couldn't the fools see that this one's surrender was planned to let the others get away?

Several of the horsemen detached themselves from the group and galloped into the woods. From the road the sound of horses thrashing around in the undergrowth sounded like wild animals wrestling. The party waited for them to return. After a long while they rode out, shaking their heads.

Well, at least, the colonel thought, we have this one. He had been musing earlier on the salutary effect of making an example of one of these rebels, and here fate had delivered to him a thin, white-faced Jew who had not run quite fast enough to get away with his companions.

Brusnowsky ordered the frightened man lashed by a long rope to the pommel of his aide's saddle. "If the Jew's so eager to run, let's help him along," he jeered, and leaned over to flick his whip at the flank of Khromov's horse. The animal broke into a canter. The rope, pulled suddenly taut around Herschel's legs, threw him to the ground. Before the lieutenant could bring the horse to a halt, Herschel had been dragged a hundred meters along the roadway.

The colonel laughed. "Just a little exercise, Jew, so you'll get the point that it's better to be quick to volunteer."

Pulled to his feet by one of the soldiers while another untangled the rope, the group started off once more toward the city. Herschel had to run to keep up, although the aide kept his horse at little more than a walk. Every time Herschel tripped on his tether, the aide stopped the horse while someone straightened the rope. Still Herschel scarcely had time to regain his breath before the colonel's whip came down on the horse's flank again and the rope tightened, cutting into his flesh and pulling him cruelly in the animal's wake. He was barely conscious by the time they reached the city. He was untied and pushed to his knees in front of the line of conscripts in the street.

"This," said the colonel contemptuously, gesturing toward the fainting Herschel, "is what happens to those of you who think you can escape from the regiments of His Imperial Highness!"

Chapter 27

*P*etya Voronov, in his usual rush to return home to Spokoinaya Zemlya after a long absence, had ridden hard and arrived from Moscow after midnight on the tenth day, good time for a journey of seven hundred versts.

Fedotov was a light sleeper. At the sound of hooves on cobbles, he came awake, immediately alert and listening. Was Karpovitch up to some new mischief, he wondered. It sounded like one horse, one rider. Not Karpovitch's style. Unfortunately the windows on this side of the house did not command a view of the courtyard. He rose and hurriedly drew on breeches and boots. He was puzzled, as no one was expected. Lightly he ran down the stairs and flung open the front doors. By this time the sleepy groom, Boris, had arrived to unstrap the visitor's saddlebags and lead the lathered horse to the stable. Fedotov recognized the horse almost sooner than the rider. It was right that he should know the roan when it had been born right here at Spokoinaya Zemlya!

"Petya! My boy!" Fedotov shouted in delight, enfolding his nephew in a bear hug. "We didn't expect you! Why didn't you let us know you were coming?" He held Petya at arm's length. "You look tired but fit. You've filled out in these last months! Come in, come in! Here, let me carry your saddlebags! I'll heat water for tea right away!"

"I couldn't wait to come home!" Petya exclaimed. His first glimpse of Spokoinaya Zemlya after all these months had miraculously revived him, his exhaustion slipping from his shoulders like a discarded cloak. Shyly, he reached out a hand to his uncle.

"But your mama, Petya, is she all right? You were supposed to have a long visit with her and Prince Trubetskoy—?"

"They're fine. I was there a week, and if I'd had to stay a day longer I would have lost my mind! After a while Mama said, 'I can see your heart is not in Moscow; you'd better go find it!' I rode off the next day. I have missed this place more than you can imagine!"

"So much has happened here," Fedotov said, "but it'll wait until to-morrow." In the light from the hall lamps he could see now that Petya was white with fatigue and his eyes red-rimmed. "You should be in bed, but first I'm going to fix you something to eat!"

"Not in my kitchen, you're not!" Maria Feodorovna said, coming into the great hall, already tying an apron over her nightgown and wrapper. "I thought I heard you, you young rascal! Didn't they feed you in the Hussars? You're thin as a rail!"

Petya kissed her on first one cheek and then the other. "Uncle says I've filled out."

"What does he know?" She drew Petya after her into the kitchen.

It took no time at all for Maria Feodorovna to boil water and slice bread. By the time the tea was brewed, she had prepared an omelet and set the food on the kitchen table before the young count.

"I'm ravenous!" he confessed. "I hated to waste time eating when I could be traveling."

While Petya ate, they talked, sometimes all at once, eagerly exchanging bits and pieces of news they would come back to in more leisurely fashion tomorrow. As if for reassurance that they were really together, from time to time a hand reached out to touch another's. Close-knit, a family, they were happy to be reunited after a long separation. Although young Petya should have been in bed, none of the three could bear to be apart so soon, and so they lingered, drinking tea and conversing in diminishing bursts of speech, until the sky began to lighten.

That's when the dogs began to bark, not in the desultory way that indicated some small animal was nearby, but frantically, as though something was amiss.

"What now!" Fedotov exclaimed, rising to open the kitchen door for a look outside. "What's this? What's this?" he said, astonished.

Two Jewish boys, their *payos* flopping as they ran, crossed the yard and practically fell across the doorstep into the kitchen. Both were breathing heavily, faces flushed and eyes dilated with fear. One was bleeding from a deep cut in his leg. Tears were making pathways down the dirty cheeks of the fat one, who appeared to be on the edge of hysteria.

"*Gospodin* Fedotov! We must see him!" the younger boy gasped as soon as he had the breath to talk.

"I'm Fedotov. What is this about? Who are you?"

"We're from Yoysef Mandelkern's. There are soldiers in Polotsk rounding up all the boys and men! We were on our way to get you when they captured Herschel." He stopped a moment to wipe the sudden moisture from his eyes. "They almost got us too—at the village just down the way!"

Fedotov and Pyotr exchanged glances. Now, what could this be about?

Fedotov frowned at Petya. "I'll have to go see what has happened. Did you hear anything in Moscow or St. Petersburg that would account for this?"

He shook his head.

*P*etya had insisted on riding out with Fedotov, and they wasted no time in getting started. Maria Feodorovna was left to bandage Mordecai's leg and to find someplace for the exhausted pair to sleep.

By the time Petya and Fedotov had arrived at the nearby village, the soldiers had already departed with the captured men in tow. A few of the women had followed them, but most, numb with shock, were still aimlessly standing in the street, talking to each other in hushed tones of fear. Big-eyed children were clutching at their mothers' skirts, too frightened even to cry. When the villagers saw that it was not returning soldiers who had ridden into their midst but the young master and the steward, they clamored around the horses, vying for the chance to tell how they had been surprised in their beds.

"It was over so quick, Master! There wasn't no chance to fight 'em off before they was roped together and on their way," one of the women told them. "Where did they take them? They ain't going to hurt them?"

"What'll we do with no men to feed us!" a young girl, heavily pregnant, wailed.

"Go back into your houses," Petya said kindly. "We'll bring your men home for you."

They did not stay to commiserate, fearing that they might miss the recruiting party. Fedotov led the way, spurring his horse to a gallop.

In Polotsk it was not difficult to locate the place where the conscripts had been assembled. The melancholy sound of lamentations, angry murmurings, and curses hung over the square in front of the cathedral. The recruits—in fact they were prisoners—were ringed by soldiers with bayonets fixed to their rifles. They were milling about in great disorder, many of them barefoot and wearing only nightshirts; few were completely clothed. Fedotov recognized faces in the crowd, but in the mass confusion, it was impossible to know how many were from Spokoinaya Zemlya. He did not, however, recognize Herschel in the bloody figure with blackened eyes who slumped, apparently lifeless, between two of the soldiers.

Positioned on a slight rise at the far end of the square, a thin-faced man sitting on a fine ebony gelding drew on a cheroot while waiting impatiently for the soldiers to form the conscripts into a ragged line.

"There's the bastard!" Fedotov said, pointing him out to Petya. "That's the officer in charge!"

Petya spoke in a low voice. "Uncle, let me talk to him."

Yevgeny Sergeivitch stared at the boy for a long moment. No, he realized, not *boy* anymore. Sometime during the months at the Officers' Training School, Petya had passed into manhood. The thought struck Fedotov with the force of revelation. He nodded, acquiescing to Petya's claim to mastery. The two rode across the square toward the officer on the black horse.

"Sir!" Petya hailed him with a smart salute. "I am Lieutenant Voronov of the Second Hussars." The colonel, his eyes arrogant and appraising, barely lifted his arm to return the salute. "*Count* Pyotr Voronov of Spokoinaya Zemlya."

"What is it, young man? We are busy right now."

Fedotov's hand tightened on the handle of his riding crop, but he did not move.

"Your name, sir?" Petya asked, every bit as narrow-eyed and arrogant as the colonel.

"Brusnowsky, Leonid Nicolaevitch Brusnowsky."

"I believe you have some of our people here." Petya motioned toward the men in the square. "I would like them released at once."

"I'm sure you would, Lieutenant." Brusnowsky said, studying the smoldering end of his cheroot.

"My family, sir, has always served the tsar faithfully and well," Petya said carefully. "My grandfather was decorated with the Order of St. Alexander Nevsky at the battle of Balaclava, and my father was a member of the tsar's personal guards. My stepfather is Prince Mikhail Trubetskoy, who served in the late tsar's cabinet."

"And?" Brusnowsky asked insolently.

Petya drew a sharp breath. "In recognition of my family's long service to the imperial family, the servants of Spokoinaya Zemlya have always been exempt from military duty. I'm sure, Colonel, that including our men has been an oversight which I shall be willing to overlook—"

Brusnowsky threw his cheroot to the ground. "Look, Voronov—or whatever your name is!—get this into your head! You petty little aristocrats think you still count for something, but you're dead wrong about that! Times have changed and you landowners have no chips to bargain with!"

"That is not quite so!" Petya said, his face red and his eyes hot. "You had better release my men at once, or else—"

"Listen, sonny, you can beg or threaten until your balls fall off and it won't make any difference! I have my orders to bring back conscripts, and that is exactly what I am doing. I'll see you in hell before I let you stop me!"

Fedotov moved forward. "We'll just see about that!" he growled. "These men belong to us! What do you want anyway, Brusnowsky? If it's gold, that can be arranged—"

"Get out of my way!" the colonel said, edging his horse past them.

Fedotov reached for the knife in his boot.

"Are you crazy?" Petya cried, leaning over to grab his hand. "Come on, Uncle, let's go home. Nothing can be done here. We'll have to work it out with military headquarters in Moscow." Petya groaned. "I can scarcely bear to think of riding back to Moscow! But at least we won't suffer the trip like these poor devils will."

"As soon as you've had some sleep, we'll leave."

"All right," Petya said, overcome by weariness. "My mother's husband will help us. And surely someone in Moscow will remember my father and grandfather."

When Malkeh's letter, bearing the sad news about Herschel's capture, arrived in Kiev, Berel and Chaim agreed that they should thank God that they had been spared that horror.

It was one of the few things lately that had their wholehearted agreement. Since coming to Kiev, strain had crept into their friendship. At first the shared excitement of being together in a great city seemed to strengthen their bonds. In those earliest days there had been between them the special closeness that travelers who are thrown together on a far journey feel for each other. But as their lives took divergent paths, and the strangeness of Kiev became mundane, their relationship faltered for lack of shared interests. They quarreled with increasing bitterness. Berel harped on Chaim's having strayed from his Jewish roots, and Chaim complained that for all the change city living had made in Berel, he might just as well have stayed home. After a while argument was replaced by polite silence.

Berel and Chaim had lived fairly comfortably in the house of Reb Shloyma Pinsker for almost two years. In all that time neither of them gave a thought to Reb Pinsker's daughter, Zipporeh. To them, she was merely a pair of willing hands serving their food and taking away empty dishes, a pleasant enough pair of hands, clean and quick, but nothing more than that. In fact, her looks and personality were such that as soon as she was out of sight, she faded from thought.

One afternoon during the summer of their second year, Berel was alone, bending over his work in the dimness of the ground floor tailor shop. Pins held between his teeth, he was carefully fitting lapels to a coat he was making. He held the jacket up to the light. The collar lay flat, perfect and ready to baste. He spit out the pins and reached for a needle to thread. His concentration momentarily broken, he became aware that something was different about the house. He cocked his head, listening. Usually there was the clatter of bowls and dishes drifting down from the kitchen upstairs. Sometimes Zipporeh would be picking out a tune on the piano. The power sewing machine would be making its own special racket. Not today. Today what had claimed his attention was the absence of any kind of noise. He scratched his head, frowning. After a minute he remembered that Frau Klara had mentioned she might stop in for a glass of tea with her friend Beilke Weitzman. Reb Shloyma, he knew, had been called by the burial society to sew a shroud for a pious man who had died that morning. As for Zipporeh, she went everywhere with her mother. What a joke that he was nervous because the house was too quiet!

Berel finished basting the garment and laid it aside. It was a hot day, and he had decided to close the shop and go upstairs for a nap. In the unlikely event of a customer on such a warm afternoon, he would certainly hear the tinkle of the doorbell from upstairs. He locked the front door and tried the handle. When he turned, he was surprised to see that Zipporeh had entered the shop by the interior stairs that connected the living quarters with the business.

"Ah, Zipporeh. I thought you went out with your mother."

"I didn't want to go."

Berel busied himself, straightening the shop. One by one he picked up the precious pins before making a scoop from newspaper and brushing the remainder of the sweepings into it. Zipporeh leaned back against the cutting table, watching him. He hung the scissors on their hooks, secured the thread on the spools, and laid the tape measures in the drawers. All the while he was uneasily aware that Zipporeh's eyes were following his every move.

"Uh, Zipporeh, was there something you wanted?"

Her reply was so soft that he didn't hear it. He rechecked the lock on the front door and pulled the curtains across the street window. The oil lamp under which he had been working provided the only illumination. "What did you say, Zipporeh?" he asked absently.

"I said yes."

"What?"

"I said yes, there is something I want—Berel."

Puzzled, he turned to look at her.

Slowly Zipporeh pulled out the hairpins that secured her coiled braids. Her heavy hair, the color of straw and rather pretty when it wasn't forced into tight plaits, cascaded across her shoulders.

Berel stared at her uncertainly.

"You asked whether there was something I wanted, and I said yes." Thrusting her flat chest forward, she slowly undid the top buttons on her starched shirtwaist. "I want you, Berel." Advancing toward him, she laid hold of his sleeve.

Berel licked his lips nervously, watching her. Her movements were both shy and wanton at the same time. He didn't know her. "Zipporeh—you're not yourself."

"Yes, I am," she said, her eyes glittering. "I love you, Berel! I have from the day you first came! I know that I'm not pretty like other girls, but underneath I'm no different than they are!"

Helpless, Berel shrugged.

"Besides," she continued eagerly, "I'm my parents' only child, and someday my husband will inherit everything—this shop and the house and money. You'd like that, wouldn't you, Berel?"

"Please, don't talk like that."

The tears came, an unbelievable abundance of tears. They welled up as though her pale eyes were oceans, rolling in great streams down her face until they fell off the end of her sharp chin. Her nose turned red, and she snuffled while she searched for a handkerchief.

"Don't cry, Zipporeh," Berel said, taking a step back, away from the enormity of her misery.

Suddenly she was angry. "It's not, after all, that you're such a good catch, Berel! You don't even have a family!"

Berel sighed. "Come on, Zipporeh. Let's forget this whole thing." He blew out the lamp to signal the end of the conversation.

Making a sudden move through the darkness, she threw herself upon him, clinging to him with all her strength, her arms about his neck and her face pressed against his chest. "You know I'm a good housekeeper, Berel—everyone says I'm a real *balabosteh*! I'll bring you a big dowry and prospects for an inheritance. What else do you want?"

Berel was silent.

"Oh, and I'll be so good to you in *those* ways—" She pressed a loose wet mouth to his to prove the point.

Horrified, Berel twisted out of her grasp and backed up the stairs. Nothing in his life had prepared him for anything like this.

"Please, Berel!" she wailed.

With more unkindness than he intended, Berel blurted out, "I don't want you for my wife!"

Zipporeh came after him up the stairs. Her hands clutched his arm, the fingers biting into his flesh. "All right, not as your wife, then! But, for God's sake, have pity on me and take me as a woman!"

"Let go of me! You're mad, Zipporeh!"

"You're my last chance, Berel. I am thirty years old, and I've never had a man. Come with me, we can do it now—in my bedroom while Mammeh's at market and Papa is out! For the sake of God, Berel, if not for me! It is a mitzvah!" Her hands in the darkness found his penis and began to rub him there.

Berel felt sick. He flung Zipporeh's hands away from him. "Lunatic!" he whispered, and pushed past her, down the stairs, and into the street.

He did not creep back into the house for hours, not until he was sure that everyone was asleep for the night.

Afterward, Berel could never bring himself to look into Zipporeh's face without guilt, aware always that her red-rimmed, suffering eyes were following his every move. Almost as bad, Reb Pinsker was making arch remarks about how good it would be to have a son-in-law with him in the business, and Frau Klara was preparing all of his favorite dishes. With every day that passed, Berel felt the trap closing around him more tightly.

He tried to talk with Chaim, to explain how he felt, tried to persuade him to leave Kiev with him. But Chaim was satisfied with his life. He had adjusted to the hard physical labor and the noise and was making a place for himself at the mill, earning a full five rubles a week already. Why should he have to start over again someplace else? Besides, marriage with Zipporeh shouldn't be such a bad deal for Berel. Though far from perfect, Zipporeh Pinsker might be the best wife he could hope to find. And, as he told Berel, life under the Pinsker roof could not be anything but improved by such an arrangement.

"But I don't love her!" Berel protested.

Chaim recalled to Berel *Bobbeh* Frumma's words: "What has love to do with marriage?"

"For me, it has everything to do with it."

"You don't get offers like this every day. You should think it over carefully, Berel."

"Did you think it over carefully when you chose Nadja Ivanova over Chava?"

"That's not the same thing!"

"Why? Because I don't yet have a woman I love? That doesn't mean I never will!"

"Berel, you're hopeless! I can't talk to you anymore."

"Really! Maybe if you ever listened to what I tell you—oh, never mind!"

A heavy silence settled between them. Finally Berel said, "I am not marrying Zipporeh Pinsker. I've thought about it, and I'm leaving Kiev. I hope you'll come to Odessa with me, Chaim, but whether you do or you don't, I have to go!"

"You're a fool, Berel," Chaim said, turning away, "but I suppose I'll miss you."

That same night Berel packed his few possessions. He understood that he would be leaving Kiev alone.

*C*haim's lack of sympathy had come as no surprise to Berel. In the time they had lived in Kiev, Chaim had grown hard and somewhat callous. Berel laid the blame at the door of Elihu Goltz, Chaim's friend at Brodsky's mill.

For Chaim, Goltz represented a whole other world, one filled with passwords, slogans, and secret meetings, a world of dim cafés where earnest university students discussed "socialism" over endless cups of coffee and where factory workers were recruited for the new Jewish Workers' Union, called in Yiddish *Algemeyner Yiddisher Arbeter Bund* or just "The Bund."

The day that Goltz invited Chaim to accompany him to a clandestine meeting of a select group of Brodsky workers was a proud one for Chaim. It meant that his friend had accepted him completely.

They were eating their midday meal of bread and cheese in the relative quiet of the mill yard when the older man asked quietly, "Well, Mandelkern, you've been around for a while now. What do you think about what you've heard?"

"Heard?" Chaim asked cautiously, fearful of appearing stupid.

Goltz grinned. "Don't play dumb! There's no one around to hear us!"

"Well, what I hear sounds fine—" Chaim said, uncertain what he was being asked.

Goltz clapped him on the shoulder. "I somehow knew you had a head for politics!"

"Yes, sure," Chaim said. "You can count on me."

Goltz moved closer and said directly into his ear, "Meeting at Mintz's room, right after work on Friday."

On *shabbes*? Chaim wondered, not daring to ask Goltz, who had made his views on religion clear more than once. "Sure. Fine, Goltz." Anyway, he thought, Berel wasn't around anymore to shake his head and give lectures about keeping the Sabbath.

Chaim began accompanying Goltz regularly to Bund meetings. He noticed that they followed a pattern and were attended by a stable group that included a dozen or so men from the sugar mill. Occasionally others were added, as he himself had been, but seldom did anyone drop away. A few were rough types, uneducated laborers, but many more were intelligentsia, having, like Goltz, graduated from a *gymnasium* and spent time at a university before economic problems forced them into the mill. Eager young men and women Bundists harangued the Brodsky workers to organize themselves to demand higher wages and better working conditions. They sang stirring songs about brotherhood and freedom and the glory of labor. Chaim was full of pride, swept up in the sweetness of this new comradeship. He began to exchange knowing glances and friendly backslaps when he passed others of the group in the plant. Rather self-consciously he began to pepper his private conversations with phrases like "exploitation of labor" and "strength through union."

In truth, Chaim was less infatuated with the "movement" than with Goltz. He adopted a swagger like Goltz's, began to wear a dark cap like Goltz's, learned to drink black coffee as Goltz did and to smoke the dark brown *papirosi* that Goltz rolled. The new friendship more than filled the void that Berel had left, and Chaim thought he was happy.

In the meantime, his lot at the mill had consistently improved over the months. Since he was a steady worker and good with his hands, he had become a mechanic's assistant, charged with helping to maintain the equipment, an important job that could lead to further advancement. He might in time be promoted to mechanic or even become an engineer.

Mr. Brodsky walked through the plant most evenings, surveying his domain and talking with the foremen while making notes in a little leather-bound notebook. The mill owner was a short, slight man, unimpressive to look at. Always he dressed in a dark suit with a high starched collar, a black overcoat that swirled about his short legs as he walked, and a dark western-type fedora. He was nearsighted and the thick, rimless spectacles he wore gave him the fierce, glassy stare of a hawk.

One day he stopped beside the machine where Chaim was working. He asked a few questions: What were the main things that went wrong with the equipment? Why were the machines so frequently in disrepair? Did the problem rest with the men or with the machines? Was there a solution? Chaim glanced at the impassive foreman who accompanied Brodsky to gauge how much he should say. Finally, stuttering slightly from nervousness, Chaim pointed to an unhoused cogwheel and suggested a slight modification that would protect the belt from being worn through by the wheel—it would cost only a handful of kopecks to make the adjustment he had in mind, and in the end it would save both replacement costs and repair time.

The owner nodded, writing in his notebook. Finished, he started to move away.

"But, sir," Chaim added bravely, "the biggest problem with the machines is that the men are exhausted, and then they get careless—"

Brodsky scowled. "Yes, milling sugar is hard work. So what are you suggesting? It's the fashion now, isn't it, to demand shorter hours—all kinds of coddling? You are perhaps one of those agitators who want to put me out of business?"

"No, sir," Chaim said. "I am only saying that I have noticed that after a day off, or early in the morning and after the midday rest, there are fewer accidents with the machines. A morning and afternoon rest period would pay in the long run." Brodsky trained his hawk eyes on him. Suddenly overcome by his own audacity, Chaim added lamely, "You asked me why the machinery broke down."

The mill owner smiled ever so slightly. "What is your name?" he demanded.

"Mandelkern, sir, Chaim Mandelkern."

Brodsky wrote it down. "You don't know anything about business, Mandelkern!" He walked on without a backward glance.

After they were gone, Goltz flashed Chaim a grin across the machinery. "What are you, some kind of socialist or something? Brodsky's got your number now, boy!"

But Chaim knew that Goltz was pleased with him, and for the rest of the day he was warmed by Goltz's approval.

The engineers came to study Chaim's suggestion for the machinery modification. Changes, not exactly what Chaim had suggested, were made. The plea for additional rest periods was ignored. It was only what Chaim had expected.

Chapter 28

The road to Moscow was a descent into hell for the long, ragged columns of conscripts. They were a diverse lot, peasants with manure still clinging to their boots, shopkeepers unused to any kind of physical rigor, Jews with ritual fringes hanging below the nightshirts in which they had been taken, young boys weeping for their mothers.

So grievously injured was Herschel Rosen that he might well have died on the way to Moscow. Unable to see from eyes that were mere slits in his swollen face, coughing blood, and painfully dragging a leg in which a long cut had begun to fester, he begged his comrades to leave him to die, but they would not. Polotsker arms supported his body while Yiddish voices encouraged him to persevere.

In the long torment of the day, there was only one period of respite, at midday. When word was passed down the line, the weary men dropped to the ground at the side of the road, hungering more for rest than for food.

Herschel collapsed the moment sustaining arms released him, falling to the earth where he stood. How soft it felt beneath his bruised cheek, softer than goose down, sweeter than linen; just to drift out of consciousness, out of pain and grief, was sweet.

But they would not let him be. Someone was shaking him insistently. Herschel resisted. "No! Don't wanna—"

"Sit up!" The voice was stern. "You'll die if you don't eat. Cabbage borscht, never mind what the fat is—"

Herschel's vision was blurred, and he felt detached from the swollen ball of his head and from the filthy collection of his other body parts. He did not want to come back for the watery soup with the sickening layer of pork grease floating on its surface.

"Get up, Rosen! You'll eat now."

He struggled to sit up, responding to the authority in the disembodied voice, the same voice that talked to him and kept him conscious while he walked. He could not remember the voice's name, though he thought he knew it from home.

An arm lifted Herschel, cradling him against a strong chest. A metal utensil was held to his mouth, and the voice ordered him to drink what it held. The name—what was it? Life and death, it seemed to him, lay in his ability to remember the owner of the voice. He pushed weakly at the bowl. The name, the name!

"Eat!"

Herschel could barely open his eyes, but he forced them as wide as possible, looking at the man for a clue to his identity. Important. He shook his head to clear the cobwebs. He had made trousers for the man, had seen him in shul. The name trembled on the brink of memory but would not come. He closed his eyes, exhausted from the effort.

"Not yet. You must eat a few more spoonfuls, and then you can rest."

Dutifully he took another mouthful. He wanted to retch but was afraid he might dirty the arm that held him upright. The name came to him suddenly—Yaakov, the baker Yaakov. That was it, the surname didn't matter. So the baker had been taken, too! Who would care for his wife, his children? Yaakov! He said the name aloud.

"Yes?"

Herschel bent his head to the bowl. He gagged on the thick grease and spilled what little his stomach contained on the grass. At this sign of weakness, tears flooded his eyes.

"Try, Herschel, try. To eat is to live—"

"Let me go, Yaakov! Let me die!" he cried. Had he not lost everything he cared about—Chaya Leya, Yoysef, his home, his future? At the very moment when happiness was a fingertip away, catastrophe had found him.

Yaakov shrugged, holding the bowl to Herschel's mouth once more, coaxing him to swallow a little more. "That's it. They want you to die. Take your revenge. Eat and live."

Herschel clung to his new friend's hand. He said his name again. "Yaakov."

He kept down almost half his ration before Yaakov left him in peace to rest upon the earth. He was immediately asleep.

Too soon the order to re-form the line came. Herschel, shaken awake by Yaakov, stumbled to his feet. His right leg would not bear his weight, and he was forced to hop on his left. Idly he wondered whether there was infection, if he would lose his leg. If he could remember long enough, he would ask his friend—why did his name keep eluding him?—to look at it. With Yaakov supporting him on one side and a husky Russian *mujik* on the other, Herschel was borne along, his right leg trailing in the dust.

*B*efore he met Marta Pirumova (if that was truly her name), Vassily had had no experience with women. He was shy and wary, and it was she who took the initiative from the start. It had always been thus, between them, even on that rainy day when she had peered at him through the window of the coffee bar and he had accused her of spying on him. Marta, a spy! It made him laugh later to remember how suspicious he had been!

By the time Marta had finished her coffee that fateful day, the downpour had turned to violent thundershowers.

"Well," she had said, taking hold of his arm at the doorway of the café, "I certainly won't find a taxi in a storm like this! Why don't we go to your place and wait for the rain to stop?"

He would always remember how the thunder had seemed to roll along the sidewalk, following them, the rain coming down in great flat sheets. Strong gusts of wind had pushed against them, hindering their progress. None of this had fazed Marta in the least. She had turned her head toward the heavens and laughed in high glee. If Vassily had to choose only one image by which to always picture Marta, it would be of her upturned face laughing in the teeth of the storm. Her face was like a rain-washed flower, fresh and vibrant with clear colors, her skin creamy with golden undertones, her lips berry red, and her eyes almost black but shiny.

By the time they had reached Vassily's boardinghouse, they were thoroughly soaked. Shyly he had suggested that she wait in the vestibule while he ran upstairs to get a towel.

"A towel's not going to do much for me!" she had laughed. "Just look at me! My clothes are dripping ice water all over the carpet! I've got to get out of them before I catch pneumonia!" She took Vassily's hand. "Lead on, Vassily! I don't know which room is yours."

Luck was theirs that day, for the landlady did not, as was her custom, open her door to see who was on the stairs. Perhaps the claps of thunder had obscured the sound of their entrance.

If Vassily was embarrassed by the poverty of his living quarters—a plain square room with ugly wallpaper faded a uniform beige except where splattered with grease stains, the only furniture an iron bedstead, a battered wardrobe, a chair, and a table. Marta seemed not to notice.

She dropped her cloak on the bed, sitting to pull off her boots and lisle stockings. Vassily stood stiffly with his back against the door, uncertain where to rest his eyes. Marta, unabashedly divesting herself of her wet clothing, took no notice of him. Her actions devoid of self-consciousness, she stood to shrug out of her shirtwaist and skirt and let her sodden petticoat drop to the floor.

"Well, silly, aren't you going to get out of your wet things?" She laughed, turning to look at Vassily, who was still clinging to the door frame.

The sight of her quite overcame him. He saw how her bosom rose from the décolletage of a lacy camisole and how even her ridiculous ruffled drawers could not hide legs that were long and slim. She picked up Vassily's towel and began vigorously to dry her hair. As she bent forward, he could see the delicate nape of her neck and the pink shell shape of her ears.

Regretting that the silk robe from the St. Petersburg days was shabby, he placed it delicately around her shoulders.

Marta looked up at him, and her eyes were liquid. She raised her arms, inviting him.

He moved uncertainly toward her, a question on his face. She reached up and brought his head down to hers. The mouth she offered for his kiss was soft and moist.

"Marta—" His voice came low from his throat.

They stepped back to look at each other, and he felt that his vision had never been so acute, recording the shimmer of the perspiration on her upper lip and magnifying the blotchy patch of color that had emerged on her throat.

Taking great pains over every button, she unfastened his shirt and softly stroked the black hair of his chest. For Vassily, it was agony, it was ecstasy. He groaned. She pulled him down beside her on the bed.

Passive under her touch, he felt her fingers drawing light circles around his nipples before moving down ever so gradually to unfasten his breeches. Her hands continuing to move in long, slow rounds, her head resting against his bared belly, he felt her rain-dampened hair move against his skin and then the light flick of her tongue in his umbilicus. Helplessly he allowed her to remove his shirt and pull his breeches off.

Her own remaining clothing she stripped away in haste, and they fell back together upon the bed. Her legs were already clasped around his hips as she opened to him.

That was how their affair had begun, on a day of thundershowers in a room that was both cold and dingy. It did not matter; Marta seemed to carry her own light and warmth within herself.

After a few weeks, it was Marta's idea to move into Vassily's room with him. She had money from home, but she said she preferred the anonymity of Vassily's quarters to the pension where she had been staying. Her clothing and her fripperies overflowed his cupboard, and the scent of her perfumes, creams, and powders overwhelmed his senses. Conventions and money meant little to Marta. Whatever she had, whether it was food, sex, or money, she shared freely. Vassily had never known that there were women like her in the world. There were some eerie times, though, when an earthy turn of phrase or a subtle lift of her chin bore a disturbing resemblance to poor dead Olga.

Within a short time the presence of Marta had become central to Vassily's very existence. He decided that there were worse places to wait for the revolution than in Berlin.

*A*t a forced-march pace of twenty versts a day, it took them over a month to reach the Moscow cantonment. To the credit of Lieutenant Colonel Pavlov, who had been forced by Brusnowsky to leave Gorodok to escort the men, none died along the way. For the conscripts the journey was a nightmare of aching limbs and blistered feet, sunburned skin and head lice, hot days, freezing nights, near-inedible food. Pavlov had at least issued the men clothing, blankets, and canteens for water; a few rudimentary medical supplies were available from a wagon marked with a red cross.

Gradually the swelling around Herschel's eyes subsided and the flow of blood from mouth and nose became a mere trickle. Yaakov reassured him that there seemed to be no internal damage.

"I don't care!" Herschel said, sullen. "I would rather die than be in the army!"

Yaakov, a big man strong from shoveling loaves of bread in and out of the ovens, struck him across the mouth. "It is a sin to talk like that!"

Herschel fought back tears. He was filthy and lice-infested, racked with dysentery. Throbbing bruises showed green and yellow and black on his face and arms. But the wound on his leg was the worst of his miseries. Each night Yaakov inspected the leg for signs of blood poisoning, bathing it in fresh water from his ration while gently stripping away the ragged tissue and cleaning out pus so that healing could take place. Grateful for Yaakov's ministrations, Herschel tried to keep himself from crying out and distressing the baker while he worked over him. The wagon with the red cross had run out of bandages the first week, but Yaakov badgered the guards for clean rags. Each dawn, as soon as he had finished reciting the *shaharit*, Yaakov wrapped the leg afresh, securing it for the day's march.

Little by little Herschel began to pick out familiar faces in the ranks. Besides Yaakov, there was Shimon Bronsky and Noyach Perloff whom he knew from the shul, Menashe Kakhovsky from whom Malkeh sometimes bought milk and butter, little Ahronchik Katz, whose bar mitzvah he had attended a month or so back, others whom he knew only by sight. Some of the peasants he recognized as being from Spokoinaya Zemlya. Gradually the Jews and the Russians had separated themselves out. Jew and peasant might be in the same awful situation, yet mutual distrust distanced them from each other.

After the first few days the men did not talk much as they walked; each had his own private grief and pain, and besides, marching required all one's energy. Nevertheless, one day Herschel asked, "Yaakov, what do you think is going to happen to us?"

Yaakov sighed. "It is in God's hands."

"Yes, but what will they do with us? Hardly any of us will make a soldier!"

Yaakov was offhand. "Oh, they'll probably put me to work in a kitchen someplace, and you'll be making uniforms for the tsar's army instead of caftans for the rabbi."

"Do you think so, Yaakov?"

The baker laughed shortly. "No. It makes too much sense."

Although Herschel's injuries were slowly improving, his inability to retain food had weakened him greatly. Three days out of Moscow, he could drag himself no farther and he collapsed in the line. Yaakov carried him to the grassy verge.

"I can't make it, Yaakov," Herschel said faintly.

"We're almost there. See, we're following the Moskva River already. I'll carry you."

"No."

"If you don't get up, maybe they'll shoot you."

"I don't care."

"*I* care."

The baker hoisted him over his broad shoulder. Herschel closed his eyes. Dreamily he marveled that Yaakov had enough strength to carry him. Later Noyach and Shimon took turns with Yaakov.

Arriving at Moscow Barracks on the last day of October, Herschel was pushed onto a stretcher and taken, protesting, to the infirmary. He reached out desperately for Yaakov, afraid that he would die without him. "I'm all right, I'm all right!" he whispered to the orderlies, struggling to rise from the litter. "Let me stay with him."

They paid no attention. The older orderly shrugged. "These Yids!" he said to the other man. "They speak Russian so funny, who can understand them?"

Yaakov shouted to him from the line. "We'll be together, Herschel! Just get strong!"

But it did not work out that way. There was a policy in the Imperial Army to disperse men of the same region to different units and to send them to separate geographical locations if possible. Breaking up ethnic groups, people who spoke the same language and had the same culture, hampered rebellion in the ranks.

For three weeks Herschel lay on a white cot, where he was fed nourishing broths and given strong medicines for the dysentery; his leg wound was stitched, and two broken ribs strapped. Away from familiar Jewish faces, he felt disoriented, restless, and anxious. Though exhausted from all that had happened, his only sleep was that induced by opiate drafts from which he awakened cold and drenched from the sweat of nightmares. Again in those dreams he relived the pain and humiliation of being dragged, weeping, behind a horse, no more important to the officers on their mounts than a turd in the road. How could one human being do that to another? No less disturbing was the other dream which began well enough with Chaya Leya's sweet, plump body in his arms, and finished when he bent to kiss her lips, at which point she faded and he was left clutching empty air.

Sometimes he imagined things. He thought once that it was his mother who came through the door to soothe him after a bad dream, but his mother had died when he was three years old, so how could that be? Once, staring out the window, he thought he saw the strong figure of Yevgeny Fedotov striding angrily along, his riding crop beating a tattoo on the side of his boot. The vision was so real that he crawled from his bed and rapped on the windowpane, but by that time the figure was gone, just another vision from a drugged dream.

When Herschel was pronounced fit to serve the tsar, he was released from the hospital and issued a proper uniform and equipment. He searched the camp in vain for his friend the baker, but Yaakov was long since gone. They all were, all the men who had marched with him from Polotsk to Moscow. A week after he left the infirmary, Herschel was herded onto a train en route to an unknown destination.

There was deep gloom in Polotsk. No one knew what had happened to the men and boys who had been taken. A delegation from the shul was chosen to travel to Moscow, prepared to do whatever was necessary to get information and to purchase releases. When they reached army headquarters, money changed hands but little was learned. By that time, the conscripts from Polotsk had been billeted at posts throughout the empire. The delegation had been too late in coming, or perhaps it would not have mattered. There was a feeling of urgency in the air, a premonition of bad times to come, and the old ways of doing things, the system of bribes and options, was no longer certain.

Eventually most families received letters from the sons and fathers who had been taken. Herschel was not heard from.

The house of Yoysef Mandelkern had known neither rest nor peace since the night of the terror. At first there was numbness and disbelief, then anger, and finally despair.

Although he knew Herschel would not come, Yoysef went sometimes at night to sit by himself in the tailor shop, straining to see the road in the darkness. Watching and waiting had become part of the family's life along with fear. Yoysef made up reasons to walk with Simcha to *cheyder* and watched through the window for him to return, as though somehow his vigilance could protect him.

Through the weeks that Yevgeny Fedotov was away in Moscow, the women stayed close to the house, huddling together and talking in voices that were hushed.

Dvoreh was sorely troubled. "Why does God permit such wickedness? Does He not see all?"

Dully Malkeh said that they must have faith in His purposes even when they did not understand them.

Dvoreh shrugged, knowing full well that her mother was not given to passive faith. Chaya Leya turned a fierce look upon Malkeh. "Would you say that, Mammeh," she asked, "if it had been Simcha who was taken and not Herschel?"

Malkeh turned away, pain like a knife in her breast.

"Well, would you?"

Malkeh refused to answer. Looking into her heart, she knew that she had thanked God that her sons had been spared conscription. She was sorry for Herschel, but better him than Chaim or Simcha. Maybe it was not right, but a mother always feels more for her own.

"Perhaps Pyotr Voronov and Fedotov will be able to get Herschel released," she offered.

"Oh, yes," Chaya Leya said with heavy sarcasm, "I'm sure they really care what happens to Herschel!"

Sitting idle for a change in the silent house, Chaya Leya had plenty of time to think about herself, about her mother, and about Herschel. That she had never been a favorite of her mother she had long accepted as true. She had not been blessed with the intelligence of a Yaakov or a Simcha nor with the beauty of a Channah or a Dvoreh. Nor had she inherited her mother's ambition and spirit. Only God knew how hard she had tried to make up to Mammeh for her failings. Had there ever been a child as dutiful as she? Not that Mammeh had ever noticed! Redemption might have come from marrying well, a man from an educated and upper-class family, but perverse as fate had always been, she had fallen in love with the orphaned child of poor parents. In Mammeh's eyes she could not even do that right! Gradually Herschel had replaced Malkeh as the center of Chaya Leya's universe, becoming for her mother and friend, brother and lover all at the same time.

Chaya Leya fixed her sad gaze on her mother's face. Malkeh, feeling her daughter's eyes upon her, turned to look in her direction. Chaya Leya's face was thoughtful. Somewhere in these last few days she had arrived at the conclusion that the ties between her and her mother had finally come undone.

Despite their discouragement, the Mandelkerns waited for Fedotov and the young count to return, clutching at the hurried trip to Moscow as their sole source of hope. The Voronovs were an important family with important connections, they told each other. And hadn't Yevgeny Sergeivitch proved himself a powerful friend in the past?

One afternoon, many weeks after the raid, Fedotov returned. He had pushed both himself and his stallion to their physical limit. His beard and his clothes were matted with dust, and he could scarcely stand for weariness. He came first to the Mandelkerns, before returning to Spokoinaya Zemlya. The women knew what had happened in Moscow before he ever dismounted; his grim expression told all.

Chaya Leya was upon him at once, grabbing at his coat and bombarding him with questions. Malkeh gently pushed her aside and would not allow Fedotov to speak until he had swallowed some scalding tea with brandy.

Malkeh had never seen him like this. She was familiar with his black rages, but this hopeless resignation was new and frightening. When he could talk more easily, he told them that when the conscripts had arrived in Moscow, he had not been allowed to see them. They were "quarantined," he had been told. Where would they be posted? Wherever they were needed. That was the sum total of the information that could be pried out of General Shulavov's office no matter how many rubles were offered. Nor had Pyotr or his stepfather had more success.

"What now?" Malkeh asked.

The steward passed a tired hand over his face. "I don't know," he said, slumping forward in his chair. "The War Ministry in St. Petersburg, perhaps. Tomorrow I'll draft a letter for the count to send."

"You are exhausted," Malkeh said. "You should go home now and rest."

"Yes. Yes," Fedotov said, rising. He turned to Chaya Leya and took her hands in his for a moment; there was sympathy and tenderness in the gesture. At the door he turned, saying in a wondering voice, "You know, it might have been Semyon!" He used the Russian name by which he called Simcha.

"God was good to us and looked after Simcha," Malkeh said, her voice trembling.

The words dug deep into Chaya Leya. She felt each one like acid burning its way through her skin to eat into her very soul. She turned on her mother. Her eyes were cold and her lips curled back from her teeth. "God was good, was He? He was good to save Simcha and destroy Herschel?"

Malkeh's hand flew to her mouth. "I never meant—"

"But you did, Mammeh! You never cared much for Herschel, did you? Just another mouth to feed until he could help Papa. A nobody. A shadow in the corner of the house. You don't really care what happens to him, do you, Mammeh? That he loves me and I love him doesn't count for anything with you!"

Malkeh moved to Chaya Leya's side, embracing her as though her arms could contain her daughter's pain. Chaya Leya shook her off and ran from the room.

Helplessly Malkeh looked at Fedotov standing in the doorway. She shrugged, embarrassed. "Please do what you can, Yevgeny Sergeivitch," she whispered.

"I am no worker of miracles," he said gruffly, then added, "The girl loves him."

"Yes," Malkeh sighed, "God help her, she does."

Chapter 29

*L*ife in Kiev might have continued pleasantly for Chaim if it were not for the arrival of Stepan Pokrovsky and his involvement in the affairs at the Brodsky mill. No one knew where exactly Pokrovsky came from or what his connection was with the Bundists. One day he was just there at a meeting, a dark-bearded fellow with big yellow teeth and eyes so pale they were almost colorless, a man older than the rest and clearly accustomed to taking charge.

When Pokrovsky began to speak that first time, it was all the usual dry stuff. Chaim was wondering where he could get boots like Goltz's when suddenly his attention was sparked. Pokrovsky was talking action, action with violence "if necessary." Chaim glanced around the room. Some of the older men were moving uneasily in their chairs. Chaim craned his neck to see Goltz. His friend was sitting forward in his seat, his mouth parted and his eyes alight. It must be all right, then, what Pokrovsky was saying, Chaim thought, and yet—

Pokrovsky became a regular attendant at the meetings. Sometimes he just sat and listened, a smile tugging at his thin lips, the strange pale eyes ever watchful. Sometimes he strode to the front of the room to speak. What he said made Chaim afraid. Chaim tried once or twice to discuss this with Goltz, but Pokrovsky seemed to have some kind of hypnotic hold over Elihu Goltz. "The Bund has just moved into a new phase," he explained.

Something more personal had begun to bother Chaim as well. Gradually Pokrovsky was preempting Goltz's time. Instead of Chaim and Goltz enjoying their leisurely Saturday strolls along the Dnieper, Goltz was likely to be having a strategy meeting with Pokrovsky. The lazy evenings spent talking in a café suffered a similar fate.

Their favorite place to meet after work was small and poor, crude wooden tables placed close together, the air blue from the smoke of many *papirosi*. Since the mill was close by, the customers were mostly Brodsky workers. The schnapps was homemade, potent, and cheap, and, except in the unlikely event that he needed the table, the proprietor didn't bother a customer who lingered for an hour over a single drink. Goltz and Chaim were regular patrons two or three evenings a week. Leaning over the tiny table so they could hear each other, they exchanged desultory gossip from the mill and small confidences. Within Goltz the conflicting viewpoints of cynic and dreamer were always at odds. Chaim, a much simpler man, thought his friend the most interesting person he had ever met.

Now the cozy evenings at the Café Metropole were no more. The first time Pokrovsky happened into the café while they were there, Chaim assumed it was coincidence. Goltz hailed him and made room at the table. Soon the two of them were deep in conversation about the Bund leadership, their talk peppered with allusions to people whom Chaim did not know. Goltz seemed to have forgotten him. Chaim sat back in his chair and watched the two of them, thinking they seemed as intimate as lovers.

When they parted, Goltz warmly urged Pokrovsky to join them anytime, an invitation he accepted with alacrity. Now Pokrovsky always seemed to be there with them. In his presence Chaim felt himself to be virtually invisible. Nursing hurt feelings, Chaim thought to withdraw from these evenings, but his need for Elihu Goltz's friendship was so great that even to salvage his pride, he could not bring himself to do it. The only place left where Chaim still had Goltz more or less to himself was at Brodsky's.

Chaim was consumed with jealousy. He hated Stepan Pokrovsky so much that he could not bear to look into his face. He began to stay away from Bund meetings. At first Goltz remarked on it, even mildly reprimanded him, but later Goltz seemed not to care one way or another. When Chaim did attend, he noticed that the tenor of the meetings had changed. It wasn't just talk now. Pokrovsky was urging the Brodsky workers to strike the plant, and if dismissed from their jobs, to put the factory to the torch. "Sugar," said Pokrovsky with an evil smile, "should burn well."

Was he serious? Chaim looked around the cellar meeting room. Goltz's face was grim but determined. Some of the men looked flushed and excited, a few, like Chaim, scared.

The next day at the plant Chaim made an opportunity to pull Goltz aside, where they could talk for a moment unobserved.

"You can't be serious about this!" Chaim exclaimed.

"Dead serious. Next meeting we'll set the strike date."

"From what I hear from other men at the shul, things are good here—the wages, the Sabbath holidays." He sensed that his friend was pulling away and he took hold of his arm. "And remember, Elihu, Brodsky's a Jew, one of ours—"

Goltz roughly shook Chaim's hand off. "If you love Brodsky so much, you're no friend of mine!"

"You can't mean that," Chaim said, appalled, staring at him. "It's Pokrovsky, isn't it?"

"Go to hell!" Goltz said, walking off.

At the next meeting, for which a large group had assembled to vote yea or nay for the strike, Chaim sat listening to overheated rhetoric for the better part of an hour, growing more agitated as the evening drew on. Unexpectedly, for he felt himself to be no leader of men, he found himself on his feet. "Brothers, comrades," he said, his voice soft and a little quavery, "once we start down this road, there will be no turning back. Before we take the first step, hadn't we better consider the consequences? Do you really think that Brodsky is going to say, 'You're right, men—of course you can have shorter days and higher pay'?" There were a few titters. "I think he's going to tell us to get the hell out of his factory, and then he's going to hire all new workers. How are we going to live then? Are there so many jobs open in Kiev?"

"We'll shut down the refinery, then he'll have to deal," Pokrovsky said, fixing Chaim dispassionately with his colorless gaze.

There was a murmur of approval for Pokrovsky's words.

"Listen," Chaim pleaded, desperation giving emphasis to his words, "it sounds all right, but it's not that simple. Wreck a crushing machine or set fire to a shed, and the police will be on us like a flash!"

"We're not afraid," Goltz said, flushed and steely-jawed.

"Not afraid? Talk for yourself, Elihu. *I* don't want to spend twenty years in Siberia—or, worse, end with a hangman's noose around my neck!"

A palpable current of uneasiness ran through the room at the mention of the police.

Pokrovsky, hulking, dark, and commanding, stood to speak. He lifted a hand for silence. "Have you forgotten that in union there is strength? Brodsky can't operate his mill without experienced hands, and the police can't arrest every Jewish laborer in Kiev! I say, we hang together or we hang separately!"

"Those are nonsense sayings!" Chaim shouted. "Don't listen to him!"

His words were lost in the crowd's response to Pokrovsky's ringing call for action. When the vote was taken, only Chaim and a few others voted nay.

After that meeting, everything seemed to come crashing down around Chaim. No longer did the other Brodsky men greet him with a grin or slap his back in passing. As the others withdrew from him, he became uncertain and afraid, and he was desperately lonely. He had few acquaintances and no friends outside of the mill. The Pinskers were unfailingly pleasant, but they had subtly distanced themselves from him following Berel's departure. He could use some of Berel's listening and commonsense advice, and he was lonesome for his friendship. But Berel had been gone several months already, was pleased with his life in Odessa according to the letter he had sent—while Chaim had never felt so lost.

Having been dropped from membership in the Bund, Chaim now found himself completely on the outside, isolated. Elihu Goltz, his erstwhile friend, cut him dead, and then others began to give him strange, angry looks. One day when he knelt to fix a broken spring in one of the beet-crushing machines, the operator whispered in his ear, "Goddamn ass-licker! Spy! You'll get yours along with Brodsky!"

Chaim, frightened, moved away. He tried to talk to Goltz. "Look, I may not agree, but I'm not a spy!"

Goltz disdained to reply, coldly turning his back to him.

Day by day, things grew more tense in the sheds. A sense of impending catastrophe lay heavily upon Chaim. Excluded, he did not know when the strike was coming. He began to have nightmares in which Stepan Pokrovsky was coming at him with a knife in his hand. He had headaches and pains in his legs. Then he developed a bad cold and was unable to get out of bed to go to work. He lay, burning with fever and beset with bad dreams.

Frau Pinsker took dutiful care of him, but he did not seem able to get back on his feet. After the fever broke, a terrible lassitude settled upon him. He was weak, unable to eat, unwilling to get up to go back to work. He lay on his cot, staring at the ceiling and wondering what had gone wrong. If only he had kept quiet at the meeting—but that hadn't been a real choice. One of Papa's Talmudic quotations was, "Know from whence you came, whither you are going, and before whom you will have to give an account and reckoning." Whatever the consequences to himself, when he had seen so clearly the disaster awaiting his friends, how could he hold his peace?

Pokrovsky was the one who had set this horrifying chain of events in motion. Until he came, the Brodsky men were content with their songs and slogans and discussions about a time when there would be "pure socialism." Lying in his attic room with nothing else to occupy his mind, Chaim wondered about the mysterious Pokrovsky.

Chaim rose from his bed one morning and began rolling his clothes into a bundle. Sometime during the night, perhaps in his sleep, he had made the decision not to go back to the mill. He had taken a wrong turning. He hoped Berel would trust him again.

*V*assily had fallen hopelessly in love with Marta Pirumova. He scarcely knew anymore where he left off and Marta began. Not even as an infant at the breast of his mother had he been so bound to another human being. Serafina's body, after all, had belonged to Vassily's father, her breast lent him for only a few months' time; the whole of Marta's marvelous body was his whenever he wanted it! And Serafina's distracted attention had been parceled out among so many—Ossip, Lyuba, Olga, himself; Marta was single-mindedly for him, his needs, his desires, his every thought supreme.

And she was lovely! When they promenaded along the Kurfürstendamm and Unter den Linden, people—men and women both!—turned to stare after her. Always she seemed unaware of this attention, her eyes only for him, responsive only to him!

Lying in bed after making love, they would talk. Vassily had few secrets from her. She knew that he was not "Vassily Golovine," the name he used in Berlin, nor yet "Vassily Chernov" from Minsk. He had gradually told her the sad history of his peasant family, dead because of the indifference of the aristocratic landowner and, more especially, because his steward was cruel. That selfsame steward who had maimed the father had exploited the son, he said. "How that bastard congratulated himself for 'educating' me and putting me to work!" Vassily told Marta. "He acted as though he had done something wonderful! Wonderful? He got a lot of work out of me for cheap wages, and he could always trot me out to show his friends his tame peasant!"

"I know how that must have hurt you," Marta commiserated, gently touching his torn earlobe with her lips.

Vassily had not even held back from her the circumstances of his escape from Spokoinaya Zemlya with the countess's necklaces and tiara. "The bitch had so many jewels," he told her, "she probably hasn't yet missed what I took!"

"It was only what they owed you," Marta had said.

In her turn, Marta told him about her stultifying middle-class family, her father who was a merchant in furs, her mother, who felt she had married beneath her because *her* father was a university professor, her older brother, who was trained to the law and lived a stuffy life with a stuffy wife and two stuffy children, and her two little sisters, who showed signs of becoming as snobbish as their mother. She herself had been lucky to find out who she really was before it was too late to escape.

"Tell me about that," Vassily said. His head rested comfortably on her belly, and she lit a brown *papiros* and put it between his lips before she replied.

"It is not a very entertaining story," she sighed. "I was such an ugly duckling when I went to study at Kazan University. I was fat—"

"That's not possible!"

She smiled. "And pimply, and my mother made me wear these terrible dark dresses with starched petticoats—and high-laced boots!"

"I can't imagine it."

"I was a terribly earnest and serious student, and so it was only natural that I should join the Marxist circle. We looked on Plekhanov as our prophet and took Mikhailovsky's *Russian Wealth* as our bible! The people in my study group opened my eyes. I began for the first time to look around me. We talked a lot about the poor, downtrodden peasants and factory workers, but, truthfully, I didn't know any of those kind of people, so it was all theoretical, don't you see?"

Absently Vassily stroked her thigh.

"But I got to thinking about the servants we had at home, how they worked seven days a week and were supposed to always be there for us, even in the middle of the night, just in case one of us might want anything! And I thought about Sonia, the little chambermaid—younger than me, she was— who got pregnant and Mama put her out of the house without a thought about whether she had money and a place to go. And Vladimir, the coachman, who couldn't drive anymore because he got old and had cataracts— what happened to him when Papa replaced him with a younger man? I had never given it a thought! I could go on and on, but you see where I'm leading."

"So you opened your eyes and saw that there was injustice in the world, and that's how you became a revolutionary?" Vassily said with an edge of irony.

"Something like that." She moved slightly to adjust to a more comfortable position. "Actually, I was greatly influenced by the leader of our circle. His name was Julius Ehrenthal."

"Sounds like a Jew!" Vassily said.

"Hmn."

"And because you discovered the revolution, you emerged from your cocoon, becoming the beautiful butterfly you are? I don't see the connection."

"No, *lubymiaya*, not because I discovered the revolution. Because I discovered love."

"Who was it?" Vassily asked, frowning.

"What does it matter? It was long ago."

Because Vassily cared so deeply for Marta, he could not bear to think of her with another man, even one from the time before they knew each other. He tortured himself with thoughts of this first love of hers. He supposed it had been the Jew Ehrenthal, but since she refused to answer questions, he could never be sure. He knew he should let the subject drop, but he could not seem to do so. He worried it like a dog with a bone.

"If you carry on like this," she told him, "I will never tell you anything again!" She was angry.

"Forgive me," Vassily said. If she should ever become so angry that she would leave him, how would he live?

*T*he little Berlin colony of fugitive Russians were greatly heartened when they received news that Lenin had been released from his Siberian detention. Deported from Russia, he and his wife had joined fellow rebels, Plekhanov, Zasulich, Axelrod, Trotsky, and Martov, in Geneva, from there to plot the further course of revolution.

Vassily was jubilant. "We'll be going home soon, Marta! You don't know how I hate this dreary city and all these dull fat Germans!"

Marta's eyes filled with tears. "Until now I scarcely dared think of home! Do you remember how beautiful the blossoms are in the spring, Vassily? Like soft warm snowflakes floating into the canals—"

"Marta! Before we go back, let's get married!" He put his arms about her waist, drawing her to him.

At the word "married" Marta pulled back, her eyes clouding and her mouth trembling a little.

"What is it? Marta, what did I say wrong?"

"I don't want to get married!"

Vassily's expression turned dark. Thick black eyebrows drew together over narrowed eyes and his skin mottled in angry red patches. "I see," he said, turning away from her.

Bitterly Vassily realized that he should have known how it would be! Marta came from a family of great wealth; anyone could see that from her manners and her clothes and the way checks regularly appeared for her.

Perhaps at some level she believed that she meant it when she talked about a "classless" society, but when faced with marrying into the peasantry, her true feelings had surfaced and her fine liberal words were revealed as empty, not applicable to someone like Marta Nicolaevna Pirumova!

Marta had recovered herself. "It's only—oh, my dear, you know how I feel about you. I would lay down my life—anything—but *marriage*? It violates everything I believe in! Why can't we go on as we are? Why must we complicate things with meaningless legal ties?"

A strain of peasant paranoia ran deep in Vassily's blood. Watching closely for her reaction, he said, "You think I'm not good enough for you!"

She turned white, then as suddenly the color flamed in her cheeks. He did not know how to interpret her stricken look. Did it mean that he had caught her? Or was it that she was distraught because he had wronged her?

"If that's what you think of me, Vassily, then you are *not* good enough for me!" She turned on her heel and walked out of the room, slamming the door behind her.

In that instant Vassily knew only that he needed her, wanted her. He ran after her, catching her before she reached the bottom of the stairs. "Don't go, Marta! Don't go! We don't have to marry. Marriage is bourgeois. You're right. Only don't leave me!" He held out his arms to her.

He was babbling, but Marta seemed scarcely aware. Weeping and smiling at the same time, she buried her face in his shoulder.

Chapter 30

"What about us?" Chaim asked Berel indignantly. Perhaps following him to Odessa had been a mistake.

"Us? Where was 'us,' Chaim, when I begged you to leave Kiev with me?" Berel asked hotly.

"Yes." Chaim reddened. "I feel bad about that. I wish there were some way I could change it." What a mistake he had made! And he had not even been fully aware of what he had lost until Elihu Goltz had deserted him.

Berel had shamed him. All during the tiring and lonely seven-week journey—from Kiev to Kirovograd in the wagon of the peddler Gershon Wolf, from Kirovograd to Pomoshnaya with another peddler, by foot from Pomoshnaya to Nikolayev, and finally from Nikolayev to Odessa in a peasant cart loaded with manure—Chaim had looked forward to a reunion with Berel in which everything would return to the way it had been. And now, on only his third day in Odessa, Berel was reminding him of the past, and spoiling the future.

On this first *shabbes* afternoon in Odessa, Berel had taken Chaim to show him the sights. They had climbed to the top of a tall hill from which the city descended in terraces to the shores of the Black Sea. From this prominence they could look down on the broad boulevards radiating like spokes from the center of the city. Berel had proudly pointed out some of the landmarks—the astronomical observatory, the opera house, the government center. Looking down on it, the city seemed orderly and sparkling clean, the regular grid of its precisely patterned streets patchworked with the green squares and rectangles of numerous parks.

Chaim's eyes had kept going back to the harbor, huge after the river ports they had seen, and with many large ships riding at anchor. "Just look at the size of that harbor!" he'd exclaimed.

Berel was less interested than Chaim. "Yes, Odessa is the center for the export of grain." He made a half turn from the direction of the harbor, lifting his arm toward an impressively large building with pillars and colonnades. "That's the Central Synagogue. Did you know that after Warsaw, Odessa is the largest Jewish community in Russia?"

Chaim refused to be distracted. "See those ships in the harbor? That's from where we'll leave for America!"

"I don't know that I'll be going to America, Chaim," Berel said after a pause. "I am happy here."

"What's the matter with you, Berel!" Chaim said, disconcerted. After the police *oblavy* in Kiev and then the threatened violence at Brodsky's mill, his desire to escape Russia had taken on real meaning. As usual, he had presumed that Berel felt the same. "Don't you remember how we planned to go to New York to make our fortunes?"

"I remember what *you* planned," Berel said, smiling over Chaim's fantasies of buying his parents a chicken farm in New York City and arranging splendid marriages for his sisters and a university career for Simcha. "But you see, Chaim, your dreams are not mine."

"So what do you want?" Chaim asked.

Berel hesitated. While Chaim had been spinning tales of wealth, Berel, ashamed that he wanted so little from life, had never shared his own dreams. Prodded now by Chaim, he said slowly, "All I want is to belong somewhere, to have a wife who loves me and children to fill my loneliness."

That was when Berel told Chaim that the love of his life was his landlady. "Soreh Glanzer means everything to me," he said, feeling inadequate to do justice to her perfection, failing even to convey the depth of his feeling.

"You haven't—you haven't asked her to marry you, have you, Berel?"

Berel dolefully shook his head. "How can I? She is rich, and who am I to look so high for a wife? Still, I will never leave her!"

Chaim stared at his friend. In the two and a half years since leaving home, Berel had grown tall and filled out. Chaim suspected that it was from all the good cooking urged on him by Frau Pinsker and now by the new landlady. He had the sour thought that women find skinny men an affront and a challenge. Surveying Berel with a critical eye, Chaim thought there was no doubt that Berel was looking good these days. He could see why women might find him attractive. His skin was clear and healthy, his beard had grown in luxuriantly, and even his flyaway hair had surrendered to a modicum of control. When Zipporeh Pinsker was so besotted in Kiev, it should have given Chaim an inkling of how Berel had matured, but in Kiev Chaim had had other things on his mind, and anyway, poor Zipporeh Pinsker would have thrown herself at the feet of any kindly stranger. This was a different thing from Zipporeh. This was an older, more serious Berel, and he was telling Chaim that his heart had been captured. Zipporeh had never threatened their relationship; the new woman might.

There were other uncomfortable things already apparent to Chaim. Arriving in Odessa, Chaim found that his and Berel's positions had reversed. It was Berel who had the money, Berel who knew the city, Berel who led the way. By then Berel had been in Odessa for some eight months, had regular work as a cutter in a shirtwaist factory, had made friends, and had established himself in a pleasant boardinghouse on Yekatarinovskaya Street. Chaim, on the other hand, had arrived practically destitute. Always careless with money, he had saved little before he fled Kiev without collecting his last wages from Brodsky's mill. When he arrived on Berel's doorstep, it was with the palm of his hand outstretched, so to speak. This was an adjustment that would take some getting used to.

Let down and depressed after this conversation, Chaim and Berel returned to the boardinghouse. Upon Berel's insistence, Chaim had moved in to share Berel's room. "After all," Berel had said, "it will cut my rent in half."

"Not if I can't pay anything!" Chaim had pointed out.

"You'll find a job. Odessa's not Kiev."

S oreh Glanzer ran a superb boardinghouse. The rooms sparkled from care, the meals were wholesome, and the tenants indulged. Soreh was a woman of thirty-three years, a widow for ten of them. Her husband had been a house painter who had fallen from a scaffolding and broken his neck. Having been left a little money, Soreh Glanzer had thoughtfully considered her choices, brushed aside several suitors, and decided to solve two problems at once by investing in the large house on Yekatarinovskaya Street; owning a boardinghouse not only permitted her to make a living but at the same time provided her with a ready-made family. Soreh had a gift for the business. She was a cheerful energetic woman who lavished on her boarders all the care and interest that she would have devoted to children had she been so blessed. Berel Levy, orphaned at the age of nine, was a natural recipient of her bountiful affection.

Soon Berel was spending his evenings in the cozy parlor, sitting companionably with his pleasant landlady, reading aloud to her from the Yiddish newspaper while she mended or crocheted. The elderly Widow Beilson usually came down from her room to join them for an hour or so before retiring for the night, and sometimes Zusya Abramowitz, the other boarder, if he had nothing better to do. Even after he moved in with Berel, Chaim never became a regular in the parlor, although it was not from any dislike he felt for Soreh. What was not to like when she was a neat, smiling woman whose round, open face and soft brown eyes reminded him of his sister Chaya Leya? The evenings were just too staid, too settled for a man almost twenty-one!

"You should get out more," he told Berel. "Meet girls. Get some experience with women before you settle down. I can't see why you want to spend all your time keeping Soreh Glanzer company. You said yourself, there's no future in it!"

Berel brushed aside Chaim's advice. He was content, he said, and Chaim should give him no further thought because he was perfectly happy to stay at home.

As Berel had said, Odessa was not Kiev. In a bustling commercial city where 140,000 Jews thrived, it was no problem for Chaim to find work. Within a week he had been employed by a large clothing store. The work was ridiculously easy after the sugar mill and the pay princely by Brodsky standards. Chaim was happy with his job; being a tailor was in his blood.

Chaim was making friends, but cautiously, having learned a lesson from Kiev. When Nathan Boersky, the other tailor at Melnikoff's, invited him to join the local Bund, he declined, bitterly reflecting that politics and friendship do not mix. Even more to the point, he distrusted the stirring speeches that he now knew were capable of evoking dark and ugly emotions. Chaim's caution was validated when a month later he saw in a newspaper the account of a trial that had just concluded in Kiev. There had been a consiracy, the newspaper reported, to burn down the Brodsky Sugar Mill. A trap had been laid, and the conspirators had been brought to trial and convicted. An agent provocateur for the police known to the conspirators as Stepan Pokrovsky, not his real name, had testified at the trials. All had been convicted and sent to labor camps. A leader of the conspiracy, one Elihu Goltz, had been sentenced to twenty-five years exile in Siberia.

Chaim was shaken by the news. Goltz! Goltz! Why didn't you listen to me! he thought. Twenty-five years! Men died of Siberian hardships before five were out! Thank God, he told himself, it wasn't *me*! The thought shamed him.

Chaim was depressed for a long time. To cheer him up, Soreh's neighbors, Judah and Feyga Kaestler, took him to a meeting of the Yiddish Lit-

erary Society of Odessa. Chaim was not a reader, but then the society did
not have all that much to do with books. Society meetings, as Judah Kaestler
had assured him, were a place to meet young females of liberated thought
who were unmarried *and* unchaperoned. Club functions included picnics and
bathing parties on the Black Sea and excursions to museums and parks. It
suited Chaim perfectly.

There was one young woman in particular who claimed Chaim's interest, Emma Dubrovnitz, whose good looks were enhanced by the glamour
of her being an actress in the Yiddish Theater—minor, it is true, but an
actress nonetheless. After Chaim met her, he never missed a meeting of the
literary society or a play in which Emma was performing. Sometimes she
even let him walk her home after a rehearsal or a performance. Emma was
a free spirit as well as a beautiful woman. She was fervently for destroying
class barriers and dramatic when she talked of the plight of impoverished
masses enslaved through economic persecution. Did Chaim know that men
and women were forced to work in sweatshops for wages so small they could
not feed their children? Why, children sometimes starved in the streets! Emma's little nose quivered and her cheeks turned pink at the thought. "I say
death to the bosses! I say let the revolution come!"

Chaim laid a cautionary finger across Emma's adorable little mouth
and looked nervously around him.

Emma tossed her curls. "I'm not afraid of *them*! Let them do their
worst! I will never keep quiet as long as I am oppressed!"

Oppressed? It was not until Chaim knew Emma much better that he
learned that her father was a banker, and she had known neither want nor
discrimination in her entire life. No wonder she was unafraid!

Chaim liked it better when Emma talked about sexual equality and the
right of women to enjoy the same freedom of expression as men, very heady
ideas indeed! But it confused him to find that when he tried to kiss her at
the door to her family's apartment, she was insulted and indignant. Perhaps
her parents had different ideas.

Chaim adored Emma for her pert little nose, her face that was shaped
like a heart, and her eyes the color of violets. He was not the only young
man so bewitched. When he waited for Emma at the stage door, he could
be certain that one or two of the other young men were also there hoping
for a nod or a favor from her. He quickly learned that if he had a bouquet
of flowers or a little gift in his hand, he was more likely to be accorded the
privilege of Emma's company for a light supper in one of the cafés near the
theater.

"Emma, Emma, why won't you at least let me hold your hand?" a
desperate Chaim asked after he had known her for some time.

"I don't want you to get ideas," she said, giving him an enchanting
sideways glance from beneath sweeping lashes.

"But I love you!" Chaim pleaded.

Emma had a tinkling laugh that descended the scale like tiny bells. "Oh, I know what you men are like. You say you love me today, yesterday it was someone else, tomorrow another girl! How can I believe you?"

Chaim would have fallen to his knees if they had not been walking on the public esplanade that edged the sea. "If I ask you to marry me, will you believe me then?"

Emma was horrified. "Oh, Chaim! My father would never agree to my marrying a tailor!"

Still, she teased and she tantalized, held out hope and then withdrew it, let him kiss her and then would not see him for a month. Chaim was out of his mind with desire. He tried to forget her by going with other young women, Raiza Schwartz and Esther Chernin from the book club, and Feyga Katz's cousin, Etke Bloom. But Emma had merely to beckon him with a bashful glance from her violet eyes and all other women were forgotten in an instant.

He tried to talk to Berel about his problems with Emma, but Berel was no help at all. These days he behaved like an idiot, grinning all the time with no apparent cause. It should not have come as a surprise, then, when one night Berel confessed that he and the Widow Glanzer planned to marry. For Chaim it was an unpleasant shock.

Chaim's face suffused with color and then paled as he stared dumbfounded at Berel. "Marry Frau Glanzer!" he exclaimed. "How can you think of it! She's years and years older than you, Berel!"

"She's thirteen years older than me, as a matter of fact," Berel said with equanimity.

"But why? Why should you do such a thing?" Chaim stuttered, feeling a sudden anger well up in him. "Is it that she makes a good home, is that it? She's sort of like a mother to you?"

Berel shook his head, smiling. "I know it's hard for you to understand. At first it was hard for me, too, to believe that a woman like Soreh could love me! When I think now that I might never have spoken if she hadn't encouraged me!"

"You mean, she actually asked you?"

Berel nodded happily. "My Soreh's a remarkable woman!"

Chaim was stunned. He needed time to think this through. Finally he said, "I guess I've left you alone a lot. You're lonely! I'll spend more time with you. You are my dearest friend!"

Berel answered, "You are my brother, Chaim, but I have not been lonely."

"I know then!" Chaim shouted in exasperation. "I know what you're up to, Berel Levy, and it doesn't do you credit! You are marrying her for her money!"

"No," Berel said quietly, and his voice was surely deeper, stronger, and more confident than it had been before. "I love her. We love each other. We want to be together all the rest of our lives. We are going to be married."

Chaim did not accept Berel's marriage plans with good grace. Not that Berel and Soreh Glanzer, wrapped in quiet joy, took any notice of his disapproval. They had decided to be married in late September, after Yom Kippur. Following the wedding, which would be simple as befitted the circumstances of a widowed woman marrying a man with no family, they would go to a nearby seaside resort to be alone for three days. It was arranged that Feyga Katz would come to cook and clean for the boarders, and Chaim would look after things in general. On their return, Berel would move into Soreh Glanzer's bedroom. Only then she wouldn't be Soreh Glanzer, she would be Soreh Levy, Berel's Soreh.

Chaim tried to write a cheerful letter to his parents, giving them the news, but all he managed was a desolate little note: *My dear Mammeh and Papa, Berel has had the good fortune to talk our rich landlady into marrying him though they come each from a different life. It is a winter and spring marriage, as the Widow Glanzer is well past thirty years. I hope they can be happy together.*

He did not hope so at all. But Chaim's anger and hurt could not diminish the gaiety of the wedding celebration. Even Chaim had to admit that Soreh and Berel made a handsome couple. Soreh was plumply pretty in her new blue dress with flounces and a lace fichu, and her bosom was provocatively soft and full with a gold watch swinging gently upon it. With her shiny dark hair piled high and her cheeks pink with excitement, she seemed radiantly youthful clinging to the arm of her tall bridegroom. Berel's eyes never left her, and the incandescence of his gaze lit the whole room.

Chaim could not shake off his loneliness. Berel, always called *shlimazel*, now had a bride and love, and he, Chaim—well, nothing had gone right for him, not with Nadja, nor Chava, and certainly not with Emma. Who would ever have guessed that Berel would be the first to marry! Now Berel was lost to him, Soreh Glanzer forever standing between them. It was not fair!

Berel was putting Soreh's shawl around her shoulders. They were married only two hours and already there was something possessive about the way Berel was leading Soreh toward the door, shaking hands with the guests.

Coming to Chaim, Berel released Soreh's arm and embraced Chaim. "My friend!" he said. "I have so much to thank you for, even for bringing me from Polotsk to Soreh. Nothing will ever change the love I feel for you."

Soreh held out her hand to Chaim. "You will always be Berel's brother, Chaim, and mine, too, if you will allow it."

Chaim mumbled something and hastily kissed the bride's cheek, touched hands with the groom. "Go with happiness," he said over an agonizing lump in his throat.

When the newlyweds had departed, Chaim fled the festive house still overflowing with neighbors and friends. Let the other guests finish the brandy, the appetizers, and the honey cake laid out in abundance. After all, why shouldn't *they* be merry? What had *they* lost when Berel married Soreh Glanzer?

Chaim went first to the theater to see if he might escort Emma home. She had already left. One of the stagehands told him Emma had gone off in a carriage with a rich young gentleman. The faithlessness of those he gave his heart to was almost more than he could bear.

Perhaps he would find someone he knew in the popular little café where their crowd often gathered to drink small cups of thick sweet Turkish coffee. Emma and her "friend" might even now be sitting there at a table, and he could let her know that he was hurt by her insensitivity on this of all nights!

Chaim made his way to the Café Constantinople, adjusting his face to the sneer he would turn on Emma Dubrovnitz if she should be there. At the café, though, the only familiar person was an inconsequential pasty-faced engineer he knew from the literary society. In his loneliness, Chaim sat down at the table with this nebbish, and ordered a schnapps. Some company was better than no company, he supposed. The two of them had a somewhat desultory conversation, Shepsel recounting a long, involved story about a misunderstanding he had had with the superintendent of his factory. Chaim did not listen, but it was enough for Shepsel that Chaim nodded once in a while. At last Chaim rose, disappointed that no other friend had arrived; it was as though with Berel's defection, everyone else for whom he felt something had also dropped from the face of the earth. Nebbish, still not done with reciting the litany of his misfortunes, was disappointed when Chaim left.

In the next two hours Chaim stopped in several more cafés, sipping schnapps or vodka as he went. He saw no one whom he knew. It was almost midnight when, without quite knowing how he had come there, he found himself on the waterfront. Slightly unsteady on his feet, Chaim groped his way along the uneven street, keeping a supporting hand on the rough fronts of the buildings. In what direction, he wondered, was the Widow Glanzer's place?

Fog had collected off the water, obscuring the ships anchored in the harbor. The lanterns on the pier produced wavering halos of light without providing much illumination. Foghorns out at sea made a mournful noise that prickled the back of Chaim's neck. It was cold, and dimly he realized that he had left the house without a coat.

He looked around him. Streets, little more than alleyways, threaded their way in a confusing maze away from the docks. He was not familiar with this part of the city. People had always told him to keep away from the waterfront because the men on the docks were rough and liked trouble. He was beginning to feel just the merest twinge of uncertainty. He closed his eyes, trying to picture the layout of the city, to get his bearings. Muzzy-headed as he was, it was hopeless.

The fog was dense and becoming more so by the moment. Chaim squinted, trying to see more clearly through the mist. It seemed to him that there were shapes within the fog's shifting layers, shapes that moved—were, in fact, moving toward him! He stood still, waiting to see what would emerge. He was not exactly afraid, more bemused, as if he were watching himself in a dream. Two or three silent men came out of the fog bank. As their hands reached out and took hold of his arms, Chaim did not struggle. He had had too much to drink. It was a relief in a way to resign responsibility for himself. With a sigh, he let his body go limp and knew only that he was being half dragged and half carried somewhere. But he did not care. He just did not care at all.

Chapter 31

There was never a time when Chaya Leya had not loved Herschel Rosen. His image was inextricably woven into the tapestry of her memories—his face, radiating light and warmth whenever as a child she hovered at his elbow, his clever fingers fashioning scraps of fabric into dolls and stringing empty spools into necklaces that he placed around her neck. Her mother had thought him a surly boy because with Malkeh he was always silent and watchful, but then, Chaya Leya reasoned, a boy made sensitive by years of living on the *tzedokeh* of the community would have been aware that Malkeh had opposed Yoysef's choosing him as his first apprentice. An entirely different aspect of himself, shyly loving, was what Herschel turned toward Yoysef and the Mandelkern children.

Except for Papa, Herschel was the one constant presence in Chaya Leya's life. It was *Bobbeh* Frumma's and Herschel's faces that had hovered over her bed the time she almost died of diphtheria, Herschel as often as *Bobbeh* spooning gruel into her mouth when she was too weak to feed herself. And when Mammeh turned away from her after the twins died, it was Herschel who had comforted her, assuring her that Mammeh's anger had nothing to do with her. In the year of the famine, it was Herschel who had shared his scant portion with her and the other children. "I'm not hungry," he had insisted. But this was not true; Herschel had been starved for all his life.

She had always known he loved her and was waiting for her to grow up to marry her. Ten years older than she, he had a long time to wait. Other young women flirted with him, and Pinchas the Matchmaker once came with a marriage offer, but Herschel only smiled, watching while Chaya Leya outgrew her long braids, developed breasts and a waist, and lost the soft contours of childhood. There was never anyone else for him.

Chaya Leya was sixteen before Herschel held her hand, seventeen before the two of them began slipping away from the house after the evening meal to walk by the river, sometimes putting chaste arms around each other's waists.

Yoysef saw how it was with them sooner than Malkeh did, but then, Chaya Leya did not often occupy Malkeh's thoughts. He was pleased. Herschel could not have been dearer to him if he had been a born son. He had watched Herschel grow from a frightened fourteen-year-old into a sensitive, responsible man and was satisfied with what he saw. Someday Herschel would inherit the business; he could trust Herschel with his daughter as with his shop. It was good.

Herschel needed all the courage he could muster to speak to Chaya Leya's parents. For weeks he rehearsed what he would say. Nights he dreamed the scene and watched dream turn to nightmare as Malkeh ordered him from her house. What chutzpah, after all, for a man with neither parents nor education to ask for the hand of the Mandelkerns' elder daughter!

One soft spring evening Chaya Leya and Herschel walked to Napoleon's Wall. Sitting on the grassy knoll, watching the new moon climb in the sky, Herschel pointed out the constellations. "See," he said, "there is Ursa Major, the Greater Bear, and there's the hunter Orion. And over there is the North Star—you can always use it to find your way home. Beautiful, aren't they?"

"When are you going to speak to Papa and Mammeh?" Chaya Leya asked.

"And that's Ursa Minor—" he continued as though he hadn't heard.

"Herschel, I asked you a question."

"Don't push me! I'll know when the time is right."

"But I want to be married. Then I can be with you all the time," she protested, twining her hands with his.

"We *are* together all the time," Herschel said, "almost as though we are married."

"Almost!" Chaya Leya scoffed. "We have to sneak away to be alone."

"All right, all right!" Herschel sighed, combing his reddish-brown beard with anxious fingers. "I will talk to them—"

"When?"

"Soon."

Chaya Leya's eyes softened. "It's only that I so much want to belong to you," she said shyly. Her fingers followed the line of his jaw, thinking how determined he was except when it came to this.

Herschel groaned. "Chaya Leya, you know they may turn me down!"

"Don't be silly," she said, planting little kisses on his chin, the tip of his nose, his ear, his mouth. "Speak to them tonight!" She interrupted his automatic protest. "All right, Herschel, tomorrow at the latest!"

But there always seemed to be reasons for Herschel to wait. All the excitement of Chaim's betrothal to Chava took precedence. And then *Zeydeh* Avrom's illness. And after that, everyone was upset over the disappearance of Chaim and Berel. There seemed never to be an auspicious time for Herschel to ask for her in marriage.

The delays were making Chaya Leya mutinous. On a morning when her father and the apprentices were still lingering over their morning tea, she slipped into the tailor shop. Herschel, as always, was the first at work.

"I couldn't sleep last night for thinking about you and me," she said despairingly. "Are we ever going to get married?"

"Let's wait until things are more settled," Herschel pleaded.

"Things will never be settled enough for you." Chaya Leya was angry. "Besides, I don't see what difference it makes!"

"Believe me," Herschel said, "it does."

"Sometimes I think it's enough for you to hold hands in the moonlight! Sometimes I think you don't want anything more. Maybe you're not only afraid of Mammeh, you're afraid of me too!"

"You don't know what you're talking about," Herschel protested hotly. He threw the garment he was holding on the floor and grabbed Chaya Leya, kissing her in an entirely new way, passionately and urgently, the way a mature man kisses a grown woman. "Does that feel like I'm afraid of you?"

Chaya Leya gasped. Her breasts seemed to thrust forward of their own accord, and her belly caught fire.

"You'd better go," Herschel said, putting her away from him. "Your father will be here any minute."

She did not argue.

After Chaim's first letter from Kiev assured the family that the boys were safe, there was no longer any excuse for Herschel. Prodded by Chaya Leya, he found Malkeh and Yoysef alone in the front room after supper; Chaya Leya had seen to it that Dvoreh and Simcha were occupied elsewhere. Herschel had dressed in his Sabbath suit for the occasion.

He had prepared a proper speech, rehearsing it with Chaya Leya, but in the end he was so nervous that he blurted out, "I want to marry Chaya Leya!" then stopped in hot confusion.

Yoysef embraced him, smiling broadly. "I thought you would never get around to asking!"

Malkeh hesitated. She and Herschel had gotten off to a bad start with each other, she wasn't entirely sure why. Perhaps Yoysef's exuberant affection for the boy had tapped an unsuspected vein of jealousy within her, but whether it was for her children or for herself, she wasn't sure. She remembered she had been sharp with Yoysef when he first told her about Herschel, asking, "Don't we have children enough, Yoysef, that you must take in yet another?"

"There is room for another," Yoysef had answered mildly.

There had been other apprentices since Herschel—poor little Zelig, Berel, Mordecai, Motka—but Herschel was always different from the rest, always playing a role in the family's life. It was unthinkable that Mordecai or Motka would ever be more than employees in the shop, but Yoysef, over Malkeh's objections, had made Herschel his partner. Now Herschel was to become in fact a member of their family.

Malkeh spoke coolly to Herschel. "Of course, we have seen for a long time how you and Chaya Leya feel about each other. The two of you have chosen to go outside our tradition to decide for yourselves, without a matchmaker, without family discussion, dowry arrangements— So be it! I will not stand in the way of your betrothal. But, Herschel, you are already a man grown, and Chaya Leya is still a child, barely twenty years old. Let the wedding wait for at least a year."

Herschel was so elated that the feared rejection had not materialized that he had gratefully wrung Malkeh's hands and embraced Yoysef. "Thank you, thank you!" he had babbled before rushing out to find Chaya Leya.

She was somewhat less pleased. "A whole year! Why? To get to know each other?" Chaya Leya fumed. "I've known you since I was four!"

"Not that. Because you're too young."

"That's crazy! *She* was *nineteen* when she and Papa married!"

"Let's not start our marriage by making an enemy of your mother," Herschel pleaded. "What does another year matter?"

"Herschel, you are thirty years old already!"

"And I'd wait another thirty years for you."

A wedding date was set for a Sunday Passover the following year. Exciting preparations fully absorbed Chaya Leya and the other women of the family, mitigating her bitterness over the long delay. Still, the weeks and months of waiting seemed long. Of course, being betrothed they could be more open about their feelings for one another. This proved a mixed blessing. Touched hands could set off tremors of desire for which there was no outlet. Herschel was firm. "It will be sweeter for having waited," he assured Chaya Leya.

"Passover is months away!"

"Time passes."

But long before Passover, the recruiters came through Polotsk, and when they left, Herschel was with them.

*A*fter the shock of the raid wore off, the Mandelkerns settled again into a kind of half life, each trying to come to terms with what had happened. The sewing machine wheel turned in the tailor shop, Yoysef instructed Motka and Mordecai with his usual kindness and patience, and attended to his prayers, although with a somberness that was a constant reproach to God.

Chaya Leya seemed dazed. Dvoreh and Simcha tiptoed around her, their quarreling muted by tacit agreement. Quietly Dvoreh assumed more of the responsibilities for the household. Since the night the army had destroyed their peace of mind, she had tried harder, helping with the morning meal and beginning the day's chores before Chaya Leya, who often did not fall asleep before dawn, arose. No one seemed to notice that Dvoreh had abruptly grown up.

After Yevgeny Fedotov returned from his fruitless trip to Moscow, Simcha resumed his lessons. He also was changed, subdued by the sudden inexplicable violence of recent events.

Impatiently one day, Fedotov reproved him. "Semyon, you are not paying attention! How will you learn algebra if you sit staring from the window?"

Gloomily Simcha said, "I won't need algebra to work in Papa's tailor shop and it won't help me if there's a pogrom or when the recruiters come to take me—"

"What's this? What's this?"

"I hate being a Jew! Why couldn't I have been born a Russian like you? What sense is there in learning anything if someday someone is going to take it all away from me?"

"I don't want to hear you talking like that!" Fedotov said fiercely. "We can't always control what happens, but we are in charge of our hearts and minds, and we can resolve to survive!" He took hold of Simcha's shoulders and looked deep and long into his eyes. "You are not going into your father's tailor shop. You are going to the university. For the rest"—he shrugged— "which of us knows our future? Perhaps the time for such bad things is over, or soon will be. You must prepare yourself as if they are, Semyon."

Simcha put his skinny boy's arms around the man's waist. "Oh, *Gospodin!* Why couldn't you have been my father!"

Fedotov pulled the boy's head into his chest and stood there, stroking the fair hair and frowning out the window.

*I*t was during that strange, uncertain period that the Yiddish Women's School graduated its first class—four young girls who had completed a two-year course in reading and writing both Russian and Yiddish, penmanship, the daily prayers, simple sums, geography, and the rudiments of natural science. There was a ceremony, muted, of course, by the catastrophe that had overtaken the community. Nevertheless, the parents of the graduates were bursting with pride, as were Malkeh and the teachers, Hodl and Gittel, when they kissed each of the four on both cheeks before distributing the elaborately scripted certificates of completion. For Malkeh, for a few hours that evening, the burden of a heavy heart was lifted.

*P*assover came and went, and the day arrived when Chaya Leya and Herschel would have stood together under the marriage canopy. Dvoreh woke at dawn to find Chaya Leya's place in the bed empty. White-lipped with anxiety, she hurriedly dressed and went to look for her sister. All the way to the river, Dvoreh was conscious that her mind was repeating "please God, please God, please God" over and over again. She ran and stumbled, picked herself up, ran again. Chaya Leya had not been herself. Throughout the Passover seders she had been wooden, her eyes vacant and her face white and strained. As the wedding date approached, she had been increasingly distraught. Dvoreh suspected that her sister had not slept more than a few hours in all of the past week. Desperate to find her before something bad happened, Dvoreh pushed herself to the limit of her strength. Please God, please God, please God! She didn't know why she was so sure it would be the river.

Chaya Leya, when Dvoreh came upon her, was standing still, looking out over the water. The Dvina was broad here, and deep. The sun's early morning rays were just beginning to reflect on the black waters, tinting them pink and gold. In response to the quickening light, the ducks were beginning to rouse themselves; they quacked lazily, undecided whether to go into the water.

Silently Dvoreh put her arms around her sister and drew her close.

Tears were running down Chaya Leya's face. "Do you know what day it is?" she asked.

Dvoreh nodded.

Chaya Leya said, "Why Herschel? He never hurt a living soul in all his life! Why is God punishing him?"

"Not God, the tsar."

"In just a few hours now the rabbi would have blessed us and made us man and wife."

Dvoreh nodded. "I know."

"They say, *Man tracht unt Gott lacht.* Man plans and God laughs!"

"Chaya Leya, were you going to—if I hadn't come, would you have—"

"Drowned myself?" Chaya Leya smiled wanly through her tears. "Why would I do that when I know he's alive? I don't know why he has not written to me, but believe me, Dvoreh, I would know it if he were dead!"

For a while longer the two young women stood looking out over the river.

"Come home now, Chaya Leya," Dvoreh said.

"Not yet. You go ahead."

Dvoreh looked uncertain.

"Don't be silly! I won't kill myself, I promise! Go on, Dvorehleh, you are shivering."

Turning often to look back at the lonely figure of her sister, Dvoreh slowly made her way home.

*T*hree months after Chaya Leya and Malkeh had roused him in the barn where he and the apprentices slept, Herschel was on his way by troop train to a border post between Siberia and Manchuria, where men were needed to secure the Trans-Siberian Railroad. A year earlier, a Chinese nationalist group, the Boxers, had torn out a large section of track on a new branch line to Port Arthur. The Russians regarded this as an intolerable affront. Port Arthur, recently acquired from the Chinese government, had strategic importance because it was the Russians' only ice-free port on the Pacific. Whatever men and resources it would take to control the Boxers and protect the rail line, the government in St. Petersburg intended to commit them.

Herschel and his companions knew little and cared less about their mission in the Siberian wasteland. They could barely cope with the information that they were to be stationed thousands of versts from home with only a narrow river as barrier between them and Chinese terrorists who waited to kill them.

Traveling in unheated freight cars that had been fitted with bunks, it was a journey of seven weeks from Moscow to Blagoveschensk. Often the train was shunted onto sidings to allow faster trains to pass. Sometimes the troop cars were detached and left sitting for hours or days at some remote station, waiting to be hooked onto another train going in their direction. Luckily, it was not yet winter. Still, the farther east they traveled, the colder were the nights. Men sickened and died and were buried among strangers in hamlets where the train stopped for fuel or water.

After the privations of the train trip, Blagoveschensk Camp looked luxurious to the conscripts. On arrival, they had been vetted and distributed among the various companies to whom the post was home. Herschel was led to a long, low barrack room that smelled of rifle oil, leather, and sweat. Curiously he examined his surroundings. Iron bedsteads, each provided with a thin palliasse and two rough blankets, lined the walls, twenty-four to a room. The only other furniture was a rude table, stools, and most oddly, parallel bars for exercising. On one wall was a rack for rifles, their bayonets fixed, on the other wall portraits of the imperial family. In a corner the company's icon was lit by a red glass lamp that burned constantly.

A red-faced sergeant-major had issued Herschel a winter uniform, a long gray greatcoat, two pair of pants, two shirts, strips of material to bind on the feet in lieu of socks, boots, and a *bashlyk*. Among the new arrivals there had been a lot of laughing barter as articles of clothing were exchanged among them for a better fit. There was a canteen, the sergeant-major told them, where they could purchase other necessities, but the pay they could expect to receive was two rubles, paid every four months.

"Two rubles!" the newcomers grumbled.

"Well, what do you expect?" the noncom said tersely. "You get your clothes, your bed, your food, medical care—do you think that's worth nothing?"

In the next few days Herschel tramped every inch of Blagoveschensk Camp. He found the disciplinary quarters, sick bays, the canteen, chapel, and workshops. In a short time the strangeness of camp life wore off, and the days resolved themselves into a boring routine punctuated by a series of bugle calls—to get out of bed, to muster for roll call, to sit down for meals, to report for drill, to prepare for inspection, to signal free time, and finally for lights-out.

There were perhaps fifty or sixty Jews in the whole of a camp of some fifteen thousand men. For the most part, they knew one another by sight. To discourage friendships, few shared the same barracks. Herschel tolerated the loneliness better than some. There was, after all, some advantage in having been raised by a series of strangers.

It was not until he reached Blagoveschensk that Herschel had the opportunity to write a letter. After that he wrote to Chaya Leya every week. There was never an answer. Weeks passed, then months. Perhaps she had forgotten him, married another? Not possible, not Chaya Leya.

One of the men in his barracks, an ex-student bombmaker whose family had been able to get his exile to the gold fields changed to regular army service, laughed when Herschel complained about receiving no mail.

"You can bet that your letters never got there, and your family don't know where you are!"

"But how could that be? I send them from the camp postal office!"

"Oh, Herschel, Herschel, you've a lot to learn! You give the postal clerk your letter, yes?"

"Yes." Herschel nodded.

"Then he weighs it on a scale, and he tells you how much money you need for stamps."

"Yes."

"And you give him the money and leave, right?"

Herschel was puzzled. "So?"

"So he pockets the stamp money and throws your letter in the fire. We're out on the edge of the world here, Rosen. We left civilization behind when we crossed into Siberia!"

"But—"

"Say that the clerk has a good day and decides to actually post your letter, what makes you think that the censors in Moscow will forward it to your people?"

"So what can I do then to let them know I'm alive?" Herschel was in despair.

The student radical smiled. There was always a solution for every problem, he said. Herschel could bribe someone in the administrative office to give him a sheet of the official stationery used for bereavement letters. The paper and envelopes were identifiable because they were edged in black. No superstitious mail clerk would interfere with such a letter, and the censors would have no reason to open it. God knows they saw enough death notifications from Blagoveschensk to pass still another through without examining it.

"You think it will work?"

"I know a dozen men who have done it already!"

Herschel followed his companion's advice. He had been in Siberia four months and was desperate to get word home.

When the letter arrived in Polotsk, Chaya Leya took one look at the black-edged envelope and dropped to the floor in a dead faint.

*C*haya Leya was just three months past her twenty-second birthday on the morning when, on her way to Herschel, she stood on the crowded platform of Moscow's central railway station. Never before had she been in a building so vast. Its glass-domed ceiling soared high above the jostling crowds and was partially obscured by the steam rising from engines that hissed with a readiness to be off and away.

The terminal was very noisy, and Papa had to raise his voice to make her hear him. "You must get on the train now, little one, if you are to settle yourself for the journey." His arm around her exerted a gentle pressure, propelling her toward the iron steps where the conductor stood waiting to hand her up into the car.

The tears already starting to spill, Chaya Leya hung back, overcome by the enormity of what she was about to do. "Oh, Papa, no—no—" she whispered, clinging to the lapels of his coat.

Yoysef could not hear her for the din, but he could see the anguish in her face, and he wanted to whisk her away from this place. Home. They could board a different train and be home again in just a few days, a letter to Herschel on its way: *Chaya Leya has changed her mind about coming to you.* Everything the same then. All the family except for Chaim together in Polotsk. To clear his head, Yoysef shook it and repeated more firmly, "It's time, my dearest daughter. It's time." Tenderly Yoysef turned the frightened girl to him and kissed her gently on the forehead. "Herschel is a good man or I wouldn't let you go so far."

"I know, Papa, I know," Chaya Leya said.

"So God go with you. If ever you need me—"

"Oh, Papa, I love you so much!"

Wordlessly Yoysef hugged her to him. Girls grew up to leave their fathers for other men. Chaya Leya was grown now. She must go to her man, to Herschel, who also loved her. It was said, Yoysef mused, that God chooses a woman's mate before she is born, the same for the man. That had surely been the case with Chaya Leya and Herschel. Her life and Herschel's had been entwined from the first moment they had looked into each other's eyes. God's will, no doubt about it.

The conductor helped Chaya Leya mount the steep metal stairs, and Yoysef handed up her food basket and the little traveling case that Yevgeny Fedotov had presented to her as a parting gift.

Standing in the tiny vestibule at the end of the railway car, Chaya Leya looked down at her father where he stood beside the tracks. Good-bye, Papa, she thought. Will I ever see you again? Will I come home someday with Herschel and our children to visit you and Mammeh in the little house with the tailor shop in front and the garden behind? Will I know whether Simcha is accepted at the university and when Dvoreh is married? Oh, Papa, do you know how much I care for you all?

The porter touched Chaya Leya's arm, pointing toward the compartment she had been assigned. It would be her home for the first leg of her journey, which would take her as far as Krasnoyarsk in the heart of Siberia, five days' travel if they were lucky and there were no breakdowns in the equipment en route. To reach her final destination, Blagoveschensk and Herschel, would require almost four weeks if all went perfectly on schedule! Three changes of train. A ferry, a barge, and a paddle-wheeler! It was not a journey to be undertaken lightly, and never one for the faint of heart.

Chaya Leya dared not think too much about hardships that lay ahead. She forced herself instead to concentrate upon the journey's end, when she would see Herschel after the longest time they had ever been apart. Would he look different after all that had happened to him? Would they be married the day she arrived? And, frightening thought, would there be difficulties bribing the officers to let him escape? She lightly touched the gold sewn into her corset cover.

Turning her thoughts to the more immediate, she tried to imagine what her travel companions would be like. She was the first passenger to arrive in a sleeping compartment for four. She hoped the others would be pleasant and clean.

As it happened, Chaya Leya's only travel companion when the train pulled away from the Moscow station was a fat, perspiring elderly woman who had been to a family funeral and was now returning home to Omsk. As soon as she heaved herself into the compartment, she simply nodded to Chaya Leya, too breathless yet to speak. Chaya Leya watched her set about her preparations for the journey, drawing a huge goose-down pillow and a travel shawl from her satchel, and bouncing up and down on the plush train seat to find the most comfortable place to settle her bulk. She had countless boxes, packages, and bundles that quite filled all the spare space inside the compartment. It was a good thing that no one else joined them, for surely there would not have been room for two more passengers. When she had finished her arrangements and recovered her breath, she announced that her name was Olga Semyonova Chassky. She was pleasant and courteous but remarked that the funeral festivities of the past week had quite tired her out and she planned to have a long nap.

Chaya Leya peered out the window as the train backed and jerked to an uncertain start. On the platform outside, a few people were still scurrying to find their cars, vendors were holding up newspaper-wrapped packets of piroshki and baskets of little green apples, and family groups were waving and shouting last-minute messages. Yoysef made a lonely figure in the bustle below, standing alone, easy to pick out in the crowd because he stood a full head taller than anyone else. Perhaps Chaya Leya should not have insisted that she say good-bye to Mammeh in Polotsk. It would have been easier for Papa to have had her with him. Selfish! Chaya Leya had always been selfish as far as Papa was concerned, wanting him to herself!

When the train began to move forward, Yoysef ran alongside until the train picked up speed and outdistanced him. The words of encouragement and endearment that he called to her were lost in the noise of the clacking wheels. Pressing her face to the glass, she tried to keep him in sight for as long as possible, determined to imprint his dear features and straight figure forever in her mind's eye. Too soon he dropped behind, grew smaller as the distance increased, and finally faded entirely from view.

Long after there was nothing left to see, Chaya Leya kept her face against the glass. When finally she turned away from the window, she had leaned so hard there were red ridges on her forehead and nose, and her cheeks

were smudged from grit and tears. It did not matter. There was no one to
see her. The widow from Omsk had sunk into a heavy snoring slumber, her
head lolling back on the seat and her legs spraddled before her. The tears
Chaya Leya had not shed in all the weeks of preparation came now in a
great torrent.

Afterward, drained, she drifted, thinking about the events that had led
her to this perilous journey. If things had been different, she would have
lived beside Herschel in a little house close to her parents, he working alongside Papa in the tailor shop, she taking her place as housewife and mother
beside her mother and aunts. In time her children would have rolled and
played on the floor of the tailor shop, the boys eventually apprenticed there
while the girls learned to cook in *Bobbeh* Frumma's kitchen and to read and
figure in Mammeh's school. The chain of generations would have been visible, unbroken. But all that had changed in the space of an hour in the middle
of one dreadful night.

Chaya Leya's dry lips moved. When she was a child, alone and bereft
after the twins died, Papa had taught her a psalm to repeat whenever she
was afraid. She had not thought about it for years. How did it go?

I will lift up mine eyes unto the hills, from whence cometh my help.
My help cometh from the Lord, which made heaven and earth.
He will not suffer thy foot to be moved; he that keepeth thee will not
     slumber.
Behold, he that keepeth Israel shall neither slumber nor sleep.
The Lord is thy keeper; the Lord is thy shade upon thy right hand.
The sun shall not smite thee by day, nor the moon by night.
The Lord shall preserve thee from all evil; he shall preserve thy soul.
The Lord shall preserve thy going out and thy coming in from this time
     forth, and even for evermore.

The journey was truly begun.

Chapter 32

*B*erel was frantic. A thoughtless Chaim might go off for a few
hours without leaving word, but this was different. In Chaim's
room he had found nothing missing, not even a coat. He had talked with
Chaim's acquaintances and with Mr. Melnikoff, who was irate that his
best tailor had skipped work. There was nothing to explain Chaim's disappearance.

Soreh told him, "We cannot bear this burden alone. You must let the parents know."

Berel sighed. "Every day I expect to see him walking through the door with a good reason for being gone."

Soreh took her bridegroom's hand. "It has been a week already."

"How can I give them news like this!"

"How can you not?"

Berel wrote a careful letter to Polotsk, couching his phrases in such a way that Chaim's mother would not be unduly alarmed. Even so, he was greatly relieved when he learned by telegram that Reb Yoysef would arrive as soon as a train could carry him here.

When Yoysef disembarked in Odessa's central railway station, he was red-eyed and sooty from long days and nights sitting up in the train's cheap "hard-class" section. On the platform, he embraced Berel.

"Reb Yoysef," Berel said, taking his things, "you are tired. My wife expects you. We will have a glass of tea, and then you can lie down."

Yoysef shook his head. "Later. I can't rest until we've done what we can to find my son."

Together Yoysef and Berel retraced the ground that Berel had already covered. In the next three days they talked with each guest from the wedding party. When had Chaim left the house? Did he say where he was going? How were his spirits? The answers were vague. Everyone had been drinking schnapps and having a good time. No one recalled Chaim's departure.

They talked with everyone they could think of who might know something. Only the engineer, Shepsel Kaplan, had seen Chaim after he left the house on Yakatarinovskaya Street. The two of them had had a pleasant chat, Shepsel said, nothing appeared out of order with Chaim.

Emma Dubrovnitz was a little self-conscious with Chaim's stern-faced father. With a flutter of coquetry, she mentioned that Chaim was despondent because she would not take his proposal of marriage seriously. "Men," she said, "are such boys! Why, once when I was peeved with him, Chaim threatened to throw himself into the sea!" Then, realizing what an awful possibility she was suggesting, she covered her mouth prettily with one tiny hand.

Yoysef smiled slightly. No danger that Chaim would throw away his life over a silly girl like this, he thought.

On the fourth day there was nothing to do but go to the police station. Yoysef described his son and diffidently asked if perhaps there was an accident report involving someone of his description?

The disinterested policeman flipped through papers on his desk. "No," he said at last, "there are no reports on anyone like that. Probably dead by now. Lots of thieves in a port city, rob a man and throw his body in the water. Sometimes the bodies float to shore, sometimes not."

Yoysef's face went ashen, and he clutched the edge of the desk.

"Or maybe," the policeman continued, "a man runs away with another man's wife, you know? They just disappear—like that!" He snapped
his fingers to indicate how fast, how complete such a disappearance could
be.

Berel shook his head.

"No? Well, it happens more often than you'd think. Or they steal
money from their employer and have to run for it. Did you check that?"

Yoysef had, in fact, talked with the haberdasher Melnikoff. "My son
had no difficulties with his employer," he said quietly.

"Well, then, that's all I can tell you. If his body turns up, we'll let you
know—that is, if we can identify it. Corpses rot quick in this weather."

Yoysef and Berel turned toward the door. There was no help here.

"One other thing," the policeman said almost as an afterthought. "It's
been known to happen that a man will be kidnapped aboard one of those
foreign boats that come into port here." Yoysef's face had brightened before
the policeman added, "Sometimes it's better to be dumped in the ocean than
shanghaied aboard one of those freighters."

"Thank you for your assistance," Yoysef said with what presence he
could muster. Followed by an equally shaken Berel, he stumbled from the
station.

On the last morning, Yoysef went to the offices of the newspaper and
paid for an advertisement offering a reward for information about the whereabouts of one Chaim Mandelkern, white, twenty years old, dark brown eyes,
dark hair, of a tall and husky build, speaks with the accent of the Byelorussian region.

With nothing more to be done, Yoysef spent the rest of the day packing Chaim's belongings so that Soreh could rent the vacant room. Among
Chaim's things was the wobbly-legged calf carved one winter by Yoysef
himself. When he saw it, he put his face in his hands and wept.

What would he tell Malkeh? She had taken the initial news of Chaim's
disappearance badly, standing still as a statue, Berel's letter clutched so tightly
that Yoysef had been almost unable to wrest it from her fingers. The color
and warmth had drained from her so completely that to Yoysef's touch she
felt frighteningly lifeless. She had not cried out or lamented, just drew in
upon herself. It reminded him of the time after the epidemic.

On his return from Odessa—God forgive him—Yoysef lied. Putting on
a cheerful face, he said, "You know how Berel is, a worrier, manufacturing
catastrophe out of nothing before he knows the facts. It turns out that with
Berel married, Chaim decided it was a good time to see something of the
world, so he signed on aboard a big ship, and he's at sea now."

"You *know* that, Yoysef, truly *know* that for a fact?" Malkeh asked
doubtfully.

"Of course I know that!" Yoysef said, blustering.

"Then swear it, Yoysef."

"I swear it on the Book, Malkeh, on the name of the Holy One Him-self." If he had already committed a sin with a lie, could the second sin of bearing false witness matter?

*M*alkeh felt that her family was scattering like straws in a wind-storm: Chaim gone—God alone knew where he might be!—and Chaya Leya en route to Siberia. Who would have dreamed that her children would go so far from home? She had never even been as far away as Vitebsk! The two younger children were still at home, but for how long could she keep them? Dvoreh's was a restless spirit that needed the anchor of a stable marriage. And after Dvoreh? Malkeh sighed, thinking of Simcha. A long time ago Yoysef had predicted that if Simcha were allowed to study with Fedotov it would end with his belonging to neither the Jewish nor the gen-tile world. Now Simcha was fighting his bar mitzvah and insisting on going to the University of St. Petersburg!

Malkeh had lived through the weeks of preparation for Chaya Leya's departure with little show of emotion. She had been practical, packing only the essentials that Chaya Leya would need in her new life, studying the railroad timetables, making lists, sewing gold coins into her daughter's corset. She and Chaya Leya had talked only of necessary things: Should she leave the tall Sabbath candlesticks that had been in Yoysef's family for generations in favor of a newer pair that would more easily fit into a trunk? Would she take two everyday dresses or three? How many shoes or boots were needed for the climate?

She had maintained a brisk, cheerful facade for the whole period of making ready, only to have it crumble as soon as Chaya Leya was actually gone. Malkeh was left with a deep and unremitting ache inside herself. She might busy herself at the school during the day, but at night she paced the house, her steps weighted with sadness for her loss.

Chaya Leya had gone without their ever having talked. There were things a mother should say to a daughter leaving home to be married, and yet Malkeh had held her tongue. She had issued maternal instructions: "See that you sit near an older woman on the train." "Keep your money out of sight" "Ask the conductor to call you when you come to your station." But had she told her daughter what to expect in lying with a man? Had she even wished her happiness? Malkeh could not remember.

What *had* she said in parting? "Never eat gentile meat, it's unclean" and "Don't talk to strangers." Chaya Leya had gone without Malkeh ever having said "I love you." Was that the way a mother should send a daughter across a continent into heaven only knew what kind of danger and hardship?

The time had passed too quickly, Chaya Leya gone while her mother was still trying to decide what to say to her. During the lonely nights when she could not sleep, Malkeh endlessly relived the painful scene between them after Herschel was taken away. Every detail was burned into her memory.

"You don't care whether he lives or dies, do you, Mammeh?" Chaya Leya said in a whisper that tore from her like a scream. "But then, why should you care about him when you find it so hard to care about me!"

"How can you say that?" Malkeh had protested angrily. "You are my child."

Chaya Leya's dark eyes burned in a white, pinched face. "How? Tell me, why don't you, that you cared when I was sick, Mammeh! You can't say it because it's not true! It wouldn't have mattered to you if I had died. If you didn't care then, why should you now?"

Malkeh was silent, unable to find words to describe the enormity of the pain she had suffered when the twins died. Some of the rabbis say that hell is heat and flames, but they are wrong. It's a headlong plunge from bright sunlight into the icy waters of a deep black pool. Chaya Leya would not have understood such a living death, nor how a mother could be sunk in such despair that she could abandon three small children, one of whom was ill almost to the point of death. When she had recovered, Malkeh couldn't explain it herself. In the face of her daughter's present bitterness, she shook her head.

Chaya Leya took her silence for assent. "You never really came back to us, you know," she said, accusing Malkeh. "Ever after, you kept the three of us on the outside of your life. Simcha and the school were enough to satisfy you."

That had not really been so—had it? True, she had thrown herself heart and soul into the Yiddish Women's School—surely that was important!—but even with all that, she had been there for the family, had prepared the meals, baked the bread, made the holidays. Perhaps she *had* pushed too much off on Chaya Leya, taken her—Chaim and Dvoreh also—too much for granted, but didn't they *know* she loved them? Still, she might have told Chaya Leya before she left, *I noticed all that you did. I couldn't have managed without you, thank you.* But she hadn't.

As for Simcha, it was as she had told Yoysef. He was God's special gift to them, the sign of His returning grace. Had it then hurt the others all that much that she had so rejoiced in having him?

If only one could go back, she would at least have tried to make Chaya Leya understand. Now that it was too late, she recognized that what had kept her quiet was her acquiescence in her own guilt.

"Chaya Leya never knew I loved her," Malkeh told Yoysef, bereft.

"She knew," Yoysef answered.

"She didn't even want me to come to Moscow to the train station with her."

Yoysef sighed.

"Yoysef, I am so worried for her."

"Don't worry. She is strong. She is like you."

"Like me?" Malkeh was puzzled. "I don't see it."

"Neither does she, but it's true all the same."

Simcha was twelve that year, preparing for his bar mitzvah in December. Yoysef's determination was all that drove him in the painstaking preparations for the ceremony.

"I will be finished with *cheyder* after my bar mitzvah, Papa?"

"Yes, my son."

"And afterward I will be considered an adult in the community?"

"You know that, Simcha."

"And an adult is responsible for his religious observance, right, Papa?"

"What are you getting at?"

"All right, then!" Simcha said triumphantly. "I shall be bar mitzvah like you and Mammeh want, and then I will be through with all that forever!"

Yoysef laughed. "You are not thinking of converting to another religion, are you, Simcha?"

"No," the boy said seriously. "I don't believe religions help people to be better."

"Well," Yoysef said, "just get through your bar mitzvah, and we can talk about it again."

If Simcha had to be pushed to go to shul, no one had to push him to go to Spokoinaya Zemlya for his lessons with Yevgeny Fedotov. In the stuffy little estate office behind the kitchen, Simcha learned history, mathematics, science, Latin, and Greek.

"Hebrew, too, is a classical language, Semyon, read by scholars," the steward told him one day.

"I hate Hebrew! I hate going to the synagogue! It smells of old men!"

"Don't you want to grow up to be like your father?"

Simcha considered this. The color in his blue eyes darkened as he struggled with some deep-down emotion. After a long moment he said, "I love my father. But I don't want to be like him."

Fedotov looked at him curiously. "He is a good man, Semyon. Why don't you want to be like him?"

"I'd rather be like everyone else!"

The man sighed. "Everyone wants to be like everyone else. A pity!"

Simcha hated having to choose between Papa and *Gospodin* Fedotov. He agreed that Papa was a good man, but the life he lived among the Jews of Polotsk was not the one that Simcha wanted for himself; he saw that life as narrow, circumscribed by family and community expectations, by *mitzvoth* that must be performed—six hundred thirteen of them!—prayers that must be said. Papa's life ignored the sciences, literature, art, mathematics. Papa's world pretended that the fermenting forces of change had nothing to do with the Jews! How could Fedotov ever understand that he could love Papa and hate Papa's life!

The boy was unfazed by the heavy load of studies his tutor laid upon him. Often Yevgeny Sergeivitch stared across the desk at young Semyon, where he bent over his books, brows contracted and underlip caught between his teeth. He had but to squint the tiniest bit to see Malkeh sitting there instead of Semyon, her pale golden hair shining in the light from the lamp, her quick eyes on fire to challenge him.

Semyon would go far, the steward thought. Maybe even take his place alongside Pasteur and Lister. The possibilities—ah, the possibilities! Perhaps one of the first of his "kind" in the Academy of Sciences? Honored by the imperial government with a medal? A chair at some great faculty of medicine?

A pity that the child could not go to proper schools! Someday soon, though, more advanced tutors would have to be found for him if he was to be ready to take his university qualifying examinations in two years.

While Simcha concentrated on a difficult passage of Homeric translation, the steward sat with his eyes closed. His mind wandered. For the most part, he reflected, life had been kind to him. He might have been born a bastard, but the old count had seen to it that he had a position in life higher than he could ever have expected. He had work that he loved, and he had seen the land prosper under his guardianship. He had good friends, like Maria Feodorovna, God bless her, and the Jewish woman Malkeh. And although he had never had children of his own, he had been fortunate to raise two fine "sons," Pyotr Voronov and now Semyon Mandelkern. One of these days, Petya would marry—the ladies in St. Petersburg and Moscow already had their eyes on him—and in time there would be Voronov children for him to grandfather.

It was their custom for Yevgeny Sergeivitch and young Semyon to have tea together in the kitchen when the lessons were done. Maria Feodorovna had not been feeling well for a while, with a digestive problem that did not seem to respond to a dose of salts. She continued, however, to supervise the cooking and baking, more often these days from her chair near the warm oven. Hers was still the finest kitchen this side of St. Petersburg. Watching Simcha dispatch a plateful of nut-encrusted cookies gave her satisfaction. She had had no children of her own, but always she had had her boys to make over—even Andrei when he was small, and then dear Yevgeny, Petya, and now this one.

It was the best time of day for Simcha. He loved being fussed over by Maria Feodorovna, and felt important and grown up when the steward talked to him seriously about events that were happening in the world. One day Fedotov said to the boy, "Semyon, someday you will be a leader of men in a new Russia!"

"But," Simcha answered, "my mother says that Jews don't have a place in Russia."

"Times are changing, Semyon. There will be opportunities for every able person. Even Jews! The Motherland will need leaders."

"My mother says we will go to America."

The steward set down his tea glass so hard that some of the liquid sloshed out. "Nonsense! Pure nonsense! Oh, I don't discount that your mother could do something as crazy as that! She's persistent when she gets something in her head. But to think of leaving now, now when the winds of change are blowing through the land! It would be the height of folly!"

The steward got up from his chair and paced. "My boy, the time is coming when peasants and workers will join hands and rise up to demand a living wage, education, support for when they're too old to work. There's already discussion about these things."

"My mother says that when the revolution comes, there will be fighting and people will die."

"Not all revolution is bloody, Semyon," Fedotov explained patiently. "Responsible gradual change is also a revolution. But for that to happen there must be educated leaders with integrity and commitment, young men of vision!" Fervently he grasped Simcha's hand. "You will be such a leader, Semyon. Yes, you! In the New Russia, the son of a Jewish tailor will lead, and the workers will follow."

"The revolution may not wait for me, Yevgeny Sergeivitch. My mother says—"

The steward stopped him with a black look. "Your mother," he said contemptuously, "is limited by her sex and her race! Listen to me, Semyon! The barriers of class are crumbling. In time it will be ability alone that counts. You must study hard to make yourself ready."

Simcha stared into the older man's fierce eyes and was overcome with excitement. "I will, *Gospodin*!" he cried. "I will be ready when the revolution comes!"

After Simcha was gone, Maria Feodorovna said softly, "How he loves you—"

"Did you say something, Maria Feodorovna?"

"The Jewess's boy. He is so like you in his ways, he might be yours."

"Every day you sound more like one of the ancient ones, a real *babushka*! The tailor is the boy's father."

She said sharply, "I am not addled, Yevgeny Sergeivitch! I merely say that the boy reminds me of you at that age."

The steward was unaccountably pleased. He planted a kiss on her cheek, only then noticing how her flesh had fallen away these last weeks.

Simcha went home to the house behind the shop that day feverish with the desire to lead the peasants to their place in the sun. He was so full of it, he could scarcely stop talking long enough to eat his supper.

Malkeh was troubled by what she heard. After the meal she penned a note to Fedotov, asking for a time when they might meet to discuss Simcha's schoolwork. A week later Malkeh sat opposite him in his office. "I cannot allow you to fill the boy's head with dreams of revolution. Should the officials find out, it will be dangerous for you and far more dangerous for my Simcha. I beg of you, let be!"

"My foolish Malkeh," the steward said, smiling, "you see a policeman behind every bush and tree!"

"I hear things," Malkeh said stubbornly. "There are *Okhrana* agents in Polotsk. It wasn't all that long ago that one of them visited my school!"

"I don't deny that! But I teach no treason. I talk to the boy about the way society grows and develops, the evolution of society through education—"

"It will not happen that way," Malkeh said bitterly. "Not here."

"And why not, pray?"

"Because violence and cruelty are part of the Russian nature."

"*That's* treason, and it's not worthy of your intelligence." The steward's face was stiff with anger.

"You are neither a peasant nor a Jew," Malkeh said evenly. "You cannot know."

"Enough!" he roared. "You are deranged on this subject! I tell you, boys like yours are the future of Russia!"

"Not Simcha," Malkeh said stubbornly, shaking her head. "When he is older, Yoysef and I shall take our children and move to America. In the meanwhile, Yevgeny Sergeivitch, I shall appreciate it if you will confine yourself to teaching Simcha languages and science. If you cannot, I shall forbid him to come here."

"You wouldn't!" the man said, glaring at her.

"Wouldn't I? The rabbi has already talked to Yoysef about how unfitting it is for Simcha to be learning such—such—gentile things. Simcha is growing away from his own people. Yoysef and I are sick about where it will all end!"

"All *right*! All right, then!" Yevgeny Sergeivitch said coldly with withering sarcasm. "Maybe you'd like to sit in the classroom beside the boy so you can judge every word, make sure I'm not leading your son astray?"

"That might be interesting," Malkeh replied, smiling sweetly, "but I really don't have the time."

Fedotov looked into Malkeh's worried eyes and saw that to protect the boy, even if it were from an imaginary danger, she was quite capable of removing him from his tutelage. He nodded. "I will be more careful," he said grudgingly. After all, he thought, he could give Semyon a feel for Rousseau and Locke, Engels, Plekhanov, and Marx in the course of his studies in philosophy and literature.

Fedotov's word was enough to reassure Malkeh. She had enough other things to occupy her mind. No news from either Chaim or Chaya Leya had reached them. Yoysef was reassuring; the Trans-Siberian Railroad, which carried the mails to and from the east, was notably unreliable, subject to unexpected breakdowns of equipment and delays due to weather. As for Chaim, how could he post a letter from the middle of an ocean? If Malkeh noticed that Yoysef stared fixedly over her head when they talked of Chaim, she did not remark on it.

Berel had continued to search for Chaim, following up the leads from the newspaper advertisement, returning weekly to the police station to check on bodies found, questioning anyone who might have had even a casual encounter with him the night he disappeared. A waiter at a bistro near the waterfront thought he might have served a drunken man of Chaim's description, and a whore admitted that she had rifled the pockets of a coatless man when he bought her a vodka. A watchman on the docks had not been sure because of heavy fog that night, but he thought he might have witnessed a shanghaiing. These were the bits and pieces of information that Berel passed on to his friend's father. His report to Yoysef concluded on a note of hope. "These things seem to point to Chaim's being on the waterfront late that night, drunk and possibly helpless. If the watchman truly saw a man being shanghaied aboard one of the ships, that man would surely have been Chaim. Unfortunately the man could not identify the vessel."

It was not much to go on, but Yoysef had to share Berel's hopefulness. There was nothing else, after all.

*I*n December Simcha performed the rituals of bar mitzvah creditably, neither disgracing nor bringing honor to his parents' name. Following the ceremony, Simcha carefully folded his *tallis*, and laid it away in a drawer. He no longer rose at dawn to recite the *shaharit* with his father, nor did he join the men in the synagogue for the evening prayer of *mincha*. He considered his obligation to his parents had been fulfilled.

*D*voreh was past her eighteenth birthday with no wedding in sight. Pinchas the Matchmaker had exhausted all his *khossen* prospects, Dvoreh adamantly rejecting each in turn. Too ugly. Too fat. Too old. Too dumb. She would find her own mate or stay an old maid, she had said, stamping her foot just like the old Dvoreh. "No one has an arranged marriage in 1903!" she told her parents haughtily. Finally Pinchas had thrown up his hands and told Yoysef and Malkeh to call him when Dvoreh grew up a little.

The family gathered in the Mandelkerns' front room to consider this new crisis. Yenta said, "Children don't listen to the parents anymore! Remember how it was with my Moishe? The same exact thing as with Dvoreh! Now that he's so far away in New York, he's sorry that he doesn't have a wife for company!"

The assembled relatives nodded. They certainly remembered how Moishe had resisted Pinchas's efforts to find him a bride.

Yaynkel was for applying a heavy hand. "Just find a good man and tell her this is it! It's not the same with a girl as it was for Moishe!"

Golda smiled. "Is that what you are planning to do with your daughter, Yaynkel? I have a feeling that young Schifre has already chosen." Everyone in Polotsk had observed the shameless way that sixteen-year-old Schifre carried on with Yonah Brailovsky.

Yaynkel colored. "Never mind about Schifre!"

Mammeh Frumma surprised them. "Let Dvoreh be! Her Papa chose for himself, and so shall she!"

Malkeh arched an inquisitive eyebrow. "Does that mean you think Yoysef chose well?"

"I didn't say that!" the old lady snapped.

Yoysef quickly intervened. "Dvoreh might have a better chance of making a good marriage if she were in a bigger city."

"Or," Malkeh added, "she might find a job that she enjoys more than being married."

"Bite your tongue!" Mammeh Frumma said. "But Yoysef's right about one thing, a change from Polotsk won't hurt her any!"

The others were quick to agree. Mammeh Frumma's opinion did still count for something.

There were three distinct possibilities, and in the next few days Malkeh and Yoysef discussed the pros and cons of each of them, with each other, with the others, and finally with Dvoreh herself. They had all agreed that Uncle Zalman in Vitebsk would be happy to have the company of such a lively young woman but, having no wife, could not provide adequate supervision. Yoysef's cousins in Minsk, who owned an inn for Jewish travelers, could always use an extra pair of hands but might be tempted to exploit a dependent relative. The unanimous choice was Riga, where Malkeh's dear friend Eshka, the widow of the cobbler from Disna, was married for a second time to a man named Lazer Berman.

"Eshka and Lazer have married off his two daughters, and last year Eshka's Rochka," Malkeh said judiciously. "They understand what is required."

Yoysef and the others agreed. A letter to feel out the Bermans was posted.

The response was prompt and enthusiastic. The house, Eshka wrote, had been too quiet since her boys had emigrated to Germany and the three girls had settled in homes of their own. Lazer would find Dvoreh a position in a respectable business, and she would see that Dvoreh met suitable companions.

At the prospect of once again losing a child, Yoysef grew silent, working longer hours than usual at his sewing machine, neither laughing nor singing aloud, as was his way. Again Malkeh packed a trunk for a daughter. Considering that there had been no word from Chaya Leya, it was with a sense of doom that Malkeh folded each piece of clothing into Dvoreh's trunk. She had to keep reminding herself that Riga was not Blagoveschensk. Riga was relatively close, a journey of six or seven days of easy travel, and Dvoreh would come home to visit regularly. It was not the same as with Chaya Leya. But then, Dvoreh was not Chaya Leya either. For all of her bravado, Dvoreh was not as confident of her place in the world as Chaya Leya.

Malkeh wept into the trunk she was packing. Now that a tumultuous adolescence had passed, Dvoreh could be an affectionate, even a merry little thing. The house would be less warm and loving without her.

"I only hope, my child," Malkeh said to Dvoreh, "you will not have used up all your laughter by the time you're middle-aged."

"Well, if she has, she just needs to look at her funny face in the mirror, and she'll get some more!" Simcha teased.

Dvoreh scowled at him. "Must you always have something mean to say, Simcha?"

"Must you always act so dumb?" he countered.

Malkeh sighed. These two would never get along. "Enough now!" She turned to Dvoreh. "You don't seem to realize how serious life is."

"And I never shall!" Dvoreh threw her arms around her mother's waist and squeezed. "You shall take care of being serious for the whole family, Mammeh, and if I need some worry, I shall borrow it from you like a cup of sugar for a cake!"

Malkeh shook her head and continued to put things into the trunk. "Be sure to write every week," she said.

"And don't talk to strange men," Dvoreh mimicked.

"And be sure to wear a clean petticoat in case you get run over by a horse and buggy," Simcha laughed.

Dvoreh caught Simcha by the legs and pulled him to the floor. He was almost, but not quite, too big for her to be able to wrestle down. Dvoreh straddled him. "Give up?"

She had not seen her father come in. He grasped her under the arms and pulled her off her brother. "Is this my daughter who is old enough to be independent and work in a dry goods store in Riga?"

"Papa! Papa! I'm so happy!" Dvoreh said, dancing around him.

"Me too!" Simcha said, scrambling to his feet. "I can't wait till you go!"

"I feel as though my life is just beginning!" Dvoreh said. "I know something wonderful is going to happen to me in Riga! I feel it here—" She touched her chest.

"That's heartburn," Simcha said.

"Uncle Yaynkel will be here to get you before first light," Malkeh cautioned. "I think we had all better get some sleep now."

But there was little rest for anyone that night.

"It doesn't get easier," Yoysef said into the darkness of their bedroom.

"No," Malkeh agreed. "A piece of me leaves with each one of them. I feel like a person who's lost an arm or a leg. Part of me is lost but the ache stays forever. I hate it!"

"Yet you agreed with me that Dvoreh should leave."

"It was time. She needs room to grow. But I don't have to like it, Yoysef! Oh, I feel like throwing everything out of the trunk and locking her in her room!"

Yoysef put his arms about Malkeh. "But you won't. The children see you as a rock. Strong like a rock."

"A rock is hard," Malkeh mused. "They think I'm hard."

Yoysef kissed her. "Try to sleep. We will be up early."

"Do you think I'm hard, Yoysef?"

"I think you're strong, and good—and still the most desirable woman in Polotsk!" His arms pulled her against his side. "We started out as two, and then gradually there were six of us, and now one by one the children leave. It's the way of the world. Someday we will again be just two!" His arms tightened about her. "That can be something to look forward to!"

Malkeh laughed, burrowing closer to his side. Yoysef's was still a good body, lean and hard and capable of filling her with excitement.

Yoysef moved carefully so that the bedsprings did not creak, rolling over so that he lay on top of Malkeh, resting his weight on his forearms. He leaned his face down to hers in a kiss that was long and deep.

In the morning Uncle Yaynkel, who was going in his wagon to Riga on business, came early to collect Dvoreh and her trunk. Solemnly the family sat together around the table, not saying anything, their hands reaching out to touch one another. For a change, even Simcha was silent.

Malkeh thought back to the morning that Chaya Leya had left with Yoysef on the train to Moscow. It had been many months ago, and yet it was now. Looking at Dvoreh, Malkeh saw Chaya Leya. Dvoreh had risen from the table and was murmuring her good-byes in her mother's ear, but the words Malkeh heard were "You find it so hard to care about me, don't you, Mammeh? That time I was so sick, it wouldn't have mattered to you if I died."

The tears streamed down Malkeh's face, and she clung to Dvoreh, and for her, Dvoreh was both Dvoreh and Chaya Leya.

"Remember now, don't talk to strangers," Malkeh said through the mist of her tears. "And write. And—" She faltered, clearing her throat. Then looking directly into Dvoreh's clear untroubled blue eyes, she finished, "And always remember, I love you!"

Chapter 33

Long before the train from Moscow reached the end of its five-day run to Krasnoyarsk in Siberia, Chaya Leya had begun to find the confinement of the compartment well-nigh intolerable. The rough ride and the lumpy berth had left her sore and exhausted, and there was not enough water left in the storage tanks to permit her to wash her body free of the grime and soot that had seeped through her clothing and turned her skin gray. The heat was oppressive, the sun shining through the day and scarcely setting for an hour at night. It was summer, the season of the white nights. Because Mammeh had sewn the little bag of gold into the top of Chaya Leya's corset, she dared not take the advice of the widow from Omsk to strip herself of every piece of clothing not absolutely needed for decency. The best she could do was to loosen the lacings.

Close quarters made for instant friendship between the widow and Chaya Leya. The older woman, when she wasn't sleeping, was talking. Chaya Leya welcomed it. Conversation helped keep her mind from the multiple sources of her discomfort.

The widow was a marvelous source of information. She had made her wedding journey from Moscow to her husband's posting in Irkutsk in 1862, well before the railroad existed, traveling across the vast stretches of taiga by horse-drawn *tarantass* on the Great Siberian Post Road, called simply the "Trakt." If Chaya Leya thought the train uncomfortable, said the widow, she should have crossed the Trakt in a *tarantass*! Those crude conveyances, more wagon than carriage, had no springs and left one with new body bruises at the end of every day's journey! In those early days one stopped at post stations for the night, wretched, lice-infested places, and it took two months or better to reach Irkutsk. She would never forget what it was like coming upon the city rising like a mirage in the flat and endless wasteland. Suddenly it was just there, a cosmopolitan city in the most unlikely place in the world.

Irkutsk, the old lady reminisced, might have been any great city except for its contiguity with China. Grand houses in the pale pastel and rococo tradition of Venice and St. Petersburg lined the broad European avenues. But inside, the houses paid homage to the Orient. Draperies of heavy silk, carved teak tables, and graceful ivory screens took precedence over heavy sofas and spindle-legged French commodes.

Olga Semyonova, her eyes shining and her fat chin quivering with emotion, described a banquet held in honor of her husband and herself upon their arrival. The women guests, all of them wives of high government officials, had dressed for the occasion in gorgeous gowns of stiff Oriental brocades, their hair ornamented with enameled combs and strings of jade looped around their necks or set into rings, bracelets, and earrings; fans of painted silk and intricately carved ivory fluttered in plump hands covered with jewels.

"What did you eat? Do you remember?" Chaya Leya asked. Her mind had been very much on food, since she had been forced, because of spoilage, to discard some of the provisions Mammeh had packed.

"Ah, the food!" the widow said. "Will I ever forget? In the dining room a whole special table had been set with *zakuski*, and bottles and bottles of iced vodka, some spiced with lemon, some with pepper, or herbs. We had to try each kind."

"The food?"

"There was fresh caviar and herring fillets, I remember, and cucumbers in brine, smoked sturgeon, cold salmon, and little warm pâtés made of meat and cabbage and fish—too many things! We ate and we drank vodka, and then we ate some more, and the Chinese servants kept pouring the vodka—" The widow's eyes glazed over at the thought of all that food and drink. Recalling herself to the present, she continued. "I thought I would never be able to eat a bite of the supper, but when we sat down at table and I saw that gorgeous repast, my appetite revived. We started with jellied sturgeon, then came a borscht made with cabbage and meat, a *kulibiaki* of some kind of Siberian fish wrapped in a pastry shell, and the *cotelettes de Kiev*—"

"What is that?" Chaya Leya asked, innocent of the great variety of foods the old lady named.

"It is a chicken cutlet, my dear, filled with sweet butter that melts as it bakes; when you cut into the chicken, a golden stream of butter pools on your plate!" She kissed her fingers in fond remembrance. "The finest French wines, of course, a different one with each course, and coffee in little cups with cognac after the dessert."

"And the dessert was—?" Chaya Leya prompted.

"A macédoine of fruit in champagne and—"

A commotion just outside the compartment intruded on the widow's memories. "Whatever is going on out there?" she exclaimed. Her bulk made it difficult for her to raise herself to her feet.

Chaya Leya leapt up. "I'll go see!"

The conductor was holding a young man firmly by the collar of his coat. "If you don't have a soft-class ticket, you can't occupy a compartment! Either get back to third class or at the next station I'll see that you're put off the train!"

Chaya Leya was too mannerly to stare, but she darted one quick, curious glance at the pair. The culprit was young, his yellow hair tousled and his clothes wrinkled as though he had been sleeping in them. Nevertheless, he seemed coolly in control of the situation and unperturbed by the official's threats. When he saw Chaya Leya in the doorway of her compartment, he flashed her a mischievous grin and moved his arm in a salute that had in it a world of impudence. Chaya Leya blushed and slammed the door shut. "It's nothing," she told the Widow Chassky. "Just someone who got into the wrong carriage."

"It happens all the time. People are so pushy these days, always wanting to be where they don't belong!" The widow closed her eyes, and Chaya Leya was afraid that she was falling asleep again, but she was merely gathering energy to continue. "Where was I? Ah, yes, the macédoine of fruits in champagne sauce. As if that weren't enough, there was a tray of napoleons so beautifully decorated that it seemed a sin to put a fork into one!" She sighed appreciatively. "To top everything off, the servants distributed Chinese willow baskets filled with chocolate bonbons for each guest to take home as souvenirs. I have kept mine all these many years. Oh, my dear, they really knew how to entertain in those days! There we were in the heart of Siberia, and the food, the service, and the wine would have honored the table of any prince! And the women, for all the strange mixture of their dress, would not have been out of place at the court of Tsar Alexander himself!"

"It sounds very wonderful!" Chaya Leya exclaimed. "I was afraid that Siberia would be wild and rough and that there would be savage Chinese just waiting to attack white people."

The widow from Omsk put her hand over Chaya Leya's. "In some parts of Siberia that is true," she said cheerfully. When she saw that the girl was disquieted, she added more kindly, "But your husband, I am sure, will take care that you are kept safe and comfortable."

Chaya Leya wondered anew what the future held for her. After a while she resumed the conversation with the old woman. "But you are not going to Irkutsk now?"

The widow sighed heavily. "No. My husband, may he rest in peace, had a difference of opinion with the director of his bureau, and as that kind of thing goes, he was transferred to Omsk. It's an ugly, wretched place, Omsk, but I suppose I will finish out my life, what there is left of it, there."

"But, Madame, why don't you go back to Moscow? You said you have relatives there."

"Oh, I don't have the money to live in Moscow. Such a tiny pension—"

"I'm sorry."

The elderly widow took Chaya Leya's hands, crushing them in her own so that her rings cut into the girl's flesh. "Ah, well," she said, "the woman is always tied to her man's destiny, *nyet*? You yourself have had to leave the comforts of home for some Cossack outpost. It's woman's lot, my dear child. No use railing against it."

When finally they reached Omsk, three days out of Moscow, Chaya Leya pressed her lips to the widow's withered cheek and wept. It was like saying good-bye to *Bobbeh* Frumma all over again.

Except for her grandmother, all the family had been at the Polotsk train station to see her and Papa leave for Moscow. *Bobbeh* Frumma had said a private good-bye to her favorite grandchild. "It is good that you go to Herschel. I have seen how he worships you. A woman's lot in life is hard, she needs that kind of love!" *Bobbeh* Frumma had taken the gold and garnet earrings from her own ears and pressed them into Chaya Leya's hand.

"But they are yours, *Bobbeh*! You always wear them!"

"They were to be yours when I am gone. I want to see how they look in your ears while I live."

The earrings were now locked away in Chaya Leya's small carrying case. She would wear them at her wedding, and it would be as though *Bobbeh* Frumma were there beside her under the *chupa*.

Chaya Leya helped the widow from Omsk carry her parcels and baggage from the train to the platform. When she returned to the now-lonely compartment, she peered from the window, watching the widow's waddling walk as she followed the porter into the station.

Eventually others took the old woman's place in the compartment—a young couple with a baby who boarded in Yekaterinberg and left the train early the next morning in Chelyabinsk, a boorish merchant and his timid wife who were bound, like Chaya Leya, for Krasnoyarsk, a farm woman who rode with them a few hours between two tiny, unnamed settlements, a basket of eggs in her lap.

At the Chelyabinsk station Chaya Leya had her first glimpse of the *ssylno kutorzhniki*, convicts, manacled and under heavy guard; like her, they were on their way to the farthest ends of Siberia. They looked to be in desperate straits, thin, dull-eyed, and exceedingly ragged. Unhappily, the sight of such columns of men became more commonplace the farther the train advanced into Siberia. The *kutorzhniki* were on their way to prison compounds, where many would perish from hard work, starvation, and disease. There were also *ssylno poselentsy*, men hardly in better condition than the convicts but sentenced to forced labor and not prison. The plight of these men sent a shiver up Chaya Leya's spine, and she wondered what these wretched people had done to merit such harsh treatment. When she remarked on this to her compartment mates, the merchant and his wife who had boarded in Chelyabinsk, the man said, "The whole rotten bunch deserves to die or they wouldn't be where they are!"

"But what did they do?"

"Some of them are murderers, but most are traitors, damn their souls!" Leaning forward, he spoke confidentially to Chaya Leya. "The Jews are behind all this radical nonsense, of course."

Feeling cold inside, Chaya Leya turned to look out the window; it would not do to challenge him since they would have to be together for two full days until Krasnoyarsk.

The merchant dozed for a while. Turning from the window, Chaya Leya smiled tentatively at the wife. She glanced apprehensively at her sleeping husband before she nodded shyly.

Toward midday Chaya Leya ate two hard-cooked eggs, a meager slice of stale black bread, and a sour green apple purchased from a vendor at the Chelyabinsk station. Later she would ask the train attendant for a glass of tea and stir into it a delicious spoonful of Mammeh's strawberry preserves. She had found the food for sale at the stations very dear, and she knew she had to be careful to make her money last the trip.

When the unpleasant merchant awoke, he was ready for his meal. Dutifully the wife folded open the little table under the window, covering it with a snowy napkin. Out of her basket she took pickled fish, thin-sliced ham, cheese, a white bread, butter, jam, and a jug filled with kvass.

Her husband, surveying what Chaya Leya thought a veritable feast, turned dark red with fury. "Where's the onion?" he demanded.

The wife's eyes grew large, and tears began to gather in them. "I guess— I forgot the onion."

"You guess, you *guess*! One would think that since your head is so empty of everything else, you'd have room to remember one small thing! Like an onion!"

"I'm sorry, Fedor," she whispered.

"You can't eat 'sorry'! She's sorry! Let me tell you this, Sonia Andreievna! Your piddling dowry isn't enough to make up for your stupidity! Your father came out ahead on this marriage! I wouldn't want to buy something valuable—like a horse—from him! I'd send you back to your family right now, this instant, only they're probably still congratulating themselves on having gotten rid of you!"

When the unfortunate woman began to cry, the merchant made a move as though to strike her, and he might well have done so if Chaya Leya had not half risen from her seat. Lowering his arm, the merchant continued to rail at the hapless woman for her ugliness, her ignorance, her lack of charm, her inadequate dowry.

All of this over an onion? Chaya Leya thought, amazed. She wanted to flee the uncomfortable scene but dared not lest, with her gone, the man begin beating his wife. Instead, she glowered at him.

"What are you looking at?" he snarled.

"A bully," Chaya Leya muttered.

"Keep your eyes to yourself!" The merchant was now more irate at Chaya Leya than at his wife. Since there was little he could do about it, he turned his attention to the food that he wolfed down without offering any to the weeping woman.

Chaya Leya, determined to ignore him, pressed herself close to the window to watch the passing scenery. During the short summer the steppes were alive with wildflowers, buttercups and daisies, orange lilies and Queen Anne's lace, wood violets and forget-me-nots. Often the approach of the train startled a moose or a little herd of deer feeding, and they ran for cover in the larches with a light-footed grace that delighted her. There were birds to watch, swallows and marsh hawks, crows, and Chaya Leya's favorite, the swooping black and white magpies that performed lighthearted acrobatics in sight of the train windows.

For the most part, the plains lay empty of human habitation which made the occasional hamlets look like toys flung down by a willful hand and then forgotten. At this time of year the little weatherbeaten wooden houses, scarcely larger than the sheds back home, seemed rather jaunty with geraniums blooming in the dooryards and tall yellow sunflowers nodding from tiny garden plots. On hearing the whistle of the train, the villagers came from their houses or leaned on their hoes in the fields, waving at the passengers. Obviously the train provided an excitement in lives that were otherwise unremittingly drab and careworn. Most of the settlers had once been deportees, either convicts or forced laborers, but a few were peasants who had taken up the government's offer of cheap land in Siberia. How lonely and uncertain life must be for them, Chaya Leya thought with an involuntary shudder. If Herschel did not make good his escape, was it possible that he might be exiled to one of the northernmost colonies? Might she then become the occupant of a small gray house in the middle of the endless taiga, her children born to isolation and privation like she saw here? She must not think of that, not now.

It was a relief to Chaya Leya when the train came to the end of its run in Krasnoyarsk. It had been an emotionally wearying two days, and she was not sorry to say good-bye to her erstwhile travel companions. At the end she had been almost as much annoyed with the weepy, apologetic wife as with the overbearing husband.

Chaya Leya had expected to transfer without delay to the mail train that would take her on the next stage of her journey, to Irkutsk, only to find to her dismay that there would be an indefinite layover. Train service in Siberia was casual. The railroad officials could not tell the passengers when to expect the mail train, whether in a few hours or in several days. In a disgruntled and straggling body, the continuing passengers made their way to the only hotel in Krasnoyarsk. They had been told that they would know when the mail train came by the noise it made, easily audible from the hotel. No one need go to the station until the whistle blew, three blasts, stop, and a repeat of the pattern until all the travelers were aboard.

Chaya Leya worried about the unexpected expense of a hotel room. She had certainly not counted on renting lodgings! But since there was nothing for it, after she accommodated to the idea she admitted that it felt good to be off the train for a while.

After a long, delicious soak, during which she washed her hair and bathed away the accumulated dirt of five days' train travel, Chaya Leya ventured outside to stretch her legs and see something of the town. Krasnoyarsk, she knew, was a river port, but she had never imagined how crowded, prosperous-looking, and foreign it would be. Here on the broad tide of the Yenisei River, Chaya Leya saw her first junks, and in the street were many exotic peoples, not only the Oriental Tatars whom she was used to seeing from home, but Goldi tribesmen in embroidered tunics, Gilyaks in short belted kimonos, and Manchurian boatmen with queues hanging below their flat straw hats. Siberia, she was beginning to see, was an alien land, becoming more so with every verst she traveled from home, and still she was three or four weeks from Blagoveschensk. How much more different could it come to be?

As she made her way along the street, Chaya Leya recognized a few of the other passengers from the train, strolling as she was in the afternoon sunshine. There was an elderly man and his elegantly coiffed wife who had stepped down from the first-class car and had engaged the largest room in the hotel. They nodded pleasantly to Chaya Leya as they passed. There was a family, mother, father, and two small boys, whom she had noticed boarding at one of the unnamed stations on the taiga; the children, happily released from the confinement of the train, raced about the dock area, threatening to upset the piles of lumber waiting to be loaded onto river boats. And there was the brash yellow-haired man who had been ousted by the conductor from the first-class carriage. Now his bright hair, still damp from his bath, was shining in the sun, and as he passed Chaya Leya, he grinned and tipped

an imaginary hat to her. She blushed to think she had witnessed his humiliation in the train corridor, but he seemed unabashed.

Chaya Leya saw him again when she returned to the hotel. In the tiny
lobby he spoke to her. "Some of us from the train will be having our evening
meal together in the dining room. Would you care to join us?"

It was bold, his speaking to her with no proper introduction, but perhaps it was excusable seeing that they had traveled together halfway across
a continent and were now stranded in the same unfamiliar place. Chaya Leya
smiled and held up her purchases—cheese, bread, and apples.

"I am desolated, Madame," he said. *"Bon appétit!"*

Chaya Leya went to her room, and after a repast that seemed especially
luxurious for being consumed in private, she pulled the curtains against the
eternal sun and lay down in a real bed, sleeping soundly for the first time
since she had left Polotsk.

The Irkutsk mail train was ready to leave twelve hours later. Waiting
to board, there were only a few additions to the group that had disembarked
the day before. More might be picked up at stops along the route, but there
was no way of knowing. Because of the refreshing layover, Chaya Leya was
able to view the ramshackle train with a degree of equanimity if not with
total confidence.

There were only two classes on this train, a "soft," or first-class, car,
and a common-class carriage which was little more than a box car with
wooden seats. On seeing it, Chaya Leya immediately regretted having exchanged her soft-class ticket for cheaper accommodations. She was somewhat
reassured to find that a pleasant gray-haired woman and the respectable young
family she had noticed on the dock the day before would be sitting there
also. The other common-class passengers were a handful of peasants on their
way to take up farmland in the barren north, and a half dozen single men
going east in search of fortune and adventure. The young man who had
spoken to her in the lobby of the hotel was among the latter. He gave Chaya
Leya a companionable smile from across the car.

Soon the train made its lurching start. Like the *tarantass* described by
the widow from Omsk, the seats in common class had no springs, and every
bump in the roadbed was experienced as a jolt to the spine. Soot blew in
through the crevices in the walls, turning everyone a common dun color
that would eventually turn black. At first the little boys thought it a great
rollicking adventure, but eventually even they succumbed to the discomfort
and began to whine and quarrel. The young parents had their hands full.
Chaya Leya turned in her seat and spoke to the mother. "Please do not
think me forward, but perhaps you will have more room if one of your little
boys shares my seat? My name is Chaya Leya Mandelkern."

After a moment's surprise, the mother beamed at her. "And mine's
Tatiana Izwolskaya. I will be most grateful!"

The three-year-old was passed over the seat to Chaya Leya. She drew her shawl from her dressing case and made a little nest for the child on the seat, but he was restless and finally Chaya Leya drew his head down upon her soft lap.

"Close your eyes, and I will tell you a story about the firebird," she said. He happily complied, and Chaya Leya began. "Once long ago, there was a prince—"

After a while the five-year-old was hanging over the seat, listening, as well. Before the end of the story, Chaya Leya's soft voice had lulled both boys into sleep.

While the children slept and their father went to the other end of the car to play dice with some of the men, the women got acquainted, the gray-haired woman, whose name was Anna Blok, moving her seat to join them.

Tatiana confided that her husband had lost his land near Cheryabinsk to the tax collectors and was hoping to make a new start farther east. Everything had been left behind—house, furniture, linens, dishes. All had been seized in payment of taxes in arrears. How cheerful and confident she is in the face of disaster, Chaya Leya thought in amazement. And the pleasant widow, Anna Alexandrovna too. She told them she was traveling to one of the far north penal settlements to care for her son, exiled after distributing pamphlets at his university, and now desperately ill with consumption. From where do such women take their courage? Chaya Leya wondered.

It was five days by mail train to Irkutsk, and a certain camaraderie among the passengers was inevitable. The six single men, all of whom seemed so good-natured and full of fun, were going to Manchuria as laborers on the Trans-Siberian Railway because of the good pay and the appeal of life on the frontier. Chaya Leya could scarcely distinguish one from the other, Gregory from Sasha, Slava from Cyril or Stepan, the one exception, Vladimir, whom they called Valodya. She knew him by his laughing green eyes and snub nose, the tawny hair he pushed impatiently from his forehead, and the balalaika that was forever at his side. He knew a wealth of tunes—folksongs, peasant songs, classical ones—and he constantly made up new ones to amuse both the adults and the restless children.

Sometimes in those five tedious days and sun-bright nights, one or another of the young men would come to sit beside Chaya Leya, and she would share with each a bit of dried fruit or a little jam, all that was left from Mammeh's packet. Each had a life story and reasons for leaving Russia. In turn, Chaya Leya confided that she was going to Blagoveschensk to be married.

The one called Valodya told her he was from Smolensk and traveling to Harbin to work in the offices of the Chinese Eastern Railway, the branch of the Trans-Siberian that ran through Manchuria to Port Arthur. After a while he said, "I guess you've been wondering what all that fuss was about on the train from Moscow?"

Chaya Leya denied her curiosity. "Not at all."

He smiled briefly at her. "I lost my soft-class railroad ticket in a dice game before the train was even out of Yaroslavl station! For a day or two I hid from the conductor wherever there was an empty compartment, but eventually he caught me asleep and bounced me back to hard class!"

"But that's terrible!" Chaya Leya said. "How could you take such a risk with your tickets?"

Valodya sighed heavily. "I couldn't help myself. Gambling is a kind of sickness with me. This is not the first trouble I've been in. This job in Harbin is supposed to give me a fresh start."

Chaya Leya was taken aback. Lamely she said, "I'm sure it will work out for you."

Valodya gave her one of his disarming grins. Picking up his balalaika, he began to play a popular ballad, exaggerating its phrasing to expose its lugubrious sentimentality.

*I*rkutsk was everything the widow from Omsk had said. After traveling across miles and miles of virtually empty taiga, the city seemed to have sprung full-grown from the earth. In Irkutsk the Izwolsky family and the party of peasants, who had kept to themselves during the trip from Krasnoyarsk, transferred to a northern line. Chaya Leya was saddened to lose Tatiana and the little boys; in five days they had become close. The remaining common-class travelers—the six young men, Anna Alexandrovna, and Chaya Leya—were to board still another train traveling east. If anything, this one was more dilapidated than the last, and there was only a single class. The elderly couple, who seemed to have been the only first-class passengers from Krasnoyarsk, were not continuing beyond Irkutsk.

There was but a scant two-hour layover in Irkutsk, and Anna Blok and Chaya Leya elected to spend it shopping for provisions. In the bazaar they found an amazing number of luxuries, both those shipped in from European Russia and those imported from China. Chaya Leya purchased a fresh melon and dried pears and plums, salted fish, lychee nuts, a candy made of sugared coconut strips, and, in a burst of adventuresomeness, a duck that had been preserved in some special Oriental way. She supposed it was very extravagant of her, but remembering the hardships already undergone and those that might yet come, she threw caution to the wind.

The rickety train that carried them to the shores of Lake Baikal took them on a harrowing ride up grades that sometimes seemed almost vertical, across soaring trestles from which one dared not look down, and around hairpin curves. The rugged scenery was very beautiful but also awesome and frightening. At times it felt to Chaya Leya as though the little train, swaying on the very edge of steep cliffs, was barely able to keep its purchase on the track. Anna Alexandrovna came to sit beside her, and periodically they clutched each other in fear. No one was sorry when the tracks ended and they shakily disembarked on the shore of the most magnificent lake they had ever seen.

The Baikal ferry was waiting for them, and they boarded immediately. During the crossing, Chaya Leya leaned against the rail, transported to see the multitudes of colorful fish swimming just below the surface. The lake was clear but appeared turquoise and pale green from the reflection of pine trees on the water. It was cupped between steep granite cliffs rising toward a backdrop of snow-capped mountains. Although it did not look like it, there was apparently enough soil on those forbidding rocks to support the trees and shrubs that grew down to the very edge of the water. The contrast from the hot, steamy train was marked, and Chaya Leya felt cleansed and renewed. This was pristine wilderness, the air crisp and scented with fir, and the clean, cold water rippled and parted in a white furrow to allow the progress of the boat.

The young man Valodya came to stand between Chaya Leya and Anna Alexandrovna at the prow. Now that he stood beside her, Chaya Leya noticed with surprise that he was quite tall and broad through the chest and shoulders. To her earlier inspection, which had admittedly been cursory, he had appeared very young and somewhat girlish because of rather delicate facial features and the way his sun-streaked yellow hair curled around his ears.

"Do you know the legend of Starik Baikal, the Old Man of the Lake?" Valodya asked the women.

"No. Please tell us."

"The Old Man of the Lake once lived at the bottom of these waters, together with his many sons and his one beautiful daughter, Angara. Starik Baikal had picked the River Irkut to be Angara's bridegroom, but like some spirited women she was displeased. She wanted to choose her own husband." Valodya grinned at Chaya Leya before resuming. "Besides, Irkut was thin and lazy, and his complexion was muddy a lot of the time. Secretly Angara yearned to be joined with the turbulent young prince of rivers, Yenisei— you remember we saw *him* at Krasnoyarsk—and a vigorous fellow he was too! Well, Starik Baikal was furious that his daughter defied him, and to teach her a lesson he imprisoned her in the bottom of the lake until she should come to her senses. Angara, though, was as headstrong as her father, and she broke her bonds and fled to her lover, Yenisei, her father in close pursuit. Starik Baikal was a raging torrent, but Angara was a leaping, plunging rapids. She escaped, but only by the merest hairsbreadth! Filled with rage, Baikal hurled a huge boulder to block her passage from the lake. To no avail. The force of Angara's passion was greater than that of her father's wrath. She slipped down a steep gorge and was gone forever."

Valodya pointed to a stony outcropping that broke the surface of the lake some distance away. "You don't believe me? There is the boulder that Starik Baikal threw in Angara's path!"

Chaya Leya stared at the lone rock marring the perfect surface of the water.

"You do believe, don't you," Valodya said, looking at her, "that love conquers all obstacles?"

Chaya Leya smiled. "I certainly hope so," she said.

*T*he pleasant ride across the lake hadn't lasted long enough to suit the passengers. Nonetheless, they were considerably refreshed when they boarded still another train—was it really possible for it to be even dirtier and in worse repair than the last?—for the descent from Baikal to Sretensk. They had traveled barely an hour before the train hit a rock in the roadbed, breaking a crucial axle in the locomotive. While the train crew inspected the damage, the travelers stepped out into a rocky barren landscape; the only shade to shield them from the sun was provided by the shadow of the train. One of the trainmen set out to walk back to Baikal, where he hoped to find a replacement part. The passengers spread shawls and pillows on the ground and prepared to wait. Anna was worried that because of the delay the driver who was to meet her in Tsipikan to take her north might think she was not coming and leave without her.

Everyone was glum. Chaya Leya pulled her basket of food from the train and suggested that they picnic while they were waiting. Initially unenthusiastic, everyone, even the engineer, got into the spirit of the thing when they saw the mouthwatering purchases Anna and Chaya Leya had made in Irkutsk. Everyone contributed something. The man called Slava even had a bottle of champagne, not chilled, of course, but champagne nonetheless. The afternoon passed more pleasantly than any of them could have imagined possible, and toward evening they caught sight of the locomotive that had been sent with the crucial replacement part to fix what had earlier been damaged. Everyone piled back into the train, and before the first star was visible, they were once more on their way.

Anna Alexandrovna was almost a day late at Tsipikan, but the driver, knowing the vagaries of Siberian timetables, was still there, waiting to take her on to the Lena gold fields, where, hopefully, her son still survived. Chaya Leya and Anna Alexandrovna hugged, promising to write, although both knew it was a promise unlikely to be kept. For a while they had been closer than sisters, but in other times there would be little in common between them.

Valodya helped Anna to unload her baggage, and the train delayed its departure while all the passengers climbed down to shake hands and wish her godspeed. When the train pulled out, Anna Alexandrovna was climbing into a *tarantass* amid a profusion of boxes and trunks. Chaya Leya was now the only woman in a train full of rough young Russian men. The general state of weariness was such that none of them gave it a thought.

Because of the delay, they missed their connection in Sretensk and were forced to wait a whole long day and a night for the barge that was to carry them along the shallow, reed-choked tributary that emptied into the head-waters of the Amur River. Arriving at the broad, deep Amur, they would board a proper steamer for the final descent into Blagoveschensk, but in the meantime there was only a shed made of reed mats to shelter them until the next barge came. Waiting, Chaya Leya looked down at herself with disgust. Her clothes, her hair, and her skin were filthy. She had not bathed since Krasnoyarsk, eleven days ago! Her clothes hung loosely on her body; she must have lost weight in the three weeks she had been en route. Looking about her at the others, she saw that they were the same—a school of sooty scarecrows, she thought ruefully.

The barge, when it arrived, was ugly, flat, and snub-nosed, able to feel its way through the sluggish river. By the time it appeared, there were at least a hundred Chinese waiting to board. The captain allowed the seven Caucasians to go first, and they chose places to sit in the shelter of the wheel-house on the broad, open deck. When the chain was lifted for the Chinese to embark, there was a rush of bodies as each person jockeyed for a good spot near the rail. Many had brought bamboo fishing poles that they appar-ently planned to drop over the sides. The noise was ear-splitting, not only the singsong of numerous voices speaking a strange language, but also the wail of babies and the laughter of older children, the squawk of chickens and the squeal of pigs; against this background of raucous hullabaloo, nightin-gales, brought aboard in bamboo cages, trilled. Almost before the barge had left its dock, the Chinese were arranging cooking fires in containers that looked like iron soup kettles. The women were busy with wicked-looking cleavers chopping unrecognizable vegetables into small pieces. Tired as they were, the Europeans feasted their eyes on the colorful scene unfolding around them. A less pleasant sight was a man casually slaughtering a pig by slashing its throat before proceeding to cut the flesh into narrow strips. The blood ran wet and sticky along the deckboards and had a strong, hot smell. Casu-ally he threw the pig's bladder to a small child, who blew in it to make a toy. Chaya Leya hid her face against Valodya's shoulder, afraid she would be sick on the spot.

After awhile delicious odors of cooking meat and steamed vegetables rose from the kettles. Since the Russians had been wasteful of their supplies en route to Sretensk, none had food left for their supper. A Chinese woman shyly offered Chaya Leya a bowlful of rice topped with a pungent meat and vegetable mixture, but she was afraid to eat it lest it be pork. Some of the young men, including the intrepid Valodya, did eat the Chinese food and pronounced it delicious though different. For Chaya Leya, huddled in her corner of the deck, it was a strange, cold, and hungry night.

The next morning they reached the Amur River and caught their first sight of the beautiful, immaculate *Admiral Chikhachev*, which was to take Chaya Leya on the last stage of her journey to join Herschel. The *Admiral Chikhachev* was a roomy paddle-wheeler with real staterooms containing berths with mattresses and basins with running hot water. There was even a dining salon where the tables were covered with white cloths and set with crystal and china. Boarding in the late morning, the weary passengers settled in as the steamer began its slow, majestic progress downriver. They would reach Blagoveschensk on the morning of the fourth day.

Until she looked into a proper mirror, Chaya Leya had not fully re-alized the toll the trip had exacted. Standing stripped before the glass in her stateroom, she shuddered to see how her ribs and hipbones protruded be-neath the skin. Her cheeks were sunken, her eyes encircled with deep shad-ows, and her thick hair was lusterless. Hardly a way to greet a waiting bridegroom, she thought, trying to pinch some color into her cheeks. For-tunately she could look forward to the restorative power of filling meals, three nights in a real bed, and hours in a deck chair in warm sunshine.

The last night aboard the *Admiral Chikhachev* was to be a celebration to mark her arrival at journey's end; the young men would have a few more days' travel ahead to reach Harbin. Chaya Leya had unlocked her trunk for the first time since leaving home. She shook out the wine-colored silk dress that Papa had made for her dowry. Why not! She had survived the dirt, the heat, the interminable days and nights, and tomorrow she would be Her-schel's bride. It was surely an occasion for festivity.

After she had bathed in the hip bath brought to her stateroom by a Chinese manservant, Chaya Leya slipped the glowing dress over her head, glorying in the feel of the silk against her flesh. The color was perfect, en-hancing the natural cream tones of her skin and picking up the reddish highlights in her brown hair. If anything, the weight she had lost in the past weeks only made her waist narrower and showed off an unsuspected elegance in bone structure. Now the finishing touches—the tortoiseshell combs for her hair, small garnet earrings in her ears. There! She pirouetted before the mirror.

When Chaya Leya entered the dining salon, the young men rose to their feet appreciatively. Gregory Bashkin began softly to applaud, and the others took it up, Chaya Leya blushing becomingly. Valodya and Gregory vied to seat her, and it ended with her between the two of them. Chaya Leya was both embarrassed and gratified by her reception. Openly admiring, Valodya lifted her hand to his lips for a moment that was a fraction too long to be merely polite. Magnanimously he ordered Crimean wine for the whole table.

Chaya Leya, a little worried, whispered in his ear, "Can you afford it?"

"Don't worry! I was lucky at cards last night—"

Slava Kirov stood with raised glass. "A toast to the beautiful bride and the fortunate groom! *Is wami peeruyeht druzyah!* Friends are drinking with you!"

The first glass was speedily emptied.

"Thank you, thank you," Chaya Leya said, coloring.

Sasha was next. "*Na slavu!* Honor to you, lady!"

Again the glasses were drained. Valodya ordered another bottle, joking that he must somehow drown his sorrow at losing her. Each of her companions from the train must take turns honoring her with a toast—*six* small glasses of wine! Chaya Leya grew rosy from the compliments and from the wine. Relaxed and smiling, her brown eyes shiny with happiness, she looked her prettiest.

More than the wine, the male admiration was a heady experience for a girl brought up to consider herself plain. Valodya was a different person, tonight, more flirtatious than he had been on the train. He touched her hand where it lay on the tablecloth and whispered in her ear. His eyes grew hot and languorous. Dreamily Chaya Leya allowed herself to succumb to his charm. How masculine he was in his embroidered tunic, the tight breeches clinging to his thighs, his boots shiny with polish. The broad planes and angles of his face were heroic in the candlelight, and his hair and eyes glowed golden.

Later on deck in the soft light of a waning midnight sun, Valodya took up his balalaika and strummed it softly. The others had finally reeled off to bed, and the only other sound was the slap-slap of the paddle wheels in the water.

"Sing me one last song for remembrance, Vladimir Mikhailovitch," Chaya Leya begged.

He smiled, playing broken chords while he thought what it should be. At last he spun a poignant melodic line from the instrument, humming as the beautiful sad tune took shape under his fingers. Chaya Leya knew the words. It was a folksong she'd heard peasants sing many times in the fields outside Polotsk. Often, passing by, she had stopped to listen to them. She joined her pure voice to Valodya's, and the silken sound drifted into the night, down to the lapping river beneath them, and up to meet the red sun.

> *Don't sew for my wedding day*
> *The red sarafan!*
> *Look, Mother, into my face,*
> *Look at my tears!*
> *How can I leave you*
> *For distant lands!*
> *Dearest Mother, believe me,*
> *I don't want to marry.*
>
> *Daughter mine, my darling child,*
> *Will you rather stay unwed?*
> *See how rain, frost, and wind*
> *Drive beauty hence so soon.*
> *You cannot escape happiness,*
> *Nor pain.*
> *Come to my heart, child,*
> *Let us joyfully prepare!*

In a few hours' time, the steamer would reach Blagoveschensk. Herschel would be there on the dock, waiting for her. The Crimean wine made Chaya Leya ache for his dear familiar self. She looked into Valodya's face and saw only Herschel. The wine. Or the accumulated fatigue. The warmth from Valodya's body might have been her beloved's.

Her voice quavering, Chaya Leya sang another chorus.

> *Look into my face,*
> *Look at my tears—*
> *How can I leave you*
> *For far distant lands—*

"Why are you crying?" Valodya asked softly.

"Am I crying?" Chaya Leya said, putting wondering fingers to her wet cheek.

Gently Valodya folded his arms about her.

Chaya Leya pulled away. "I am promised—" she said.

His firm lips tasted of wine. His arms tightened about her.

Chaya Leya shook her head to clear it. This sudden upsurge of feeling was only the residue of a difficult journey that was drawing to an end. Tomorrow another man would hold her in his arms, a man who had shared her life since childhood. The Russian would be on yet another train on his way to Harbin. Only for this one night, in the sun that was rising after its hour of rest, could there be a space that contained the two of them.

> *Look at my tears,*
> *How can I leave you—*

Indeed, Chaya Leya thought, how can I bear it that we will never meet again?

Valodya pulled himself to his feet and raised Chaya Leya to stand beside him. "Will you kiss me good-bye?"

Chaya Leya's arms went round his neck, but Herschel stood between them.

"Ah, well," Valodya said, stooping to plant an affectionate kiss on her mouth. "After all," he said, "this is my only chance. After tomorrow we will never see each other again."

Chapter 34

*U*ncle Yaynkel, having deposited Dvoreh and her trunk at the home of Eshka and Lazar Berman, declined to stay for supper, pleading the need for an early start the next morning. He was eager to be done with avuncular duties; after two and a half days, he was as weary of Dvoreh's chatter as she was of his advice. The good-bye kiss he planted on his niece's forehead was somewhat perfunctory. He could not forgo a final admonishment for Dvoreh to behave herself in Riga. Still, when he had flicked the reins over his horse's back and the wagon had lumbered off, Dvoreh felt a loss. She was eighteen years old, and, for the first time in her life, on her own.

Eshka Berman put a comforting arm around her. "I can't tell you how happy we are to have you. Did your mammeh tell you how we met? It was years and years ago, before any of you children were born, and your mammeh came with your papa to make a new suit for my first husband—may he rest in peace—" Drawing Dvoreh into the house, Eshka's easy voice filled the spaces left vacant by Uncle Yaynkel's departure. "I think you will like your room. It was my daughter Rochka's until she married Velvel and moved away. Let me show you." She led Dvoreh upstairs to a small bedroom that seemed to Dvoreh the epitome of elegance. Used to rooms with narrow windows and walls of chinked logs, Dvoreh thought the pink flowered wallpaper and white window curtains were fit for a Voronov at least! She stood dumbstruck in the doorway for a long moment.

"Is something wrong?" Eshka asked anxiously.

Dvoreh shook her head, too awed to speak. Was all this for her? The carved wooden chest with its marble top? The tall wardrobe for hanging clothes? The brass bedstead with its billowing feather bed the same color as the wallpaper?

Dvoreh thought the Bermans must be very rich indeed to have a house on two levels, an indoor bathroom, and a bedroom like this kept just for guests. She would have liked to tell this kind woman—"Aunt Eshka," she had told Dvoreh to call her—how much she admired the room, but she was overcome with shyness.

"Perhaps you'd like to be alone to unpack and wash? I'll just go put supper on the table. You come down when you're ready."

Downstairs Eshka told her husband, "She's a bashful little thing. And nothing like her mother for looks or spirit."

"I think she is quite pretty," Lazar Berman disagreed. "All that dark curly hair and those blue, blue eyes."

"Well, she'll settle in, I suppose." Eshka shrugged.

Through his connections, Uncle Lazar arranged for Dvoreh to work at Riga's largest dry goods store, Mir Khozayki, and accompanied her on the trolley the first two days while she learned the city and the route. In Dvoreh's eyes, Riga seemed very large and exceedingly cosmopolitan. From the stop near the Bermans' house to Alexander Street downtown, the streetcar traversed several ornate bridges, and Uncle Lazar told her that the river was the Western Dvina. The Baltic could not be seen from here, but Uncle Lazar told her that there were beautiful beaches just a few miles outside the city on the Gulf of Riga.

Mir Khozayki, housed in a handsome structure of yellow brick, occupied two floors, and a basement where the employees left their wraps and lunches. The ground floor held an amazing variety of goods—bolts of wool, silk, and cotton fabrics, tray upon tray of multicolored threads, cards of buttons made of everything from bone to real silver, spools of laces, ribbons, and embroideries. On the upper level were finished household goods, linen towels, tablecloths, blankets, quilts and pillows, curtains and quilt covers, bedsheets, and the like.

The manager of the store, Yaakov Lichtman, took Dvoreh around the first day and introduced her to the other employees. "Meet Tsaya," he said. "You'll be working in ribbons and buttons with her." Dvoreh and the other girl smiled shyly at each other before the manager, followed closely by Dvoreh, walked on. "This is Nachem," he told her, not seeing the wink the balding young man gave her. A moment later: "Bashka, you can ask anything—she's been here five years!" The older woman's hand exerted a friendly pressure on Dvoreh's. Mr. Lichtman introduced her to the eight floor employees and then led her to the office to explain the system of timekeeping, the pay schedule, and the general mechanics of the business. In the office

Dvoreh met the typist, Anna, and the bookkeeper, Lev. Becoming part of such a business made this the proudest day of her life!

Everything was stimulating, exciting, and utterly fascinating to Dvoreh, every day filled with possibilities and surprises. Grateful that Mammeh had insisted she learn her sums, she slipped effortlessly into the work at Mir Khozayki. Tsaya Kaganova became an instant chum, the others lesser friends, and she carried on a mild flirtation with Nachem Feltsman from the fabric department. So immersed was she in her new life that she scarcely had time to miss Mammeh and Papa; she even forgot to be angry with the way Simcha always had everything his own way at home. After all, Simcha was still a child in Polotsk while she was in Riga leading a life of sophistication and glamour.

At home Mammeh had always scolded Dvoreh for being slow to get up in the mornings, but it was different now. She was up at first light, slipping into her freshly pressed white shirtwaist and dark skirt and puffing her hair into a pompadour like Tsaya Kaganova's before joining the stream of people on their way to business. She never tired of watching the hurrying throngs from the window of the trolley or picking out the landmarks she was coming to know—the Gunpowder Tower, the Kronvalda Garden, the several famous bridges.

Being admitted to the department store through the heavy double doors an hour before the store opened to the public, Dvoreh felt important and privileged. She imagined that she was the envy of passersby on the street, and it made her square her shoulders and hold her head high. Once inside, Dvoreh joined the other young people in their early morning banter. After only a few weeks, she felt accepted at Mir Khozayki as if she had always been part of that family.

At the end of each week the bookkeeper handed her an envelope containing her wages. Having her own money was a heady experience, though it took a few weeks to get the knack of managing it so that it lasted between paydays. It was grown up to be a "boarder" and to hand the Bermans the weekly rent that she herself had earned. It was liberating to shop with her own money for a new ribbon for her shirtwaist or a package of pins for her hair, to buy a meal in a restaurant or pay for a performance at the Yiddish Theater. No one told her what to wear, what she needed, what she could do without. Thank God she had resisted her parents' efforts to have Pinchas the Matchmaker arrange a marriage. Imagine spending the rest of her life having to ask a husband if she might have her shoes resoled or buy a new petticoat!

There were three men, besides Yaakov Lichtman, who worked at the store. Loebe, who was older and married, Nachem, who indiscriminately adored all women, and Lev Goldenburg in the office. Lev kept the ledgers, and Dvoreh saw him when she signed her name first thing in the morning and again before she checked out of the store at night. At first all that Dvoreh had noticed about him was that he was handsome, as clean-shaven as any gentile, with thick dark hair neatly trimmed and sharply parted on one side. To Dvoreh's mind, there was something noble about his looks, because of his high, broad forehead and fine gray eyes. He wore starched shirts with immaculate stiff collars and cuffs protected by a gray cotton work jacket, sleeve envelopes, and clips to keep them from being stained by the ink. His pressed jacket hung meticulously from a polished wooden hanger from morning until the end of the day, when he whisked away any accumulated dust before putting it on. Gradually Dvoreh noticed other things, his seriousness about his work, the courteous way he addressed everyone, and a certain appealing shyness of manner. Tsaya Kaganova whispered to Dvoreh in the stockroom that many of the girls were interested in knowing Lev Goldenburg better, but that he was aloof, elusive.

"I can't believe that. He's so nice!"

"To everyone."

"There's always a way to a man's heart."

"Ha!" Tsaya Kaganova scoffed.

Intrigued and feeling the power of her own femininity for the first time, Dvoreh promptly fell in love with him. She dreamed that it would be she who would finally capture Lev. A match with a professional man, a bookkeeper, should show Mammeh that in these modern times a girl didn't need a *shadken* to get a husband!

*F*ar to the east, Valodya Mirov was struggling less happily than Dvoreh Mandelkern with the twin challenges of displacement from home and the demands of his employment. Walking home from the day's work to the bleak boardinghouse where he lived among many other bachelor employees of the Chinese Eastern Railway, Valodya's thoughts were sour. If Harbin was the "Moscow of Asia," as railroad publicity would have it, then he'd gladly exchange "Moscow" for any lesser town or village—as long as it was in Europe! *Boizamoi!* How he hated the stifling heat, the bland faces of the Chinese servants, and most of all, the utter boredom of life in this enclosed Russian community! What's more, Valodya loathed his job as a bookkeeping clerk in the central office of the railway. Was this the life of romantic adventuring promised him by the family friend who had arranged the job as a favor to Papa? If only he could get away from the damned ledgers and out with the engineering crews it would be bearable, but he had been hired to fill a certain box in the administrative structure, and there was no way to break out of that box even to go to another just like it. Bureaucracies! All the worst features of Russian government had been flawlessly reproduced in the middle of Asia!

Without regard for his best boots, he scuffed his feet in the dust as he walked along Kitaiskaya Street, the main thoroughfare that bisected Harbin. Having nothing better to do, he stopped for a while at a building site to watch the Chinese coolies stacking the locally made red bricks that would someday be the Russo-Chinese Bank Building. It was said that when the structure was complete, it would rival anything in St. Petersburg for elegance, but how completely Russian, how Russianly stupid it was to erect a building that would be more at home in Europe than it would ever be in Harbin! Why in the world would anyone choose to erect a three-story brick block when they could have followed Chinese tradition of placing multiple structures, gracefully built of aromatic woods, around airy open courtyards, tile-roofed to reflect the heat of summer and to retain the sun's warmth in winter. These brick buildings didn't breathe!

In his discontent Valodya reflected that Harbin embodied all the worst traits of Russia. And why not? It was a city created by the Russian government and managed by the railroad. The chief administrator of the Chinese Eastern was also the administrator of the city, which already numbered some sixty thousand Russians, eleven thousand of them railroad employees, the rest military personnel, civil authorities, families of all the above, and employees of stores, banks, hotels, whorehouses providing services to the rest. The ubiquitous Chinese lived on the outskirts of the city in the original Manchurian village or on small outlying farms. They were the brute labor that powered the city, the household servants, and workers in the factories the Russians had built to manufacture bricks, flour, and vodka.

The raison d'être for the city was the railroad. The Chinese government had granted Russia the right-of-way for a broad-gauge railroad across northern Manchuria to Vladivostock, some five hundred versts to the east, a grant that had included the land on which the city itself stood. Valodya, like so many others, had been hired when the railroad was expanding with a new branch line, arrowing south out of Harbin to Port Arthur, Russia's newly acquired naval base. He would have liked to be working on one of the construction crews, like Slava and Stepan, the friends he had made on the train, but that was not his lot.

Valodya turned east toward the river port. The air scarcely moved and the heat lay like a giant hand upon his chest. His dormitory room at the boardinghouse would be pure hell on such a day. The water of the Sungari River, although somewhat shallow and muddy here, should at least give an illusion of coolness.

The steamer that made a biweekly connection with the Circum-Baikal loop of the Trans-Siberian had just arrived in port. Valodya was surprised to see that the dock area had been cordoned off by the police. Curious, he drew nearer. A captain of the police was seated at the foot of the steamer's gangplank, apparently examining the papers of disembarking passengers.

A policeman at the barricade eased open the tight collar of his uniform jacket. He nodded his head toward the queue from the boat. "This is a hell of a duty to draw on a hot day! I bet I'll be standing here in the sun for two hours or more!"

"What are they doing?" Valodya asked. "I came in on that ship two and a half months ago, and I don't remember anything like this."

"New procedure," the policeman said. "St. Petersburg's *always* got a new procedure! They ain't been here, and they think if they got crooks in Moscow, we must have twice as many here! We ain't caught anyone yet!" he grumbled.

"I don't think I understand."

"I don't understand very well myself. It has something to do with the army. Everyone knows a war's coming out here, and we're supposed to take a look at people coming into the city, look for spies"—he winked at Valodya—"and wanted criminals and deserters. Don't know what we'll do if we find any, but we still gotta look!"

Valodya glanced toward the line of wrinkled, perspiring passengers. They looked to be mostly businessmen or newly arriving railroad workers with a few fidgety family groups. Hardly a spy or deserter among them, to judge from appearances.

"Well, good luck!" Valodya said to the policeman, turning back toward the main part of the city.

A long, empty evening stretched before Valodya. There wasn't exactly a wealth of social activities to be found in Harbin, but it wouldn't matter if there had been. He was not only broke, he was in debt for his next two salary disbursements. What a run of bad luck he had had at cards the past week or two! Maybe Oleg, his mate from the boardinghouse, would loan him a few rubles—but even as he thought it, Valodya knew better; he was already in Oleg's debt for almost fifty rubles, and his credit was not good with anyone. If only he had ten rubles—five even—his gut told him his luck was about to turn and he could recoup his losses in an evening, maybe even get ahead! His shoulders slumped with the realization that no one was going to advance him a stake. As soon as it cooled off a bit, he would spend the evening writing a letter to dearest *Maman*. He had not been as good about keeping in touch as he had promised when he left Smolensk. Maybe he could even hint that some extra money slipped into her next letter would be appreciated. If only he could be sure that *Maman* would not show the letter to Papa—

*M*y dearest child, Malkeh wrote and then paused. It was difficult to write to Chaya Leya, knowing that her daughter would rather hear from Yoysef than from herself. But she also knew that if she gave in to her impulse to withdraw, there would never be a bridge built between them. *We were thankful to receive your short letter*—she crossed out "short," Chaya Leya might see it as criticism—*and to know that you have arrived safely in Blagoveschensk. I was happy* (she underlined "happy") *to hear that Herschel has adjusted to the army and is well. You have told us nothing about your wedding or any other plans you might have, but perhaps it was too soon after your arrival to have settled things. We will be anxious until we hear that all has gone as we hope.* Chaya Leya would surely know that they were worried about Herschel's escape.

All is well in Polotsk. Papa keeps busy in the shop. I tell him he should hire another tailor and he says yes, he must do that, but he drags his feet. In truth, he cannot accept that Herschel won't be coming home to Polotsk for a long time.

The school has a new beginning class of eight girls! Gittel now has enough experience to handle the little ones herself, although Hodl keeps an eye on things. I seem to keep busy managing all the details of running a school. I teach only one class now, some of the older women. Like your Aunt Golda when we first started, they want to learn only how to parrot the prayers in Hebrew! They say to me, "Don't bother us with what they mean!"

Speaking of Aunt Golda, she and your grandmother are pretty much the same. Bobbeh Frumma has almost completely recovered from the last little stroke she had. She would write to you herself, but her hand shakes too badly these days. Thank God, from what I hear, your grandparents in Dagda seem to be holding their own, but each year they, too, grow older and frailer.

Aunt Yenta, Uncle Yaynkel, and their children are well. Moishe writes from New York that he has found work in a meat-packing plant. Imagine! There is so much to eat in America that they have a whole factory just to cut up meat!

Malkeh closed her eyes, trying to think of entertaining or interesting news tidbits she could pass along to this daughter who was so far away. When time passes without regular contacts, connections loosen and what might have interested Chaya Leya before would no longer have meaning.

My heart is sore that we have not yet had a letter from Chaim. Papa heard from Berel the other day, and Berel has received a letter, telling him that Chaim is fine and happy aboard his ship. I think it is strange that Chaim should write to Berel and not to us, but Papa says maybe the letter he wrote us got lost in the mail. I guess anything is possible.

We hear regularly from Dvoreh in Riga, not that she tells us much more than that she doesn't have time to write! Dvoreh was never much of a writer.

Simcha is doing fine with his schoolwork, according to Yevgeny Fedotov. Incidentally, when I saw Fedotov the other day, he most especially asked after you. He and the young count always felt very bad that they could not do anything for Herschel. Finally, though, they were able to get most of the Spokoinaya Zemlya peasants released from military service, and in time for the harvest! I was at the estate just last week. Maria Feodorovna has now taken to her bed, poor thing, and I go regularly to read to her or just to visit. She is in much pain, I'm afraid, although she does not complain, and her mind is clear. Last time she told me that there is still trouble with the zemstvo. *There are constant demands from that man Karpovitch. First it was for an overseer, and then it was for hiring more men to do heaven only knows what, and now it is for letting someone from the council go over the estate's books to make sure that the Voronovs are not making too much money off the peasants! She said that our friend Fedotov almost had apoplexy over that. Count Pyotr, though, tries to accommodate, especially seeing as how there have been more uprisings lately—all, I must tell you, in the Ukraine and not here in Byelorussia. What terrible times we live in, and I can't see them getting any better!*

How bad things really were, Malkeh could not really convey in a letter to Siberia, where Chaya Leya and Herschel would be coping with problems of their own. A weight of depression settled upon her, and she rose from the table to stand looking out the window. It was not exactly a new heaviness of spirit, but one that had come upon her bit by bit. One by one her oldest children had left home, and now the older generations' time on earth was drawing to a close; too soon Mammeh Frumma, Maria Feodorovna, and her own parents would be gone. Lately Yenta and Yaynkel had been talking about going with their children to America to join Moishe. With the growing unrest, other friends and acquaintances were leaving, too. Sometimes Hodl Nachman, her invaluable assistant, talked about moving to Milwaukee, where she had cousins. All was change, all was loss, all was turmoil. Only yesterday she had been sitting in her rocking chair, not reading or sewing, just thinking, when Simcha came home from Spokoinaya Zemlya.

"What's the matter, Mammeh? You look sad," Simcha had asked, sprawling on the floor at her feet.

Preoccupied, she had not heard him come in. "You're home early, my son. No lessons today?"

"That man Karpovitch from the *zemstvo* came to see *Gospodin* Fedotov about something. The *gospodin* told me to go study in the kitchen while they talked. I was working on my Homer—you know, the translation I was having trouble with last night?—but even so, I could hear them yelling at each other. Well, Karpovitch was the one yelling at the beginning. Then I heard the *gospodin* telling him in a loud voice to get out of the house; he was so mad you could hear every word in the kitchen. He said to Karpovitch that if he came near him again, he would knock his head off. Then Karpovitch yelled he would just see about that, and then the *gospodin* said if he didn't get out that instant he would kill him dead on the spot. After that, Karpovitch went out and slammed the door so hard, the whole kitchen shook. When I took my translation to *Gospodin* Fedotov to correct, he said he had a headache and I should go home. Mammeh, what is going on at Voronov village?"

"Ah, my darling, it is what is going on all over—a struggle to take power from the landowners and give it to the people."

"But that's good, isn't it?"

Malkeh smiled slightly. "Sometimes."

Simcha shuddered. "I don't like that Karpovitch."

"He's not a nice man," Malkeh agreed. "He wants this, he wants that. What he asks for the peasants is not all bad, you know, it's the way he goes about it that's so ugly." She remembered what Yevgeny Fedotov had said only a month ago. "The *zemstvo* began by asking for favors, now Karpovitch demands, later the peasants will take what they want."

Returning to the present, Malkeh concluded her letter. *I think I have told you all that is happening here. We will watch every post for further news from you, my darling child. With dearest regards from myself and from Papa, I am your loving mother.*

Malkeh read over what she had written and decided that it would do. Yet before she had sealed the envelope, something else occurred to her and she appended a postcript. *Eshka Berman wrote me recently that your sister has a special friendship with a young man in Riga. We will have to wait to see what develops.*

*D*voreh had had to make the first approach to Lev Goldenburg or nothing would have happened between them. She invited him to accompany her to a Purim party at the home of Tsaya Kaganova's parents. The festival Purim was celebrated with special gaiety, feasting, and practical jokes, and the carnival atmosphere was such that Dvoreh felt issuing an invitation to Lev was properly permissible.

"You didn't!" her friend Tsaya squealed when Dvoreh told her she had asked the bookkeeper to take her to the party.

"Yes, I did. I'm going to marry Lev Goldenburg someday," Dvoreh said half-jokingly, "so I have to get started someplace!"

Somewhat to Dvoreh's surprise, Lev had agreed to escort her, although he was obviously taken aback. "Yes, all right," he had said. "As long as I don't have to wear a costume." Masquerades were a commonplace of Purim celebrations.

"All right, then I won't either," she agreed.

"But you would look beautiful as Queen Esther!" he had said, and then, suddenly confused, had stopped and looked down at his ledger page.

There was an awkward pause. "Perhaps I will then," she said finally.

On the night of the party, Lev called for Dvoreh at the Bermans' house. His eyes admired her costume, a long, gauzy skirt that Aunt Eshka's daughter Rochka had once worn in a school play, a peasant blouse that

Dvoreh had brought from home, and all the bracelets and necklaces that Aunt Eshka could find in her drawer. Dvoreh had brushed her hair to a sheen and left it loose, regretting that it was too curly to lay properly on her shoulders. Lev stared at her, and indeed she looked quite different from the girl in the white shirtwaist whom he saw every day at work. Recalling himself, he made the effort to be polite to Aunt Eshka and Uncle Lazar, succeeding so well they had no qualms about seeing their young charge go off with him.

They rode the trolley, transferring twice, to the Kaganov house. Away from the familiar surroundings of the store, neither could find anything to say to the other, and an uncomfortable silence grew between them. Dvoreh was beginning to regret her rash invitation.

At the Kaganovs, things did not improve. Although Lev knew many of the other guests from Mir Khozayki, he was painfully ill at ease meeting them in a social setting. Dvoreh brought him punch and hamantaschen, but he continued to sit hunched into himself as if he were cold, even after the party warmed up and the singing started. In Dvoreh's eyes, he seemed to have shrunk in stature since she had last seen him at the store. How could that be?

Dvoreh had a clear, sweet voice, soprano, though somewhat limited in range, and she loved to sing. Perched on the arm of Lev's chair, she led the others in singing *"Unter di Grininke Beymelekh"* ("Under the Little Green Trees") and *"Dos Lid fun der Ayznban"* ("The Train Song"). Her face was prettily flushed and her eyes sparkled with fun. She knew the words to all the songs of the day and seemed never to tire. She could not help but respond to the admiring looks of the young male guests. When her throat grew dry, she went to refill her punch cup. Nachem Feltsman, from the fabric department at the store, came to stand beside her at the refreshment table. His arm casually encircled her waist, and his fingers pinched her lightly just below where her corset stays ended. At first Dvoreh thought she imagined it. She shrugged off his arm.

"Ah, Dvoreh! You are such a beauty! So lush, so ripe for plucking—" Nachem said, nuzzling her neck.

Dvoreh moved away. "Have you been drinking wine along with the punch, Nachem?" she asked with a frown.

He shook his head. "I'm drunk on love!" One arm clutched her while the fingers of his other hand moved inside the neckline of her blouse.

Dvoreh turned pale and then bright red. She did not know what to do. She didn't want to create a scene at her friend's party, nor did she want to appear a silly, gullible innocent. She struggled to free herself, but Nachem's grip only tightened.

"Keep your hands off the young lady!" Suddenly Lev Goldenburg was there, hissing into Nachem's ear. Dvoreh had not even seen him leave his chair.

Nachem took a step backward, and his arm dropped to his side.

Lev took hold of Dvoreh's arm and led her back to where the singers were still gathered near the piano.

"Maybe we should go," Dvoreh murmured, blushing. "I'm not having such a good time anymore."

"The evening has just started," Lev said. "I want to hear you sing some more." His hand held hers reassuringly. "Do you know *'Ale Brider'*?"

Dvoreh nodded. When she started the first line, everyone was startled to hear Lev join in, his tenor voice smooth as cream. *"Un mir zaynen ale brider—"* he sang. "For we are all brothers and sing happy songs. We stay together, always united, caring for one another."

Lev was still humming the tune a long time later when, flushed and excited, he and Dvoreh took their leave of the others.

On the way home on the trolley, Lev took Dvoreh's hand, whispering into her ear, "You were the prettiest Queen Esther at the party!"

Chapter 35

*T*he fixer in Blagoveschensk Camp was a long-time soldier known simply as Davka. He probably had more of a name than that, but no one seemed to know it. He'd been in the army so long that he claimed he could not recall what village he was from, and he remembered Blagoveschensk in the days when it was a small Cossack outpost and not a proper fort at all. Blagoveschensk had never been a favored posting for a variety of reasons—because of its situation on the border between Russian Siberia and Manchuria, because of its bleak geography and isolation, and, of course, because of the ever-present peril of Chinese attack from across the Amur River.

Davka liked to tell stories of the days of glory when just a few stout Russians had routed the "Redbeards," as the Chinese bandits were incongruously called, and he equally enjoyed calling up the times of horror when soldiers had frozen to death in the snow, been savaged by wolves, or had died of cholera. One had to be strong to survive Blagoveschensk, Davka said with a certain pride.

Although in public the officers treated Davka with the same contempt and verbal abuse that they showered on every person of inferior rank, it was said that in private he drank cognac with his superiors, lent them money, and was privy to their secrets. No one could remember when Davka had attained this state of grace, but there was little doubt about *how* he'd done it. After all, wasn't he the fixer of all things?

Sex? Of course. Just specify preference. Women. Boys. Whips and bonds. Sheep or dogs. Voyeur or exhibitionist. It was all the same to Davka, and there was no order that he could not fill, and with discretion.

Money? The fixer seemed to have a boundless supply that he lent at "reasonable" rates to those careless officers who had gambled away their wages before the next pay train was due. It was whispered that the Cossack general himself was in Davka's debt and had surrendered his gold-inlaid saber as security. A rather farfetched story, but still—?

Davka could obtain cognac and champagne, caviar and fresh meat when there was no visible source of supply in all of Blagoveschensk or the surrounding countryside. He could so perfectly forge a supply order that Moscow had never challenged the propriety of even one, and Blagoveschensk Camp had more creature comforts than most military installations—for the officers, of course.

On the side, Davka did a brisk business in discharge papers, facilitating the complex arrangements that were necessary to effect a successful "escape." For a considerable fee, business being business.

In short, Davka was an entrepreneur with diversified enterprises, a rich man, a panderer, extortionist, thief, or philanthropist, depending on one's point of view.

Herschel had been in a fever of excitement since the arrival of Chaya Leya's letter telling him of her travel arrangements for her journey. She would leave Polotsk in mid-June to ensure the best traveling conditions. Continuing to write in Yiddish to baffle the censors, she added: *We have received gifts of* many rubles *which should make it possible for us to begin married life* as we had always planned.

Herschel's forehead creased in thought. What could that mean? They had made no special plans he could think of. *Many rubles,* she had written. Of course! She would bring gold to make his escape possible.

"I have packed my wedding linens and dowry to bring with me," Chaya Leya wrote, obliquely assuring him that she was prepared to make a home anywhere their flight should take them, even if it should be outside Russia.

At the bottom of the page she had added an awkward postscript: *On the day we picked for our wedding in the spring, I stood on the banks of the River Dvina and closed my eyes, imagining that we stood together under the wedding canopy. I think of myself truly as your wife and you as my husband.*

Herschel's heart ached. His gentle Chaya Leya deserved better than this arduous journey and its uncertain end in some faraway place. He would have liked to give her silk dresses and jewels for her ears, a home with a Turkish carpet and fine furnishings.

Herschel counted the weeks on his fingers. If all went well, Chaya Leya might arrive as soon as August, most certainly by the early part of September. He must prepare. The letter had taken so long in transit that it was July already. He must arrange a clean, respectable place for her to stay and see to a rabbi to marry them. Most important, he must set in motion the arrangements for his escape.

In his mind Herschel had been preparing for flight since his arrival in camp, observing without seeming to observe, listening to others talk, noting comings and goings. He had learned that there was a man in camp who arranged such things. When the time was right, Herschel would make his move. He must just stay alive and be strong. He had seen scores of conscripts die en route to the camp. Many more had perished of pneumonia that winter or had sickened with chronic consumptive coughs. There was dysentery in the camp. Everyone had it in some degree all the time. Herschel was better now, but it had left him as thin and dry as a reed. What's more, it was whispered that there was cholera across the river in Manchuria and an epidemic in Harbin. Thank God there had been no cholera in Blagoveschensk in over a year!

The months in the army had toughened Herschel's body and given him a knowledge of himself he might otherwise have lacked. Somewhat frail and retiring all his life, he had discovered a stubborn strength and resilience in himself, and a will to survive. The pale indoor look and the flab of unused muscles were gone, but the main change, not so immediately apparent, was in Herschel's spirit. He would endure to start his real life with Chaya Leya.

It was to Davka that Herschel Rosen went after he received Chaya Leya's letter. He found him in a small, bare office off the platoon orderly room, a small man with a shaved head, smoking a real cigarette from a foreign package, not a hand-rolled *papiros*.

"So you want to desert, eh?" Davka asked with an evil grin.

Herschel nodded, twisting his cap between nervous hands. Davka's slight appearance was deceptive. His body had the strength and tension of a tightly-coiled spring and his skin was tough as leather. His jaw was aggressive, eyes gray and hard as pebbles, neck thick and strong. An artery pulsed disconcertingly in his forehead, just above his left eye.

Davka, at ease, leaned so far back in his chair that only two of its legs teetered on the floor. Picking his teeth with a straw in feigned boredom, he returned Herschel's stare through half-closed eyes. The fixer had learned to judge men. He categorized escape prospects into three rough groupings: the big talkers who boasted but in the end had neither the money nor the stomach to make the run; the weak and the sick who might have money and courage but lacked stamina for the enterprise; and finally those few who had strength, daring, and cash, the only customers worth his time. In which group was this Jew?

Davka considered. Rosen was not from a rich family, that much was apparent from his clothes and his speech. On the other hand, the mail clerk had reported that he had received a thick letter from Russia. That might mean rubles. At the least it meant that he had connections at home, and that was promising. Where profit was concerned, one should never be too hasty in drawing conclusions.

Physical strength? Perhaps. Some of these who looked so malnourished survived better than the big, healthy-looking ones, maybe because they had adjusted to hardship early, had few expectations, and were conditioned to privation. It boded well that the soldier had survived the trip from Moscow and the first months in Blagoveschensk.

What about courage? That judgment would have to be made on intuition alone. Davka knew that it is impossible to predict what a man will do when his life is in danger. He had seen strong men reduced to trembling at the first whiff of gunpowder. He had also seen delicate boys risk themselves grandly and heroically in battle. He remembered one—what was his name? Shimansky, something like that—who had dived under the hooves of a Redbeard's horse to pull a comrade to safety. You never knew.

Abruptly Davka asked, "How much money do you have?"

"Only a little, *Gospodin*, but my—my wife is on her way with gold."

So! There were to be two of them to get out of Blagoveschensk, and one a woman! That changed the odds, the risks having just multiplied by more than two. Davka said, "I'll have to think it over."

"Just out of the camp, sir," Herschel pleaded. "Just help me get away from the camp, and I'll manage all the rest—"

"Fool!" Davka spat. "What do you know about traveling through Manchuria? Will you know without my help whether you've hired a Boxer or a Redbeard to guide you through the mountains? How are you going to get hold of identity papers so that you won't be sent back by the first soldier or policeman you meet on the road? Getting out of Blagoveschensk Camp is easy, any fool can manage that without my help. Getting to Shanghai is the real trick!"

Herschel's jaw set in a rigid line, and he glared at Davka. "We'll make it with or without you, don't you worry about that!"

Davka grimaced. "When your missus gets here with the cash money, the both of you come back to see me. I'll decide whether to help you then."

It was not what Herschel had hoped for, but it was the best he could do at the moment. Bowing slightly, he said, "Very well, *Gospodin*. But you will see that my wife and I are worthy and can pay your price."

Davka only nodded.

A period of anxious waiting set in. What would they do if Davka refused to help them? Would Chaya Leya then return to Polotsk alone? Should they try to make it out of Blagoveschensk Camp without help?

Herschel discussed the problem endlessly with his two acquaintances from the barracks, Mikhail, the former student radical who had given him good advice about the letters, and Avraham, who had arrived recently, the sole member of a Vitebsk yeshiva to have survived the journey east.

"*Boizamoi!*" Mikhail swore. "How I hate that peasant food we get day after day after day!" The three were on their way back to the barracks from the refectory, where their evening meal had been black bread, boiled buckwheat, a cabbage soup, and kvass.

Avraham shrugged. "Food is food. You eat to live—even if the food is bad, even if it is unclean for Jews."

"Do you have tea?" Mikhail asked Herschel, ignoring Avraham. He tolerated Herschel, who might be a Jew but at least was not a peasant like the others in their barrack, but he found the former yeshiva student too exotic for his taste.

"I bought some at the canteen yesterday." Since tea was not provided at meals, the three were carrying containers of hot water from the kitchens.

As if it were the continuation of a conversation—which, in a way, it was—Herschel asked, "But can you really trust Davka?"

Avraham said, "Who can you trust in this life except yourself? On the other hand, if you trust no one, how can you live?"

Herschel turned to Mikhail. "You've been here longer than I; what is he really like?"

"Did he talk to you about killing Redbeards and Boxers?"

Herschel nodded.

"How about what happened here in 1900?"

Herschel was puzzled. "What happened?"

"That was the time," Mikhail said, "when rumors had spread that the Boxers were going to sweep down and kill all the white people. Lots of Chinese lived in Blagoveschensk then, and every one of them was under suspicion. General Puyashkin and the governor issued orders that within twenty-four hours every Chinese had to be out of Blagoveschensk and across the river. The only problem was that there weren't any boats to ferry them across."

"So what happened?"

"Of course, it was before my time here. As I heard the story—and the old-timers don't like to talk about it—the troops rounded up four thousand Chinese—men, women, children, babies. They separated them into groups, and marched them into the river at bayonet point. Of course they drowned, four thousand drowned! Imagine what it must have been like!"

"But that's terrible!" Herschel exclaimed.

There were tears in Avraham's eyes, and for once he was silent. "And Davka?"

"Ah," said Mikhail, "they say that it was Davka who whispered the plan into General Puyashkin's ear."

*C*haim dreamed that he was locked in a tight embrace with a wriggling naked Nadja. Her breasts rubbed against his chest and her soft pubic bush lay wet against him, inviting him to enter her. As he held her in his arms, her body, slick with sweat, slid from his grasp, and he was left with nothing.

Chaim's eyes half opened. The smell of sweat and dried herring was so strong and his dream of Nadja so real, he felt sure he was lying on a pile of sacks in a corner of the dim shed where they had spent so many afternoons. Yet, when he rolled over to embrace her, he clutched only empty air. Awake, he was aware of other odors, the staleness of unwashed bodies and standing urine.

Chaim closed his eyes and lay motionless against the dizziness that came over him. The place where he lay seemed unsteady beneath him. Cautiously he opened his eyes again and looked around. He seemed to be lying on a kind of iron cot fastened to the wall. Its mattress was what smelled of damp and urine. In the dim light he could just make out other bunks, one on top of the other, two deep, around the sides of a long, narrow room without windows. A heavy wooden table occupied the center of the space and was bolted to the floor. Wherever he was, it was not the herring shed, not anyplace he recognized.

Feeling an urgent need to urinate, Chaim made a supreme effort and staggered to his feet, cracking his head sharply on an upper bunk as he did so. His head was already a throbbing drum, and now a trickle of blood ran down his cheek and into his beard. As he stood waiting for equilibrium to return, the floor dipped steeply under his feet, and he had to grab the side of the bed to keep from falling. In a moment the floor began to rise again. How odd it was that the floorboards rose and fell, while the walls simultaneously rolled from side to side in a motion like a rocking cradle.

A wave of overpowering nausea made it prudent for Chaim to sink back on the cot which, however, offered little solidity in an unstable landscape. He screwed his eyes shut and tried to conjure Nadja once more, but he could not close out the motion of the room, the smell, or the groaning and creaking that presaged the disintegration of the walls with every downward plunge of the floor.

Chaim lay still, using all his willpower to control his heaving stomach. Dimly he recalled the fog-bound waterfront where he had gone after an evening of unaccustomed drinking. Why had he been drinking anyway? A celebration of some sort. Ah, yes, he had been feeling very sorry for himself after the wedding of Berel to Soreh Glanzer. If only he could put his mind to it, he knew he would be able to reconstruct exactly what had happened and where he was now. For the moment, however, he was too preoccupied with his bodily needs to think clearly.

Very carefully this time Chaim lifted his head and inched off the bed, holding on to the top bunk for support. Very very slowly he groped his way across the sliding floor toward a wooden door in the opposite wall. It took a long time to traverse the short distance. He shuddered, remembering the rich food at the wedding and the cheap schnapps he had drunk later—when? Yesterday? He could taste the sour bile in the back of his mouth and throat. He didn't know if he could stop himself from spewing it up before he found a toilet.

When he pushed against it, the wooden door would not budge. It appeared to be barred on the outside. Chaim put his entire weight against it in one mighty heave of his shoulders, but it was too sturdy. Dizzy, sick, he closed his eyes against the motion of the room and leaned against the door, tears starting at the realization of how weak and helpless he was. Furiously he clenched a fist and banged. A futile gesture. The poor sound of his fists would never be heard over the creaking that continued rhythmically every minute or so as the room rocked back and forth on its downward course. He hammered until his knuckles bled. No response. He shouted for help. Did they intend to leave him locked in this heaving, plunging prison until he perished?

He had to get hold of himself. That he had been left to die made no sense. Why bother to snatch him off the docks merely to immure him between damp walls?

Chaim looked about him carefully. His eyes were beginning to adjust to the gloomy light. He identified what appeared to be a slop bucket in a corner, and he made his way to it and relieved himself. The stench that rose from the receptacle was so overpowering that he could hold back no longer, and his vomit splashed half in and half out of the container. When he had finished, his forehead was beaded with clammy sweat, but he felt somewhat better, though so weak that he feared he would fall. He crept to a bunk as far from the noisome pail as he could manage; lying as motionless as he could, he was grateful to have made it to a resting place.

He must have dozed then, for it was almost completely dark when he opened his eyes and realized that it was the sound of someone removing a heavy bar from the door that had awakened him. He lay still, holding his breath and bracing himself for any assault that might come.

Slowly the door groaned open. Someone holding a lantern before his face stood in the doorway, obscured by shadows. The light advanced toward Chaim, where he lay on the cot. Whoever was holding the lamp lowered it to look at him. They stared at each other, Chaim assessing the other man's intentions and his own potential for overpowering him if it should be necessary. The man with the lantern was a head or more shorter than Chaim, but his barrel chest, the corded muscles on his thick arms, and the tough thrust of his swarthy jaw dissuaded Chaim from making him an adversary, at least not in his present weakened condition.

The man grunted with satisfaction when he saw that Chaim was awake, and he said something to him in an unintelligible tongue. Chaim shook his head, indicating that he did not understand.

In halting and poorly articulated Russian, the man pointed toward himself. "Me—Stavros. You?"

"Chaim."

The man tried it on his tongue and found it foreign. "Hy-am." He pronounced it with two distinct syllables. He made spooning motions from his hand to his mouth. "You want eat?" he asked, feeling out the unfamiliar Russians words.

Chaim shook his head, the nausea rising in the back of his throat at the thought of food. But his mouth was dry and he asked for water, pantomiming drinking to be sure he was understood.

The man, Stavros, nodded and went out, leaving the door open but the room in darkness. Chaim lay back, reflecting. His kidnappers, then, as he had surmised earlier, did not intend him harm. After a while Stavros came back with a tin cup of water. It was warm and tasted of the cask where it had been stored, but to Chaim's parched mouth, it was good.

"Where am I?" Chaim asked. "What do you want with me?"

Stavros clearly did not understand, and Chaim tried again, more slowly. "Where?"

"Ah." Stavros grinned, white teeth flashing in a dark face. "You— ship. Greek ship. *Archimedes.*"

Yes, Chaim thought, he had already gathered that he was on a ship. Now he knew it was Greek, and he guessed that the man had given its name though he had not understood. *"Pochemu?"* Chaim asked.

Stavros said, "You work." The wide grin split his face again, and he made a motion that suggested shoveling coal.

Chaim groaned and closed his eyes again. Shanghaied, then, to fill out the crew of a foreign ship. He should never have been on the docks at night. He had been warned.

Other men drifted in, for these were the crew's quarters. There was a good deal of talking and laughing and the stealing of sidewise glances at the silent giant who was prone on the bunk. Some were smoking cigarettes hand-rolled in thin brown paper. The evening meal appeared on the table and was quickly demolished. The thick smell of olive oil, and the odor of many bodies started Chaim retching again, and he made self-conscious use of the slop bucket in the corner. This was vastly amusing to the other men, who slapped each other on the shoulders, pointed, and laughed. Stavros stayed by Chaim, either appointed or self-designated as his guardian and keeper. After each spell of vomiting, he wiped Chaim's face with a kerchief, fairly clean, and offered water to rinse his mouth before helping him back to his bunk.

It was a wretched night, followed by three more days in which he lay in the belowdecks compartment, hoping he was indeed about to die. During the day he was alone as the men went about their tasks on deck or in the engine room.

Several times another crewman, a dark fellow that the others called Pasha, came into the room and stood near Chaim's bunk, staring silently at him. He just stood there, looking, his face impassive. It made Chaim tense. If he had had the words, he would have asked Stavros about Pasha, but they had yet to establish a common language.

Lying weakly on his mattress, the hours of the day were identifiable only because of Stavros's periodic visits, carrying food that Chaim could not swallow and water that he gratefully accepted but often vomited up as soon as it sloshed into his stomach.

On the fourth morning Chaim, though wan and exhausted, felt a little better. The floor seemed more stable under his feet when he got up to relieve himself, and he even thought he felt a pang of something resembling hunger. When Stavros came to him that morning, he brought no food but helped Chaim into his boots and a filthy coat he had brought from somewhere. With a strong arm about him, Stavros helped him through the stout door and along a gloomy passage to where a companionway ladder gave access to the deck.

A stiff cold wind whipped across sparkling water and Chaim, shivering, was grateful for the warmth of the repulsive garment that Stavros had bundled around him. Fortunately the clean salt smell of the sea overcame its stench. Stavros, using his strength to hold Chaim steady, helped him to a sheltered corner of the deck and lowered him to a sitting position. The ship still rocked and plunged, but Chaim noted with satisfaction that he had apparently accustomed himself to the motion.

Chaim assessed his surroundings. He saw that the ship was not large, apparently a coastal vessel not meant for long ocean voyages. That was good. It meant he had a chance to get back on land soon. It was trim, compact, and very clean. The men working on deck were going about their tasks quietly. That seemed to indicate that the ship's master was a professional seaman and not a pirate.

After a while Stavros brought him a cup of hot strong coffee and a crust of hard bread. Chaim tentatively tasted and drank, and he felt no nausea. He was hungry, he wanted more, but Stavros shook his head, no. It was enough for now.

All morning Chaim sat on the deck and delighted in the sun, the sweet-smelling air, and the gulls that swooped and danced above the ship. The men working on deck studiously ignored him—all, that is, except the dark man known as Pasha. Chaim turned once or twice to find his glittering black eyes fastened upon him. Where the other man's eyes touched him, Chaim felt soiled.

Sometime during the morning two men were led to where Chaim sat by a pointing, gesticulating Stavros. Stavros motioned Chaim to his feet but had to help him up because his legs were still shaky. The three men, one of whom Chaim guessed to be an officer from the braid on his sleeve, stood in front of him and talked with one another in a language that Chaim now knew was Greek. Finally the officer nodded assent, and Stavros and the other man seemed pleased.

It was only then that the man in authority, the first mate as it turned out, spoke to Chaim in accented but perfectly comprehensible Russian. "You have enlisted for a term of duty aboard the *Archimedes*." He swept his arm in a wide arc to indicate the vessel on which they sailed. "We are a steamship of Greek registry, carrying cargo for Marseille. Your contract of service will be drawn up and signed by you immediately. You will be paid the same number of drachmas as any other inexperienced seaman." He appraised Chaim with sharp eyes. "You look to be strong and healthy. You will work for Constantine here in the engine room. All you have to do is follow his orders exactly. Stavros will help you learn your way around a ship." The officer turned to go and then swung back to Chaim. "One more thing. You were *recruited* for this voyage in Odessa. If you tell a different story, no one will believe you or care a fig if they do. That's all for now. You are still weak from being seasick. When you are stronger, tomorrow or the day after, you will start earning your keep."

The man's tone was so authoritative, his posture so commanding that Chaim swallowed his indignation, and his response was deferential. "Yes, *Gospodin. Spaseba, Gospodin.*"

While initially despairing, after a few weeks Chaim had to admit that there were worse things that could have happened to him than being shang-haied aboard the steamship *Archimedes* out of Salonika. Once the seasickness was gone, he felt strong and healthy, avid for whatever might come next. He enjoyed an uncomplicated companionship with Stavros and some of the others, and for the first time in his life he did not feel set apart by his religion. Somewhat to his surprise, he found that he liked life at sea.

Chapter 36

*A*fter another meeting, this time with both Chaya Leya and Herschel, and in exchange for a great deal of gold, Davka agreed to arrange everything. If Herschel and Chaya Leya had expected dark intrigue for their money, they were disappointed, for the business of escapes was straightforward. On the appointed day, Herschel merely changed his drab-hued uniform for the dark suit and high starched collar Chaya Leya had brought with her in her trunk, put Davka's bogus discharge and identity papers in his pocket, and walked through the front gate past sentries who scarcely looked at him. It was all so simple that Chaya Leya wondered why they had parted with so much money.

Davka had recommended that they cross the river and travel over the Khingan Mountains to Tsitsihar in Manchuria, from where they could make their way gradually by seldom-traveled routes to a port on the coast of China. It would be best, Davka said, for them to avoid populated areas, particularly those Russian-controlled, where there might be random army patrols or where they might come upon police checkpoints. He would arrange, for a price, for them to travel with a band of Chinese smugglers through the dangerous mountain regions. The journey might be rough, but it would likely be safe.

Herschel was by nature a cautious man. That he decided this time to choose the route of higher risk was out of character for him. It was a decision born of his anxiety for Chaya Leya. She had arrived in Blagoveschensk thin and tired after the long trip from home, and her remaining strength had been sapped by the bloody flux that had persisted for several wretched weeks following her arrival. To subject her now to long days in the mountains on foot and donkeyback seemed both cruel and foolhardy. What good would it do to elude the authorities only to have Chaya Leya sicken and die?

Taking the official-looking discharge document from Davka, Herschel studied it. It attested to the fact that Herschel Rosen, Jew, had completed the terms of his conscription, and it was signed with a flourish by his company commander and by General Puyashkin himself. The paper certainly seemed genuine, authentic in every detail. Considering the fact that most soldiers and most policemen could not read, it should do nicely. In an envelope was the internal identity card that every Russian must carry.

Courteously thanking Davka for his advice about the route but demurring, Herschel shook hands.

"Good luck, Rosen. You're making a mistake," Davka said to him in parting.

"We'll be all right," Herschel mumbled uncertainly. When he thought of Chaya Leya's face, so white that each freckle stood out in relief, he knew he could never have chanced spending weeks in rugged mountain terrain, sleeping in caves and eating off the land. More emphatically he repeated, "We'll be all right."

On Davka's advice, Herschel had set the time for their departure as very early the following morning. He confided in no one except Avraham. While he genuinely liked Mikhail, he did not have the same faith in him as in Avraham. Old attitudes do not die, he thought with regret. He would have liked to thank Mikhail for so many kindnesses but could not overcome an ingrained distrust. Mikhail had never given him reason to doubt—in fact, without Mikhail, Herschel might not have survived the terrible early days at Blagoveschensk. It was Mikhail who had interpreted the tacit rules of the camp so that Herschel would not blunder into disaster, Mikhail who helped him send word home to Polotsk and led him to Davka. It was Mikhail who saved his life.

Of the twenty-four men in the barracks, Herschel had been the only Jew until Avraham arrived a few months later. The other soldiers were conscripts, chosen by lot from the poor peasantry in various military districts. A few were men like Herschel who had been picked up at random in the same extraordinary recruitment effort that had swept Polotsk; these tended to be from towns and cities, and of a somewhat different class from the peasants. Grouped according to their place in the social structure outside, they functioned in their present situation as they would have at home. Mikhail was an anomaly, a university student from an upper-class family. The other oddity was Herschel.

Herschel's introduction into this hierarchy was traumatic. Gavril, a loud, foul-mouthed peasant from the Ukraine, had taken one look at him and released a glob of spittle on the floor at Herschel's feet. "Well, look at this! We got ourselves a *Yid* here! Must be some mistake, *Yid*! The dog kennel is the other way!"

Herschel remained impassive, continuing to arrange his newly issued clothing in a pack at the foot of his cot, as the sergeant major had instructed.

Gavril turned to the other five or six men who had come into the barracks at the same time. "Does anyone know why Hebes make such shithead soldiers?" he asked.

There was a chorus of ribald responses.

"Nah!" the big peasant said. " 'Cause they're cowards! They only like to kill little children—"

"And God! They killed God!" shouted someone.

"The Christ Himself!" Gavril agreed. "And they need blood from a child to make their Jew bread! Do you think we should have to share a room with a pile of shit like him?"

"Throw him out! Throw him out!"

The men converged on Herschel. Grabbing his pack, they threw the clothing out, trampling it underfoot before pitching it from the window. Wearily Herschel sat down on the cot, closing his eyes until it should be over. This was not the first attack upon him since he was taken from home, and he knew from experience that eventually his tormentors would tire of the game.

But Gavril was especially inventive. "First we gotta see that this is really truly a Yid! Let's take his pants off and make sure!" The peasant's massive arm forced Herschel down on the bed, and the others pulled off his trousers. Like a teacher showing a class a specimen of some vile plant, Gavril nodded. "Yep, look at that! He's one of them all right!"

In a moment he had taken out his own penis, comparing the two with salacious comments for the elucidation of the others. Then, standing over Herschel, he released his urine in a hot splashing stream into Herschel's face.

A door slammed, and there was a roar loud enough to be heard over the appreciative laughter of the men. "Enough! Get the hell off him!" A newcomer had entered the barracks and grabbed Gavril roughly from behind.

At the authority in the voice, the other men backed off.

The new arrival pulled Gavril off Herschel, who lay numb with shock in a pool of the other man's water.

"What are you, some kind of animal!" the newcomer exclaimed with an anger so hard-edged that it was like a slap in the face. "Now get out of here! Go pick up this man's things!"

The soldiers looked uncertainly at Gavril, but at least for the moment he was as intimidated as the others. Sheepishly they filed out.

Herschel's savior tossed him a towel. "There's clean water in that bucket over there."

Silent and wary, Herschel cleansed himself the best he could and pulled on the pants that had been kicked under the cot.

"My name's Mikhail. I heard a new batch of recruits had arrived. I'm a little late, but I want to welcome you to Camp Blagoveschensk."

*I*t was not the end of Gavril's bullying, but when it became clear that Herschel was under Mikhail's protection, the ragging became less overt. There were still incidents. Once when Mikhail was in the infirmary overnight, Gavril's gang set upon Herschel and beat him so badly that he had urinated blood for a week. That was the worst of the physical punishment, but petty meannesses continued. They emptied his pack on the floor just before inspection. They stole his tea. They tripped him when he walked by. Once they locked him in the barracks so that he would miss roll call.

While Mikhail saved Herschel considerable grief from the men in the barracks, he had no clout with the officers. For peasant recruits, life in the tsar's army was mostly good. For one thing, the food was plentiful, as it was not always at home, and on feast days the ration included a glass of vodka. Duties were not heavy and paydays came around regularly. The "work" consisted of drilling, taking care of the beautiful Cossack mounts, helping in the kitchens, the forge, or the other workshops—nothing like the backbreaking field work they were used to on the estates. Many of them even learned to read and write while they were serving the terms of their enlistment. On the other hand, for Jews, many of whom died of exposure, abuse, or even suicide, the army was hell on earth. The dirtiest and most disgusting tasks in the camp—emptying the outhouses, burying the dead, mucking out the stables—were reserved for Jews; if it were the Sabbath, so much the better. Disobedience could result in a flogging with the *nagaika*, the lead-tipped leather whip, even to the death. The Jews bent under any burden, mindful of the injunction to preserve life even if they must violate *halacha*, religious law.

Herschel thanked God for allowing him to live to escape. He left his cache of tea and his canteen credit for Mikhail and only hoped that his erstwhile protector would understand how grateful he had been for his friendship.

*E*arly the next morning Herschel walked through the gates of Blagoveschensk Camp without a backward glance. Chaya Leya, dressed in her traveling clothes, was waiting for him with her trunk, boxes, and dressing case at the ferry landing. They would cross the Amur River to the little Manchurian port city of Aigun, to board a train on the newly completed Circum-Baikal Loop of the Trans-Siberian. A short journey of three days would bring them to the Sungari River to meet the riverboat for a leisurely two-day descent into Harbin. From Harbin they would travel overland to Shanghai, where Herschel had heard there was a large community of Jews.

The Amur was wide here, and deep. As the little ferry made its way across the choppy waters, Herschel remembered the four thousand Chinese who had lost their lives in this river. An involuntary shudder passed through him. Davka's plan, Mikhail had said. Had Davka also betrayed Chaya Leya and himself?

"What's the matter?" Chaya Leya asked, pressing against his side.

"Nothing." He could spare Chaya Leya.

In Aigun they had a two-hour wait for the train. The station was tiny and stuffy, and after Herschel had purchased the tickets—the first successful test of his forged identity papers!—they stood outside on the platform to wait.

Herschel had a surprise for Chaya Leya that she would discover when they boarded the train. He had bought soft-class tickets with a compartment to themselves, and for just this one time they would take their meals in the dining car. It was Herschel's first decision as a husband. Chaya Leya would undoubtedly scold that it was a needless expense, but after all, it was their wedding journey!

Slowly other passengers gathered—a well-to-do Chinese family, the father in a long, padded gown of silk, a skullcap on his head from which emerged a queue, the mother wearing a dark cheongsam, and two small children incongruous in Western dress, two Russian businessmen deep in discussion, a robust British woman with a wan little girl in tow, and a very beautiful woman in furs, waiting while a man who must have been her husband purchased their tickets and arranged for their baggage. A handful of hard-class passengers, Chinese and Caucasian both, and shabbier than the others, were also standing in clusters, waiting for the train to come.

Chaya Leya was enjoying herself, but Herschel was tense and nervous. Surely by now, he thought, the sergeant-major would have discovered his absence and sent out an alarm. The military police might even now be crossing the river to search for him. He looked down at himself. Anyone could see he had not been a civilian for a while. The suit Chaya Leya had brought was too snug, and the sleeves were short; to his mind, the ill-fitting clothes branded him a runaway and deserter. He chewed his nails, and his eyes darted back and forth, observing the waiting passengers for possible threat. The husband of the fur-clad woman had now emerged from the station. The sight of him, a full colonel in Cossack uniform, set Herschel to trembling.

Chaya Leya pulled him away from the others. "You have to stop this!" she told him severely. "We don't look different from anyone else. Unless you act funny, no one will notice us."

Herschel was sheepish. Peering around him, he saw that the colonel was lighting a cigarette while staring into the distance to see if the train was coming, his wife was having a friendly chat with the Englishwoman, the businessmen were preoccupied, and the Chinese, even the children, were self-absorbed. No one appeared the least bit interested in them. Herschel's spine relaxed, and his lips essayed a tentative smile that turned genuine when his eyes, resting upon Chaya Leya, saw how flushed she was with happiness now that Blagoveschensk was almost behind them.

Herschel had been unable to find anyone in the camp or in the city to perform a marriage ceremony. Among the Jews in camp there were a number of yeshiva students and a few older men of learning, but as it happened, no rabbi. None at all. There had been one in the winter, but he had died of pneumonia before Chaya Leya's arrival. Herschel had had too many other things on his mind to dwell on this problem; first he had to see Chaya Leya nursed back to health, and second, he needed to work out the details of his escape. When the time of leaving was actually upon them, however, it pressed upon his mind.

"What shall I do?" a despairing Herschel had asked a former student at the famous yeshiva at Lvov. He had chosen this one as a confidant over his friend Avraham because of his reputation for outstanding piety and wisdom. His youth played a part in the decision, too, since Herschel figured he was of an age to understand the longing to possess one's beloved.

The young scholar considered the problem at length, pursing his lips and furrowing his brow. At last he said, "On the one hand, you have a responsibility to be an honorable man. As an honorable man, you must protect the good name of your betrothed so that none should have occasion to call her unchaste."

"Oh." Herschel's face fell.

"But on the other hand—"continued the yeshiva student.

"Yes?"

"On the other hand, is it possible for you to keep safe her reputation in circumstances where you have little choice but to travel as man and wife?"

"Not really," Herschel agreed, wondering where the argument was leading.

"If you travel separately, say as brother and sister, you will call attention to yourselves, is that not so? And if you are noticed, you endanger your lives. The Torah teaches that it is a sin for one not to take every precaution to safeguard life."

"That is true," Herschel said hopefully.

"But if you go as man and wife, will it not be a betrayal of her parents who you say were good to you? The question is, Rosen, is it your duty to protect her honor or her life?"

"Her life, of course," Herschel said promptly.

"On the other hand, what kind of future can you have together if it is built on lies and broken trust? Is that not a betrayal of spiritual life as much as risking death is a betrayal of physical life?"

"I guess so—"

"Yet," continued the yeshiva student, shaking his head, "these are extraordinary times, and the rabbis allow a certain latitude."

Herschel raised his downcast eyes, hopeful once more.

"Consider the Israelites in the desert, Herschel," said the former student, rocking his upper body back and forth as in prayer. "In the years of the Exodus, had they more priests to bless their marriages in the wilderness than you have? No. In generations of slavery in the land of Egypt, did priests exist? How then to consecrate marriage?"

"How?" asked Herschel, wishing he had devoted more time to the study of Torah.

"Why, simply in the vows of a pure heart."

"You mean—?"

"Yes, Herschel, why not? As your ancestors in the desert did, so shall you do also. Go to your loved one." The young man raised a pale hand in a sort of benediction. "And may your coming together be blessed."

Herschel wrung the student's hand and swore not to forget him.

"But listen, *chaver*, as soon as you get to Harbin," the student warned, "you'd better find a rabbi."

"You are a *tzaddik*, a righteous man," Herschel said. "I will always be in your debt."

*C*haya Leya and Herschel's marriage commenced with the leisurely five-day journey to Harbin. Herschel had explained the yeshiva student's reasoning to Chaya Leya, and after considering the matter, she had nodded concurrence. "In my mind, beloved," she had said, "we have been married since the Sunday after Passover."

Each day of this magical journey had no beginning and no end, and bliss softly blurred the outlines of reality. They made love first to the sound of iron wheels on track, later to the turning paddle wheels of the riverboat. Chaya Leya was shy but Herschel was tender, and his physical self felt almost as familiar to her as her own. They had known and loved each other for fifteen years. Together now in a new way, they explored undreamed-of capacities for expressing love. Lifelong habits of reticence melted away. They talked through the days and in the night, making gifts to each other of secret dreams while discarding secret hurts. Each day was discovery and revelation, and love lent perfection to the smallest things—the wild berries bought in paper cones at railway stops were surpassingly sweet and beautiful to behold, the wine they drank smelled of flowers and prickled deliciously on the tongue, and each morning's dawn was like a celebration of the Creation.

The train chugged its way south, crossing the Lesser Khingan Range. These smooth and rounded hills were as different from the steep granite cliffs around Baikal as the ancient Chinese civilization was from the brash Russian culture. Gradually, as the train descended to the alluvial basin of the Sungari River, the trees and mountain vegetation gave way to undulating plains of rich black soil. From the windows of the train, small farmhouses could be seen, grazing herds of sheep and goats, cultivated fields. Herschel identified millet, wheat, flax, and sugar beets. Dropping to sea level, they saw their first rice paddies. Chaya Leya was fascinated by the women with their skirts hiked up and knotted at their waists, standing knee-deep in water to harvest the rice. She waved vigorously at them, but never had a smile or a nod back. For hard, backbreaking work, the lives of these women were similar to those of the wives of the Siberian taigas. Yet while the Russian women had greeted the passing train with waving kerchiefs and laughter, the Chinese seemed aloof, disdaining even to notice the train. She said as much to the Russian-speaking Englishwoman who, with her daughter, shared a table with them in the dining car that evening.

"They are Manchu, not Chinese," the Englishwoman said, "though there has been a fair amount of intermarriage by now. You notice that they are taller and lighter in skin than most Chinese." Lady Hayes-Farnsworth had spent many years in Manchuria and enjoyed talking about it. "If they seem unfriendly, it is only because they are a proud warrior people. Manchuria is named for them, you know. By the end of the seventeenth century the Manchus had conquered the whole of the Chinese Empire—and governed it brilliantly for a hundred years or more. In fact, the Manchu dynasty still occupies the throne of China."

"But how interesting that is!" exclaimed Chaya Leya. "I thought all Orientals were the same people!"

Lady Hayes-Farnsworth smiled. "No more than Russians and English people are exactly the same stock. But tell me," the Englishwoman said, "what brings you to this part of the world? Will you be staying in Harbin or going on? That delightful Colonel Roskov and his wife are on their way to Port Arthur. Isn't that interesting?"

Chaya Leya could see that Herschel was becoming agitated at the mention of the colonel. They had avoided him and his wife the whole of the trip, although Chaya Leya thought privately that this gave away more than it hid. She said lightly, "We are on our way to Shanghai. My husband has relatives there."

Herschel stood abruptly, not even waiting for Chaya Leya to finish her tea. "Please excuse us, but my wife has not been well and must rest—"

After that, Herschel arranged that they eat at a table for two.

On the third day the train reached its termination point, and the passengers transferred to a funny bow-shaped junk that was to be their transportation down the Sungari River into Harbin.

Herschel and Chaya Leya had purchased berths, but the cabin was very cramped and it was stuffy belowdecks; they elected to sleep on deck under the star-pierced sky.

"Now, Herschel, will you relax?" Chaya Leya asked. "We are four days from Blagoveschensk, and there's no sign that we've been followed. Your papers have been checked five times already, and there has never been a question about them. The day after tomorrow we'll be in a part of China where the Russian government can't touch us! We're almost there, Herschel, *free!*"

"You're right, as always. I've been silly. Davka's papers are perfect." Herschel's arms pulled Chaya Leya close.

He lay on his back, holding Chaya Leya and naming the constellations over to himself. Big Dipper. North Star. Cassiopia. Orion.

She fell asleep with her head on his chest, hearing the regular thrum of his heartbeat beneath her cheek.

*T*he river trip into Harbin was perfect but brief. Disembarking, the passengers found the Russian police waiting to examine their papers.

"Please have ready your passports and identity cards for the captain to examine," said a police sergeant as the passengers lined up on deck to disembark.

There was a nervous rustling among the travelers, furtive examinations of papers, a whispering one to the other as if guilt were confirmed by the mere fact of a police presence.

Herschel turned as pale as death, and his forehead beaded with sweat. "My God, my God," he muttered over and over.

Chaya Leya took his hand. "Calm yourself," she murmured. "You give yourself away."

The Rosens hung back, watching, until most of the passengers had passed through the police checkpoint. They could see that the captain examined each document quickly before nodding the person through. No one had yet been detained. Surely it would be all right. After all, Davka was a master forger.

When they came to the desk, the captain did not look up, just reached out his hand for the documents. He was finished with Chaya Leya in a moment, and she stepped aside.

"This is our first visit to Harbin," she said, chattering to cover Herschel's nervousness, "and we're so excited to finally be here! It looks to be so interesting!" Why must Herschel's hands tremble so!

The captain took up Herschel's papers, passport first. "From Byelorussia, eh? What are you doing so far from home?"

"I was in the army, sir—in Blagoveschensk."

The captain looked up, his tufted black eyebrows rising. "Discharge papers, please."

Herschel fumbled in his pocket for the certificate of discharge.

Chaya Leya said brightly, "Of course, we're really just passing through on our way to Shanghai, but we want to see all the sights while we're here—"

Herschel wiped his glistening forehead with his sleeve while the police captain examined the papers.

"All right," the captain said, "seems to be in order."

Herschel swallowed hard, his relief patent.

The official handed back everything but the identity card. This he raised closer to his eyes. "This is odd," he said. "Where was it issued?"

Alarmed, Herschel said, "Odd? How, sir?"

"It was signed by Vassily Berdyaev who hasn't been at the ministry for at least two years now. It should have the signature of Boris Klyuchevsky." The captain drew a magnifying glass from his pocket and, scowling, scrutinized the offending document.

"I received this identity card with my discharge in Blagoveschensk, sir." A certain shrillness had entered Herschel's voice and made the captain look up. "It isn't my fault—"

Chaya Leya interrupted quickly. "He doesn't know anything about it. He was given the identity paper just this way." Her tinkling laughter floated over the desk. "Imagine! Issuing this on an old form!"

"Hmn," said the police captain, looking from one to the other. "Well, it's probably an error—someone saving money by using leftover forms. But you understand we have to check it out with Blagoveschensk and with Moscow. Until then, Citizen Rosen, I will have to hold you."

"But I—we have a train to catch—my wife, what will happen to her if you take me away?" Herschel cried.

"That's not our problem," the captain said, not unkindly. "Take him to the jail," he said to one of the policemen. He was well-pleased to have found a suspect.

"But, Sir Captain," Chaya Leya cajoled in a falsely lilting treble, "obviously this is nothing but a simple mistake—"

The captain shrugged. He had no illusions about bureaucracy. He agreed with the woman that a clerk somewhere had made an error, but in the meantime, while it was being clarified, at least one arrest could be claimed on the month's report.

Policemen, one on either side, took Herschel's arms.

"Wait!" Herschel cried, trying to shake them off. "I have to talk with my wife for a moment."

The captain was a decent sort. He nodded assent, and the policemen relinquished their hold, though remaining close.

Herschel's face was the color of paper when he turned to Chaya Leya. "It will be all right. They will get it straightened out." His strangled voice betrayed the words. "But you must not stay alone. Find the shul and tell the rabbi what has happened. They will take care of you until I am free. The authorities have no reason to keep me in jail."

Chaya Leya nodded, too frightened to trust herself to speak.

"Call at the jail tomorrow, missus," the police captain said in a friendly tone. He had nothing against this nice young woman.

Chaya Leya nodded. Her brain was racing ahead, considering possibilities. If necessary, there was always the option of a bribe. Russian officials being what they were, it would all work out. In a day or two they would be rolling through the Chinese countryside toward Shanghai and laughing over the whole ridiculous business.

Chapter 37

Chaim worked in ten-hour shifts in the bowels of the *Archimedes*, shoveling coal into the jaws of the furnaces that powered the vessel. The work was unskilled and unpleasant, but for someone who had been tempered in the crucible of Brodsky's sugar refinery, it seemed easy enough. Besides, he liked Constantine, the good-humored boss of the "black gang" which fired the furnaces. When he got used to them, he found the other men on the gang to be friendly.

Chaim learned to speak a little Greek and to pick out from among the crew those men he could trust and those he would do well to avoid. Stavros remained his special friend, tutor, and defender throughout the voyage. Whenever there was a prank afoot, a celebration, some fresh tidbit for the evening meal, Stavros's voice shouting "Hy-am" rang out for him. Most of the others called him Russkie. He liked the fat old man named Skouros who played a stringed Greek instrument, a bouzouki, not unlike a balalaika. And in time Chaim developed a particular fondness for the cabin boy, Theo, who was the same age as Simcha.

Mostly the sailors were a hardworking, decent sort. Chaim's only real uneasiness was with the muscular Turk whose stare seemed to follow him everywhere, on the deck, when they sat together at table, even when they lay down to sleep. One hot afternoon when the men stripped off their clothes on deck and were sloshing themselves with cold sea water, the Turk's hand reached out and stroked Chaim's naked flanks, his hot eyes caressing him, his wet mouth stretched in a lascivious grin. Chaim swung around, his face flushed, his fist raised to strike Pasha where he stood. Stavros's hand on his arm stopped him. Stavros shook his head. "No."

When they were dressed, Stavros took Chaim aside. "Pasha likes boys, not women," he said in the pidgin mixture of Greek and Russian in which the two conversed. "A sickness of the Turks!" Stavros spat on the deck, indicating his hostility to the whole of the Turkish people.

A repugnance verging on nausea rose in Chaim. Growing up he had heard such things whispered but had taken them to be the imaginings of boys not yet become men. That the Turk had chosen him for his attentions, of all the men on the ship, made him feel uneasy and unclean. "If he touches me again, I'll kill him," Chaim said slowly.

"Be careful, Hy-am. Pasha has a quick knife."

After that time on deck Pasha no longer trailed Chaim to stare at him. He took instead to taunting him for his youth and inexperience. Time and again Stavros restrained Chaim from answering back. "That Turk no good. He full of death. Let what he say pass over you."

Chaim knew it was good advice, and there were whole days when he was able to forget his nemesis. It was his good luck that Pasha was not in the engine room.

Constantine, who had first shipped out as a cabin boy younger than Theo, instructed Chaim in the ways of the sea. Standing together on deck one cool evening, he told him that while the shanghaiing of crew was common, the captain of the *Archimedes* did not himself condone it—not from any moral standpoint but because crewmen obtained this way were usually worthless. Chaim's kidnapping had been a matter of simple expediency. One of the crew had been stabbed in a waterfront brawl in Odessa, and with a cargo of grain threatening to rot before it reached Constantinople, there was nothing to do but to pick up a replacement any way they could. Constantine shrugged. It was Chaim's destiny that he had been standing on the dock at the very moment they urgently needed someone.

He clapped Chaim on the back, smiling. "Still, not too bad, eh, Russkie?"

Chaim agreed. "*Nyet*. Not too bad."

Occasionally, lying in his bunk at night before he fell asleep, Chaim thought about how far he had come since Polotsk. The old certainties passed on by parents, grandparents, and shul were not always applicable, and conversely some quandaries of his present life were not answered by anything learned at home—the attentions of a Pasha, for instance. When he thought about it at all, Chaim was troubled that there had been a loosening of his Jewish identity. The process had begun in Kiev when he had sacrificed the observance of the Sabbath for a few additional hours of sleep. Now aboard the *Archimedes* he neglected even the most minimal of religious duties. If he had had a mind to do so, he could certainly have recited the daily prayers, which he knew by heart. That he never thought of doing so was because it was more comfortable to blend unobtrusively into shipboard life. For the first time in his life he was someplace where he never heard the word "Jew" spoken. He liked that.

Soon Chaim lost track of the days so that he did not even know when he profaned the Sabbath. Not that he would have had a choice, for the devouring furnaces had to be fed every day of the week. In the matter of keeping the commandments of *kashrut*, the dietary laws, it was no simpler; constantly hungry from hard physical labor, he either ate what was put before him or he did without. With a wry smile he recalled his early enjoyment of a supper of roasted meat which he took to be breast of chicken. The flavor was intriguing, slightly smoky, and somewhat strong, which he attributed to unknown seasonings. He helped himself to a second portion. "Good chicken!" he said to Stavros.

The little man looked puzzled.

"Chicken?" Chaim pantomimed a flapping of wings.

Still, Stavros frowned.

Chaim made pecking motions with his head, accompanying it with the cackling sounds of hens in a barnyard. Stavros and the other men at table howled with laughter.

Finally Stavros wiped his eyes with the back of his hand. He shook his head. "Pig!" he said, then, snuffling, "Oink, oink."

It took Chaim a moment to gather this in. Pork! He had actually eaten the unclean meat of a pig! Chaim spit out what was still in his mouth and ran up the companionway ladder to the rail, where he vomited his dinner into the sea. How could he have ingested this vileness and not even known it! What other forbidden things had he unwittingly digested?

Chaim's greatest worry during these days was not about food or prayer but about his parents. Mammeh, he knew, would be frantic over his disappearance, certain that the worst had happened. Ever since Channah and Yaakov had died, Mammeh constantly expected the worst. God alone knew how she had reacted to his dropping out of sight on top of Herschel's conscription. He sighed. What trouble he had brought on the family!

Chaim coaxed Theo to steal paper, ink, and a pen from the captain's cabin. In secret he began to write a letter home, intending somehow to get it posted from Constantinople. The mate, Athanasius Anargyros, had told Chaim that if he continued to behave well, he would be allowed to go ashore with Stavros as chaperon when they reached their next major cargo stop. Chaim was thrilled and excited. He had watched from the railing while the other crewmen disembarked on brief shore leaves in Constanta in Rumania, and later when they took on fresh water at a small port in Bulgaria. He hungered for the feel and the smell of the earth.

The ship was to dock in Constantinople in late October and to remain there for almost a week. At the great crossroads city that straddled the continents of Europe and Asia, the grain taken on in Odessa would be unloaded for transshipment by rail west into Greece and southeast to the Arab lands of the Middle East. In its place tobacco and cotton grown in Turkey would be brought aboard to be sold or traded at later ports of call.

One bright morning the *Archimedes* approached the point where the Bosporus joins the Black Sea to the Sea of Marmora and provides an outlet into the Mediterranean. Constantinople, the City of Mosques, slid into view, its domes and minarets rosy in the light of dawn. They docked in Stambul, the wonderful natural harbor sheltered between the arms of the Golden Horn. The men of the *Archimedes* hastened to their tasks that day, unloading the grain sacks with an alacrity that was usually wanting. By early afternoon the men who were going ashore had been dismissed.

His letter to his parents pressed against his breast and his first pay clinking in his pockets, Chaim disembarked, his arm linked in that of Stavros on one side and old Skouros on the other. Theo, unfortunately, had come down with chicken pox a day out of port and was confined to his bunk. Only a skeleton crew was left behind to guard the ship.

For an hour or two Stavros took his job of chaperon so seriously that Chaim could just imagine what threats the first mate had made should Stavros lose him in the city. Athanasius Anargyros and Stavros need not have worried, for Chaim had no intention of trying to escape the *Archimedes* just yet. Unexpectedly given an opportunity to see something of the world, he had no intention of wasting it!

Chafing but dutiful to his charge, Stavros humored Chaim's desire to see the city's bazaars, mosques, and public buildings by racing him pell-mell past one public place and another. Finally he exploded. "No more! You sailor, not goddamn tourist, Hy-am! Come! I show you a t'ing or two!"

Following his tough little friend back to the area of congested quays, Chaim was dragged into a succession of dark waterfront bars filled with sailors and the women they bought, pink-shaded back rooms where a sweet-smelling substance was inhaled through water pipes, and tavernas in which dusky-skinned women, bellies gleaming darkly, gyrated to the sensual clap of the tambourine and the beat of drums. The brothels were in this area, too, halfway up the hill from the Galata Bridge. By then Stavros was drunk and offered to treat Chaim to a woman, but Chaim shook his head. The women had a greasy look under the rouge and powder, and they stirred him not at all. He had heard about body- and mind-destroying diseases that whores give their customers.

"You go! I walk around outside. Meet you at ship, no worry, I be there."

Stavros looked at him doubtfully.

"Really. I be there. My word!"

After a momentary struggle between lust and responsibility, lust won out, and Stavros nodded. "Four days, Hy-am! Ship leave in four days!" he cautioned.

"Promise. I be there."

Left free and alone when Stavros departed in the company of a dark-skinned woman, Chaim oriented himself. Constantinople was two distinct cities: Pera, the modern Levantine city of wealthy foreigners, and Stambul, the medieval city of Moslems, where people lived as they had for centuries. He had separated from Stavros at the docks of Pera, and his landmark was the Galata Bridge on one end of Yuksek Kaldirim Street and the Galata Tower on the other end.

Chaim found a plain, clean hotel that he could afford in Pera, and the proprietor told him where he would find the central postal office. Affixing the stamps that would take his letter to Polotsk, Chaim felt choked with emotion, wondering if he would ever see his parents again. Fortunately depression could not last, in the noise, color, and bustle of the city.

Leaving the post office, he explored Stambul, eating from the stalls of street vendors when he was hungry and finding a city park to rest in when he was tired. At sunset he watched the small fishing barques tie up at the wharf below the Galata Bridge, and the fishermen spread out their catch for sale, mostly mullet and tuna, while veiled women jostled to buy the biggest and freshest of the fish for their husbands' supper.

When he discovered the Great Bazaar, it became his favorite place. Here merchants of a dozen hues and costumes cried out in many languages to attract shoppers. Each street was dedicated to a particular craft, like the Street of the Quilt Makers and the Street of the Spoons. Anything that one could possibly imagine was for sale somewhere in the labyrinth of streets and arcades. The richness of the wares on the Street of the Goldsmiths bedazzled Chaim, and on the Way of the Carpetmakers he soon became surfeited on rugs woven in designs of great intricacy and executed in the richest of colors. Leather goods, pewter and brass, precious and semiprecious stones, fabrics and glassware, sacks full of spices—fresh vanilla beans from Madagascar, cloves from Zanzibar—it was almost too much. Over all hung the sweet smell of hashish mingled with the spicy odor of lamb cooking on open braziers.

When Chaim found the street of clothing stalls, he took his time in selecting a coat. The Turks being smaller, he had trouble finding one that fit across his broad shoulders.

"Mister want coat from wool of finest angora sheep?" the merchant asked in Greek, a broad, white-toothed smile creasing his dark face.

Chaim shook his head that he did not understand.

"Ah, voulez-vous un habit, non?"

Chaim shrugged.

The merchant tried Italian and German before hitting upon Russian, perhaps the least adequate of his languages. By signs and gestures, Chaim made his needs known. Negotiations took some time, as the Turk tried to pass off a garment too snug and then several others made from inferior materials; the tailor in Chaim would have none of them. Finally they came to an agreement on one of closely woven wool in a blue so dense as to be almost black, not Chaim's immediate preference but the only coat that fit fairly well and was warm without being heavy upon his shoulders. He was embarrassed; he had already taken up the better part of an hour and drunk two cups of the merchant's coffee and now wanted only to quickly conclude the deal and depart. For the shopkeeper, the longer it took, the more animated and smiling he became; he was only disappointed that the haggling over price was brief. Westerners, he concluded, did not know how to bargain. He would have sold the coat gladly for half!

Chaim was satisfied. He discarded the hated shipboard garment, stuffing it into a trash container from which some beggar would surely retrieve it. In his new coat he felt a different man altogether.

Even a place as fascinating as the bazaar eventually palled and Chaim returned to his hotel early that night, tired but too stimulated to fall asleep for a long time. It was good to be in a room by himself, good to bathe and crawl between actual sheets. Refreshed in the morning, Chaim set off early to visit the historical sights listed in the Baedecker the innkeeper had kindly loaned him.

His first stop was St. Sophia, its dome and spires dominating the landscape of the city. Once a Christian basilica, now a Moslem mosque, for a thousand years its enormous interior had awed visitors from all over the world. Chaim found it oppressively cold and bare, and he did not stay long. More to his liking was the smaller Blue Mosque. Removing his shoes and washing his feet before entering like any other worshiper, he knelt inside, where the azure-glazed wall tiles dazzled the eye. The high, thin sound of the muezzin, calling good Moslems to prayer, was somehow reminiscent of the intricate cantillation of Hebrew and gave him an unanticipated thrill of pleasure.

After his visits to the mosques, there were still three days remaining before the *Archimedes* was scheduled to sail again. He had scarcely seen any of the ship's crew since leaving Stavros in the bar that first afternoon. But then, he had not spent his time where most of the others might have been expected to spend theirs, partaking of the various pleasures of the waterfront. Since Pera's European atmosphere was not appreciably different from Odessa or Kiev, he preferred the more exotic Stambul. Here were the moldering shells of Crusader churches and monasteries, here, too, one saw parts of Roman buildings curiously incorporated into the walls of tenement flats as well as the broken remnants of Byzantine sculptures carelessly strewn in empty lots. The buildings of Stambul were in need of repair, the paint peeling off the sides of houses, and the paving stones cracked with grass growing up between—and yet it conveyed a history and vitality that captured Chaim's imagination.

Although he could not understand their language, he enjoyed being among the men who relaxed on unsteady divans in dim coffeehouses. Like them, he sipped tiny cups of heavily sweetened Turkish coffee and looked out at the life of the streets where the mysterious veiled figures of women glided past without a sound.

On two of his remaining afternoons Chaim walked across the Galata Bridge which spanned the Golden Horn. It was crowded with humanity: women on shopping expeditions, mustachioed *hamals* bent double under loads of fruit, carpets, and spices, Gypsies banging tambourines to attract an audience to performances of tame bears, street vendors selling baubles.

Chaim spent several hours in the Topkapi, once the palace of the sultans, later abandoned by them in favor of the more western Dolmahbace Palace which was at present the residence of royalty and the seat of government. The Topkapi covered one of seven hills on which Old Stambul rested, its spacious grounds sweeping down to the very edge of the sea. Chaim stood staring up at it, absorbing the beauty of its arched doorways, latticed windows, and delicate pillars. Surely it must have been here in this very palace where Princess Scheherazade, about whom Mammeh had read them, beguiled the evil sultan with her stories! If only he had the gift to tell Mammeh what he was seeing!

On the morning of the last day Chaim took himself to one of the public baths, called in Turkish *hamam*. It was rather more ornate than the *banya* in either Polotsk or Kiev, the tubs and pools of marble, the ceilings domed and decorated with gold leaf. Leaving his clothes in a dressing room outside, he went first into a cold section, where a bath attendant helped him wash and dry himself before entering the hot room to steam and relax in a deep pool of superheated water. When Chaim emerged more than an hour later, he looked at his fingernails which were truly clean for the first time in months, and stroked his beard which felt soft and silky to his touch. He made his way to Pera, where he had decided to have a final meal in one of the restaurants where there were white cloths upon the table and an orchestra played behind palm trees. A fine ending to his four days in Constantinople, he thought.

All too soon the hour for the *Archimedes* to put out to sea approached. Chaim did not know where to look for Stavros. Undoubtedly his friend was with one of the women who promised the delights of the harem for just a few copper coins, but there were many brothels near the quays. Now, as the time arrived for them to return to the ship, Chaim became increasingly anxious, remembering Stavros's warning: "You no come back, you sorry!" with a dramatic gesture suggesting hanging, his head lolling to one side, dark eyes bulging in their sockets.

With no sign of Stavros and so many whorehouses where he might still be, Chaim ran from one to another, describing his friend in pidgin Greek and gesture. Each proprietress shook her head. No, no short, broad-chested Greek sailor in her house. No one named Stavros. No, shrugging indifferently, the name *Archimedes* meant nothing. So many ships in the harbor, so many sailors, how could a person remember all the names?

As Chaim entered an alleyway where he had been directed to still another brothel, a familiar figure reeled towards him. The Turk called Pasha.

An evil grin twisted the Turk's mouth, and he stopped in his tracks, eyeing Chaim speculatively.

Chaim instinctively moved backward.

"Hah! Russkie! C'mon closer! No hurt. Not be afraid!"

Not taking his eyes from the Turk's face, Chaim remained silent, rooted to where he stood. His heart hammered against his chest, but his body felt taut, prepared for whatever came next.

"C'mon, Russkie! I make you feel nize!" the man wheedled, moving closer. "I luf you!"

"Get away!" Chaim said, contempt edging his words.

Surprisingly quick and lithe for a man so obviously drunk, the Turk sprang at Chaim. The force of his leap knocked the younger man to the ground. A heavy, muscled arm held Chaim where he lay with his face pressed against the cobblestones of the dirty street while a huge hand tugged urgently at his trousers. Horrified, Chaim surmised the Turk's intent and fear poured adrenaline into his bloodstream. Even so, he could not throw off the heavier man. Now Pasha's hand was inside Chaim's breeches, touching him where no man should touch another. Chaim could feel the Turk's sex hard and hot as a poker. Pasha's stiff penis was prodding at Chaim's buttocks, trying to force its way inside.

Chaim twisted and turned, struggling against this obscenity. Straining desperately, he managed to throw the Turk off and scrambled to his feet, pulling up his pants as best he could. Now Pasha was on his feet also, coming toward Chaim, a flashing knife in his hand. His face was contorted with rage and desire. Chaim backed away from the menacing blade that sliced the air.

In the weeks of shoveling coal, Chaim had developed considerable strength in his shoulders and biceps. Cold sober while the Turk was drunk, Chaim saw his chance and jumped the other man, his hands grasping Pasha's knife arm and forcing the wrist back until the dagger clattered to the stones. All the revulsion Chaim felt, all the pent-up anger he had swallowed at Pasha's jibes and taunts, all his horror at what the Turk had tried to do, coalesced in him. Relentlessly he pummeled Pasha, waiting for him to drop, willing him to die.

But drunk or sober, Pasha was stronger than Chaim would have believed. He fought back with fists and feet, pushing Chaim back and back, giving as good as he got. Where the alley made a tight turn, Chaim found himself trapped against a wall. Pasha's evil face was so close that he could feel the heat of his breath. With slow deliberation Pasha's hands sought and grasped Chaim around the throat. His thumbs began to push against Chaim's windpipe, pressing slowly. So this was how he would die, was it, Chaim thought wonderingly. In a dirty alleyway in Constantinople. Just another unidentified corpse when they found him. He closed his eyes against the wickedness in Pasha's wet face and slavering mouth. As his breath was choked off and his vision blurred, the words of the *Sh'ma*, unthought of for months, echoed inside his head. "Hear, O Israel, the Lord Our God, the Lord is One."

At the moment of Chaim's passing from consciousness, Pasha's hands inexplicably loosened. Chaim gasped for air, coughed, took a great gulp into his burning air passage, retched. He sank to his knees, and his eyes slowly swiveled, seeking his tormentor. The Turk's face, when he found it, wore a look of astonishment, and his mouth worked but no sound came from it. In slow motion Pasha reeled away a few steps and then, turning to face Chaim, fell heavily in a heap on the stones. A knife was buried to the hilt in his back.

Constantine, the burly boss of the engine room, stood at the entrance to the alley. His mouth was a tight line, his eyes hard. "You all right, Russkie?"

Chaim nodded, ashamed and close to tears.

"Pick up your pants, then, and let's go. Didn't you hear the whistle from the ship?"

Shakily Chaim got to his feet, hitching up his breeches the best he could. In his haste, Pasha had torn the buttons off.

Constantine said kindly, "Not your fault what happened. That Pasha a bad man. What happened, nothing to do with you, could have been anyone."

Chaim started to follow Constantine, then stopped in his tracks. "Stavros! I have to find him!"

"No time! You'll be taken as a deserter. Stavros already back at the harbor!"

"I've got to make sure. You go, Constantine!" Chaim grasped his hands. "You saved my life."

There was a blast of a ship's whistle. Constantine stood teetering on his heels, uncertain. Finally he said. "All right. I go. I try to hold the longboat for you. No more than fifteen minutes now, Russkie, understand?"

Chaim was already on his way. At a dingy whorehouse at the end of the alley, Chaim discerned a gleam of recognition when he questioned the fat woman who sat knitting in the doorway. From this slight evidence he was convinced that Stavros was still upstairs. Chaim pushed his way past the mountain of flesh that barred his way and took the stairs two at a time. In the second room he tried he found Stavros unconscious on the bed, naked and snoring.

There was no time to waste, for the *Archimedes* was blasting its final warning call. Chaim hoisted Stavros, naked, to his shoulder and ran with him down the stairs and along the alley. Averting his eyes, he skirted the body of the Turk, crumpled where it had fallen. He raced down a steep hill to the dock, holding Stavros with one arm, the other hand keeping his trousers from falling down and tripping him. Passersby made way for him, pointing and laughing.

The longboat was already skimming across the water toward the ship, but the pilot heard Chaim's shout and, turning, saw the ridiculous sight that Chaim and his burden made at the edge of the pier. Slowly the boat wheeled about and the men, cheering and hooting, hauled Chaim and a dazed Stavros aboard.

When he had sobered up, Stavros thought it all an uproarious joke, and for the rest of his life repeated the story of how the tall Russian had thrown him naked over his back and carried him like a sack of grain to his boat just before it sailed away.

After Constantinople, the ties between Stavros, Chaim, and Constantine were strengthened. No one missed Pasha, for while he was a strong hand, he was a troublemaker. It was not a good thing to have a man with the Turk's appetites in the close confines of a ship. Another seaman would be enlisted to take his place when they reached Tunis.

As the ship made its way through the islands of the Aegean Sea en route to the next port of call, Chaim began to tell Stavros about his dream of going to America.

"Too bad, Hy-am. Too bad you not on French or British ship. Not little Greek boat. Could go to America on big ship." Stavros sighed at the pity of it.

Chaim said eagerly, "Where could I sign up on a ship for America? Maybe in Tunis?"

Stavros's eyes went blank.

"Where, Stavros? Where?"

"*Ne ponemayu.* No understand Russian," Stavros said.

Chaim remained thoughtful. Their next long stop would be in Tunis, where they would take on a load of lumber, olive oil, and dates and sell their cotton and Turkish tobacco. Would there be big ships in Tunis harbor? Would he have a chance there to slip away from his comrades and sign on for a transatlantic voyage? And if he tried and failed, what was the penalty that the master of the *Archimedes* could invoke?

He was preoccupied with these questions all the way to North Africa.

Chapter 38

How odd it was, Chaya Leya thought, that the rickshaw puller knew exactly where the synagogue was. As he plodded through dusty streets toward the very edge of the city, Chaya Leya kept her eyes closed and her lips moved: "I will lift up mine eyes unto the hills, from whence cometh my help. My help cometh from the Lord, which made heaven and earth. He that keepeth thee will not slumber—" Papa's psalm. How she longed for the comfort of his strong arm and steady eyes. Papa would know what to do, but he was many weeks away, Herschel was in jail, and she was alone and frightened in a foreign land that she did not understand. Herschel had instructed her to go to the shul. But suppose no one was there? Or suppose the rabbi assumed that Herschel was a criminal and turned her away? She must not panic. Their danger was great, but, she told herself, somehow she would work things out. If she had made it this far, she could get Herschel out of jail and to Shanghai. She made a conscious effort to focus on the words of the psalm. How did the rest go? "The Lord shall protect thee from evil. He shall preserve thy going out and thy coming in from this time forth, for evermore."

By the time the rickshaw man lowered the shafts of his strange conveyance, Chaya Leya was feeling somewhat more optimistic. He had delivered her to a street of Oriental-looking houses, stopping before what looked to be a walled Chinese compound.

"No!" Chaya Leya said sharply. "Not here. Synagogue." She struggled to explain. "Jewish church."

The man nodded, beaming and pointing toward the house.

Chaya Leya felt the tears begin to prickle in back of her eyes. Suppose she could not make this man understand! Maybe he would abandon her here on the very outskirts of the city! Or perhaps he had brought her to this isolated place because he intended her harm! Her heart began to thud, but he was smiling and pointing. His head bobbed up and down encouragingly.

Chaya Leya climbed down from the rickshaw and stood looking at the high wall surrounding the place. With the Chinese still urging her toward the gate, she shrugged and took a few steps forward. Perhaps someone inside could direct her to where she needed to go. The rickshaw man followed at her heels with her trunk precariously perched on his shoulder. Oh, God, Chaya Leya thought, this is crazy! She might even be arrested for trespassing. What did she know of this part of the world? To prove to the rickshaw man that he had brought her to the wrong place, she pushed on the gate, and it swung open into a shaded courtyard. Beyond a pleasant little fountain was a structure, one wall open to the air. Her eyes widened. She could hear the sound of men's voices davening—*praying* here? in this Chinese house? in Hebrew!

The rickshaw driver gave her a grinning half bow and extended his hand for payment. Unsure what to give him, Chaya Leya held out her own hand with a handful of Russian coins on the palm. He chose some before carrying her boxes into the courtyard. Who knew what a rickshaw should cost? She was so grateful to have reached this haven that she would gladly have emptied the total contents of her purse into his hand!

When the bowing, smiling Chinese had withdrawn, Chaya Leya edged up to the building and peeked inside. A minyan was chanting the late afternoon prayer called *mincha*. If the men noticed her at all, they paid her, a mere woman, no attention. She sat down on her trunk which the driver had thoughtfully left in the shade of a tree. If it had not been for her overwhelming sense of urgency, she would have found the courtyard pleasant and peaceful, but now she was frantic for the service to end. What must be happening to Herschel at the jail now! Yet she dared not interrupt the men, and it felt like a very long time until the final "amen."

The men, bearded, somberly dressed, wearing silken skullcaps, might have been from Papa's own shul at home. Somehow she had imagined something more exotic in this faraway place! They nodded slightly but kept their eyes averted as they filed past her and out the gate.

The rabbi, white-haired and ruddy-cheeked with spectacles sitting on the end of a prominent nose, beckoned her to come in. The sanctuary satisfied Chaya Leya's notion of the foreign. In an almost bare room was a raised *bimah* furnished with a cupboard for the Torah scrolls and a long teak table for holding the unrolled Torah while it was being read. An old-fashioned lamp, surely brought from some synagogue in Poland or Russia, burned over the Ark. Two beautiful rosewood chairs of curved Oriental design flanked it. Additional chairs of plainer design stood below the *bimah* in the body of the room; seating for women was in the very back, hidden behind a trio of magnificent painted screens depicting a Chinese Noah standing on the deck of his junklike ark to welcome the embarking animal pairs. Chaya Leya would not be able to appreciate this melding of cultures until some time in the future.

Rabbi Samsonovitch listened gravely to Chaya Leya's story, waiting sympathetically when her voice choked with tears, nodding his understanding, patting her hand. He was heartsick. So many young men conscripted, so much misery in the camps, so many attempts at escape. He had met other fugitives passing through Harbin but none before with a wife. The gathering clouds of a possible war with Japan complicated everything. He had heard that the police had set up roadblocks. Spies could be shot on the spot. He didn't know about deserters. He scratched his beard. Something would have to be done with Chaya Leya while the matter of her husband was adjudicated.

The rabbi, talking to cover his anxiety, led Chaya Leya through winding streets with names like "Flowering Peach" and "Bubbling Brook" to the nearby home of a pious elderly couple, Reb Meier Koch and his wife, Tzipah. The Kochs had been in Harbin since the end of '98, he told her, one of the original Jewish families who had taken advantage of the government's program to encourage rapid settlement of the city. Jews were allowed to buy land (as long as it was not in the heart of the city), could own businesses (but not work for the railroad), and were permitted access to the countryside with relatively few restrictions. At last count there were four hundred fifty-nine Jews in Harbin, the rabbi said. Reb Koch owned the small newsstand and bookstore on Kitaiskaya, the main street of town in the Russian part of the city. Since the Kochs were childless, they made anyone who needed help their own. He was certain that they would welcome Chaya Leya.

She had scarcely attended to what the rabbi was saying. When he paused for breath, she interrupted him. "But what about Herschel?"

"Yes, yes," Rabbi Samsonovitch said, shaking his head. "We will put our heads together and decide what to do. Maybe the police realize already that they've made a mistake. If they don't let him go free, we'll just have to see. You are not to worry."

"But—"

"Ah, we are here!" The rabbi shook the cluster of bells at the gate, and a Chinese servant let them in.

Both Kochs were home. Reb Meier was a portly man past middle-age but still vigorous in appearance. He came from Kiev and prided himself on being a modern city man who had discarded earlocks, beard, and head coverings, except in the shul itself. Frau Koch was a large, comfortable woman, whose multitude of bracelets jingled whenever she moved her fat arm.

As soon as she had heard the story, Frau Koch folded Chaya Leya to her ample bosom. Of course she would stay with them in their house! It would all work itself out, Chaya Leya would see.

"Please, please won't you go with me to talk to the police? See what's happening with Herschel?" she pleaded, turning first to the rabbi, then to the grave-faced Reb Koch.

The latter said, "Perhaps tomorrow. It's better not to be thought pushy."

Chaya Leya was outraged. "Pushy! Is it pushy to ask what they've done with my innocent husband!"

The rabbi stood up, glad to leave the Kochs with this problem. He was no good with women who might at any moment turn hysterical. "I must leave to make a call," he said. Awkwardly he patted Chaya Leya on the shoulder. "Reb Koch is wise in the ways of the Russians. Lean on his advice. Everything will be clearer by tomorrow." Hastily he let himself out.

"Get me a rickshaw, then!" Chaya Leya demanded. "I will go to police headquarters myself!"

"Believe me, that's not wise. Come, you are exhausted. My wife will make us a glass of tea."

"I know it's kind of you, and I thank you both very much, but don't you see? I can't sit here drinking tea when my husband is in trouble! Please! I have to go to him! I went to the shul to ask for help for him, not for me! Just tell me what direction to take to get to the police station!"

Reb Koch sighed. He and his wife looked at each other. Frau Koch shrugged and nodded to her husband. "All right. Let me tell our boy to get us a rickshaw. Only way to get around here. We will go together."

Frau Koch clucked soothingly, "You're right to want to see what's happening with your man," she said to Chaya Leya. "When you come back, we will have a nice supper. Things always look better on a full stomach."

Of course, Reb Koch was right, and there was nothing to be learned at the police bureau. No charges had been filed against Herschel. He was being held while his status was clarified. It was all very routine. They were ushered into a cold, bare visitors' room, where they were allowed five minutes with the prisoner.

It was odd, Chaya Leya thought fleetingly. When the policeman led Herschel into the room, he had been in police custody for only a few hours, and yet already his sun-browned skin seemed to have bleached out and he had shrunk in upon himself. Of medium build, wiry rather than strongly made like Chaim and Papa, he looked frail and vulnerable. His dark hair and beard were matted as though he had been asleep, and his eyes were red-rimmed and somehow furtive. It was probably, Chaya Leya thought, the yellow lamplight playing tricks, and yet she was frightened at the change. Unmindful of Reb Koch, she embraced Herschel, covering his face with kisses. He seemed distracted. Gently he put Chaya Leya from him and turned to the older man. "For myself I am not so worried," he said. "I have been through much that was hard in my life. But my wife is yet a girl—"

"Frau Koch and I will take care of Frau Rosen, do not fear."

"I am grateful," Herschel said wearily.

The two men talked in low voices. Chaya Leya stood with her back against the wall, fuming at how easily Herschel had dismissed her. Hurt and angry, it was as though she saw him for the first time and found him just like all men—except perhaps Papa! "Girl" indeed! Hadn't the last five nights proved to him that she was a woman? And did he think it was a "girl" who quite alone had made the long, grueling trip from Polotsk to Blagoveschensk? She sniffed loudly, but the men did not appear to hear.

The warder came to let the visitors out. Herschel, devoid of any trace of the ardent bridegroom, kissed Chaya Leya lightly on the forehead. "Go with Reb Koch now. He and his wife will watch over you while I can't." Anxiety clouded his eyes. "God knows what word Blagoveschensk will send about me—"

"But Davka—" she whispered.

"—is an evil man," he finished.

Chaya Leya settled in to wait. The days lengthened into weeks, and still Herschel had not been charged or tried. The Kochs' home, behind its Chinese wall, was small, square, European; they had had it built in the image of a proper Russian house. Chaya Leya slept in a small, curtained alcove off the parlor and insisted on helping Frau Koch with the cooking and housework in exchange for her board and room. She still had a few gold coins secured in her corset cover, and once or twice a week she brought home from market a fat chicken or a bunch of autumn chrysanthemums, some pears or maybe an embroidered handkerchief for Frau Koch.

"But my dear," Frau Koch demurred, "you don't have to do this! You are wonderful company for me, and you help me with the chores besides. We love having you."

"Please. I don't want to feel I am a burden."

Every day Chaya Leya walked to the jail. More often than not, she was turned away at the door. Occasionally she was allowed inside to see Herschel, though seldom for more than a few minutes at a time.

Chaya Leya quickly learned who the influential Jews of Harbin were. She went from one to another of them, pleading for their intercession on Herschel's behalf. "Please! You must! He is dying in that jail!"

They were sympathetic, but one after the other said the same thing. "Time takes care of all problems. Be patient." And "The authorities are unpredictable, depending on how the wind blows from St. Petersburg. Wait." And finally, "The less notice the police take of us Jews, the better it is for all of us."

"You mean," Chaya Leya said scornfully, "that you're afraid Herschel's being in jail will somehow rub off on you!"

After that, she did not know where else to turn for help. Finally Frau Koch said, "Perhaps, dear child, you should consider returning to your family."

Chaya Leya's reply was stony. "Herschel Rosen *is* my family!"

A sympathetic tear slid down Frau Koch's nose and she subsided. Poor child, she thought.

Chaya Leya grew increasingly restless and worried. Fall had given way to a very cold winter. The river had frozen over and would remain frozen, Frau Koch said, until April. For all practical purposes they were cut off from the outside world. It was unlikely that information concerning Herschel's status would arrive for several months now. She supposed this was all to the good, but how the time dragged! There was little money left. It had cost dearly to buy Davka's help, and afterward Herschel had splurged on first-class tickets to Harbin. Now Chaya Leya counted and recounted the remaining coins. Not enough to keep her for any length of time. Reb Meier told her not to worry, the shul would take up a collection if she needed anything.

"I don't want pity! I will find work."

"Work!" exclaimed Reb Meier. "Well," he said, shaking his head, "that might be difficult. A young woman should not work outside her home."

"Please, won't you help me? Maybe I can work for you in the bookstore—"

He shook his head. "There's scarcely enough to occupy me alone!"

"I can do housework, sewing, anything!"

"I will ask," he said with reluctance. "But in Harbin if a woman needs help in her house, she hires a Chinese. There won't be much for you here, my child."

A vague thought, a mere flicker of an idea, had been in the back of Chaya Leya's mind since arriving in Harbin. Desperate over the Kochs' lukewarm reception to the idea of her working for money, it sprang full-blown into consciousness. Her fellow passenger, Valodya—Mirov?—the flirtatious boy from the train, had been bound for Harbin. If the rabbi and the Kochs and the other Jews would not help her, perhaps he would.

Thoughtfully Yoysef bent his head to the page before him. Writing did not come easily to him, and his letters tended to be brief and factual, the composing of them painful.

Malkeh, correcting papers at the other end of the kitchen table, asked, "What are you writing, Yoysef?"

"A letter."

"To whom?"

"To Chaya Leya," he said briefly, looking down at what he had already written. "I want to tell her that we have heard from Chaim."

"But, Yoysef, how will you know where to send it? All we know is that she and Herschel have left Blagoveschensk!"

Yoysef nodded. That was true. A letter from Blagoveschensk, months en route, had finally arrived, telling them that "all is proceeding as planned," which had to mean that Herschel's escape had been arranged. But were they already in Shanghai? Or had they perhaps been delayed someplace along the way? Might they even have beaten the winter storms and taken a ship for New York?

"Well, I will write and keep the letter until we know where to send it. She will have been so worried about Chaim."

Malkeh said softly, "Like you were, Yoysef?" She reached a hand across the table and laid it on his arm. "You know, I never believed your silly story about Chaim telling Berel he was going to sea."

Yoysef looked up at her, astonished. "You didn't?"

"No. And I was sure you had lied when the letter came from Constantinople and you cried."

"Ah, Malkeh," Yoysef said, "I didn't want you to worry. And I was right, wasn't I, because everything turned out fine."

"Do you think me so weak, then? No, don't answer me, I know what you thought. In all that time, Yoysef, we could have helped each other."

Yoysef kissed the palm of her hand. "Will you forgive me?"

Malkeh laughed. "Well, *I* will, but I don't know about God! As I remember, you swore on the Holy Book—"

"I knew He forgave me when we heard that Chaim was safe."

Smiling, Malkeh returned to her papers, and Yoysef leaned over to reread what he had written: *My dearest children. We have had the most wonderful news! A letter has come from Chaim, posted from Constantinople! Did anyone ever think that a Mandelkern would get to Constantinople? Or for that matter, to China? Chaim is on a Greek ship, and he writes that the next port will be Tunis in North Africa! He is fine and happy, both. How I long to hear that the two of you are also!*

"Malkeh, did you not write Chaya Leya after Mammeh died?"

"I did, but I think my letter missed her in Blagoveschensk. Why don't you tell her again?"

Your bobbeh *died peacefully in her sleep one day last summer. Mammeh wrote you but perhaps her letter didn't get to you. Do not grieve overmuch, dearest Chaya Leya. She was very old and very tired. I like to think that somehow she is looking out for you, her favorite grandchild. I have sold the house where she and Zeydeh lived to a very nice young family, and your aunt Golda has moved in with us. She has the room you and Dvoreh shared. I rather think that neither you nor your sister will come home to live again.*

Yoysef paused. According to Eshka Berman, Dvoreh had been seeing the same young man for several months now. It was time for him to make a commitment, Yoysef thought. Malkeh was fretting about it, too, although she didn't say much. When the weather was better, he and Malkeh would pay their younger daughter a visit in Riga, see what was going on, meet the young man. Maybe he just needed a little push.

Your sister was home for the High Holy Days. She is very happy in Riga. The whole time she was home she was singing and dancing, just as if these were not the most solemn days of the year! She even forgot to quarrel with Simcha.

As for him, he is working hard. He insists that he is going to take the entrance examinations for the university next year. For myself, I see no sense in it, but these days he listens very little to what I have to say. Gospodin *Fedotov spoke to me about Simcha when I was at Spokoinaya Zemlya last. He says he is brilliant—for whatever good that will do him! Brilliant Jewish boys belong in yeshivas, not universities!*

Incidentally, Maria Feodorovna is very ill. Mammeh goes to see her often. It is hard to watch a good person suffer, yet she clings to life.

I don't know what news you get of Russia. Perhaps you know that there has been a wave of killings in the government. First the Minister of Education was assassinated, and now the Minister of the Interior. A group of radicals "take credit" for it—as if the taking of a God-given life is to anyone's credit! It is a time of sickness in the land, and that can only be bad for people like us. I pray God that you will soon be away. Your loving father, Yoysef Mandelkern.

O ften Vassily and Marta talked about returning to St. Petersburg. All the time that Lenin had been exiled in Siberia, Vassily had felt somehow lost, rudderless, waiting always for his hero to come home and take charge. Then they had learned he was back, settled with his wife in Geneva, but saying little and doing less. Rumor among the Russians in Berlin was that their erstwhile leader was spending his days puttering among his geraniums. Had they broken him, then, in Siberia? Where was the fiery Lenin of old? Vassily felt himself crushed, as though a verity on which he had built his life had been an illusion. He had been willing to die for this man. Was Lenin now just a dupe of the Jews who surrounded him, the Martovs and Axelrods, the Trotskys?

But how could Vassily have doubted! In July at the Social Democratic Party Congress in Brussels, Lenin had outmaneuvered all his opponents to establish his Bolsheviks as the predominant faction of Russian Marxists. Vassily had been exuberant. While pretending to be weak and broken, the old fox had pulled off a coup, wresting control from Martov and the rest! He had bided his time only until he had gathered strength and was ready to take over the organization.

Hoping soon to get direction from Geneva, Vassily spent most of his mornings at the cellar where the Russian fugitives gathered. Here, over endless glasses of tea, the exiles talked grandly of all they would do when finally they returned to the Motherland. All any of them were waiting for was word from Lenin.

Marta, finding these discussions boring, grandiose, and, worst of all, fruitless, had stopped accompanying Vassily. Especially after a night of particularly imaginative lovemaking, she preferred to spend the mornings alone in bed.

On a morning in the fall of the year, she was sitting naked in the middle of the unmade bed while she dried and combed her long dark hair. Luxuriating in the feel of its silken weight against her bare breasts and shoulders, she felt the heat of renewed desire rising from her belly to the hardening nipples of her breasts. It was tiresome that Vassily was gone off when there was much she longed to do to and even with him. Although Marta knew herself to be a woman of moods and fickle nature, tiring often of lovers, there was an intensity and darkness in Vassily that drew her. She would not be ready to move on until she had mastered whatever it was that drove him.

As if in response to her wish, Marta heard a step upon the stair. Ah, Vassily was home early! She would send him to the bakery for cream cakes and let him lick the *schlag* from her fingers between their tastings of each other. She rose from the bed and unlocked the door for him.

But it was not Vassily. On the threshold stood a man dressed in the dark, rough clothing of a laborer, a worker's cap pulled down over his hair. Though she had not seen him in nearly three years, she recognized him in an instant.

"Julius!" She threw her arms eagerly around his neck.

He kicked the door shut. A smile played around the edges of his mouth as he held her at arm's length, the better to see her. "Ah, Marta! Waiting for me, were you?"

She broke away. "You bastard! When the *Okhrana* was looking for you in Kazan, you left me to take the heat!"

"Nonsense!" he said matter-of-factly, throwing his cap on the bed. "You didn't know anything to tell them. They let you go, didn't they?"

"After two days of interrogation!"

They stood looking at each other. His narrow, aristocratic face with its high-bridged nose and intelligent gray eyes gave the workmen's clothes the lie. Except that his hair had grayed completely, he looked no different from when they had last seen each other. In a hundred sexual dreams that charming, half-mocking smile had aroused her to passion. Even as the tip of his tongue wet his lips, Marta reddened, remembering that she was naked. She picked up her wrapper.

"What are you doing here?" she asked coolly.

"I heard you were in Berlin. I've been standing outside for the past two days, waiting to make sure your boyfriend wouldn't walk in on us."

"He'll probably be away until the middle of the afternoon."

"I know." He drew her to him, and his lips went directly to the special place below her ear that made her thighs tremble with desire.

There was something about one's first lover, Marta thought dreamily, the princely presence that awakens the sleeping maiden to the possibilities of sex. What would it hurt just this once, for old time's sake—

"Lock the door," she said.

Vassily was passionate, rough, with an edge of suppressed violence that always excited her. Julius Ehrenthal was sensual, tuned to unspoken wishes, playing a woman's body with an exquisite attention to nuance and timing. She had forgotten what he was like, why she had once adored him.

They made love once—"for practice," he said, laughing—and then again, taking a long time to build to a heroic climax that shattered Marta's sense of her independent self.

"I loved you, you know," she said afterward, leaning over him to trace the line of his eyebrow with her fingertip. "I would have done anything for you. I would have followed you anywhere, been anything you wanted. I would have been faithful— Why did you leave me in Kazan?"

"You've always wanted to play Juliet, haven't you, Marta?" he said with a sardonic grin. "But the time was never right for it." He rose on one elbow and glanced at the clock. "I'd better go before I have to slide down the drainpipe. I'm getting too old for that kind of nonsense!"

Marta, marveling at the perfect whiteness of his body, watched him dressing. "You didn't tell me what you were doing in Berlin."

He shrugged. "Same as you. Waiting until it's time to go back to Russia."

"But where have you been since I last saw you?"

"Oh, here and there. St. Petersburg. Smolensk. Kiev. London. Geneva. You know better than to ask someone like me where he's been!"

"Are you with Lenin, then?"

He did not answer.

"Will I see you again?"

He stooped to kiss her on the chin. "Every chance I get, " he answered, picking up his cap.

Chapter 39

Chaya Leya arose early. She washed her long hair with an infusion of camomile to brighten the color, brushing it afterward until it shone with reddish lights. Drawn into a neat knot at the nape of her neck, it made her look very much the young matron. Wearing her best dark woolen dress, its lace fichu freshened and pinned with the gold brooch Mammeh had given her, she needed only to put on her shawl and plain black cloak and pick up her gloves and reticule. Her winter cloak was regrettably shabby, but it was fiercely cold outside, and there was no choice. Frau Koch looked up from her sewing. "Are you not leaving for the jail early today, my dear?"

"A little," Chaya Leya said, drawing her shawl over her head and fastening it under her chin.

"I don't know why you put yourself through this when the weather's so bad! You haven't been allowed more than fifteen minutes with your husband the whole of this month!''

"I'll be all right. Hwang found a sleigh for me at the corner." Hastily she bent to brush her lips against the old woman's cheek. Please, she thought, no more discussion; she did not want to lie.

Lying in bed at night, Chaya Leya had planned how she would locate Vladimir Mirov and what she would say to him. If he were still in Harbin and working for the Chinese Eastern Railway, the central headquarters office would have a record. It was six months since they had said good-bye on the dock at Blagoveschensk, but it seemed much longer. So many things had happened, so many versts had been traveled, so many days had gone by. She was nervous at the thought of seeing him, but her need outweighed her reluctance. That kiss on the deck of the *Admiral Chikhachev* had been an accident, meaning little beyond friendship to either of them. She wasn't even sure he would recognize her, or she him.

She motioned for the sleigh to leave her in front of the big ugly building on Kitaiskaya Street. Brushing the snow from her cloak and removing her head covering, she steeled herself to enter the central office of the Chinese Eastern Railway. It is not for myself, she thought, but for Herschel that I must do this.

She found herself in a dark, drafty room lit by smoky lamps and whatever pale sunlight could get through the high, dirty windows. After the bright whiteness of the outdoors, it took her a moment to adjust her eyes to the gloom. A number of young men were standing behind tall desks, dipping their pens into inkwells and entering figures in large bound ledgers. One of them was Valodya Mirov. The stiff-collared shirt and dark linen jacket did nothing to disguise that bright tangle of hair!

Chaya Leya's entrance caused a stir. Not many women came to the offices of the railway. Looking up to see her standing there, Valodya was momentarily disoriented. During the long, lonely hours of nights in the graceless boardinghouse where he lived, he had thought of her often enough. Becoming acquainted on the train from Krasnoyarsk, she had interested him solely because she was so different from any of the females he had known in Smolensk. He had never before met a woman as natural and unpretentious (and as plain and freckled) as a boy. *Maman* and his six sisters, other women of his class, were mistresses of artifice and flirtation, but he could talk to Chaya Leya without empty compliments and double entendres. What's more, she had never once complained of the rugged travel conditions nor asked for special accommodation because of her sex. He remembered the impromptu picnic, her inspiration, while they had waited for the replacement part from Baikal. And then at the end, when he thought that everything about her had been revealed, she had magically transformed herself by means of a red silk dress into a woman as feminine as any he had ever known.

"Madame! What in the world—?" he exclaimed, coming toward her with his hands extended to take hers. His lips grazed her fingers.

At the warmth of his greeting, relief swept through Chaya Leya and quick tears sprang to her eyes. Aware that the scratching of pens and murmur of low conversation had ceased, she withdrew her hand from Valodya's. "Please, can we talk someplace more private?"

"Of course. We are almost through for the day. I'll be just a moment."

Chaya Leya sank down on a bench while Valodya replaced his work smock with a proper jacket and carried his ledger to a large open safe to be stored. After he had pulled on his boots and taken an overcoat lined with fox fur from a hook near the door, he led her across the street to a dim coffeehouse, empty at this hour. She was grateful when he brought her a cup of the hot, thick brew.

"But, my dear girl, what are you doing in Harbin? Are you passing through? Where is your husband?"

Briefly Chaya Leya told him what had happened to them, shy at first but gaining confidence from the interest and concern in his eyes.

"I have seen this happen before," Valodya said when Chaya Leya told him of the delays in the handling of Herschel's case. "They are waiting for instructions from St. Petersburg."

"But it is such a minor matter, and he has already been in jail over two months! Surely no one can think it is Herschel's fault if someone issued him an identity card on an out-of-date form!"

"You are being reasonable; the government isn't. They have been nervous since Minister of the Interior Sipyagin was assassinated. Officials can be irrational when they're worried."

"You don't think there's a chance they might sentence Herschel to prison!" Chaya Leya was thoroughly alarmed now.

Valodya was hasty with reassurances. "Of course not. It's so trivial a matter."

"But they treat him like a common thief!"

"Well, they do when someone's waiting to go to trial. It doesn't mean anything. But tell me how I can help."

Chaya Leya stared into her coffee cup, swallowing hard. She had never found it easy to ask for favors. "I—I—I mean *we* never counted on being so long on our way to Shanghai. I—" She stopped, then blurted out, "I am almost out of money."

"Oh," Valodya said, quickly calculating how long he might put off his creditors. "I have just had a bank cheque from home. I can surely make you a loan." He picked up her hand that was lying on the table, folding it into his.

"No!" she said, turning crimson. "Is that why you think I came to you? I need to find work, and I thought you might help me. If you can't, then just forget I said anything."

"Shh! Did I say I wouldn't help? You know I will!"

A job? Valodya thought. The young ladies of his social acquaintance did not get jobs! Where would he even start to help her with this? What salable skills could she have? Her education hardly prepared her to be a governess, and neither women nor Jews were hired by the railroad. The boardinghouses, of which there were many for single railroad employees, were always short of western help, but those places were too rough for a girl like her. The shops? The dressmaking salons? He frowned. If only she weren't of that unfortunate race! He chewed his bottom lip while he considered. At last he said, "I'm not sure what to advise you. Can we meet to-morrow after I've had time to think a bit? On Saturdays I work only until midday. There is a small railroad museum near the river. It will be warm there, and we can talk some more."

Chaya Leya agreed. Frau Koch liked her to sit in the little parlor and read to her on *shabbes* afternoons, but she would say that she had been promised a visit with Herschel. She felt already as though a load had been shifted from her shoulders. Valodya would help. He had said so. He was worldly, from a great city. He had been to a university. Certainly he would know how she should proceed. She squeezed his hand, smiling into his face.

Her trustfulness only increased his nervousness. He stood. "Let me see you home—but, tell me, where *are* you staying?"

She explained about the Kochs. He must not ever, she told him, come to their house. They would be outraged if they knew she had been, unchaperoned, to visit a gentleman, and, worse still, one not of their faith! It would be time enough to tell them about him when she had a job.

Smiling a little while he shook his head in disbelief, he agreed. They clasped hands on it before he escorted her from the café.

He flagged a passing sleigh for hire and handed Chaya Leya into it. Evening was falling, and it was even colder than before. He stood on the curb, watching until she disappeared into the gloom. What had he gotten himself into with his glib promises? It would be damned difficult to help the girl. He was crazy to try. It crossed his mind that getting mixed up with Jews and criminals couldn't help his career any.

Still, he found himself humming as he turned toward his boarding-house. He had not felt so exhilarated in months!

*W*hen Chaya Leya went to work for the family Kutuzov, people smiled knowingly. There had been other housekeepers in the house on Nicholas II Avenue, but none had stayed longer than a month. It was not just that Madame Kutuzova was delicate and quite incapable of directing a household, nor that the Chinese servants were both disrespectful and dishonest, not even that the house was incredibly slovenly. What drove housekeepers from the Kutuzovs' was the problem of six ill-behaved little boys, aged six months to nine years. Chaya Leya had heard all about the Kutuzovs, but it was a job, the only one offered, and she needed the money.

Anatoly Kutuzov was the chief engineer of the Chinese Eastern Railway. Like other official families, the Kutuzovs had brought servants with them from home, but Harbin was neither Moscow nor St. Petersburg, and there were not rewards enough to keep a European staff content in such a godforsaken place. A constant stream of maids, governesses, and housekeepers rode the trains back to European Russia every week that the weather permitted.

Chinese servants were easily hired, but they lacked knowledge of Western ways. Then, too, if the Chinese were unsupervised, the "squeeze" could get quite out of hand. Valodya had explained all this to Chaya Leya when he had first suggested housekeeping as a line of work. It was not the fault of the Chinese, he said, they simply did not know what was expected. That's why European housekeepers were so greatly in demand among the railroad families. Chaya Leya should have no trouble finding such a position if she did not feel demeaned by the work.

Demeaned! Chaya Leya beamed in delight. She could think of no occupation for which she was better qualified. When did Valodya think she might start?

He had laughed at her enthusiasm. "I'll just let it be known around the railroad office that you are open to an offer. You'll be at work within a week, I'm sure!"

It had not been quite so easy as Valodya had led her to believe. There was the matter of her religion, of course, and the fact that her husband was in jail. Those things made people very uneasy.

The first position which Valodya found for Chaya Leya was in the establishment of Superintendent Malanov. That had worked out badly from the beginning. Madame Malanova had given Chaya Leya a stuffy, windowless little room behind the cellar kitchen, a space formerly used for storage. It had no heat except that which came through the kitchen wall, and the only furniture was a lumpy cot and a small wicker chest. The pay was less than Chaya Leya had been led to expect, the cost of board and room being deducted. For those minimal wages, Madame expected Chaya Leya to be available at all hours of the day and night, whenever, in fact, she was summoned by the tinkling of a large brass bell.

One morning at the end of the second dreadful week, Chaya Leya was feeling especially weary and dispirited. The night before she had had difficulty dropping off to sleep, the air being close and the mattress uncomfortable. When finally she had fallen into the dreamlessness of total exhaustion,

Madame's bell had awakened her. It was past midnight, but Madame desired a tisane to calm her nerves. Chaya Leya, flooded with rage, prepared the infusion, and bore in up to Madame as directed, in her own special porcelain cup. Only when Madame became drowsy was Chaya Leya dismissed to return to her own bed. She was unable to fall asleep for the remainder of the night.

In midmorning Chaya Leya was summoned from the kitchen to bring breakfast on a tray to the mistress's chamber. It would not do for the Chinese maid to carry it upstairs since Madame complained that the sight of an Asian face before breakfast made her nervous. Besides, she wanted to give Chaya Leya her instructions for the day. When finally Chaya Leya was permitted to return to the kitchen, she immersed herself in preparations for the one o'clock dinner for which Superintendent Malanov and two guests would be present. Chaya Leya was demonstrating to the Chinese cook the art of making a custard, when the bell tinkled again. Leaving the cook to carefully stir the milk to a simmer, Chaya Leya obediently climbed the stairs to Madame's bedchamber. Madame demanded that the French marmalade instead of the strawberry preserves be brought for her breakfast rolls. Chaya Leya returned to the pantry to make the exchange, and carrying the little glass pot of marmalade, she took herself up to the bedroom once more. In the meantime, Madame's tea had cooled in its glass. Wearily, Chaya Leya made the trip to the kitchen for a jug of boiling water. She had quite forgotten to check the custard, and the milk had scorched in the bottom of the pan. Never mind. She would start over.

After she had prepared fresh tea, the mistress of the house said, "Lay out my clothes for the day, and then you may go."

In the kitchen a peaceful hour passed before there was another furious jangling of the bell.

"Yes, Madame?" Chaya Leya asked, breathless from climbing the stairs for the fifth time that morning.

Her employer was livid except for a white line around her thin mouth. She could not find her amethyst brooch. "You stole it!" Madame said coldly.

Chaya Leya looked at her mutely, scarcely taking in the words.

"I should have known better than to hire a jailbird! *Jailbird! Jailbird!*"

Chaya Leya said reasonably, "Let me help you look for the brooch, Madame."

"I am going to call the police. And then you can join your husband in his jail cell!" Madame Malanova cried, increasingly hysterical.

"Look, Madame, you have overturned your jewel case. Perhaps the brooch fell to the floor." Chaya Leya went down on her knees and began picking up fallen pieces of jewelry.

"Don't touch anything! *Get out! Get out!*"

In shock, Chaya Leya stood absolutely still for a moment, considering. "Yes," she said. "I am leaving."

Abandoning the half-cooked dinner—let Madame explain it to the superintendent and his guests!—Chaya Leya packed her belongings and returned to the Kochs.

The Kochs were not sympathetic. They had been shocked and dismayed by Chaya Leya's abrupt decision to go to work—*and* in a menial capacity, for gentiles! Reb Meier now said that what had happened at the Malanovs just proved his point. Frau Koch, observing Chaya Leya's white face and obvious distress, relented and roasted a plump hen for her supper.

At the table, Reb Koch continued in the same vein. "You see what comes of being so headstrong. That man Mirov gave you bad advice. It is not for nothing that we Jews keep to ourselves, Chaya Leya! If you insist on going to work, let it be with some Jewish family."

He had more to say, but Frau Koch interrupted with unusual sharpness. "Leave the child alone, Meier! Can't you see she's exhausted and upset!" She turned to Chaya Leya. "Eat your supper, and go rest yourself. You don't have to go to work, Chaya Leya," she added, glaring at her husband, "but whatever you decide is fine with me."

Chaya Leya was not sure that Reb Koch might not be right, but it was a moot point. No Jewish family would hire her, tainted as she was by Madame Malanova's accusation of theft. It changed nothing that her former employer had found her brooch still pinned to a dress she had worn and had sent an unapologetic message demanding that Chaya Leya return to work at once.

Chaya Leya refused. Madame Malanova said that since she had "broken her contract," she had forfeited the ten days' wages owing her. Valodya was furious, but Chaya Leya refused to fight the Malanovs. She would rather take charity than enter that house again, she insisted, reflecting that it might come to just that, charity, since she was down to her last gold coin.

With some reluctance, Valodya told her about the Kutuzovs. He warned her against them, but at their first meeting Chaya Leya felt drawn to pretty, fluttery Madame Kutuzova and to the children who were sturdy and handsome in their own right. When she picked up the baby, Yuri, and felt his velvety cheek against her own, the bargain was sealed.

*L*ater those years in Harbin had the quality of a tale not lived but invented in someone's imagination, engrossing at the time it was read but only a fading memory after the cover was closed. How could it all have happened? Life is made up of small circumstances that taken together shape its direction. Thus, the trial of Herschel Rosen, Jew, was linked to the uneasy climate of the Imperial Court in St. Petersburg in which delicate negotiations were taking place with Japanese envoys. Thus also, Chaya Leya's dizzying leap from the narrow life of the Jewish community to that of the upper-class gentile world was determined by a chance meeting on an east-bound train. And finally, the oddly knit relationships of the Harbin years were born in the fear of war and woven from the disparate strands of Her-schel's despair, Vladimir Mirov's loneliness, and the impact of sudden inde-pendence on a young woman alone for the first time.

It was almost summer before Herschel was brought to trial. Because of the delays in adjudicating his case, he had been moved from the jail to Harbin Prison. He assured Chaya Leya that life was not too bad inside the prison, better than at Blagoveschensk Camp and more pleasant than in the jail. The inmates were Russian nationals, mostly petty criminals, some with larger offenses like grand theft or murder; Chinese offenders were turned over to the Chinese authorities. With a little money, Herschel had been able to buy a job in the kitchens, where the food was plentiful and the working condi-tions relatively easy. Chaya Leya came every visiting day, carrying fresh fruit and other edibles and leaving money to purchase his continued comfort. When she left, she took with her Herschel's soiled clothing to be brought back washed and pressed.

At the prison, visits were allowed once a week, on Sunday mornings, for an hour. Prisoners who had visitors were brought under guard to a large high-ceilinged room on the outer perimeter of the grim yellow brick block. The room was light and airy, not unpleasant. The windows were not barred and, in fact, looked out on the warden's flower garden. The visiting area was sparsely furnished with chairs and a table or two, but with all the inmates and visitors milling about, furniture was not missed. It was always very noisy during the visiting hour, which, on the one hand, had the disadvantage of forestalling tender communications but, on the other, advantageously masked confidences.

Chaya Leya put on a cheerful face for her visits and entertained Her-schel with local gossip and funny stories about the Kutuzov children and her misunderstandings with the Chinese servants. She often mentioned her Rus-sian friend, Vladimir Mirov, who continued to help her in so many practical ways. Herschel was alternately proud of Chaya Leya's independence and worried about her. His feelings were so at war with each other that he both urged her to return to Polotsk and in the same breath cried that he could not survive without her visits.

With Herschel in prison, Chaya Leya's life had established a flow and rhythm of its own. She was getting by, perhaps better than might have been expected. There were hours, even whole days, when, preoccupied with prob-lems at the Kutuzovs', she did not think about Herschel's peril at all. If there was much that troubled her about her present situation, she consoled herself that it was not to be for long.

Every morning at five Chaya Leya rose from her bed at Madame Irina's rooming house, splashed herself with cold water from the pitcher, and dressed. After her experience at the Malanovs', Chaya Leya had refused to stay in the Kutuzov house. Nor would she remain living with the Kochs. Dear as Frau Koch always was to her, Reb Meier could not leave off lecturing, and Chaya Leya found his disapproval depressing. She loved having a place of her own, even if it was only a drab room in a boardinghouse. There were disadvantages, of course. It meant that she must spend some of her earnings for lodging, and it also necessitated her daily flights in the cold light of early morning across the square, north on the Ulitza Kitaiskaya, and then north again on Nicholas II Avenue to her employer's house, a very long walk in winter.

On Chaya Leya's first day on the job, she had arrived to find the older boys rummaging in a cold kitchen for a scrap to eat, the baby wet and screaming in his crib, two middle children wrestling on the floor, and a weeping Madame, still in her dressing gown, bouncing a feverish two-year-old on her hip. The Chinese cook was standing idly by the cold stove, picking his teeth with a straw from the broom.

Chaya Leya reached for the sick child so that Madame could tend the hungry baby. She patted his back, crooning softly in his ear until he relaxed against her, his hot little face pressed into her neck. Curious about the new housekeeper, the two boys who had been fighting in the middle of the kitchen floor sat up to stare at her.

"Oh, dear, oh, dear!" Madame Kutuzova wailed. "Whenever my husband is away on a surveying expedition, everything falls apart! The servants won't listen to me, and the children act their very worst!" In the next breath she added, "I'm so glad you're here to take care of things. I feel better already!"

Although intimidated by his hostile stare, Chaya Leya turned to the cook. "Please start breakfast now. The children are hungry."

The cook shrugged and held out an empty cereal container.

"Yes, well, we shall buy some more later. Is there bread, eggs?"

Unhurried, he unlocked the larder cupboard with a key hanging from a cord at his waist. He removed a loaf of stale bread.

Chaya Leya sighed. It would have to do. She pointed to the cold samovar. "We shall have some tea, please."

By this time all the little boys and Madame Kutuzova were standing around the two of them, silently watching the scene unfold.

The cook did not move. "Not my place," he said, grinning insolently.

Chaya Leya handed the two-year-old back to his mother. She picked up the empty water pail and thrust it into the cook's hands, coldly pointing toward the door. Moving ever so slowly while watching Chaya Leya from between the slits of his eyelids, he went out of the kitchen.

"Now then," Chaya Leya said with more cheer than she felt, "I will just slice the bread. It will make quite a nice breakfast, won't it?" She examined the larder, removing butter, a jar of preserves, eggs, milk, a tin of tea. "And later we shall make a list of what we need to stock the pantry. Perhaps you big boys can gather some twigs to start the fire in the oven, and later I will bake some fresh bread." She chattered on to cover the silence. "I shall have to get to know everyone's name. Mine is Chaya Leya Rosen. Is that hard to say? You have to make a little coughing sound on the 'Ch'!"

By the time the kitchen table was cleared of clutter, and the bread sliced, the cook still had not reappeared.

"I'm afraid you've offended him," Madame Kutuzova said, wringing her hands.

"Nonsense!" Chaya Leya said with more confidence than she felt. "I'll just go see what's keeping him."

She found him sitting in the shelter of the porch, smoking a cigarette, the empty pail beside him.

"Why haven't you drawn the water for the tea?" she snapped.

"Not my job. Water boy's job."

"So where is the water boy?"

The tall cook shrugged again. Shrugs seemed to be the primary mode of communication with him.

"I'll get the water!" Chaya Leya said, grabbing the pail and heading for the pump. She had been in China long enough to know that she was losing face, but the cold, hungry children seemed more important at the moment.

Struggling with the heavy water pail, she inched past the cook, who was sitting, gazing dreamily at the curling smoke of his cigarette.

In the kitchen she filled the samovar with water and placed charcoal in its central tube. When the water came to a boil, eggs went onto the top ledge to steam. The teapot was located and filled with tea leaves and boiling water to make a strong brew which would be kept hot on top of the samovar and mixed with boiling water as needed for the individual tea glasses. While the water heated, she cleaned the ashes from the neglected oven, relaid the fire, and lit it to warm the kitchen. By the time she was through, her face was smudged and her skirt filthy from the soot. Still, with the prospect of a warm breakfast ahead, life seemed to have returned to the room. The baby was dry, fed, and sleeping, Madame was sitting in the rocking chair with the sick child in her lap, the two eldest had gone outside to gather kindling, and the other children were quietly playing in a corner.

"How many servants are there?" Chaya Leya asked Madame Kutuzova. "And who is in charge?"

"Oh," she said vaguely, "six or seven, I guess— They take orders from the cook."

"Well, I think you should make clear to them that they will have to take directions from me."

Madame looked aghast at this suggestion. "Oh, I couldn't—maybe when my husband gets home—"

"I see. When will that be, do you think?"

"Oh, I don't know, a month or two, I guess."

Chaya Leya's heart plummeted. She could see that things could be very difficult at the Kutuzovs. Again she told herself that she could tolerate anything—for a short time. The important thing was to be able to support herself and save some money so that she and Herschel could continue on their way to Shanghai the minute he was released.

*V*alodya Mirov had become a part of Chaya Leya's life. He had developed the habit of stopping in at the Kutuzov kitchen for a glass of tea after he left work in the evening, waiting until Chaya Leya was ready to leave so that he could walk her home to her boardinghouse. It was not safe, he said, for a pretty woman to be alone on Kitaiskaya Street at night. If, having left her, he was spending his evenings at the gaming tables, she was not aware of it. She might have been distressed, but she would have thought it no business of hers.

She was glad to have someone to talk to about her problems with the Chinese staff. After the return of *Gospodin* Kutuzov, it had been made clear to the servants that they were to obey the new housekeeper as though she were the master himself. Things were better for a while after that, but gradually the cook reverted to his old cheekiness, and the rest of the staff, following his lead, treated Chaya Leya with contempt, doing pretty much as they pleased.

"Well," Valodya said, "maybe you expect too much. You have to judge the Chinese by Chinese standards, not European rules."

"I can't believe that all Chinese are like them! Besides, I've checked, and the cook is doubling the food bills, and all of them are helping themselves to whatever they like from the pantry!"

"Oh, Chaya Leya." Valodya laughed. "That's just part of their wages. It's expected. It's the Chinese way!"

But Chaya Leya was stubborn and began to keep careful track to have facts to present to *Gospodin* Kutuzov. She had learned almost immediately that it made no sense to talk to Madame about any of this. Charming though she was, Marina Kutuzova did not want to deal with problems.

The little boys made up for some of Chaya Leya's aggravation, particularly the baby, Yuri, who was deliciously fat and cheerful. She had discovered that the reputation for wildness was not completely earned. The boys were high-spirited, curious, and endlessly inventive. Since they were and their pretty mother couldn't cope with so much vitality, they were left a good deal on their own, and their restless boredom turned at times to destructive behavior. But Chaya Leya had mothered spirited children before. She made rules and gave them boundaries they could live with. Gradually the situation with the children improved.

By a sort of natural progression, Valodya and Chaya Leya had begun spending Sunday afternoons together. Now that spring had arrived, a favorite way to pass the time was to watch the river junks pass by from the grassy embankment high above the Sungari, Valodya strumming his balalaika, Chaya Leya resting her back against a tree trunk in dreamy contemplation of the river. On some Sundays, after Chaya Leya's visit to the prison, they went to hear the Railroad Band play concerts in the square. Often they took one or another of the little boys with them. Then they looked like a proper family indeed.

Once Madame Kutuzova took Chaya Leya aside and quite delicately asked about her relationship with Valodya. Chaya Leya laughed. They were friends, no more. What else could they be? She was a married woman. Madame nodded and said no more.

When Herschel's trial date finally arrived, he was confident that the court would take into account that he had already served many months and had a record of good behavior. Valodya accompanied Chaya Leya to court and sat beside her. The room was a replica of what existed in European Russia—dark-paneled, gloomy, with a raised box for the prisoner and a table for his advisers, another for the prosecutor. The magistrate, only one for minor cases, three for major, sat on a high platform, looking down on the defendants and witnesses. There was a small area in the back of the room for observers.

"Why do you look so glum?" Chaya Leya asked Valodya. "Are you worried?"

"About your husband? Hardly. He'll be free tonight, and then you and he will be leaving Harbin, I suppose."

With a sudden pang, Chaya Leya realized that what he said was true. "Well, of course," she said. "We are going to Shanghai, and then maybe to America."

"And I—" Valodya said, his green eyes sad, "I will remain here quite alone. Won't you miss me even a little?"

Chaya Leya took his hand. "I'll never forget you. You've been like a brother to me."

Valodya laughed bitterly. "A brother, eh? Just what a man with six sisters wants to be! Well," he said jauntily to cover his hurt, "maybe I'll get lucky and your husband will be sentenced after all!"

Two other cases were heard before Herschel's, and in his judgments, the magistrate proved both tolerant and lenient. That gave Chaya Leya confidence.

When Herschel was led into the room for his turn, Chaya Leya was proud to see how respectable he looked in the neat suit that she had pressed for him. The judge was fiddling with his pince-nez and lining the papers in front of him into precise piles. The clerk read out the charges in a bored voice and asked Herschel if he was guilty. Maybe, Chaya Leya thought, they should have paid someone to represent Herschel in court. Since it was such an obvious open-and-shut case, it had been Herschel's decision not to spend money unnecessarily. Listening to the charges read out in this awesome setting, Chaya Leya had second thoughts, and her hands began to sweat.

Now Herschel replied in a clear, quiet voice that he had been guilty of buying identity papers from an "unofficial" source. Since the police had already established that the identity card was a forgery, Herschel and Chaya Leya had agreed it best for him to confess to this charge. Davka's discharge papers having held up, there was nothing to prove the far more serious crime of desertion.

Why had he bought forged papers? the magistrate asked.

Candidly, Herschel replied that he had needed to travel from Blagoveschensk through the Chinese territories to Shanghai. His own papers had been lost when he was conscripted, and if he had waited for replacement documents to arrive from the ministry in St. Petersburg, winter would surely have set in, and he could not have made the journey. This was the story Chaya Leya and Herschel had rehearsed. He begged the court to understand how pressed he was to take his bride out of Siberia before the snows came. He added balefully that everyone knew how slow the ministry was in everything it did!

People in the audience nodded, but the magistrate was frowning. In a cold voice he asked Herschel if he was criticizing the government. Herschel, realizing that he had made an error, hastened to retract, but it was too late.

There was not much more to the trial than that. The judge yawned and remarked that it was time for his noonday meal. Almost as an afterthought he turned to the prisoner. "Six years," he said casually on his way out for his dinner. "Six years for knowingly buying a forged document, for contributing to the moral decadence of government officials by the passing of bribes, and"—fixing Herschel with a stern eye—"for denigrating the just and due processes of the government of your homeland. For these crimes, Herschel Rosen, I sentence you to six years, minus the time already served, confined to Harbin Prison. At that you are lucky, young man, because if it had been desertion, you would have been shot!"

Everyone stood. Chaya Leya could not believe what the judge had just said. Policemen were already leading the numbed prisoner from the room. Chaya Leya stared wildly about her. This had to be a mistake! It was not supposed to happen like this! As the courtroom emptied, Valodya was taking her arm. She shook him off. "It's your fault!" she hissed. "You gave him bad luck! You wanted him to be sentenced!"

"Chaya Leya! That's silly! I was making a little joke—I never dreamed—"

Chaya Leya stalked out, Valodya at her heels. "I never want to see you again," she cried, hurrying past him.

*A*fter the stunning conclusion of the trial, Herschel sank into emotional torpor. He withdrew from Chaya Leya and whatever comfort he might have received from her, leaving each of them isolated in private misery. By the verdict of a Russian court deprived of the right to manage his own life, Herschel was frightened and confused, swept back in time to when his parents had died of cholera and he, just three years old, became in a day's time a charge on the community. He'd known neither love nor safety until Yoysef Mandelkern took him into his house. He had vowed never to be that helpless again. Stronger men have broken when their integrity is breached, so why not Herschel Rosen, who already knew what it was to be defenseless in the hands of strangers? Six years! A lifetime!

As for Chaya Leya, at twenty-three she was an innocent alone and ignorant of the twistings and turnings of her own heart and mind. Overwhelmed by the prospect of a six-year separation from home and family, crushed by Herschel's turning away, she understood only that she had been abandoned when she needed loving. For the first time, Herschel was thinking only of himself, and she reacted to his tears and sighing silences with anger.

It was a bad time. Rabbi Samsonovitch and the Kochs came to see Chaya Leya in her rented room. A collection had been taken up by the Jews of Harbin to send her home. It was a good time of year, Reb Koch reminded her, to travel; a wire could be sent to her parents through the office of the railroad so that she would be met in Moscow.

"I don't want the money," Chaya Leya said angrily. "How dare you do this behind my back! I am not going home. If Herschel is here, I need to be here."

"But it is for *six years*! How can you stay alone for six years?" Frau Koch said, greatly agitated.

"I'm not alone. I have a job. I have friends."

The rabbi said reasonably, "It is not good for a young woman to be so far from family."

"That's for me to decide!"

"I'm going to write your father!" Reb Meier threatened.

"Yes, you do that, but it will not change anything. I am not going." Chaya Leya looked from one kind, distressed face to the other. They were concerned about her, but their concern only made her feel more like a child than ever. "Please. I would like you to leave now."

After they were gone, Chaya Leya broke down. They were right. There was nothing for her here. Herschel didn't want her. What reason could she have for staying? But they had had no right to decide for her—and to ask for contributions as if she were a beggar! She would not go home if only because of that! Besides, she was too depressed to contemplate the long journey, let alone the thought of facing Mammeh and the family at its end.

Marina Kutuzova was sympathetic. After sentence was passed, she had held Chaya Leya in her arms and mingled her tears with Chaya Leya's. But in time, although Madame was too kind to say so, she quite lost patience with her housekeeper's depressing effect on the entire household. The servants had become more lax than ever. And the children were becoming intolerable once again.

Chapter 40

*D*voreh and Lev, the handsome bookkeeper at Mir Khozayki, had begun walking out together after the Purim party at Tsaya Kaganova's. When leaving for work in the morning Dvoreh now had an added reason for looking her best. A rosebud from Eshka Berman's garden pinned to the lapel of her jacket, a little spritz of lavender water on her wrists, a bit of lace fastened to her collar—Lev's acute gray eyes took it all in. Not that he said anything—certainly not at the store—but Dvoreh saw the admiration in his eyes and it was enough to keep her glowing through the day.

On *shabbes* and on Sundays, when the store was closed, they took long walks together. Dvoreh loved the Old City with its winding streets and medieval churches, its castle, and the remnant of an ancient city gate; for his part, Lev preferred to ramble through the public gardens. On occasion they attended a play or musical recital sponsored by the Society for the Promotion of Culture Among the Jews in Russia. Sometimes, too, acquaintances from the store invited them for an evening. But mostly they were content just to be with each other. Being alone together offered moments of discovery. Lev learned that Dvoreh hated fish, Dvoreh became aware that Tchaikovsky depressed Lev, Lev noticed that one of Dvoreh's blue eyes was smaller than the other, Dvoreh remarked on the way Lev's dark hair grew in a widow's peak, Lev instructed Dvoreh on the intricacies of banking, Dvoreh teased Lev that he didn't understand a joke. And always there was magic in touching hands and an electricity when, by accident, hip bumped hip.

Eshka Berman fretted that spending so much time alone might lead to a premature intimacy, but Dvoreh's worries were quite the opposite. Lev, for all his seeming worldliness, had proved to be shy, their relationship confined to a chaste holding of hands and once in a great while, the brush of lips across a cheek or forehead.

In October, when Dvoreh and Lev had been seeing each other for some months, Yoysef and Malkeh came to Riga to visit. Although Lev had not yet spoken of marriage, it was not too soon for cautious parents to look things over. Dvoreh's letters home were full of Lev, Lev, Lev—on every page, Lev. When Eshka wrote to Malkeh she mentioned the young man's prospects and the respectability of his family, the father a professional man, a dentist no less!

Dvoreh's parents were prepared to like Lev Goldenburg, and their first impressions were positive. His diffidence and good manners charmed them even more than his clean good looks and the fine cut of his clothes. In these times when young people tended to be loud and brash, they found Lev becomingly deferential and modest. That he was also well regarded by his employers was apparent from his shy allusions to increasing responsibilities and steady advancements at Mir Khozayki.

"It may be a good match for Dvoreh," Yoysef told Malkeh. "I like a serious man."

"God knows our daughter can be flighty," Malkeh agreed. Her face softened. "Anyone can see they love each other."

Malkeh spent a wonderful week in Riga. In the early days of marriage there had never been money for holidays, and later there were too many responsibilities. She was excited by the city, and pleased to find Dvoreh in high spirits. The Bermans were warm and hospitable, and it was good to be reunited with Eshka, to whom she could open her woman's heart. For a change she had no worries of home. Simcha having been left in Golda's care and the school in Hodl Nachman's, Malkeh felt carefree and unburdened for the first time in years. For Yoysef, too, it was a welcome change after the pressures of the rush of work before the High Holy Days.

The only unsettling thing about the visit was that Lev seemed oblivious to the opportunities Yoysef made for a private talk about the future. Still, it seemed a good sign when the Goldenburg parents invited Malkeh and Yoysef to spend an evening. Surely they would use the opportunity to settle questions of dowry and wedding arrangements.

Only somehow it had not worked out as expected. Time and again Malkeh had opened with the Goldenburgs the subject of the young people, only to find the conversation deflected; looking back afterward, she could not even say how that had happened. "What is it with them that they don't want to talk about the wedding?" a frustrated Malkeh asked Dvoreh after their return to the Bermans' house.

"Oh, Mammeh, you're pushing!"

"Don't they like you?" Malkeh persisted.

"I think they do. It's just that they feel differently about marriage than you and Papa. They think there's no rush and that too many people get married without being sure of their feelings. Lev agrees with them. His sister Sonia was twenty-four before *she* was married. I guess *you* would call her an old maid!"

"I guess I would," Malkeh agreed, shaking her head. She had been more than a little perplexed by the evening. Reviewing it in her mind, she felt uneasy, as though everything had been just the merest bit off track.

Lev's father, a short red-faced man, had dominated the visit, talking incessantly, his plump little hands gesturing widely to emphasize his remarks. The mother, in contrast, had seemed vague and detached, scarcely attending her husband's ramblings. The sister, two years Lev's senior, had sat quietly on the sofa playing at cat's cradle with Reuben, the youngest child, a boy of twelve; her husband was not with her and Malkeh gathered that he did not get along well with his wife's parents. Also absent was the older sister, Leya. The mother had dismissed her in two brief sentences—she was living in the Ukraine and she had not been home in years. Lev and Dvoreh sat apart from each other at opposite corners of the room. Malkeh could sense Dvoreh's discomfort.

Dr. Goldenburg, the dentist, had an opinion about everything. The Bundists? Bad for the Jews to call attention to themselves. Anyway, why should Jews concern themselves with labor problems when things had never been better for them—already six percent of the doctors and dentists in Riga were Jews, just think of it!

All those so-called revolutionaries? Just a bunch of troublemakers with nothing better to occupy their time. If young people spent half as much time working and studying as they did protesting, the world would be a better place!

The Imperial Court? So what if the aristocrats lived well while people were hungry? For reasons of His own, God had made princes and paupers both, hadn't He?

Dr. Goldenburg's rapid disposal of enormous problems dizzied Mal-

keh. At times a tart comment rose to her lips, but a warning look from
Yoysef quelled it. Silently she sipped the sweet wine and nibbled at the food,
following the lead of the mute members of Lev's family. Mrs. Goldenburg
busied herself passing plates of *mandelbrodt* and fruit and refilling wine-
glasses. Studying her, Malkeh saw that Lev looked a great deal like her,
except that, unlike Lev, there was a curious opaqueness in Mrs. Goldenburg
that made it impossible to guess what she was thinking.

Odd, Malkeh thought, a very odd family. And yet to all appearances,
this was a solid and successful group of people. The room where they sat
together was sumptuously furnished with horsehair sofas and Biedermeier
tables (imported from Germany), the polished floors covered with Turkish
carpets. That there was nothing really *personal* about the room—not a book
or a bibelot—was, after all, a matter of taste. Or was it? The family members
were just like the house, superficially attractive but bland and impersonal. It
was difficult to carry on a conversation with any of them, impossible even
to begin to know them.

When the two families said good night, nothing had been settled about
Dvoreh and Lev. Malkeh came away feeling faintly chilled. She discussed her
uneasiness with Eshka in the morning.

"Well, Malkeh," Eshka said reasonably, "you have to remember that
the Goldenburgs have always lived in Riga while you come from a provincial
city. And then, too, the father is a professional man while Yoysef is a tailor.
You don't have a great deal in common. You have to face that and not hold
it against them. It's a good sign that they asked you for a visit at all," Eshka
concluded.

"Maybe so, but why didn't they mention a betrothal?"

Eshka pursed her lips. "It was up to you and Yoysef to bring it up, I
think."

"Not where I come from," Malkeh retorted.

"That's exactly what I mean! You don't understand big city ways."

Before they left for home, Yoysef, prodded by Malkeh, invited Lev for
a talk, and the two walked out together into the brisk evening air. Yoysef
returned some time later, bewildered.

"*Nu?*" questioned Malkeh, the one word encompassing everything—
anxiety, hope, expectation.

"So '*nu*' nothing!"

"He didn't speak about Dvoreh?"

"Oh, yes, he did, he did. He talked about what a fine young woman
she is and how he respects her."

"But love, Yoysef, didn't he speak of loving her?"

Yoysef squirmed. "Not exactly. He said that everyone thinks a great
deal of Dvoreh."

"Did you ask him what he intends?"

"It was not easy," Yoysef admitted, reluctant to own up to his failure.

"But you did?" Malkeh persisted.

"I said that Dvoreh is twenty and should be settled in a home with a family already."

"And he said—?"

"He agreed. He said Dvoreh would make a wonderful wife."

Malkeh's face brightened. "Well then?"

Yoysef frowned. "Well, but that was all! He was as quiet as if there wasn't anything left to say. Finally I asked him outright if he was interested in Dvoreh."

"Yes? Go on."

"Well, he didn't exactly say yes, and he didn't exactly say no."

Exasperated, Malkeh demanded, "What *did* he say?"

"He talked about how important security is in marriage."

Malkeh snorted, "If we'd waited for 'security,' I'd still be a spinster in Dagda!"

"Well," Yoysef said uncomfortably, "he's a very thoughtful young man. Unusual." He turned a questioning face to Malkeh. "It's a good thing to be serious about life, don't you think so?"

"Excellent, but it won't make us any grandchildren!"

Disappointed, Malkeh and Yoysef returned to Polotsk the next morning.

Eshka kept in touch. The young people spent all their free time together, she reported in her letters. Most of Dvoreh's other friends had drifted away. The two seemed truly to love each other, so she was at a loss to understand why Lev had not spoken. She had heard that the parents' marriage was an unhappy one. It was rumored that once Mrs. Goldenburg had spoken with the rabbi about a divorce, but, of course, what grounds could she have when he had given her four children, a fine house, and was home with her every night? Anyway, maybe that explained why Lev was so cautious about declaring himself.

Dvoreh was as bewildered as her parents had been. Lev loved her, she was as sure of it as she was sure of her own feelings. There seemed to be a clear though tacit understanding that she would be his wife—sometime. They had spent an afternoon looking at bedroom suites and talking about how they would furnish a flat. They had talked about children. But when it came to action, Lev was vague; pushed, he became irritable.

Dvoreh's best friend, Tsaya Kaganova, had met a young man at the Cultural Society and was married within three months. Nachem Feltsman from fabrics decided to settle down and married Anna Berg from notions. Still Lev made no move to make their own ties permanent.

Worried letters continued to come to Dvoreh from her mother in Polotsk. Has Lev spoken? What are your plans? Are you seeing any other young men? We need to talk things over, please come home.

Dvoreh could not bear to face the puzzlement of her parents, Simcha's teasing, the questions from her aunts and her uncle. She made an excuse about being needed at work to avoid going home for the Passover holiday. Later she realized it had been a mistake, because although she threw herself into helping Auntie Eshka prepare for the seder, she knew that the feast was not her feast, these kind people not her flesh and blood, their customs not those bred into her at home. Lev would be spending the holiday with his family. Inexplicably the Goldenburgs had not invited her. Lev made no excuses. "My mother thought you would rather be with the Bermans," he said.

Tears flooded her eyes. "I would rather be with you!"

He had given her chin a brotherly kiss. "There will be other seders. Anyway, Auntie Eshka is a better cook."

There was nothing to be done about it. Like a stranger who had just happened into this house, Dvoreh sat, closed in silence, between the Bermans' son-in-law Velvel and Uncle Lazar. Across the table was Auntie Eshka's daughter, Rochlea, her two-year-old beside her, Aunt Eshka fussing over the child from the other side. The candles made the damask glow, the first cups of sweet wine were poured, and an expectant hush fell over the table. It had always been Dvoreh's favorite holiday, of all the year's festivals a time for families to be close to each other. She had expected that on this Passover she would be bringing Lev home with her to Polotsk, to make him part of her childhood, the house where she had been raised, the family that had formed her.

Uncle Lazar began to read the story of the exodus from Egypt from the Haggadah. As the youngest person at table except for the baby, Dvoreh was obliged to ask the questions that formed the framework for the service: "Why is this night different from all other nights? On all other nights we eat either leavened bread or matzo; on this night, only matzo. On all other nights we eat all kinds of herbs; on this night we especially eat bitter herbs. On all other nights we do not dip herbs at all; on this night we dip them twice in salted water. On all other nights we eat in an ordinary manner; tonight we dine with special ceremony. Tell us, then, why is this night different?"

She could not do it, the words stuck in her throat. The hot blood rose to flood her face, and she tasted bitter bile in her mouth. "I'm sorry. Coming down with something. Going to be sick." She shoved back her chair and fled the room.

When Auntie Eshka came upstairs with a bowl of chicken soup, Dvoreh pretended to be asleep.

hatever else it was, it was not lack of attraction that kept Lev silent and apart from her. Dvoreh's face caught fire even now when she thought about that time, that one time when she and Lev had come together in love. There could be no mistaking that outpouring of passion for anything else.

It had been early on a Sunday in May when Auntie Eshka and Uncle Lazar had taken the train from Riga to Sigulda to spend the day with Rochlea and Velvel and the baby. They had left before dawn, carrying baskets of fresh-baked cookies, herrings from the gulf, and jars of golden chicken fat with cracklings. Sleepily Dvoreh had waved them good-bye from the doorstep, and then gone back to bed. She must have been more tired than she realized—it had been inventory week at the store—and she did not waken until past nine o'clock, when a knocking at the door roused her from sleep.

She knew immediately that it was Lev, for they had made plans to take the local train to the seashore at Jurmala. Leaping from her bed, Dvoreh drew on her wrapper and went to the window. "A moment, Lev, give me a moment!"

Hastily Dvoreh cleaned her teeth and her face in the cold water from a pitcher on her dresser and pulled a brush through the tangled dark mass of her hair.

The knocking came again, imperious, impatient. Lev was never happy to wait.

"A moment! A moment!" she shouted from the window.

Dvoreh had been about to draw on her skirt and shirtwaist when the second knocks on the door changed her mind. "I'm coming! Dear God, don't break down the door!"

A glance in the mirror satisfied Dvoreh that she was decently covered and reasonably tidy, and she hurried downstairs to open the front door.

Lev stood on the doorstep, his stylish straw hat in one hand, a sack of fresh warm *bublitchki* in the other. He looked dashing in his fawn-colored suit and sparkling shirt, a hero from a romance, even with the bagels in hand. He had been frowning at the delay, but now his jaw dropped ever so slightly, and his face was lit by surprise.

Dvoreh clutched her wrapper close to her. "I overslept," she said guiltily. "Come in, and we'll have tea with *bublitchki*, and I'll get ready to go. It'll take only a minute to heat the water for the tea."

Lev had not moved from the doorstep. His eyes seemed to swallow her whole. Dvoreh was conscious of her unbound hair, the swell of breasts and the cleavage at the neckline of her wrapper, the uncorseted curves of her figure. Embarrassed, she wished that she had taken the extra moments to clothe herself.

"Come in, Lev," she said crossly. "Let's not give the neighbors something to talk about." As he hesitated, she added, "It's all right. I'll just start the water heating and go upstairs to get dressed."

Lev entered the dim hallway, putting the bagels and his hat on a chair and looking about him. "Eshka? Lazar?"

"They went to visit Rochlea and Velvel for the day. I told you."

"No, you did not," Lev said, his face stern.

"Well, I thought I did," Dvoreh said. "What difference does it make?" She turned to go into the kitchen and Lev caught her by the arm.

"I've never seen you with your hair down," he said. "Turn around and let me look at you."

"No, honestly," she said nervously. "I have to get dressed."

Lev's hands gently turned Dvoreh toward him, and his eyes were bright when he looked at her. Carefully he reached out a hand to touch the crown of her hair, then the smooth curve of her cheek. "You are very beautiful," he said softly. "Very lovely."

Dvoreh stood still, her breath catching. Her arms, which had been holding her wrapper closed, dropped to her sides. The neck gaped open, revealing the line of her breast beneath the fine lawn nightdress. Slowly the robe slipped down on her shoulders.

Lev's hand moved to cup itself around the small breast, feeling the delicate flutter of her heart beneath his touch. Without moving his hand, his dark head bent down as his lips met and covered hers. Her arms went around his neck, pressing him close and closer still, waiting breathlessly for the barriers between them to come down. She had longed for such a moment.

When he lifted his head and took a step back from her, Dvoreh could see that his eyes were wet. "Lev, my dearest," she murmured, "what is it?"

He shook his head. "I am so grateful."

"Lev, I love you!" Dvoreh said, her head pressed against his chest.

"It's for that I'm grateful," he said, and he was smiling slightly. "You are my princess—no, my fairest Queen Esther." His fingers traced a delicate path on her throat before his lips softly caressed her. The hands that drew aside her robe so that his finger tips could touch the slight swell of her belly were gentle. Dvoreh cried out. He raised questioning eyes to hers. They stood like that for a long moment before Dvoreh released her breath in a faint sigh and nodded ever so slightly.

He took her hand and led her upstairs to her bed.

After the sweet frenzy of their lovemaking, Lev had drawn apart from her, lying as far from her as the narrow bed permitted.

"Lev, Lev, my dearest love, what is it?" she had asked him, alarmed. Her bare arms tried to gather him to herself, but his body had gone rigid.

He would not lift his face, half buried in the pillow, to look at her. "We shouldn't have! Oh, God, we shouldn't have! What have I done!"

When Dvoreh would have reassured him, he pushed her away and sprang from the bed. "That was a bad thing we did, Dvoreh. Suppose there's a child?"

"Suppose there is," she said, confused that in a matter of seconds he had become a stranger. "There's nothing to keep us from marrying, is there?"

Lev was hastening into his clothes, putting the wrong buttons through the buttonholes, careless about his tie. "There's no choice now. The sooner the better," he said, tight-lipped.

"Wait a minute!" Dvoreh said, sitting up in bed. "Is it that you don't want to marry me but you think you should because of what we just did together?"

"You'd better get dressed, Dvoreh. Someone might come to the house." His eyes refused to meet hers.

She drew back as far as she could against the headboard of her bed. A moment ago she had not been ashamed of what they had done in love, but now—? Why was Lev acting like this?

"For God's sake, put on some clothes!" he said, his voice agitated.

"Well, maybe I don't want to marry you, Lev Goldenburg! Why don't you just take your bagels and leave! I'm sure your mother would appreciate them."

"I *said* we'd get married, didn't I? Isn't that what you've been after since you got to Riga?" He stooped to tie his shoes.

Furious, Dvoreh picked up the pillow, throwing it hard and fast so that it caught him in the back of his head. "Get out," she said. "Get out of this house! I don't want ever to see you again!"

"All right, if that's the way you want it!"

She heard the front door slam when he let himself out.

But she hadn't meant it, and he knew that she hadn't.

*A*fter that one time there were no occasions when they were quite so alone together. Lev saw to it. Dvoreh had been hurt at first, feeling rejected as a person and flawed as a woman. For a time she had wondered if there might be something wrong with her body, something that had repelled Lev, but close inspection in the bath revealed no apparent defect to her. If only there were someone she could talk to about what had happened. But, of course, that was impossible. Mammeh would be shocked, her friend Tsaya would think her wanton, Eshka Berman might put her out of her house. If only she could confide in Chaya Leya, who always had answers for everything, but her sister was far away and out of touch. Time eventually calmed Dvoreh's anguish, and she made her peace with Lev's odd behavior, rationalizing that it was but another sign of how he loved her and wanted to care for her.

When news of their betrothal reached Polotsk, Malkeh wept tears of

joy, and Yoysef was relieved that at long last Dvoreh was settled. Once the
decision had been announced, the Goldenburgs had seemed accepting. There
was no rush to have the wedding as Lev had feared, and a date in December
was chosen. Dvoreh should have been deliriously happy, but she was not.

*M*arta smiled as she coiled her long black hair into a complicated
French knot and fastened it with slender pins. For the first
time since they had returned to St. Petersburg, she was happy and relaxed,
all because the morning post had brought her a letter from Geneva. Being
home in Russia had made her afraid, afraid that changes in name and appearance would not protect her, afraid that an acquaintance from a past life
would hail her on the street, afraid that her dossier was active in an *Okhrana*
file even after a four-year absence. Since coming back, she had been nervous
and jumpy, not unlike Vassily, who seemed to breathe in anger and suspicion
from the very air.

The decision to leave Berlin had been Vassily's. "It's time to go home,
Marta," he had told her one day. "The revolution won't be fought in
Germany."

"But Lenin himself is in Switzerland!"

"All the more reason for us to carry on for him in Russia."

Marta had felt clammy perspiration in her armpits. "I don't know that
I'm ready to go home yet, Vassily. I like Berlin."

He had glared at her. "*You* would like to sit things out at Étienne's!"
He named the restaurant of her favorite indulgence.

"I'm as committed to the revolution as you are!" Marta was stung.
"I'm just not sure the time is right yet—"

Vassily had grasped her roughly by the wrist. "When I leave here, you
leave here, Marta." There was no mistaking the menace in his voice.

"Don't talk to me like that!"

There had been a time when any sharp retort from her had intimidated
him. Not now. "I'll talk to you as I please," he had said coldly.

Vassily had begun immediately to make plans for their departure. There
were no further overt objections from Marta. There was no point, she had
thought, in unpleasant arguments. When the time actually came, she would
simply tell him that she was remaining behind. She had never confided in
him her recollection of that shattering flight from Kazan when she had been
terrified that at any moment the *Okhrana* would rearrest her and subject her
to another interrogation. She was not brave enough to go back, she'd thought,
knowing that four years ago it would have taken only a little more time in
the custody of the secret police, a little more pain, and she would have
confessed to anything they wanted. She had had nightmares for months after

her release. Now she had begun to sleep badly again, just since Vassily had begun to talk of going back.

That Julius Ehrenthal was still in Berlin played a not insignificant part in her indecisiveness.

After his visit to the boardinghouse, they had begun meeting in Julius's flat instead of in the room where Marta lived with Vassily. She had had many other men, but no one had ever satisfied her as Julius Ehrenthal did.

She thought about her last tryst with Julius before leaving Berlin. Next to her in the bed Julius had lain asleep, snoring softly. She gently reached out her hand to touch him, letting his crisp, silvery chest hair curl around her fingers. Without waking completely, he had pulled her to him. Her head had found the familiar hollow in his shoulder and nestled there for a moment. After a few minutes she'd pushed herself up, sighing audibly. The little Swiss clock on the bedside table read three o'clock, time to leave if she was to get home before Vassily. She had swung her legs over the side of the bed.

Julius had opened his eyes, looking at her lazily. "I hate to send you back to him—"

She'd leaned down to nuzzle his neck.

"If you keep that up, I won't be able to send you back. I suffer every time I think of you and him together."

"Maybe," she said lightly, "there's something to be done about that."

He hadn't responded. Instead he had left the bed, padding barefoot to a table in the middle of the room moving aside a tower of papers and magazines to find his packet of French cigarettes.

"Actually," she'd said to provoke him, "he is rather sweet, you know."

He had frowned, lightly a cigarette and inhaling deeply. He watched her fasten her stockings with pale pink garters. When she stooped, looking for her shoes beneath the tumbled bed, he'd admired the curve beneath her petticoat.

She remembered, smiling now, how he had moved across the room to her and without waiting to be asked had fastened the row of tiny buttons on the back of her dress.

"Marta, be careful. After all, what do you know about this man?"

"That he's good in bed—" Marta teased.

Julius had not been sidetracked. "Only that he was taken from a peasant family and given an education and work on an estate. That he cooperated with the local *zemstvo* to spy on the aristocrats. That he took part in a bloody pogrom in '92. And that afterward he ran away and set himself up in a new life on stolen money. Don't you see, he's not exactly your typical revolutionary!"

"I don't know any typical revolutionary," she'd said, "do you?"

"Don't be flip, Marta. The man is amoral. And he's the worst kind of anti-Semite! He doesn't know you're a Jew, does he?"

Marta shook her head. "It hasn't come up." She stood before the mirror, fastening two tortoiseshell combs in her hair. "Suppose," she had said casually, "that I leave him?"

Julius moved up behind her, his arms circling her, their eyes meeting in the mirror. "To do what?"

She turned to look at him directly. "I thought maybe—" She stopped in confusion, began again. "Vassily is planning to leave in a couple of weeks for St. Petersburg." Her eyes had asked a question of him.

He shook his head. "Marta, Marta!" he'd chided. "You know what my life is like—a couple of months here, a few weeks there, half the time living underground—uncertainty, hardship—"

"I don't care!" she said, throwing away her pride as she'd vowed she would never do.

Gently he disengaged from her. "It's late, Marta. Vassily will suspect something. You'd better go now."

It had been a bitter blow to Marta, but not really a surprise, to recognize that her attachment to her old lover was stronger than his to her. That had been the case four years ago; it was the case after they had resumed their relationship in Berlin.

Going home to Vassily, she had hated herself for the face of weakness she had revealed to Julius Ehrenthal. Never again, she had promised herself, never again. She hoped it would punish him to some small extent if she *did* leave with Vassily. Shrugging slightly, she had decided that she might as well go to St. Petersburg; there was nothing for her in Germany.

*W*ith Marta's money continuing to support them, they had settled into two bleak rooms on a back street in St. Petersburg. It had been possible to enjoy life in Germany, but in Russia pervasive paranoia and constant tension exacted a toll. Walking down the street, one always thought, Is that man behind me a police spy? Is he following me? The use of false names was the norm unless one had known someone for ages, and even then one searched the other's eyes uneasily. One changed addresses often, did not invite acquaintances home, responded in fear to any knock at the door.

The quarrel yesterday had been typical. "I can't help it!" Marta had wept, apologizing to Vassily for snapping at him over something inconsequential. "I have a past here, just as you have. I'm afraid to leave the flat, and I'm afraid to stay home. It's making me a nervous wreck."

"What did you do, Marta? Bomb the Lubyanka? Put poison in the tsaritsa's tea?" Vassily said unpleasantly.

"Why can't you understand? I hate it here! I'm afraid all the time."

"A real dedicated Bolshevik, aren't you?"

"Oh, leave me alone!"

"Gladly." Coldly he put on his jacket and went out, closing the door with exaggerated force.

The letter from Geneva, coming as it did in that very day's post, had changed everything for Marta. Because Julius had taken time from his important life to sit down and write her a letter, she felt herself strengthened. Bending toward the mirror, she approved the fresh color of her complexion, the gloss of her blue-black hair, the liquid gaze of her nearsighted dark eyes. Four years ago she had been a student, pudgy with baby fat and given to outbreaks of pimples. Even if the *Okhrana* was still looking for Marta Braun, even if she should cross the path of a former classmate, no one would recognize her for that person. She was Marta Pirumova now. How silly she had been to be afraid!

Vassily had not come home as he usually did for the midday meal. He was still in a temper, she thought, still sulking after their quarrel. Or perhaps he was at a meeting. He had lately become interested in the Socialist Revolutionary Party, which paralleled Lenin's Bolsheviks in its fervor if not exactly in its aims. He had met a fellow named Arkady Runich who, like Vassily himself, seemed to hang around the fringes of the organization. They had become friends of a sort. That Vassily would waste his time with a dull fellow like Runich just proved how desperate and impatient he'd become after three months of inactivity. Marta hoped he would not come home angry today to take out his frustrations on her. His mood had turned dark lately. Many a night he paced the floor until dawn seeped through the drawn curtains. He had changed toward her, becoming short, and on one frightening occasion striking her.

Marta's feelings for Vassily were complicated. When she had first met him in Berlin, she had been restless, at loose ends. He was handsome and something of an enigma, certainly a change from other men she knew. He had told her he came from a wealthy merchant family and had been a student in St. Petersburg. She hadn't believed it for a moment. He had too many rough edges. Because she'd been intrigued by the mystery and generally bored with her life, she had set about seducing him. It had not been difficult. She had found him a surprising lover, excitingly unpredictable—she never knew whether he would be rough or tender, masterful or passive. Living together, a genuine friendliness had grown up between them; did not both look to Lenin as to a father? And when he had confided in her the terrible events that had shaped him into the man he had become, a deep and abiding empathy had added still another facet to their relationship. Now she was worried about him, concerned that he was so troubled.

Marta moved to the wardrobe and drew from its hiding place among her camisoles and underdrawers the letter Julius had written partly in French and partly in Russian, his hand and his language equally elegant. Fight it though she had, she loved him even though in some deep place inside herself she knew that she would always be secondary to his real mistress, the revolution. Her lips brushed the page as though Julius's touch was still upon it.

Ma chérie, mon amour,

That you and V. have arrived safely and are settled in St. Petersburg both pleases and saddens me. I am filled with elation to think of you at the heart and core of the great cataclysm which will soon take place. But how I wish that it was I, instead of V., with whom you share the climax of our work.

Souviens-toi la villa on the Black Sea where we first made love? Has a sky ever been so full of stars, a passion so true and pure? *Hélas*, time for us has always been too short—a few days at the dacha, a few months in Kazan, a few weeks in Berlin. But the memories always in my heart!

À Genève, there are constant arguments among the leadership about method and direction. How it all wearies me when I long so for action instead of talk. I will be glad to be away soon again. There is work to be done in Brussels, then London. Who knows where I might turn up—even at the door of your flat one day?

Do not lose faith in our cause. I know you will never lose faith in me,

Your own J.E.

Je t'aime toujours.

Chapter 41

Chaim did not jump ship in Tunis. Stavros had pointed out that the experience aboard the *Archimedes* would qualify him for a berth aboard a transatlantic steamer, a much better plan than being a deserter in a foreign port.

This made sense to Chaim. Besides, he did not know what the punishment might be for desertion. He could not quite believe what Stavros had said about hanging. On the other hand, Skouros, who had been at sea a long time, had told him that when he was a cabin boy, a deserter had been dragged back to the ship in chains, lashed to the forward mast, and flogged to death. Sometimes, Skouros said, he thought he could still hear the sailor's screams in the shrill of the wind at night. The first mate, Athanasius Anargyros, was not someone Chaim could imagine with a whip in his hand, but on the other hand, he was the kind of man who would live by whatever he saw as the code of the sea. It made one cautious.

Chaim was even more afraid of Captain Mihlotoulos, whom he had seen only at a distance, standing on the bridge. The cabin boy, Theo, said that the captain was a moody man who had once scalded him by flinging at him a pot of coffee that had displeased him.

It was easy for Chaim to promise Stavros that he would stay with the *Archimedes* for the term of his contract. With Pasha gone, life aboard ship had settled into a pleasant routine. The other Turks had continued their teasing and tricks for a time, but gradually these had tapered off. Chaim did not know why this was so until one day Stavros stood him before the gleaming brightwork on deck so that his image was reflected. Chaim stared at the black-bearded giant who glared fiercely back at him.

"No pick fight with that one, hey?" Stavros laughed.

From Tunis the *Archimedes* sailed to Marseille, which Skouros told him was the most wicked city in the world. The waterfront streets swarmed with French toughs, pimps and thieves, sailors of all nationalities, and half-naked women. The whiskey was raw, the wine watered, and the whores diseased. Chaim was not altogether sorry to be on the gang assigned to load the French cargo they were taking into the hold—great casks of wine, salted cod, sardines—and to stand watch while most of the crew went ashore.

It had become difficult for Chaim to refuse to join Stavros at the whorehouses. The little man had first thought that Chaim had no money and offered him a woman as a gift. No, Chaim said, it was not that. Was he then perhaps a virgin, afraid to take a woman? No, Chaim said, blushing, not so. Could he then be one of that strange breed, like Pasha, who prefers other men? No, no! Then what in the name of Lord Christ was the matter with Chaim, a grown man, at sea without sex for many months already! It wasn't natural!

Since the truth, that Chaim found the women on the docks unappealing, might well offend Stavros, Chaim lied. Putting on a solemn face, he confessed, "Stavros, my friend, to atone for a sin, I have taken a vow never to lie again with a woman until she is my wife."

"Ahh," breathed Stavros, nodding. This he understood. "A vow, a religious vow." He put a consoling hand on Chaim's shoulder. "What a misfortune! Well, my little brother, if you should ever decide to break your promise, I will see that Father Stephan gives you pardon, for the need of a man for a woman cannot truly be considered a sin."

On the third day that the *Archimedes* was in port, when Leonidas relieved him on deck, Chaim decided that he and Theo should spend a little time looking around Marseille—no harm surely in a little sightseeing. At the last moment Constantine joined them and the three set out for a little taverna owned by a Greek countryman whom Constantine knew, a place where there was always succulent souvlaki for a meal and plenty of ouzo to wash it down.

The café was some streets east of the waterfront in a poor, working-man's section. The shabby basement room was so crowded with burly Greek-speaking dockworkers and warehousemen that the three newcomers could scarcely edge their way inside. They were beckoned to a table in the corner by their shipmates, Skouros and Stavros, who were already drunk. The room was cozy with the warmth and smell of thick blue smoke, the soft sound of spoken Greek, and the friendly press of male bodies packed closely together. Chaim felt the fatigue drain out of him. Stavros pressed a glass into his hand and motioned him to drink up. The liquor had a biting taste that warmed his belly and relieved the ache that had settled in his back and shoulders after a day spent hoisting crates. The second glass tasted less bitter.

At one end of the crowded room a man began to play a bouzouki and another a zither. By the time the dancing began, Chaim was stamping his feet and clapping his hands with the rest, enjoying himself immensely. He did not object when Skouros and Theo lifted him to his feet and wedged him between them into a line of dancers. Chaim was flooded with love for these men, all of them! He had loved Berel like a brother and had known hero worship for Elihu Goltz in Kiev, but this—this was something else entirely. Ah, he was lucky to be a man, he thought, virile and potent, among others like himself!

Another thimbleful of ouzo to toast his comrades from the ship! And still another to salute the musicians who played so sweetly one could weep. And then more dancing, the men weaving and dipping and passing a handkerchief among them in the sinuous line of the dance. The oily liquor was beginning to taste quite pleasant to Chaim as he rolled it around his tongue. It reminded him of the fennel weed he and Nadja had chewed after making love.

After a while Stavros drifted away and then Constantine also. Chaim was not even aware when they left, only that at some point just Skouros, young Theo, and Chaim himself remained. Much later they stumbled into the street, arms laced together.

At the end of the little street was a dingy, open-faced booth where an artist used needles to draw red and blue pictures, dragons, vultures, and women, on the bodies of sailors. The three from the *Archimedes* paused to watch a mermaid worked into the bicep of a Swede. When the artist was finished, the sailor flexed his muscles so that the hips of the mermaid wriggled and writhed obscenely. Theo giggled. "If that were your arm, Hy-am, the bottom would really bounce!" He pressed Chaim's arm muscles with envy.

Chaim demurred but Skouros and Theo pressed him to roll up his sleeve for the tattoo artist.

"*Ah, c'est magnifique, bien!*" exclaimed the Frenchman, closing his eyes in feigned ecstasy. "*Merveilleux!* Perfection!"

"Yes, yes," chorused Skouros and Theo, "a real sailor must have a tattoo on his arm!"

The needles hurt only a little, and when the artist was done, Chaim had a completely bare female torso on his forearm, her bosom and bottom voluptuously rounded by the swell of his biceps. He kept his sleeve rolled up as they walked, and flexed his muscles now and again to see the lady's buttocks swell. By this time the ouzo was having an effect on his coordination and vision and Chaim was beginning to think he might call it a night and return to the ship. He didn't exactly know how it happened that when he awoke, he was lying naked across the mattress of a strange bed. The morning light streaming through an uncurtained window had awakened him and he threw his arm across his eyes to block the glare. As he did so, he glimpsed the naked female figure on his arm and eased himself to a sitting position for a closer look. He rubbed a tentative finger across the tattoo. It did not rub off. He scrubbed at it more vigorously. No effect. With a groan, Chaim buried his face in the pillow.

After a while, the door opened on an enormously fat old woman, her wrinkled face grotesquely painted, the soiled wrapper scarcely covering the sagging mountain of her flesh.

"Ah, très bien! Vous êtes bien éveillé!" she said in French. When Chaim looked blank, she repeated it in Greek. "You are wide awake, I see." Her demeanor took on a threatening cast. "You pay only for an hour, not all night, *mon ami*! Now you owe many francs!"

"Yes, all right," Chaim said. "Where are my pants?" His embarrassing nakedness did not faze the old woman.

She picked up his dungarees from the floor and handed them to him. Wondrously there were still a few francs in the pocket. Having no idea about the value of the French coins, he emptied everything into the hand of the stern madam. She did not seem displeased, and after a final exhortation to get up and get out, she left him alone to dress.

All sense of exhilaration was gone, and Chaim was left with the enormity of the sins he had committed. He had drunk himself senseless, he had lain with a whore although he could not remember it, and he had had himself tattooed, all three anathema to an observant Jew.

When he had made his way back to the ship, Chaim carefully washed his body, working strong yellow soap into his skin until his flesh was red and burning. Dressed in clean clothing, he faced east, toward where he imagined Jerusalem might be. After he had recited the morning prayer as well as he could now remember it, he broke down and wept.

For weeks after Marseille, every time he urinated Chaim examined his body for signs of disease. He was tormented because he could not remember the woman he had slept with. Perhaps she had been clean, and he was lucky, but he could not recall anything about it! What was worse, he might not know if he was sick for a long time. Constantine had told him that there were diseases a man got from whores that showed up years later.

There was at least one other souvenir of Marseille that he knew he could never part with—the naked lady permanently engraved on his arm!

*T*he *Archimedes* did not put in at Salonika, its home port, during the eighteen months that Chaim served aboard her. It was a cargo vessel whose factors ordered it from one port to another, here to unload its freight of tobacco, leather, and cotton, and there to take on olives, oak, and wine. It wandered restlessly between the ports of the Mediterranean and the Adriatic, selling, buying, transporting goods from one place to another for the profit of its Greek owners. For the period of the voyage, the *Archimedes* was the universe for its crew, and its men a kind of family.

Chaim jealously stored up memories of the adventures he had had, the men he had met, the places he had been—Algiers and Oran and Tangier in North Africa, Salerno, Cosenza, and Reggio in Italy, Cagliari in Sardinia, Cadiz, Algeciras, and Malaga in Spain! There was magic in the names. In Naples Chaim bought Mammeh a gold-rimmed cameo brooch carved delicately in the likeness of a woman, her hair pulled high the way Mammeh wore hers on the Sabbath. Since he had no sure way to send it, Chaim wrapped it carefully in a cotton handkerchief and put it in the bottom of his sea bag. Someday he would himself pin it on the collar of Mammeh's black dress.

Chaim was too involved in the life of the ship to dwell on thoughts of home and family. It was not until the *Archimedes* returned finally to its home on the Aegean that he experienced the acute pain of loneliness. For when the ship neared the sheltered beaches and coves of Greece, Chaim's comrades of the sea became strangers to him. It was their homeland, not his, and here all had homes and friends and a past. Even the Turks, who would be traveling home overland from Salonika, could look forward to being reunited with their families.

Approaching their final destination, Stavros and the others took from their sea chests wrinkled suits of clothes, unworn since the beginning of their journey two years before. Beards and mustachios which had grown luxuriant at sea were carefully shaved or trimmed, and hair that had hung braided down the back like a Chinese queue was cut to a respectable length. The piratical crew of the *Archimedes* disappeared, cast over the side or into trash bins with the ragged jerseys and greasy overalls. Chaim wondered, as he stared at his erstwhile companions, where these respectable farmers and villagers had been all that time at sea.

Stavros, preening and turning before Chaim in his tight striped suit and shiny shoes, apologized self-consciously. "My woman, she like to show off. Big sea captain husband, home with lotsa drachmas to spend!"

Chaim marveled, "You have a wife, Stavros?"

Stavros looked surprised. "Of course, wife. Children"—he held up five fingers proudly—"even mother-in-law."

"But in every port—I mean, you never mentioned that you were married!"

"Married, sure! What kind of man you take me for, Hy-am!"

So were Skouros and Constantine married men. Theo had a mother who would be waiting for him on the dock, Leonidas a sister. Alexis and Nikos had sweethearts they were longing to see. Even Anargyros had a wife who tended an inland farm. The only ones who would have no one waiting were the sprinkling of foreign sailors who had signed on along the way, and Captain Mihlotoulos, who was something of a misogynist.

Chaim was to remain with the *Archimedes* while she was in port. He and some few others had been engaged to work on repairs. Sadly Chaim bid good-bye to crewmates, promising this one and that one that he would come for a visit but knowing all the while that he would not. Last of all he embraced Stavros, tears in his eyes as he clasped the short Greek to his chest.

"You good sailor, good man, good friend," Stavros said. "We sail again together some time, yes?"

Chaim said yes, they would sail together again, but he did not believe it. Stavros kissed Chaim on both cheeks before he ran down the gangplank. The last Chaim ever saw of his friend he was surrounded by children, a small, black-clad woman clinging to his arm and leading him away from the dock.

The most miserable days of Chaim's life set in after his shipboard friends left the *Archimedes*. He felt exceedingly sorry for himself. He was angry and bitter toward these sometime friends of the sea. He fantasized about how different things might have been for him. He might have been a partner in Papa's tailor shop by this time, married to Chava, maybe even father to sons! But maybe, too, Chaim reflected sadly, he might have been conscripted like poor Herschel, and God only knew where he would be now! Dead perhaps of dysentery or cholera in some army barracks. Or forced to fight in one of the tsar's little wars, where a bayonet might pierce his heart.

Athanasius Anargyros, although he was officially on leave, was charged with seeing that the repair work on the *Archimedes* was completed on schedule. It was truly the ship that was home to the first mate and not the rocky farm where his long-suffering wife lived alone with her goats and chickens while her man was at sea.

One morning the officer came to Chaim, where he was busy polishing and oiling the machinery in the now-silent engine room. "Go wash yourself and pack your sea bag," he ordered in his cool, precise voice. "Then come to me on deck."

The months on board the *Archimedes* had trained Chaim to obey speedily and without question. He wondered, though, as he packed his canvas bag, why he was being dismissed. It was good, he thought, that he had saved a part of his pay, for he knew that he would have to support himself until he found other work.

On the deck the first mate inspected Chaim. At last he said, "Well, you are strong and fit enough. Pity you look so—rough. Still, there's no time to waste getting all that hair off your head and face."

Chaim said. "Yes, sir," without knowing in the least what Athanasius Anargyros was talking about.

"Pick up your stuff, Russkie, and come with me."

Struggling with his heavy bag and hurrying to keep up as the mate of the *Archimedes* strode down the gangplank and along the wharf, Chaim followed. When they reached the place where a gleaming white-hulled ship rose steeply from the water, riding high at anchor and with its distinctive flag fluttering in the breeze, Athanasius Anargyros stopped. He pointed toward the ship with a long lean finger. "That is the *Oceania*, British ship. Bound for New York and San Francisco by way of Cape Horn. I've told their captain you've a strong back, clean habits, and are willing to work hard. They are picking up extra crewmen here. If you still want to go to America, this is your new berth. What do you say?"

Chaim studied the clean lines of the *Oceania*, so much larger and prouder than the *Archimedes*, and his heart swelled. It was a vessel that would ride the waves of the Atlantic with ease and deliver him safely to New York and the fortune he knew was awaiting him there.

While Chaim was stammering his thanks, the first mate was already hallooing the ship. A uniformed officer peered over the side at the pair on the dock. Recognizing Anargyros, he spoke to him in a strange language, and there followed a brief conversation in that unknown tongue. English? After a few moments, the mate of the *Archimedes* nodded his head, and, turning to Chaim, held out his hand.

"Go on board now, and God keep you, Mandelkern," he said. Then he was gone.

They sailed on the tide.

Chapter 42

*Y*ou can admit pain as a permanent guest in your life, Chaya Leya thought finally, or you can get on with living. Six years in Harbin. That was the sentence the court had handed down—to her, no less than to Herschel. So be it.

Having taken the positive path herself, she was furious with Herschel for surrendering. For most of her young life, he had been her mainstay and her strength, and now with the need for fortitude at its greatest, he had given himself over to despair. Well, all right, then! If he chose to drown, she need not choose to throw herself into the flood after him!

Her options, she saw, were either to return home to resume her place as a child in the family, or to make an independent life in Manchuria. The latter was not chosen without trepidation. But then, she knew she could always go home.

Madame Kutuzova was delighted that her housekeeper's spirits seemed to have taken a turn for the better. Things had been quite tiresome for a while, but now Madame could stop worrying her head about the household and leave Chaya Leya to straighten out its problems.

In just a few weeks' time the situation at the Kutuzov house had deteriorated considerably. Cook was more surly than ever, the other servants both indolent and rude. Despite Valodya's often expressed theory that "squeeze" was self-regulating, that had not proved to be the case, and the pilfering was approaching the magnitude of grand theft. When Chaya Leya conducted a casual inventory of the pantry and cupboards, she discovered that not only had food disappeared in alarming quantities, but also towels, linens, and even clothing. It was the first test of her resolve. She was not yet ready for a confrontation with Cook, and she drew back while she considered the implications. She had always been afraid of him.

Everything came to a head on the day of Madame Kutuzova's tea to greet the wife of the superintendent who had recently arrived to replace Alexei Malanov. The party had been carefully planned, but Madame was nervous to the point of distraction. The advancement of her husband's career rested on her ability to conduct such events with grace and poise. For reassurance, she had kept Chaya Leya by her side half the morning.

"Suppose the children misbehave? Remember how Boris's snakes got loose from the cage last week!" Marina Kutuzova had worked herself up to a fine frenzy.

"I had Lee replace the lock on the cage and move it to the shed."

Chaya Leya led Madame to the chaise longue. "Why don't you just rest until it's time for your bath?"

Madame's open, childlike face looked up at Chaya Leya. "You are good to see to all of this." She grabbed her hand. "I don't know what I would do without you!" Chaya Leya turned to the door, but again Madame stopped her. "I only hope that the boys won't be quarrelsome!" she fretted.

"They'll be fine. I'll see that they are clean and dressed in their best, so that when the guests arrive, the ladies can see how handsome and well-behaved they are. Then *Gospodin* Kutuzov's assistant, Feodor, will collect them for an afternoon's outing. You won't have a thing to worry you!"

"Oh, yes, I remember now."

Chaya Leya moved toward the door.

"And the food—is everything ready?" Madame had asked the same question several times already.

"Cook should be starting on the tea sandwiches now. Please, Madame, do not trouble yourself."

"Yes, you're right. I'll leave it up to you."

Chaya Leya had worked alongside Cook for a week, baking pretty filled cookies and making the base genoise (following the recipe in Madame's cookbook) that, filled and decorated at the last moment, would become petit fours. The bread for the tea sandwiches was waiting in the larder to be thinly sliced and spread with butter and various fillings. Little imported *cornichons*, olives, candied fruits, spiced nuts, and bonbons had been put into silver dishes. The dining table had been set with the best lace cloth, and the silver tea service had been polished to a soft glow. Champagne for a toast was chilling on a block of ice. Only last-minute tasks remained to be done. Madame wasn't the only one a little nervous about the party; beneath her calm, Chaya Leya was also. What did she know of tea parties and napoleons and fancy French condiments! Luckily Cook, who had worked for other railway families, seemed to take it in stride.

It was an hour before the guests were scheduled to arrive, just time to check on the kitchen, send the boy up with hot bath water, and make a final inspection of the table. But what was this? The kitchen, when she came down from Madame's room, was inexplicably cold and silent. The silver trays for the tea sandwiches were empty, and the samovar had not yet been filled with water. Sharply Chaya Leya called Cook's name. Where could he have gone to? It was almost time for the guests! She called again. Again there was no response. Her heart began to turn over slowly in her chest as she sensed rather than knew that catastrophe was imminent. She shouted for the other servants. Within a short time, one of them, the water boy, Wei Fan, appeared.

"Where's Cook? Where's kitchen helper Chu? Why aren't things ready here?"

"Don't know, Missy. Not my job."

"Yes. All right. Take some hot water upstairs to Mistress."

He nodded.

"Then help the children wash themselves and see that they're dressed."

"Not my job—"

She cut him off in midsentence. "Keep quiet! Your job is to do as I tell you! Hurry up now!"

She could not imagine what had happened to Cook. Grimly she began to search for him. She found him in the pantry, sitting on the floor, propped against a sack of rice. His face was flushed, his eyes bloodshot. For a moment she thought he might have suffered a stroke, then she saw the empty bottle of champagne by his side.

"You're drunk!" she snapped. "How dare you!"

He grinned stupidly at her.

"As soon as you can walk, I want you out of this house. And take your pack of thieves with you!"

"You not mistress!" he cackled, slurring the words. "You can't make me go. You nothing but servant girl!"

"I can and will make you go! You be out of here by tonight, or I call the police!"

Chaya Leya turned her back on him, closing the pantry door firmly against the string of Chinese oaths he was delivering.

So much to do yet! Working at breakneck speed, she assembled sandwiches and petit fours, boiled water for tea, arranged the food in dishes, scrutinized the boys. Looking back later, she would never know how she had managed it, but the most important preparations were complete before the first guest stepped down from her rickshaw. A serene Marina Kutuzova sailed through the gathering without a single worry line to mar her beautiful and composed face. Afterward the ladies commented on how well dear Marina had carried off the afternoon. It had been a truly magnificent party!

When the guests were gone, Chaya Leya told Madame that she had fired all of the servants. It was then, when it no longer mattered, that her employer collapsed.

Now that Simcha was fourteen, he spent almost as much time at Spokoinaya Zemlya preparing for his university entrance examinations as he spent at home. Times being unsettled, Fedotov had not been able to arrange for an additional tutor and was sometimes in the position of being himself only one lesson ahead of the boy, particularly in modern languages like French. Unreasonable as he knew it was, he had loathed the language since his childhood, when Andrei's mother had excluded him by conducting all family conversations in French.

Malkeh, too, was often at Spokoinaya Zemlya these days to see to

Maria Feodorovna, who was confined to her bed. The old lady's once plump body had shrunk in upon itself and was now as small and frail as a child's. And like a sick child Maria Feodorovna had become querulous and difficult. Nothing pleased her. The food was fit only for pigs. There were wrinkles in the bedsheets—how could a body rest! The servants were noisy as they went about their work, she could hear them bumping the furniture. They were probably careless with their cleaning too. She complained endlessly.

"And," Maria Feodorovna said, the tears seeping from the corners of her eyes onto the wrinkled yellow skin of her cheeks, "no one cares about me anymore!"

It was her illness talking. Malkeh came almost every day to feed her chicken broth and soft-cooked eggs, coaxing the old woman to swallow what she held out to her on a spoon. She bathed her, taking care not to hurt her, changed her nightgowns and rubbed her back with good-smelling oils. The inevitability of her end cruelly gripped Malkeh's heart. So grievously ill was the old woman that the doctor did not understand how she still lived. Malkeh understood, though. Maria Feodorovna was determined to hold on to life until she saw Petya's bride installed in the house as the next Countess Voronova. Fortunately, the wedding date was fast approaching.

Malkeh and Yevgeny Fedotov were often together at the old woman's bedside. The steward's thick hair was graying and in the last few years his face had developed deep worry lines. With the peasants ever more demanding and agitators keeping feelings high, it was increasingly trying to manage the estate.

Sometimes sitting beside Maria Feodorovna's sickbed, he read aloud to pass the time, stories he thought she might enjoy and articles from the newspapers. Occasionally after the old housekeeper dozed off, Malkeh and he shared a glass of tea in the kitchen before she started for home in her little horse-drawn cart.

The old housekeeper had had a bad afternoon. Fedotov had administered a large dose of laudanum, and after she slept, he and Malkeh crept out of the darkened bedroom. Chastened by Maria Feodorovna's turn for the worse, they sat silently at the big kitchen table, lingering for whatever comfort they might give each other.

Life was one long preparation for being apart, Malkeh thought. Maria Feodorovna would be gone soon, as so many of those dear to her were gone—the stillborn child she had never known and the twins she had adored had disappeared into the earth, Mammeh Frumma and Papa Avrom, Golda's Dovid, and little Zelig also. It was man's destiny to return to dust. Separations of minds and hearts were even harder to bear. She thought somberly of the children run off or sent away, Chaim, Chaya Leya, Dvoreh. Even

Simcha, whose presence was still in their house, had left Yoysef and her long ago. It had begun with his insistence that he be called Semyon. "I am no longer Simcha," he had claimed, whatever that meant.

Then, after his bar mitzvah it had become: "There is no God" and "I am not a Jew." And now, "I will never be a tailor. Like anyone else, I will go to the university!"

But Simcha, she had thought, was not like anyone else; he was the son of a provincial Jewish tailor.

Whose fault? Yevgeny Fedotov's because he had turned the boy's head with dreams? Hers because she had nurtured his pride and pleaded with Yoysef to let him fly?

"What is it, Malkeh?" Fedotov asked, breaking into her silence. "You have been sitting there for fifteen minutes, staring into space, and sighing as though your heart would break."

"Do you really think that Simcha will be accepted at the university?"

"He will pass the entrance examinations very high."

"That isn't what I asked you."

He understood her. "Most universities take a small percentage of Jews. Petya will recommend him. The Voronov name still means something."

They sipped their tea. Yes, Malkeh thought bitterly, influence, not ability, is what it will take. She and Fedotov were responsible. They had made it so that Simcha had a foot in both worlds and a home in neither. Yoysef had been right when he had wanted to keep the boy close.

Busy with their own thoughts, they didn't look at each other. Finally Malkeh asked, "Will you be going to St. Petersburg for the young count's wedding?"

He nodded. "I will go as late as possible—because of her."

"Yes." After a while she said, "I should be getting home—" but made no move to rise.

"Stay a while."

"All right."

The shadows were falling in the kitchen. A great sadness was upon them. After a long time, he said, "A good thing that your boy is out of Odessa."

"Why is that?"

The steward picked up the newspaper that he had earlier let fall in Maria Feodorovna's rocking chair. "Read what it says here. The paper speaks of 'Jewish cartels' controlling the price of grain in the Ukraine."

Malkeh turned pale. "It sounds like 1892 all over again!"

Fedotov's jaw was a hard line. "It sounds like an organized hate campaign. Listen to what the editor of the *Odessaya Novozsti* wrote last week: 'Since Jewish bankers and merchants keep prices high, honest Russian merchants are forced out of business. This is the major cause of unemployment in Odessa and in the whole of the Ukraine. Does one alien segment of our great country have the right to gain a stranglehold on the economy?' "

"How many times do we have to go through this?" Malkeh whispered.

"Whenever there is trouble, the government will find a way to divert attention from itself. The cabinet wants to blame someone for the strikes and demonstrations. The people need a scapegoat for unemployment and inflation."

"Why us? Why are we the ones you hate?" Malkeh's eyes were on Yevgeny's tired face.

He slapped down his newspaper. "What are you talking about! I don't hate Jews!"

Malkeh's eyes had turned dark. She could not stop herself though she knew it was wrong. "You knew there would be a pogrom in '92, and you did nothing to stop it."

Fedotov stood up so suddenly his chair scraped the wall. "My God, Malkeh! Have you felt that way these last twelve years? I did all I could!"

"You didn't stop the army from taking away Herschel and the others!"

"What do you want from me, Malkeh! What am I supposed to be, one of your saints?"

"A righteous man, that's all!" she said coldly, biting off the words. Where had this terrible flooding anger come from?

"This has always been what has stood between us, hasn't it? You love the man—admit it, Malkeh!—but you won't trust the gentile."

"Yes," she whispered sadly. "It is always there." She began to cry quietly and hopelessly. "I have never felt more afraid and alone in my life!"

Frustrated, uncertain, Fedotov stood looking down at her.

"I hate everything that's going on. It's as if my life is out of control and everything's spinning away from me!"

He knelt by her chair, took her hands down from her face. "Ah, Malkeh, do not fight me. We need each other. We have always needed each other."

High society had gathered for the marriage of Ekaterina, youngest daughter of Prince Alexander Volkonsky, to Count Pyotr Voronov. As the two knelt before the priest, there was an appreciative murmuring among the guests. They were so beautiful, she radiant in her white gown, he resplendent in the uniform of a captain in the Hussars.

As the priests held the marriage crowns above the heads of the young couple, Yevgeny Fedotov could scarcely swallow for the lump in his throat, and his vision was blurred with tears. The years had passed too quickly. He thought of Petya as a fat-legged two-year-old, delightedly trying to catch hold of a pheasant in the poultry yard, and as a towheaded youngster striving to match strides as he made the morning inspection of the estate. He remembered a twelve-year-old learning to jump his horse over the ditches and a university student, a cadet in the Officer's Corps. Nor could he forget Petya defying the peasants who wanted his uncle's life, nor his laboring as hard as anyone to save the grain during the drought.

Although Andrei was rarely in his mind, the fleeting image of his half brother, Petya's father, came to him now. Andrei had wanted gold, but threw away the real treasure, he thought.

*A*rmed with the delegated authority of *Gospodin* Kutuzov, Chaya Leya wasted no time in procuring a new Chinese staff of her own choosing. She had given careful thought to the needs of the household, so the first employee she selected from a railway-approved list was an amah for the children. The woman, Meiping, was a widow whose own children had been adopted by her dead husband's brother. She was small and quick, and when she looked at the little boys it was with warm, knowing eyes. Even without a language in common, she and Chaya Leya understood each other at once.

Chaya Leya enlisted Amah's help in hiring others. First came Big Chang, the cook, a good-natured, fat-bellied man whom Chaya Leya liked immediately for his clean fingernails and mirthful grin. Amah admitted, "Chang, Amah's first uncle."

Chang, of course, had to have a water boy, wood hewer, and general errand runner, and so his son, Little Chang, came to work also.

The sweeper arrived next, Li Feng, Amah's third cousin.

The laundress came about the same time, a jolly woman, fat for a Chinese; she had two giggling daughters to assist her in lifting the laundry baskets. The laundress was Amah's sister.

Finally Amah selected as lady's maid for Madame, young and pretty Ayi, who may or may not have been Amah's own daughter.

Later the gardener, Wu Lei, arrived, as well as a rickshaw puller, a porter, and several others. All were related in some way to Meiping. Although it seemed to Chaya Leya a veritable army of people, they joined the household so gradually that each new presence was scarcely noted, and when it was, Amah insisted that the new employee was needed for a specific duty. While *Gospodin* Kutuzov might otherwise have complained about the size of the staff, Amah so regulated wages and skim-off that the household expenses were actually no greater than before. Kutuzov was therefore pleased, Madame was delighted with the new order in her household, and, between Amah's gentle rule and the way they were spoiled by everyone else, the children thrived in the best of all possible worlds.

*C*haya Leya continued to be irrational about Valodya Mirov. She had liked him, perhaps too much. Now she accused him of having the "evil eye."

For his part, Valodya did not know whether to laugh, to reason, or to weep. He tried all of those things in turn. When he found that he could not move Chaya Leya, he stayed away. Yet he was miserable. Over and over he reviewed the course of their friendship, looking for causes, for flaws. He remembered that at the beginning of the journey from Irkutsk, she had been nothing more to him than a casual flirtation, a way to pass a boring trip. Even when she turned up in Harbin later, needing help, it had been little more than a titillation of his male ego to renew the acquaintanceship. And after the fiasco at the Malanovs, he had felt responsible for how things were working out with the Kutuzovs.

When he had already lost her, Valodya realized that in the months before the trial, Chaya Leya had become his closest friend. He had told her more about his family in Smolensk than he had shared with anyone else, ever. When he would have flung down his pen and quit his tiresome job, it was Chaya Leya who helped him commit to something for the first time in his life. After a time, encouraged by her, he had talked to Engineer Kutuzov directly about transferring from the accounts office to the surveying team—and had actually been accepted!

Now that Chaya Leya had turned her back on him over some superstitious nonsense about his green eyes, Valodya was hurt and sad. He did not know what to do with his Sundays or his evenings. He missed seeing the young housekeeper, her face rosy from the heat of the ovens and her lap full of children. He had no one to tell about the day's happenings, no one to whom to pass along a good joke. Damn the girl anyway! Because of her he couldn't even succeed at the local brothel! The thought of her round, freckled face and the gentle curve of her hip kept coming between him and the trollop! The only thing that diverted his attention was the gaming table. Once again he ran up a debt, again wrote surreptitious letters to his mother, begging for money. If word got back to Engineer Kutuzov about the extent of his indebtedness, he would lose his job, maybe even be shipped back to Smolensk in disgrace. Yet choices did not seem his to make.

*O*n a Sunday in August when Chaya Leya left Harbin Prison after the visiting hour, she felt limp from the humid heat of the day and soul-weary from her encounter with Herschel. She was sick to death of his brooding silences, sick of his eyes refusing to meet hers, and sick of his refusal to help himself. The Herschel she had loved all of her young life was now a stranger.

She had nothing to look forward to but an empty afternoon in her little room at Madame Irina's boardinghouse. Lately the walls had seemed to close in on her, making her breathing quicken and her heart pound. Nothing helped, not even the words of Papa's, which had always eased her mind in the past. Maybe she should give up her solitary room and move into the house on Nicholas II Avenue, or admit failure and go home to Polotsk. If she stayed in Harbin, she might end by hating Herschel. But how could she abandon him when he was so alone, when there was no one else for him?

Her head ached, and the air was so heavy that it pressed upon her chest. Perspiration collected in her armpits and crotch and ran down the backs of her legs. Her everyday cotton gown tangled around her heavy limbs like a winding sheet, and she longed to tear it off her body. If only it would rain.

As Chaya Leya heard the prison gate clang shut behind her, she hesitated a moment to let her eyes adjust to the strong sunlight. Glancing about her without interest, she noticed a figure lounging against a far wall. There was something familiar about the slouch of the shoulders, and she squinted to see better. Green eyes looked back at her. Although she was too far away to see such details, she imagined the golden flecks in their depths, the thick lashes. Her breath almost stopped and the palms of her hands became slippery with sweat. Those eyes, the color of tall mountain trees, of a meadow pond, fresh and cool—oh, to give in and let herself sink into them! How had eyes like that ever seemed evil to her?

The man made a half movement, tentatively raising his arms, then dropping them to his sides. So uncertain was the motion, so boyish, it made Chaya Leya's heart lurch. The green eyes did not waver. Starting toward her at a half run, he stretched his arms out wide, and Chaya Leya came headlong into them.

*H*er life now became a lovely dream in which a largely unknown stranger named Chaya Leya ate and slept, talked and made love. It was as though she possessed no past, no husband, no family. Her only connections were with her employers and with her Russian lover, Valodya Mirov. Perhaps he, too, had shed his own history to live the same dream.

Valodya rented a little house for them beyond the city, where the Chinese lived. It had three small whitewashed rooms, and the owner had left a few shabby pieces of furniture. Chaya Leya had not questioned the house, nor had she hesitated to share it with Valodya. She had emerged from her period of travail a different person, having learned that to plan, to consider, to project were in vain, and only the present moment was sure. It was not what she had been raised to believe, but she thought Papa would understand, for hadn't he said, "Be righteous but follow where your heart leads"?

For Chaya Leya, living every day in the same house with Valodya was more the reality of marriage than the few days spent at Herschel's side en route from Blagoveschensk to Harbin. Herschel and Valodya had become one person in her mind. Evenings under the lamp she embroidered Valodya's shirts and mended Herschel's. Her eyes, straying from her work, took pleasure in the way the lamp burnished Valodya's hair; sometimes though, Herschel's darker silhouette merged with Valodya and they became one and the same in her sight.

Dreamily slipping in and out of a past that had contained no Valodya, she might allude to something that had happened in childhood, realizing only when he looked at her quizzically that she had spoken to him in Yiddish. Sometimes she awakened weeping in the night, and Valodya told her she had called out Herschel's name in her sleep. These were the times when she was not sure which of them held her close, only that the arms were strong and loving.

In happy times they constantly surprised each other. Valodya's sighing love lyrics contained an unexpected edge of sly humor, and within Chaya Leya's practical nature lay the innocent soul of a child. He wrote her songs while she baked him rich *babka*s. She sewed him a *rubashka* of finest cambric; he bought her a small pendant of jade the same color as his eyes.

Now on visiting days, Valodya walked with Chaya Leya, carrying the clean clothes and food she had prepared and waiting at the gate until she emerged. On the way home, his comforting arm guided her steps.

For a short time they enjoyed an encapsulated existence. Although both went out to work each day, the world of the railway and the Kutuzov house and that of Harbin in general were apart from what each thought of as their real life; *that,* they thought, could never be penetrated from the outside.

When the Kutuzovs first heard rumors that their housekeeper had moved out of her boardinghouse and was living with a man not her husband, *Gospodin* Kutuzov was outraged. His face engorged with blood, eyes almost popping out of his head, he railed against the immorality of eastern outposts. "You must dismiss her at once!" he stormed while Madame sobbed. "*At once,* I say! I will not have my sons and wife exposed to a—to a—*tart!*"

"Oh, please." Marina Kutuzova wept, the tears rolling in rivulets down her pretty pink cheeks. "Please, Tolya. I know what she is doing is wicked, but I don't think I can manage without dear Chaya! And the boys—oh, oh, *oh!*" She dissolved in a fresh spurt of pain.

Kutuzov lowered his voice, momentarily chastened. Replacing a housekeeper in Harbin was an almost insurmountable problem. "Married to one man and living with another! Do you realize how sinful that is?"

"Yes, yes, my darling, I understand," Marina agreed. "But you know, dearest Tolya, in St. Petersburg and in Moscow we have acquaintances who have 'alliances.' Even here in Harbin—"

Kutuzov exploded. "Marina! You're speaking about people of our class, not your housekeeper! One thing doesn't have any bearing on the other."

"Of course you're right as always. But"— Madame lifted a tear-stained face to her husband—"but we cannot get along without her."

That was a basic fact that could not be ignored. "All right, then," Engineer Kutuzov said. "But it's on your head, I warn you, Marina."

"I take full responsibility," she said, beginning to smile through her tears.

The Kochs, Rabbi Samsonovitch, and the entire Jewish community of Harbin were scandalized. Reb Koch took the unheard of initiative of visiting the house on Nicholas II Avenue to talk with Chaya Leya. She led him into the secluded kitchen garden, where there was an arbor with a shaded bench. Big Chang carried a pitcher of lemonade out to them and tactfully withdrew.

"I don't have to tell you, I'm sure, that what you're doing grieves us."

"I'm sorry for that," Chaya Leya said, handing Reb Koch a cool drink.

"I knew that something bad would happen when you took a job with gentiles and moved away from your people! Gentile ideas of right and wrong are not Jewish ideas of right and wrong."

"On the contrary, Reb Meier," Chaya Leya said, smiling tightly. "I don't think Madame and *Gospodin* Kutuzov would agree with you about that!"

Reb Koch took her hands into his. "I can understand how it happened—an innocent young girl away from her parents for the first time, the shock of a husband in prison—you must have been afraid and lonely. I understand that, I do. You can hardly be blamed for his taking advantage of you—"

"Everything you say is true, except that Valodya didn't take advantage of me. If he had not always treated me kindly and with respect, I would not be with him."

Reb Koch dropped her hands. "You're a wicked girl!" he said angrily. "You know, do you not, that you are an adulteress? In biblical times you would have been stoned!"

Chaya Leya said slowly, "I know that you have come to see me out of concern. But Volodya and I are hurting no one."

Reb Koch sprang up from the bench, knocking his lemonade to the grass. "You seem to have forgotten you have a husband!" he thundered.

Chaya Leya shook her head. "Herschel turned away from me long before I went to live with Valodya. And, in case it makes a difference, I should tell you that no rabbi ever married Herschel and myself."

Leaving Reb Koch with his mouth agape and nothing to say for a change, Chaya Leya walked into the house and shut the door behind her.

Later Rabbi Samsonovitch paid a special visit to the little house on the edge of the Chinese quarter but fled without talking to Chaya Leya when he saw through the window that the tall gentile was there. It was all too much for an old man! Too much.

*F*rau Tzipah Koch came by herself, stepping down daintily from her rickshaw. She embraced Chaya Leya warmly. "My husband doesn't know I'm here," she confessed with a conspiratorial smile, "but I had to see for myself how you are."

"I am truly fine," Chaya Leya said, "happier than I've been in a long time."

Frau Koch nodded. "Yes, I can see."

"Aren't you going to lecture me? Tell me what a disgrace I am? How God will punish me?"

The old woman shook her head. "I'll leave that to others." Her little eyes sparkled mischievously. "You've really turned the shul upside down and given us something to talk about for a change!"

They sat for a while in companionable silence. Chaya Leya had always liked Frau Koch, and now she was grateful for her unwavering friendship.

"There are two things you should think about, though," the old lady said. "Your husband—Herschel, that is—is going to know about this sooner or later. As an act of kindness you should talk to him before someone else does."

Chaya Leya lowered her eyes. After a time she said softly, "Yes, you're right. I will."

"Also, I wanted you to know that my husband has felt himself obligated to write a letter to your father."

Chaya Leya's face flamed. "How could he do that! What business is it of his!"

Frau Koch touched her sleeve gently. "Please. It is not meant as punishment. Meier feels responsible. It is your parents' right to know if you're in trouble."

"But I'm not!"

"In our view."

"Thank you for letting me know."

The old woman heaved herself out of her chair with difficulty. "I must go now. Mostly what I came to say, my dear child, is that my door will never be closed to you. Whenever you want, please come to see me."

That was the only time during that strange time when Chaya Leya wept. Perhaps she seemed indifferent to right and wrong, but then nothing in her life had prepared her to be so alone. Without Valodya she might not have found the strength to do what she must each day.

C haya Leya took Frau Koch's advice to heart. As hard as it was, she could not put off telling Herschel about Valodya. It was a wrenching experience.

Herschel turned his face to the wall but said nothing.

Enraged by his silence, Chaya Leya cried, "Have you nothing to say to me, Herschel?"

He shook his head.

"Do you truly care for me so little?"

"No. I understand. I have nothing to offer you now, nothing but five more years in this godforsaken place! You are right to leave me, Chaya Leya. You are young, full of life, why shouldn't someone else give you happiness? I understand."

She was stunned. Could he ever have loved her and still discard her like this? She had hoped that telling him would shake him from his lethargy, make him fight for her, something, anything but this limp nothingness! "Do you understand, Herschel, that your wife has left you for another man?" she asked.

"Truly, you were never my wife. We owe each other nothing."

Chaya Leya was momentarily struck dumb. "You make me out a whore, and what we felt for each other nothing!"

With a painful smile he answered, "No. It is you who has done that."

Herschel's words lingered. Chaya Leya finally spoke. "Will you say that you forgive me, then?"

"You're forgiven." It was more sneer than blessing.

So cold. He was so cold! Sadly Chaya Leya picked up his parcel of dirty clothes and the empty food basket and signaled the guard that she was ready to leave.

If he beat his head bloody against the cold stones of his cell after she was gone, Chaya Leya never knew.

Chapter 43

*H*ome once more in the Motherland, the stark contrast between the condition of the poor and the flaunted excesses of the aristocracy hardened Vassily's resolve and his commitment to the revolution. An anger that had been largely formless, pieced together from childhood anguish, envy, and vengeful fantasy, coalesced into a cold, hard, and purposeful rage.

He saw the wretched souls who lived as they could on the streets of St. Petersburg, and he felt compelled to speak to them. "Auntie, where is your village?" he would ask. "Ah, Chagoda? And why are you here?" He would nod his understanding as the beggar spilled out a familiar story of increased taxes, redemption payments that could not be met, eviction from house and land followed by starvation, disease, dying children. Vassily did not need to hear such stories. He had lived them. And still he asked, gathering evidence, compiling a weighty dossier in the recesses of his mind.

One late spring afternoon Marta and Vassily strolled, arm in arm, along the Nevsky Prospekt. The companionship they had enjoyed in Berlin had suffered from Marta's nerves and Vassily's distraction. Avid to play a role in the movement, thus far he had been permitted nothing more daring than handing out leaflets in working-class cafés. With his new friend, Arkady Runich, and with Marta, when she was so inclined, he attended clandestine meetings of the Socialist Revolutionary Party, the S.R., coming away stirred by the speeches but increasingly restless for action. Arkady's claim that the S.R. was responsible for the wave of assassinations that had swept the country Vassily found hard to believe.

The weather being soft and warm following several days of rain, Marta and Vassily had decided to walk instead of hiring a *drozhki* to carry them to the meeting. They talked of inconsequential matters—where they would eat their evening meal, the price of oranges in the fruit stalls, the program at the Maryinsky Theater. Marta was careful to lift the skirts of her new gown as they walked, for there was water standing in puddles and she did not wish to soil the hem.

When Vassily paused on the curb to put a few coins into the outstretched hand of a crippled peasant, Marta impatiently preceded him into the intersection. Did he have to try to support each one of them! Was it really necessary to hear every last life history? Frowning with irritation, she was paying scant attention to her surroundings. She did not see a powerful bay stallion, ridden hard by a man in uniform, rounding the corner as she stepped down into the street. Who would have expected a galloping horse in this place of sauntering pedestrians and slow-moving carriages!

Vassily looked up in time to see horse and rider bearing down upon Marta, who as yet was unaware of her danger. In one swift movement he jumped into the street and roughly pushed her out of the path of the horse. Even so the stallion grazed her side, and she lost her balance, falling heavily in the muddy street.

Passersby stopped in their tracks. The rider of the bay reined in sharply. The high-strung animal snorted and pawed the ground, spattering the crowd and the injured woman with street filth. Frightened, outraged, in pain from a twisted ankle, Marta began to scream. Vassily, terrified by her shrieks, knelt beside her. "Get up, Marta! Get up!"

"I can't! I can't!" she insisted.

The careless rider indifferently surveyed the scene, did not dismount. The horse was lathered, but the man himself was cool and untroubled.

Vassily sprang to his feet. "You son of a bitch!" he shouted. "You could have killed her!"

The rider, a handsome man, muscular beneath his gleaming white dress uniform, stroked his beard with one hand and flicked his whip lightly but did not speak.

"It's a public street, damn you!" Vassily's rage was compounded by the other's apparent ease.

The crowd, silent now, drew nearer.

The officer reached into the pocket of his meticulously tailored breeches and brought out a handful of coins. "Let that take care of the woman's trouble," he said carelessly, tossing the money into the street. He swung his horse about to move off, but now the way was impeded by a press of bodies scrambling for the windfall.

When the shower of coins landed all about her, Marta was sitting in the muddy street, nursing her rapidly swelling ankle and crying quietly. Startled, she looked up to see that Vassily's crippled beggar and fifteen or twenty other ragged peasants, who surely had not been there before, were running into the road in a frenzy to retrieve the money. Screaming for Vassily to help her, she only just managed to scramble to her feet before being trampled by the mob. The hem of her gown was muddied and torn in the melee.

Vassily seemed transfixed. His teeth were clenched, and a froth of spittle had collected at the corners of his mouth. He was staring at the horse and rider; the image of arrogant profile and scornfully curled lip etched into his brain forevermore. This dog of an aristocrat expected gratitude, did he, for a handful of kopecks thrown into the filth of the street! He'd show him what to expect! In an instant Vassily sprang forward, grabbing the rider's leg to bring him down off the horse. The officer slashed at him with his whip, catching him across the cheekbone.

Marta began to scream in earnest then. Vassily scarcely heard her over the surge of blood pounding in his head. All of his being was focused on his hatred for the enemy in the beautiful white jacket. Always his enemy had been so rich and proud and indifferent! He was a small child again, watching the broken body of his father carried unconscious into the one-room hovel that was his home. He was his father, surprised by the feared and hated steward, whip raised to mutilate him. He was the schoolboy bearing again the brunt of Father George's scorn at the tiny village school: "You think to rise above your origins, boy? God made you what you are—filthy scum! Forget anything more!" He was the jealous clerk in the estate office, reaching out to feel the fine leather of Pyotr Voronov's boots to be told, "Don't touch! You will leave finger marks on the leather!"

A loose cobblestone from the road was in his hand; he didn't remember picking it up. He smashed it into the aristocrat's thigh. It did not unseat the bastard, though he cried out in sudden pain. Using his whip to open a path through the people scrabbling in the dirt on hands and knees to grab a coin or two, the man moved off without a backward glance. Half sobbing, cursing, his hair falling across his forehead, Vassily ran after horse and rider. The heavy cobble left his hand, arcing toward the man's patrician head. But too much distance had already opened between them. The stone fell short of its mark as the rider cantered away.

Indifferent now to the pain in her twisted ankle, Marta reached Vassily where he stood in the center of the road, cursing the horse and rider as they disappeared. He had not moved. He was dazed, the vein in his forehead pulsating, his arms hanging heavily at his sides. The ringing in his ears was subsiding now, merging with the shouts of the crowd; the blackness before his eyes was fading, and Marta's dim face swam toward him. Urgently she tugged at his sleeve. "Run, Vassily, run!"

He seemed not to comprehend. Marta took him roughly by the sleeve, pulling him behind her as she shoved her way into the milling crowd. Her sharp eyes had noticed a partly open gate a few houses from where they stood, and, skillfully eluding the policemen who were converging, she dragged Vassily into the sheltering courtyard and pulled the gate closed behind her.

"*Boizamoi!*" gasped someone on the sidewalk. "Did you see that? That man must be deranged! He tried to kill the Grand Duke Sergei!"

*A*fter a few months Chaya Leya became aware that Valodya had changed in some indefinable way. He seemed ill at ease, unable to concentrate. Now, instead of spending the evenings sitting with her under the lamp, scribbling his verses and strumming the balalaika, he pored over his newspaper or wandered like a restless spirit from room to room. More and more often lately he left the house, not saying where he was going or when he might be back. If she asked, he most often said that he was worried about the news and was going into town to talk with some of the men. Sometimes he did not return until long after she had blown out the lamp. When he crawled into bed beside her, he stank of smoke, sweat, and strong wine. She worried sometimes that there might be another woman, but how could she know for sure? When they made love, he seemed as ardent as ever.

Marina Kutuzova told Chaya Leya that her husband was worried about the worsening situation in Asia, but neither of the women had more than a passing interest in the negotiations with the Japanese over the future of southern Manchuria. Governments made treaties, and people carried on the best they could. Chaya Leya had other worries. On four occasions in the past month, needing to buy flour or some other necessity, she had gone to the cracked leather purse where she and Valodya kept the household money. Each time she could not imagine why the money seemed to go so quickly. She thought about the garnet earrings and gold brooch that she had lost lately, and recalled other times when it had seemed to her that her purse was lighter than it should be. "Maybe we have a thief who enters the house while we're away," she had said worriedly to Valodya, more than once.

"Nonsense! What thief would bother with us!"

"But jewelry and money are disappearing—"

"Everything costs more in the wintertime—that's why the money doesn't seem to last."

"But my earrings, the pin?"

He had kissed her lightly on top of the head. "My darling muddle-headed little Chaya Leya! You don't remember where you put them, is all."

But where could she have mislaid her jewelry in a tiny three-room house? And as for the higher costs of food in the winter, at the Kutuzovs, where she kept the household ledgers, she noted that the costs were not anywhere near so high. Then what was the explanation? Did it have something to do with Valodya's evening outings? She shook her head to clear away such an uncharitable thought.

Valodya told her at supper that night that he would go into town.

Heaven knew she did not want to become a nag, yet she couldn't stop herself from saying, "You've been out almost every night this week."

Valodya's face darkened, but when he spoke, it was in a light, half-joking vein. "You almost sound like a wife!"

This reminder of her status closed her lips, as intended.

Valodya played listlessly with the food on his plate. He loved Chaya Leya, and he hated himself when he said something that caused her pain. He seemed to be doing that a lot lately. "Look," he said, "these are serious times. I can't just sit here pretending that nothing is going on! Down at the Railway Club I hear about things, talk to the other men—" As she sat there, just looking at him helplessly from wide, innocent eyes, he exploded. "Dammit, Chaya Leya! I can't talk to you about politics! You couldn't care less if the Japs are arming and the tsar is itching for a nice little war out here!"

Chaya Leya, her hands clasped tightly together on the tabletop, said nothing.

Desperate to break the silence, Valodya continued to talk, though he knew that she wasn't listening to him. "Those asses in St. Petersburg actually think we can win a war in Asia! Can you imagine the problems of running a supply line across Siberia! And in the wintertime!"

A single tear slid slowly down Chaya Leya's cheek. "If you stay home, maybe you can explain it to me," she said timidly.

He pushed back his chair. "I've got to go. I promised to meet Oleg and some of the other fellows from the office."

She continued to sit at the table while he put on his overcoat and heavy boots.

"Oh, by the way, I'll just take five rubles out of the purse—we're taking up a collection for Viktor's new baby."

Chaya Leya looked up. "Isn't that a lot of money for a present? We seem always to be running short these days—"

"I can't be the only holdout, Chaya Leya!" he snapped. "Please don't niggle so about money!"

As he left, Valodya told himself that a man shouldn't be tied hand and foot to a woman. Still, he decided that if he won at cards tonight, he would buy her a special present.

*E*ventually even Chaya Leya had to agree that something threatening was happening in the world. Many of the Chinese had suddenly disappeared from Harbin, gone to cover in the countryside. It was said that the Chinese relied on a sixth sense when it came to events in the West. So far, the Kutuzovs had been lucky that none of their help had left, although each morning when she arrived, Chaya Leya performed a silent roll call.

A firm order had evolved at the Kutuzovs, and when Chaya Leya let herself in before dawn each morning, she expected to find a kitchen bustling with activity. Little Chang would have drawn the water, and the cook, Big Chang, would have the samovar at a boil and be starting a kettle of *grechnevaya kasha*, for the children's breakfast. As often as not, Meiping would have arrived before Chaya Leya or the family stirred. All would bow to each other for the sake of politeness, and Chaya Leya would join Meiping for tea. After a while Big Chang might sit down with them so they could go over the menus and any special plans for the day.

Though she knew she needed to ask whether the servants planned to stay or to go, Chaya Leya did not know how to start. As close and warm as she felt their relationship to be, there was still a distance between the Chinese and herself. Carefully she observed, "The Grekovs have lost their cook, I understand."

Two pairs of black eyes looked back at her.

"And last week the Basilys' entire staff disappeared." There was a long pause. "*Gospodin* Kutuzov thinks there may be a war with the Japanese." Silence. Chaya Leya was not good at being direct with them. "If war comes, what will you do?"

The lines around Meiping's eyes crinkled with silent laughter. "What should we do, Missy?"

"Will you go away?"

Meiping shook her head. "This my home. Upstairs my children. We not go!"

Chaya Leya breathed a sigh of relief. "Ah, that is good, then," she said, returning to her meal with a good appetite.

*C*haya Leya began to fear that Valodya and *Gospodin* Kutuzov were right, that something terrible was coming that would disrupt all their lives.

One afternoon as she was working in the dining room, counting the silver teaspoons, she overheard the *gospodin* in the adjoining parlor reading Marina the text of a speech that a high government official had made in Moscow. " 'Russia'," he read, " 'has been made by bayonets, not diplomacy, and we must decide the questions at issue with China and Japan by bayonets and not by diplomatic pens.' What warmongering nonsense! I tell you, Marina, they are all idiots at home!"

"Do you think we will be safe here, Tolya?"

He sighed. "I wish to God I knew! I should have insisted that you take the children home last summer. Now there's no way out until spring."

"I would never dream of leaving you," Madame said, with more determination than Chaya Leya would have expected.

"Thank you, my dear. But the Chinese Eastern Railway is a crucial link to our naval base at Port Arthur—that makes Harbin a logical target for the Japanese."

Shivering, Chaya Leya put away the silver chest. Back in the kitchen it would still be warm and safe.

*A*ll through the early days of winter there were rumors of a massive Japanese military buildup, and tension in the city increased tenfold. Now that things were coming to a head, Valodya was exhilarated.

"If it's going to come, let it come and let's get it over with!" he said more than once.

He no longer went out in the evenings but stayed at home, reading the newspaper, mending his boots, and meticulously tending his weapons—hunting knife and rifle. He was in a constant state of excitement, talking about battles to come, about who the best generals were, and how they should deploy the troops to protect the city. Chaya Leya felt even more frightened than when he had silently taken their household money and disappeared into the night.

In the first week of February, a severe snowstorm paralyzed Harbin. For two days it raged, and by the time the blizzard had worn itself out, the snow was piled in such deep drifts that it was impossible to get out of the houses. The double-hung windows were frosted with a solid coating of ice, and the doors blocked as if boulders held them shut. Chaya Leya and Valodya found themselves captives in a dimly lit cave of ice and snow. On the fourth day, February the tenth, Valodya managed to get the door open and broke a path through to the street. It was yet another two days before Harbin learned that while the city was imprisoned within walls of snow, on February the ninth, Japan had attacked the Russian fleet at Port Arthur.

The long-awaited war had begun. Harbin was in its direct path.

*V*alodya and Herschel went south to the war within weeks of each other. Valodya had volunteered in April when the first relief troops came through Harbin en route from Siberia to Port Arthur. Herschel departed in early ·June in a group of prisoners and exiles who had been released in order to join the fighting.

Valodya never mentioned to Chaya Leya that he meant to volunteer. He just arrived home, saying that when the Harbin Battalion left at the end of the week, he would be with them.

"But why, Valodya, why?" she had wept. "You told me yourself that you didn't believe in the war! Why should you go?"

"I have to. When the Japanese attacked Port Arthur, it changed everything, surely you see that?"

"But you might be killed! You said Russia can't win a war in Asia!"

Her hands clutched his coat. Angrily he tore himself away. "Would you have me sit here safe in Harbin while Russia is defeated by a country no bigger than our smallest province?"

"Yes! Yes, that's exactly what you should do! Vladimir Mikhailovitch, we are talking about your life!"

He turned his back to Chaya Leya. "Please. I must go, don't you understand?" He swung around to her once more, the slightest of smiles tugging at his mouth. "Anyway, I'm a gambler! I like to play the odds!"

"I don't want you to leave."

"You see everything in terms of what you want. Maybe I want the same thing—to stay here with you—but I can't. It's a matter of honor."

"Honor!" she said, spitting out her distaste. "A man's word!" She had sobbed until she had no more tears.

At the end of the week, Chaya Leya, her face puffy from lack of sleep, packed Valodya's things. On the last night they made love sadly, and she slept finally with her arms wrapped tightly around him as though to hold him safe.

In the morning there were no more tears or entreaties. "Do you have everything?" she asked tonelessly.

He put down his glass, the tea untasted. "I guess so."

This is the last morning meal we will share, she thought. This morning the last time I will waken to see his head on my pillow. When he walks through the door it will be for the last time.

He carried his bundle a few steps toward the door before turning back. "I have the thought," he said, "that I might never see you again. You will not forget me?"

"Forget you! I could sooner forget the sun and the green grass growing!" Her eyes rested on him, memorizing the contours of his face, the roughness of his bright hair. "Every day I will pray for you to come back."

He stood a moment more. "I have loved you, Chaya Leya."

She closed her eyes against the past tense. When she opened them, he was gone.

The shock of the undeclared war and the violence with which it had erupted shook the confidence of the people of Harbin. Every day they expected to hear the tramp of Japanese boots on the southern road and to see a cannon trained upon their houses from the surrounding hills. Escape from the city was no longer possible since every means of transportation was needed to move troops and supplies forward to the Liaotung Peninsula and to carry the wounded back to safety.

In St. Petersburg the court derisively referred to the Japanese as "ugly little monkeys." But try as they would to diminish the enemy, Japanese soldiers were in fact dogged in battle, giving no ground, and bearing up under fearsome punishment. Moreover, the Japanese had been equipped and trained by allies among the Western powers while the Russians in Manchuria were neither well-supplied nor well-led.

The Russians, caught unawares despite ample warning of impending attack, were at an enormous disadvantage. The Japanese had one hundred and eighty thousand men in Korea with more readily available just across the narrow strip of water in Japan. The Russians had one hundred thousand troops in all of Manchuria, and those were scattered among many outposts.

Aid from European Russia was a myth. All rail traffic came to a halt at Lake Baikal, where men and war materiel had to be offloaded and transferred to sledges to cross the winter ice, then reloaded on the other side onto trains which might or might not run. Delays of precious days and weeks at this bottleneck threatened the whole war effort.

Sea transportation was no better. Ships based at the naval port of Kronstadt sailed through the Baltic, out to the North Sea, through the Straits of Dover, around the coast of Africa to Madagascar, and thence across the Indian Ocean into the Pacific before finally arriving in the South China Sea. It was a formidable and lengthy journey, and at its end the only access to Port Arthur snaked between Japan and Korea through the Straits of Tsushima, a passage so narrow that ships had to go through it in single file. The whole defensive enterprise was a military nightmare for General Kuropatkin, commander of the Russian forces in Asia.

Harbin prepared for a siege. A bulwark of sandbags was thrown up around the southern edges of the city and militia patrolled the train tracks and the riverbanks. Railroad clerks, mechanics, and storekeepers rushed to join the Cossack troops quartered in the city. Borochev, the military commander of Harbin, had commandeered supplies of rice, grain, and beans. These were cached in government warehouses alongside kegs of herring, pickled vegetables, dried meats, and barrels of fresh water. Each family was assigned a ration and was warned that hoarding was a capital offense. Nonetheless, *spekulanti* thrived, as they always do in wartime.

Until the first wounded arrived, the populace saw the war only as nuisance and inconvenience. The condition of the injured men in that first trainload horrified the citizens, who had crowded onto the train platform to give them a heroes' welcome. These maimed men were the lucky ones. Many hundreds had died on the field in the stunning defeat suffered at Liaoyang. As trains continued to roll into Harbin, the wounded overflowed the existing military hospital, and another makeshift medical facility was established in an abandoned go-down on the river. And still they came.

Civilian refugees, Russian and Chinese both, followed the military trains. They walked up the tracks with their pitiful bundles, their frightened children following behind. The despairing eyes and the near starvation of these families were more demoralizing than the gaping wounds of the battle veterans. Harbin set up kitchens to feed the civilians and rude shelters to house them. The women of Harbin tended the sick and the homeless alike. Even Marina Kutuzova, prettily helpless in the best of times, took her turn ladling food and knitting imperfect but functional sweaters and scarves.

With the threat of invasion, Chaya Leya gave up the cottage she had shared with Valodya and moved in with the Kutuzovs. Shortages and food lines had become a heavy burden for everyone, and the officials had decreed that Chinese servants could not be trusted to collect rations for Russian families. It was Chaya Leya who now stood in food queues, often coming away after a half day's wait with only a small portion of rice and a half *funt* of dried beef or salt cod. Fortunately Big Chang was ingenious at turning these unlikely ingredients into edible fare by the addition of dried mushrooms and pungent soya sauce.

Things improved with the coming of warm weather. Farmers from the outlying areas carried cabbages, greens, and onions into the city, and there were fish to be caught in the river. Little Chang's early morning duty was with bamboo pole at water's edge.

Chaya Leya found herself unwell from the winter's restricted diet. But she did not feel better even when the weather warmed and fresh food appeared on the table. Always quick and full of energy, she now dragged herself through the days, sometimes too fatigued even to strip off her clothes when she fell into bed at night. Then there were the frightening spells of vomiting that overtook her without warning. Often now she was too weak and sick to go to the commissary for the family dole, and eleven-year-old Boris, the oldest of the children, was sent. Still a child, he did not pay enough attention to the weighing of the rice, especially if his brother Mischa went along for company.

Chaya Leya had not laid eyes on Herschel in some months. He had refused to see her after that day she had told him about Valodya. She had continued to carry food to the prison and to bribe certain officials to allow him privileges, but she did not press him to talk to her. Nevertheless, on the day in June when a contingent from Harbin Prison was scheduled to leave for the front, Chaya Leya was at the station to see him off.

The heat and the jostling crowd on the platform had raised a clammy sweat on her back and under her breasts, and she felt as though all the bodies pressing in upon her were depleting her air. The heavy smell of close-packed humanity assaulted her like a physical presence, and the noise of farewells, the shrieks and the laughter, hammered at her. Her head swam even as she forced a cheerful smile to her lips and waved a vigorous good-bye to the men going off to war. She kept her mouth tightly shut, pushing the bile back in her throat. She would not faint. If only she could get a breath of fresh air—

Chaya Leya caught sight of Herschel before he saw her. Clean-shaven now against the heat of southern Manchuria, dressed in his new drab-colored uniform, he seemed taller and stood straighter than before, the military pride instilled at Blagoveschensk reasserting itself.

"Herschel! Herschel!" she called, trying to make herself heard above the noise of the crowd.

He turned, saw her, and an inner light broke over his thin, narrow face. In a few determined strides he had pushed his way through the crowd to her side. Without hesitation he pulled her close against him and kissed her with a roughness that was new between them.

Taking a step back, the better to see her, he said, "You're too thin and too pale. Why isn't Valodya taking better care of you?"

Shakily Chaya Leya began to laugh. "You sound like Papa!"

"So where is he?"

"Gone to the front, in April. I'm living with the Kutuzovs now."

"That's good," he said awkwardly. "They'll take care of you."

The sergeant-major in charge of the men was already blowing his whistle to signal that it was time to board.

He pulled her to him and bent to kiss her on the lips. Before releasing her, he whispered fiercely in her ear, "Whatever happened doesn't matter. You're mine. You always have been. I'll be back for you. Wait for me."

She held herself stiffly upright until the train had churned off into the distance, but as soon as it was out of sight, Chaya Leya slumped against one of the shed's iron pillars. She felt so ill that she wondered if she could make it back to the house on Nicholas II Avenue. Luckily for her, Big Chang was even at that moment coming along Kitaiskaya Street with his basket of vegetables, on his way home from the bazaar. He glimpsed her leaning, half fainting, against the wall of a building, and he went to her at once. His arm was strong and sturdy to lean on—she would not have gotten home without it. When they reached the privacy of their own courtyard, he lifted her in his arms and carried her inside, where he set her carefully into a chair and sent Little Chang scurrying to fetch Amah. When Meiping came into the kitchen, Chaya Leya was weeping into her hands, and the Chinese woman gathered her into her arms, rocking her as she would have rocked one of the little boys. Later Amah gave Chaya Leya an herb draft to sip and wiped her face with a cool damp cloth.

"Oh, Meiping, what am I to do!" Chaya Leya whispered. "I'm so sick and alone."

"Not sick, I think. Baby coming."

"Baby!" Chaya Leya's eyes widened. Yes, of course, why not? She and Valodya had been together for many months with no thought of consequences. A baby! How long had it been since her monthly flux? She had not given it a thought. At least three months, perhaps more. A child! But what of the father?

"I'm afraid for Valodya—and for Herschel too! Will they come back, Meiping?"

Amah stroked Chaya Leya's hair. "Is joss, Missy. Gods alone know."

Chapter 44

*A*lthough Simcha was fifteen, almost everyone he met at the University of St. Petersburg thought him at least two years older, and he did not hesitate to tell people that he was nineteen. He had always looked and acted older than his years.

The first days and weeks in St. Petersburg would have been lonely for most boys his age, but Simcha had lived within himself for most of his young life, aloof from his surroundings. It was a habit acquired as a small boy who had no affinity for the others in *cheyder*. In those days, while other boys might spend summer afternoons teaching themselves to swim in the Dvina, Simcha was occupied in eavesdropping on his mother's classes. Other youths had a best friend, a confidant, of their own age; Simcha thought of Yevgeny Fedotov, the steward of Spokoinaya Zemlya, as his.

Although greatly stimulated to be at the university, Simcha characteristically took his time in moving into his new world, carefully studying the institutional system and patterning his behavior after that of the older students. On Fedotov's advice he had enrolled in the humanities curriculum with the intention of transferring at some later date to the Medical Institute. That he planned to train as a doctor was fine, the steward had said, but first he needed to educate himself to be a man of culture and understanding.

Simcha was slow in making the acquaintance of other students. An occasional classmate walked out of the lecture hall beside him, discussing some point that had just been made, and other students nodded at him in the noisy basement tearoom where he sometimes sat between lectures, but he was seldom invited to join them. He was quite unaware that because he had grown accustomed to wide-ranging arguments and challenges with Fedotov, those same kinds of exchanges were perceived by classmates as cocksure and abrasive. Nor did he realize that his level of knowledge, beyond that of most students trained in *gymnasia*, made both his fellows and some of his professors uneasy.

*W*hat kind of name is Mandelkern anyway?" Valery Maximov, one of Simcha's classmates, asked him one day. Maximov was one of the few who sometimes invited Simcha to join him for tea.

Simcha shrugged. "I don't know. Just a name."

"I don't think I've ever known another Mandelkern," Cyril Tokarev, who was sitting with them, mused.

"And I've never known another Cyril Tokarev either," Simcha said sharply.

"Names are funny," Tokarev said. "It almost sounds Jewish."

"So what did you think of Professor Malinkov's analysis of the laissez-faire theory?" Valery Maximov asked quickly. In a very few moments the three were enmeshed in a discussion based on the morning's lecture.

Later, when Simcha was walking home to the boardinghouse where he lived, Maximov caught up with him. "Why don't you join me at the Blue Lantern Coffeehouse tonight? There's to be a poetry reading."

Simcha considered. It was the first social invitation he'd received since he'd been in St. Petersburg. He was elated and wary at the same time. "All right," he said, suddenly shy.

"Shall we go together? Where are your rooms anyway?"

Simcha said quickly, "It will save time if I meet you at the Blue Lantern. What time did you say?"

Uncomfortably he thought that he did not want Maximov to know where he lived. Earlier he had been uncomfortable with Tokarev's questioning his name. He had not often given any consideration to Russian anti-Semitism. Perhaps he thought it would be no problem in the intellectual world of the university. He wished now he had enrolled as Semyon Fedotov, but almost at once had the grace to be ashamed of himself.

Papa, when he brought Simcha to St. Petersburg, had found a tiny room for him in a somewhat run-down boardinghouse a few blocks from the university. Yoysef, rather than Simcha, had decided that it was clean enough and respectable. Besides those assets, it provided kosher food at a cheap rate. Simcha had agreed to his father's choice, caring little where he lived and nothing for the other boarders, a couple of Jewish students at one of the city's technical institutes, and several men who worked in the neighborhood. It was a poor room by anyone's standards, but there was space enough for his books and a table to study at, and nothing more was required. His *real* life was at the university. Nothing outside its great lecture rooms meant anything to him. The huge halls rose from the lectern and blackboard towards the ceiling in tiers. A little nearsighted, Simcha tried always to come early to position himself toward the front, though some lecturers insisted that he and certain others sit at the rear.

From his first glimpse of the solid stone buildings, Simcha had thrilled to the university's graceful buildings and parklike setting amid green lawns that extended to the very banks of the River Neva. Inside, the rooms were painted in pale green and rosy pink with ornamental gilt cornices and crystal chandeliers that dated from the time of Catherine the Great. Why should he care that his own room was small and dark when he could come every day to this princely place!

Examining his appearance in the mirror before leaving to meet his new friend at the poetry reading, Simcha was satisfied that he looked no different from Maximov, or any of the others. His father had made him a sober, dark suit, cut in the Russian fashion, and Fedotov had presented him with a fine leather portfolio for carrying his papers. His mother, having studied pictures of students in the newspapers, had made him a plain white linen tunic to wear belted, and had bought him boots and a peaked student cap.

Except for his surname and "*Ivrai*" printed on his identity card, there was nothing to mark him as other than Russian. As he had often been told, his fair looks were pure Slav. To his regret, he was not as tall as his father and brother, but nevertheless was broad through the chest and shoulders, his trunk solidly joined to strong legs. He had a high forehead and reflective eyes of the same clear blue as his mother's, a serious thin-lipped mouth, a straight nose. Only at home was he known by his Yiddish name, Simcha— for the rest of the world he was "Semyon." It was no artifice to assume a Russian name; since he did not believe in God, he no longer considered himself a Jew.

The Blue Lantern was packed with too many bodies and the air was thick with the haze of cigarette smoke. Maximov had been waiting for him on the sidewalk outside. Valery was apparently known at the coffeehouse, and a place was made for them at one of the tables. The reading had not yet commenced.

Maximov made the introductions: "Semyon, this is Adam and Vadim," nodding toward a slight dark-haired man in a student cap and another who appeared to be albino. "Adam and Vadim, this is Semyon."

Adam and Vadim were both graduate students in the economics faculty. The four of them chatted a little self-consciously until the poet, a gangly, middle-aged man dressed in black, stood up to read. Simcha found the poetry callow but his tablemates fascinating. At eighteen, Maximov was the leading student and by far the brightest star in the philosophy seminar where Simcha was also a participant. Professor Mishkin made sly comments about Valery's radical ideas, but it was taken as a joke; after all, Valery came from an old Cossack family with a history going back many generations. Adam Markovitch was apparently a Jew, older, maybe even as old as thirty. It was hard to tell anything about him because he had a hard, closed face and wary eyes. As for Vadim Golub, Simcha was too distracted by his white hair, colorless skin, and pink-rimmed eyes to try to comprehend what he was like.

After the reading, Vadim went home, saying that he needed to get some sleep, and Valery, Adam, and Simcha went on to a small, quiet café for schnapps. By the time they said good night a couple of hours later, Simcha felt he had made two friends for life.

All things considered, it was odd, Simcha thought later, that he should have become involved in the revolution through a personal relationship with a Cossack and a Jew. From his first attendance at a meeting of the Social Democratic Party, where he went with Valery and Adam, Simcha felt himself at home and at peace. In the superheated atmosphere of the movement, he found an acceptance that enabled him to shed the loneliness of a lifetime. Never able to embrace the xenophobic mentality of Jewish Polotsk, and excluded from the Russian intelligentsia because he was born a Jew, Simcha had lived his life as a stranger among others. Until now.

My dear friend and teacher (Fedotov read in the letter that had just arrived from Semyon). *If, as you taught me, "All roads lead to Rome," then surely they must all lead away from St. Petersburg, because from the ideals and the energy concentrated here, the Cause of Freedom will spread and be won.* (So, the steward thought, scratching his beard, you have caught revolutionary fever, have you? Well, that's as expected—if you don't carry it too far.)

You were so right when you told me that when I came to the university I would find people like myself to keep as friends. I have made two dear comrades, Valery Maximov and Adam Markovitch. Together we are working in an organization (Be careful what you commit to paper, Semyon!) *dedicated to a democratic future for all. Everyone tells me I have a real talent for persuasive writing if you know what I mean.* (What exactly are you doing? Speeches? Pamphlets? Yes, you would be good at that.)

We go often to a coffeehouse called the Blue Lantern. Most nights we sit up until very late talking about the world we want to see. When there is so much need around us—the homeless who live as best they can on the streets of St. Petersburg—there is no time to waste before getting on with the Great Task. (Must you see everything in capital letters?) *Last weekend there was a spontaneous rally near the statue called the "Bronze Horseman"—I'm sure you know the one I mean—Peter the Great, the most famous monument in St. P. The police came around but they didn't do anything. Since they can't put everyone in jail, they prefer to infiltrate and catch the leaders! Next weekend Valery and I plan to go talk to the workers as they come out of the Putilov Locomotive Works.* (About what? Yes, and when do you study?)

I can't thank you and Count Pyotr enough for making it possible for me to come here. This is the most wonderful city in the world! (You haven't mentioned your classes, your reading, your teachers!) *I kiss you on both cheeks! Your pupil and friend, Semyon Mandelkern.*

Simcha's comments might be offhand, but stories of street violence in St. Petersburg filtered back to Polotsk. Likewise, his assurances that the police were not interested in rank-and-file radicals proved premature. Cossack troops had been brought in to put down the disturbances. In rounding up the rioters, the Cossacks had behaved with special brutality to students, flogging the men and raping some of the women. The Minister of the Interior, Vyacheslav Plehve, under whose department the police operated, took no measures to control the troops. It was Plehve's stated intention to instill mortal fear in those who opposed the government.

Feeling that this new twist was beyond them, Malkeh and Yoysef went to Spokoinaya Zemlya to discuss what should be done about Simcha with Fedotov and Pyotr Voronov.

Malkeh was agitated by all she was hearing. "We've got to get Simcha home! He could get hurt in a riot! By accident even! They say people in the streets are throwing stones, and the soldiers are hitting people with their rifle butts. Even if Simcha is innocent, he could be arrested. The whole city has gone crazy. I'm sure I don't know how the university can keep running! Simcha is too young to be in St. Petersburg alone. My God, he could get killed!"

Yevgeny Fedotov was irritated. "You're working yourself up over nothing! You can't believe everything they write in the newspaper! Anyway, Semyon has a good cool head on his shoulders—"

"How do you know? How do any of us know what he's doing?" Malkeh cried. "He's barely fifteen! I want him home!"

Fedotov's mouth clamped shut in a hard, rigid line. "You have always fought against Russifying the boy!"

"We're not talking about that now," Yoysef said mildly.

But Fedotov had gone too far to stop. "Jews!" he snapped. "You won't be content until Semyon's bound to the ghetto! What shall he be, a tailor or a rabbi?"

Malkeh turned white. "How dare you?"

Yoysef said simultaneously, "There are worse things."

Pyotr Voronov intervened. "The news is certainly exaggerated. Of course there's unrest in the cities, but when have things ever been quiet in Russia? At the universities it's only high spirits. Believe me, it will all blow over."

"Do you really think so?" Malkeh asked, grasping at straws. She wanted Simcha to have his chance, but he was so vulnerable. How could a boy that age, his first time away from home, take care of himself properly?

Pyotr smiled. "When final examination time comes around, all these diversions will be forgotten. You'll see."

Malkeh nodded but she and Fedotov continued to glare at each other from opposite ends of the table.

Yoysef said, "Well, all right, then, let's wait a little. But at the first sign of more trouble, I shall go get the boy myself."

What none of them in Polotsk knew was that the assembly halls and lecture rooms of the university, even though they were in the very shadow of the Winter Palace, rang with the cry to take up arms and rise up against the government.

*J*n September, both Dvoreh and Simcha came home for Rosh Ha-shanah. Dvoreh stayed a week, scarcely speaking to anyone and emerging, red-eyed, from her room only when it was absolutely necessary. Most days Simcha was off and about his own vague business—what, he never said, though often he was at Spokoinaya Zemlya. If he noticed how moody Dvoreh was, he paid it little mind.

The parents were perturbed by her unhappiness.

"What is it, Dvorehleh?" Yoysef had asked in a troubled voice. "What is wrong? Please talk to us."

Dvoreh merely shook her head, averting her face.

Malkeh's eyes were dark with anxiety but her tone was sharp. "You are acting like a child! Either tell us what's wrong or set it aside."

"Mammeh, you know nothing about anything!" Dvoreh said, her eyes overbrimming and her dark brows knitted in her small, pale face. Unable to meet her mother's worried gaze, she flew from the room, banging the door shut behind her.

After a time Dvoreh opened up to confide that the wedding had again been postponed. Had there ever been a longer betrothal since the biblical Jacob waited fourteen years to marry Rachel?

First the wedding, originally scheduled for the previous December, had waited until Lev's brother, Reuben, was bar mitzvah. Then Frau Goldenburg had suggested that the date be put off until after Passover, when the weather would be more pleasant. And then the Goldenburgs decided that the ceremony might just as well wait until summer, when the elder sister planned to come from Kiev for a visit. At each of these suggested delays, Dvoreh had protested but Lev had given in. "We'll be married a long, long time," he told Dvoreh, "so what difference can a few months make?"

"Lev," Dvoreh said, looking fearfully into his face, "tell me the truth. Have you changed your mind about marrying me?"

"Of course not! I'll tell you what, Dvoreh. Some beautiful German pieces came into Slomisky's just this week. Why don't we begin to pick out our furniture?"

Dvoreh had allowed herself to be diverted. She and Lev had spent hours choosing furniture, dishes, linens. They did not actually buy anything, of course, because, as Lev said, they had no place yet to keep it. Dvoreh's only acquisition, one she did not mention to Lev and certainly not to Frau Goldenburg, was her wedding dress and veil, which, carefully wrapped in muslin, hung in the back of her wardrobe. The coarse white muslin began to look to Dvoreh like a shroud.

Then in June came the crowning blow. Dr. Goldenburg, while working on a patient in his office on Alexander Street, had a massive coronary and died on the spot.

It was a surprise to everyone that the successful little dentist had left behind a mountain of debts. He had been quietly speculating in land at a time when land values were going down. To Lev fell the responsibility for paying off the creditors and the tax collector, and for providing support for his mother and younger brother. He was, after all, the elder son.

"Two can manage better than one," Dvoreh had pleaded. "My wages and yours will be enough to pay off everything!"

"No," Lev had said resolutely. "I will take care of Mammeh and Reuben. After we are married, you will not work!"

A whole new cycle of frustrations and postponements began then, grinding Dvoreh's hopes into the ground. It was in this sad state of mind that she went home for the observance of the New Year.

The afternoon before her return to Riga, Dvoreh found her mother alone in the kitchen. Malkeh was sitting in her rocking chair, idle for a change, just rocking. Her face was lined and sad.

Dvoreh sank down on the floor by her mother's feet. "Mammeh, what shall I do?"

Malkeh shook her head. "No one can tell you that, Dvorehleh. Are you sure that you love him?"

Dvoreh nodded slowly. "I think so—only now I get the feeling that he no longer wants me."

Malkeh rocked slowly, back and forth, back and forth. Neither of them spoke for a long time.

"Is there something wrong with me, Mammeh?"

"Wrong?"

"I mean, something that would make a man change his mind about me?"

Malkeh put her hand out to stroke Dvoreh's soft curls. "I think any man would be lucky to have you for a wife." She sighed. "Life does not always go in straight paths, my darling child. Maybe you should leave Riga. Come home for a while. If this match is meant to be, Lev will come after you."

"Do you think so, Mammeh? I love him. I can't imagine living without him!"

"Think about it. A separation may be good for you both."

But the next day Dvoreh, without coming closer to a resolution, returned to Riga and the question of the unsettled relationship with her betrothed.

*A*t home on this, his first visit since he had entered the university, Simcha realized what his life could have been had he been less fortunate! How had he ever stood the provincialism of Polotsk! How small the city was, how cramped the house behind the tailor shop, how boring, boring, boring were his relatives, even Papa and Mammeh! As for his old nemesis, Dvoreh, she did nothing these days but cry and blow her nose. He couldn't even get a rise out of her. If anyone asked him, she'd be better off dumping this Lev Goldenburg!

Mammeh had invited all the relatives for Rosh Hashanah dinner. Uncle Yaynkel had talked about nothing but going to America. He had already sold the shop, and the family was in the process of packing for an October departure, although it was clear to see that Aunt Yenta was having second thoughts. Mammeh had mistaken Simcha's irritation with his uncle for envy. She had patted his hand and said, "Finish your education, my son, and then you, too, can travel to America." As if he would ever consider leaving St. Petersburg and the part he had yet to play in the glorious revolution! For what? To live in a sinkhole of capitalistic exploitation? America! Uncle Yaynkel was as much a fool as ever. He thought he was going to take up an easy life in New York, when he'd be lucky to find some second-rate job. And for this he'd exchange his shop and his house for a cot in his son Moishe's tenement flat? Oh, yes, Simcha had read in *The Spark* how things really were for immigrants in the New World even if his family had not! He could almost bring himself to feel sorry for his aunt and uncle and cousins.

The letters that Simcha had sent home from St. Petersburg had been increasingly brief, at least since spring. Without elaboration he had written that he had passed his examinations well and looked forward to continuing his studies. This was something of an exaggeration. His extracurricular pamphleteering had taken up so much of his time that he had constantly missed lectures and shamefully neglected his reading. Sitting for his first examinations of the new school year, he had barely made passing grades. Ashamed both for his performance and for his lies, Simcha gave himself excuses. After all, how much could be expected of him when half the time classes were disrupted by student demonstrations and the other half by police actions? At that he had done better than his friend Valery Maximov, who was about to be dropped from the university altogether. As for the evasiveness of his letters, what was the point of worrying Mammeh and Papa? Besides, if they should ever guess at the truth, they would never let him return to St. Petersburg, and this was an intolerable prospect.

Face-to-face with Yevgeny Fedotov, it was a good deal harder for him to hide the truth. His old mentor questioned him closely about his classes, his professors, and his reading.

Simcha was wary with Fedotov. "Well, sir, I studied so many of the great thinkers with you—Locke and Rousseau and—well, I decided that the philosophy lecturers in St. Petersburg had nothing to offer, so I stopped going." He did not intend to confess that he had been dropped from the philosophy seminar. Besides, he had hated the reactionary Professor Mishkin with a passion.

"I see." Simcha was uncomfortably aware that he probably did.

"You were a superb teacher, *Gospodin*," Simcha said nervously.

"Hmn."

"I was ahead of all the other students—"

Fedotov nodded. Possibly. Young Semyon had been an exceptional student. Still, a sudden suspicion jarred him. "It couldn't be, could it, that your evenings at cafés and the 'persuasive writing' you do for the movement have something to do with it?"

Simcha was shamefaced. "That too."

Fedotov rubbed the bridge of his nose thoughtfully. "Perhaps you should tell me just what organization you belong to and what your role is."

"I belong to the Social Democratic Labor Party," Simcha said proudly.

"And what is your perception of this group?"

Simcha said carefully, "The people who belong want, like you yourself do, to see reforms in the government. We are pushing for a constitution with basic guaranteed freedoms."

"As it should be," the steward said. "As it should be. But what exactly is your part, Semyon?"

"I write an occasional paragraph or two for a pamphlet, *Gospodin*, and once in a while I run the printing press. How much can a student do, after all?" He half hoped that Fedotov would see through his mealy-mouthed half truths and demand candor. He would like to confide in Fedotov, if he dared.

But the steward wanted to believe him and was therefore reassured by Simcha's answer. Fedotov had worried that Semyon had gotten mixed up with Socialist revolutionaries, but, unlike the S.R., the Social Democrats did not call themselves a "fighting organization" and were not dedicated to assassinating officials and burning down estates. He was thankful for that, at least. Semyon needed both years and an education to mature him. Then, and only then, Fedotov thought, would his old pupil be prepared to step into place as a philosopher-leader of the revolution, a place for which Fedotov had so carefully prepared him.

Gazing into Semyon's candid blue eyes, Fedotov nodded in satisfaction.

Chapter 45

*T*he encounter between Vassily and the Grand Duke Sergei brought him to the attention of Yevno Azev, chief of the terrorist arm of the Socialist Revolutionary Party.

"Dumb, dumb, dumb!" Azev said when he heard about the attack on the tsar's uncle. "The fool was in the open, he was recognizable, and he had about as much chance of hitting the duke with a cobblestone as shitting in a teacup!"

"You're missing the point," the other man in the room said mildly.

"And what is the point I miss?" Azev grinned, for he knew he missed precious little. He was a tall man, thin, balding, affecting black clothing. His people called him "The Bat."

"You weren't there. The man was a bundle of raw rage. He didn't know what to do with it and lost his head. But if it were channeled—"

"The streets are full of anger, Arkady, every peasant burns with it. Scratch a Russian and the hatred of someone or something shows through. Anger is only a tool. What we do requires a cool head."

"I've had an eye on this man since he arrived in St. Petersburg."

"Yes?"

"He goes by the name Vassily Chernov."

"Not his real name, I assume."

"He used the name Golovine in Berlin. One of our informants recognized him as a hanger-on of Ulyanov's a few years back. He was tipped off and escaped before he had a chance to join the others for a free vacation in Siberia."

"So he has a strong sense of self-preservation and not much loyalty. What else is there to recommend him?" Azev asked with a slight smile.

"In Berlin he seems to have been marking time until he could return to Russia. He picked up with a young woman there who is still with him."

"What do you know about her?"

"Nothing really. She's pretty, pleasant, has a good education. They may have known each other earlier."

"So who is your rock thrower, Arkady? Who is he really?"

"I don't know. The police have a dossier. Years ago he was at the university and spread the story that he was related to the Chernovs from Minsk—but they don't claim him."

"He had money?"

"Apparently."

"From the upper classes, then?"

Arkady shrugged.

"I don't need to remind you what we are looking for—idealists but not hotheads, Arkady."

"Something on the street the other day triggered him. You should have seen it. I was following him and the woman—they never knew I was there. A man with a trigger can be used. At will."

Azev stretched out a hand toward the one called Arkady. "Give me a cigarette."

The younger man lit a cigarette and placed it in Azev's hand. "If he really has reason to hate the grand duke Sergei for some reason—"

"And since the grand duke is high on *our* list—" Azev left the thought unfinished. "Well, what's the hurry? Investigate. And the woman—see that we know as much about her as about him."

*V*assily could scarcely believe his great good luck when he was told by the leader of his S.R. group that he had been picked for a special assignment with an elite and secret unit. He would shortly be called to a meeting to discuss it in detail. In the meanwhile, he should say nothing to anyone.

At last! After all these long months of waiting, he was going to be allowed to actually do something more than pass out leaflets! It was what he had prepared himself for, what he'd come home to Russia to do. He thought of all those life stories he had heard on street corners and in doorways, and his anger boiled up strong and hard. The "elite and secret unit" had to be the combat section; it couldn't be anything other than that!

Vassily was full of excitement when he returned to the flat he shared with Marta. He picked her up and swung her around and around until, laughing, she protested that he was making her dizzy. Actually, she was delighted to see him in such high spirits. After the incident on the Nevsky Prospekt, he had become more angry and morose than ever, and she had decided that soon she would have to leave him; she had just not determined how or when she would do it.

"What has happened? Tell me! It's something good, isn't it?"

He shook his head, his finger on his lips. "I'm not supposed to tell." He hugged her to him. "Marta! Tonight let's go to Chez Mère for supper! I know how you love French food!"

"But you hate that place!" Marta frowned. She well remembered the last meal they had eaten there. It had been Vassily's saint's day, and Marta had ordered an elaborate meal to celebrate the occasion. At first he had been happy, making jokes about the frog's legs and the snails sautéed in garlic butter. She loved to introduce him to luxuries—it was such fun to watch his reactions! She had made a game of feeding him the velvety cream soup from her own spoon, so sensuous— When they got home, they would make wonderful love, she had thought. She had poured more champagne, watching him from under her lashes to see how the wine was affecting him. She had to be careful because sometimes drinking exacerbated a bad mood. He had only toyed with the fish course, trout from some cold stream in the Caucasus, and Marta had had the waiter take it away. By the time the leg of venison was brought to the table to be carved, his mood had become black. Gesturing at the bloody meat, he growled, "What we wasted tonight would feed a peasant's family for a week!"

"Perhaps you're right, my love," she said as lightly as she could, "but then, it's doubly a shame if we let the restaurant throw away what we've paid for!"

His hand banged down on the table. "Where did you learn to think like that, Marta? From your aristocrat parents?"

"My family aren't aristocrats," she answered evenly. She pushed her chair back. "Shall we go, Vassily?"

"Oh, no! I'm going to sit here and watch you eat every bit of what you ordered!"

He glowered at her while he forced her to eat the venison and then, choking, the watercress salad. Whenever she started to rise from the table, he grabbed her wrist, twisting it until her choice was to scream and create a scene or to sit.

When she finally gagged on the charlotte russe, Vassily allowed her to stop. He was in a white-hot rage by the time they left the restaurant. There had been other times when he had hit her, but that night it was the worst beating yet.

Wary despite his obvious good humor, she said, "I don't think I want to go out tonight, Vassily. But tell me what has happened?"

Surely, Vassily thought, they couldn't have meant Marta when they told him not to tell. Why, Marta was as close to him as his very skin! "I've been picked for a special secret assignment," he said, his eyes glowing.

"So tell me, what is it, Vassily?"

"I don't know yet! But it's something big, I just know it!"

"But that's wonderful, my darling! I know how unhappy you've been waiting for something to happen!"

"Well," he said proudly, "something's going to happen now!"

*J*t was not until sometime later that Vassily learned that that unprepossessing fellow, Arkady Runich, his fellow supplicant on the fringes of the S.R., was actually one of the combat section's inner circle. Arkady gave Vassily to understand that the mysterious and legendary Yevno Azev, whom he had yet to meet, had some serious reservations about him.

"Why?" Vassily asked Runich desperately. "What do I have to do to prove myself?"

"Azev will think of something," Arkady said slyly.

"I'll do anything he says. Just give the word, and I'll finish off Minister Plehve for him!"

A frown narrowed Arkady's eyes. "What makes you think we need someone to do that?"

"Oh, come on! Plehve's going to be killed, everyone knows that!"

"Where did you hear that?" the other man asked casually.

Vassily realized suddenly that he had ventured onto thin ice. He temporized. "Oh, I just thought, it makes sense—"

"Vassily Yulevitch, stop thinking, stop trying to make sense. Just follow orders, period."

"I'm sorry."

Vassily was disconcerted. He had heard whispers. General Bobrikov, the butcher of Finland, was to be assassinated. And after him, the minister of the interior, Plehve. He had wondered, with a little shiver of excitement, if perhaps his "special" assignment had something to do with one of these missions.

Marta was not home when Vassily arrived at the flat, and he was irritated. Probably out shopping, as usual. She seemed to have an endless supply of rubles. When he had pressed her, she said that she had a legacy from a grandfather. She did not like to talk about it. He wondered, not for the first time, where this money was kept.

Vassily had been with Marta for over two years. He thought he knew her. Certainly he knew the contours of her lovely body, the way it arched upward toward him in lovemaking. He knew how she looked when she slept, her rosy mouth pressed against the pillow, one plump bare arm thrown free of the covers, her black hair loose and wild. He knew how she loved the feel of silk against her skin, the pleasure she took in her bath; he pictured her white teeth biting into a fleshy peach, leaving a trail of juice across her chin.

He wandered aimlessly about the flat. He wanted to tell Marta about the encounter with Arkady Runich, get her advice on how to handle Azev.

A thought nagged at him. Suppose there was no inheritance from a relative. Suppose she had another lover, or more than one, who supplied her with jewels and clothes and bank notes? It had been ridiculously easy for him to seduce her—he couldn't even remember who made the first move. Would she be so easy with other men? He gritted his teeth and disciplined himself to put such thoughts from his mind. He went mad if he visualized her in the arms of someone else.

He had not been himself lately. Once or twice he had hit her, surely a small thing in the village, but Marta was not a village girl. The only real beating—and it was richly deserved!—had been that night after the restaurant. He had had a lot on his mind—she said she understood that. But since he'd blackened her eye that time, sometimes, when he looked up suddenly, he found her staring at him with a questioning coldness.

What had started him thinking about all this? Oh, yes, the source of Marta's money. It seemed an endless supply. If there was a bank account, there would be a record. Where would a woman keep such a thing?

He knew a great deal about Marta Pirumova—one did after two years—

and yet he knew nothing. She did not talk about her family. She did not talk about her years at the university. She said little about her flight to Berlin, or how she had lived before that rainy day in the dingy café.

He shook his head to clear it. This business was making him a little crazy. He wasn't sure that he hadn't ruined everything at the S.R. by talking about killing Plehve. He had to give his mind a rest. Tonight he would suggest to Marta that they go to the Ukrainian restaurant that she liked, he would order Crimean wine with their meal, and she would grow giggly and relaxed, and after dinner they would come home and make love the rest of the night.

He flung himself down on the bed. A nap to pass the time until she came home. But he could not seem to clear his mind for sleep.

If Azev decided not to accept him into his section, what would happen to him? He wanted it badly! He would really be someone important then! Arkady had never told him what Azev's reservations were. Maybe it was that he had once followed Lenin, but what was wrong with that? They were all agents of the revolution, weren't they? Maybe he'd have remained loyal to the Bolsheviks if Lenin hadn't surrounded himself with so many of those damned Jews!

Restlessly Vassily rose from the bed. The door to the wardrobe cupboard hung open, and he looked inside as though there might be a clue to Marta's whereabouts. She had so many dresses, Vassily thought, it was no wonder the doors wouldn't stay shut. He stood inhaling the scent of her skin and the faint perfume that clung to her frocks.

"If she has a bankbook, it will be in one of her pocketbooks," he said to himself. There were several on a shelf, and he opened each one, finding nothing more than a handkerchief, a few hairpins, loose coins.

Or it might be among her underthings. Unconcerned, taking his time, he began to shake out her camisoles.

*M*arta Braun stood in the fitting room in the salon of one of St. Petersburg's leading dressmakers, Madame Suzette. Madame was making infinitesimal adjustments, fastening pins in the neckline of the evening dress the young lady had ordered. For such an elaborate gown, she must be going to a ball at the Imperial Court, the couturier thought. Madame prided herself on knowing all the great ladies of the city, yet she did not recognize this one. But she was certainly a pretty little thing, perhaps someone's newly acquired mistress.

The dark-haired woman had been in the shop several times for fittings on this one garment. The seamstresses were at their wits' end. The customer refused to be satisfied—the seam did not lie right, the neckline gapped, the shoulder was uncomfortable, one complaint after another. In exasperation

Madame herself had gone to see what the trouble might be. And there was nothing wrong with the fit, nothing at all! Still, customers must not be challenged, and so Madame was placing pins here and there.

One of the shop assistants knocked timidly on the fitting room door. "Come," called Madame, her mouth full of pins.

The assistant came close and whispered in her employer's ear. Madame looked surprised, and then, spitting out the pins, she almost laughed out loud. Ah, so that was it! Now it was clear, this business of the girl's demanding daily fittings on a gown that was perfect. What a delicious story this would be to tell! An assignation, and in *her* shop!

"You will excuse me, my dear," she said to Marta. "I have an urgent matter to attend to in the workroom. I have quite finished, in any case, and you may remove the gown and leave it on the chair there—whenever you are ready to leave."

With a gleam and the faintest intimation of a smile, the shop owner bustled from the dressing room. "You will not be disturbed," she said, closing the door.

Marta struggled to get out of the dress without scratching herself on the pins.

"Here, let me help you," a male voice said. "I've had experience."

Marta turned to fling herself into the arms of Julius Ehrenthal. He bent his head to hers in a long kiss.

After a while he said. "It will be hard to explain the scratches from these pins. Let me lift the dress over your head."

The dress disposed of, they touched each other tenderly with their fingers and their lips. When finally they drew apart, each spoke at once.

"Is it safe?"

"You are so beautiful!"

"I've been here every day since I got your message."

"How the French love a tryst!"

Reassured that it was not a dream, their breathing slowed and thoughts took form.

"Julius, how do you dare come back to Russia?"

"I'm all right for the moment. The secret police think that Lenin's Bolsheviki are safer than the S.R. They'll allow me to try to organize support. They like to divide and conquer. That's why I came—to meet with some of the others." Smiling down at her, he added, "Besides wanting to see you."

"What is going to happen, Julius?"

He grinned at her. "What do you want me to say? Lenin will prevail in the end, and we'll all live happily ever after?" In a change to a serious mood, he said, "When I leave, Marta, you will come with me. You might like New York."

"New York! Are you joking? You are going to New York?"

"For a little while. You won't like being married to me, I warn you, Marta."

"Married! You mean it?"

"Well, I need to stop thinking about what kind of trouble you'll get yourself into. I've been worried about your boyfriend Vassily."

"These last months with Vassily have been—difficult."

He said gently, "I can imagine. Get dressed now. In three days' time, meet me here at Madame Suzette's. We will be out of Russia by nightfall, and you will never have to see Vassily again. Three days."

"I feel as though a weight has been lifted from my heart," Marta said, nestling in his arms. "Can't I go with you now?"

Julius kissed her. "I wish you could. But I have men to meet in great secrecy. They would not understand why you are with me. It could ruin everything." He lifted her chin so that he could look into the depths of her dark eyes. "Only three days! You're shivering, Marta! Get into your clothes now."

On the following day, Vassily was called to meet with Yevno Azev for the first time. Arkady Runich stood behind Azev's chair. Runich had always been friendly, but today his eyes refused to meet Vassily's.

Vassily felt nauseated. There was a chair beside Azev's, but he had not been invited to sit.

"I understand that you have volunteered to assassinate our good friend, Minister of the Interior Plehve?"

"Yes," Vassily said faintly, "I want to prove myself."

Azev sneered unpleasantly. "Oh, I'll see that you do that, one way or another!" He turned to his aide. "Do you think anyone will miss the bastard, Arkady?"

Who? Vassily's heart missed a beat, and he gasped. So he had been found out!

"No, sir," Runich said.

"Not even the tsar?"

"What do you think, Vassily?" Arkady asked slyly.

"I don't know," Vassily mumbled. They were playing with him, teasing. He felt hot, and his knees had begun to tremble. Get it over with, he thought. If you know something, come out with it!

"Well, maybe the tsar," Azev continued thoughtfully. "After all, look at all of the services that our dear minister performs for him."

They were talking about Plehve, and he had almost betrayed himself! Marta had warned him that his suspicions would destroy him.

With relish Azev recounted some of those services: "He confiscated the wealth and lands of the Armenian Church—what a windfall that was to the treasury! Then he got busy and Russified Poland and Finland; true, it meant killing a lot of Poles and Finns, but what of that? And, of course, he has always been vigorous in carrying out the policy against the Jews—you've heard of Kishinev? No? No matter. They *say* the massacre there wasn't his doing."

Vassily asked shakily if he might sit.

"You do look somewhat pale, Vassily Yulevitch! Are you ill?"

"No, no, tired. A very late night."

He leaned his head against the back of the chair. He could not stop thinking about Marta. She had come home to their flat at dusk, flushed and happy. She'd reminded him of a sparrow, nervously fluttering about to divert attention from a nest with fledglings. He had confronted her. "I was looking for your bankbook among your underthings, Marta," he had said. That had taken the roses out of her cheeks all right!

As though it were the continuation of a conversation, the man in black asked, "So if it were up to you, how would you kill the minister?"

By my bare hands, Vassily thought, so I could feel the tiny neck bones breaking between my palms. "By a bomb, sir?" he asked.

"He is well guarded. It would be hard to get close enough."

Vassily realized that the interrogation was a test. He must think carefully. If only he felt better. "It is well known that he has women. There is a certain brothel— He could be gotten at through a woman."

Azev gave Vassily a cool, searching look. "A man's lust often exposes him to danger, don't you think so, Vassily Yulevitch?"

Vassily averted his eyes. His head ached.

"Take you, for instance—do you think a woman might betray you?"

Vassily bit his lips. Marta, Marta! he cried soundlessly. Why did you do it? He saw her writhing beneath him, her lips pulled back from her little white teeth. Except for her terror, they might have been engaged in an act of love!

"What do you say? I don't hear you!" Azev asked.

"I don't know."

"You didn't know that Marta Pirumova is the Jewess Marta Braun and the mistress of Julius Ehrenthal? What kind of a fool are you!"

There was no escape for Vassily from Azev's flat black eyes. "I didn't know until yesterday! How could I suspect?"

Azev motioned Arkady to light him a cigarette. "Do you work for the Bolsheviki?"

Vassily licked his dry lips. "No. I loved Lenin, but then he turned to those Jews—"

"Like Marta."

"Will you kill me?" Vassily blurted out, looking into Azev's face.

His thin lips curled scornfully. "Why should I do that? I have use for you. I want you to make the Bolsheviki an offer to work for them. Tell them you're on the inside of the S.R. combat section and for love or money—I don't care which—you will keep them informed. We will let you know what we want you to tell them. They may even tell you things that would interest us!"

"A double agent—?" Vassily whispered. That was a dangerous game.

Azev laughed aloud, a harsh, barking sound. "An old Russian habit—"

Vassily took a deep breath.

Azev puffed on the lit cigarette that Arkady handed him. "Yes, we Russians like to work both sides at the same time. For all you know, I may be with Plehve's secret police!"

Arkady guffawed.

Vassily's voice shook. "Yes, sir."

"So it is understood, Vassily Yulevitch, that you will work for us by pretending to work for them."

"Yes, sir. I can do that."

Azev nodded, smiling.

Vassily felt himself dismissed. Gratefully he rose from his chair. His forehead was beaded with sweat, but he dared not risk exposing his nervousness by mopping his face with his handkerchief. He edged toward the door, keeping his eyes on Azev all the while.

"Oh, by the way, you are quite right that the way to reach Plehve is through his whore. We have decided on the date, July fifteenth. You will act as cover and backup for Comrade Sazonov, who will actually throw the bomb."

"I am grateful, sir."

"That is your *second* assignment. Do you know your first, Vassily Yulevitch?"

Vassily shook his head.

"The first is to kill Marta Braun."

Vassily felt his knees buckle. He was afraid that he would be sick on the spot. He turned away so that Azev and Runich would not see his face. "I've already taken care of that," he said.

Chapter 46

*T*here was something irresistibly romantic, Simcha thought, in the notion of a peaceful religious procession of priests, workers, and families winding its way through St. Petersburg to the Winter Palace to present a petition to the tsar. Having once been at a meeting where the organizer of the march, the Ukrainian priest, Father George Gapon, spoke, Simcha could understand his enormous success in bringing the workers of the city into his Assembly of Russian Factory and Mill Workers. In his black cassock with the heavy crucifix swinging on his chest, his wild black beard flapping and eyes burning, Father Gapon had been a towering figure that night, a fiery orator, a leader of men. It was only after he had stepped down from the platform that Simcha had realized that the priest was in fact a rather ordinary-looking person, if anything, somewhat short and slight of build. The motivation for the march to the Winter Palace was to let the holy tsar, the Little Father, know what abuses existed in the factories so that he could dismiss those corrupt officials and greedy mill owners who were responsible.

The more cynical revolutionary leaders sat back, waiting to see what the government would do about Father Gapon and his ragtag marchers. Simcha's party, the Social Democrats, advised its members to stay away from the demonstration. Simcha attributed this sour attitude to the rivalry that prevented the various radical groups from taking any kind of unified action. Nevertheless, he was torn, craving the excitement of being part of the procession but fearful that he might be subject to organizational discipline if he went. Early in January, he had still not made up his mind what to do, and the event was scheduled for Sunday, January ninth, at the beginning of 1905.

Simcha wished there were someone he could discuss this with, but there was no one. Valery Maximov had been arrested in one of the autumn riots and had subsequently been expelled from the university. Although he swore that he would continue working for the revolution no matter what, the arrival of his father and elder brother to take him home to Rostov had put an end to all that. Adam Markovitch had moved to Moscow to establish a new party cell, and even Mischa Golub, his acquaintance with the albino coloring, seemed to have disappeared from St. Petersburg, no one knew where. Simcha had never been lonely before he met Valery and Adam, but once one admits people to his life, he thought, one feels alone when they are no longer there.

Leaving the cellar where he had supervised the typesetting of his most recent literary effort, Simcha realized how much he craved companionship. He could, he supposed, drop in at party headquarters. Earlier in the day there had been a girl, an artist, working on some posters there; she had followed him with her eyes and smiled at him quite a lot. She wouldn't still be there, he thought. But if she was, maybe she might want to go for a cup of coffee at the Blue Lantern.

Perhaps if his mind had not been on the girl, he might have paid more heed to his footing. During the day the sun had been warm enough to melt the thin layer of snow still on the sidewalk, but now that the temperature had dropped, the melted snow had solidified into a solid sheet of ice. Abruptly Simcha's feet slid out from under him, and he fell flat on his back. He sat up, carefully feeling himself all over to be sure that nothing was broken. He decided that he was more jarred than hurt. He had to rise but it was difficult to get a foothold on the slippery pavement. A man coming toward him on the street quickened his pace when he saw Simcha struggling to stand.

"Here, let me help you," the stranger said, putting his hands under Simcha's arms to raise him. "Are you hurt?"

It took Simcha a few seconds to recognize that the samaritan was vaguely familiar to him; he had probably seen him at revolutionary gatherings. An older man, he was perhaps thirty, maybe even older, a man with a thin, intense face and a nervous nail-biting habit. "I think not. Just very cold!"

"Well, that can be fixed," the man said. "There's a little café around the corner where we can get something hot to drink."

That suited Simcha, who had begun to shiver from the bitter cold.

Proceeding arm in arm for mutual support on the icy sidewalk, they made their way to a small coffeehouse on the next street.

Simcha's rescuer turned out to be a pleasant fellow and a sympathetic listener. They discussed Father Gapon's march, which was scheduled for the following Sunday.

"I haven't decided whether to go or not," Simcha confessed. "What do you think?"

The older man was thoughtful. He said, "Technically I guess the demonstration is illegal." He pursed his lips, considering. "On the other hand, the police have had plenty of time to warn off Gapon, and they haven't done it, so from that standpoint it should be safe enough."

"But word has come down that we're not to participate."

"That's true, but that's because Gapon's organization excludes socialists." As an afterthought, he added, "And Jews, of course."

"I see."

They ordered second cups of coffee and talked of other things. The man told Simcha that he had once met Lenin personally, had in fact delivered a package to him. Of course, it was years ago when he was himself not much older than Simcha.

"Really!" Simcha's eyes widened with interest. "What's he like?"

"Very compelling," the man said. "It was a long time ago."

They sipped in silence. After a while, Simcha's companion commented, "It would be interesting to observe what happens at the Winter Palace on Sunday. It may turn out to be a historic event, like my meeting Lenin that time."

Simcha turned this over in his mind. "Someone should be there to record it for Archives."

"Do you write then?"

"An occasional article for small papers, pamphlets, things like that," Simcha said with becoming modesty.

"I read something I liked recently," the older man mused. "Let me think—what was it called? *Towards a Better Life*?"

"I wrote that! *Towards a Freer World*," Simcha amended.

"Your work's as good as that of some older journalists," Simcha's new acquaintance said, admiringly. "You might be the one to write a firsthand report of the Gapon March for *Novoye Vremya* or *Iskra*!"

"Do you really think they would publish something like that?" What a coup that would be for a fledgling writer!

"I wouldn't say it if I didn't."

Sipping the last of the coffee in his cup, Simcha turned it over in his mind. It might even be his duty to go to the demonstration as an objective observer for his party. The more he thought about it, the more he liked the idea.

They shook hands at the door of the coffeehouse before going their separate ways.

"By the way," the man said smiling, "I couldn't help but notice your Byelorussian accent. Where do you hail from?"

"Polotsk. Do you know that part of the country?"

"I was born there. I've been gone so long, I've probably lost my accent." They casually shook hands.

"By the way, my name's Semyon."

"I'm Vassily."

In these dangerous times, it was not the practice to exchange surnames.

*P*etya Voronov usually breakfasted at dawn with his uncle, Yevgeny Fedotov. It was a time that both men looked forward to, before the house came awake and the problems of the day had to be addressed. It was their time to exchange thoughts, bits of information, plans, speculations. Later, when Ekaterina awoke, Petya might have a second meal with her, but that was different from this quiet early-morning time shared by the two men.

When Maria Feodorovna had been alive and well, she had always prepared the food but had never joined them. Now that she was gone, none of the servants stirred this early. Carefully, Fedotov himself brewed the tea, strong, the way he and Petya liked it. Petya cut the bread. When Maria Feodorovna was alive, the bread was fine and white as cake. This stuff was stale and hard.

"We must get a new cook, Petya," Fedotov said.

Petya sighed. "Ekaterina tried to talk to this one, but she didn't want to press it after that scene with Karpovitch last week!"

Fedotov grunted. It was a sad state of affairs when an estate owner couldn't fire an incompetent servant without conferring with the village council. He picked up the tray of bread and tea and carried it into his office, where a space had been cleared on the desk.

They drank their tea, not talking for a while. Finally Petya said, "I think I may be called up soon, Uncle."

"What! There is no war!"

"In a way there is. While you were in Polotsk last night, Nicholas Bruchensky came by. He was heading home from St. Petersburg and stopped to give me the news."

"Which is?"

"A general strike. No trains running, no streetcars, no mail—"

"I wondered where our newspaper was."

"The banks are closed, even the Imperial Ballet refuses to dance."

Fedotov took another swallow of hot tea. "So what's it about?"

"Bruchensky didn't know the details. Something about the police arresting delegates to a railway-union conference. After the protest started, it spread like wildfire."

"I see." He looked over the top of his glass at Petya. An incredible weariness was in his eyes. "How foolish of the police. But then, I don't blame them for being nervous after what happened to Grand Duke Sergei Alexandrovitch. These radicals spoil chance for true reform with their bombs." He broke off a morsel of the bread and put it in his mouth, chewing carefully. "We really *must* do something about the cook! Would Ekaterina mind if I took care of it?"

"Hardly. She hates that kind of unpleasantness." Just thinking of his young wife sound asleep in their bed upstairs brought a soft smile to Petya's face.

"But why do you think you may be called for duty? The police can handle the strike, can't they?"

"Nicholas says that it's spread into the military—soldiers in some of the units, even officers, are laying down their arms. It's rumored there are full-scale mutinies." The two men finished their tea in silence.

All morning, as Fedotov went about his chores on the estate, he thought about his country. How naive he had once been to imagine that Russia would peacefully evolve into a constitutional monarchy with a representational parliament and guaranteed rights for all its citizens! He had clung to that dream for a long time, even in the face of bureaucratic implacability, even, too, when there was clear evidence that the tsar believed wholly in his own divinity. The dream was fading, but hope dies hard.

Toward noon the Mandelkerns' sleigh came through the gates. Throwing the reins to the stableman, Malkeh hurried into the house, stamping the snow from her boots at the kitchen door.

"Malkeh! What is it!" Fedotov had come from his office when he heard sleigh bells.

"Simcha has dropped out of the university!"

Fedotov was thunderstruck. After all the rigorous preparation for admission, after a year already completed, Semyon had simply dropped out!

Just like that? Without talking it over? Without a letter in his own hand explaining himself?

"How do you know?"

"Yoysef's cousin was passing through St. Petersburg and as a favor to us stopped at Simcha's rooms. His impression was that Simcha has not been in class since the fall! Simcha told him he had stopped attending lectures to run an underground printing press."

"Damn!" Fedotov said, hitting the wall with his fist.

"We should have brought him home when we first talked of it," Malkeh said bitterly. "How could we expect a child to keep his head when grown men can't?"

Fedotov motioned for Malkeh to sit and sank back into a chair himself.

"You knew what he was up to, didn't you?" she accused. "He must have written to you—maybe you even talked about it when he was home in the fall!"

He was defensive. "It was nothing out of the normal for a boy his age to be interested in politics. I had no idea how deeply he was involved!"

"You're the one who filled his head with ideas of revolution! I said no good would come of it!" She began to weep. "All I wanted was for him to become a doctor or a lawyer or a professor—to have a good life."

"A pretty exalted dream for a Jew in Russia! At least your son understands that the changes he fights for are what will free *all* people."

"Wonderful! A sixteen-year-old boy fights injustice by dropping out of school and joining a rabble! You should have told us when you knew what he was doing. *We* are his parents."

The steward looked down at his hands, saying nothing.

"Suppose Simcha is arrested?"

"A good possibility," Fedotov said glumly.

"They may send him to Siberia."

"They may well hang the young fool instead." He shouldn't have said it out loud.

Malkeh drew back, her eyes stark with terror. "You must go talk to him!"

"Yes," he said slowly, but there was no hope in his voice. "I think it will do no good. We sent a dreamer to St. Petersburg, but the times were wrong." He pressed a hand to his forehead. His head had begun to ache fiercely. "I will go find him, but you must prepare yourself that it will come to nothing."

"I will go with you!"

Fedotov smiled thinly. "There was a time when I'd have welcomed taking you to St. Petersburg without your husband."

Malkeh flushed and turned partly away. "Then go with Yoysef. He is Simcha's father, after all!"

"The Bolsheviki say there is no father, there is no mother, there is only the common humanity of the revolution."

Malkeh's eyes swam with tears, and she longed to rest her head against his breast for comfort. Even angry, she never doubted that he cared for Simcha as much as she and Yoysef did. "But you will try, Yevgeny Sergeivitch, my friend, my dearest friend?"

He nodded. "I have no choice but to try."

The morning of the march dawned bright and clear with no wind. God, they said, was smiling on the marchers. The temperature was five degrees below freezing, not exceptionally cold for the month, and the sun shone. The people, dressed in their Sunday best beneath padded jackets, had assembled on the outskirts of the city, where Father Gapon and his helpers formed them into five columns. The lead column was to be headed by Father Gapon himself and the others also by priests in vestments. Shambling along behind the clerics on their way through the city, the ragged lines were augmented by more marchers along the way. The police cleared a path for them, and passersby made the sign of the cross and bowed as the priests carrying icons passed.

The workers had been warned to carry no arms, not even a penknife. They were to sing religious hymns and to carry holy icons and pictures of Nicholas and Alexandra. So that there would be no excuse for police interference, there was to be no evidence of anything that could be construed as revolutionary—no red banners, no placards with slogans, no stirring revolutionary songs, not even a red handkerchief!

Simcha linked arms with a young father and an older man in one of the first ranks behind Father Gapon. There was a festival atmosphere, an air of peaceable euphoria. People smiled and joked with one another. To Simcha, caught up in the excitement, all the women looked rosy-cheeked and pretty in their bright flowered shawls, all the men brave, heroic, and enormously tall. Someone started to sing the hymn "How Glorious Is Our Lord in Zion!" Other voices took up the melody. The black-skirted priests hoisted the icons high so that all could see. When the marchers emerged into the great avenues leading to Palace Square, the voices, now 200,000 strong, swelled as "God Save Our Noble Tsar" carried on the cold, still air. There was an uplifting feeling of solemnity and holy purpose. The young man walking beside Simcha took his little girl from his wife's arms so that the child could ride on his shoulders and remember what it was that she saw on this historic day. Simcha admired her fat pink cheeks and the yellow curls that escaped her knitted cap and kerchief.

The cheering of the crowd was deafening. The young man said, "Surely, the Little Father must hear our voices in the heart of the palace itself!"

No one of them was aware that on Friday the tsar had removed himself to Tsarskoe Selo with his wife and his children. Except for servants, the Winter Palace was empty.

During the night the police had erected barricades in the intersections to prevent the marchers from entering Winter Palace Square. Some of the soldiers behind the barriers ordered the demonstrators back and fired their rifles into the air in warning. But by this time the front ranks, pushed forward by others from behind, could not have stopped if they wanted to. They moved inexorably in a solid phalanx through the barricades and into the square.

Father Gapon had planned to read a proclamation aloud before giving it into the hands of the tsar. Copies had been passed through the ranks of the marchers, most of whom were illiterate. Most thought the intent was to throw themselves upon the mercy and protection of their monarch. Reading Father Gapon's petition aloud as he marched with the others, Simcha was startled by its demanding tone, more inflammatory than anything he had ever turned out on his press! "Sire," it began, "we workers and dwellers in St. Petersburg have come to Thee, Sire, with our wives, our children, and our helpless old parents to seek truth and protection. We have become beggars; we have been oppressed; we are weighted down with unbearable toil; we have suffered ... Now we have stopped working and we have told our masters that we will not work again until they ... reduce the working day to eight hours ... minimum pay of a ruble a day ... no more overtime ... The officials have brought the country to complete ruination and have involved it in a detestable war in Asia ... We workers have no voice in spending the huge sums taken from us in taxes. These things beset us, Sire, and have brought us before the walls of your palace ... Do not refuse to help your people ... Break down the wall between Yourself and your people and together with Yourself, let them rule the country ... order elections ... to be carried on by universal, equal, and secret voting ..."

Now Simcha's column was within the square itself. At the barricades there had been troops who had hesitated to fire on unarmed people, but here there was a company of Preobrazhenski Guards under the command of Prince Vasilchikov. A volley of flame engulfed the first rank of marchers, destroying any semblance of order; Father Gapon and his protectors fled at the first shot. An elderly man bearing aloft a huge portrait of Tsar Nicholas fell, his chest streaming blood from a gaping hole. The face of the young child carried aloft by her father flowered like a rose, the white bone emerging from red petals of laid-back flesh. The guards came on, riding into the crowd, sabers slashing and plunging, trampling the marchers beneath their horses' hooves. There was nowhere to hide. Those who escaped the cavalry were cut down by the covering fire of riflemen.

Simcha battered his way back through a solid wall of panicked people who clogged the narrow entrance into the square. It was no better in the avenue into which he emerged. Crack shots from the guards unit had been concealed in strategic locations, and the people in the street were caught in a deadly crossfire. Desperately Simcha's eyes swept the area, seeking a route of escape. Resisting the flow of humanity that would have swept him into the line of fire, he edged his way along a high wall, feeling with his hands for a gate, a weakness in the stone, a foothold by which to climb over. At a place where the brickwork had recently been repaired, Simcha found what he was looking for—a narrow crevice in the stone. It was very small. He stripped off his bulky coat. With great difficulty, scraping himself on the jagged edges of the aperture, he scrabbled through, emerging on the other side in a compost pile in the kitchen garden of the palace. Behind the thick wall the sounds of bullets and the death screams of the helpless were muffled. He was alone. The palace staff, frightened at the appearance of Father Gapon's mob, had hidden themselves in the cellars.

Simcha was sick behind a tree. Then, shivering uncontrollably, he burrowed deep into the compost, where he was hidden and warm. Here he settled himself to wait until it was silent outside.

Chapter 47

Chaya Leya's baby, a dainty and unusually beautiful little girl, was born in a third-floor bedroom of the Kutuzov house on November 21, 1904, with Meiping and Madame Kutuzova in attendance. Although Madame had sent for a doctor early in the afternoon of Chaya Leya's labor, she was informed that he would not come unless there appeared to be a problem the women could not handle. Harbin's handful of physicians were hard pressed to deal with both civilian emergencies and the severely wounded arriving weekly from the battlefields to the south.

"No matter," said Madame cheerfully. "If there's one thing I've had lots of experience with, it's having babies!"

Meiping agreed. "Amah also. Five babies"—she held up the fingers of one hand—"five."

"Now, Chaya, you must get right into bed," Madame instructed.

"Not Chinese custom," Amah said politely. "Sometimes baby born in rice field, mother working."

"She needs to rest, to keep up her strength," Madame was positive.

Amah gazed past Madame's head in a successful attempt not to engage her in controversy.

Except for an occasional cramp, and the backache, Chaya Leya was surprised at how simple it was to bear a child. Even the tactful bickering of the two women added a dash of spice to the occasion. With Amah tight-lipped in the background, Marina Kutuzova had her maid put fresh white sheets on Chaya Leya's bed and bring up one of Madame's own dainty ruffled nightgowns.

"There, you see! You will be ever so comfortable while you wait for the little one to arrive." Madame smiled complacently.

"I'm too nervous to stay in bed," Chaya Leya protested.

"I have just the thing for nerves! I'll go down to the kitchen and show Big Chang how to brew up a proper tisane!"

As soon as Madame left the room, Chaya Leya let Amah take her arm and walk her back and forth along the third-floor corridor. All that was left for her to do was wait.

"This is easier than I thought," she said to Meiping.

The older woman smiled and nodded.

In an hour, Meiping was still smiling and nodding, but Chaya Leya had changed her mind. Mild cramps had become regular sharp stabs that caused her to grab her abdomen and double over. Still Amah kept a firm grip on her charge with an arm about the waist, leading her up and down the long hall. "Blood need to move, good for baby, good for mother." Fortunately Madame was not there to disapprove, having gone downstairs once again to have dinner with her husband.

"How long?" Chaya Leya gasped after a particularly hard pain. "Shouldn't it be soon now?"

Meiping cast a practiced eye over her. "It come, I think, 'bout morning."

"Morning! I don't think I can bear it that long!"

Amah smiled. She had a talent for it, Chaya Leya thought with irritation.

Toward midnight Chaya Leya lay flat upon the bed, moaning and holding Meiping's hand in a grasp of iron. Madame Kutuzova had been faithful about massaging her back while it still seemed to help, but now she sat on the opposite side of the bed with a basin of cool water in her lap, periodically leaning over to wipe Chaya Leya's face and neck with a damp cloth. Gently Meiping disengaged her hand from Chaya Leya's and went to the foot of the bed to gauge the progress of the labor. Little Chang had brought a kettle of boiled water and clean towels, and Meiping washed her hands carefully before the examination. Good. The opening was stretched, and she could feel the baby's head in position in the birth canal. Meiping and Madame looked at each other, exchanging a positive nonverbal message.

The pains were coming very close together now, almost too much to endure! "When, Amah, when?" Chaya Leya panted.

"Little while."

"Scream if you like!" Madame encouraged. "It'll feel better!"

Meiping disapproved. "Not Chinese way."

"She's not Chinese. Go ahead and scream, Chaya."

"Noise frighten little boys."

"Well, that's something else." Madame subsided.

Chaya Leya grasped her belly, crying, "Mammeh! Mammeh!" Hot tears rolled down her cheeks. Madame stroked her hair, comforting.

"Little while," Amah said again. "I get ready now. Hot water. Knife—"

"Don't leave me! It's coming! It's coming!"

"Not yet. Soon. I be here."

"Is the baby all right?" Chaya Leya turned anxiously to Madame. "Am I going to die?"

Madame patted her hand. "Everything's perfect." Reassured, Chaya Leya lapsed once again into an undifferentiated haze of pain.

At a little before one in the morning, Amah laid the squalling infant, still wet and sticky from the birth, on her mother's belly. Chaya Leya looked down upon her child. Tears of joy and weakness fell upon the baby's head. Conflicting emotions tugged at her, and she both pitied the infant's helplessness and felt herself the captive of that tiny fist.

When the baby had been cleansed and swaddled, Chaya Leya could see that her skin was the color of pale ivory. A down-soft crown of reddish-gold fuzz covered her head, and the sleepy eyes tilted at the corners like her father's. "I shall call her Channah," she said dreamily, "Channah after my sister who died when she was little."

"Isn't that bad luck?" Madame asked.

Chaya Leya shook her head. "It's our custom. My sister was very beautiful and very smart. The child honors her memory."

Amah busied herself removing the birth debris and arranging the bed with fresh linens. "I call her 'Bright Flower.' Never saw hair color of poppy before."

"That's a good name too," Chaya Leya said.

"What about her father?" Madame asked gently.

Chaya Leya considered. "Well, perhaps she can also have the name 'Valentina' for him. Channah Valentina." She touched the infant's cheek gently with her finger. "Would you like that, little one?"

Madame sat beside the bed, smiling at the picture they made, like an icon of the Madonna and Child, she thought.

"Thank you for what you did for me today," Chaya Leya said shyly to the two women.

"Do you know, Chaya, that toward the end you called me *Maman*? Women always want their mothers at a time like this. You must miss her very much, I think."

Chaya Leya did not answer. Her eyes rested on the sleeping baby. Just like this must Mammeh have looked down at *her* with awe and wonder. Just so must she have examined *her* infant body to count the fingers and the toes and to wonder whether the ears were like Papa's. Like this Mammeh must have put out one of her fingers for *her* to grasp in a tiny hand. Oh, Mammeh, she thought, if only I could see you smile on her! Looking down at her baby, Chaya Leya's heart overflowed with love and happiness, and for once, when she thought of her mother, bitterness was absent from her heart.

The outbreak of the war with the Japanese had completely cut off the civilian mail service between Manchuria and Russia. The last letter from Chaya Leya had been written shortly after Herschel's trial and sentencing. What had become of Herschel in the intervening months, how Chaya Leya was managing with him in prison, the impact of war on their situation— all of this was fertile soil for Yoysef's and Malkeh's worried imaginations.

"At least we know that Harbin has not been attacked," Yoysef sighed. "All the fighting is farther to the south."

"Surely the war can't last long!" Malkeh said worriedly. "Yevgeny Fedotov says that as soon as our navy gets to Port Arthur, it will be all over for the Japanese."

"Alevai," Yoysef said soberly, "may it be so."

Into this great silence exploded Reb Koch's letter to Yoysef. The fact that a letter written so long ago could have arrived in Polotsk was itself a minor miracle.

The *poshtalon* who brought the letter to the house merely shrugged when he handed it over. "It's probably been sitting in a sack someplace for the past year! From your daughter, is it?"

Yoysef turned the letter over in his hands, shaking his head. "It seems not to be." But who else could be writing from Harbin?

If the letter had indeed been from Chaya Leya or Herschel, Yoysef would have waited for Malkeh to return from school so that they could read it together. As it was, he was grateful that he had had a chance to digest its astonishing contents beforehand.

Dear Reb Yoysef Mandelkern, he read. *Permit me to introduce myself to you—Meier Koch, formerly of Kiev and now a bookseller in Harbin and the gabai of the shul. Perhaps you already know me and my wife from your daughter's letters.*

It is with a grievous heaviness of heart that I take up my pen to write you this letter. I believe that you and your wife are good people of sound religious beliefs and high moral standards. I would therefore not give you pain lightly, but having searched my heart through many days of prayer and nights of wakefulness, I have decided that it is my duty.

As you know, Reb Mandelkern, my wife and I were happy to shelter your daughter in our home after Herschel Rosen was arrested. In fact, my wife grew quite fond of her. It was not our choice, I assure you, that Chaya Leya accepted employment as a servant in a gentile household and left our home! Frau Koch and I would have been happy for her to remain as a guest in our house for as long as she wanted and needed us. It is our way to shelter the stranger. Despite our disapproval of her employment, do not think for a moment that the Jewish community of Harbin turned its back on your daughter. After Herschel was sentenced, I counseled Chaya Leya strongly to return home to Polotsk. A collection was taken at the shul to purchase her ticket home. She refused both the money and the counsel. I am sorry to say that you have raised a most headstrong child.

Since then, things have gone from bad to worse. It is my sad duty to inform you that your daughter is now living—like a wife, is the only way I can put it in all delicacy—with a gentile man who works for the railroad, one Vladimir Mirov. When I remonstrated with her, pointing out that she is engaged in adultery, she told me that she and Herschel Rosen were never married! You can imagine my distress!

I am at my wit's end to know how to deal with this situation. I suggest that as soon as possible you journey to Harbin and take your misguided daughter home. Please be assured that I condemn her actions rather than herself, with which point of view our revered rabbi agrees. In other words, I believe her to be weak rather than criminal. Please advise immediately what your intentions are. Sincerely, Meier Koch.

If Yoysef had not known from Chaya Leya's letters of the kindness of the Kochs, he would have put it down as the work of some gossipy crank who had misinterpreted facts. As it was, he did not know what to make of the news.

Malkeh, when she had read it, was more forthright. "It's nonsense! The whole thing is a pack of lies! Chaya Leya could no more behave like some *nafka* than a swan could turn into a goose! Not married to Herschel? Living in sin with a Russian! Can you believe that for a moment, Yoysef? If ever there was a match made in heaven, it was Chaya Leya's with Herschel! And if she's working as a servant, it's probably because it's the only job she could get, and what's wrong with that? Oh, I could scratch this Reb Koch's eyes out for saying such things about my daughter! If he were here, I'd spit in his face!"

Yoysef smiled thinly at Malkeh's passion. "Still, if the letter had come earlier, I'd have left for Harbin on the next train," he said.

The people of Harbin awaited a stunning victory, confident that the largest army and navy in the world would quickly administer the death blow to the Japanese. How could it be otherwise? Although the war had begun badly for the Russians, they were confident that as soon as the expeditionary forces arrived from Europe, the Japanese would be summarily dealt with!

What was largely unknown in Manchuria was that a desperate situation at home had claimed the government's attention. The "Bloody Sunday" of Father Gapon's march had shattered any last illusions the people may have had about the tsar. Confidence in the government had crumbled. Violent strikes closed factories, peasants in the Ukraine seized estates, soldiers and sailors mutinied, and even the usually conservative middle class called for the establishment of a constitutional government. Tsar Nicholas obstinately refused the counsel of those who advised making concessions to the people in the interests of peace.

In the context of this larger turmoil, the invasion of Port Arthur was an annoyance, a "little war." Preoccupied, the government was slow to ship armaments and foodstuffs to Manchuria, and military units, which would otherwise have protected Russian interests abroad, were busy keeping order at home.

For Chaya Leya, waiting in Harbin for letters from the front, it was as if the trains that had borne Valodya and Herschel away had dropped them into some nether world from which none emerged. For months she had haunted the railway station, trembling with fear as each carload of wounded was unloaded on the platform. She breathed a prayer of thanks each time Valodya and Herschel were not among the dead and mutilated. Reason told her that there were other places where bodies were brought for identification and burial, but as long as there was no physical evidence of death, she could believe in life for a while longer.

To a soldier with a dirty, blood-encrusted bandage wound around his head, she asked, "Vladimir Mirov? Do you know him? With the Harbin Battalion?"

He turned sightless eyes toward the sound of her voice. "It was awful," he said in a hollow voice. "You can't imagine."

"How about Herschel Rosen?"

He shook his head. "There were so many—"

She continued along the platform, stopping to lean over a litter where a fairly alert soldier was lying wrapped tightly in blankets despite the warm day. "Vladimir Mirov? Herschel Rosen?"

"Don't know," he mumbled.

A medical officer, stooping to examine the soldier, gently motioned her to leave. Before she turned away, the officer had pulled away the blankets and she saw that where the chest wall had been, there was now a gaping, festering hole. Hypnotized by the horror of it, she stood staring into the wound where maggots crawled.

*L*ater in the day a man with ragged stumps where once there had been legs said to her, "Never heard of no Rosen or Mirov. But maybe they'll get lucky like me!"

"Lucky?" Chaya Leya asked faintly, looking at the empty trouser legs pinned together at the ends.

"Sure. Listen, I took a bayonet wound in my chest at Mukden. Just missed my heart or I'd be a dead man. You think I got sent back to the hospital? Medic put a plaster round the hole, and the next day I was back in the line. 'What are you, some kind of malingerer?' the sergeant said. 'We need everybody we got!' I was so weak from losing blood, I thought I'd pass out on the field, but I didn't dare or I'd get killed proper. Those Japs as soon carve you up for souvenirs as look at you! Next day, same thing. Fellow next to me blew off a couple of toes, I ain't saying it was on purpose but coulda been. Him they send back to hospital 'cause he can't walk. I think, hey, that's the way to do it. Nice clean hospital bed, nurses, food without bugs in it! And in time getting to go home!"

"Well, it looks like you've made it," Chaya Leya said, swallowing hard.

"Well, it wasn't any party, I'll tell you. We was to relieve Port Arthur. Then somebody set off a bomb or something, and next thing I know, I'm bleeding something awful—I never seen so much blood! No pain, so I start to get up to run away, you know? Only there's nothing there to stand on."

Awkwardly Chaya Leya patted his shoulder. "I'm sorry," she said. "I hope you'll be home soon."

*O*n a fine spring day Chaya Leya was enjoying the sun on her back while she weeded the little kitchen garden where she had planted sorrel and carrots, radishes, parsley, and lettuce. Everything grew well in the rick dark loam of the region. Channah was lying on a quilt near her mother, quietly examining her bare toes and fingers against the sunlight. She was a good, happy baby who ate everything, slept soundly, and enjoyed any and all attention.

"So, what do you think of having a good sorrel borscht for supper tonight, Channah? With black bread and sweet butter, and some of these little new lettuces?"

At the sound of Chaya Leya's voice, Channah hiccuped engagingly.

"Yes, I think so too! I'll just pick some of these leaves for Chang!"

Intent on her task, she barely registered the sound of the back gate opening and then clicking shut. But a moment later a scraping sound on the gravel caused her to look up. A soldier, uniform tattered, leaning on a crutch, was limping toward her.

There were so many convalescent or newly demobilized soldiers in Harbin that most people were quite used to seeing them at their back doors.

Chaya Leya got to her feet, brushing loose dirt from her skirt. "Oh, you're hurt! Come inside and sit. Are you hungry?"

"I'm looking for a lady named Chaya Mandelkern," he said.

"I'm Chaya Mandelkern." Her heart began to pound wildly.

The soldier held out a dirty, creased scrap of paper.

A letter, she thought, a letter he's been carrying around in his pocket for a long time! The bold upright script, though barely visible through the dirt, was well known to her. Valodya, she thought, a message from Valodya.

With trembling hands she unfolded the single sheet of paper, and Valodya's green eyes seemed to look over her shoulder, the light from his golden hair illuminating the page. For a moment she could not see to read, and she swayed slightly.

The letter-bearer cleared his throat.

Recollecting herself, Chaya Leya said, "I can't thank you enough for bringing this." She thrust the letter into her apron pocket and picked up the baby. "Come into the house, please. Let me fix you some food."

After the soldier had gone, with as many ruble notes in his pocket and as much food in his stomach as Chaya Leya could spare, she sat down in the rocking chair. Meiping had carried Channah upstairs for her bath, the boys were off someplace with Chang, and there was an unusual silence in the kitchen. She drew out the letter. It had been many months en route. Dated August 1, 1904, it had been written from Anshan.

My dearest Chaya,

We move south to the battle zone tomorrow morning. After almost four months of boredom, in a way it will be a relief to finally see action. We have been in one miserable makeshift camp after another. One, near Fuyu, was in the middle of a swamp. The heat was terrible, and the mosquitoes ate us alive. Half the men were sick with malarial fever, the rest with dysentery. To make things worse, the food that reached us from Moscow had spoiled en route, and the medical supplies never did arrive! The camp here at Anshan is somewhat better. It is sort of a halfway point between Harbin and the battlefields, which means that the men are either waiting to go into combat or have been injured and are on their way to the rear.

I could never have imagined the things I've heard here about how fiercely the Japanese fight. To the death. Surrender, someone told me, is not a word in their language, and suicide is preferable to defeat. When I left Harbin, I thought of the war as a sort of outing. In my heart I probably believed what we were told, that the Asians are an inferior race. I was wrong about everything. I have seen too many mutilated bodies on their way home. I would rather die than live like that, without arms or legs, blind or stone deaf, half-human.

Fear and repugnance started out from the page. Chaya Leya could almost smell the sour sweat of his anxiety.

We go to Liao-Yang, south of Mukden. The Japanese are there in great numbers—a hundred fifty thousand, they say. The battle will be decisive. If we win, Port Arthur is saved, if we lose—but we dare not lose!

If I do not return, and that is a possibility we must face bravely, you must wait for your husband to finish serving his sentence and then go with him to America as you had planned. The money we put into the Russian-Manchurian Bank together is yours and will help you on your way. I wronged Herschel Rosen, but the times were strange. He is a good man, and he loves you. As do I, in my own inadequate way. Valodya.

Postscript: I need to make a confession. It was I who took your garnet earrings and your gold brooch and the money. Gambling has always been a weakness of mine. Perhaps what I now face is the greatest gamble of my life! Pray for me. V.

The words fell like the tolling of the deep-throated bell in the cathedral at home. She would never see him again. Valodya knew it too. The certainty of a final parting had lain between them on that last morning in the little house they had so briefly shared.

The next day, although she was fearful of churches and the intimidating black-frocked priests of Russian Orthodoxy, Chaya Leya went to the church and paid the priest to light candles and say prayers for Valodya's safe return.

"You are not of our faith, my child?" the priest asked her.

Chaya Leya shook her head. "But my—friend—he is. He would wish you to pray for him."

"Will you not stay awhile and say your own prayer for your—friend as well?"

"Thank you; I will."

Chaya Leya stood in the dim interior of the church, reaching out to the God that Valodya prayed to. She stared at his body on the cross behind the altar. How he suffered, his limbs twisted, his lips drawn tight over teeth clenched in pain. She realized that she had seen his face before, often, among the soldiers unloaded from the boxcars returning from the front. She closed her eyes. The scent of incense made her ill. She did not feel a connection with the figure upon the wall. The place was alien to her. The Russian God, she thought, did not listen to Jewish prayers.

For Herschel, Chaya Leya could speak to God while she worked on the household accounts, shelled the peas for supper, or sat quietly nursing her baby. He was the One who dwelt in the hills of the psalm. "O Lord, God of Israel, keep Herschel safe and bring him home. Amen."

While Chaya Leya waited for word of her men, her thoughts were dark. What did she want for her future and Channah's? She didn't even know what choices she might have. Herschel had made his intentions clear before he left, but, of course, he had known nothing about a baby. She had no idea what Valodya would want. In fact, the longer that Valodya was gone, the dimmer he grew in her thoughts and in her heart. She owned no picture of him. She avoided walking by the little house they had shared during their brief idyll. And to recall him to herself she had to reread his brief letter or to wear the jade pendant he had given her—or, of course, to look into the face of his child. Overwrought and plagued by uncertainties and self-recrimination, Chaya Leya was restless during the day, and her nights were filled with terrifying dreams.

Luckily, Channah was a sunny, undemanding child, content to play with a string of wooden beads or to watch Yuri and Gregor playing at cocks-and-hens and other games. Sturdy and rosy, she was alert and active. Her hair was a mass of thick rose-gold ringlets, and her eyes were large and long-lashed, neither green like her father's nor brown like her mother's, but a combination of the two, hazel, with green and golden lights.

One afternoon Chaya Leya took Channah to visit Frau Koch at a time when she knew Reb Meier to be at the bookstore.

The old lady drew her into the house, obviously delighted to see her and the child. "Are you all right? Are you getting enough to eat? What do you hear about the progress of the war?" She took the baby from Chaya Leya's arms and kissed the child on both fat cheeks. "What a dumpling she is! Why haven't you come to see me before!"

"I thought it might embarrass you if I came."

"I'm too old to be embarrassed! Let's sit down and have some tea, and you can tell me what is happening!"

Over tea and a kind of odd butterless, sugarless cookie Frau Koch had devised in a time of wartime shortages, Chaya Leya unburdened herself.

The old lady dandled Channah on her knee and, to the child's delight, fed her bits of cookie. "I believe," she said slowly, "that nothing happens by accident."

"It bothers me that I can't explain it. It's as if those months with Valodya were a dream I had. Now that I'm awake I scarcely remember what it was about."

"This child now—God's precious gift to you!—came in a time of great need and enormous loneliness. Maybe that's explanation enough."

"But will Herschel look at it like that? Can he put the past behind him?"

Frau Koch reached across the table and took Chaya's smooth hand into her old mottled one. "The question is not whether Herschel can, but whether you can."

Chaya Leya laughed shakily. "Your husband said I should be stoned for an adulteress!"

Frau Koch chuckled. "Men's talk! Put your trust in God that He knew what He was about when He gave you Channah."

*P*ort Arthur fell, and anticipation of victory turned to despair. There had been fighting south of Mukden with heavy losses on both sides. Neither the Battle of Liao-Yang nor the offensive on the Sha Ho River had been decisive. Still, total defeat no longer seemed impossible. And where were the reinforcements from home?

When word finally reached Harbin in April of 1905 that the Baltic fleet had left Madagascar on the last leg of its journey from Kronstadt, the people knew that the prayers murmured before lighted candles and the vows made to the Virgin of Kazan had been heard. The pealing bells of St. Basil's were a signal for wild rejoicing in the city. *Gospodin* Kutuzov opened the last bottle of cognac from the cellar while Madame and Chaya Leya hugged each other and the boys danced excitedly around the grown-ups.

"It's the mightiest fleet in the world! Better than the British!" Anatoly Kutuzov said, rubbing his hands together. "And there is no finer seaman in the world than the Russian sailor! It's taken a long time for our boys to get here, but now the war will be over in a matter of days!"

"To the quick downfall and damn—damnation of Admiral Togo!" Marina Kutuzova said, trying to rise to her feet but already too tipsy to do so.

"To the end of the war and the return of our men," Chaya Leya added quietly.

Admiral Rozhdestvensky, commander of the fleet, chose not to circle the Japanese islands to the east but to proceed more directly through the Tsushima Straits between Japan and Korea. The formidable array of ships— eight battleships, twelve cruisers, and nine destroyers—steamed one after another through the passageway, flags bravely flying. Japanese cannon hidden in camouflaged emplacements on either shore loosed their balls. The first battleship was hit and listed in the water. Hit again, it sank. The second was close behind the first. The captain saw the danger but once in the slot, there was no possibility of retreat and no room to maneuver. The second ship foundered. Then the third. One by one, the Japanese guns picked off the ships of the Russian fleet as they made their way through the straits.

The fiasco at Tsushima was the true end of the war. In September 1905 a peace treaty was signed. Russia lost to Japan her leases to Port Arthur and Dairen, the southern branch of the Chinese Eastern Railway, and half of Sakhalin Island. It could have been far worse, but for the Japanese it was enough that mighty Russia had lost face at the hands of a tiny Asian country.

*C*haya Leya's letter giving her parents the news of the grandchild born the previous November arrived with the first reestablished mail service from Manchuria. Chaya Leya a mother, Malkeh thought with tears in her eyes, and her not there to support the back of a daughter in her first labor, not there to bathe the birth blood from the little one, nor to hold the child close to her breast on the very first day of her life.

"A little girl, Yoysef, and named after Channah—" Malkeh said wonderingly, her eyes soft and young.

"A blessing on our house."

Golda, who had lived with them since Mammeh Frumma died, said, "I shall bake a honey cake!"

"And we will announce her name in the shul." Yoysef planned.

"I will write to everyone! Immediately! Tonight!" Malkeh said. "I will get letters off to Dvoreh and Simcha, and to Chaim in care of the shipping company, and to Yenta in New York, and to my own mammeh and papa in Dagda, and to Berel and Soreh in Odessa . . ." Malkeh's voice gradually trailed off, and her excited face fell.

"What is it, Malkeh?" Yoysef was always attuned to her.

"It's only—I never realized—the family is not together anymore."

Yoysef put his arms about her. "It's the way of the world."

"No," Golda said, "it's the times. When Mammeh and Papa were alive, they were the center of the family; everything moved around them. It was like that in all the families we knew. The children lived close by and shared the good times and the bad. And families never took an important step without everyone having a say."

"You're right, Golda. That's what I was feeling! Now we're all like straws in the wind."

"You are both too gloomy!" Yoysef said. "And this is a day of celebration! I am going to open a bottle of *bromfen* so that we can all drink to the health of young Channah!"

Malkeh was awake for a long time that night, thinking about the new baby, remembering her own babies and wondering where her grown children were tonight. Scattered. Chaim was somewhere on the high seas, even now on his way to New York, perhaps to settle in America. Dvoreh, lost and unhappy, in Riga, still hoping to make a life with her reluctant bridegroom. Chaya Leya, cast free from the supporting bonds of home, bearing a child alone in a far-off land, some mystery surrounding the child's parentage. And Simcha, the repository of so many hopes and dreams, was the most insubstantial of them all—a bit of chaff, tossed here, tossed there by any wind that blew.

It was not what she had intended. She had told the children, "Hold fast to each other, be one family!"

A single stalk of wheat, she thought, is a poor, pitiful thing. But bind it with others, and it becomes a firm, strong sheaf. A family should be like that.

*C*hannah, a never-ending delight to Chaya Leya, served unexpectedly as a source of connection with Malkeh. As she bathed the
plump little body, she thought, this is what Mammeh did for me when I
was a baby. Mammeh must also have put her lips to the wrinkles in a fat
neck and drawn the good soapy infant smell into herself.

Playing peek-a-boo with the child or steadying her on her fat legs,
Chaya Leya thought, Mammeh must have played this game with me, helped
me stand, taken my hand.

When she sat at night over her sewing, there was in her mind the
picture of Mammeh sewing a Sabbath dress for a small daughter.

Occasionally she thought of that earlier Channah, and of Yaakov. Now
a mother herself, Chaya Leya began to have some dim sense of what it must
be like to watch a child grow and then to lose it in a day.

Had the news of Channah's birth even reached Polotsk, she wondered.

*T*he Kutuzov kitchen on a snowy afternoon just before Channah's
first birthday was a cozy place. Big Chang was chopping vegetables for a good-smelling pot of soup simmering on the stove, and Amah was
humming as she mended a child's shirt under the lamp. From time to time
Chang distributed scraped carrots or pieces of celery among the children.
Chaya Leya occupied the rocking chair with Mischa, Dimitri, and Gregor
sprawled at her feet. The baby, Channah, was playing a game with Yuri on
the floor near the oven, stacking wooden blocks into a tower to knock down,
both of them laughing uproariously to see them scatter. Boris and Sasha, the
older boys, were having a game of chess at a table in the corner, half listening
to Chaya Leya read a story to their brothers.

"In a certain land," Chaya Leya read, "in a certain big village, there
lived a peasant who was neither poor nor rich. He had a son and bequeathed
to him three hundred rubles, saying, 'Here, my son. I give you my blessing,
with three hundred rubles when you come of age.' The son grew up, came
of age, and—"

A knock on the kitchen door caused her to look up and lose her place.
It was not usual to have a visitor at the back door so late in the day.

Big Chang moved toward the door, the cleaver still in his hand.

At first the man in the doorway seemed like any other of the discharged soldiers who had wandered through Harbin since the end of the
war, looking for a handout while waiting for transportation home. What
was unusual was that with winter upon them, the trickle of returning men
had almost completely tapered off.

The soldier seemed to fill the doorway, not because of his actual size,
but because of the gray army greatcoat that engulfed his body and hung
almost to the floor. A great bush of a beard and hair that hadn't been cut in

months added to the impression of size. On closer inspection, one could see that the face beneath all that hair was pale, the eyes hollow with the soul-sickness that all the battle veterans seemed to have. The man was actually thin and wasted to the point of emaciation.

Chaya Leya slowly stood, the book of fairy tales sliding unnoticed from her lap to the floor.

Channah held out her chubby arms to the newcomer, waiting confidently to be picked up. Just learning to talk, she imitated little Yuri Kutuzov. "Pa-pa," she gurgled, and then, becoming less tentative from seeing the smile on the strange man's face, she triumphantly shouted, "Papa!"

Chaya Leya whispered, "Herschel!"

He lifted the baby from the floor and held her against his thin chest, weeping and smiling at the same time.

*A*lthough Chaya Leya continued to wait patiently for the trains from the south, though she trudged daily along the road along which people straggled home from the war, though she wrote letters to General Kuropatkin's command and pored over the death registry, nothing was known of the whereabouts of Vladimir Mirov. That wasn't unusual. All was chaos in the aftermath of war. Still, as winter passed into spring, and spring into summer, and the war had been over for a long time, Chaya Leya began to lose hope.

After his return from the war, Herschel had gone to live at Madame Irina's boardinghouse. Slowly Chaya Leya and Amah had nursed him back to health, and his body had filled out and grown strong from Big Chang's nourishing food. When he was sufficiently recovered, Reb Meier Koch found him a job clerking in a dry goods store. Herschel came often to the Kutuzovs', sometimes with gifts for the children—a basket of red apples, shiny tops and balls, a soft doll for Channah. He seemed content to sit in a corner of the kitchen, his dark eyes following Chaya Leya as she went about her tasks. Faltering from embarrassment at first, they learned to talk to each other again, and gradually old habits of sharing took over—with the one exception that Herschel never talked about what he had seen at the Sha Ho River offensive or in the pillaged city of Port Arthur. Channah adored him from the start. She invariably held out her arms to him. "Papa," she would say, "Papa." Chaya Leya did not correct her.

"Chaya Leya," Herschel said to her one evening, "it's summer again. The fighting's been over a long time, and those who were going to come back have been home for months now. It's time that we were on our way to America."

"Valodya—"

Herschel put his hands on her shoulders and turned her toward him.

"You must understand something, Chaya Leya. If he had come back, I would never have let him have you."

She looked at him quickly. "Do you forgive, then? The child—?"

Herschel grinned. "Channah calls me Papa. Children know."

She smiled painfully. Sometimes children were wiser than their parents.

Eventually Chaya Leya had to concede that there was logic in what Herschel said. There was nothing to hold them in Harbin, and it was time for them to get on with their lives. Valodya would have wanted it. He had told her to use their money to go to America with Herschel.

It was at Herschel's insistence that Chaya Leya agreed to be married before leaving Harbin. "After all," he said, "this time I don't want any question about it. It's for the rest of our lives!"

Rabbi Samsonovitch performed a simple wedding ceremony at the home of the Kochs. Chaya Leya wore a new blue silk gown, a gift from Madame Kutuzova, and because red was the color of luck and happiness, she carried a bunch of red poppies picked for her that morning by Meiping. Herschel placed a thin silver band on her finger as a symbol of their consecration to each other. There were no guests except for Reb Meier and his wife. After the ceremony a beaming Frau Koch toasted them in homemade berry wine and fed them honey cake—to assure that the marriage should remain sweet and true.

*T*he next morning Chaya Leya, Herschel, and Channah boarded the train to Shanghai on the first stage of their journey to San Francisco.

It had been difficult saying good-bye. Madame Kutuzova and Chaya Leya clung to each other. More than an employer, Marina Kutuzova had been a friend to her. Tears in her eyes, Chaya Leya turned to bow to Big Chang and Little Chang, Li Feng, Ayi, the laundress and the gardener and all the others in order of status. She had intended to say good-bye to Amah with equal ceremony—in the Chinese way—but she couldn't do it and hugged her instead, weeping at the thought that she would never look into that wise, kind face again.

"I will light joss sticks for a safe journey," Amah said. "Good fortune will follow your footsteps."

For better than three years Chaya Leya, the Kutuzovs, and the Chinese servants had lived under one roof, sharing one another's lives. They had an extended family, supporting Chaya Leya's transition from girlhood to womanhood. They had shared her joy when God gave her Channah, and their love had helped her live through despair and bitter loss.

"*Do svidanya,*" Chaya Leya said, kissing each of the little boys in turn. "*Do skorova svidanya.*"

Herschel picked up Channah in one arm, the basket of food that Big Chang had prepared in the other. "The rickshaws are waiting."

Everyone trooped out to the street behind them. "May God go with you!" Madame said softly.

The boys ran for a little way after the rickshaws before turning back.

*I*t had been a beautiful warm day in 1906 when the train bore Chaya Leya, her husband, and her child away. It was almost two years more before Valodya Mirov, released from a Japanese prison camp, stopped briefly in Harbin on his way home to Smolensk. There had been many changes in the city since the war. The house on Nicholas II Avenue was occupied by a different family, and the offices of the Chinese Eastern Railway were closed. He asked many, but found none who remembered the Kutuzovs or their Jewish housekeeper.

He often thought to himself afterward that it was in the nature of dreams to fade away.

Chapter 48

*T*he terror of the massacre of Father Gapon's marchers was compounded for Simcha by the hours spent burrowed in a self-dug grave of foul-smelling compost. His first impression on emerging from his hiding place was of sharp biting cold, and the second of an odd, dead silence. He didn't know how long he had been there, but it was already dark. He wished he had not been forced to leave his overcoat behind when he escaped. Once more he crawled through the crevice in the wall that surrounded the kitchen yard of the Winter Palace; this time he was so numbed from the cold that he did not feel the jagged edges of the bricks that scraped his skin raw as he squeezed through. The street, when he emerged, was unlit except for the wavering light from a lantern in a sentry box at the intersection. He could see the shadows of one, perhaps two, soldiers inside. Although he knew he should observe the movements of the sentries before making his dash past their shelter, it was too cold to remain motionless; he would just have to hope that the intense cold would keep the soldier or soldiers inside. Swiftly, keeping his head low and his knees bent, he moved past the sentry box, expecting at any moment to be challenged. His shoulder blades prickled with the anticipation of a bullet in the back, but nothing happened. Keeping in the shadows of buildings, he made his way through the deserted streets. Once when a group of soldiers passed, half running in close order drill, he pressed himself into a dark doorway, hoping that the chattering of his teeth would not give him away. Another time several mounted men clattered by. There were no pedestrians on the streets, and he assumed, correctly, that there was a curfew. He wondered how long he had hidden in the palace garden, but he had no way of telling.

Thankfully his boardinghouse was not far. When he reached the building, he scarcely had strength left to creep up the stairs and unlock his room. Not bothering to remove his boots, smelling of rot, the toes of his feet stiff from frostbite, he fell into bed and pulled the quilts up around his neck. For two days he huddled there, shaking with chills and fever and a malaise that he did not recognize as despair. Too ill to eat the food the landlady left at his door, he took nothing but a little water. It was dark in his room, silent, warm. In the cocoon of his quilts he could block out thought. But if he slept, he dreamed, and the dreams were terrifying. The face of a plump-cheeked toddler was blown off again. The ecstatic graybeard who had carried an icon lay in the dirty snow, holding his pink intestines in his hands. Sharp hooves trampled and swishing saber blades cut down people where they stood frozen in bewilderment. Again and again in his sleep Simcha felt the hot steam of a rearing stallion's breath on his neck and felt himself falling beneath the horse's belly.

On the third day a knock was followed by the door bursting open. "Ah, Semyon, my young friend," cried the dark-bearded man, rushing to the bedside to grasp Simcha's hands in his. "I have been so worried for you! You could have been killed! And to think that it was I who encouraged you to follow that fool Gapon! It's taken me all this time to find where you live!"

Simcha raised his head weakly from the pillows. "Who—?" The face swam into focus, and he thought he recognized the man who had picked him off the ice a week ago.

"Vassily Chernov. I had a devil of a time finding you, but finally I persuaded someone to remember the Semyon who writes the pamphlets." The older man deftly arranged the quilts to cover Simcha's shoulders. "But you are so pale, and your hands are like ice! What have you had to eat? Nothing? I will take care of that at once! Just rest while I see to it!"

Simcha could hear Vassily's boots on the stairs. He was oddly comforted by the sound. Because he was so weak—undoubtedly that was the reason—a tear slid down his cheek.

In a short while Vassily was back, balancing a tray. He set it down on the foot of the bed and helped Simcha to sit, adjusting the pillows behind him. Carefully, delicately, he fed chicken broth, spoonful by spoonful, to the sick boy. Simcha had not realized that he was hungry. Afterward the man examined Simcha's body, clucking over the frozen toes to which, however, circulation was painfully returning. When he was satisfied that Simcha was relatively intact, he tucked the covers tightly around him and sat down by the bedside. With Vassily there beside him, Simcha slept, this time without dreams. When he awoke, Vassily was still there.

The man smiled at him. "You are a little better, yes? You have a little color in your face now, God be praised! Are you hungry again? Well then, just some hot tea and lemon—I will get it."

For the next day or two, Vassily seemed always to be there whenever Simcha opened his eyes. He carried up bowls of soup and glasses of steaming tea, held the chamber pot, and bathed away the smell of sweat, dirt, and fear. At the end of that time Simcha felt strong enough to care for himself.

It was the beginning of the most important friendship that Simcha had ever had. Here was a man, as old as Pyotr Voronov, who called him comrade and treated him as an equal. Most important, he filled the void left by the departures of Maximov and Markovitch and soothed the hurt inflicted by Yevgeny Fedotov, who arrived in St. Petersburg to berate him for dropping out of the university. Vassily listened when he talked. He seemed to understand how hard it is to live up to expectations of parents and teachers.

Vassily's organizational ties were vague but his revolutionary zeal was unquestionable. While Simcha was impelled by lofty idealism, Vassily was driven by rage. Taking Simcha into the factories where workers were treated like slaves, making him listen to the stories told by displaced peasants, he opened Simcha's eyes to the real meaning of revolution. Simcha's pamphlets changed, became more impassioned, and his mentors in the Social Democratic Party were well-satisfied.

Simcha admired Vassily, and in time he loved him. He wondered sometimes whether he talked too much about himself. He didn't want to bore his friend. On the other hand, Vassily always seemed interested in his family, his home, his growing-up years. Simcha attributed this interest to homesickness for Byelorussia.

"No wonder that we are such good friends," Simcha said, "when we are from the same province!"

"It was a happy accident that we met," Vassily agreed.

Seldom did Simcha succeed in turning the conversation to Vassily's own background.

"Who are your people, Vassily Yulevitch? I mean really?"

Vassily essayed a little laugh. "Ah, Semyon, in the revolution, you never ask a question like that!"

"Yet you ask me all the time, and I tell you about my family and about my teacher and about Spokoinaya Zemlya. Why is that different?"

"Maybe because you have nothing to hide."

"But you do?"

Vassily smiled slightly but did not answer.

"Hymie, m'lad, tomorra at this time the finest city ye've iver seen'll be knocking your eye out! I kin hardly wait! We'll come upon her all of a sudden, an' there she'll be, rising out of the water all shining an' sparkling! Ye've just niver seen anything like it!"

Chaim pulled his knitted cap more closely over his ears and turned the coat up around his face against the chilling wind. It was dark, no stars, and the moon was hazy behind clouds. The *Oceania* rode easily on the swells. She was a fine ship.

"Ye'll fall in love with Frisco, Hymie, mark my words."

Chaim did not look at the man who stood at his elbow. When he spoke, his tone was sour. "You say same in New York." Chaim spoke in heavily accented English, but his companion was used to it.

"So I did," the second man agreed, "but 'twas only to please ye, Hymie, 'cause ye was so raring to git there. Do ye think ye'd have heard me if I'd said New York is a dirty stinking hole fit fer no sailor nor ither human being neither! Ye would not 'ave! Ye had yer head made up from the start, ye did, that New York were going t'be yer paradise. Well, ye had t'see fer yerself, ye did!"

"So why I believe you now?"

The two men were standing on the deck, Chaim preparing to turn over the watch, the other to accept it.

"Ooh-ooh! Such a cynic we got here! 'Tis yer gloomy Russian soul speaking! Don't take me word, Hymie. Ye'll see soon enough." The speaker, tall as Chaim but scarecrow thin, clapped Chaim on the shoulder. "Better go below an' git warmed up an' ter bed. 'Tis surely chill enough up here ter freeze yer balls, God ferbid!"

"*Spokony nochee*, Jamie," Chaim said.

" 'Twill be a big day tomorra. Ye won't fergit it!"

It was late, past midnight, and Chaim was alone in the galley. He had found the makings for tea and now sat waiting for the kettle to boil. He knew that Jamie's advice was good and he should be in bed, but he was not sleepy. Maybe when he had thawed out a little, sleep would come.

Chaim reflected that so far the new world had been a great disappointment to him. When he had signed on the *Oceania* it was for the purpose of reaching New York City. The captain had understood that from the beginning but was glad to have a strong, dependable seaman for however long Chaim was willing to stay. It had been a leisurely voyage via Naples, Le Havre, Toulon, and Falmouth. But for Chaim the days in new ports followed by the monotonous passage across the Atlantic Ocean meant only that he was that much closer to his destination, New York, the object of his dreams since he and Berel had first seen the great ships in Odessa harbor.

He badgered the crew to tell him about America and spent hours poring over a book with pictures loaned him by Jonas Gore, the first mate. The others took to calling him the "American-That's-Never-Been," but it was friendly joshing which Chaim did not mind. True, he had been wary when he first signed on, the British ship so large and fine, the crew smartly turned out in uniforms that were so—English. When he got past the language barrier, the men were not so different from the Greeks and Turks aboard the *Archimedes*, a mixture of good ones and bad ones, friendly ones and indifferent ones, a few who were hostile because he was different from them. He had an ear for languages and picked up the rudiments of English fast, and he found friends to help him among the crew.

In the warm galley Chaim stood and stretched. He did not know whether he would even get off the ship in Frisco tomorrow. It was just another dirty port with plenty of dishonest Americans waiting to take advantage of innocents. He had seen how it was with Americans in New York, he thought bitterly.

Chaim closed his eyes against remembered pain, but he could not stop thinking. Leaving the *Oceania* in New York harbor, Chaim had shouldered his seabag, waved good-bye to his shipmates, and headed in a direction away from the docks. Like sailors everywhere, the crew were looking for a bar and a good time. He, on the other hand, was going to scout the city and find a place where he could settle down.

What he found was a con man who, pretending to be a government agent helping him exchange his foreign currency for American money, had fleeced him of his savings.

What he found was a Jewish woman from his homeland who exploited immigrants by overcharging them for a place to sleep in lice-infested blankets.

What he found was a thief who, when he went outside to the toilet, took the opportunity to rifle his seabag and steal the cameo he had bought for Mammeh so long ago in Naples.

What he found was disillusionment and bitter resentment against the country he had dreamed would give him warm welcome.

When he returned to the *Oceania* two days after he'd left it, there was no trouble getting his place back. The first mate was genuinely sorry for Chaim but happy to have the use of his experienced hands and strong back for the duration of the voyage. Back aboard, Chaim withdrew into himself. He did not go ashore in New Orleans or in Galveston, and he refused for a long time to talk with anyone about his misadventures.

Chaim did not hear Jonas Gore come into the galley and started awkwardly when the mate spoke to him. Gore had finished his duty, and he busied himself brewing tea and filling mugs for the both of them. Sitting down beside Chaim, he gratefully stretched his legs before him.

"Tomorrow you'll see one of the grand cities of this world, Mandel-kern!" Gore said, pouring a little rum from a flask into his tea and Chaim's. Nodding at the rum, he said, "Good to fight off the chill!"

"Jamie say nice city." Chaim's tone was noncommittal, and he lowered his head to the fragrant cup.

"It's not New York this time," the officer reminded him gently. "You've got to put that behind you. New York's like every big city. Like London and Paris and Athens, all of them the same. Everyone's out to get his and to hell with the rest! But San Francisco"—he smiled into space— "Frisco's as rough and tumble as a whore—even when you know she's not particular about her favors, you'll always be longing to come back for more!" Gore poured himself and Chaim a little more rum. "I can never wait to get to San Francisco, and I hate to leave her behind when we sail."

Chaim kept his eyes down. Gore, he saw, was smiling at some secret pleasure of his own. Chaim did not want to look forward to San Francisco. He had to remember New York if he was not to be so gullible again.

Sitting now beside Jonas Gore in the galley, Chaim thought again about his life. He had never set out to be a seaman; he had been kidnapped into a life at sea. After that, sailing was but a means toward the end of getting to America. Now he had been in America, and he had hated everything about it.

He wasn't sure what he should do now. It would be easy to just drift. He supposed he could return to Russia, maybe even go home to Polotsk, but he was not the same person who had left. A man of twenty-two is not a boy of sixteen. So what should he do? Make his way back to Melnikoff's shop in Odessa? That was a possibility, except that Berel's life with Soreh left no room for him. Anyway, he thought, looking down at his rough, callused hands, he was no longer a tailor. So be it! Let it be a choice, then, and not an accident. Let it be an end in itself and not a means to an end. Chaim slapped the table with the flat of his hand. Jonas Gore was startled.

"Sorry, Mr. Gore," Chaim said sheepishly. "Just thinking."

"I guess so." The first mate rose and took his cup to the sink. "I think it's time we both turned in." He laid a friendly hand on Chaim's shoulder.

Chaim said in a rush, "I like stay with *Oceania*, sir. Learn steer maybe. More than shovel coal."

"Yes, yes," Jonas Gore said. "We'll see about it. But to tell you the truth, I don't see you spending your life as a seafaring man. I think you're a man who needs roots, has been looking for a place to set them down for a while now. Anyway, Mandelkern, you don't have to decide tonight. We'll talk it over after we've left the States."

"Good night then, sir," Chaim said.

"Good night."

Gore was whistling as he left the galley. As he went down the passageway toward his cabin, Chaim heard him say, "God! April's a wonderful month to be in Frisco!"

Jamie O'Donnell surprised Chaim that first day in San Francisco. When they left the *Oceania*, Jamie linked his skinny arm in Chaim's and led him past and away from the dance halls and bars of wicked Pacific Street. Ignoring the jibes of their crewmates, the Irishman led Chaim through a series of crooked streets into a wide, cobbled thoroughfare bustling with activity. The great energy of the city hit Chaim with almost physical force. Over the street hung a cheerful din, a mixture of clanging bells from the cable streetcars, a simultaneous pounding and hammering from a cluster of construction sites, and the cries of newsboys who shouted the latest headlines from the *Call* and the *Chronicle*. The sidewalks were crowded, men with leather satchels and women with reticules moving purposefully toward their destinations.

The *Oceania* had made port at dawn, led through the gray fog-shrouded harbor entrance by a pilot tugboat whose falsetto whistle had been a ridiculous echo of the basso tones of the booming Bay foghorns. All hands had been busy during those early hours with securing the ship and unloading the cargo.

It must have been ten o'clock before Chaim came up on deck to a skyline that, released from the early-morning fog, sparkled against the brightest blue sky he had ever seen. The ship had settled into a snug berth in a wide, calm bay. Looking north, Chaim could see the encircling arms of the Golden Gate through which they had steamed in the morning darkness. Straight ahead was a city built on hills, faintly reminiscent of Naples because of the bright-painted houses spilling down steep slopes toward the waterfront. To the east the taller buildings of the business district created a jagged silhouette against the sun. A wide strip of green woods—a park perhaps—bisected the city and softened its angular lines. The whole was cupped in a hollow with rounded green hills rising behind and the silvery ocean lapping the other sides.

Chaim studied the view in silence, looking for ugliness. There were scarred hillsides where someone had burned off the growth in his haste to build, and even at a distance Chaim could see that the structures at the water's edge were carelessly ramshackle. Perversely satisfied, he scoffed to himself, "Americans! Also builders!"

Chaim was coaxed by Jamie to leave the ship. "You'll regret it the rest of your life if ye miss this, lad!" Jamie continued to badger him through the morning's labor. But in the end it was the soft green hills and the longing to smell fresh-turned earth that finally enticed Chaim to set foot on shore. He had capitulated in his halting English. "Ve try again, *nyet?*"

The street where Jamie and Chaim walked appeared to be a main boulevard. It had a newer, rawer, and more open look to it than the streets Chaim had seen in New York. Much appeared to be unfinished, and he and Jamie were often forced into the street to avoid piles of lumber and mountains of bricks waiting to become buildings. Businessmen about their errands seemed to have leisure to call advice to the construction crews, and those who were accidentally jostled by the upward-peering sailors were good-natured about it, looking them directly in the face, not avoiding their eyes in the way of men in large cities. Almost against his will Chaim felt his jaw relax and his spirits brighten.

"And vehr ve go?" Chaim asked Jamie as he was led along Market Street.

"Trust me! I'm thinking on a plain hotel south of Market, with clean beds for just a few coins. We'll just call at the Opera House on the way and see what's to be had for this evening."

Chaim stared dumbfounded at Jamie.

Discomfited by Chaim's look, Jamie bristled, "Would you rather be working on a case of the pox in a whorehouse with th' ithers? Or getting rolled in some saloon?"

"You not?" Chaim grinned.

Jamie stopped in his tracks, glaring at Chaim. "Ye dumb Russian!" he yelled above the clank of a passing streetcar. "Don't ye know what's good for ye!"

Chaim put his big arm around Jamie's thin shoulders and propelled the sputtering Irishman forward. He figured that he would mind the opera far less than he'd mind an angry Jamie O'Donnell.

Jamie halted in front of a poster plastered against a board fence. His eyes glowed with excitement. "Would ye just look at that!" he exclaimed, pointing.

Chaim could not read English. The picture on the poster showed a man dressed in pale knee breeches and a fancy jewel-encrusted jacket that stopped short at his waist. He carried a triangular hat and a sword under one arm, and a cape swirled jauntily from his shoulders. He was presenting a rose to a beautiful dark-eyed woman whose bare shoulders and bosom rose enticingly from the décolletage of a deep red dress.

"Vaht it means?" Chaim asked.

Jamie carefully sounded out the bold lettering on the poster. "First per-for-mance ever in San Francisco! The Metro-pol-i-tan Grand Opera Company of New York pre-sents Madame Olive Frem-stad an' Signor Enrico Caruso in *Carmen*!"

Chaim looked curiously at the intriguing picture.

Jamie explained. "It's opera you sod—play-actin' with music! Caruso's the greatest singer in the world, an' he ain't even an Irishman!" Jamie took Chaim's arm companionably. "Ye'll like it, I promise ye, an' tomorra we'll sample the fleshpots of Frisco! But tonight—tonight, we go unsullied t' th' opera!"

Although the house had been sold out for weeks, only a little before they arrived at the box office someone had turned back two seats in the very center of the grand tier. After he translated the cost from American money to pounds, it seemed fearfully expensive to Chaim, but Jamie was ecstatic.

With the extravagant tickets safely pocketed and Jamie whistling the "Toreador Song" in happy anticipation, the two made their way to the plain hotel where Jamie had stayed on earlier visits. The Valencia was a four-storied frame building in the area known as "South of the Slot." The "Slot," Jamie explained patiently, was exactly that, the narrow cleft between the streetcar rails that ran on Market Street from the Ferry Building toward Twin Peaks. The area on this, the south side of Market, was one of wooden homes, cheap lodging houses, and hotels, all of which had an unfinished flimsy look, as though they had been erected hastily in a time of boom, which in fact they had. Still, the buildings had been painted in brave colors and had the same clean brash look that Chaim had noticed in the rest of the city. Their luck held here, too, for two beds were available on the second floor, bathroom down the hall, no cooking in the room, and payment in advance.

Chaim thought that everything that day augered well, the spank of the brisk breeze off the Bay, the crystalline air that gave everything a knife-sharp focus, the friendly smiles of passersby, and, of course, luck in obtaining last-minute opera tickets and the only two beds left at the Valencia Hotel.

In the early evening Chaim and Jamie, bathed and with their good coats brushed, made their way to the Opera House on Mission Street between Third and Fourth. It was only a short walk through the now-chilly dusk. A festive crowd stood on the broad steps and in the foyer, visiting, preening, and hoping to have their attendance reported in the next morning's *Chronicle*.

Jamie became expansive. He extracted a thin cigar from his breast pocket and puffed on it with all the aplomb of a civic leader. "Ye see, boyo," Jamie whispered to Chaim, "it's all in knowin' how to pretend. We c'n pretend t'be society same as the rest of 'em. Wouldn't be surprised a-tall to find our names in the society pages tomorra. See how the ithers are lookin' at us!"

Chaim nodded but thought uncomfortably that probably the smiling looks behind fans had to do with their shabby suits and Jamie's cheap cigar. Most of the audience were in evening clothes. Chaim's experienced tailor's eye took in the stylish cut of the men's evening jackets, the stiff-ruffled shirtfronts and glittering studs. The women, elegantly coiffed, their gowns rustling delicately as they moved, were like princesses.

Chaim was grateful when the warning bell sounded and they could lose

themselves in the throng threading their way to seats in the gradually darkening theater. By the time they had settled in their chairs, the conductor had
bowed to the applause of the audience, lifted his baton, and filled the audi-
torium with the opera's opening strains.

The performance was sheer magic. Chaim succumbed to the soaring
tones of Enrico Caruso and was drawn into the melodrama unfolding on the
stage. The music touched him deep inside and left him sad for what might
have been. After all, he knew something about a passion that altered the
course of one's life! When the final notes died away on the stage, Jamie had
to nudge Chaim to bring him back.

Afterward Jamie and Chaim strolled along Market Street. Chaim could
not throw off a certain melancholy, but his silence went unnoticed as Jamie
chattered about other operas he had seen, the best and the worst of the singers, the run-down condition of La Scala and the magnificence of Covent Garden.
At last Jamie's light-hearted imitation of that immense Wagnerian soprano,
Madame Fremstad, languishing in the arms of a Caruso half a head and many
pounds lighter than she, broke Chaim's mood, and he began to chuckle.

Jamie told Chaim that he dreamed of becoming a famous Irish tenor.
On watch sometimes Chaim had heard Jamie singing to the stars, his sweet,
sad voice caressing the rich Irish words, the sounds floating out to sea.

"Maybe still time, Jamie, to be singer," Chaim said, consoling his
friend, "like Caruso."

"Sure, an' I'm only a boy yet. Two an' twenty, like ye!"

The two young men linked arms, smiling. They were walking like that
when a horse-drawn cab stopped beside them and a familiar voice called out
to them. It was Mr. Gore and First Officer Oliver Gideon, the ship's purser,
who were returning to their hotel from some occasion of their own. Could
they give them a lift?

"Well, sir, we're just going t'have a bite of supper somewhere," Jamie
said respectfully.

"We're going back to the Palace Hotel. They have a very fine dining
room there," Jonas Gore said.

"Fine!" Neither Jamie nor Chaim had realized until that moment how
hungry they were. Now they clambered into the cab, and the four continued
on together.

The carriage left them in an ornate covered courtyard. Chaim drew
back. The hotel was too grand, fit for a tsar!

"Oh, go on," Jonas Gore said, "every newcomer to San Francisco
should have supper once at the Palace!"

They said good night to the two ship's officers in the pillared lobby.

Mr. Gore was right about eating in the Palace Restaurant. It was an
evening to savor for a lifetime. Chaim never forgot any part of it. As an old
man, he could recount, course by course, the wonderful things he and Jamie

ate that night. There were the oysters on the half shell to start with, washed down with champagne, then the pâté maison and a sherried terrapin soup; the smiling waiter explained that it was turtle soup. Chaim nodded but thought he was being teased. Finally the main course, pink roast beef with puffy potatoes, swirled into little crowns, and a weedlike vegetable called asparagus. To finish, there were whole strawberries—imagine strawberries in April!—drenched with a raspberry liqueur and capped with a fluff of cream, and then coffee, brandy, and cigars. It was the magical cap on a magical day.

It was almost two o'clock in the morning when Jamie and Chaim turned their footsteps toward the Valencia, a short walk but a world away from the Palace. They were happy men, and Jamie sang softly as they walked, a happy Irish song about the beauty of Killarney.

What a letter Chaim would write home about San Francisco! He decided to mail the opera program. Mammeh and Papa would not be able to read the English words, but there was a picture of the Opera House printed on the cover. Back in their room at the Valencia, Chaim carefully set the program aside while he undressed for bed. Just before he lay down he asked Jamie to read him what was printed on the cover of the program so that he could tell Mammeh in the letter he would write in the morning.

"Well," said Jamie patiently, squinting at the printing, "it says 'Metropolitan Opera Company' on th' top here. Then th' big words in th' middle of th' page are 'Enrico Caruso an' Madame Olive Fremstad.' At th' bottom there it says 'San Francisco, California.' "

Chaim pointed to another smaller line. "Vaht iz dot?"

"The date. April 17, 1906." Jamie yawned. "Blow out the lamp, Hymie, an' let's get some sleep!"

Chaim sighed with contentment as he lay back on his pillow in the dark. Another two days of shore leave stretched before him, and he wondered if they could possibly be as exciting as the first.

*J*t seemed to Chaim that he had only just closed his eyes when he was forced abruptly into consciousness. A roaring sound, not unlike hurricane-force waves crashing against the hull of a ship, filled the room, rattling the windows and rocking the lamp back and forth on its pedestal.

"Tidal wave!" Jamie screamed, sitting upright in his bed and clutching the blanket to his skinny chest.

Chaim looked toward the window through which seeped the first gray light of dawn. He could see nothing through the glass to account for the deafening racket that had invaded the room. A crazy clanging of bells accompanied a deep rumble rising from the bowels of the earth. The floor began, at first gently, and then violently, to roll beneath them.

"Sweet Jesus," prayed Jamie, hands clasped and eyes fixed on the ceiling, "on this Your Judgment Day, forgive an' spare this poor sinner!"

Chaim was hurtled from his mattress but managed to get to his feet, clinging to the bedframe even as it assumed a life of its own and careened wildly across the bucking floor. He was slammed with stunning force against the wall. When the thundering noise ceased as suddenly as it had begun, Chaim heard himself shouting into the sudden stillness. He made himself stop, took a deep breath. Less than a minute had passed since the first jolt had thrown him from the bed. In the silence, only the sharp tinkle of breaking glass and the terrified murmur of Jamie's Hail Marys could be heard.

Chaim tried the door handle even as he ordered Jamie to get off the bed and come outside with him. The movement of the building had shifted the door frame just enough that the door stuck fast. By then Chaim could hear other people in the corridor on their way toward the stairway and the blessed outdoors. He shouted and pounded the door, but either no one heard or there were none willing to pause to help a stranger. Calling on Jamie to help him, Chaim put his shoulder to the jammed door.

"Hail Mary, full o' grace," mumbled Jamie, his eyes dark and glazed in an ashen face.

A wave of desperate fury swept Chaim. "God damn you, you son of a bitch!" Chaim swore in Russian. "Help me or die here!"

In the next second there was a sharp crack like an explosion, and once more the building began to buckle and sway. Death was with them in the room, and fear lent Chaim strength. Using his shoulder as a battering ram, he thrust powerfully against the door. It gave with a splintering sound and Chaim was catapulted into a hallway where there were other people clinging to the walls and each other and screaming in terror.

The hotel seemed to be disintegrating around them, like the houses Chaim had built of sticks as a child. The light fixtures snapped like twigs in a windstorm, the hall mirrors crashed to the floor, and the stairway, crowded with fleeing people, swayed and then ever so gently collapsed, a stairway no more, just a heap of kindling littered with bodies. All around in the darkness there was noise, confusion, choking dust, and the sour smell of fear.

When the floor gave way beneath him, Chaim was conscious that he was falling in a kind of slow motion. A wind seemed to be roaring through his head, shutting out the screams and curses that had filled the air a moment earlier. In that moment of falling, he knew without much emotion that he would be dead when he landed.

Part Three

A Sheaf of Wheat

1906–1923

Chapter 49

*B*erel was only dimly aware that a terrible earthquake had occurred a continent away in far-off San Francisco. Settled now in
New York, he was too preoccupied with the day-to-day struggle to keep
food on his table and a roof over the heads of his wife, Soreh, and their
infant son, Isaac, to pay attention to the news. Of course, he had no way of
knowing that his friend Chaim had been in the western city when it was
stricken. It would, in fact, be several months before an exchange of letters
between Berel and his old master, Yoysef Mandelkern, would inform him of
Chaim's whereabouts.

The pogroms of 1905 had driven Soreh and Berel Levy from Odessa.
The troubles had followed a familiar pattern, not unlike what had transpired
in Polotsk in 1891, only played out on a larger scale. The usual factors had
been involved. High taxes, restrictive agricultural policies, and massive unemployment had stirred up the peasants. The atrocities of Bloody Sunday
had prompted the liberal middle class to demand reforms. And the unpop-
ular war with the Japanese in Manchuria had aroused antigovernment feelings in all segments of the population.

In Odessa, Jews had committed the crime of being too successful, both
in the professions and in commerce. A hate campaign, fomented by the
government, sprang to a vigorous life of its own, sweeping through a disgruntled population like a firestorm.

Berel had been nervous but Soreh shrugged it off. She had lived in
Odessa all of her life, and although there was nothing new about anti-
Semitism, there had been no violence since '81. Surely this, too, would pass.

Berel was not so sure. "Maybe we should sell the boardinghouse and
use the money to move to America."

"America!" Soreh had laughed. "Where would Frau Beilson and Zusya
Abramovitz go if I moved away! They are like family, not boarders!"

Berel sighed. "You can't be a mother to all the world, Soreh." When
she turned away, Berel knew that his had been an unfortunate turn of phrase.
He gathered Soreh into the circle of his arms and laid his cheek against hers.

"You'll have a houseful of babies yet," he promised her. "We've been married only two years. Be patient!"

"Besides," Soreh said, dabbing at a tear, "how can I leave this dear little house!" She looked around her at the snug, sunny rooms, the wooden floors polished to a high shine, the carefully tended garden just outside the windows. "I've put my life into this place! Leaving it would be like deserting an old friend!"

"Still, Soreh, it is only a house. Promise me you'll think about it. I don't feel safe here anymore."

"You worry too much, beloved! You don't understand the Odessa mentality. Believe me, this will blow over."

Despite Soreh's reassurances, Berel was uneasy on a morning in late April when he set out for his job at the shirtwaist factory. Only the day before an older man who worked on the bench beside him had been set upon on the street and beaten so badly that his nose had been broken in two places. As if that were not bad enough, there had been a rash of fires, rumored to be deliberately set, and the city fire companies had refused to answer summons from Jewish districts. Worst of all, a week earlier the great synagogue, the pride of every Jew in the Ukraine, had been desecrated by vandals who had broken windows, slit the velvet Torah covers, and written "Yid Bastards!" on the walls. Berel was increasingly worried about leaving Soreh home alone, but she continued to go about her life as though nothing extraordinary was happening.

Actually Soreh was not quite as sanguine as Berel imagined. There had been incidents. The flower seller at the corner of the square had said she had no flowers to sell her even though there was an abundance of fragrant blooms in the stall. And yesterday the dairyman hadn't made his usual delivery and Soreh knew that she would never see him at her door again.

Always an open, cheerful woman with a ready smile, Soreh's spirit had been sorely oppressed by the cold hostility that seemed now to press in upon her from every side. Perhaps she *should* sell the house. But where would Frau Beilson go? Perhaps now that her granddaughter was married . . . Berel might be right about leaving, until things settled down again.

Soreh was thinking about her husband as she sorted the winter clothing, brushing each garment before folding it away in a trunk to store for the summer. There were some, she knew, who had called her foolish for marrying Berel. He was so much younger, they said, he would surely one day find a woman his own age and leave her. Besides, why should a prosperous widow want to tie herself to a man who had neither means nor prospects? But the marriage hadn't been a mistake. Marrying the house painter, Nahum Glanzer—he should only rest in peace!—had been for practical reasons, but when she married Berel Levy, it had been for love. In two years, except for the heartache of not having conceived, she had not had a moment's regret. Berel was strong and constant, loving and gentle, a good husband in all ways; she never failed to thrill to the feel of his arms around her, the silky softness of his beard against her cheek. Perhaps if Berel were home from work early, they would make love before supper. It was a perfect day for it, since Frau Beilson was away visiting the granddaughter, and Zusya would be late, his factory having gone on overtime.

Soreh was so intent upon her thoughts that she was scarcely aware of the buzz of men's voices from the street in front of the house until the sound burst upon her with an angry roar, and she realized that someone was frantically banging on the door, trying to get in. Berel! Home a little early, she thought gratefully. From the sound of it, he must have been pursued through the streets by a gang of hoodlums—lately there were more and more happenings of that kind. Possessed by the certainty of her own wishful thoughts and panicked by the shouts of angry men, she hurried to open the stout front door for Berel to come in. In the instant that the door swung open she knew she had made a terrible mistake. Desperately she tried to slam the door between herself and them, but seven or eight ragged, dirty men swept past her into the spotless little hallway. They were led by a burly giant with hair so light it seemed almost white. Though not dressed much better than the others, he seemed altogether fitter and cleaner than the rest, and Soreh imagined that he was probably a government agitator or a police agent. Passing by her, the white-haired man deliberately brushed against her, grinning at her with his sharp teeth bared.

When they had disappeared into the other rooms, Soreh still stood motionless in the hallway. From the dining room there was a sound of breaking china. Soreh's beautiful pink and gold plates, long saved for and purchased a few at a time, were being systematically smashed. She raced into the room, flinging herself upon the men while trying futilely to grab a cup here, a saucer there. This excited the marauders, and they began on the bowls and vases. Roaring with laughter, the men broke out the dining room windows by hurling cut glass through them. Through the roaring in her ears, Soreh heard the leader shout, "Should Jew dogs live better than you, brothers?" and the men answered back with curses.

Soreh closed her eyes, resigning herself to how helpless she was to stop the destruction. She pressed back against a wall, dazed by the sight of men so drunk with vodka and power that the damage they wreaked was mindless. She could not stifle a moan as a knife whipped out of a boot to rip upholstery, shred wallpaper, and slash photographs.

The first intruders had been joined by others thirsting for a share in the fun. Soreh recognized some of the clerks from shops on the boulevard. The men had found the bottle of schnapps and the Sabbath wine, and the bottles were being passed back and forth among them. Some of the men had their own jugs of vodka. Maybe, Soreh prayed, they would drink themselves into a stupor before they completely broke up her pretty little house.

Slowly Soreh edged her way toward the big downstairs bedroom that she shared with Berel. If she could reach the bedroom unnoticed, she could quietly lock herself in until they were gone. No one paid attention to the small woman inching her way out of the dining room. Once in the hallway, Soreh turned and scuttled for the safety of the bedroom. She was barely a step from the open doorway when she was seized from behind and a voice, quiet with menace, said in her ear, "Don't struggle, my plump little bird. There's no one to help you!"

Soreh, her arm doubled painfully behind her back, was forced into the bedroom, the door kicked shut and bolted.

"Isn't this where you wanted to be, my pigeon?" said the smooth voice as the man propelled her, stumbling, toward the bed.

Struggling made the pain in her arm unbearable, and Soreh knew that if she persisted, her assailant would not hesitate to snap the bone like a dry stick. When he released his hold for a moment, Soreh rubbed her forearm to restore circulation, but the respite was short. The same strong arms picked her up and threw her across the bed. Soreh looked up at him with eyes dilated by fear and loathing. It was the fair-haired leader who had grinned at her with white wolf's teeth when the crowd had thrust through the open doorway into the house. The only sounds were of breaking glass and roistering voices that filtered through the bedroom door. Soreh and her tormentor stared into each other's eyes.

Then he was upon her, his hands tearing at her clothes, and Soreh was fighting him, her nails reaching for his eyes, his ears, any soft place where she could hurt him. With unexpected strength Soreh jabbed her knee into his groin, and he swore a mighty oath and brought his hand up to strike her across the face, not once but several times, each deliberate blow harder than the last. "There will be worse to come if you do not lie still. Behave, and it will be over soon."

Lying beneath the blond man's crushing weight, her face stinging from his blows, Soreh knew that struggle was futile. It would just give him satisfaction to use his superior strength to hurt her. He was the kind of man who enjoys punishing women. There was only one thing she could do, and that was to disengage, making herself limp beneath him. She lay still, refusing to close her eyes. She intended to burn every detail of his face into her memory so that someday she could find him and kill him with her own two hands. An inner rage helped her survive the next few minutes. As though the violated body belonged to someone else, Soreh experienced his violent penetration of her, his breath hot and thick upon her neck; she was relieved when the great spurt of his seed inside her signaled that he was done with her.

When the muscular man finally lifted himself off the bed and stood to fasten his clothes about him, it was for him as though nothing had transpired between them. Soreh pulled her skirt down but otherwise lay inert on the soiled coverlet. On the way to the door the white-haired man lit a cigarette. Before he left the room he spoke. "If I were you, I'd get out of the house before we set it on fire."

He was gone then, closing the door quietly behind him.

Soreh rose from the bed. She rebolted the door. There was water in the pitcher on the corner stand. Numbly she washed herself, scrubbing hard with soap at the parts he had touched. By the time she had finished she could smell smoke. The threat to fire the house had not been idle, then, but why should she have assumed otherwise? Opening a drawer in her cupboard, Soreh found the small purse in which she kept her household cash—it wasn't a great deal. Thinking more clearly now, she felt behind the clothes for her little jewelry case and emptied its contents into her pockets. Everything else was gone or would be soon. Perhaps the sale of the jewelry would be enough to help them start life.

As smoke billowed beneath the door, Soreh opened the bedroom window and dropped to the ground below.

The house was burning hard when Soreh walked away, deliberately forcing herself to look forward and not back. She was almost at the intersection when Berel turned the corner, running hard. On his way home from the factory, he had seen mobs in the streets, the flames leaping toward the sky, and he had known with dreadful certainty that it was his house that burned, his wife who was in danger.

Soreh threw herself into Berel's arms, laughing and crying with tension and near hysteria. "Oh, Berel!" she cried. "How lucky we are! There's nothing at all to keep us from going to America now!"

God's ways, Chaim thought, were beyond the understanding of man. On the day of the earthquake when he had been lying, injured and in pain, on a cot beneath a tarpaulin shelter in Golden Gate Park, he had felt that his life was no longer worth living. Jamie O'Donnell was undoubtedly dead in the ruins of the Valencia Hotel, no telling what had happened to Jonas Gore and his other shipmates, and for all he knew the *Oceania* had sunk in the harbor. Sick with the torment of broken ribs, dizzy from concussion, he was still aware that he was alone and stranded in a foreign city, and with fires raging all around him, no money in his pockets, no coat or shoes against the cold. When he had tried to rise, he had been shaken by a pain so vigorous that he had fallen back on his cot, certain that his own death was just a matter of time.

Yet look how it had all turned out! Twenty-four hours later the doctor had said he was well enough to leave the makeshift hospital in the park, and a volunteer had found a thick flannel shirt and shoes that were only a little too short for his big feet. The same volunteer had arranged transportation to an aid station that, he said, would be able to help Chaim get back on his feet. In that unlikely place, he had met Raizel, the pretty, dark-eyed ... Silently he corrected himself. Not "Raizel," though that was the name given her by her parents, but "Rosalie" according to her own wishes. The fact that Rosalie had been in San Francisco at all during the earthquake made Chaim feel that their union was *beshert* by God Himself. On the very eve of the disaster, Rosalie, from Sacramento, a sleepy valley city some ninety miles to the northeast, had come to San Francisco to visit cousins and see about hiring a manager for her inherited haberdashery business.

From Golden Gate Park Chaim had been taken by wagon across the city to a large wooden building still standing amid neighboring scenes of destruction. More than a little stunned and depressed, he had scarcely noticed the Hebrew lettering and the six-pointed Magen David above the main portals of the structure. Instead, his eyes had been drawn to the huge red cross and hand-lettered sign on the side door. He pushed through the door into a large room bustling with cheerful activity and smelling comfortingly of coffee. Mattresses had been spread on the bare floors, where a dozen or so people, mostly elderly women, small children, and a few injured, were resting. Along one wall a table held mounds of bread, platters of cheese, and baskets of fruit. A thin woman with white hair was filling tin mugs with milk for the children and coffee for the adults.

Near the door where Chaim had entered were several information desks where men and women wearing armbands sat with pens and long strips of paper on which they either wrote things down or consulted for information. Chaim wondered if someone here might have information about the *Oceania*. For the moment he felt too tired and confused to conjure up the English words needed to ask.

Chaim had been standing uncertainly in the doorway when he felt a soft hand in his, drawing him into the room and toward one of the desks. He had looked down into widely spaced dark eyes in a smiling face. The woman was young, her complexion fresh, pink, and clean. She spoke to him in English. "You should register at the table here so that your family can locate you. Would you like to make inquiries about anyone?"

Before this onslaught of incomprehensible words, Chaim had found himself faltering. Haltingly he had asked, "Vehr—iss—dis place?"

The woman had looked up at him, surprised. "Not American?"

Chaim shook his head.

"What is your name?" she had asked loudly with exaggerated slowness. "Chaim Mandelkern."

She seemed pleased. "This is a shul—Sherith Israel. It is being used as an emergency aid station, and I'm a volunteer." The dark eyes had smiled into Chaim's. "My name is Rosalie Riskin. I'd like to help you."

Help him she did. She took him to a man with an armband who found him a place to sleep in a tent dormitory. In the next few days Rosalie accompanied him to the field stations as well as to the large central hospital at the Presidio. Some of Chaim's shipmates must have lived through the earthquake as he had, but where were they?

Rosalie also went with him to the docks. They found the waterfront cordoned off and guarded by militia. Fire had not broken out anywhere near the harbor, but just in case, fire-fighting equipment stood at the ready. A soldier told them that many of the ships that had been in port, worried about the danger of aftershocks and fires, had put out to sea with or without their full crews. Chaim had had to conclude that the *Oceania* was one of these. He thought with fleeing regret of his seabag with its veritable treasure in back pay, and of his clothing, including the warm coat from the Grand Bazaar in Constantinople.

Rosalie guided him to Portsmouth Square, where the dead had been laid out in ranks, waiting for identifying information to be logged by the coroner's office before the bodies were consigned to common graves for quick burial. Rosalie helped him make the necessary inquiries. An Oliver Gideon had been identified from seaman's papers found on the body, but there was no record of a Jamie O'Donnell, a Jonas Gore, or the half dozen other comrades Chaim asked for. Finally, tired and dispirited, Chaim had concluded that he was now a man without a past. He confided to Rosalie that it was as if his life had begun in San Francisco, USA, at the moment of the first shock, April 18, 1906.

When Chaim was a little stronger, he and Rosalie had joined a throng of sightseers streaming up Russian Hill from where the view of the devastated city was best. They could see the haze of smoke from the still-smoldering blazes. Large sections of the city had been destroyed either by the quake or by fire, all of Chinatown, much of the Hayes Valley, the South of Market area, part of the downtown. Standing on the hilltop, Chaim's breath caught in his throat to recognize the full violence that had been done to the city. Rosalie was crying openly. Silently they held on to each other.

It was perhaps more a feeling of rightness than of romantic love that drew Rosalie and Chaim to each other. The natural disaster had shown each what a dangerous and unpredictable place earth is. Life now seemed more precious, more intensely real than before, and there was an urgency to get on with things. Both essentially alone and adrift in the world, Rosalie and Chaim had married each other three weeks later. Virtually overnight Chaim's status had changed from seaman to businessman, from immigrant to resident, from bachelor to husband. Even his name had changed, Rosalie insisting that Chaim Mandelkern was too much of a mouthful for an American; thereafter he was to be known as "Hy Mandel."

Rosalie had installed Chaim as manager of Riskin's Gentleman's Store on "J" Street in Sacramento, and they had settled into married life in the big, dark, three-storied home that belonged to Rosalie now that her father was gone. Chaim had been amazed that a small store like Riskin's supported such a house. In business since the Gold Rush, Riskin's was a habit with older Sacramentans. Besides, the economy was flourishing in those golden days at the end of 1906. Rosalie was pleased that whatever her bridegroom's other failings, he seemed to have a natural talent for the clothing business. The profits rolled in as never before. Chaim began to make changes in the store. A plate-glass window was installed in the front wall, the floor space was enlarged, a second employee added.

Once or twice Rosalie had protested that some portion of the income be invested against the possibility of future hard times. "I admit the place could use a little remodeling, Hy, but on the other hand, remember that my father did exceptionally well without fancy improvements."

"Times change," Chaim assured her. "I work good shop in Odessa— Melnikoff's—see stores in Europe. This place too small, too dark."

"Sacramento is conservative. Besides, we should have a nest egg."

"Nest egg?" Chaim puzzled. He patted Rosalie's hand. "Times good, improve business; times bad, cut down. I be one to worry. You too nervous."

Rosalie backed down.

Both Chaim and Rosalie were mystified by marriage. What had seemed in San Francisco like the natural evolution of a relationship made in heaven now seemed like the forcible binding of two beings from separate planets. Their backgrounds were so widely different that they had no way of evaluating, nor certainly of appreciating, each other's past experiences. And their personalities—Chaim's open and expansive, Rosalie's aloof and narrow—had inevitably clashed. A deep and abiding sexual attraction between them might have eased their way, but sadly, it was lacking.

Rosalie shuddered when she thought of their marital relations. Hy approached the sexual act without the reverence that her romantic novels and girlhood imaginings had led her to expect. He was not worshipful, not grateful that she allowed him access to her body. Sometimes, in fact, he even joked and laughed in bed! Insensitive to her respectable upbringing, he wanted to look at her body, and he touched her with his mouth and his hands in ways that disgusted and frightened her. She supposed he had learned those ways when he was a sailor in foreign ports—where that disgusting picture of a naked woman had been tattooed on his arm! Certainly no proper Jewish bridegroom would treat a wife like a whore.

They had married at the San Francisco home of Rosalie's only living relatives, Oscar and Emma Weintraub, the cousins she had been visiting when the earthquake struck. It was a small but elegant ceremony with a few family friends in attendance, conducted in a Jewish Reform tradition strange to Chaim. After a wedding supper prepared by the cousin's cook from the best ingredients to be found from limited post-earthquake supplies, they had gone to spend their wedding night in the Claremont Hotel in the Berkeley Hills.

Firmly closing the door of their opulent room, Chaim had taken his bride into his arms, exhilarated by the faint odor of perfume rising from her skin and reveling in the delicacy of her bones felt even beneath the whale-bone stays of her corset. Alone at last with the woman he had taken for life, he stooped to cover her mouth with his own. There had been embraces—restrained and not too many—during their whirlwind courtship, but this was different, a lover's kiss. He was surprised to find her lips sealed against him and cool to the touch. Her hands pushed against his chest.

"Honestly, Hy, can't you wait until I've at least taken off my hat!"

Chaim stepped back, bewildered. Well, he thought, she is young and innocent. He would have to take great care with her, but still he was not concerned. After all, hadn't he been taught the art of pleasing women by that expert of sensuality, Nadja Ivanovna?

Chaim smiled and released her. He walked across the room to turn the spread down on the double bed. When he glanced back at Rosalie, he saw that she was sitting rigid on the edge of a straight satin chair, her eyes avoiding the bed. She had not taken off her hat nor discarded her coat. Nervous, he assumed. There was something endearing about that. He knelt by the side of her chair, speaking quietly and reassuringly. "Von't you take off hat? Here! Let me help with boots—" He slipped the shoes from her feet, gently rubbing her cramped toes. She suffered him to do this in silence. "Is late, *malenkaya*. I t'ink go to bed now?"

Color flooded Rosalie's pale cheeks, but she rose at once with an air that was both purposeful and resigned. "All right." She dragged her little dressing case into the adjoining bathroom, locking the door behind her with a loud click.

Feverishly Chaim threw off his clothes, standing before the mirror to observe what Rosalie would see when she returned. Yes. It was a good body, graceful despite its size. The shoulders were heavily muscled from shoveling coal and the chest was broad, covered with dark hair that made a trail across a flat midsection to end in gentle curls about the genitals. The flanks were narrow, no extra fat anywhere, and the legs strong and well shaped. He peered into the glass, wondering whether he should shave again, decided not, thought about whether he should let his beard grow now that he was out of the engine room. Without the bush of a beard, he saw that his complexion was fresh and ruddy, and he rather liked having a naked chin.

What was taking Rosalie so long in the bathroom? Gently he tried the handle on the door, confirmed that it was locked. "All right?" he called through the partition.

"Oh, for heaven's sakes!" she exploded.

Chaim retreated to the bed, pulling down the top covers and climbing in. After another all but interminable wait, the bathroom door opened. Rosalie stood in the opening. Feeling disappointment, he saw that she had changed to a high-necked nightgown and matching robe. Gingerly she approached the bed.

"Blow out the lamp," she ordered Chaim.

"No. I vant see you!"

"Please," she said. "Otherwise I'm not going to take off my peignoir."

He had no idea what a peignoir might be, but he understood that she did not intend to disrobe in the light. "I like look at you, Raizel."

"Rosalie!" she said automatically. "That's disgusting!"

He sighed. There was so much to teach her! He blew out the lamp and after a long while she lay down beside him. The nearness of her sweet-smelling body aroused him, but when he reached for her, his fingers encountered voluminous folds of cloth. He leaned forward, brushing her nearest earlobe with his lips while his hands began to gently lift her gown out of the way. When his fingers made contact with flesh, she shrieked. From there, it got worse. She wept and protested as though he were some kind of mad rapist and not her husband of three hours! His passion cooled to match her resistance, and he sat up in the bed. "Raizel," he said firmly, "luffing is part of being together. Vhat you vant I do?"

"Yes, I know, Hy, I know," she sobbed, "only you must give me some time to get used to it! I didn't know it would be like this!"

Chaim lay down again. She was a good religious girl, he thought, a virgin. He must remember and be tender. He took her shaking body into his arms, stroking her through her nightgown. With infinite care and patience he calmed her, managing in the process to push her gown up around her hips. When at long last he mounted her, she lay beneath him with tightly closed eyes and clenched teeth. At the moment he pushed into her, she moaned piteously and then lay still as a corpse. As soon as he rolled off, she turned on her side, moving as far away from him as she could possibly get.

This was their wedding night.

In the months ahead, Rosalie made an adjustment to the physical side of marriage, stoically enduring Chaim's embraces but always relieved when the act was finished and she could turn over and go to sleep, knowing that it might be a week or more before her husband would approach her again.

She enjoyed playing house in the old mansion. Every day she dusted the inherited furniture and once a week she lovingly rubbed it with lemon oil. She bought cookbooks and made elaborate meals that Chaim ate without comment. She invited women friends for mah-jongg games and couples for supper parties. If only she had a baby, she thought, she would surely be content with her life.

Rosalie was used to thinking of Chaim as having sprung to life full-grown after the earthquake. It had therefore been a surprise to her when one evening at supper Chaim had said to her, "I haf invited my friend Berel Levy to come from New York."

"Berel Levy? Who is he?"

"I haf told you I get letter from Berel one, two months ago."

"Oh, yes. The boy you ran away from home with, isn't it?"

Chaim nodded. "Him, his woman, baby, in New York almost year now. Business could use Berel."

Rosalie said carefully, "Well, but if we need another salesman, wouldn't it be better to hire someone who—can speak to the customers?"

A gleam of amusement showed in Chaim's eyes. "Like me?"

"Well, your English is improving Hy," she said, granting that he did have a gift for languages. Rosalie began to gather up the dishes from the table. "I just don't see that we can use a greenhorn in the business," she said judiciously.

Chaim scraped back his chair, standing so that he towered over her. "You call me greenhorn all time, Raizel! Someone tell me not nice name give someone. Berel is friend—honest man, hard worker, good tailor. He having it hard in New York. I wrote him come."

"But—" Rosalie started.

"No but!"

Rosalie could barely bear to think of the soon-to-be-arriving Levys. She had felt the need to explain to her women friends that bringing the newcomers to Sacramento was an act of charity on the part of her overgenerous husband.

The weekly mah-jongg game had gone on so long that day that they were still playing when Chaim came home from the store. Rosalie heard his key in the lock, sensed that he had stooped to pick up the mail that had dropped through the slot in the hall and that he had taken off his jacket and was hanging it in the front closet. Now he would be glancing through the letters and advertisements that had come in the afternoon mail delivery.

"I guess it's later than we thought!" she said to the three other women. "We'd better finish up or none of our men will get supper tonight!"

"Let's just call it a day!" one of the others said, throwing in her tiles.

"Just because you're the big winner!" grumbled another. "I guess I owe you twenty cents."

"It won't break you."

They had begun to sort the ivory tiles and put them back into their wooden case when they heard Chaim's whoop of exultation from the hallway.

"What in the world—?" Rosalie's forehead creased.

Chaim came into the living room then, waving a sheet of paper, his face aglow as Rosalie hadn't seen it since their wedding day. She half rose to her feet.

Chaim hastily acknowledged the other women before turning to his wife. "See what Mammeh writes, Raizel!"

"Rosalie!' she corrected him sharply. "You know I can't read that foreign language!"

Chaim shook his head. "That foreign language is yours too. Yiddish."

"I still can't read it!"

The three women were gathering up their jackets and pocketbooks in preparation for leaving.

"Mammeh writes most vunderful news! Chaya Leya—my sister—with Herschel and their little girl on way from Shanghai! Be here soon. Can you believe?"

Rosalie shook her head, dismayed, wondering how many more immigrant friends and relatives she could expect to put up. "Please don't feel you have to rush off," she said to her friends.

"No, really, it's late," one of the women said nervously. "Good-bye, darling! That's lovely news, Hy. We'll be dying to meet your family! We'll let ourselves out, Rosalie. It was a gorgeous afternoon."

Rosalie walked her friends to the front door. When she returned, Chaim was staring misty-eyed into the distance. "Long time I haf not seen Chaya Leya—six, seven years already! Or Herschel! What a lot we all got to tell! How I haf missed them!"

For a moment, Rosalie felt jealous, of whom she wasn't sure. Of Hy, who, unlike her, had close ties with family and friends? Or of the unknown sister who was so beloved?

Chaya Leya stood on the deck of the S.S. *Pegasus* as it moved sedately through the Golden Gate on its way to dock in San Francisco. Her husband Herschel stood beside her at the rail, one arm around her, the other holding up two-year-old Channah for her first glimpse of their new country.

"First thing, we'll let Chaim know we're here!" Chaya Leya exclaimed. "I hope Mammeh wrote to him!"

"I keep thinking of Chaim as he was the last time we saw him," Herschel said, "and now he's grown-up with an American wife and a house and a business!"

They were silent, remembering the boy who had run away from home over a love affair with a Russian maidservant. Finally Chaya Leya said, "So much has happened to all of us, hasn't it, Herschel?"

A small boat came alongside the *Pegasus*, bringing immigration officials to examine the documents of the first- and second-class passengers. If the papers were satisfactory and the owners of them not visibly impaired, they could go ashore immediately when the ship docked. For those traveling steerage—Chinese coming to work on the railroads, in the garment trade, and in service industries—it would be a different story. They would be taken to a large warehouse owned by the shipping company, the Pacific Mail Steamship Company, where they would undergo a lengthy interrogation and a thorough medical examination.

Chaya Leya was nervous. Interactions with government officials inevitably reminded her of Herschel's arrest at Harbin.

Herschel's arm tightened around her, and he whispered in her ear, "This time the papers are not Davka's!"

They both began to laugh. Channah, responding to her parents' good humor, chortled happily and held out her arms to the man from immigration.

Chapter 50

*L*ev could not seem to move past the initial shock of the death of his seemingly indestructible father. What made it all so unreal was the discovery that the little dentist had left behind him a mountain of debts and a house that had been pledged to creditors. There had not been sufficient cash even to pay for a cemetery plot or for the widow's weeds that Frau Goldenburg had immediately ordered. Lev had paid for everything, including the substantial death duties, from his own bank account, it being the case that the schoolteacher sister had little to contribute, and the sister in Riga nothing at all, her husband being unemployed and she herself once more pregnant.

Lev grew ever more pale and gaunt. He slept little and ate less. At Mir Khozayki, he performed like an automaton, sitting hunched over his columns of spidery figures long past the time when the store was closed and all the other employees had gone for the day. He seemed to have retreated inside himself to some private place of suffering from which no amount of effort could coax him. He scarcely noticed Dvoreh even when she brushed up against him in the office. He refused to enjoy with her the last brisk days of autumn, pushed aside the small delicacies she had carried to work in her lunchbox, no longer met her at the tram stop on Alexander Avenue or visited on *shabbes*. When Dvoreh went home to Polotsk for a week that September, he seemed largely unaware of her absence.

Dvoreh was determined that Lev's behavior not continue unchallenged. Remaining behind when Yaakov Lichtman, the manager, locked the big front door one evening in October, she placed herself firmly in a chair next to Lev's, feet flat on the floor, arms folded, and her face pale and serious.

"You'll miss your tram," Lev remonstrated.

"There'll be another."

Dvoreh watched Lev enter the day's receipts in a ledger, checking and rechecking against the sales slips. He was clearly distracted by Dvoreh's presence and frowned up at her from time to time. Good, she thought, at least for a change he knows I'm here. When the last entry had been blotted dry and the big book closed, Dvoreh asked quietly, "Are we ever to be married, Lev?"

What he answered plunged slivers of ice into her heart. "This is not the time to talk of marriage."

They had been betrothed for well over a year, waiting first for one thing and then another. She understood that he was suffering, and her heart told her that she could help him if he would only allow her to come close. She wanted nothing more than to hold him in her arms while her body thawed what was frozen inside him; gradually her love could heal him. Why, then, did he refuse her comfort—unless it was that he no longer loved her.

Dvoreh blurted out, "I already have my wedding dress and the veil!" It wasn't what she had meant to say. Somehow the thought of that beautiful wispy veil nestled in its layers of tissue paper gave her pain beyond all other things.

Lev was cold. "I've lost my father and become responsible for my family, and you talk to me of pieces of gauze and lace!" he shouted.

"Lev, my dearest friend," Dvoreh cried, dropping to her knees beside his chair and gripping his hands in hers, "can't we face things together—not just you alone but us two against whatever troubles there are?"

"No!" Lev said. "Stop pushing me, Dvoreh! I've got so much on my mind! I need time to figure it all out—"

"But, Lev—"

"I can't be husband to you and Mother both! Can't you understand that?" Agitated, he rose from his chair, toppling her in the process.

She scrambled to her feet. "No! I don't know what you're talking about."

"Responsibility! So heavy for one man!" His eyes were red-rimmed, desperate. "There isn't money for us. Everything I saved, gone, everything gone."

"I don't care about money," Dvoreh said, putting her arms around him and leaning her dark head against his shirtfront. "We'll manage."

Roughly Lev pushed her away. "You've been at me since I first met you," he said savagely. "You're always grasping at me, making demands I can't meet. Do you think I want a lifetime of accusations and nagging? Do you? Do you think I want always to be on my guard against the snares you lay for me?"

"Snares?" Dvoreh was puzzled.

"You came to Riga to find a husband, didn't you, Dvoreh? And with your shameless ways you trapped me into promising marriage! I know how it is! First it's just being together that's important, then it's buying a house, furniture, finally it's children. I know the things that enslave a man for life!"

Dvoreh stared at him, stricken.

Lev turned a white face to her. "That time you invited me to the house and didn't tell me that Eshka and Lazar had gone away for the day—and you stood before me in your nightdress with your hair down around your shoulders, and when I kissed you, you opened your mouth against mine. Where did you learn such whorish tricks, Dvoreh? In the streets of Polotsk or in Riga?"

Dvoreh struck him hard across the mouth with her open hand. "How do you dare talk to me that way!" she said furiously. "If I am shameless, Lev, what are you? If not you, who was with me in my bed that day?" Her eyes flashed. "I release you from any commitment!"

She spun on her heel and left him where he stood.

That same evening, Aunt Eshka hovering nervously, Dvoreh packed her trunk to return home. It was all over with Lev. Strangely, after the anger had passed, what she felt was only relief that a burden had been lifted. There had been too many unfulfilled promises, too many postponements, too much disappointment, and now she longed only to be home within the comforting circle of her parents' and her aunt Golda's love.

The next morning when she gave notice that she was quitting her job, the other clerks, Bashka and Nachem, Anna and Loebe, clustered anxiously about her. They scattered when Lev, his face dark with anger, came rushing from the office.

"What are you doing!" he shouted. "We are getting married soon!"

Dvoreh began to shake so that she had to find a stool on which to sit.

Swallowing hard, she whispered, "It's clear to me now that you have never wanted to marry me."

"That's not true!" he said, his eyes wild with fear.

"Yes. Yes, it is."

"Stay, and we'll get married tomorrow, today even—I didn't mean what I said last night!"

Dvoreh shook her head. "If we marry now, you'll always feel I forced you."

"What will you do? Where will you go?"

"I don't know. Home for a while. Away from here."

"Don't you love me?" Lev demanded, unaware that an early-morning customer was staring at them, open-mouthed.

"I thought I did."

"So you're punishing me for what I said when I was upset? You know I didn't mean any of it!"

Dvoreh reached out a hand and touched his cheek. "Let's see how we feel after we've been apart for a while, Lev. I'll keep in touch with you."

*I*n a handsome house in Sacramento, Rosalie handed Chaim a letter recognizable by its beautifully sloped penmanship and the row of colorful stamps printed in the Cyrillic alphabet.

Even before Chaim was settled in his chair, he had eagerly ripped open the envelope. Letters from home were reaching him with gratifying regularity. The contents were predictable: Papa reported with newspaperlike brevity on the whereabouts, health, and status of each member of the family; Mama wrote about the political situation, the school, happenings at Spokoinaya Zemlya; Aunt Golda cautioned him about eating properly and dressing warmly against the cold, sometimes including a headache remedy or a list of herbs to be mashed into a paste; rubbed on red flannel and pinned about the neck, it would cure sore throat, she wrote. Chaim had stopped translating Aunt Golda's "receipts" for Rosalie when he found her repeating them to the vast amusement of her friends.

Today's letter was entirely in Mammeh's hand, and he frowned as he read.

"Something the matter, Hy?" Rosalie asked, sinking into a chair across from his.

"I don't know," he said absently. "Mammeh writes that Dvoreh has broken off with that bookkeeper fellow in Riga. She's come home to stay."

"Oh? I thought that was supposed to be such a great love match?"

"Well, there were family problems." He looked into the distance. "Mammeh thinks Dvoreh needs a change."

Rosalie sat up straighter in her chair. What was Hy not saying? Was this another relative coming to stay?

"I see. Your mother wants her to come to us, is that it?"

Chaim nodded.

"You know how I feel about people helping each other, Hy," Rosalie said, "but is it really the best thing for a young girl to be so far from home?"

Chaim said reasonably, "Dvoreh has brother, sister, old friends like Herschel and Berel here. Not like coming to strangers."

"Yes, but—"

"Mammeh wrote Chaya Leya too. Not worry, Raizel. If Dvoreh come, she stay there." Chaim's face grew hard, remembering the discomfort of Berel and Soreh under his and Rosalie's roof. "To tell the truth, Chaim," Berel had said after only a few days in Sacramento, "Soreh's set her heart on living in San Francisco. She thinks it better for little Isaac. Don't worry. I'll find work, and it will be good being close again to Chaya Leya and Herschel."

Chaim could not fault Rosalie. She had behaved toward the Levys with proper politeness. Maybe it was just that all of them—himself, Chaya Leya, and Herschel too—were just too "old country" to fit conveniently into Rosalie's world. He could understand how she might feel and still be sick at heart that it was so.

"One thing," Chaim said now, looking down at the letter, "Mammeh writes that money is big problem. Government not allow rubles out of country. I haf to send *shifskart.*"

"What?"

"I forget." Chaim hated the constant struggle with English. Despite a growing proficiency, it was a relief to be able to speak Yiddish or Russian with Chaya Leya and Herschel and Berel. "Ticket for ship. We take train to Frisco Sunday, talk things over with Chaya Leya and Herschel."

"San Francisco," Rosalie said automatically, "not 'Frisco.' All right, though I'm not a bit sure that coming to America is a good solution to an unhappy love affair."

*D*voreh was also unsure that going to America would solve her problems. "How can I go so far from Lev?" she wept.

"I thought," Malkeh said with a certain amount of impatience, "that you had decided it was better to separate."

"But not forever! Maybe I'll go back to Riga. Lev—"

"Forget Lev Goldenburg!"

"I can't. I love him."

"Dvoreh, he doesn't want to be married."

"That's not true. In every letter he write he says he wants me back."
Dvoreh, sitting on the floor beside her mother's chair, put her silken head
in the old woman's lap, a child wheedling a reluctant parent. "I can't help
myself, Mammeh. I can't imagine life without him."

Malkeh's face creased with pain. That her child was obsessed with this
poor, frail man was clear; yet she could see no happy ending for the relationship. "Let me suggest this, Dvorehleh—go to America, to Chaim and his
wife. Or to Chaya Leya and Herschel, if you'd rather. In the meantime, Lev
will take care of his obligations to his family and will follow you."

"He'll never have the money! His mother spends every kopeck!"

"So you'll work in America and save the money to send for him."

"And if he doesn't want to come?"

"Then it is not meant to happen. Have faith that God in His wisdom
arranges all things."

Dvoreh looked up at her mother with just a hint of the old mischie-
vousness. "God? And all the time I thought it was *you* who asked Chaim to
send the passage money and got Count Voronov to arrange my emigration
papers!"

Malkeh laughed despite the heaviness that lay upon her heart. "I serve
as God's hands," she said, only half joking.

*I*n San Francisco, Chaim, Chaya Leya, and Herschel sat together
at the round oak table in the cramped dining room. After a year
in America the Rosens felt well-established in their simple frame two-flat
building. Harriet Street was one of several narrow streets in a neighborhood
of Italian, Irish, and Jewish immigrants, the mixture of cultures part of its
overall charm for Chaya Leya. The flat, large by some standards—two bedrooms, a sunny living room, tiny dining room, kitchen, and bathroom—was
near a streetcar line and close to the businesses of lower Market Street.

Chaim's visits had become something of a habit during the months
Chaya Leya and Herschel had been in San Francisco; however, Rosalie seldom accompanied her husband on the ninety-mile train journey from Sacramento. Chaya Leya had guessed, correctly, that her sister-in-law did not
feel comfortable with her recently acquired Old World relatives, and while
she was sorry for that, since she would have liked to be friends with her
brother's wife, she didn't know what to do to breach Rosalie's aloofness.

They had not seen Chaim for some time now. He had sent them a
scrawled note that said he was tied up with business matters. Chaya Leya
hoped that he had not been affected by The Panic of 1907, but Herschel said
that that was very unlikely since Chaim was a careful businessman.

Today when Chaim came to visit, he was definitely not himself. He
did not perform his usual trick of making candy or a coin materialize from

the ear of three-year-old Channah—"Hannah" as she was called in America—did not thrust a sack of oranges into Chaya Leya's hand or carry beneath his arm a sheaf of *Jewish Daily Forwards* for Herschel. He sank into a chair, leaning his head upon his hands, to all appearances thoroughly disconsolate. Alarmed by the gauntness of her brother's face, the worry lines etched deep, Chaya Leya shooed Hannah into the bedroom to play with her dolls, woke Herschel, who was taking a Sunday nap, and put the kettle on the fire for tea.

Chaim was despairing. "I have lost it all, all!" he said, speaking in Yiddish. "The store is gone, they foreclosed on the house to pay what I borrowed, there is no money left. Do you know what that means?" He looked from one to the other, his eyes red from sleeplessness. "I've lost the money Rosalie's father left her. This week we sold the furniture to have money to eat. Rosalie found a flat to rent and is looking for a job as a saleslady or a type-writer. How can a man respect himself?" He stared bitterly into his tea. "All I can find are odd jobs on the riverfront—that is, when there aren't enough Chinese to unload the ships. And still it's not enough money for everything! 'File for bankruptcy,' the bank tells me. 'We won't lend you money to keep the store open, but if you want to be a bankrupt, you don't have to pay your bills'! Is that not *meshuggeh*, tell me I'm lying!" His eyes swung from Herschel to Chaya Leya, searching faces soft with pity for answers. "America! What went wrong? What? Rosalie and me, we had everything. A house with oranges growing in the yard, a store, a bank account. And in just a few weeks it is all gone! All!" He stared about him in bewilderment. "What did I do wrong?"

Chaya Leya put her hand over her brother's. "You'll build up a business again, Chaim."

Herschel's long face was somber. "You were not buying stocks, were you, Chaim?"

Chaim shook his head. "No, I'm a different kind of fool! I thought I could turn Riskin's into a department store! Times were good. The bank fell all over itself to lend money. I spent everything we made and borrowed more besides. What did I understand about signing a paper to use a house, a business for 'security'? The bank said it was just routine! Routine, ha! I guess I wanted to prove to Rosalie that an immigrant from Russia could be a success! Fool that I was!"

Thoughtful, Herschel stroked his chin. "Don't blame yourself. Who could know that a panic on the stock market could mean something to people like us," he said. "I still don't even understand what a stock market is!"

"I'll tell you what it is. It's rich men speculating with other people's money!" Chaim snorted. "I should never have come to this cursed country! It's no better than it was at home!"

"Russia, America, people are all the same," Chaya Leya commiserated. "The rich can afford to gamble. If they lose, what's the problem for them? They raise prices or lower wages, and if the ordinary people end up in the streets without bread, so what's new?"

"All of a sudden the bank calls in the loans," Chaim told them, "and I have no cash to pay because business is bad, customers are out of work, and nobody comes into the store to buy. It might have been all right if they'd given me some time. Everyone says the Depression won't last forever. Mr. Leland Stanford they would have given time to—no one would have called in his loans! Mr. Julius Kahn and Mr. Weill, rich German Jews like that, they can ride out a business failure. But if you're plain Hy Mandel, a newcomer from Eastern Europe, it's another story! There're no breaks for us. That's the way of the world at home and here both!"

Chaim glared at his listeners, his face dark red and mottled. "Let me tell you something, and you mark it down somewhere so you'll remember. I am going to make a success. I am going to be one of the rich ones. When there are any loans to be called in, I'll be collecting them. I'll be buying up businesses for pennies on the dollar, not the other way around. Remember what I say!"

Herschel had been sitting quietly, swirling the tea leaves around in the bottom of his glass. The silence stretched out. Chaim's bravado faltered, and the others didn't know what to say. The clock ticked loudly, the tea-kettle hissed, and Hannah could be heard in the next room crooning to her dolls.

Finally Herschel said, "I have a little money—"

"What money! The few cents you make from buying and selling junk from a pushcart on the street?" Chaim spat. "Don't make me laugh! I need real money. Pennies he offers me!"

Chaya Leya spoke sharply. "Chaim! A hungry man says thanks for groats to fill his belly! This panic hasn't exactly been good for us either, and we have a child to feed, besides another on the way!"

Chaim felt the rebuff like a blow. Flushing, he looked down at the backs of hands clasped tightly on the tabletop. When he looked up, Chaya Leya and Herschel saw tears on his cheeks. "I'm sorry," he mumbled. "It's just that—well, Rosalie's taking it so hard. I'm almost crazy trying to figure some way out."

Chaya Leya murmured, "It's hard for her to lose her father's house and business both. It means a lot to her—more than just a store and a place to live—"

"I'll have a bigger one someday!" Chaim said, defiant, but the tears would not stop.

Herschel cleared his throat. "We have almost two hundred dollars put by that we can let you have. And you know that Berel and Soreh would give you the clothes they wear if it would help. Ask them. We're not rich, Chaim, but in a family we eat from one pot."

Chaim needed ten thousand dollars to clear his debts and restore his credit, but this time he did not answer back. Two hundred dollars must be a fortune to Herschel and Chaya Leya. Saved coin by coin, it *was* a fortune. Chaim was ashamed. Unable to speak without weeping, Chaim grasped Herschel's hand and gave Chaya Leya a weak smile through his tears.

He had leaned on Chaya Leya since he was born, and later Herschel had been a source of good sense and strength in his life. He had to feel sorry for poor Rosalie, who had never been part of a whole rich family structure. Would it change her attitude toward them to know that Chaya Leya and Herschel had offered all they had? If she scoffed at the paltriness of the sum, he would not be able to stand it. Perhaps he would not say where he'd found the money. Or perhaps he would. She should know what a family is.

After a while, Herschel's little pile of crumpled bills in his pocket, Chaim put on his jacket, kissed Chaya Leya, and hugged Hannah. He had, he said, things to take care of before he took the evening train back to Sacramento. At the door he turned and embraced Herschel, leaning his head for a moment against the other man's shoulder. With his eyes closed he could almost have been in his father's tailor shop, and for that moment at least, he felt safe.

When Chaim left Chaya Leya's flat, he took a streetcar to the northwest part of the city, transferring once and finally stepping down from the car on Fulton Street. The fog was spilling in from the Golden Gate and had already obscured the narrow front of a modest four-flat building in midblock. Chaim took the steep outdoor steps to the front door two at a time. Though he pressed the doorbell, he did not wait for the buzzer from upstairs but let himself in with a key already in his hand.

The door of the second-floor flat was thrown open, and the tall, auburn-haired woman stood waiting, her arms held open to him.

"Ah, Manya, love!" Chaim exclaimed in Russian, kicking the door shut behind him in the same instant that he took her into his arms. He held her so tightly that he could feel the hammer strokes of her heart and inhale the soap-clean scent of her skin and her hair. So different from Rosalie, he thought, pressing the woman to him with his hands against her firm, round buttocks. Different as a field flower is from one of those artificially perfect blooms that florists sell.

"You help me to live through the weeks, my pigeon. Whatever happens to me, you make me know I'm a man," he whispered.

The woman stopped his words with her mouth against his. Her lips were moist and full, and they moved over his face and throat, exploring him like an unknown country although in fact she knew him well.

Chaim's chest seemed to swell with the fullness of his desire. He wanted to hold her so close she would become part of him, to incorporate her into himself so that she would be with him even after he returned to Sacramento. Although Manya was full-bodied and almost as tall as he, Chaim easily swung her up in his arms and carried her, already moaning with longing, to the bed in the other room.

There was comfort here, and aside from sex, there was much he wanted from her; he needed advice and compassion from her overflowing abundance. Maybe he would take the morning train home instead of returning tonight. Rosalie would hardly miss him, and he could tell her he had been delayed following up a job lead. If he stayed there would be time for Manya and him to talk over supper, and when finally he lay down to rest, he could lay his head upon her heavy breasts and maybe sleep without nightmares. Ah, Manya! Manya!

Even as Chaim stripped off his clothes and tumbled into the woman's waiting arms, he smelled the good borscht simmering on the stove.

*C*haya Leya and Herschel sat at the table after Chaim left.

"*Chai?* Another glass of tea?" Chaya Leya asked, heaping a teaspoonful of preserves in the bottom of Herschel's glass and filling it without waiting for a reply. She refilled her own glass as well before she said carefully, "Two hundred dollars was all we had, and it took us over a year to save it."

Herschel nodded, not meeting her eyes.

Chaya Leya said, still in an uninflected voice, "Business isn't so good these days, and if it doesn't get better, I don't know how we'll feed the horse, much less Hannah and the baby that's coming."

Herschel looked out the window, where the fog curled on the ground like scraps of gray dust under a bed. At last he said, "I was the first of your father's apprentices—just an ignorant rag-poor orphan worth nothing in the eyes of the world. I came to him without a kopeck to my name and Yoysef, not a rich man, mind, taught me a trade, made me his partner, and gave me his daughter in marriage." He shook his head in wonder. "How many men, do you think, would have acted like that? How many?" He bowed his head, supporting it in his hands, and his voice when he spoke again was low. "Do you understand now?"

Chaya Leya sighed. "Chaim will someday be what he says, a rich man, and you, Herscheleh, you will only be a saint!"

Later as they lay close and snug in their bed, the mixture of moonlight and fog making eerie patterns on the walls, Chaya Leya could not sleep for thinking about Polotsk and her parents.

There was a day she remembered as clearly as though it were happening even now before her eyes. She was a little girl in the year of the great famine, huddled in a dim corner of the front room, playing dolls with Dvoreh to keep her mind from dwelling on her hunger. Nonetheless, she could hear the growl and feel the empty cramping in her stomach. Although her parents were talking quietly at the other end of the room, Chaya Leya could hear every word that passed between them. Mammeh was nagging at Papa to dismiss the apprentices. "They eat too much," she said, "and with times so bad they don't earn their keep." She was being reasonable, pointing out that the boys were young and strong and would make out all right foraging in the streets and in the fields like so many others. The family's store of food was frighteningly small to keep them all alive until spring.

Papa had kept shaking his head. Mammeh had cried then, pointing out that Papa's first obligation was to his four small children and to his elderly parents. Papa had shrugged. And then Mammeh had become very angry, accusing Papa of harboring the sins of stubbornness and pride. Mammeh as well as Papa could always quote biblical injunctions when she needed to rally support in an argument. But whatever she said, Papa had continued unmoved. "No. And no! *And no!* However bad things get, no one will be put from this house."

It was one of the few times that Chaya Leya remembered Papa's taking a stand against her mother. Perhaps that was why the recollection had remained so sharp all these many years.

Finally spring had come, and there were mushrooms and berries in the woods, the fish flourished once more in the ponds and the river, and the vegetables they had planted sent out green shoots that promised an abundant harvest. Papa had been right after all, that while the cruel winter would pass and the hunger be forgotten, sins of conscience last forever.

If Herschel had set himself the task of being like Papa, he had done the job well. But was Chaya Leya, then, to become her mother? In this time of trouble she had thought first of Hannah, Herschel, and the baby growing in her stomach. Like Mammeh so many years before, she did not have faith enough or love as Herschel had.

Chaya Leya turned heavily in the bed. Unable to sleep, she tugged at Herschel's shoulder. "Herschel, are you sleeping?"

"Yes," he said, his voice muffled in the pillow.

"Herschel, listen to me," Chaya Leya said, "even now as we lie comfortable in our bed, Dvoreh is on her way to New York without money for a railway ticket to bring her to San Francisco."

"Yes, yes, we've gone over that a hundred times!"

"Dvoreh will be stranded in New York, yet we could loan Chaim two hundred dollars."

"That," Herschel said slowly, "is a different matter." Resigned that Chaya Leya would not permit him to sleep yet, Herschel pulled himself up against the headboard. "Two hundred dollars is cheap for a life—Chaim's life. You still don't understand, do you? It's *because* two hundred dollars is all we've got in the world that it means something. Giving our last cent tells Chaim that we trust him enough to gamble our future for him. If *we* have that much confidence, don't you see, he'll have to prove himself worthy of it! Our faith will give him back his own. I know two hundred dollars isn't anywhere near what he needs, but who can tell? With our two hundred, and another fifty from Berel and a twenty here and a fifty there, he might just be able to raise enough cash to save himself."

"And Dvoreh? Don't we owe something to her too? Didn't we encourage her to come to America? Can we leave her in New York like a piece of unclaimed baggage?"

"It's not quite as black as all that, Chaya Leya," Herschel said reasonably. "Moishe and Lily will meet her at the boat, and she can stay with them—or with Yenta and Yaynkel—for a while. Not so terrible a fate! Dvoreh will get a job and save money to come west, and we will help. In no time she'll be here. How expensive can a railway ticket from New York be?"

"Expensive enough! It took us a year to save two hundred dollars when times were good!"

"We'll do the best we can."

"Chaim says it is terrible in New York, a real hell, crowded with people who talk Yiddish like saints and behave like devils! Suppose something bad happens to my little sister?"

"Berel and Soreh were in New York two years, and they didn't find it so terrible. And Moishe is all right, isn't he? He has a good job in a meat-packing plant, and an apartment."

Chaya Leya considered this in silence. "My conscience troubles me, Herschel."

"It's too late for that," Herschel said, yawning. "Why does your conscience bother you?"

Chaya Leya pulled herself into a sitting position, not easy considering her pregnancy-awkward body. "Herschel," she said urgently, "I wrote letters home to Dvoreh about how grand everything is here and how well we're doing—and, you know, maybe I exaggerated just a little."

"We all do that." Herschel slid down in the bed. The hour was late. "Good night, Chaya Leya. Tomorrow I have to make an early start." He pulled the pillow over his head.

"There's something I haven't told you, Herscheleh—"

"What?" he asked, giving up any pretense of sleep.

"I have some money. In the cracked china pitcher. I mean beside the two hundred dollars you gave Chaim."

"Oh?"

"I've been doing some piecework while you're away with the horse and the wagon. Millie O'Hara from next door got me started. I sew jet beads on evening dresses for one of those fancy stores downtown. I have seventeen dollars—in only six months! If I put by some of it for emergencies, I can maybe send Dvoreh a little toward her ticket. Will you find out tomorrow how much it costs?"

"You're a wonder, Chaya Leya!" Herschel said, pulling her down beside him, his hand caressing the taut round of her belly. "I'll stop at the Southern Pacific ticket office tomorrow."

Chaya Leya's lips nuzzled the soft place between her husband's shoulder and ear. "Do you suppose Dvoreh will ever be as happy with anyone as I am with you?"

"People earn their happiness. Anyway, God will decide. All *you* have to decide is to go to sleep now. It's late." Herschel yawned again, and the sound was heavy with significance. "Good night, Chaya Leya." His tone was firm.

"Good night, Herschel."

On the *Darmstadt* out of Hamburg, Dvoreh Mandelkern slept soundly, dreaming that Lev's arms held her tight and secure.

Chapter 51

There were some who would call it hallucination, but Vassily knew otherwise. Other roomers in the house wondered when they heard him talking to someone at night. But it was the kind of boardinghouse where lodgers keep their eyes lowered when they pass in the dark hallways and would never dream of exchanging the simplest greeting. If they had asked, he might have told them, "Yes, she is with me still. I tell her things I have saved up all day to share with her. We have been together since Berlin, a long time now, and things have never been better between us. Now that certain irritations are gone, I find her to be quite perfect. And she is completely mine."

He needed no other woman to make him happy. Of course, there was that troublesome dream. It always started happily enough. They were in the shabby room they had shared in Berlin, and the rain beat upon the windows as it had the very first time they were together. She stood naked before him, her body flushed and moist from her bath. When he gathered her into his arms, the scent of jasmine from her special French soap aroused in him a powerful eroticism. *Marta! Marta!* he cried in the dream, burying his face in the wealth of soft dark hair that tumbled about her shoulders and half covered her perfect round breasts. Her body curled against his in perfect yielding, and even as they fell upon the bed, she whispered love words in his ear. *Liebschen. Beloved. My soul.* He luxuriated in the silkiness of her hair, her voice. *Lubymaya. My own. My dearest one.* He covered her body with his own and felt the slim pelvic bones pressing against him. He gloried in the feel, the smell, the warmth of her body. He felt himself rising toward a pinnacle of experience, and then—*Julius,* she said.

Struck through the heart, he lifted himself away from her. As the loose red mouth laughed, his hands reached out, tightening about her throat to squeeze off the taunting laughter. How dare the Jew-whore make fun of him! When at last the thrashing body lay still, the face black, the tongue protruding, he would awaken with cold sweat pooling on the sheets.

He was often afraid to sleep. Yet he knew he must rest if he were to keep his wits about him. He had managed to convince the Bolshevik leadership that he had information to sell about the rival Social Revolutionaries. Most of what he passed them was useless or false. What fools they were, easy to dupe, and they actually paid him for lies! Occasionally Arkady Runich gave him a nugget of genuine, if essentially unimportant, information to share, just to reinforce his credibility. He grew bored with the game; it was too easy.

Vassily pressed Yevno Azev constantly to allow him to play a larger part in the terrorist activities of the S.R. That was where the real excitement lay! Had he not done well in his assignments thus far?

Azev shrugged. "Sazonov did Plehve, not you."

"But I was there in case he lost his nerve or something went wrong."

"You were sick in the gutter afterward," Runich said in disgust.

Vassily flushed. "I didn't expect him to be blown into little pieces!"

"I know, you're fastidious. Strangulation *is* cleaner, I suppose." Azev could be cruel.

"What about the grand duke? I was there for that!"

"Kalyaev threw the bomb."

"Give me a chance! I'll prove myself."

"We'll see."

Afterward Azev said to his lieutenant, "We can't trust him to keep his head."

"What's the worst that can happen?"

Azev, considering, motioned for Runich to give him a cigarette. "Has he got the nerve, do you think, to kill Stolypin?"

Runich caught his breath. First Minister Stolypin, the force behind both the agrarian reforms and the police strategy of meeting violence with even greater violence, was their most important target to date. "I don't know. He panicked with Plehve and hung back when Kalyaev killed the grand duke."

"Stolypin's policemen are picking off our people like flies! The bastards scarcely bother with trials anymore!" Azev spat on the floor in distaste. "Instant executions! What do you think, Arkady? Chernov has the capacity—as we saw with the murder of Marta Braun—but he's an impulsive rather than a thoughtful killer."

"We can always send someone dependable with him."

"If he's killed in the attempt, it's no great loss." Azev said, exhaling a great lungful of smoke. "He might even pull it off."

Simcha's revolutionary education, begun so long ago by Yevgeny Fedotov, was now augmented by Vassily Chernov. The irony of that was not lost on Vassily. He was vastly amused at the notion that his influence outdistanced that of his old enemy.

What was being called the Uprising of 1905, starting with Bloody Sunday in January and culminating in the general strikes later that year, had been put down by the militia. Out of the turmoil, however, the tsar had been forced to make concessions that set at least a few constitutional limits on the monarchy. On the whole the people were optimistic. Most of them craved relief, not revolution.

"It's like my old teacher said," Simcha exulted to Vassily, "a revolution *can* be evolutionary!"

They had been drinking tea and playing chess in Vassily's meager room. Simcha was the better chess player, but he had been too cocksure of himself and Vassily had taken the game from him.

"What drivel! The trouble with your old teacher—and with you—is that you haven't suffered!"

Simcha bristled. "I lived through the famine!" he growled.

Vassily laughed. "How old were you? A year? Two? Still at your mama's tits?"

"Well then, what about you? You told me once the Chernovs were rich merchants."

"They are, Semyon, they are! But my people were peasants. Five of us lived in a one-room *izba* on an estate where the steward beat my father so badly he never worked again. My mother sickened trying to take his place in the fields, and my sisters died young—one of hunger, the other of tuberculosis; she was a child prostitute."

Simcha was appalled. "But didn't the estate owner take some responsibility? I know at Spokoinaya Zemlya Fedotov and the count think of the peasants as part of their family."

Vassily's mouth twisted in a cynical smile. "Like the black slaves in America? Like our own serfs?"

Color flooded Simcha's face. "Can't you ever accept that there are good landowners as well as bad ones? Fedotov broke his back to make things better for the peasants! He improved their living conditions and opened schools and tried to show the men how to get better yields from their fields—"

"A real saint!" Vassily said sarcastically.

"And didn't put them off the land when they were too old to work—"

"Is that what he told you?"

"And loaned them money to pay their taxes, and—"

"And collected big rents, and charged high interest, and ruled them with an iron hand."

"Go to hell!" Simcha said, rising so abruptly that the table tottered and the chess pieces slid to the floor. He stamped out of the room.

Vassily heard the boy's feet on the stairs and the reverberations from the slamming of the outside door. He threw back his head and roared with laughter.

*A*fter that day they did not see each other for quite a while. Simcha avoided the places where they were accustomed to meet. He did not visit their favorite coffeehouse on the Fontanka Canal, did not stroll along their preferred stretch of riverbank or go to the Saturday-night poetry readings at the Blue Lantern. He was as angry as though Vassily had spit upon his family. What upset him most was that partly Vassily was right. There was an edge of arrogant paternalism in Fedotov's reforms, a basic assumption that peasants, being too backward or too stupid to think for themselves, needed a benevolent master to manage their lives. Still, Simcha thought defensively, Fedotov and Pyotr Voronov were well ahead of other landowners in what they wanted for their people. There it was again—"their" people, as though, as Vassily had said, peasants remained the possessions of their landlords despite the 1861 Emancipation Act.

Every day when Simcha went to work in the dank cellar where he churned out articles to reflect the current party line, and then took his turn setting the type and running the crude hand press, he half feared, half hoped that Vassily would appear with a grin on his face and an apology on his lips. But he didn't come. So be it, he thought, hurt. If Vassily didn't want to be his friend, he would find others who did!

It was during the period of estrangement from Vassily that Simcha met a young woman so fiery and flamboyant that even her frizzy brown hair seemed to vibrate with electrical impulses. For a long time before they ever spoke he had noticed her—how could he not?—at weekly party meetings, usually surrounded by two or three pale youths with pimply cheeks and shabby coats. As they seemed always to come and go as a group, he had never had the opportunity to get to know her, but he kept hoping that her flirtatious eye would someday settle upon him; just in case, he took special care on meeting nights to brush his coat and clean the printer's ink from under his nails.

On a particular hot evening in June, she wore a thin embroidered blouse and a dark red skirt daringly hiked up to midcalf in the style of peasant women who pin their hems to keep them clear of the dirt while they work in the fields. In the same peasant style, her wiry hair was bound back in a flowered scarf tied at the back of her neck. Simcha could scarcely take his eyes off her. The trim ankles alone were enough to turn a man's head. When he looked up, it was to see a pair of bright gray eyes laughing at him from behind glinting spectacles. He blushed furiously.

The meeting seemed endless that night, the speaker excruciatingly doctrinaire, the burned-out house on the outskirts of the city airless. When the meeting concluded at long last, she walked boldly up to him and stuck out her hand. "I'm Vera. Who are you?"

"Semyon," he stuttered. "Semyon Mandelkern."

"You're not supposed to use your right name, silly!" she laughed. "How old are you?"

"Eighteen," he said, exaggerating by two years.

"I'm twenty." Vera was twenty-one. "You write all those stirring proclamations, don't you?"

"Me and some others," he said modestly. He could think of nothing further to say, and they stood looking at each other in silence.

"Well, good night, then, Semyon. I'll see you around."

"Wait!"

"Yes?" she half turned toward him.

"Would you like to go for coffee?" he asked shyly.

"Can't. The boys"—she nodded toward three young men standing at the door—"are waiting to walk me home." But she didn't move toward them.

"I could use some help running the press tomorrow. We've got a big run of leaflets to get out."

She surveyed him carefully, hands on hips. What she saw apparently satisfied her. "All right."

*V*assily had not terminated their relationship as Simcha had feared. Rather, he was too busy to socialize, for Azev had finally given him his chance. And what a chance it was! He was told that he had been chosen to assassinate Minister Stolypin, who, next to the tsar, was the most powerful person in all Russia. He had been given the authority by Azev to call upon the assistance of anyone he chose and had been guaranteed full access to the weapons arsenal and bomb-making laboratories of the S.R. The date and the time of execution were left to his discretion.

For a month that summer, Vassily trailed his victim, studying his habits, his vulnerabilities, and his personality. It was very easy and at the same time, incredibly difficult—easy in that Stolypin disdained to surround himself with bodyguards, difficult because the man was flat and dull, rather like a blank page. A tall, white-haired man who carried himself with exaggerated rigidity, Stolypin seemed devoid of emotions. If he had vices, they were carefully concealed. Vassily guessed rather than knew that if Stolypin had personal attachments, they must be only to tsar, wife, and children. Although he socialized with the well-born and powerful of St. Petersburg, he had no discernible friends, no mistress, not even a close relative.

Vassily studied the house the Stolypins occupied. It was modest by the lavish standards of St. Petersburg society, a three-story wood and plaster structure with wide second-story balconies flanking a portico. A cobbled drive made a semicircle in front of the house, allowing for visitors to dismount at the front door. Terraced flower beds in back of the house sloped down to the River Neva. If the house was under guard, it was not apparent, although it was always possible that the gardeners and the housemen were employees of the secret police. The minister was punctilious. He left for his offices at seven o'clock each morning and was always home by four-thirty in the afternoon. He spent evenings, when there were no diplomatic functions to attend, working in his study at the back of the house. He took tea every evening at five o'clock in the front parlor with his wife and children. It was all regular as clockwork.

By August twenty-first, Vassily's preparations were complete. His plan was simple. He, Soloviev, and Kresky, dressed in policemen's uniforms, would drive up to Stolypin's front door in a carriage of the plain black variety favored by the police. They would boldly dismount as though they were visitors with legitimate business with the minister. If they were intercepted, Vassily had concocted a story about checking on a rumored assassination plot. If they were not, Vassily would immediately arm the powerful bomb he carried in a briefcase and hurl it with all his might through the window of the ground-level parlor. The bomb was equipped with a sophisticated delayed-action fuse that would hopefully give the conspirators time to jump into the waiting vehicle and speed away before the explosion.

Vassily and the two other men had gone over the plan many times and foresaw no problems. There was little that could go wrong, the plan being both simple and straightforward.

Shortly after five o'clock on the appointed day, the three S.R. men, convincingly disguised, stepped down from their carriage. One of them carried an official police briefcase. They were not challenged. Only one detail was different from what they expected. Instead of being in the parlor taking tea with their parents, the children, a small boy and an older girl, were playing some sort of game on the balcony. As the carriage rolled up the driveway, the children looked up from their game and waved. To show them a friendly face, Vassily raised his hand and grinned back.

Soloviev nudged him. "There's something wrong. Stolypin may not be home."

"We'd better postpone," Kresky echoed.

Vassily already had his hand on the bomb. He had imagined the scene a hundred times, and he knew his part letter-perfectly. Stolypin *was* home they had seen him turn into his driveway at four-thirty as usual. Postponement was out of the question because the minister was scheduled to leave the next day for his dacha on the Baltic.

Kresky was tugging at Vassily's sleeve. Soloviev already had his foot on the carriage step.

"No!" Vassily cried to his comrades. *"Now!"*

He lobbed the bomb through the parlor window. There was the crash of shattering glass. If the timing mechanism worked as it should, the conspirators had thirty seconds to get out of range of the explosion. Vassily raced down the driveway, his eyes sweeping the grounds for someplace to shelter. The horses had bolted with the noise of splintering window glass. The other two were not behind him. He turned his head to look back. Kresky had slipped on the cobbles and Soloviev was stooped, trying to drag him to his feet. Fool! Vassily thought; time was running out and the two of them would blow up together! Vassily dived into the shrubbery at a distance he deemed safe from the anticipated blast. After it was all over, there would be great confusion, and he would be able to slip out the gate and lose himself in the streets beyond.

The bomb worked exactly as planned. There was a tremendous blast, and the whole front of the house disintegrated before Vassily's eyes. He was close enough to feel a stabbing pain in his eardrums, close enough, too, to see the surprised look on the faces of the children as the balcony slid into the driveway below. They disappeared at once, buried in the rubble of the collapsing house. Anyone sitting in the ground-floor parlor had to be dead. Peering through a thick cloud of dust, Vassily saw no sign of Kresky and Soloviev, but considering their proximity to the explosion, unless they had wings, they were now just minuscule bits of flesh and bone. A large crowd of people—where had they all come from!—were screaming and running every which way. It was time for Vassily to make his escape. Turning for one last look at what he had wrought, he stood for several long seconds, glorying in his handiwork. But then—? It could not be! One of the men who had come running from the rear of the house was tall and white-haired. Already he was digging frantically through the rubble to free the bodies of the children.

Failed, then! He had failed! Vassily had to fight the urge to run back and fall upon the minister, to beat his head bloody upon the stones. Others had died, the two S.R. men, of course, and servants were carrying bodies from the damaged house; the two children were under mounds of stone and plaster and wood. But Stolypin lived! It wasn't right!

Telling Marta about it later in his room, Vassily wept for his failed mission. Looking to her for comfort, he said, "It wasn't my fault, was it, Marta? Was it?"

Her large dark eyes looked wet. *You shouldn't have hurt the children, Vassily.*

"It wasn't my fault!"

You'll pay for that, you know.

"Shut up!" he shouted, raising a hand to strike her.

The outlines of Marta's body shimmered and blurred, and even as he watched in horror, she slowly dissolved before his eyes.

Chapter 52

*B*y the time the *Darmstadt* docked in New York harbor, Dvoreh had been en route from Polotsk for over four weeks. Chaim had sent the *shifskart* on the Hamburg-America Steamship Line, steerage, for the fare was dear. With the precious exit papers (obtained for her by *Gospodin* Fedotov from Police Chief Morozov), steamship ticket, and a ten-ruble banknote in her pocketbook, Dvoreh had traveled alone by train from Polotsk to St. Petersburg. Simcha had met her at the Finlandia Station to help her transfer to the emigrant train that would deliver her, after several days' travel, to the shipping line's *Auswanderer-Hallen*, the point of embarkation situated in the suburbs of Hamburg.

For a change, Simcha had been quite nice, although he could not refrain from sharing his views of America. What he'd said hadn't mattered a great deal to Dvoreh since she was accustomed to discounting his views.

"But, of course, you are not going with any illusions, are you? You are leaving because of Lev," he had added abruptly.

Her eyes became teary.

Awkward, boyish, Simcha had put an arm around her shoulders. "Come on, Dvoreh, there's four hours before your train for Hamburg leaves. Let me show you the sights and buy you some supper at the Blue Lantern!"

Later that night, squeezed upright on a bench between two other women within the confines of the Hamburg Line's special railroad car, Dvoreh had plenty of time to reflect on her decision to leave Lev. Many a frantic letter had come from Riga, Lev promising to work things out and begging her to return. She had to admit that her resolve had faltered under that barrage of letters. And then he had come to Polotsk, and she had faced the full realization of what a separation from him would cost her. With his arms clasping her to him, she had been ready to capitulate until he said, "We will have to live with Mammeh only until Reuben finishes at the university—" She had known, then, that nothing had been resolved.

Later when they parted he wept, and her own cheeks were wet when she said, "I do love you, Lev, but we will never be happy in Riga. When Reuben and your sisters take their rightful turns in caring for your mother, then you will come to me in San Francisco. I will wait for you, I promise."

The train journey to Hamburg was very wearing. The women had been segregated in a car separate from that occupied by single men, husbands, and male children. At night they had to sleep sitting upright on the narrow benches or else lay on the floor amid the baggage. The only food available was what they had had the foresight to bring with them. Dvoreh was grateful that Simcha had had a basket of food and a bottle of water prepared for her to take with her from the restaurant where he had bought their supper, otherwise she would have had either to depend on the generosity of others or to have gone hungry and thirsty.

From time to time the train was shunted to a siding while other cars carrying emigrants from Austria, Hungary, and Bohemia were added. Since the journey was anything but direct, it took several days to reach Veddel, where they would be processed and await passage. In this embarkation center as large as a village, the Hamburg-America Steamship Line housed and fed the steerage passengers, medically examined them, fumigated their persons and baggage, and interrogated them for the official passenger lists. It was all most confusing. Some of the emigrants had to wait as long as three weeks for their assigned ship to leave, but Dvoreh was lucky. The *Darmstadt* was on its way two days after she reached Hamburg.

The ship sailed with nine hundred passengers, three hundred fifty in comfortable second-class and luxurious first-class accommodations, the rest in steerage in the lower parts of the ship. For passengers traveling alone, dormitories had been set up, narrow bunks stacked in double tiers around the sides of whitewashed rooms. Meals—tepid soup, boiled potatoes, herring, and black bread mostly—were shared out around a table in those same quarters. Those passengers in "married accommodations" were scarcely better off than those in the dormitories, the cabins cramped and airless. For the two weeks required for the crossing they all had much to endure.

But all that was behind her now, Dvoreh thought as the *Darmstadt* came within sight of land: the seasickness, the discomfort of being too close to too many other unwashed bodies, the bad food, the inevitable quarrels, all behind her! Soon her darling cousin Moishe would claim her, and she would be on her way to Chaya Leya and Chaim in California.

The last meal of stale bread, rancid butter, and thin, lukewarm coffee had been passed out at dawn. As a parting gift, the Hamburg-America Line had given each steerage passenger an orange, the only piece of fruit any of them had seen during the entire voyage. Like everyone else, Dvoreh had been too excited to eat and had stuffed the orange into her handbag. She had waited in line for a turn at the sink in the women's washroom so that she could wash herself in cold saltwater before putting on the fresh clothing she'd saved for her arrival. She had tied her suitcase securely with rope and checked her pocketbook to be sure she had her ten-ruble note and the piece of paper with Moishe's address on it. There was nothing further to do then except to find a place on deck from which she could watch for New York to come into view.

By midmorning the liner had moved into the Upper Bay. On the left rose the Statue of Liberty and ahead was the soaring skyline of the city. Immigration officials had come aboard earlier to process the first- and second-class passengers who would be free to disembark as soon as the ship docked. Those in steerage would be taken by ferry to Ellis Island for processing. Even now they could see the outlines of a sprawling building that covered most of the land space of that small island.

Ellis Island! The name struck terror into the heart of immigrants! On "The Isle of Tears" they would be judged, and their fate would be sealed. The majority would be admitted, but some would be detained until they could be sent back to the point of embarkation. The thought was enough to send chills chasing along the sturdiest spine.

On the ferry later Dvoreh lugged her heavy suitcase to a place near the rail. With no room to pack it, she was wearing the heavy coat Papa had made her, and was suffering from the heat of a late summer morning. It was somewhat cooler while the boat was moving. Immigration officers had separated the passengers into groups of thirty, the number assigned the group pinned securely to each person's coat. When they reached Ellis Island they were taken off the ferry in order, by group. Dvoreh's group—thirty-seven—stood in line for an hour or more, waiting for their number to be called. They had had neither food nor water for many hours, there were no toilet facilities, no place to sit down, and no shelter from the strong overhead sun. Dvoreh was finally forced to carry her coat. She was glad that she had saved her orange from breakfast. She decided to savor the thought of its sweet juiciness for a little while before eating it. There was no way of telling how much longer they would have to wait.

Ahead of Dvoreh in the line was a stout, perspiring woman whom she knew well from the voyage. She had had the bunk next to Dvoreh's and had kept everyone awake with her moaning and complaining. At mealtimes she had grabbed the largest slab of bread, the best piece of herring. She had elbowed her way to the front of lavatory lines and refused to hurry at the sinks. A thoughtless and thoroughly unpleasant person. Now she began to cry, the fat tears making streaks down her flushed cheeks and plopping onto the bosom of a shirtwaist that became limper by the moment. "Oh, oh, oh!" the woman whimpered. "I just know they'll send me back! And what will I do then? I sold everything to pay for my passage!" She wrung her hands. "What shall I do? What shall I do?"

"You don't know that they'll send you back," Dvoreh said reasonably. "Why do you think they'd want to?"

"Because—" she sobbed, "because—there's no one to claim me!"

"What do you mean? Don't you have a husband or someone to guarantee you?"

The woman shook her head. "Just before I left he wrote me—that he was leaving me—for someone younger—and I decided to come anyway—because there was nothing for me in Kishinev! But now the Immigration will know I'm alone—and what will I do? What will I do?"

There was something enormously pitiable about the woman, so alone, so frightened. Dvoreh whispered fiercely, "You'll stop crying is what you'll do. And you'll tell the Immigration that you have a husband. And they'll find him and make him do right by you! He can't just abandon you!"

The woman looked up at Dvoreh with reddened eyes. "Do you think so?"

"Yes, I think so. Only you mustn't act like such a scared rabbit!"

"Yes, I know you're right— If only I didn't feel so faint! I'm absolutely famished. And so thirsty, I know I'll collapse!"

Dvoreh sighed and extracted the orange from her bag. "Here!" She thrust the fruit into the woman's hand. "Suck on this!"

It was a relief to Dvoreh when her group was shepherded down the gangplank. She had not yet found her land legs, and she stumbled a little on the firm ground. Just ahead was a massive building of red brick trimmed with limestone, four magnificent towers reaching into the hot blue sky. The immigrants moved up the walkway, entered the building, and were swept in a mass up a steep flight of stairs to the huge registry hall. Despite the size and loftiness of the room, the noise was incredible, people talking in every imaginable language, children crying, and uniformed officials shouting names and instructions in various tongues. The room was a maze of passageways defined by waist-high metal pipes, and the passengers from the *Darmstadt*, funneled into one of these, were hurried along in single file by guards. At the end of the passage stood a blue-uniformed official, a doctor, who watched sharply as the immigrants moved toward him. Dvoreh and the others were not aware that this was their first test in the new land. If the doctor perceived that a person's breathing was labored, he chalked an "H" on his back (for possible heart disease), an "L" for lameness, an "X" for mental defects, and so on. As the line snaked past the first doctor, a second physician sharply eyed the immigrant for telltale signs of tuberculosis, leprosy, or skin diseases.

At the third turn of the line was the most dreaded examination, in which the under part of the eyelid was turned outward with a buttonhook while a physician looked for telltale signs of trachoma, an eye disease for which a person was deported without question. Her heart pounding in her chest, Dvoreh watched some of her shipmates branded with the terrifying chalk marks and herded into a screened pen to be held for more detailed medical evaluation. The weepy fat woman whose husband had left her was still beside her, however, at the next phase of examination, interrogation by the Immigration inspectors.

They sat on uncomfortable wooden benches for a long time, periodically moving along as the line progressed. Dvoreh rehearsed with the fat woman what she should say if asked about her errant husband.

She was hot and perspiring, her mouth dry, partly from anxiety and partly from thirst. She wondered why she had been stupid enough to give her orange to the ungrateful, complaining woman who hadn't even said thank you for it! She licked her lips, imagining the sweetness of orange juice trickling into her mouth. How could she have deprived herself of that!

It was midafternoon before those who remained from Dvoreh's group had moved into the last of the benches before the desk of the inspector and his interpreter. The fat woman, wet with sweat and chewing on her fingernails, went first. Dvoreh leaned forward, hoping to hear the questions, but she was not close enough. She could see that the woman seemed at the edge of breakdown. Her interrogation took a very long time, and from the stern looks of the official, it didn't look good for her. He was peering at her and tapping the side of his nose with his eyeglasses. Finally, though, he leaned back in his chair. The interpreter was handing the woman a landing card! Without so much as a backward glance at Dvoreh, she rushed off.

The immigration officer stumbled over Dvoreh's name but did not falter in his queries, which were translated with equal speed.

"What work do you do?"

"Saleslady in a department store, sir."

"Do you have a job waiting for you?"

"No, sir."

"Who paid for your passage?"

"My brother in California, your honor. Chaim Mandelkern."

"Is anyone meeting you?"

"My cousin. Moishe Fleischman."

"Where are you going?"

"To San Francisco, if it please your honor."

"How much money do you have?"

"Ten rubles."

"Show it to me."

Dvoreh fumbled in her pocketbook and withdrew the bank note.

"Where did you get it?"

"I earned it, working."

"Can you read and write?"

"Yes, sir."

The official looked her hard in the eye for a moment and then nodded curtly. The interpreter gave her a genuinely warm smile and said, "Welcome to the United States—" he consulted the landing card that the official had stamped and handed to him "—Miss Deborah Mendel Kern."

Dvoreh pushed open the big swinging doors that led to the outside room where relatives awaited the arrivals. Moishe and Aunt Yenta were both standing there. She almost collapsed in Aunt Yenta's arms.

*H*erschel and Chaya Leya's two hundred dollars evaporated like steam from the teakettle that perpetually simmered on the kitchen stove. And Berel and Soreh's seventy-five, and Manya's one hundred forty, and all the smaller amounts that people who knew and trusted Chaim had dug deep to find. It would be years before any of them saw their money again. It was especially hard for Chaya Leya and Herschel, who were dogged that year by bad luck. First Herschel's horse had broken a leg and had to be destroyed. Then unexpected complications with the delivery of the new baby had required the services of a doctor. Afterwards Chaya Leya needed magnifying glasses in order to continue with the exceedingly close work of sewing bugle beads on evening dresses. When Chaya Leya tried to save on coal during the coldest part of the winter, baby Becky developed croup and Hannah and Herschel deep chest colds. Chaya Leya's teapot savings were quickly exhausted. To her credit, she did not throw up to Herschel his extravagant gesture in loaning their bankroll to Chaim.

Chaim had used the loans to pay off creditors. Rosalie was against it. "The bank told you that if you declare bankruptcy, you aren't liable for debts. Then you can use the money to make a new start."

"I no understand," Chaim said.

"You *don't* understand," Rosalie corrected him.

"I just—I am just poor immigrant sailor. Seem to me, I owe people money, I pay it, *then* I borrow money from bank, start new business."

"You really are a greenhorn!" Rosalie said bitterly. "That's not the way we do business in America!"

"It say in Torah, righteous man pay his debts." Chaim was unyielding on this point.

Most days Chaim left the tiny apartment in the early mornings to look for work. There wasn't much in that time of deep economic depression. He took any job that was offered—manual labor on construction sites, stevedoring, once even delivering handbills for a concert. Evenings he plied his tailoring trade, mostly alteration work given him by Rosalie's friends. Unaccountably Rosalie liked this least of all, regarding it as "made" work and charity.

Chaim said mildly, "It not charity if customer get something for his money. They no—they cannot—get work so cheap other place."

"Don't you know that they give you work only because it makes them feel good?" Rosalie sniffed. "They can feel like they're better than us."

"Well, better *off* anyway." He grinned. Infuriated, she left the room, slamming the door behind her.

Chaim could not be hard on Rosalie. She had taken the first job of her life, typewriting and filing for Hershkowitz the lawyer, and she was finding it hard. She hated the dark rooms above a grocery store where they now lived. She hated the borrowed money from Hy's immigrant friends and his sister. She hated his working side by side with Chinese on the docks and with Irish ruffians on the building sites. Most of all she hated the pity of friends who kept up with her these days only because the name Riskin had once meant something in Sacramento.

Looking into Rosalie's eyes Chaim felt like a criminal. Every day he walked past the store that had once been theirs. For a long time it was empty, the big plate-glass window that he had installed reflecting empty sunshine, the bright sign, RISKIN'S GENTLEMAN'S STORE, beginning to tarnish. He could no more forgive himself for losing the store and the house than Rosalie could. How had it gone so wrong when all he had wanted was to gain Rosalie's respect! He shouldn't have been in such a hurry! His mistake had been in thinking that if you understood clothing, you understood business. He should have taken time to learn about banks and investments, business loans and mortgages—and stock markets that could "crash" in faraway New York and leave him penniless in Sacramento, California!

The business failure wasn't the only cause of Rosalie's discontent, only the handiest post on which to hang it. She found fault with his clothes, his speech, even with his body from which she withdrew to the opposite side of the marriage bed. The issue might appear to be money and status, but even in the earliest months of marriage Rosalie had been critical, restless, and dissatisfied.

Chaim could not truly say that problems with his wife had driven him to the relationship with Manya Aksakova. He had not been looking for anyone. Meeting Manya in the waterfront bar in Frisco, where he had gone in hope of hearing something about the *Oceania*, was accidental. These days, guilt, and the fear that Rosalie would find out about Manya, only added to the tension that shimmered between them like a taut electrical line.

It had promised so much, his marriage. Rosalie was crisp, pretty, American. He had been attracted to her the first time he saw her at the shelter where he had come for help. He had wanted her. It would not have mattered if she were poor, if she came from an inconsequential family, even if she were not of his faith. But none of those things had been the case, and even though the courtship had been rushed, Mammeh and Papa would have approved the match. So what was there to do if it was not working out? Mammeh would have said that a person should look well how he makes his bed, because he's going to have to sleep in it a long time!

It was not in Chaim's nature to dwell on problems. His mind was filled with the day by day challenge of making a living, and he was sustained by dreams of reopening Riskin's more successful, more resplendent than ever before. He pictured an emporium providing hand-tailored suits (he could duplicate anything made in New York or London!), custom shirts, and fine leather shoes. He had walked the length of Post Street in San Francisco, going into the finest haberdasheries, observing the styles, feeling the textures of garments between his fingers, making mental calculations of cost and markup. He knew he could do it better.

It was a blow when Chaim saw the sign come down from over their store, new lettering applied to the windows. He had always thought to reopen Riskin's, it never having occurred to him that someone else could move in. When Robertson and Kline leased the premises, the shock was almost as great as the initial loss.

Rosalie was devastated. She had lost everything—her parents, the house where she had been raised, the prosperous establishment where she had spent part of her childhood playing "store" with empty boxes in the back room, and the status of being the Riskin heir. All she had was pride, and it was that alone which enabled her to rise above the pity of acquaintances who whispered to each other that Rosalie Riskin should have known better than to marry a Russian newcomer, no matter how flashing his eyes or how broad his shoulders!

It was a pity that Chaim did not recognize the sense of loss and deep loneliness beneath the pride. Preoccupied with his own losses, he was completely unaware of how he failed his wife.

In time Chaim's dream of a new business enterprise centered on a property located adjacent to the elegant Travelers' Hotel. He dragged a reluctant Rosalie to see it, and even she had had to agree that the location was perfect. It was the first time in a long while that Chaim had seen her eyes brighten with anything other than tears or malice. They scraped together enough money to give the landlord a deposit to hold the property while they tried to negotiate a business loan.

At the bank, Chaim met with Mr. Alcott, the assistant manager. Rosalie had considered accompanying Chaim to the bank. His English was adequate to the task but his accent might prejudice the outcome of the meeting. Still, it would look bad for a businessman to appear to depend on a woman, she thought, and they decided that Hy should go by himself.

Chaim explained plans for a chic new shop clearly and persuasively,

laying a rough sketch of the proposed remodeling on the desk between himself and Alcott, and concluding by handing him an estimate of financing
requirements. Rosalie had worked out the figures, and the ledger sheet was
in her neat, precise hand. They were asking to borrow eighty percent of the
total outlay, the remainder to come from investors and from their own
assets.

Mr. Alcott tapped his jaw with a long, impatient finger. "I see you
have everything worked out here," he said.

"Yes," Chaim said eagerly. "All I need is money. You loan at two
percent annual, I think, simple interest."

"Well, yes, the bank does—to good credit risks."

"What means that? I am good credit. I owe no money. No man say I
don't pay what I owe."

"Well, that's true, Mr. Mandel," Mr. Alcott said gravely, "but your
last business did fail, after all."

Chaim half rose from his chair. "Not business what failed, Mister.
Times hard and whole country in depression. Bank failed me! If bank waited
a little—! How could I pay right away? No business had money then!"

Mr. Alcott cleared his throat. "That's not strictly true, Mr. Mandel.
Yours was not the only loan we handled, but yours was one of the few
businesses that defaulted. But we are not talking of the past, are we?"

"I'm glad not," Chaim said, sitting back in his chair and making an
effort to smile. "I come make bank an offer—is that how you say? I need
five thousand dollars open a store next door hotel. The bank make two
percent on money."

"Or we could lose our investment."

Chaim understood that the serious negotiations had begun. He said,
"All right. It's 'cutting close'—I say right? you understand?—maybe we manage on forty-eight hundred."

"Well, I don't know," the assistant manager said, a slight smile on his
thin, colorless lips.

"With two percent interest quarterly."

Mr. Alcott shrugged.

Chaim amended quickly, "*Three* percent interest—one more than usual
rate. Cover any 'risk' to bank!"

"And what security do you have to offer?"

Chaim said quickly, "Good name! Riskin's been here over fifty years!"

Alcott smiled thinly. "If you fail, we can't foreclose on a name!"

"Best business deals built on trust."

"Well, Mr. Mandel, I'll have to discuss your proposition with the bank
president. Why don't you come back in a few days—say, a week from tomorrow?"

"Let me see him now," Chaim said. "Let me explain—myself explain. He see how good this can be!"

"That's not how it's done." Mr. Alcott was patronizing. "Come back next week, and I'll give you the decision." His voice was as smooth and empty as his face.

Chaim was reluctant to leave things so indefinite, but Mr. Alcott had risen from the desk and held out a cool, dry hand. "Good-bye," he said. "A week from tomorrow at two o'clock?"

He had been dismissed. Dammit, dammit, he thought. The owner of the property might not wait, might rent the desirable location to someone else. He had lost Rosalie's store to this same bank. He should not have come here. There were other banks—

Mr. Alcott had already turned away.

Feeling impotent, Chaim murmured, "Thank you. I come back. You try, please."

Chaim and Rosalie were nervous. They went back time and again to look at the space. It was perfect. Rosalie checked all the figures again—one thousand five hundred dollars for minor remodeling, thirty-five hundred for the smallest inventory they could start with, two hundred for various city and county fees and for advertising, the rest to be put aside for emergencies. They would barely squeak by. At night they lay side by side, not touching but going through a list of possible investors, figuring options, talking business.

A week later Chaim returned to see Mr. Alcott. "I'm sorry," that gentleman said after a cursory handshake, "but we decided not to go ahead with your request. We had to consider your business history," Mr. Alcott said, rubbing his nose, "and your lack of experience. Maybe you had better wait until you've been in this country a little longer, Mr. Mandel."

The second bank concurred. And the third. As with the original store, Chaim was forced to watch someone else lease the shop next to the hotel. Rosalie was furious, perhaps less with the bankers than with Chaim. Surely, she thought, he could not have presented their case well, could not have adequately explained the drawings and the figures she had so meticulously drawn up. He had to have botched it!

Although she managed to bite back the words, Chaim knew what Rosalie thought, and he smarted under her unspoken criticism. They were careful not to argue these days. There had been arguments in the past, bad ones, but now there was so much anger on both sides that neither dared risk further confrontation.

"If only *I* were the man in the family," Rosalie had said one time, "things would be different!"

"Yes? Well, if you treating me always like ignorant nobody, I never be man to you, Raizel!" With heavy emotion, Chaim's English suffered a relapse.

"And don't call me Raizel! I'm not one of your shtetl girls!"

"If you wass, you know how to be wife!"

Stung, Rosalie retorted, "And if you were a real man, you could give me a baby!"

"Maybe nobody telling you, you haff to make luff to make babies!"

"I wish I'd never laid eyes on you! I hate you!" Rosalie had burst into tears. "You—you greenhorn!"

"Better greenhorn than cold bitch!"

It was better, Chaim reflected, that they not hurt one another that way again. Each had taken his own unspoken anger and retreated to a neutral corner. Conversation, never rich between them, had dried up, and in their marriage bed sometimes Chaim could not perform. About that, Rosalie's feelings were complicated, a mixture of rage that Hy could not give her a child, and relief that she would not often have to endure his lovemaking.

After the fiasco at the bank, Chaim decided to invest in a horse and secondhand wagon, cheap overalls, bandannas, boots, and straw hats, and to peddle these goods at outlying farms in the delta and in the northern farming communities around the Yuba River. He did not talk it over with Rosalie first, and when she heard of his plans, she was outraged.

Peddling had been Berel Levy's idea. It was on a Sunday afternoon during one of Chaim's frequent visits to San Francisco. Chaya Leya and Soreh Levy had cleaned up the dishes after a substantial Sunday dinner and put the children, Chaya Leya's Hannah and Becky and Soreh's Isaac, down for naps. With Chaya Leya's good roast chicken and potato *kugel* under his belt and the prospect of being with Manya yet ahead of him, Chaim was relaxed. He enjoyed a solitary cigar—neither Berel nor Herschel smoked—and sleepily watched the smoke curl toward the ceiling.

Chaim had been thinking about later pleasures and not his business problems, so he was startled when Berel said, "Look, Chaim, your father was not too proud to strap his sewing machine to his back and go from village to village. From his peddling, he built a business. The farmers here aren't so different from those in the old country. They need clothes and things they can't always go to the city to buy. Why not take the merchandise to them?"

"Because Rosalie would die of shame."

Chaya Leya smiled thinly over her sewing. These days she always seemed to have a dress and some saucers full of beads in front of her. "Rosalie already dies of shame when you work with the Chinese unloading the ships," she pointed out.

Soreh Levy added, "Berel talks always of how you worked like a *mujik* in Brodsky's sugar mill. That was so high class?" Soreh had become plumper than ever since Isaac's birth and her jowls jiggled when she spoke.

"I was younger then, and alone. I had no one to think of but myself. Rosalie is proud."

Herschel said wryly, "Shame is only in your mind. Earning a living honestly—what can be shameful?"

Chaya Leya leaned across the table and squeezed her husband's hand. "Doesn't Herschel go on the streets? Does he enjoy being a junkman? He does it for us, so that we will have a future."

"But that's different," Chaim protested. "I—well—"

Chaya Leya said sharply, "I know. Herschel doesn't have an American wife, and you do."

*T*he first day that he drove his wagon into the country, Chaim did not know what to expect. He was nervous. He had been up before dawn and on his way shortly afterward to pick up the horse and wagon kept at the livery stable on the edge of town. Rosalie had been dutiful but grim. She had risen from bed to make his coffee, but in the shadow of her chill countenance, the coffee did nothing to warm him, and he had no appetite to eat anything.

If he had been less apprehensive as he drove his wagon into the first farmyard that morning, Chaim would have been struck by the beauty of acre after acre of peach trees in the first glory of their rosy flowering. As it was, his thinking did not go beyond the problem of getting past two ferocious farm dogs that had set up a frightening clamor. His foreboding was not allayed when a stout, sour-faced woman in a faded housedress appeared at the door of the farmhouse.

"Whacha want?" she called from the door. Her voice sounded sharp and unfriendly.

Chaim gestured toward the wagon bed. "Got overalls and shirts and things to sell. Your mister home?"

"Eatin' breakfast. Climb down an' come in," she said curtly. Then noticing Chaim's wary eyes fixed on the dogs, she added, "Pussycats!" Chaim still hesitated. The woman's arm shot out and pointed toward the house. "Git!" she yelled, and for a moment Chaim thought she meant him! The dogs retreated to the porch, where they curled up in the shade under the steps.

Her husband and two farmhands were at the kitchen table with heaped plates and steaming cups of coffee in front of them. Busy with their food, only their eyes acknowledged the stranger. There was no rudeness implied. They had already done half a morning's work and were very hungry.

The farmer's wife announced loudly, "Peddler from town." She motioned for Chaim to sit beside the men.

Clearing his throat, Chaim began the spiel he had rehearsed while driving out to the country, but the men scarcely lifted their heads from their food. The woman said, "Later, Mister." She set a plate of eggs and meat, biscuits, gravy, and fried potatoes before Chaim. "Eat first," she said, pouring coffee that smelled like heaven itself.

Chaim said, "But—!"

"Aincha hongry? All men're hongry," she said.

The heavyset farmer at the head of the table looked up from his plate and grinned. "For sumthin' or t'other!"

Chaim felt warmed by the sly smile and open affection, and at that moment realized that he was indeed hungry.

After the best breakfast Chaim had ever eaten, the farmer, his wife, the two hired hands, and the dogs gathered around Chaim's wagon while he showed what he had for sale. When the farmer would have demurred, the wife nodded her head. "We'll take two pairs of them britches an' one of them stout shirts." Chaim had just learned a retailing lesson he was never to forget, about women as primary customers.

By the time Chaim had left the farm, he had sold four pairs of overalls, six workshirts, underwear, socks, and a pair of rubber boots. Not bad for his first sale! In honor of the occasion he had given each of the men a red or blue bandanna handkerchief and the wife a broad-brimmed straw hat to wear in the fields. The farmer's wife told him to come back anytime. Even if they didn't need anything, there would always be a good meal waiting for him.

Chaim found that first experience more the norm than not. Almost without exception he was gladly received, the more isolated the farmstead, the gladder the welcome. As he relaxed, he found it pleasant to drive through the beautiful countryside of northern California, fragrant and beautiful in the spring, hot but abundant in the summer, and golden before the rains of winter turned the sere hills green. He began to know what the farmers wanted and to stock merchandise accordingly. And he did his best to anticipate the unique tastes and requirements of particular customers. Soon Farmer Watkins was telling them at the grange that Hy Mandel had found him the perfect high boots for mucking out the pig yard, and Mrs. Farmer Pierce was relating how the peddler from Sacramento had brought a little silver spoon as a gift for the new baby, and young Sheldon remarked on his first four-in-hand silk tie for his wedding to the preacher's girl. The peddler from the city also offered credit so that the farmers need not wait until the harvest was sold to get the things they needed.

In return, his customers not only fed Chaim and gave him produce to carry home, they were eager to buy what he had for sale. The city was far away and farm families were not always comfortable in stores that served an urban clientele. Besides, salesmen in those city places did not always know the difference between ordinary galluses and fancy pants suspenders!

Chaim's joy in making an independent living without recourse to banks and bankers was not shared by Rosalie. She was never to reconcile herself to Chaim's going out to peddle behind a horse. It might have been in exactly this way that her father of blessed memory had made his start in life, but times were different now. The best she could say of it was that at least it was no longer necessary for Chaim to take in alterations work from her friends. And there was money every month to pay the rent.

*W*ithout the funds to continue her journey west, Dvoreh "Kern" went to work as a seamstress at the Komfort Pajama Company at a salary of three dollars a week. Not that she often received a full three dollars at the end of her eighty-hour week. There was the system of fines to contend with—fifty cents for looking out the window, twenty-five cents for giggling, fifty cents for whispering while working—plus the payment for the thread in the sewing machine and a weekly rental charge of five cents for a tiny space in which to put her coat and her lunch sack. Many weeks Dvoreh carried home less than two dollars. Out of this she paid a dollar and a half for her food and a place to sleep—actually two chairs pushed together in the front room of the cramped one-bedroom railroad flat that was home to Moishe, Lily, and their twin sons. Little wonder, then, that the coins she was saving for the rail fare to San Francisco grew with agonizing slowness.

In the adjoining building on Ludlow Street lived Moishe's parents with their four younger children. Dvoreh's Uncle Yaynkel, unable to find work in a kosher butcher shop and without enough capital to establish his own, had gone to work in the same slaughterhouse as Moishe and lamented the day he had left Russia. In Polotsk he had owned a shop, a horse and wagon, a comfortable house with a garden, even a piano. He had been able to afford to set a fine table for the *shabbes* meal and dress his wife in black silk and pearls for the High Holy Days. And look what had become of him here! Living in a filthy, rat-infested tenement house, forced to labor on the Sabbath—God should only forgive him!—his wife doing piecework to supplement what he earned, his daughter Chava working at the Triangle Shirtwaist Factory when she should be in school, ten-year-old Reuven delivering milk before dawn, and eight-year-old Zusya already an accomplished thief, stealing coal from the wagons in winter and ice in summer! *Ah klog auf Columbusen!* A curse on Columbus and his New World! Yaynkel lived for the day when he would have saved enough to take the family back to Polotsk!

Yet, in Dvoreh's eyes, all was not hardship and tragedy on Ludlow Street. There was a vigor to life on the Lower East Side. The streets provided a constantly shifting background against which high drama unfolded. One had only to watch and to listen to learn everything there was to know about living. Pushcarts crowded the main streets—Canal and Hester, crossed by Orchard, Ludlow, Essex, Norfolk, and Suffolk—their owners hawking their wares in a mixture of Russian, Polish, and Yiddish dialects interspersed with a kind of bastard English but carrying the unmistakable accents of home. One could buy almost anything on those streets: live chickens, fish, meat, pickles, produce, eggs and honey to make the Sabbath bread; children's underpants (five cents), women's stockings (six cents), men's workshirts (nine cents); glassware, pots and pans, dishes and bowls, tablecloths and curtains. Living so close together in tenement blocks—as many as four thousand people on a single street—one bumped into friends and acquaintances while shopping or just enjoying the hurly-burly of the street. Dvoreh found it endlessly entertaining.

Landsleit, a stream of people from the old country, arrived daily, adding to the excitement of life. "How are things in Minsk? Did you know Petcha, the woman who ran the dairy on the edge of town? You're related to Lame Velvel! No! Really?" There were reunions, husbands and wives, fathers and children, lovers. Both tragedies and comedies could be written about what went on.

There was no shortage of celebrations. There were weddings and bar mitzvahs, rituals associated with the births of sons, seders for Passover, masquerades for the Feast of Esther, banquets for Rosh Hashanah. As poor as the immigrants were, there was always money enough for occasions.

Of all her relatives, Dvoreh had always loved her older cousin Moishe best. Now she had also formed a warm friendship with his wife, Lily, who was still, after three years of marriage, the same friendly, apple-cheeked girl who had first met Moishe at the Henry Street Settlement House.

Always Dvoreh looked forward to the end of the week when, after working six thirteen-hour days in a row, the celebration of the Sabbath was like a party. Hurrying home on Friday afternoons, Dvoreh's mouth already watered in anticipation of Aunt Yenta's golden chicken, with its glaze of shining fat. Aunt Yenta might have to piece the table together with makeshift boards and stretch it from the kitchen into the bedroom, but the tablecloth was lace, and the candlelight as warm as it had been in Polotsk.

On other evenings, Dvoreh might attend classes in English, performances at the Yiddish theater, or visit with girls from the factory. A cloak cutter named David Persky had begun coming around to see her. Lily teased that there would soon be a wedding, but Dvoreh smilingly shook her head. David was attractive, but a promise was a promise.

The coach fare to San Francisco was $13.64. Not a great deal of money, perhaps, but eternally just beyond Dvoreh's reach. She had needed heavy lisle stockings for the winter, boots for walking to and from work in the snow, gloves. After she had been at Komfort for six months, she was given a raise of fifty cents a week; still, the coins in the old pickle jar where she kept her savings did not mount as fast as she hoped.

With spring arrived a new restlessness. Nine months already she had been in New York, almost a year since she had said good-bye to Lev, and she was beginning to despair of ever reaching California. Lev's letters were filled with sadness. Nothing had changed in his situation, nor, she thought, was it likely it ever would as long as he willingly shouldered the burden of his family by himself.

Dvoreh was thinking dark thoughts when she came home from work one unseasonably hot afternoon. She found Lily in the kitchen, rolling out *lokshen* on the kitchen table. "*Oy*, what a day! Those boys of mine are never quiet for a minute! Moishe's mother says they're just like he was! Only I've got two of them at once!"

"Where are they now?" Dvoreh asked, noticing the unaccustomed quiet in the flat. "I'll read them a story while you fix supper."

Lily shook her head. "They are next door with their *bobbeh*. She is making candies for Passover already! Oh, I almost forgot. There's a letter for you from your sister!"

Dvoreh picked up Chaya Leya's letter from the shelf above the sink and carried it into the front room to read. A crisp ten-dollar bill fell from the envelope and floated to the floor. A fortune! Dvoreh had to work three weeks to earn ten dollars! Her eye ran quickly down the sheet of paper. *My beloved sister,* she read. *I never thought it would be so long until I could send you money, but you know from my letters how it has been with us, one thing after another! Finally, though, everyone is well, and I have been lucky to have some extra work from Madame Celeste. If you have been able to save a little, too, perhaps this will be enough to buy your railroad ticket. I long to hug you to me! How many years it has been since we've seen each other, and how I've missed you! Hurry! Hurry! Your loving sister, Chaya Leya.*

Dvoreh shook the coins out of the pickle jar, counted them once, twice, three times. Even after she'd bought the new dress for Passover, there was still five dollars and eighty-seven cents in the jar. And that was not counting the ten-ruble bank note she had stubbornly kept hidden as a symbolic gesture of her pledge to bring Lev to America.

With her five and Chaya Leya's ten, she now held in her hand enough to buy a railway ticket to California!

Chapter 53

*D*voreh came a far distance and waited a long time to marry Lev Goldenburg, longer and farther than she could ever have imagined on the day of their betrothal in 1905. At that time, who could have foretold that the wedding would not be celebrated until 1912, and then take place thousands of versts from home in San Francisco? Who could have imagined that it would be Chaya Leya and Chaim standing at Dvoreh's side under the wedding canopy and not Mammeh and Papa?

Herschel could not help but think of the biblical Jacob waiting seven years for his beloved Rachel and then waiting seven years again. He said as much to Lev.

"I know this bride is the right one though!" Lev said with a smile. Glancing across the room at Dvoreh, he saw that in the time of their separation she had become even more desirable than before. The shadow of her uncertain adolescent self, so prominent when first they knew each other, had quite disappeared, replaced by a thoughtful and purposeful young woman. Had she been so beautiful in Riga, he wondered, and thought not. The intervening years had honed her in many ways.

On the morning of the wedding, Dvoreh rose from her bed with her heart overflowing with happiness. Since arriving in San Francisco, she had lived with her sister and brother-in-law, sleeping on a makeshift bed in the front room, much as she had done at Cousin Moishe's in New York. Harriet Street was a far cry from Ludlow Street, altogether quieter and cleaner, a street of blue-collar workers, most of them immigrants from a variety of European countries. Trees grew here and flowers in pots on windowsills. Sometimes, though, Dvoreh missed the color, the excitement, and the babble of Yiddish voices from the Lower East Side. Nothing ever happened on Harriet Street.

Chaya Leya, sitting on her bed, twisting the pale yellow hair of seven-year-old Hannah into a plait, heard Dvoreh's voice rising sweet and clear from the bath. Two nights ago the four of them—Dvoreh and Lev, she and Herschel—had gone to the Curran Theater, where Rudolf Friml's *Firefly* had opened. The tickets had been a kind of extra wedding present for Dvoreh from Chaya Leya. It was one of the Friml melodies that drifted through the door. Unconsciously Chaya Leya's hand tightened, and Hannah said a loud "ouch," turning to see how it happened that her mother had pulled her hair.

"Sorry," Chaya Leya murmured, planting a kiss on the little girl's neck before slipping an elastic over the end of the braid. She rose to knock on the bathroom door. "Dvoreh! You'll wake the neighbors!" she called through the door.

"I can't help it! I'm so happy!"

It was just a silly superstition, Chaya Leya thought, but there was that old saying, "Sing before breakfast, weep before dinner."

"Well, hurry up and come have some coffee and a roll!"

"Right away! I'm starved!"

Nothing must spoil Dvoreh's day, her sister thought. She had worked hard for it. She thought about Dvoreh's long days in the alterations department at the Emporium Department Store, the extra money she earned making dresses for women in the neighborhood, the way she never went anyplace that cost anything, never bought things for herself except the barest necessities. Since the day when Lev had written that he had made up his mind to leave Riga to come to her, Dvoreh had been single-minded in her determination.

Chaya Leya took stockings and underclothes from the bureau drawer for five-year-old Becky and for Jenny, who was three. She would wait to dress them until the last minute. Her mind occupied with thoughts of her sister's long courtship, she set up the ironing board and put the flatiron to heat on the stove. Neither she nor Herschel had had confidence that the long distance romance would actually lead to a wedding. Then suddenly Dvoreh had told them that Lev would be arriving within the month!

"What happened? I thought he couldn't leave his mother?" an astonished Chaya Leya had asked.

"He couldn't for the longest time! But when his younger brother dropped out of the university and eloped without a thought for anyone, Lev told Reuben he'd better find a job because he was finished supporting them all!"

Chaya Leya had eyed her sister. "You had nothing to do with that, I suppose?"

"I'd been after Lev to take a stand for years!"

He had arrived two weeks before, and Chaya Leya had to admit that he was a figure out of a Yiddish romance novel, handsome, polite, well-spoken, charming. A bookkeeper, a professional man besides—the first in the family!

Chaya Leya sipped a glass of tea while Dvoreh, who had taken to American ways, drank her coffee. It would soon be time to leave for the shul. Hopefully Chaim and Rosalie would arrive soon so that they could all go together. Berel and Soreh were to bring Lev, who had been staying in their house since his arrival.

"I miss Mammeh and Papa," Dvoreh said suddenly, pushing her breakfast aside. "Can you imagine Mammeh's sending me her pearls?" She fingered the round beads. They were smooth and warm to the touch. Memories of how they had always gleamed in the light of the Sabbath candles brought home and parents close.

"None of us has given them much pleasure, I'm afraid." Chaya Leya said pensively. "Come! We're getting too serious! Get dressed, Dvoreh! I've pressed your gown."

That morning as she stood beneath the silken *chupa*, its corner poles held by Berel, Herschel, and two family friends, Dvoreh's blue eyes were brilliant, and her face shone with joy. Lev stood close, leaning over her, his dark head bent to hers, his arm brushing her side. The women guests sighed. It was truly a romantic tale, handsome groom, lovely bride, and a courtship fraught with obstacles!

The ceremony was followed by lunch at the Mark Hopkins Hotel. Chaya Leya had shaken her head over the extravagance—the newlyweds could scarcely afford a pot to boil water! Still, she had to concede, there was something to be said for giving this particular marriage a spectacular beginning.

Toasts were drunk, wishes were made, the wedding cake was cut with ceremony. Laughing, Dvoreh fed some of her portion to her groom. Lev leaned over to kiss her. It was an incandescent moment when the bride and groom seemed alone with each other. Many of the women swallowed over lumps in their throats. In an unusual display of feeling, Rosalie Mandel reached for Chaim's hand, and a fat teardrop rolled down Soreh Levy's cheek. Sitting to the left of the bridal couple, Chaya Leya was overtaken by a sudden frisson, and she closed her eyes against the blinding happiness of her sister, praying God to keep her safe.

Herschel laid a tentative hand on his wife's arm. "What are you thinking?"

"How did you know I was thinking anything?"

He smiled.

Chaya Leya sighed. "I've had funny feelings all day. It is only nonsense—"

"What?"

"You know, Mammeh believes in the evil eye. Too much pride, too much happiness tempts the devil. Sometimes I feel the same."

"My foolish girl! God inscribes our fortunes, not the devil."

"I know that only in my head," Chaya Leya said slowly.

C haya Leya forgot her uneasiness. Good fortune followed the footsteps of the new couple. Lev found a job he liked in Kurilov's Jewish Bookstore on upper Geary Street, and Dvoreh was promoted to head alterations lady at the department store. When the flat above Herschel and Chaya Leya's fell vacant a few months after the wedding, it was claimed by Lev and Dvoreh, and everything was perfect.

It was a wonderful living arrangement. The sisters ran up and down the stairs between the flats as if it were one house, one family. When Chaya Leya baked *challah*, it was for both, and when kitchen curtains went on sale at the store, Dvoreh bought for both. Lev and Herschel got on well, and the Rosen children—Hannah, Becky, and Jenny—were spoiled shamelessly by their aunt and uncle upstairs. *Shabbes* was always at Chaya Leya's table, other meals shared casually. Berel and Soreh Levy and little Isaac were as close as relatives. On Sundays both households joined with landsmen from Minsk and Vitebsk for picnics in Golden Gate Park or, if it was warm, at the beach. When it was cold, which was likely in San Francisco, they gathered at the Rosens. There was only one thing needed to make the young Goldenburgs' lives complete, and in December Dvoreh discovered that she was pregnant.

"God is good to us," Dvoreh told her sister. "He's so ashamed of giving us a hard time at the beginning, He is trying to make it up to us!"

"That's blasphemy," Chaya Leya said.

The years since the economic recovery of 1909 had been good to everyone. Herschel, who had started out on the streets as a rags-bottles-and-sacks junkman, had foreseen that the growing population of the city would create a demand for secondhand goods. While still peddling from a wagon, he began to buy and resell used furniture.

One evening Berel remarked, "From a wagon, Herschel, you can only handle furniture a piece or two at a time, never a whole living room or bedroom suite. If you had a store, you could go to sales and pick up a whole house of furnishings to resell at a profit."

"You're right about that," Herschel said thoughtfully, "but I can't afford the rent on a store."

"You could if you had a partner. Soreh and I have been talking it over. I am tired of working for someone else. And we've been able to save a little money."

"Is that so?" Herschel asked slowly.

"Will you think about it?"

"I will."

Out of that conversation, the Fillmore Used Furniture Depot, H. Rosen and B. Levy, Proprietors, was born. It had achieved a modest two-year success when, without warning, the bottom dropped out of the economy again.

It was 1913, scarcely six years after the panic of '07. The usual gaiety of the Rosens' dining table died, and discussions grew somber. What, they asked each other helplessly, did it mean? Was there to be no stability for them in America? Things were worse by far than it had been in 1907. For the first time, there were bread lines and soup kitchens in the city.

Apologetically Mr. Kurilov cut Lev's wages at the bookstore. Business had fallen off to almost nothing. Who bought books when there wasn't enough money for food? Lev didn't mind. The absence of customers gave him more time to read, and Dvoreh had a good steady job.

She had resumed full workdays after the birth of the baby, in order to make ends meet. It tore her heart out to be away from Ruthie, but there was nothing else to do. Chaya Leya calmly absorbed the infant into her household, and the domestic life on Harriet Street went on undisturbed.

Herschel and Berel's enterprise was not lucky. Day by day, business grew worse. There were times when scarcely a customer crossed the threshold, and few who came bought. Determined to delay as long as possible the day when Herschel would be forced back to peddling and Berel to working as a cloak presser, the two families cut expenses to the bone. Despite persistent headaches that made close work torture for her, Chaya Leya again worked late into the nights over her embroidery frame, enduring the strain because she knew that her work provided the children's clothing and Hannah's violin lessons.

Soreh rented out the family's two bedrooms to roomers. She and Berel slept on a mattress in the front room and their little boy on a cot in the kitchen. From Odessa, Soreh knew the boardinghouse business well, and there was plenty of demand for beds in San Francisco, where many men came alone until they could save the money to send home to the old country for wives and children. For Soreh, taking four strangers into her flat was not a hardship. The extra work was all part of a business she enjoyed.

When Herschel came home from the store one afternoon late in August, Chaya Leya could see at a glance that it had been a bad day. He looked like an old man, bearing his worry like a garment around his thin shoulders. "I don't know how much longer we can keep the store," he said quietly.

Chaya Leya kissed him. "Sit down and rest yourself while I fix supper."

Herschel sank into a chair and closed his eyes. What was he going to do? He had not felt so vulnerable since the time he was a prisoner in Harbin. He pushed aside those thoughts. In Harbin he had almost lost everything to despair, but then was not the same as now. Now he had a family, friends, a loving wife. Resolutely he straightened and reached for the *Jewish Daily Forward*, snapping it open at the front page.

Chaya Leya was in the kitchen cutting up vegetables for a salad. For a change, the flat was quiet. Hannah was at her music lesson, Becky and Jenny playing next door at the Malones', and an hour before Dvoreh had taken the baby upstairs. Chaya Leya was worried about Herschel. He had looked so defeated lately. She, too, remembered Harbin. She would ask Madame Celeste for more work. If they could weather the next few months, things would improve. The new governor, Hiram Johnson, had been elected on the promise that better times lay just ahead. If they could just hold on to the store.

Chaya Leya was setting the table in the kitchen when Herschel came to the door, waving the newspaper. "Tsarist times have come to America. The police are killing peasants."

"What are you talking about?" Chaya Leya asked, astonished.

"It says so here. Read!" He thrust the paper toward her.

Chaya Leya put down the cutlery she was holding and took the paper in her hands, scanning the article quickly. Twenty-eight hundred migrant farm workers, recruited by newspaper advertisements and handbills, had reported for work at a ranch near Wheatland, California, to pick hops. When the pickers arrived, though, jobs were available for fewer than half, and a near riot broke out as desperate men vied with one another for a place in the searing August fields. One underbid another. Organizers for the I.W.W. arrived to represent the workers, but the union men had been expected. A sheriff's posse emerged from the sheds with rifles at the ready. Frustrated and confused by the appearance of weapons, the hungry men sprang at those with guns, and the jittery sheriff's deputies began firing into the crowd. Within minutes the dust raised by the milling mob made it impossible to tell who was a worker, who a union organizer, who a sheriff's deputy or a rancher. In the ensuing melee, hundreds were injured, some to die later; four were dead on the spot. It took the National Guard to restore order.

"It's Bloody Sunday all over again."

"It's not the same," Chaya Leya said slowly. "In Russia they would have killed everyone. Here they arrested this union man, this Blackie Ford who came to talk for the workers, and took him to jail."

"You'll see, they'll hang him yet," Herschel said darkly. "Then someone'll decide it's the Jews' fault, and there will be a pogrom."

"It's not like that here," she repeated stubbornly.

"People are the same everywhere."

Chaya Leya sighed. They had brought history like a yoke with them from the old country. Herschel would not eat supper this night.

*I*n February of 1913, just before the Depression hit, Chaim had exchanged his career as peddler for that of retail merchant. His new venture was an altogether different thing from "Riskin's Gentleman's Store." This was a workingman's store, geared to the needs of farmers and to the men who worked on the docks, railroads, and construction sites. Chaim had had a large sign made for above the door: HY MANDEL'S it proclaimed in bright red and white letters. IF YOU'RE JUST PASSIN' BY, AT LEAST STOP AND SAY "HY!" Similar signs had been stuck here and there on the shoulders of the road leading into town.

The store was in Stockton, fifty miles from Sacramento, a rapidly growing river port in the heart of farming country. It was the perfect place for a workingman's store. Chaim had already signed a lease before he discussed the new venture with Rosalie.

Hurt, she had shrugged. "Do as you want. You will anyway!"

"I'm asking your advice, Rosalie," he had said, keeping his temper in check.

"Since when have you ever taken my advice? You didn't listen to me when you borrowed money on Papa's store. You didn't consult me when you took charity from my friends. You didn't ask me before you bought that awful horse and wagon and went out on the road like a common peddler. Why should you ask me now?"

Chaim sighed. Trying to talk to his wife was hopeless.

She also refused to move to Stockton. "Sacramento is my home," she said. "And besides, I have my job with Hershkowitz."

"You know you do not haff to work now I make good living."

"If it's as good as the last living you made, I'll just wait and see how it turns out."

There was no answer to that, and he turned away.

With the improvement in Chaim's fortunes, they had rented a small house in Sacramento, and Rosalie remained there, Chaim sleeping in the room behind his store during the week. More and more now when he spent time away from the business, it was in San Francisco instead of Sacramento.

By summertime, Chaim was glad that Rosalie still had the job with the lawyer Hershkowitz. The Depression was in full flower, hitting hardest the farmers who were the backbone of Chaim's business. His customers had little cash money, and Chaim, no less than Herschel and Berel, was faced with disaster. During his peddling days he had earned a reputation as the farmers' friend by extending credit. Now he was at a crossroads. He could either carry his customers or turn them away as most other businesses were doing. Because he could not find it within himself to do otherwise, he chose to give credit. Mostly he was paid faithfully, whatever the customer could afford; even a quarter a month was something. But some months what he took in did not cover the rent, and he grew desperate with fear.

When Chaim thought he would have to reverse his policy in order to keep the store, Rosalie surprised him. "Giving credit is a good plan," she said to him. "Times will get better, and the customers will stick with you. Just don't get carried away."

Chaim was so grateful for this unexpected support that he would have promised her anything. "You good woman, Raizel."

Letting the Yiddish name pass uncorrected, she explained dryly, "It's strictly a matter of business."

Although he would never have known it from her outward indifference, Rosalie had given a great deal of thought to her husband's venture. After all, she was not Morris Riskin's daughter for nothing! She had grown up around her father's store, listening to his conversations with the "drummers" who came to sell him merchandise, privy, from the time she was twelve or so, to the reasons behind her father's business decisions. If there had been a son, Morris Riskin might have relegated Rosalie to a more traditional female role, but she was the only child, and he was lonely for someone to talk to. She was always around the store after school and on Saturdays; even when he tried to send her off to play with other girls, she preferred to stay with him. Lonely, unsure of herself, Rosalie regarded the store as her home and her father as her closest friend. She had never made real friends among the girls at school.

To keep Hy's afloat, Rosalie now sold the last of the jewelry her mother had left her, which permitted Chaim to continue his credit policy. His reputation for fair and square dealing with the working people grew.

*J*t was so quiet in the bookstore that Lev Goldenburg had the opportunity to read through the stock. Kurilov's was in the old-fashioned tradition—dim, musty, its stock haphazardly placed, books on top of books in no discernible order. The exception was a special collection of books on an upper shelf. Now that Lev had found these, he no longer bothered with the others. These were volumes devoted to kabbalah, the esoteric mystic theology born among Jews of the Middle Ages and kept alive by succeeding kabbalistic schools. What Lev found in these books was difficult to comprehend, arcane, but full of the promise of deep meanings. Unable to fully understand content, he eagerly absorbed the images and symbols that were rich within the doctrines. His head swam from his reading, the very words on the pages mysterious. Wonderful ringing phrases reverberated: "the world of souls"; "cosmos of the unknowable Divine"; "creation by emanations from the Godhead"; "Descenders of the Chariot." Determined to master it, he practiced mystical meditation but was always disappointed, always unable to achieve the goal of ecstatic union with the infinite, the "Most Hidden of the Hidden." Feverishly he searched the books for help, turning to kabbalistic exercises to induce the state of mind where ascent to the Godhead might occur. These aids to contemplation made use of the letters of the alphabet, particularly those that comprise the names of God; others relied on the manipulation of number combinations. He practiced faithfully, and persevered, but still he failed.

Lev became ever more certain that in an earlier transmigration of soul he had been one of the "Masters of the Mystery." His affinity for the teachings of Isaac Luria, Abraham ben David, and Rabbi Isaac the Blind convinced him that he had sat at the feet of mystics in some earlier life. He would have liked to ask Kurilov for help, but he sensed a reluctance on the old man's part. His employer had earlier cautioned Lev against delving into mysteries he was not prepared for. "The rabbis tell us," Kurilov had said gravely, "that only one who is over forty, who is a talmudic scholar, and who is married, should risk speculations about what we cannot know."

"What is the danger?" Lev scoffed.

The elderly bookstore owner combed fingers yellowed with age through his wispy beard. "There is a talmudic story, Lev, about four eminent rabbis who, through fasting and prayer, are finally enabled to enter the celestial regions. The first looked about him and died. The second looked and went mad. The third became an apostate. Only Rabbi Akiva, who was a true saint and a holy *maven*, entered the Palace in peace and came out in peace. The point is that there are things in heaven and on earth that we are not meant to know! Leave well enough alone, my son."

Lev was somewhat chastened but could not stop. He raced to work in the mornings so that he might read—so many books, so much he did not know. He began to hate the interruptions of customers coming into the shop and was short with would-be buyers. He tried to engage some, who looked to be scholars, in discussion about things that he had read, but they looked at him strangely and turned away. Mr. Kurilov warned him about his shortcomings, and for a while, at least, Lev was more circumspect. Now that this wonderful world had opened to him, he could not afford to lose a job with access to books he could never afford to buy!

The study of kabbalah now became the focus and center of Lev's life. It explained to him as nothing else ever had the presence of evil in the world, and it provided him with amulets against the malevolence he felt to be all about him.

In growing agitation, Lev tried to talk to Dvoreh about what he was learning. But these days Dvoreh was tired from the long hours she spent at the store, and was preoccupied at home with caring for Ruthie. She paid scant attention to Lev's talk about books he had read.

As the white fogs of summer settled upon the city, Lev seemed to be more high-strung and excited than ever, and even Dvoreh had to take notice.

"Is something the matter, Lev?"

Exhausted, Dvoreh had gone to bed early in the evening, awakening some time past midnight to find Lev still awake, pacing back and forth in the living room.

"I've just figured it out!" he said, his eyes glittering. "I know now what happened at Papa's grave!"

Although Dvoreh had drawn a shawl around her when she rose from the bed, a coldness like a sudden gust of wind passed over her.

"What happened at your father's grave?"

"It was a spell, you know, Dvoreh. When my father died, he went to the lower world—you knew that, didn't you? And when we went to put the headstone on his grave, there were demons in the graveyard who put a spell on me."

Dvoreh put her hand on Lev's arm. "Come to bed, it's late, Lev."

He shook off her arm. "I realized it tonight. Because of the numbers. After Papa died, I couldn't make the numbers come out right anymore. The demons prevented me because they didn't want me finding the right combinations to reach God." Lev caught his wife's hand in his. "Oh, Dvoreh, you can't know how terrible it was for me after Papa died. I would sit in the office at the store and add up the day's receipts, but once I had the sums, I wasn't sure of them. I would have to keep adding them over and over again. Sometimes I didn't go home from the store until after dark, and then I was still worried that the numbers weren't right. Sometimes I went back to the store after supper and started again. It was the demons, you see. I know it now since I've been studying kabbalah."

"Your hands are cold. Let me make you some tea."

"Yes, that would be nice," Lev said, following Dvoreh into the kitchen and sitting at the table. "I've never told you what happened at the graveyard, did I?"

"No. No, you didn't," Dvoreh said carefully.

Waiting for the kettle to boil, Dvoreh poured some brandy into a glass and pressed it into Lev's hand.

"What's this?"

"Just a little *bromfen* to warm you and help you relax so you can sleep."

Over tea and brandy, Lev began to talk about his father, the dentist, who had speculated with the family's money and lived a lie until his death made it all clear.

Lev had fallen into a black rage when he learned the extent of his father's fecklessness. He refused even to say kaddish. Young Reuben was horrified, although Lev's mother merely shrugged, indifferent as always. Neither would Lev go to the cemetery to tend the grave, and Mrs. Goldenburg didn't seem to mind that either.

How cool and bland his mother was, hardly noticing all that Lev did for her. Every cent of his earnings went into the house for her support and Reuben's, but never once did she imply by a soft look, a touch of the hand, or a word, that her son's assumption of responsibility was anything more than her due. There were times when Lev had to grit his teeth to keep from shouting at her: "Look at me! I'm giving up my life to care for you! At least acknowledge that I exist for you!"

But if he had given in and cried out, what good would it have done? Would that smooth, immobile face that he had watched with temerity all of the years of his life have expressed shock, grief? Would those flat eyes have registered surprise even?

At year's end it was time to raise a headstone. Lev was cold in his refusal. He said that every kopeck of his savings had gone to pay his father's debts and the taxes. For all he cared, Dr. Goldenburg could lie in an unmarked grave like the pauper he was!

Lev's sisters paid for a plain small marker, but the older sister in Kiev didn't care enough to come north for the raising of the stone. If Mrs. Goldenburg was affected, it wasn't apparent. She merely told Lev she would need money for a black hat, and wordlessly he handed over the rubles.

It was a gray day when the headstone was placed. Shortly after the family arrived at the bleak Jewish cemetery on the edge of the city, it began to rain, a cold, steady downpour. Automatically Lev covered his mother's new hat with his umbrella.

As Lev stood at the foot of his father's grave, eyes riveted on the raw granite block, the rabbi's mournful voice filling his ears, he felt himself pulled out of his body and moved forward toward the grave. He could observe himself, a shadow shape advancing over wet grass, while at the same time his corporeal self stood among the little band of mourners, his arm with the umbrella rising stiffly above his mother's hat. At the head of the grave, he felt himself sinking into the ground, tasting the gritty sand in his mouth, the heavy mud sealing his eyes closed. It was—peaceful. He was where he belonged, lying next to his father.

From far off he could hear the rabbi's final blessing, and only wished that now everyone would go home and let him rest where he lay in the earth. He had been tired for so long! But it was not to be. His mother took hold of the arm that held the umbrella over her and turned away. From the quiet of the grave Lev had to smile that his mother did not notice that the real Lev was in the ground. At the same time he knew he was being pulled back to life. Slowly the sodden group moved away from the field.

Later they said that Lev had fainted in the graveyard from an excess of emotion, but he knew that that was not true. In any event, he must have caught a chill standing in the rain for so long, for he was feverish for several days afterward. In his bed he had talked excitedly about being buried in the cemetery. Mrs. Goldenburg roused herself to give him tea and broth and to put cool towels on his head. After a day or two the ravings of his delirium disappeared, and he was better. Lev could scarcely remember all that had happened. A dream he had had, perhaps.

At the end of a week Lev went back to work at the store, but he found it difficult to concentrate. Always so meticulous in his accounts, he had become inexplicably fearful that he might make a mistake. He forced himself to recheck his work numerous times and, still doubtful, anxiously asked the manager to go over the figures himself. No one could reassure Lev about his computations. Finally the store's owner found something else for him to do.

Dvoreh poured the last of the brandy into Lev's glass. "That all happened a long time ago," she said soothingly. "Your father's dying in debt was a shock to your mind. That's all."

"No, Dvoreh," Lev said sadly, "it was demons. I understand now." But the agitation was gone from his voice. The brandy had done its work, and now Dvoreh led him to bed and sleep.

Chapter 54

*R*osalie was greatly pleased when Chaim was invited to join the Stockton Merchants, Manufacturers, and Employers Association. Chaim had come home to Sacramento especially to tell her about the invitation. Tentatively at first, then with more assurance as he found her receptive, he had been talking to Rosalie about the business. Her astonishing understanding and support for his credit policy had broken down a barrier between them, and he realized how isolated he had been. Sometimes she saw things he missed. Her grasp of business possibilities was wider than his; moreover, she was quick to sense opportunities.

"Why, every important businessman in town belongs to the MMEA," she said, glowing. "It means you've been accepted!"

Chaim frowned. "I don't understand these things too good."

"Too *well*, Hy. Well, what did they do at the meeting you went to? Is it like a social club, or what?"

"They talk," Chaim said. "They talk business."

"Yes?" Rosalie prompted him.

"They talk bad about unions." Chaim was troubled.

"Well, you're not *for* them. Don't you remember the time you worked in the mill in Kiev, and that awful man came in to organize a strike, and your friend went to prison—"

"This is not same," Chaim said. "Brodsky was hard man but decent." Chaim struggled to think through what he wanted to say and to find the right words to say it. English often confounded him with its complexities. "Here, I see bosses paying wages won't feed family. I see children work to buy bread. I see people get sick, dying even, from how they work. These Wobblies say union make things better for worker."

Rosalie said, "If employers have to pay higher wages, they'll raise prices; if you're so worried about working people, do you think they'll be any better off then?"

"I not know," Chaim said uneasily. "I just not know."

Rosalie stood up and moved around the living room, unnecessarily straightening the doilies on the polished tables and wiping nonexistent spots from the ashtrays. Without looking at Chaim she said, "You—you wouldn't do anything silly, would you?"

"Silly?"

"Like speaking up for the unions at a meeting."

Chaim laughed shortly. "Who is going to listen foreigner like me?"

That fall, four hundred two members of the Stockton Merchants, Manufacturers, and Employers Association voted to keep Stockton an open-shop town. To make it stick, the MMEA asked every member to contribute money to a kitty, to be used to hire out-of-town strikebreakers if the unions proved militant. One member voted "nay."

"But why, why?" Rosalie wept when she heard. "The other businessmen will ruin you!"

Chaim lit a cigar. "My customers cannery workers, longshoremen, foundry workers, farm laborers. Big on unions. They look for union label on what they buy. Mandel's only union store in town."

"*If* the others don't run you out!"

"Besides," Chaim continued, sucking on his cigar, "is advertisement.

If Hy Mandel votes aye with four hundred, nobody care. If Hy Mandel votes nay against four hundred, tomorrow name gets in *Stockton Record* and *San Francisco Chronicle*."

"Yes, because someone's burned down the store or hit you over the head with a blackjack."

"I can take care of myself," Chaim said. "Not worry about that!"

"I'm not so sure," Rosalie said. She looked up at the ceiling for a long time. "Those are not the real reasons you voted against the MMEA, are they?"

"I, no—I don't—like people tell me what I sell, who I hire, what I pay. I don't like idea if people not agree, bring in someone beat them up. Like pogrom."

"Go on," Rosalie said. "What else don't you like?"

"Mr. Alcott from bank invite Kreisler from MMEA to Sutter Club talk about union busting. I not like that."

"A feud against bankers, is that it?"

"I hate that bastard Alcott!"

"You are not only a greenhorn," Rosalie said coldly, "you are also crazy if you think you can fight the whole business establishment."

*F*or this special dinner on a Sunday in January, Chaya Leya had saved for a month to buy a small turkey. Now it was roasting to a glistening crispness in her oven. That morning she had baked a tall chocolate layer cake to eat with the ice cream Herschel would pick up at the last minute at the sweet shop on the corner. The celebration was for Hannah, who had won the Citywide Music Competition for Children in Public Schools, the prize a year's scholarship to study violin at the San Francisco Conservatory of Music.

Chaya Leya finished arranging the celery and carrot sticks in a cut-glass dish before taking off her apron to join the company. She had heard Berel, Soreh, and Isaac come in a little while before. Just as soon as Chaim and Rosalie arrived from Stockton, they would have dinner.

Dvoreh was alone in the front room, her head against the high back of the rocking chair and her eyes closed. Chaya Leya could hear the children playing a noisy game in the bedroom.

"I thought Berel and Sorel were here. And where's Herschel?"

"The three of them walked down to the candy store to get the ice cream. Herschel is going to ask the man to pack a burlap sack and some salt around it so it will hold."

Chaya Leya nodded. "And Lev?"

"He was finishing his bath when I came downstairs with the baby." Dvoreh looked drained. "I've just put Ruthie down to sleep, and I can help you now."

"No," Chaya Leya said, smiling at her sister. "You just sit there and rest. You don't get enough of that!"

Chaya Leya took the chair near the front window and picked up her crocheting. She was frowning. Dvoreh worried her. She was looking thin and haggard, and her color was not good.

"Are you feeling all right?" Chaya Leya asked abruptly.

"Why shouldn't I be?"

"I don't know. You look sort of—I don't know, peaked."

There was a little silence. When Chaya Leya looked up from her crocheting, she saw that her sister was crying. She threw down her needlework and knelt by the side of Dvoreh's chair. "What is it?" she asked gently, her arms around her sister.

"Oh, Chaya Leya!" Dvoreh was sobbing in earnest now. "I'm pregnant again!"

Chaya Leya felt herself flinch. What a time to have another baby! They were in the midst of one of the worst depressions the country had ever known. With Lev working only a few hours a week, Dvoreh was the mainstay of the family. And Ruthie wasn't even six months old yet! What could they have been thinking of!

"Well," Chaya Leya said, swallowing hard. "Well, Dvorehleh, babies are to smile over, not to cry about!" She drew a clean handkerchief from her pocket. "Wipe your eyes before the others come back and see you crying."

Dvoreh obediently took the handkerchief but continued to sob. "I don't know how we'll manage. I can't keep burdening you with my children, but I can't pay anyone either!"

Chaya Leya rocked Dvoreh back and forth in her arms, murmuring, "Aiy, aiy, aiy" as if Dvoreh were herself a child. "I always said I wanted six, just like Maria Kutuzova!"

"But not someone else's!"

"Ah, Dvoreh, a child is a child." Chaya Leya rose to her feet. "It will all work out, you'll see."

Dvoreh blew her nose and dabbed at her eyes.

"No more tears now!"

Shakily Dvoreh stood up. "Thank you, Chaya Leya."

"I wish they'd get here already! The turkey will be overcooked." Chaya Leya went to watch by the window. "Let's not say anything about the baby just yet. It will just upset Rosalie."

"I didn't plan to." Dvoreh went into the bathroom to wash her face.

Chaya Leya sat down to wait. She waved to her neighbor, Mrs. Glass, from the front window. The train from Sacramento must be late, she thought.

A baby! The timing couldn't be worse, and yet her heart quickened a little at the thought of another little one. Mammeh said that a child was a gift from God.

Ah, here they came at last! They must have walked from the ferry building. How shabby Rosalie's coat was. Money must be short for them too. Chaim was carrying a box wrapped in fancy paper under one arm. He should not have spent money on a present for Hannah. Biting her lower lip, Chaya Leya hoped that Becky and Jenny, who were still little, would understand why it was Hannah and not they who got a present. Chaim looked up at the window and saw her. Grinning, he reached into his coat pocket and held up two other small packages for her to see. Chaya Leya smiled. They understood each other perfectly.

For today they should all put worries aside and enjoy one another. Being here together was miracle enough to celebrate, and today, besides, there was the joy of Hannah's triumph. "They're here, Dvorehleh!" she said as her sister, looking better, emerged from the bathroom. "We're going to have such a good time!"

Herschel, Berel, and Soreh returned with the ice cream—chocolate, per Hannah's request—on the heels of the newcomers from Sacramento. Lev, hearing the commotion in the hallway, came downstairs, looking elegant and smelling of after-shave lotion. There was a flurry of greetings. The San Francisco family had seen less of Chaim since the Depression had worsened, and it had been many months since Rosalie had been to the city.

"You are looking wonderful, Rosalie!" Chaya Leya said to her sister-in-law, making an effort to speak English correctly. Indeed, Rosalie did appear more animated than usual.

"Thank you, Chaya," Rosalie said coolly.

"Raizel is helping me keep books for the store," Chaim said in Yiddish, not without pride.

"A real partnership!" Herschel said heartily, also in Yiddish.

Chaya Leya, leading everyone to the dining room table, said, "Let us try to speak only English today." There was no sense in antagonizing Rosalie by making her feel an outsider.

In fact, everyone spoke the language of their adopted country passably well. Chaim, Berel, and Soreh had already received citizenship papers, Chaya Leya and Herschel would be eligible soon, Dvoreh somewhat later, and Lev had filed his declaration of intention. It was emotionally nourishing to speak the expressive languages of home and childhood when they were together, but not at Rosalie's expense.

The dinner was a feast. Afterward nine-year-old Hannah played for them the Joachim adaptation of a Paganini etude, the performance of which had won the conservatory prize. Hannah's red-blond head was bent lovingly over the violin tucked under her chin. Her hazel eyes, almost green at times, were closed, and the chiseled planes of her face already showed signs of her turning into a real beauty. Chaya Leya's breath caught sharply in her throat. At times Hannah's resemblance to poor, dead Valodya Mirov was unnerving.

When Hannah made her carefully practiced bow to the family, she shyly tucked herself into the curve of Herschel's arm. He poured a little sweet wine into a glass for her and lifted his own high. "For the next Jascha Heifetz!"

"Oh, Papa!" she giggled. "That's not possible! He's a boy!"

"To Hannah, then, who will be only herself!"

After Hannah had grown bored with adult talk and run off to play with the other children, Chaya Leya took a thick letter from the china cupboard and bore it to the table. "It came yesterday," she explained. "Shall I read it aloud?"

"Of course, yes. Read it!"

"It is in Yiddish," she said, glancing apologetically at Rosalie. "I can translate maybe."

"Don't bother," Rosalie said stiffly, rising. "I'll just go in the other room and play with the baby for a while."

Dvoreh said nervously, "Ruthie's sleeping."

"Well, I'll just go and freshen up. We have to catch a train at six."

It was an awkward moment, and just when Chaya Leya had hoped to make Rosalie feel at home.

"Go ahead, read the letter," Chaim said.

Chaya Leya took the thin sheets of paper from the envelope and began to read. There were a few brief sentences from Yoysef about the relative state of health of the household, and then Malkeh had picked up the pen and continued:

I have just returned from Dagda, where your bobbeh *and I buried my papa. God be thanked, he was not sick a day in his life! One morning he left his tea on the table, saying he was a little tired and would lie down a bit. He did not complain of pain or sickness. But when my mammeh went into the bedroom to ask him a question, he was dead.*

Chaya Leya paused in her reading, her eyes seeking Chaim's. She had known from the sharp intake of his breath that he, as well as she, was remembering the kindness of their plump, loving grandfather during the lonely days when their mother had withdrawn from the world. She had cried her fill yesterday, but Chaim needed time to come to terms.

He lived a long life. As near as we can tell, he was somewhere near eighty-four years old, in length of days a veritable Abraham! I wanted Mammeh to come stay with us in Polotsk, but she said she had made other arrangements. Your grandmother was always independent! And so, after the funeral, she sold the house and moved to Vitebsk! It seems that Uncle Zalman had asked her to come live in his house! I wouldn't be surprised if in time she marries him. After all, there is a biblical injunction about the responsibility of a brother-in-law to marry the widow of his brother, and I have always thought that Uncle Zalman had a special affection for Mammeh. Well, it is not seemly to speculate about that so soon after we buried Papa. On the other hand, Mammeh is almost eighty and Uncle Zalman must be seventy-seven or seventy-eight. Neither of them should be alone in the time that remains to them. It pleases me to think that in Uncle Zalman's house, Mammeh will have the kind of good life that Papa, he should rest in peace, could never provide for her.

I had plenty of time to spend with Mammeh in Dagda. It's been three years now since the government closed my school, and I can't seem to come to terms with it. Was it not a paradox that at the same time the ministry made it compulsory for Russian children to go to school, they closed the Jewish schools?

I spend my days now taking care of your papa and Aunt Golda, whose health is not good, and I work in my garden. Since food is not plentiful in the Gostinny Dvor, I have dug up most of the flower beds and planted them in vegetables—potatoes, carrots, and onions mostly. From time to time our friend Yevgeny Fedotov comes by to leave off a piece of beef or a duck (not kosher but we eat it anyway!) and, best of all, a tin of tea! I nurse what he brings us carefully, I miss it so terribly when we run out! He brings me books, too, from the library at Spokoinaya Zemlya. Did I ever tell you that the first time I saw that library, I wondered that anyone could possibly read all those books! Well, now I have read most of them myself and I have started over again with my favorites. Fedotov used to have a standing order with a shop in St. Petersburg to send him the new books as they were published, but now, he tells me, the shop is out of business—burned down! What foolishness! What few books there are these days are printed somewhere else.

A few weeks ago Simcha was home for a short visit. He is working in St. Petersburg, but God only knows what exactly he is doing. I ask him, but he says only that it pays enough so that he can live. He speaks a great deal of a girl he knows—everything is "Vera and I did this" and "Vera and I did that"—but actually he tells us little about her.

Chaya Leya looked up from her reading.

"Obviously, she's not Jewish," Chaim said.

I guess you have read in the newspapers about the massacre of the striking miners at the Lena Gold Fields in Siberia? That has set off another wave of strikes. The whole country is paralyzed with one strike after another. No wonder food is scarce, clothes too.

Herschel said, "I wonder how that got through the censors!"

"Maybe they're on strike too," Berel smirked.

In your last letters, my children, you beg us to come to you in America. But how can we come and leave Simcha alone here? You in America have each other. Simcha, whom I think will never leave Russia, has no one but us!

So that is the way it is with us, my dearest children. Keep each other close in your heart, and remember us who are far away. Your loving mother.

"Not exactly a cheerful letter," Dvoreh said, shaking her head.

Chaya Leya rose to get the teakettle from the stove. The letter had dampened high spirits. Rosalie had wandered back in, and Chaim was looking at his pocket watch. The children in the other room had begun to quarrel over the pieces of a puzzle and the baby to scream hungrily. Lev went to the older children, Dvoreh to pick up Ruthie.

Chaya Leya said, "I know things are hard for all of us, but not so hard as for Mammeh and Papa and Aunt Golda. Why don't we send them a package?"

Chaim nodded. "I can get wholesale shoes and shirts, underwear."

Soreh clapped her hands. "We can mail sugar and canned milk and tea. Lots of tea."

Dvoreh had come back in, holding the baby on her hip. "We have a box of books upstairs. Last month when Mr. Kurilov couldn't pay Lev, he gave him a lot of leftovers."

Warming to the subject, Chaya Leya offered, "We'll send pictures and letters from everyone, even the children. I'll send wool for sweaters and scarves."

Chaim was looking out the window. "People I know talk about war breaking out in Europe," he said gravely.

"They should get on the next boat!" Dvoreh cried. "They shouldn't wait!"

"Mammeh sets her own course—" Chaya Leya sighed.

"—and Papa follows it," Dvoreh and Chaim added together.

Chapter 55

"Wake up, Uncle!" Pyotr Voronov said, using one hand to draw back the heavy draperies to let the thin February sunshine filter into the bedchamber.

Yevgeny Sergeivitch was not asleep. The ear-shattering artillery salute from the fortress of Saints Peter and Paul had awakened him early, reminding him unhappily that he was in St. Petersburg, faced with two more days of pomp and ceremony before he could retire once more to the peace and quiet of Spokoinaya Zemlya. He had chosen to remain with his eyes closed against the torment of a migraine that was already sounding a drum roll in his head. Now he opened his eyes a slit to peer at his nephew.

Petya looked disgustingly bright even after the previous night's banquet at the palace that his stepfather, Prince Trubetskoy, kept for visits to St. Petersburg. He set the glass of steaming tea on the table, and seated himself comfortably on the edge of the bed.

"I wish Ekaterina had come with you instead of me!" Fedotov grumbled, reaching for the tea glass.

"You know she couldn't risk it with the child coming."

"Still, I'm about as welcome at the Imperial Court as some pox-ridden peasant."

"Nonsense! Our family has always been loyal to the tsar, and truly, Uncle, if anyone has a right to call himself Voronov, it is you. So sit up now and stop behaving as though coming to St. Petersburg with me has been a terrible imposition."

Groaning, Fedotov pushed himself into a sitting position and drank down the scalding tea in great drafts. It assuaged his raging thirst and to some extent settled a queasy stomach. At his age, he should know better than to drink so much vodka! "I'm damned if I'll go to the cathedral this afternoon for any memorial mass! There are some things I draw the line at."

"All right, Uncle," Pyotr said comfortably. "Spend the day as you like. Only don't forget that we're going to the Marinsky Theater later and then on to the Mirskys' for a late supper. I asked Pavel to press your evening clothes."

Fedotov clutched his head. "Do I have to go?"

"You've been in the country too long. A little exposure to culture will do you a world of good." He grinned wickedly, ignoring the older man's expletive. "I'd better get dressed or I'll be late for the royal procession."

"I'm surprised they're doing it," Yevgeny said. "They've hidden themselves away at Tsarskoe Selo for months now."

"It's a grand opportunity for reconciliation." Remembering the newspaper that was folded in his pocket, the young count threw it on the table before leaving the bedroom. "You might want to read the tsar's proclamation to the Russian people."

The early-morning rifle fire and cannon volleys, the whirl of social events, the special mass at Kazan Cathedral—all were to commemorate the three hundredth anniversary of the first Romanov ruler who had ascended the Throne of All the Russias. Fedotov ran his eye down the columns of newsprint, reading rapidly. Nicholas praised his subjects for cleaving to the Orthodox faith and for their sacrifices in the face of economic difficulties. He alluded to significant achievements in agriculture and industry, literature and art, and ended with compliments for the heroism of the men in the armed forces. The words had a precise correctness, and no soul.

Fedotov stretched. Ah, it was good of Petya to let him off from the scheduled formalities of the afternoon. How he loathed ceremony! As he grew older, anything that took him away from home was a bore and a nuisance.

Newly energized by anticipation, he threw off the bedclothes, suddenly in a hurry to bathe and dress for an errand of his own.

A rather thin scattering of people lined the streets, waiting for Nicholas, Alexandra, and their children to ride by en route to the great cathedral, where they would honor the dead heroes and celebrate the past victories of the Romanov regime. Despite the bitter cold, it was good to be outside and strolling in the fresh air. Getting out of those stuffy rooms made his head feel somewhat better. As he walked, Fedotov scanned the faces of the people, many of them worn down by years of strife and hardship. There were none of the usual homeless on the streets, probably cleared by police from the parade route. Here and there were family groups, some better dressed in good furs—the ever-optimistic middle classes. Some of the well-fed were probably police agents placed to whip up the enthusiasm of the crowds.

"They're coming! They're coming!" someone at the curb shouted, and the people pressed forward. In the back rank someone had begun to sing the national anthem, and a few joined in.

Fedotov found a doorstep, from which he had a fair view of the street. The imperial carriages moved slowly, the tsar and tsaritsa in the lead, the children in the carriage behind, then the imperial grand dukes and grand duchesses, followed by all the lesser aristocracy. Nicholas did not acknowledge the people in any way. His face was closed and stern, and his wife's haughty. The pale little tsarevitch Alexsei, heir to the throne of the Romanovs, raised a frail hand to the crowd. A cheer rose from the people. *Bozhe tsaria khrani!* God save the tsar! Soon the procession had passed out of sight, gone to pray at the Kazan Cathedral. They had better pray well, Fedotov thought, moving on toward his own destination.

He had no trouble locating the run-down house where his former pupil rented a flat. Semyon might well prefer not to see his old teacher, but as long as he continued to send his address home, he would be forced to tolerate these periodic intrusions from his past. Yevgeny was deeply troubled by the disturbing transformation Semyon had undergone during his years in St. Petersburg. Being sent from home so young had served him ill. But everyone could be wise after the fact.

Fedotov's knock was answered by a young woman still dressed in a wrapper and slippers. Slovenly, the steward thought; it was almost noon. Yet for all that, she was rather appealing, he conceded, trying not to stare. She looked defenseless until she fished in her pocket and put on a pair of wire-framed spectacles. A mass of springy brown hair and appraising gray eyes set off her small, oval face.

"Yes?" she asked without courtesy.

"I've come to see Semyon Mandelkern."

"He's not here."

"I think he is." Yevgeny pushed past her just as Simcha emerged from the other room.

"Fedotov! What are you doing here?" No more "*Gospodin*," Yevgeny noted with a mixture of amusement and distaste.

"As you see, I have come to visit you."

Simcha gestured toward one of the two chairs in the sparsely furnished room. He declined to sit, repelled by the sticky dishes on the table, the piles of clean and soiled laundry on the floor, dust and grime and piles of papers everywhere. The girl, bestowing upon him a spiteful look, disappeared into the bedroom.

"I noticed a coffeehouse a few doors away. I should like a cup of coffee." The girl's malevolence hung on the air of the room and made talking difficult. The steward was certain that she was listening at the door.

"I'm—busy."

"A cup of coffee and a few minutes' conversation. For the sake of old times."

Simcha shrugged. "All right. I'll get my coat and hat."

"Thank you."

Yevgeny Fedotov could hear Simcha and the girl arguing in the bedroom. He wondered if she had come for the night or whether she lived here. The room, bare of personal objects, gave no clues to their relationship. Well, he thought, Semyon had grown up. He calculated that he would be twenty-three or so now.

It had been some time since Fedotov had last seen his young friend. After Simcha had dropped his studies to work full time on his "writing" career, Fedotov had made an ill-conceived trip, at Malkeh's behest, to caution the boy to be careful. Semyon was still young then, impressionable, malleable. He had seemed to take in everything that Fedotov said, and when they parted, had promised to stay away from dangerous activities. But he would not agree to come home. Fedotov blamed himself for not convincing him. Knowing that St. Peterburg was a hotbed of revolution, he should have insisted! But what then? Their relationship was shaky enough without issuing unenforceable ultimatums.

Now the boy had developed a man's thicker chest and body. The wide blue eyes, which Fedotov remembered as curious and thoughtful, were wary now and refused to meet his gaze directly. He was clean-shaven, but his hair needed cutting, hanging in a shaggy mane around his ears. His clothes were wrinkled, probably grabbed from one of those piles on the floor. Altogether he looked shabby and unkempt—not so different from the homeless peasants who lived in doorways. When they went outside, Fedotov saw that his coat was thin, and the woolen scarf pulled across the lower part of his face did not quite hide the blueness of his lips.

In the café Fedotov ordered black coffee. Sometimes coffee helped his headaches, and he hoped that would be the case today. Simcha had tea and a couple of piroshki, which he wolfed down as though he had not been eating regularly.

"So, then," Yevgeny said after a while, "what are you doing these days?"

"I am working for a newspaper."

"Journalism is a very worthy profession, Semyon. Your parents will be pleased. May I tell them which paper?"

"They wouldn't know it."

"I suppose not."

"Look, Yevgeny Sergeivitch, why did you come here? Did my parents send you to talk to me?"

The steward's head was pounding and he could barely tolerate the glare of bright sunlight reflecting on the snow outside. Little colored lights danced behind his eyes. He would have to hire a carriage to take him back to Pyotr's house, and he'd have the devil's own time managing that on a parade day like this! He said slowly, "I thought we were friends who would like to see each other. It's why I came with the count to St. Petersburg. Was I wrong, Semyon?"

Simcha grimaced. "You are trying to make me feel guilty. Next thing you'll be on me about why I didn't stay at the university! Just tell my mother that I'm fine and happy, all right?"

Yevgeny lowered his voice. "And working for an underground newspaper?"

Simcha agreed, "Working for the revolution! And why not, Yevgeny Sergeivitch? The tsar hates the workers and encourages anti-Semitism. He wants to see Russia cleared of Jews!"

"And," Yevgeny Sergeivitch whispered, "in the end he will pay for it—when the Jews help topple him from his throne."

"Exactly."

A wave of nausea choked the steward. "Can you find me a carriage? I am ill."

Simcha rose. "I will try," he said with an unwelcome leap of concern. "Perhaps you should come back to the flat—?"

Fedotov shook his head.

Before Simcha disappeared to look for a conveyance, Fedotov asked, "Shall I tell your parents about the woman in your flat?"

"Why not?" He was defiant, swaggering. "You can tell them her name, too, if you want—Vera Politsovskaya! We live together as lovers."

Fedotov sighed. "Of course," he said, nodding. "You are no longer a child."

The conflicts that made Vassily's mind a battleground were increasingly confusing to him. At the same time that he wholeheartedly wished for the destruction of anyone connected with his enemy, he had feelings of genuine fondness for Semyon Mandelkern. He had begun to suffer again from strange pressures in his head. He could not sleep without nightmares, and the benign Marta of daydreams at night changed into a frightening and malicious presence.

He sometimes forgot why he had cultivated Semyon in the first place, forgot that he was a Jew, forgot that he was the *particular* Jew, in fact, who was the son of the whore who had caused his father's downfall, and the protégé of his sworn enemy. The trouble was that Semyon, too young at the time to have remembered Vassily from Spokoinaya Zemlya, looked up to him, confided in him, even loved him. If things had been different, they might have been friends of the closest sort. They *were* friends of the closest sort. It was bewildering. Damn Semyon anyway! He hated him, though Marta's mocking voice insisted that he loved him.

They strolled together that summer day, arm in arm, along the Nevsky Prospekt. It was safer to talk in the street than in buildings where eavesdroppers might lurk. Even so, Vassily had taught Semyon to spot suspicious characters who walked too close behind, or who hid their faces in open newspapers and took pains not to look at them. They were alone today, but if anyone had been following them, they would have parted at the next corner, shaking hands like casual acquaintances.

Today their conversation could have been attended by the chief of the *Okhrana* himself. Simcha, his brow puckered and his expression sour, was talking about Vera. "And so," he concluded, "she has been acting impossible! All because Fedotov insists on writing me letters. She thinks we should move so that he can't find us again. Vera says I should completely cut ties with home. But how can I do that? My parents—I just can't! What do you think, Vassily Yulevitch?"

The older man shrugged. "What did Fedotov want?"

"What he always wants—for me to go home, to give up politics."

Vassily stroked his beard. "I guess he wouldn't like it if he knew just how active you really are!"

Simcha looked about him, but there were no pedestrians within earshot. He murmured, "We attack the Panovsky weapons factory on Tuesday. When we set fire to the plant, it will be the biggest fireworks display since the coronation!"

"You really shouldn't be telling me."

Simcha was surprised. "But why not?"

"Ha! Some conspirator you are!" Vassily dropped his voice. "The fewer who know your business, the safer you'll be."

Simcha said affectionately, "You worry about me too much! Besides, it's not like I'm telling the whole world! Just Vera and you, my two best friends."

Vassily frowned. "It's better to trust no one. *No one!*"

"What's the matter with you?" Simcha was becoming irked. Vassily, who should have been enthusiastic, was behaving oddly.

"Just be careful."

They fell into an uneasy silence and shortly afterward said good-bye. Vassily walked as far as Simcha's flat, but declined to come upstairs. He didn't much like Vera, and anyway, he had another errand to perform. He sighed. His chief in the S.R. would be very interested in the Bolsheviks' plan to fire the Panovsky plant on Tuesday. What difference, anyway, could it make if Yevno Azev knew? S.R. and Social Democrats had the same basic objectives, didn't they? Lately, though, there had been disturbing rumors about Azev. Twice in the years since he had led the S.R. combat unit, key members of the team had been arrested. As fantastic as it seemed, there were some who wondered if he might be an agent for the police.

*T*hey had chosen a moonless night for the operation. Friendly hands had promised to unlock the factory's back gate for the five who comprised the party. Simcha had chosen the team for this, his first operations venture, carefully—Fedor, the ex-wrestler; Nihita, who was only sixteen and fearless; Alexander, the burly printer who worked Simcha's press these days; and Valentin, the fiery orator. The guards who normally patrolled the factory grounds were said to be sympathizers; they had promised to be occupied elsewhere on the premises this night, but to assure their loyalty, "gifts" had changed hands. A Panovsky worker, a secret party member, had smuggled a rough sketch of the compound to Simcha, so that he knew exactly where he must lead his men to reach the warehouse where rifles and ammunition, cushioned in straw, and packed in wooden crates, were stored for shipment. Like the front gate, the sliding doors to the warehouse would be left unlocked. Each of the five were to carry matches and oil-soaked rags wrapped around lengths of wood. Once inside, they would ignite the torches and hurl them among the stacked boxes. If all went as planned, they would have ample time to get well away from the building before fire reached the ammunition.

That was the plan. They easily found the back gate and slipped through it. The bulk of the looming warehouse was visible as a darker shadow. As expected, no guards were visible, and the barking of dogs was distant. In single file, the five men crept silently across the factory yard. Everything was working as it should. Still, Simcha was on edge. The back of his neck prickled, and he could feel sweat soaking his shirt. He heard the harsh rasp of heavy breathing and was unsure if it came from him or from Sasha, who was directly behind him. Except for that, all was silent, the yard black and silent. He signaled the men to hurry. One by one, stooping low, they arrived at the sheltering wall of the warehouse. Simcha slid back the doors, relieved that they had been greased to move noiselessly. The party moved inside. Simcha leaned against a wall, his knees weak and his heart beating fast. What happened next was not particularly clear. Bright lights burst upon them from every direction, there was noise from shots being fired, and suddenly there were men everywhere, standing between them and the doors. While Simcha was still trying to assimilate all this, a heavy object came down on the back of his head; he slipped to his knees and was sucked down into darkness.

*J*t was Yuri Marozov, the director of the police bureau in Polotsk, who brought the news of Simcha's arrest to his parents. For the remainder of her life Malkeh would never forget anything about that dreadful day—June 23. The weather had been stifling for several days, and they had risen at first light to get the day's work done before the temperature grew unbearable. Malkeh had set Golda the task of chopping beets for a cold borscht. She was singing in her high, thin voice, a fly droned in the window, and the hum of Yoysef's sewing machine came through the thin partition from the shop. At the unexpected arrival of the policeman at their door, Malkeh carefully set aside her paring knife and pan of vegetables. Ushering Marozov into the front room, Malkeh asked Golda to get Yoysef from the shop.

When Yoysef came, the official told them about Simcha. Later Malkeh realized that she had heard little of what he said. A roar like that of waves crashing on rocks came between her and the policeman. She saw his mouth moving but couldn't take in what he was saying. And yet she knew why he was there. She had been expecting it for years.

Yoysef asked the necessary questions. When was he arrested? What charges had been brought? Did he have a lawyer? Where was he being held? Could they see him?

Marozov, after satisfying himself that the parents knew nothing about their son's activities, gave them what little information he had. For all that they were only Jews, he reflected later, they displayed a certain dignity. Only the aunt seemed not to understand what had happened. The father, very tall and straight for a man his age, had replied to Marozov's queries in a firm, clear voice and asked only what he needed to know. The mother had said not a word, but her remarkable eyes had met his directly, reading there that the sentence for arson at a weapons factory must be very severe.

The next morning Malkeh, Yoysef, and Yevgeny Fedotov boarded a train for the capital. Malkeh continued to hold herself under a control so tight that only those who knew her well could recognize that she was on the edge of hysteria. Fedotov had reserved a first-class compartment and ordered the conductor to bring tea at once.

Yoysef glanced warily at his wife. "Maybe it is not as bad as it sounds."

"It's worse." Malkeh's voice was toneless.

Fedotov busied himself adding sugar to the tea. He agreed with Malkeh.

"We don't even know if they will allow us to see him," she said in the same flat voice.

"Of course they will!" Yoysef said heartily. "We're his parents. And besides, whatever Simcha intended, nothing whatsoever happened. No one was hurt, no damage was done! They can't prove anything except that he was in the factory when he wasn't supposed to be. We'll see that he has an advocate. It will be all right, you'll see it will!"

"It won't be all right."

Fedotov offered her tea. She shook her head.

"You must have something!" Yoysef said. "Since that policeman came yesterday you've taken nothing at all, not even a glass of water!"

Not bothering to answer, she closed her eyes and leaned her head back against the plush seat.

Yoysef flashed a look of appeal toward Fedotov, but the steward shrugged.

It was a long, silent journey. From time to time Yoysef picked up one of Malkeh's pale, limp hands and held it. Intermittently he urged her to drink a little tea or take some food. He brought a cool cloth from the lavatory and pressed it against her forehead. She paid no attention to any of these ministrations.

Once she said, "Did you know that the last time he was home we had an argument about that friend of his, that Vassily?"

"No."

"He was never the same after he met him. It was always 'Vassily says this' and 'Vassily says that' and every other sentence was one of those awful revolutionary slogans! Was Vassily arrested too?"

"I don't know."

In the afternoon Malkeh fell into a restless sleep, and Fedotov motioned for Yoysef to come with him into the corridor.

"Yoysef Avromovitch, you must prepare yourself for the worst. The boy has committed an act of treason—"

"Can they prove that?"

"Are you joking? They arrested him inside the factory with incendiary materials! Someone in Semyon's confidence must have betrayed him. Of course, I will find someone to represent Semyon in court, but it will likely make no difference. The trial may be over already."

"Siberia?"

"If he's lucky."

The blood rushed into Yoysef's face, turning it an unhealthy brick-red color. "My God! You can't mean—"

"What do you think? Pull yourself together, man! You've got that woman in there to think of."

*A*rriving in St. Petersburg at nine o'clock in the evening, it was too late to do anything but find lodgings and agree on a time to meet in the morning. Malkeh and Yoysef went to Simcha's flat.

A woman they did not know opened the door. "Who are you?"

"His parents," Yoysef said tersely. "Who are *you*?"

"A friend of Semyon's," she said, allowing them inside. "I live here."

"Where are they holding him?" Malkeh demanded.

"At Peter and Paul Fortress!" Vera's face crumpled, and she began to weep in great gulping sobs that made her seem much younger than she had first appeared to be.

Malkeh said sharply, "Stop that! Has there been a trial?"

In response came a new freshet of sobs. Malkeh took the girl by the shoulders and shook her. "Stop, I say!"

Scarcely able to talk, the girl shook her head. "There are hundreds of cases waiting to be heard, so many that they say they may not bother with trials; they may just turn the prisoners over to a firing squad!" She seemed close to collapse. "Vassily says they will execute Semyon, and soon!"

"That's a lie!" Yoysef shouted at the weeping girl.

"I want to talk to this Vassily," Malkeh said.

"He's doing everything he can." Vera's lip trembled.

She was so young, so vulnerable, that Malkeh had a fleeting urge to clasp her to her breast. This girl, this Vera, was a part of Simcha's life that his mother could never know anything about. Malkeh did not move.

*L*ittle could be done. It was as Vera had said. The dungeons were full, the court docket clogged, and there were rumors of summary executions. They were allowed neither to visit nor to send communications of any kind. Yevgeny Fedotov had hired a lawyer. Feeling that Simcha's friend, Vassily Chernov, might have information for them, they were disappointed to be unable to talk with him. As bad luck would have it, he had been struck down by illness and was quarantined in his house.

After a week filled with empty activity that led nowhere, Malkeh and Yoysef returned to Polotsk. They had grown to know Vera a little in the days they had spent together. The girl loved Simcha, Malkeh thought. Something warm and alive had existed between them that made it possible for the parents to overcome their biases and took the edge from Vera's abrasiveness. When they left, she went with them to Finlandia Station. "I will never give up!" she promised. "And I will let you know if anything changes."

This time Malkeh drew the girl to her and kissed her cheek. "Goodbye, my dear. I understand what my son must feel for you."

Yevgeny Fedotov stayed a few days longer to follow up additional contacts suggested by Petya and his old friend, Marozov, and then he also went home. "There is nothing to do but wait now," he told Simcha's parents. "I talked to some people in the Interior Ministry about leniency, but no one will promise a thing."

Chapter 56

*T*he heat shimmered in bluish waves along the ground, softening the tar in the streets and reflecting off the sidewalks. People with no need to be out and about stripped down to the least number of clothes that decency permitted and stayed indoors behind drawn curtains until the sun went down. Even in night there was no relief, only the accumulation of the day's heat gone stale. Sweat pooled in the hollows behind knees and collected in armpits, faces blotched, and hair became limp from humidity. Shirts and dresses, fresh from the iron, were wrinkled in moments. Tempers frayed. Babies screamed with discomfort, and adults quarreled over little things.

In the dim interior of Mandel's Workingman's Store, Chaim and six other men huddled in close conversation. Chaim had discarded his jacket and unbuttoned his shirt collar. Two were dressed like Chaim, but the other four men wore rough blue workshirts open over hairy chests, sleeves rolled high on muscled arms.

The air in the store was fetid, made worse by a strong smell of perspiration. The tall piles of overalls and workshirts which hid the men from the view of passersby on the street also held in the stale air. A couple of the men sat, fanning themselves, in the straight chairs that Chaim kept for shoe customers. Two others were seated on the counter beside the cash register, and one was stretched out full-length on the floor. Chaim took up a position in mid-group, squatting on the shoe stool.

"Hy," said a tall, heavily built man in dungarees, mopping his forehead with a red kerchief, "I done like you asked about findin' out how may of them come into town. Best I kin figger, must be a couple dozen."

A second man whistled. "We gonna need more bodies than jus' us."

"Can the union help us?" asked one of the businessmen.

"Union's kinda layin' low right now. We ain't the only fish they got fryin'," the first speaker said.

"When you figure they gonna make their move, Hy?"

Chaim scratched his chin. "Soon now. Maybe tonight. Couple dozen men, you say?"

The first spoke again. "Frisco toughs. 'Course, they ain't no match fer us!" He laughed, playfully punching Chaim's arm with a beefy fist.

"Who's got most to lose if unions get closed out?" Chaim asked. "Get those men over here. Plenty dock hands and Irishers from where the new warehouses are going up—they love a fight and are big for the I.W.W., farm workers—let them know what's happening. Spread the word everywhere. We got to set up watch now on all businesses that came out against the MMEA. And it's got to be from tonight on. If the association brought in men from Frisco, they're not paying them to sit around Stockton. There be action pretty quick."

"Those guys are bragging all over they gonna wipe up the town with us!"

"Oh, God!" exclaimed one of the businessmen, turning pale. "We haven't got a chance!"

"We'll see about that," Chaim said, his face grim.

"Maybe we should just give in now. There are four hundred members of the MMEA!" It was the slighter of the two shop owners speaking.

"Less now," Chaim said, grinning, "since some of you decided to join me. We got twenty-five with us, pro-union."

"Still—" The man was visibly nervous, running his finger around the inside of his collar. "We never expected it would come to a—a war, Hy! Someone's likely to get hurt!"

The big man who had punched Chaim with his fist began to laugh. Chaim put a restraining hand on his arm. It wouldn't do for the merchants and the workingmen to start a fight between themselves.

"I only talk for Hy Mandel," Chaim said, his voice rising and his accent becoming increasingly pronounced. "Hy Mandel don't like getting pushed around by bankers and men who think because they're rich they own this city. Hy Mandel is just one of the guys out here working to make an honest dollar. My customers are same. Decent men, work hard. We don't want no one telling us we can't sell or buy union, can't join a union, can't hire union workers." Chaim turned and fixed the two uneasy businessmen with a cool look. "Now we got fight on our hands. Not our doing! Association hired criminals to scare us off. You want to let them get away with it? If they do, it won't be end of it. You give them idea that force works and they begin to use it against anyone who thinks different from them."

"Well, I understand what you're saying, Mandel, but—"

"My wife, Rosalie, she born American, she say Americans make up own minds about what they want—like no one should tell them whether to buy union-made pants or not, things like that. Where I came from, not so many things to decide."

"Ain't you a good Americun?" one of the dockers asked the timid businessman.

He capitulated, realizing that he had been backed into a corner. "All right. I'll get word to the others to prepare themselves for—for whatever comes. If you'll organize some muscle power to back us up, Mandel. We're not fighters."

They shook hands on it.

When everyone had gone, Chaim sat down and considered the situation. The appearance of the city rowdies had scared his supporters. He did not blame them. They scared him too. That may have been the whole point, to get them to surrender without a fight. The MMEA would like to keep its skirts clean if possible. Chaim would have quite a job keeping the opposition firm in its resolve. He lit a cigar, considering whether he should provoke an early confrontation. Their best chance would come in the opening rounds, when no one expected serious resistance.

*R*osalie had been livid. "I guess it's typical of you to side with the bums and the roughnecks."

"My customers, Raizel, don't forget that."

"*Rosalie*, damn it!"

Chaim stared hard. Lately her ladylike speech had slipped a little. She blushed under his scrutiny. "The point is, you're on the losing side, Hy. Why can't you be like the others? Oh, what's the use of talking to you! You have no head for business!"

"You want to be invited to Sutter Club, yes? That what bothers you?"

"No, that's not the reason. Not that I wouldn't like to be invited to better places! I'm just afraid you'll get yourself killed!"

"You would care?" he asked curiously. Rosalie's recent interest in the business had confused him.

"Don't flatter yourself! I just don't want it to all go bust again, that's all!" she snapped.

*A*n uneasy night and another day passed before the strikebreakers made their move. If they had waited just one more day, the demoralized group of merchants would almost certainly have broken ranks.

Giving his final instructions to his hirelings, Kreisler, of the MMEA, told them to start with the Workingman's Store, figuring that when the ringleader, Hy Mandel, collapsed, the other holdouts would fold like wet cardboard. Mandel's store, the one they usually called "Hy's," was the crucial center of the opposition.

"You don't have to go easy on that Jew Mandel," Kreisler told them. "If he gets hurt—well, all the better." He shrugged. "We need to teach him a lesson. If troublemakers like him don't like the way it is here, they ought to go back where they came from!"

"We'll fix him for you, boss!" a beefy longshoreman named Tyminski promised.

"You bet!" another man agreed. "In the old country, we knew how to take care of guys like him!"

*T*hat night, their second on watch, Chaim and a dozen others sat waiting in the darkened store. They were armed with sticks, bottles, and fists that were callused and as hard as nails.

Just past midnight there was breaking glass and the crunch of a crowbar on wood, forcing the front door. The waiting men tensed, watching Chaim for a signal. He crouched behind the long counter, his eyes on the enemy, who were kicking in the door or climbing through the broken front window. The light from a street lamp was enough for him to see that they had left no reinforcements in the street.

"Hey! Call *this* merchandise!" one of the men said, holding up a shirt from a pile on a table.

Still, Chaim did not move.

The men came deeper into the store, spilling display goods from the counters and tables and sweeping boxes from the shelves.

"Looks like the Jew-boy got scared an' ran home t'hide!" laughed another.

By this time, the intruders, twenty or so of them, were well away from the door. They seemed to have no leader and milled about aimlessly. Seeing no one, they let down their guard. Chaim marveled at their stupidity. He motioned for some of his men, keeping behind cover, to edge quietly around the interlopers to take up positions between them and the exit.

"Hey, look!" one of the outsiders said, plopping a cap on his head. "How do I look?"

"Like a kike storekeeper!"

When the thugs were surrounded, Chaim tightened his hold on his club, took a deep breath, and then leapt shouting into their midst. There was immediate panic as Chaim's dockers and construction workers sprang from their hiding places, weapons raised menacingly. No one had told the roughnecks that Hy Mandel was a giant of a man who had learned to fight on the roughest waterfronts in the world. He laid about him with his club and his fists, his ferocity inspiring his supporters. Men grappled and fought, overturning tables and crashing against walls, the fallen still fighting as they pulled their opponents down with them, rolling over and over on the floor. In the thick of it all was Chaim Mandel, massive as an oak, sweating and cursing in an unknown language.

Suddenly there was the flash of gunfire, and a man dropped where he stood. In the sudden shocked silence, the heavy thud of the body hitting the floor seemed louder than anything that had happened before. Chaim shouted for someone to bring a lamp from the back room, and when it came, he knelt by the body. One of the intruders was dead, shot through the head.

"Get him out of here!" Chaim said coldly. "And don't come back. Go on, get out now!"

Muttering among themselves, confused at the turn things had taken, the men from the MMEA filed out into the street, bearing the body. They held a worried conference before dispersing by twos and threes. When Chaim next looked, the corpse was gone. Later the sheriff would come to arrest someone, but when he searched Chaim's men, there was no sign of a gun. Chaim shook his head in answer to the question. "No. I told everyone, no knives, no guns."

After the sheriff left and the excitement died down, they took stock. Everyone was bruised and had injuries of one sort or another. Chaim had a long deep knife wound in his forearm and a broken nose.

One of the men bragged, "Well, we sure whupped them bastards!"

Chaim was angry. "No call to use gun. This no war. Those guys were longshoremen no different from you. Probably needed work is all."

There were no more deaths, but the struggle was far from over. It became harder and meaner than ever, the out-of-towners intent on vengeance. Pro-union businesses became targets, and despite Chaim's best efforts to organize protection, windows were broken, merchandise doused with water and gasoline, fires set. As the days dragged on, it became clear that the situation was hopeless. The laborers who formed the backbone of resistance were physically spent from days and nights on watch and injuries had thinned their numbers alarmingly. The twenty-five anti-MMEA businessmen were paralyzed with fear. It was bad enough to have one's store trashed, but when threatening signs began to appear on the lawns in front of their homes, when their wives were harassed at the grocery and the children at school, it was time to call it quits. On the fifth day the MMEA brought in reinforcements. Chaim counseled his people to give up. Stockton would remain a nonunion town for a while longer.

Chaim returned home to Sacramento with a heavily bandaged arm and a swollen nose.

Surveying his sorry condition, Rosalie said, "I told you how it'd be, Hy. You didn't have a chance against them, and you only got yourself hurt."

Chaim was stubborn. "We almost won, Rosalie, it was a near thing!" His grin was crooked beneath his painful nose. "They just had too much money. They could have kept bringing in new men forever!"

"Almost won? When they terrorized the whole town? How much is it going to cost you to replace the window and repair all the damage to the store? How about the other businesses and all the people who were hurt? Almost won, did you?"

"You should have seen how we stood up to them! We could have won."

Rosalie was oddly touched by her husband's spirit. His dogged determination in the face of disaster was what had attracted her to him in the first place. Almost tenderly she reached out a hand and touched his cheek. "Come, Hy, you're exhausted and sick! Let me put you to bed!"

"Not so bad now." He let himself be led to the bedroom. "Store be closed now seven, maybe eight days, get everything fixed up." He sat on the edge of his twin bed and let Rosalie pull off his shoes. "I go to city tomorrow, see about new fixtures, get more merchandise."

"Why do you have to go now? You need to take it easy for a few days, let your poor nose heal!"

"I rest there. Business not wait on me!"

*A*lthough Chaim visited his wholesalers in San Francisco, it was not primarily business that took him to the city. It was Manya Aksakova. "Mistress" didn't seem to be the right word to describe Manya. The word implied an inequality between them that was simply not there. She and Chaim had become lovers in 1907, not long after they had met in an Embarcadero bar, a rough sort of place frequented by sailors. After the earthquake Chaim had begun to stop there regularly, sure that someday someone would have news of the *Oceania*.

One afternoon the bar was presided over by a striking red-haired woman who must have stood at almost six feet. She illuminated the drab bar like an explosion of electric lights. Not because of her brilliant plumage alone but because she seemed to radiate energy and light from inside.

"What you want, mister?" she had asked that first day. Her voice was low and husky and thick with accent.

Without a moment's reflection, Chaim spoke in Russian: "*Ott kudova vih?*"

Her wide smile revealed very even white teeth. "*Moskva!* I'm a Muscovite!"

"God sent you here! We are countrymen!"

In the first instant that their eyes met, he had known that he would not leave the bar without her. He had sometimes since wondered about the inevitability, the fatedness, of their pairing. He could no more have walked away from Manya than he could have willingly stopped breathing. There was never a choice, not for him, not for her.

The Russian woman had come to California as maid to a wealthy Moscow couple. In San Francisco, where her employer, a dealer in furs, had business, his wife had taken a chill and died. Manya had declined to return to Russia. There was nothing for her to go back to.

When they met, Manya was still new to the bar, but it was a job for which her size and her easy good humor suited her. Chaim tried to figure out exactly what it was that had attracted him so powerfully. There was, of course, a superficial physical resemblance to his first love, Nadezda Ivanovna, mostly the red hair. But Nadja had been a small, plump child while Manya was a handsome woman of generous proportions. They looked nothing alike. Nadja had had green eyes, a pert nose, a few delicious freckles; Manya's face was square and large-featured, her skin very white, and her eyes the deep blue of the Caspian Sea. What the two women had in common was an extraordinary warmth and openness, and a fierce sense of independence. What each gave, she gave of her own accord and on her own terms.

Manya and Chaim had entered the relationship with their eyes open and had been together for six years. Chaim was happy with the way things were and saw no reason why anything should change between them. She cooked Russian dishes for him and spoke to him comfortably in the language of the old country. He could take off his shoes and smoke a cigar in her flat, drink a vodka or a schnapps, lie down and take a nap. They made love more than once in a night, hungrily, and sometimes during the day, on the floor, on the couch, in the bathtub. She made no demands—except that sometimes she wanted to keep him with her longer than he could stay. He did not feel guilty with her. He had never made a secret of his marriage, or of the problems within it.

"So why do you stay with her?" Manya had asked one night when they were lying side by side, tired but peaceful in the aftermath of love. "She doesn't want you. You don't make love with her. She gives you no babies. What holds you?"

"I don't know, I don't know." He closed his eyes, trying to think his way through this difficult question. "I—maybe I feel sorry for her. She's so alone."

Manya laughed, and there was a little edge in it. "And am I not alone?"

He shook his head. "Not in the same way." Chaim was an inarticulate man, unaccustomed to probing beneath the surface of his thoughts. How, then, to explain how it must feel to be Rosalie, a woman who has never been at home in the world and who is empty inside.

"I don't understand."

"I don't understand very well either."

"You feel you owe her something because you lost her father's money?"

"Yes, there's that. And I owe her something because I married her, and she has never been happy with me. Can you understand that? All I know is that there is no way I can leave her."

Manya sighed deeply. "Poor Chaim! Like a bird in a net!" A little later she added sadly, "And poor Manya."

Except that one time, they never spoke of a future. Someday, a grateful Chaim thought, when times were better, he would make it up to Manya— take care of her, buy her things. He couldn't yet. In Stockton little problems had begun to creep up with the business; fire inspections that required expensive renovations, a faucet left running all night damaging merchandise, a steep raise in the rent. The MMEA was not a graceful victor.

The labor troubles of 1913 affected Chaim's future directly and profoundly. For one thing, when the economy improved, as eventually it did, Chaim's customers did not forget that Hy Mandel had given them credit when more established businesses had shunned their trade. And many a union man remembered that in one small city in California, there was a man who had led an unequal fight against an entrenched establishment—for them!

Chaim was already a legend to his customers. He had worked with his hands, carried bricks on his back, and been poor on the road. He had been denied by the banks and in debt to his friends. He had been to the brink of financial ruin and come back. Like them. Now they repaid him by making "Hy's" a workingman's store in more than name only.

In another way, not immediately apparent, the bad times of 1913 had an impact in Chaim's future. In nearby Sacramento, Hiram Johnson, who had won the governorship of California in the 1910 election, and later been on the unsuccessful Progressive Party ticket with Teddy Roosevelt in 1912, had his eye once more on the gubernatorial election of 1914. Johnson had entered politics with a reputation as a fighting liberal, nemesis of the powerful political bosses and of the railroads. Immensely popular once, his reputation in California had waned after the lost presidential race.

In the summer of 1913 things had looked bleak indeed for Johnson's hopes. Al McCabe, his aide and longtime friend, was not one to give up easily. There was a golden campaign issue to be mined someplace, if only he could locate the vein. The old Johnson charisma was not dead, it just needed a vehicle.

Sitting in an office that overlooked the lush lawns of the state capitol, McCabe drew a pad of paper toward him and began to write down the major public concerns of the day. Defense preparedness. Economic protectionism. Maternal and child welfare. Occupational safety. Women's suffrage. He checked them off. Johnson's political platform would make reference to all of these. But they weren't sexy issues. What was needed was a burning cause specific to California, the kind Johnson had run on in earlier races. He needed villains, like Abe Ruef, the boss of San Francisco, or the S.P. Railroad. And if not villains, he needed heroes.

McCabe, his brow furrowed, thumbed through the morning newspaper, hoping for a flash of inspiration. Business conditions were improving, something to be touched on in the campaign. The Balkan situation was growing sticky—not a local concern. He flipped another page, staring down at an editorial about the inroads the I.W.W. had made in California's economy. He turned another couple of pages, and then, thoughtful, turned back to the editorial page, reading the essay carefully. It made reference to two events: the riots in Wheatland which had provoked a confrontation between ranchers and labor organizers, and the shutout of unions in Stockton by the powerful Merchants, Manufacturers, and Employers Association. This was more like it! It grabbed the imagination. All it needed to be surefire was some skillful management!

McCabe sat back in his chair, chewing the end of his pencil. The labor movement was sweeping the entire nation. California might kick the union organizers out of towns and hop fields today, but tomorrow was theirs. If he was right, and he thought he was, a strong support of labor should sweep him into the governor's office. And after the governorship, why not Congress, why not the presidency itself? Yes. He would talk to the "governor" and begin to work the theme into the campaign. Just as they took on the Southern Pacific in 1910, they would take on the likes of the MMEA in '14. There were plenty of villains and heroes in this issue, and from among them he would find a symbol for the voters to relate to. McCabe knew in his soul that it would work.

*O*vernight Chaim found himself lionized by the press for his prounion stand. People wanted to take his picture, shake his hand, give him medals. What nonsense! He had just been trying to save his stake in the Workingman's Store!

Even more strange, the candidate for governor of California, Hiram Johnson, mentioned him by name in a speech, then in many speeches. Johnson called him "a hero in our second American Revolution"! If the newspapers had not printed what the candidate said, Chaim would never have believed it. Rosalie was ecstatic at the publicity. Chaim demurred. A man had been killed in his store in July. What kind of hero did that make him?

His denials were written off as charming modesty, and his remarks were quoted in the papers. As canny Al McCabe had known, newspapers need heroes. Candidates need heroes. Workers, too, need heroes.

One day in the late fall, one of the young fellows who worked down the street at the newspaper office came running into Chaim's store.

"Hy, there's a telephone call for you from Sacramento!"

"Telephone?" Chaim had no telephone in his establishment. In fact, he knew no one who owned such an instrument.

"In our office! Someone wants to talk to you from Sacramento!"

Sacramento! Raizel! Had something happened to Raizel? Chaim's knees went weak. He ran out the door, not even remembering to lock up and put his BACK SOON sign in the window!

The offices of the *Stockton Record* were less than a half block from the store. Directed to the telephone by one of the reporters, Chaim grasped the unfamiliar instrument with white-knuckled hands.

"Hello? Hello?" he shouted into the telephone. "This is Mandel speaking!"

"Mandel," the rasping voice of Al McCabe said over the telephone wires from Sacramento, "Mr. Hiram Johnson, who will be the next governor of California, wants you to know he appreciates what you did down there in Stockton."

"Who is this?" Chaim asked, confused. "Is Raizel sick? What's the matter?" His heart was in his throat.

"Wrestle?" It was McCabe's turn to be confused. "I'm McCabe, Governor Johnson's campaign manager. I'm calling to thank you for your stand on unions."

Chaim shook his head to clear it. The telephone call had nothing to do with Raizel? Thank God for that! Now, what was this man talking about? "Maybe you didn't hear we lost the fight," Chaim said.

"But not the war. Listen, Mandel, Mr. Johnson will be in the governor's office again real soon, and you know who'll help put him there?"

"Who?"

"The labor vote, Mandel, the union vote, the voters you represent."

Chaim didn't know what to say to this madman. Voters! Labor! It was more of the same nonsense that was in the newspapers.

The voice dropped, became confidential. "Mr. Johnson has his eye on you, Mandel. You've become a goddamn idol! He personally told me to call you and tell you that California's going to be the strongest prolabor state in the whole nation! And let me tell you the governor's going to ride that all the way to the White House!"

"That will be nice," Chaim said, cautious.

"Yeah, and remember this, Mandel. Hiram Johnson never forgets anyone who's done him a favor."

Slowly Chaim hung up the telephone and walked back to his store. He must remember to tell Raizel about talking on the telephone. She might understand what it was all about. He sure didn't.

Chapter 57

Simcha and the others were held overnight at the Central Police Bureau for preliminary questioning. After wearying hours of answering questions that seemed always to contain a trap, Simcha was hustled into a wagon and taken the short distance to the Fortress of Saints Peter and Paul. The conspirators had been kept apart from each other since their arrest in the Panovsky warehouse, and Simcha did not know whether the others had been similarly treated. He did know that it boded ill for him to be taken to the fortress, the most dreaded of all Russian prisons.

Tottering between two heavily armed policemen, sick from shock, exhaustion, and a probable concussion from the blow to his head, he was escorted across the Troitsky Bridge to the great barred gate of the island fortress, where he was delivered to two prison gendarmes. Gazing about him, he felt an upsurge of hope. There was nothing frightening or forbidding about the handsome buildings of gray stone. The whole island seemed to float in a rosy mist that lifted from the surface of the surrounding waters of the River Neva. The ornate gate that had swung open for his entrance was flanked by classical marble statues, Venus on one side, Mars on the other, and a bas relief that mixed religious and historical figures; he recognized Christ embracing Peter the Great. Just beyond the gate was an ordinary street and a square with a small, elegantly proportioned church topped by a single slender spire of gold. Looking up at it, Simcha could see a figure on top—as near as his blurred vision could make out, an angel holding up a cross. The church, as every citizen of St. Petersburg knew, held the tombs of the tsars.

He was half dragged across the square, past a row of army barracks, a parade ground, and a building with heavily barred windows which he assumed was the prison, except that his warders did not stop there; afterward he had a fuzzy recollection that the Imperial Mint was said to be within the walls of the fortress. Just beyond the mint was the larger of the two actual prison buildings, the one called the Trubetskoy Bastion; more important political prisoners were held on the western end of the island at the Alexis Ravelin. The two-story prison compound, entered through a rusty gate, had seventy cells above ground plus an uncounted number below. The wings formed a rough triangle around a ragged garden.

A massive door led into the building. Two things about the place immediately communicated to Simcha the inexorability of his plight—the absolute silence and the lack of natural light. Taken briefly to the warden's office before being led to his cell, he was warned that speech was strictly forbidden. Nor could he expect his guardians to speak to him. The only place where talking was allowed was within the interrogation rooms. That was the primary reason for the ominous quiet, the others being the thick walls and the fact that the guards were required to wear felt boots which could not be heard on the stones of the corridors. The whole effect was one of oppressive weight bearing down, more frightening by far than if the building had resounded with the cries and moans of prisoners. At least that would have communicated something human!

The cell Simcha was assigned was not in the dungeons. However, it was small and damp, the walls a depressing gray, the window set high in the wall and triple-barred. No light came through the aperture because it had been painted over with lime. The bed and the table were bolted to the floor. An oil lamp, protected by iron mesh, was high in a niche in the stone wall. When the heavy wooden door slammed shut, Simcha succumbed to raw terror. Years before, he had read Dante with Yevgeny Fedotov, and he knew himself now to be in one of the pitiless circles of hell. Staring at the door, he was startled to see a disembodied eye observing him through a Judas window.

Simcha threw himself down on the iron cot and escaped into sleep. Awakened sometime later by the creak of the door on its iron hinges, he sat bolt upright and, disoriented, called out, "Who's there?"

A guard carefully set down a tin bowl of watery soup before he walked over and silently slammed Simcha's head against the cell wall. A little reminder of the rules. The pain was excruciating, and Simcha fainted. When he came to, he was alone, and the food was gone. There was no way he could know then that it would be twenty-four hours before there would be more.

Simcha learned the rule of silence quickly. If he so much as coughed, he could see the eye appear at the Judas window. He began almost to long for the interrogations, they being the only time he heard the sound of another human voice. After a while even those stopped. When the application of the knout failed to elicit information about the Bolshevik organization—after a while he would have been glad to name names if he knew any—he was left alone.

In the months before his trial, Simcha had plenty of time to reflect on who might have betrayed him. He had told no one what was planned except Vera and Vassily, and given the chance, he would not hesitate again to entrust his life to either one of them. Vera's loyalty was beyond question. In the two years since she had forsaken all others to become his lover, she had been faithful and true. A man, he thought, cannot be mistaken about someone he has held in his arms through hundreds of nights. And Vassily—if he could not believe in a man who had been his closest friend for eight years, whom could he believe in?

Vassily had warned him repeatedly to keep his secrets close. Now Simcha could see that too many others had been privy to their plans for the Panovsky plant. Dmitri, for instance, the party leader who had given them the assignment. The security guards. The two factory workers who had produced the map and unlocked the gates. His hand-picked team—Fedor, Nihita, Alexander, Valentin; if one of them was not the actual betrayer, could not one or all have carelessly shared information? He wondered what had become of them. Were they here somewhere within the stone walls of the prison? There must be other prisoners, many of them, but he never saw them, never heard them. It was eerie.

Eventually he gave up speculating about what no longer mattered. He focused his mind instead on what had set his feet on the road to this prison cell. It was not, he realized now, the words set down by Lenin and Trotsky and paraphrased by him in inflammatory leaflets so much as the empty eyes and bloodless lips of those who begged on the streets and the sound of their voices telling of evictions from the land, conditions in the factories, illnesses and beatings and the deaths of children. Even now, remembering them gave him courage and strengthened his resolution.

In a prison cell time seems scarcely to move. To keep from going mad, he set chess problems for himself, working them out in his head. He remembered long passages from Pushkin's *Eugene Onegin*, stretching his mind to remember ever more of the long narrative poem. He declined irregular verbs in French and German, Greek and Latin. And he devised ways of keeping himself oriented in a world that seemed to have no boundaries. The bells that chimed regularly from the church spire, for instance, were clearly audible. At frequent and regular intervals, probably on the quarter hour, the bells rang in the tones of one particular liturgical phrase. On the hour—at least he *thought* it must be on the hour though time had little meaning here— he recognized the hymn, "How Glorious Is Our Lord in Zion"; by coincidence it was a favorite of Vera's that she had often hummed. Once a day the bells chimed "God Save the Tsar," probably at midnight, because it was at the opposite end of the day from when his one meal was brought. The guns of the fortress were fired at noon, or so he thought. Lacking the sun and the stars, who knew when was day and when was night? For all he knew, it was conceivable that food was brought in the middle of the night to keep the prisoners disoriented.

Every day when he was fed he scratched a mark on the wall with the handle of his spoon. That's how he knew that his trial date was approaching. He had been told during interrogation that he had been assigned an advocate who would appear for him in court, but he had yet to see him or to receive a message from him. It was all part of a plan—to give the prisoner hope and then to snatch it back.

*V*era was frantic for news. She haunted the Interior Ministry until she was forcibly put out on the street. She wrote petitions to the tsar and pleading letters to Empress Alexandra. She sent a telegram to Lenin in Geneva demanding that the organization take action on Simcha's behalf.

She did not understand Vassily Chernov. Because he was Simcha's great friend, she had counted on him to be an ally.

"Semyon knew what the risks were," he told her carelessly. "Play with fire—no pun intended—and you get burned."

"What are you suggesting, Vassily, that we desert him?" Vera asked, unbelieving.

"I'm saying there's nothing to be done. *Nothing!* You can't help him! All you're doing is putting the *Okhrana* on your trail."

"I have nothing to hide. And even if I did, I'd risk it for someone I love!"

"Ah, yes, love!" Vassily said cynically. "You had other lovers before Semyon. You'll have other lovers after him." He cupped her face between his hands. "You are a pretty thing, you know, Vera? Perhaps we should comfort each other."

Vera's lip curled with scorn and revulsion. "I have to believe you are joking, Vassily Yulevitch," she said, "because otherwise I'd have to kill you."

Vassily laughed.

Vera added softly, "And if you betrayed him, I still might."

*S*everal times a week Vera crossed the Troitsky Bridge and stood at the gates of the fortress, staring transfixed at the quiet streets and the thick green grass of the square inside. Some of the gendarmes were beginning to recognize the good-looking woman who came to the gate, asking for news of a certain prisoner. She was wasting her time, of course, because there was no way anyone was going to give her information, even if they had it; it was all right with them if she chose to hang around.

Vera was not wasting her time as much as they thought. She was acquainting herself with the habits of various members of the guard unit and observing their routines. She had no specific plan in mind, but she hoped an opportunity would arise to let Semyon know he was not abandoned. It was as if he had disappeared into a deep black pit. If there was a way to reach him, she intended to find it.

Eventually Vera chose to approach a young gendarme whom the others good-naturedly called "rube" and "hayseed." He was a boy of perhaps twenty, fresh-faced and towheaded. He went off duty afternoons at four, and most days he returned to his barracks. She had observed, however, that on Fridays, payday, he crossed the bridge and stopped in a small bistro for a glass of kvass or a beer. On one of these payday afternoons, when he came in, Vera was sitting quietly at a table, sipping coffee. She nodded pleasantly and smiled at him, but since she did not approach him, he did not feel compromised by her presence. After that first time she was frequently there when he came, always drinking coffee at a solitary table. After a time Pavel sat down at the table beside her. "Do you mind?"

She shook her head.

In the way that people make small talk, she led him to tell her about himself. "Where are you from? I think you are not a native of St. Petersburg," she said.

"No, no!" He laughed. "I was raised on a farm. Outside Kostroma."

"How interesting! I know that part of the country myself!"

She seemed interested in everything about him, where he was from, who his parents were, whether he had a girl, what he thought about various things. All quite harmless. The captain of the guard himself could not object to their conversations. Pavel was flattered by the rapt attention of this attractive city woman.

A few weeks later Vera asked Pavel if he would mind, since it was already dark outside, walking home with her. Feeling every inch the gallant, he leapt to comply.

As they strolled, Vera's small hand tucked into the crook of his arm, she said, "As you know, sir, my—brother—is a prisoner in the fortress. All a misunderstanding, of course."

"I'm not allowed to talk about the prisoners in the fortress, miss."

"No, of course, not." They walked a little faster, the silence stretching out. Vera made a long face and gave a mighty sigh. "You see, our mother is very ill, dying really, she'll be gone any day now. And she longs with all her heart to get a message to Semyon. To tell him before she dies that she forgives him for his crimes. She won't be able to die easily until she has a chance to let him know."

Pavel said curtly, "Prisoners can't get messages."

Vera's face was piteous. "Oh, I understand that! I just wanted to ask your advice. I don't know what to do to ease our mother's passage to heaven!" She crossed herself. "If I could just get a note to him in Mother's hand—"

"No! You can't! Don't even think about it!"

"Please, Pavel. What if it were your mother?"

He stopped abruptly in the middle of the street. "I'm going to turn around and go back to the barracks now. I'll forget that you asked me to do something like this. You know, you could be arrested!"

"But you wouldn't do that?" she said in her most enticing voice.

"I'll forget it just this once." His soft young face grew hard. "I like you, but I won't carry any message for you. I won't do anything I'm not supposed to do."

"I'd be so grateful," Vera coaxed. "You don't know how grateful I can be."

"Forget it! Listen, miss, there are lots of prisoners in the fortress. So many they're going to have a mass trial. Some are going to be executed, and some will be exiled, and the really unlucky ones will be sentenced to serve terms at the fortress."

"When will that be? Tell me, Pavel, when will the trial be?"

"It's a secret. I'm not supposed to talk about it."

"Tell me!"

"October thirtieth."

"Thank you, thank you!" Vera said, kissing him on the cheek. "My— mother—will feel better for knowing."

*A*fter the trial, the lawyer, Krupchik, was allowed a visit with Prisoner Mandelkern. It was the only time they ever saw each other.

The advocate carefully explained about his client's being tried in absentia.

"That's against every rule of justice!" Simcha protested.

"These are extraordinary times."

"And how did I plead?" Simcha asked sarcastically.

"You *were*, after all, found in the warehouse with matches in your pocket."

"And the verdict?"

"Guilty as charged." Krupchik cleared his throat. "The sentence was ten years."

"Where?"

"Here."

After four months in the lightless prison, Simcha's skin was pale as parchment. It seemed impossible that he could be any paler, but at the news of his sentence, whatever color remained bleached out. Ten years of gray walls and constant twilight, of dampness, lice, and one wormy meal a day? Ten years of never setting eyes on a person you cared for and who cared for you? Ten years of utter and complete silence!

The lawyer cleared his throat. "Many of those charged with crimes against the state received the death sentence."

Simcha bowed his head. Ten years in hell, he thought, overcome by the enormity of what had befallen him.

Krupchik laid a hand on Simcha's thin shoulder. "Be grateful, you young fool, that you had a friend to get you a lawyer and another who found out the trial date. Your execution order was already signed when I went into court! You could be living now under a death sentence!"

Simcha gave a hollow laugh. "But I am, sir, I am. The difference is that for them it will be over in a moment."

The guards came then, shuffling silently in their felt boots, to lead him back to his solitary cell. Hearing the massive doors clang shut behind the prisoner, Krupchik wasn't sure he had done his client any favor.

These days Malkeh was usually at home, busying herself with some small household task or working in her garden with Golda beside her. It was a pity that she no longer had an outlet of escape from her deepest worries. The school, which had served the purpose for a long time, had been boarded up by order of the Ministry of the Interior, the pupils warned to stay away at risk of instant arrest. It was only one in a general closure of Jewish institutions. Yeshivas had gone first, *cheyderim* next, then all the secular Jewish schools. "Centers of subversion" they were called by the Ministry. A ridiculous charge, Malkeh thought indignantly, unless teaching someone to read was treason! She had grieved for a long time before coming to terms with her loss. Her friend and fellow teacher, Hodl Nachman, never got over the trauma of watching the police lead the terrified children into the school yard to stand at attention while a bonfire was made of the books. Two years later Hodl still burst into uncontrollable tears and woke nights shaking with anxiety. "I was certain," she told Malkeh, "that the police were going to throw the children on the pyre!"

Malkeh wished that she had some real task to occupy her mind. Housework and gardening kept her hands busy but left her mind free. She had given up trying to read. The horrifying picture of Simcha crumpling under a volley of shots stared up off the page at her, and she had to throw the book down.

Fedotov said the trial would surely be soon, but more than four months had passed since Simcha's arrest, and they had heard nothing. Suppose Simcha had already died in the prison? Even here in Polotsk, the name "Peter and Paul Fortress" struck terror into the hearts of the populace. Let him live, God, she prayed. As long as his heart still beat, there was hope.

Today Yoysef had taken the horse and wagon and gone to the country to see if he could buy cheese and eggs. He had taken Golda with him to give her a little outing and to provide Malkeh some relief from the constant attention that poor befuddled Golda needed.

Malkeh, her skirts tucked up and her forearms bare, was on her hands and knees, scrubbing the kitchen floor, when the steward, getting no response to his knock, pushed open the door.

As soon as she looked up and caught sight of her old friend, Malkeh knew that the news was bad. She stood up and carefully rolled down her sleeves, taking care not to look at him again.

He was perhaps too brutal in the telling, but there was no easy way. "I have received word from the advocate. There was a trial. Simcha was sentenced to ten years' imprisonment."

Not so bad as it might be, she thought; people survive Siberia, and after a while, family visits were permitted. "Exile or the penal colonies?"

Fedotov was shaking his head. "He'll serve his time at the fortress."

There was a silence thick with denial. She clutched Yevgeny's coat. "Tell me you're lying to me! Tell me you're playing a trick to frighten me! They couldn't have given him ten years for a crime that was never committed!" She saw his pitying eyes. "No! I won't have it! No, no, no!" Her voice rose in a hysterical crescendo, and her fists beat against his chest.

Fedotov took her hands in his and pulled her toward him. "My poor Malkeh! What a mess we have made of things!"

She wrenched herself free of him and ran out of the house.

Leaving his horse tethered in the street, Yevgeny ran after her. Her fear drove her faster than he could run these days, and he did not catch up with her until she had flung herself breathless on the knoll called Napoleon's Wall. She lay facedown on the bare earth, beating her forehead against a sandstone boulder.

Roughly he grabbed hold of her and lifted her from the ground.

"Let me go! You did this to him! You killed my son!"

Struggling to get his breath, Fedotov struck her across the face.

There was a moment of shock and astonishment, and then she crumpled against him. Holding her with one arm, he stripped off his coat and wrapped it around her. "Like you, I wanted the best for him," he said brokenly. "I was blinded by his intellect. I never stopped to think—"

"I know." Tiredly her head fell to his chest and burrowed there. He stroked her hair.

It was like this that Yoysef and Golda, driving home from the country, found them. Silently Yoysef helped Malkeh into the wagon and waited while Yevgeny clambered in behind her.

*A*s a convicted criminal, Simcha was moved the next day to one of the underground cells. He had imagined that nothing could be worse than his first four months. How naive he had been! Underground, the slime of the Neva crept up through the floors, and sometimes water rats appeared through holes in the stones. The iron stovepipe that was supposed to heat the cell was either completely cold, in which case he curled up in a tight ball on his cot, or was so hot that he was forced to strip off his clothes.

It was inevitable that he would sicken. One day he awoke from sleep—was it nightime? was it day?—with a raging headache and pains in his limbs that made any movement agonizing. All that day and the next, he lay on his bed, first shaking with chills and then burning with fever. Or was it just the iron stovepipe with its alternations between hot and cold?

He was too sick and too weak to get up to eat the food that the guard shoved through the door. He could scarcely swallow water. He lost all track of time. He had fearsome nightmares—or were the rats really gnawing on his feet?—and he knew he must be thrashing about and shouting when three guards converged to hold him down. Simcha heard them talking as if from a far distance.

"He's delirious. Better get the doctor. It could be cholera."

"God help us if it is!" said another, making the sign of the cross. "It'll kill us all!"

One morning eleven days later he awoke in a clean bed in a white-washed room. He thought he had died and gone to the other world.

"Mammeh?" he called weakly. "Mammeh, are you there?"

A male orderly came to the side of the bed. "Awake, are you? You've been calling for your mother since you got here!"

"Where am I?"

"In the army infirmary."

"I don't understand—"

"Had to isolate you so you wouldn't give the whole place cholera. There was no choice."

"Ah." It was too much to take in. Simcha closed his eyes and slept for another twelve hours.

When he had finally recovered enough to reflect on what had happened, he realized that contracting cholera had undoubtedly saved his life. In the infirmary he was cleansed from filth and lice, put into clean clothes, given nourishing food. By the time he was taken back to the prison, he felt strong and rested, and had put some flesh on his bones. The doctor insisted that he not be returned to the damp underground, and so, when he left the hospital, he was taken to an upper-level cell that in comparison seemed luxurious. Also, the doctor had said that he must have sunshine and exercise if he were not to suffer a relapse. His prison routine was thereafter punctuated by twice-weekly visits to the tiny garden, where he was allowed twenty minutes of open air.

It wasn't much of a garden, but to Simcha's hungry eyes, it embodied all the glories of nature. The sky over his head was blue, the sun was warm on his back, and the overgrown lilac and cranberry bushes were fragrant. When he grew tired of pacing the perimeter, there was a half-broken wooden bench on which to sink down.

One day when he was being led back from his outing, the door to the cell next to his own stood open while the guard emptied the prisoner's slop bucket. Simcha's eyes eagerly swept the cell, his eyes meeting those of another man. A message, nonverbal, passed between them. We are not alone, it said. We will beat them by surviving!

That night when Simcha lay down to sleep, he was conscious for the first time of a presence on the other side of the wall. He had the sun now. He had a place to walk. He had fresh air. And, unseen or not, he had a companion nearby, just on the other side of a stone wall. Whatever else was happening, nothing could take that away from him!

*I*n the capital of Bosnia on June 28 that year, 1914, the Sarajevo cell of the Black Hand Society, to prove their devotion to the cause of panslavism and their hatred for Austria, assassinated the Archduke Franz Ferdinand, heir to the throne. It was the spark that ignited a war that was to sweep all the major countries of Europe, plus Great Britain and the United States.

Tsar Nicholas ordered a general mobilization of his armies on July 29, and on August 1 the kaiser declared war upon Russia.

Isolated in his cell, Simcha heard the great guns of the fortress firing off one salvo after another. No sooner had they stopped when the chimes from the Peter and Paul Church played "God Save the Tsar." It was all most extraordinary! The guns were supposed to fire at noon, the chimes at midnight, twelve hours apart. As if that were not puzzling enough, there was the sound of hurried footsteps—actual footsteps!—in the corridors outside his cell, and then the guard was shouting through the Judas window. "We're at war! We're at war! God save the tsar!"

*B*efore August was over, Count Pyotr Voronov was called to report for military duty to General Samsonov's command in Warsaw. Now that the Austrians and Germans were advancing on Poland, Generals Rennenkampf and Samsonov, each at the head of a large Russian force, were scrambling desperately to head them off.

The prospect of adventure stirred Pyotr more than he cared to say. While he was comfortable at Spokoinaya Zemlya, content with the easygoing life of the landed aristocracy and happy with his pretty wife and three fine sons, there was a certain sameness to his days that he was forced to recognize as boredom. He had sometimes longed for some grand event that would change his life, and now he had it.

Yevgeny Sergeivitch insisted on accompanying Pyotr to Moscow, where he was to join his battalion on its way west to Poland and Samsonov.

On the platform of the railroad station, the two men waited while the troops were loaded into their designated cars.

"Do not worry, Pyotr Andreivitch," Yevgeny said, "I will take care of Ekaterina and your sons while you are gone."

"I know, Uncle. I am not worried."

"Remember what I taught you on our hunting trips. Keep your weapon clean and your ammunition dry."

"I'll remember."

"And always keep clean stockings in your musette bag. The difference between victory and defeat sometimes depends on who has dry feet."

Pyotr turned away to hide a smile. Yevgeny Fedotov would not have seen it in any case, tears having obscured his vision.

He continued. "Always be fair with your men and share what you have with them—" Fedotov's voice broke. Wars! What did they accomplish except to kill off the young men! Pyotr did not understand what lay ahead, he thought of it as an excursion. "Your men's loyalty may save your life when your rifle can't."

The conductor ran along the platform, blowing the departure warning on his whistle. The upper bodies of uniformed men leaned from the train's windows as they shouted last-minute messages and waved farewell. Here and there a couple on the platform clung to each other in a last embrace. "Time to go! On the train with you!" the conductor said, trying to hustle the men into the cars. But as soon as his back was turned, lovers embraced once more. Frustrated, the conductor blew his little whistle so hard that his cheeks inflated and his face turned red. "All aboard! All aboard!"

"They can't start the war without us, brother!" one of the soldiers called out.

Someone on the train began to sing the national anthem. The women on the platform wept into their handkerchiefs.

"Go now," Yevgeny Sergeivitch said, giving Pyotr's shoulder a little push in the direction of the train.

He closed his eyes for a moment, vowing that he would keep the Voronov estate intact at least until Petya came back from the war. No one could promise more in these terrible days. If Petya did not come back? He would not think of what would happen.

The two men shook hands gravely. Pyotr mounted the steps, and the conductor folded them up behind him.

While the steam built in its boilers, the train began its slow backward and forward movement. Petya and Yevgeny stood staring at each other, one from the train vestibule, the other from below. Suddenly Pyotr jumped to the platform and threw himself into the arms of the older man. They held tightly to each other for a moment.

Yevgeny Sergeivitch tried to speak, but the unaccustomed words of love stuck in his throat. He kissed first one cheek and then the other, then the first again, clasping his nephew close to his heart. When he released him, Pyotr had to run to catch the slow-moving train.

Fedotov watched while the train edged out of the station and picked up speed. "Let whatever divinity may exist look after you," he whispered, drying his eyes on his sleeve.

Chapter 58

*P*yotr Voronov came home from the war a different man. He had aged ten years in less than three. The easy self-assurance and the charming insouciance of the aristocrat had been replaced by the hard demeanor of a field officer accustomed to making harsh decisions that will be immediately obeyed. By nature temperate and optimistic, the war had made him cynical, and given to brooding silences.

Pyotr was initiated in war at Tannenberg in East Prussia. Assigned to serve in General Samsonov's Second Army, under the direct command of Colonel Igor Konstantinovsky of the 24th Infantry Division, he had scarcely become acquainted with his men before orders were given for them to take to the field against the Germans.

Germany had entered Russian Poland from the north, the Austrians from the south, intending to sever Poland from the main body of Russia. Russian General Rennenkampf's First Army had already engaged the Germans in two successful, though costly, encounters, pushing their line back toward Prussia. Overconfident now, General Rennenkamp fell easy prey to the German ruse of a seeming retreat. He ordered General Samsonov to advance north from Warsaw to head off the "retreating" Germans before they could cross the Vistula River; he, in the meantime, pulled back to rest his men. Samsonov's Second Army, without knowing it, was about to be engaged in a major battle.

At field headquarters on the day before they were scheduled to move out to engage the enemy, Pyotr asked Colonel Konstantinovsky for the details of the battle plan.

Igor Konstantinovsky had been in Poland for six weeks longer than Pyotr. A gray-haired lawyer from Kiev, he probably knew less about military regimen than his captain, who at least had had training as a cadet in the Hussars.

"Have you inspected your troops yet, Captain?" he asked now, a sardonic smile hovering about his thin lips. "Inventoried your supplies?"

"I have only just arrived, sir."

"I suggest that you do so at once."

Pyotr went back to the company he expected to lead into battle the next day. He asked his sergeant for a census of the men in his command and an assessment of their level of field competence.

The sergeant shrugged. "Sir," he said finally, "what we have here are peasants straight out of the villages, most of them sent here without any training. This will be their first battle."

"I see," Pyotr said. It would not do to admit that he didn't see how he could take untrained men into war.

The sergeant, himself a fifteen-year veteran, added, "Most of them never heard of Germany or Austria. They don't know why they're fighting. They don't even know they're Russian!" A couple of men were lounging nearby, and he called them over. "What's your nationality, brother?"

The soldier looked blank.

"Your country?"

The man beamed. "Ah, my country! Why didn't you say so? I Kaluga!"

"He's from Kaluga Province," the sergeant explained to Pyotr. "And you?" he turned to the second man.

"I Tambov, sire."

"Are you Russian?"

The first man shrugged his shoulders. "Kaluga," he said again.

Pyotr absorbed this silently. "Well, Sergeant," he said, dismissing the men, "that's very interesting, but there's nothing we can do about it for now. Let's check the artillery and the ammunition so that at least we know how we are prepared in that regard."

"Yes, sir." The sergeant handed Pyotr a list of the company's weapons.

"But—" Pyotr said, puzzled, "this doesn't add up. There are too few artillery pieces. There aren't even enough rifles for all the men in my command!"

"Yes, sir," the sergeant said, "but, of course, these *mujiks* don't know how to shoot a gun or put a shell in a cannon anyway."

Pyotr took the list and went to find the colonel from Kiev. "Before we can fight, I must have adequate weapons!"

The colonel shook his head. "There are none."

"But what are the men to use?"

"Their hands, their fists, stones and sticks, whatever they can find! Look, it's the same everywhere. There are no roads or railroads to bring up supplies. It's not just guns that we're short. There's too little bread and damn little fodder for the horses! Everything's a mess and confusion here on the front!"

"But what are we to do?"

"The best you can, Captain."

Greatly disturbed, Pyotr returned to his men. He lined up his company and demonstrated how to fire a modern rifle and how to load a howitzer; he didn't bother to show them the use of a machine gun, since there weren't enough to bother about. His men, as the sergeant had indicated, were illiterate peasant farmers; many of them knew how to use a breech-loaded shotgun but few understood newer weaponry. When he would have allowed the men to practice with actual ammunition, the sergeant reminded him that there was too little to waste a single shell.

That night Pyotr wrote letters to his wife, Ekaterina, and to Yevgeny Sergeivitch. Heeding his uncle's advice, before he went to bed he packed clean socks in his musette bag. Then, falling to his knees before the small icon Ekaterina had given him, he prayed fervently that he would not let his men down the next day.

In the morning they marched out, advancing with difficulty through a terrain of lakes, marshes, and forest. They stopped frequently to consult the maps. If they missed the road at any point, they could become hopelessly mired.

Ludendorff and Hindenburg led the German defense. Unlike the Russians, they knew the countryside and its road system well and chose to engage the Russians near Tannenberg. They had had plenty of time to situate their forces and to bring up heavy artillery from Konigsberg, and moreover had been prepared for the Russian advance by intercepting the Russians' uncoded telegraph messages.

The enemies came together near noon. At the first volley from German cannon, Pyotr's men panicked and scattered, many of them foundering and sinking in the bogs. With difficulty the sergeant and Pyotr rallied the frightened men and regrouped them into a ragged formation. It was a choice of being shot by their sergeant or facing the enemy.

The Germans had deployed a large concentration of heavy field guns in a wedge formation, using them to batter their way forward while leveling everything that stood in the way. To the poorly equipped and untrained Russian soldier, the monstrous guns belching fire and iron were terrifying. Behind the wedge the infantry advanced, their weapon blasts echoing those of the heavy artillery.

The Russians had the benefit of numbers, the Germans of equipment and discipline. When Pyotr's men realized they had no place to retreat, they fought fiercely. Pyotr himself was everyplace, encouraging the men, deploying strength where it was needed, leading his sector's assault. But all was chaos. No one seemed to be in overall command of the Russian forces, and there were times when they inflicted more damage on one another than on the enemy.

The battle raged for several days. Each day the men in Samsonov's command expected reinforcements from General Rennenkampf's First Army.

Telegrams were sent, making explicit their perilous position, but help never arrived. In the early evening of the fourth day, their food and ammunition exhausted, Colonel Konstantinovsky rode into Pyotr's sector. His uniform was torn and muddy, his face and mustache black from gunpowder. "Fall back! Fall back!" he shouted to Pyotr before wheeling about.

The intrepid sergeant had been killed earlier in the day. Pyotr gave the command to retreat. It was more than a rout, it was a massacre. Three corps were decimated, a huge number of Russians taken prisoner, and artillery that couldn't be spared had been captured by the German forces. Crushed by the extent of his defeat, General Samsonov strode alone into the dense Tannenburg Forest and shot himself.

Later Pyotr counted his company's losses. Too many. Had he done everything he could to safeguard his men? How could he have taken green troops into battle! That it had not been his decision was no comfort. Too exhausted to wash himself or to eat the rations his corporal brought him, he fell on his cot and slept for twenty hours.

After Tannenburg the Russians suffered a second rout at the Masurian Lakes. In the next week Hindenburg drove toward Warsaw, reaching the outskirts before finally being repulsed by the desperate Russians and Poles.

The winter of 1914 passed in hard fighting that ranged back and forth across the Polish plains. Of necessity, Pyotr's surviving men learned much and quickly about the art of war. They learned to hold their positions until otherwise ordered, regardless of the risk, and grew accustomed to the sudden and gruesome ways in which men die. They became adept in using the fixed bayonet when there was no ammunition for their rifles, and most important, learned to follow orders. As peasants they already knew how to fight on an empty stomach.

A major problem was a constant need for replacements, all of whom had to be trained and prepared for battle. There were precious few officers to do the training. Before the end of 1914, the Russians had lost two-thirds of their leaders to Austrian and German riflemen ordered to aim first at officers, identifiable by their uniforms. Pyotr Voronov was himself wounded in the shoulder during the big offensive at Lodz. Taken to an aid station where a bandage was applied, Pyotr refused to be evacuated to a hospital. He had heard what medical care was like in those places—a flesh wound like his could end in septicemia, amputation, gangrene, death. His arm in a sling, he returned to his men in the field.

Lodz was one more disaster for the Russians. A quarter million Germans, under Hindenburg, faced twice that number of Russians. The Russians, long on manpower but short of rifles, bullets, food, warm coats, and boots, crumpled beneath the onslaught of the well-trained and well-equipped Germans.

In the field, the Russian army fought heroically, sometimes brilliantly.

But there were problems with the logistics of moving men and supplies, bureaucratic incompetence, mixed priorities. The rumor swept the ranks that railroad cars were being sent on regular runs to the Crimea to bring fresh flowers for Empress Alexandra's boudoir, when there was insufficient transportation to carry supplies to the front. Pyotr didn't doubt it. He had seen for himself the stupidity of St. Petersburg—called "Petrograd" now to sound more patriotically Slavic.

At Lodz, at the end there were no bullets for the rifles; the men searched the horizon day after day for the expected supply train. When the news was telegraphed that the train was near, the troops envisioned warm clothes, food, cartridges for their rifles. Inexplicably the train never arrived in Lodz. When it became clear what had happened, there was a near riot. Instead of sending equipment and food, Russian officials in occupied Galicia had appropriated precious railway cars to transport priests to the region's Uniate Christians to Russain Orthodoxy.

*A*t the start of the second year of the war, a critical food shortage, affecting civilian and military populations both, was even more critical than the lack of clothing and ammunition. The general mobilization of 1914 had taken the peasants off the land, and there was no longer a ready labor force to sow, tend, and harvest the crops.

At Spokoinaya Zemlya, Fedotov swallowed his dislike and went, hat in hand, in a manner of speaking, to have a talk with Igor Karpovitch of the *zemstvo.*

"You need me now, I see," the short, barrel-chested man swaggered.

"The army, and the people who live here, need the food we grow. It is my—suggestion—that I—that we—ask every woman, child, old one, and cripple to come work with me to plant grain, potatoes, root vegetables, whatever we can, and then to tend the fields through the summer, until we harvest the crop."

"So you can sell it and make more money for your masters, Yevgeny Sergeivitch?" Karpovitch sneered.

Fedotov kept a tight reign upon himself. "So that the people will not starve next year. So we will have enough to send the troops in Poland."

"So why do you come to me?"

"Please let us not play these games, Karpovitch! Nothing will happen unless you tell the people it's all right to come work our fields!"

There was a smugness on Karpovitch's face. He couldn't stop himself from rubbing his hands together. "And if I don't want to?"

"I'll let it be known that you alone are responsible for the people's hunger. I'll also report you to the military district. You can believe me that I mean this."

Karpovitch frowned. "Look, I'm as patriotic as you are, so don't give me any of that shit!"

"Then you will help me get the message out to the people that if they work, they share in the harvest?"

"All right." He was sullen. "But I'll be watching to see that you don't skim off a little extra profit for yourself!"

The vein in Fedotov's forehead began to pulse. "You bastard! My nephew, Pyotr Voronov, is fighting out there! The people of Spokoinaya Zemlya are *our* people!"

"You can bet that I'll be there to keep watch on you, Fedotov!"

The steward was grim. "If you come, you'd better bring a hoe."

On the first day of spring planting, Malkeh, Yoysef, and Golda, dressed in their shabbiest clothes, were among those who reported for work in the fields. In ordinary times it would have made Malkeh laugh to see the odd assortment of people who had answered Fedotov's call. Besides strong-looking young women, there were men rejected by the army because they were missing the index fingers of their right hands or had been sent home because of wounds to left feet, there were children of all ages, and there were stooped *babushka*s, and old men. In the crowd Malkeh saw dignified Rabbi Nachman with his wife and Hodl, many other Jews. Most had family members in the army.

An unsmiling steward greeted them, showing them how to drop the seeds into furrows that had already been prepared, how to pat the dirt down around them, how much water to give each hillock. They would, he said, work one field at a time. "My foreman and I will keep track of who has worked and for how many hours. It is our national duty to send as much food as possible to the front. The rest we will share out proportionately in accordance to how much time you have given. I shall expect you to be consistent, not to come one day and then decide you're too tired the next. I have to be able to count on your willing hands and your strong backs. Jews will not work on Saturdays. Christians will not work on Sundays. If I don't need you, I will let you know. Is all that clear?"

Afterward the foreman gave each group a sack of seeds and assigned them to a particular section. He or Fedotov stood watch until certain that the process was understood.

The spring sun felt good upon Malkeh's back, and the loam was warm between her fingers. She had placed Golda between Yoysef and herself so they could keep a watchful eye on her. They moved along the row in unison, Yoysef making a little nest for the seeds, Golda dropping them in, Malkeh mounding the earth over them; at the end of the row Yoysef would work his way back with the water bucket. After a while they might, for the sake of variety, switch tasks.

It was quiet and peaceful in their section of field, and it was good to have a repetitive job to do that required no thinking. Butterflies fluttered through the air, pausing now and again to light in the elderberry bushes that outlined the borders of the fields. Bees made a pleasant droning sound as they circled close to examine all this human activity.

Malkeh thought about the last time people had worked together to save what they could for Spokoinaya Zemlya. Had it really been twenty-five years since then? She remembered how Dvoreh and Chaya Leya and Chaim had carried water on poles from the River Dvina. Simcha, of course, had been an infant. Malkeh's heart was squeezed by a spasm of pain. It had been almost two years now that Simcha had been in that awful place. He was like a stone dropped in a well, she thought, with not even a ripple to mark the place or a splash to break the silence.

She mounded the soil over the seeds, concentrating her gaze on the rich earth. Her tears had long since dried up; sometimes she thought her heart had too. A hand, not Yoysef's, touched hers, and she turned her head. Fedotov was kneeling beside her at the furrow, dropping the seeds, three at a time, into the holes while Golda rested.

"He won't make it, will he?" she murmured.

"I don't know." Fedotov knew she meant Semyon.

They worked to the end of the row together, and then Golda returned.

"Why are we planting here instead of our own garden, Malkeh?" she asked.

"We talked about that on the way here, remember, Golda? About the war?

"Oh, yes," she said vaguely. They worked in silence for a few minutes. "What war is that, Malkeh?"

*P*yotr's division, which, after Lodz, had been reassigned to General Dimitriev's Third Army, had spent the icy winter of 1915–1916 starving and freezing in the Carpathian mountain passes. Without reinforcements, plagued by insufficient food, and little ammunition, offensive action was out of the question. The best they could do was to try to hold the Russian line. It was a time of unparalleled hardship for the men. Frostbite was a constant threat, and it was not unheard of for a whole company to freeze to death.

By this time Colonel Konstantinovsky, the green lawyer from Kiev, and Pyotr, the dilettante hussar officer, were not only stripped of excess flesh but also of illusions about the Russian chances for success. Neither man thought he would live to see the outcome.

Few of Pyotr's original company remained. Battle losses had been as high as fifty percent. Desertions were epidemic. Men simply threw down their empty rifles and walked home. Some mutilated themselves, a shot in the foot better than the uneven struggle against the enemy, the verminous food, the endless cold, and the tedium. The few soldiers who had been with Pyotr since the beginning accorded him a respect that bordered on reverence. Unlike some, they said, Captain Voronov did not lag behind but led the charge, and his heroism was legendary. Unlike other officers, Captain Voronov did not hold himself aloof from his men either. More often than not, when he could be dining in the officers' mess, he ate black bread and groats and shared his sugar ration with the common soldiers. In the mountain passes at night, he didn't sleep but passed among them to check for frostbite, himself rubbing circulation into toes grown white and, on more than one occasion, putting his own socks on the feet of a frostbitten soldier. Pyotr was amused but did not refute the stories. He knew that people need to believe in someone. He only wished that he had that luxury himself.

The anxiety of battle gave way that winter to boredom. There was nothing to do in the mountain ravines but wait for spring to release them to renew the struggle. Pyotr shared a tent with another captain of infantry, Vitaly Goremkin. While Vitaly removed himself from the winter's discomforts in sleep, Pyotr wrote—love letters to his dearest Ekaterina, thoughts on war, soldiering, and the future of the human race to Yevgeny Fedotov, accounts of battle strategy that he hoped his sons would someday find of interest. And he read. Andrei Belyi's novel *Petersburg* which had appeared as a serial in 1913, Dostoyevsky's *The Brothers Karamazov*, Lermontov's *Borodino*, Tolstoy and Chekhov and Turgenev—whatever he could get his hands on. By spring every piece of reading material in camp was tattered from being passed among so many hands.

By April the Germans had a third of a million men plus plentiful guns and artillery in position opposite the Third Army. The battle, when it was finally joined, was brutal. The Russian Command Headquarters was criminally incompetent. When General Dimitriev urgently telegraphed for cartridges, reporting that his men were fighting with empty guns, he was told to be more economical. "It is clear," the return wire said, "that your troops are being negligent with supplies." Somehow Dimitriev's troops managed to hold out for a month before abandoning their hopeless position.

The tattered Russian forces now began a steady retreat, pushing their way through Galicia, the Privet marshes, Pinsk, and into the great heartland of Russia. The peasant-soldiers were fatalistic. Igor Konstantinovsky shared with Pyotr a joke that was making the rounds among the men: "We will retreat to Siberia. When we get there the enemy's army will be so tired of chasing us, it will have shrunk to a single German and a single Austrian. The Austrian will, as usual, give himself up as a prisoner, and then we will kill the German."

In the defense of Molodechno, Pyotr almost sacrificed his life against a German cavalry charge. He was hit in the face and upper body by a spray of bullets and fell beneath a riderless horse. He should have been dead, but somehow the bullets missed vital organs, and he managed to roll away before the flying hooves of the horse could completely mangle his leg. Unconscious, he was slung over the shoulder of one of his men and carried to shelter. Transported to hospital after the battle, he would not allow the medics to cut open and scrape his leg wound free of possible infection. Encouraged by the patient's cocked revolver, the doctors were persuaded simply to cleanse the wound with antiseptic and bandage it securely. There was nothing anyone could do to save Pyotr's right eye, which had been irreparably damaged by flying metal debris.

His injuries gained for him his discharge. Having received a field promotion and the Medal of St. George before being mustered out, Major Voronov's war was over. He walked, accepted rides in farm wagons, and sometimes briefly rode on trains as he slowly made his way home. It was the autumn of 1916. In places where there had been people to plant the fields, the grain was tall and golden. Pyotr thought of Spokoinaya Zemlya and wondered if his fields, later to ripen than these southern ones, would soon be ready for scything. He had no doubt that Yevgeny Fedotov would have seen to the nurture of the Voronov lands. Gladdened at the thought of home, he hastened his limping footsteps to the north.

Here and there Pyotr's path crossed that of retreating Russian soldiers who were making their way to secure redoubts before the inexorable advance of Hindenburg's troops. On a bright afternoon in August he saw such a company standing idly by the side of the road, watching as tongues of flame leapt through a dry grain field.

"Hey!" he yelled, hobbling up to the officer in charge. "Can't you see that the field is on fire!"

Unbelieving, he saw torches in the hands of some of the soldiers. "You are burning the wheat?" he asked, incredulous.

"Headquarters policy, Major," the lieutenant said. "We have orders to leave nothing standing that the enemy can use!"

"But—the people! What will our people eat?"

The lieutenant shook his head. "I'm sorry, sir. I just follow orders."

Pyotr was transfixed. He stood by the side of the road until the flames had died, and the field was flat and black. Thinking of the hunger to come, tears oozed from his one good eye and ran down his cheek.

Chapter 59

*T*he United States came late to the conflict that had swept Europe.

Most Americans felt that European quarrels had nothing to do with them, but now in the fall of 1916, when German U-boats had stepped up attacks against American shipping, the nation was locked in somber debate. While Congress weighed the evidence, the country prepared for war.

The opinions at the Rosens' table on a Saturday night reflected the uncertainties of the American people.

"Did you read in the paper about the Huns?" Berel lowered his voice so that the children, who had gone into the bedroom to play, would not hear. "In some village in France, they speared babies with bayonets. The *Forward* said so!"

"Like Cossacks," Soreh Levy said, shuddering. "Ah, God, what we have seen in one lifetime!"

Berel scowled. "The United States should declare war! If we don't stop the kaiser now, the next thing you know, he'll be over here!"

Chaya Leya cut thick slices of fragrant honey cake and passed them around the table. "I don't think war ever solves anything," she said quietly.

Herschel was troubled. "I wish we knew what is happening at home. What has it been now, over two years since we've heard from Polotsk?"

Dvoreh picked her younger child, Saul, off the floor and held him in her lap. "I have been so worried about Mammeh and Papa and Simcha."

Chaya Leya nodded. Who could know what was happening in Russia? Few letters were getting through, and the reports in the newspapers were muddled and contradictory. There were rumors of shortages of food and fuel, of increasing anti-Jewish propaganda, of strikes in the cities and wholesale desertions from the Imperial Army. She had never been more worried in her life.

Soreh Levy poured tea into the glasses. "I say the *mishigass* is Europe's. Let them keep the madness over there! It is no business of ours!"

"The Germans have made it our business by attacking our ships," Chaim said reasonably.

"We should not go to war over a few ships," Soreh maintained.

Herschel said mildly, "You sound like Chaim's friend, Senator Johnson, Soreh."

"Some friend!" Chaim felt a disclaimer was necessary. "I've never even met the man."

"Can't we talk about something else?" Chaya Leya pleaded. "All this talk about war gives me a headache!"

Chaim lit a cigar. "Well, I can say one good thing about all this—it's been a shot in the arm for business."

"The new store in Sacramento is doing well, then?" Herschel asked.

"Business is wonderful in both stores."

Herschel nodded. After a long dry period, things were picking up at the furniture store too. It made him ashamed that it took a war for a man to make a living.

O nly Herschel and Chaya Leya had been close enough to war to fear it. They talked far into the night about what they would do if war was declared and Herschel called to serve. For weeks already Chaya Leya's mind had been relentlessly drawn back to the days when Valodya and Herschel had gone off to defend Port Arthur and only Herschel had returned.

"It's not the same, it's not the same," Herschel told Chaya Leya, holding her close.

"If there's an enemy and people get killed, it *is* the same!"

"President Wilson says there will be no war for America."

"And you believe that?"

"Go to sleep now." Herschel pulled the quilt up around Chaya Leya's shoulders.

"I can't! When I close my eyes I have bad dreams!"

"I will hold you in my arms while you sleep."

Night after night in Chaya Leya's dreams, Valodya's tawny head, encrusted with blood, lay on barren earth, his hand outstretched, as if for help, and his sightless eyes staring upward at the sun. She would awaken from the nightmare in a cold sweat, her nightgown twisted around her body and her face wet with tears.

"If only I could have buried him properly," she mourned, "but we don't even know how or where he died."

Herschel was gentle. "Wherever he is, he is at peace. Leave him that way."

Only once had there been word from any of their friends in Harbin. Letters posted to the Kutuzovs at the house on Nicholas II Avenue were not acknowledged; neither were inquiries sent to the Moscow headquarters of the Trans-Siberian Railway. Had the letters arrived at their destination? Was it that the Kutuzovs had returned to St. Petersburg? Been posted elsewhere? There was no way to tell. One brief letter had come—in 1907 or '08, thereabouts—from dear Frau Koch, and then nothing. A letter sent to the Mirov family of Smolensk, asking for news of their son Valodya, had been returned,

marked "incomplete address." Herschel reminded Chaya Leya that a country in turmoil is bound to have uncertain mails. Silence, he said, did not
necessarily spell disaster.

Chaya Leya did not believe that. Lately she had felt Valodya was slipping away. Only the nightmare kept his face before her. Her anxiety grew
daily. If Valodya could go off to war and not return, why not Herschel?

Even though Chaim had long ago ceased to wonder about the promise
of his "friend," Senator Hiram Johnson, the senator had not forgotten him.
Months before war was declared, Al McCabe came to see Chaim at his store
in Sacramento. Contracts were to be let for the manufacture of army uniforms. Senator Johnson wondered if Hy Mandel would like to submit a bid.

"Uniforms! What you talking about? I'm in retail!"

"Chance of a lifetime, Mandel." McCabe grinned. "I did some checking on you before I came out from Washington, heard you were once a
tailor."

"Sure I was tailor, good one, too, but I don't do that no more."

McCabe handed Chaim a sketch. "Could you make me a suit of clothes
like this one, do you think?"

Chaim studied it. "I can sew anything!"

"How many yards would it take?"

Chaim, interested despite himself, examined the picture and made a
mental calculation. "Oh, say two yards and a little bit for jacket, a yard for
pants. Depends on size." Chaim closed his eyes, thinking how he would lay
out the pattern on the cloth. "Of course, cutting more than one from a
length of cloth, there'll be less waste."

McCabe was pleased. "Well, say the uniform was made out of wool.
How much would it cost you to make it—on average?"

"Depends on quality of the wool. And how many I'm going to make.
The cost of fabric and findings is going to be lower if I buy in quantity."

McCabe waited. Chaim's eyes narrowed, considering. "One suit from
medium grade wool probably costs seven or eight dollars to make. Ten suits
you could turn out for under five apiece, fifty maybe only three or four
dollars. I'd have to figure it out on paper."

McCabe nodded. "Do you know anything about power machinery?"

Chaim scratched his head. "A little. Papa had power machines in the
old country, not fancy like here, though. I worked an industrial machine
once—oh, it must have been back in 1908 or '09—I had a job making pajamas.
The factory went bust, and I lost job."

McCabe slapped Chaim on the back. "I think you've got what it takes,
Mandel. I trust you. Work out the costs. Senator Johnson will be expecting
your bid for ten thousand uniforms. Union label, of course."

"Ten thousand!"

"Well, just for a start." McCabe laughed. "The government expects good quality, but it's okay if you cut some corners to give yourself a fair profit. That's the name of the game, profit. Okay?"

Chaim said slowly, "I don't know, Mr. McCabe. I got two stores. I make good living. What do I know about manufacturing?"

"You gotta think big, Mandel! I told you a long time ago that Hiram Johnson doesn't forget his friends. He's giving you your big break. Don't muff it, okay?"

"Okay?" Chaim echoed. "Yes, I guess so—okay."

*C*haim could not have prepared the bid without Rosalie. Working from the sketch McCabe had left behind, Chaim prepared a sample pattern and calculated the fabric requirements for an average-size uniform. But when he had finished this preliminary work, he was not sure how to proceed.

Rosalie said, "You've got a lot of questions to answer, Hy. Where are you going to make those uniforms? Can you get your hands on machines to do the job? At what price? How many skilled men, or women, will you need to turn them out? What will the fabric cost wholesale?"

"Ten thousand! I think maybe we forget it!" Chaim said helplessly. "Stores are doing fine, is maybe enough for us!"

Rosalie spoke sharply. "Don't talk like a greenhorn! This is your chance to be a success in life! First you ask a real estate agent to find you a factory site. Then you go up to the woolen mills in Oregon, see what they've got in stock and bargain for a good price. When you get all the information together, preparing the bid is easy!"

"Rosalie, please! In first place, who take care of stores while I run around?"

"That's why you have a manager and salesmen."

"Raizel, I'm not knowing how to do this!"

"If I can figure it out, you certainly can!"

"Come with me, Raizel. Help me do this thing."

She considered. "Well, I guess I can do that," she said slowly. Then, warming to the idea, "I think I'd rather like that!"

*R*osalie Mandel had made good use of the time she had worked for Hershkowitz the attorney. She was quick and shrewd, and in the lawyer's office she had learned to order facts and present a convincing case. She liked business and had learned from her father to drive a hard bargain. That training worked for her in preparing the proposal they later submitted to the U.S. government.

Rosalie had been at Chaim's side during every step. Working into the nights, they had developed cost estimates, calculating, revising, arguing, starting over. They drew close for the first time in all their married years, the excitement of competition a potent stimulant.

On a night in Portland, they lay between the clean white sheets in a bedroom of the best hotel in the city. Although it was late, Rosalie was still not ready to lay down the argument they had been having over supper. "You shouldn't have given in so easily, Hy! I know they would have come down in price."

Idly Chaim lifted the hem of his wife's prim nightgown. Ever so gently he touched her. Tonight she did not shrink from his touch.

"Now, if you can just get twenty-five jackets from a bolt instead of the twenty-three you project—"

Tentatively he stroked her thigh.

"And if we can get a little better price at the Pendleton Mills—"

He began to ease the nightgown up over her hips. "Do you really need this thing on, Raizel? Room has steam heat."

"I guess not," she said absently, leaning across him to the bedside table for pad and pencil.

Chaim reached up and pulled her down on him, his arms circling her waist. As she struggled to loosen his hold, Rosalie was mesmerized to see the naked torso of the tattooed lady wriggle on his biceps.

"Raizel," he whispered, "lie down against me."

Staring at the tattoo, she let her body sink into his. There was a pleasant hardness to his muscles, and after a while there was that other hardness pressing against her lower abdomen. His arms locked about her, he smoothly reversed their positions. He was kissing her smooth white forehead, the tip of her nose, her pointed chin, and she was kissing him back, tasting the saltiness of his skin and mouth.

"Ah, Raizel—" he murmured.

"Rosalie," she said automatically.

His hand reached over and switched off the light.

The Department of the Army liked the Mandel proposal and promptly awarded Chaim his first government contract. Almost as if fate were leading them, they found that the old pajama factory where Chaim had worked briefly was vacant and for sale. They mortgaged the two stores in order to make an offer on the derelict factory. It would serve well enough to turn out that first order, and if they were successful, it could be renovated later.

On the suggestion of Al McCabe, Chaim engaged Hamilton, McGrory, a firm of management consultants, to establish the manufacturing operation. Young Brent Hamilton, son of the senior partner, came himself to work with Mandel. Yale educated, bred to the Social Register, Hamilton could not understand Hy Mandel nor could Hy Mandel understand Hamilton. After six frustrating months Chaim terminated the contract. "I'll manage factory myself," he told Rosalie.

She scoffed. "What do you know about running a factory? You can't even balance a checkbook!"

"I don't have to," Chaim said calmly, "you do it. I bet you could do better job than that Hamilton fellow."

"Of course I could," Rosalie said.

"Well, then?"

"The government people might not like dealing with a woman," she warned.

"They get used to it."

"The factory workers may resent me."

"Is okay, I handle."

"Well, let's give it a try!"

They just about broke even on that first army contract, but they learned from their mistakes. By the time the contract was renewed for twenty-five thousand pieces, Rosalie had found a mill selling a perfectly adequate cloth at approximately half the cost. In the meantime, Chaim was working out problems in the manufacturing process itself.

The work at Mandel's divided itself naturally. Chaim stayed on top of all the manufacturing operations and Rosalie ran the office. The two stores, doing well because of the war boom, were put under the management of Sam Taylor, a man experienced in the retail trade. As Rosalie became increasingly adept in business dealings, she acquired a polish that was the perfect foil for Chaim's shrewd but rougher presence. Together they were formidable. Their marriage gradually evolved into the association of business colleagues.

*W*ar finally came to the United States in April 1917. As the over-forty father of three children, Herschel received a deferment from the draft. Berel was rejected because of weak lungs, and Lev didn't pass the medical examination either. Chaim was eager to fight and volunteered but was turned down because by that time his business was considered essential to the war effort. Of them all, only their cousin Moishe Fleischman in New York was inducted, spending ten dull months in supply procurement in New Jersey and two months in the trenches of France, where he lost a leg. "Could have been worse," Moishe said after the war was over. "I could've lost a hand, and whoever heard of a butcher without a thumb on the scale!"

*C*haim went to San Francisco for several days every month. He never explained these trips. Rosalie supposed that he went to see his sisters and his friends, the Levys. She had never wanted to go with him, yet she was resentful that he no longer asked her. She was not proud of it, but she had always been a little jealous of Chaya Leya—for the affection she seemed to attract without half trying and for those beautiful little girls and adoring husband. She felt excluded from Hy's close relationship with Herschel and Berel, irritated, that he felt responsible for his younger sister and her odd husband.

She was often lonely when Hy was gone, but if she had been able to bring herself to tell him, he would have been surprised to learn that she missed him.

*B*y this time, Chaim's and Manya's lovemaking had lost its edge of excitement. What it had gained in ten years was the comfort of the familiar. Not that there weren't occasional surprises, but the contours of Chaim's body, the feel of his firm flesh, the clean smell of his skin were like extensions of Manya's own person, the same for him with her. Like a long-married couple, they no longer took sex seriously; it was part of the texture of the life they had made together, no more and no less important than anything else. There were times when Manya needed Chaim's vigorous mind more than she needed his body, and others when the thought of Manya's borscht drove Chaim mad with a longing quite apart from sex.

On a Friday in March, Chaim came to Manya's flat on Fulton Street earlier than usual, shortly after midday, in fact. Recently, on Chaim's insistence, Manya had reluctantly agreed to accept financial support from him and had quit her job at the bar. Now she filled her days visiting among the little group of Russians who had settled around Clement Street. With some of the other women, she helped out at the Russian Orthodox Church, arranging flowers, laundering altar cloths, and polishing the metal censers until they shone. But on that Friday, because she expected Chaim, Manya was at home, making pirozhki that they would eat later with the thick cabbage soup already simmering on the back of the stove. When she heard his key in the door, she emerged from the kitchen, flushed and with a streak of flour in her hair. As Chaim lifted her off her feet in a hug, he thought she had never looked prettier.

"You are so early!" she exclaimed. "I would have been finished if I'd known!"

"I love to watch you cook," he said, following her into the steamy kitchen.

He sat at the table while she finished filling and shaping the dough. Her sleeves were rolled above her elbows, and her arms were plump and white and smooth. Chaim felt a strong stirring in his groin, and he rose and came around behind her, circling her waist with his arms. He nuzzled her neck where it emerged beneath the coil of thick red hair and felt beneath her apron for her nipples. She turned to him, her floury arms reaching around him and leaving their imprint on his coat.

"Leave the pirozhki!" he said, his voice husky.

"Yes." In one swift movement she scooped up the baking sheet and shoved it into the ice box.

In the bedroom they made love with exceptional passion, their limbs tangled and slippery. Afterward, Chaim kissed her tenderly in her flour-streaked hair and drifted into a quiet sleep, his arm still holding her close beside him. When he awoke later, Manya was still lying at his side, very still, her eyes, open and thoughtful, fastened on the ceiling.

"Haven't you slept at all?" he asked.

"I want to talk to you," she said.

"So talk!" Chaim smiled, looking into her serious face. There was no answering smile. Chaim sat up, leaning his back against the headboard. "Well? What is it, Manya?"

Her voice was dreamy. "I'm pregnant, Chaim."

"Pregnant!" Chaim was astonished. "But you can't be after all these years!"

"But I am. I have been quite sure for weeks now, and yesterday I saw a doctor."

Chaim was bewildered. "But Rosalie said I couldn't make children!" In an abrupt movement, Chaim moved away from her. "Manya! Has there been someone else! Tell me! Is there another man?"

Manya sat up, holding the sheet to her full breasts. A red stain started at her throat and spread upward across her face. "You can ask me that? Is that all you think of me?"

"But I—I am not able—"

"What nonsense! A man full of life like you! If I hadn't always taken care, we'd have had half a dozen by now!"

Conflicting emotions contorting his face, Chaim swallowed hard. "But—but what are we to do, Manya?"

"Do? What is there to do? The child will grow within me and when it's time, it will come into the world." Manya's arms reached out to him. "Come and hold me, Chaim! I am crazy with wanting you. Do you suppose that having a baby makes a woman feel like this?"

The next morning when Chaim prepared to leave, he paused in the doorway. "What are we to do?" he asked again, troubled.

Manya took his face between her hands. Her eyes almost on a level with his, she searched his face. "What do you want to do?"

He groaned. "Oh, God! I don't know. I don't know!"

"There is time. It's more than six months before the baby comes. Things will come clear of themselves."

Chaim kissed her gently. "I love you, Manya."

She smiled a little sadly. "I know."

*B*ack home in Sacramento, Chaim was moody and withdrawn. He snapped at Rosalie when she tried to talk to him about a business decision that had to be made.

Rosalie put down her coffee cup. "What's the matter with you, Hy? Are you not feeling well?"

"I'm fine," he said shortly. He threw down his napkin and got up from the breakfast table. "I think I'll go for a walk."

When he left the room, Rosalie stared after him. A walk?

Chapter 60

*T*sar Nicholas II was forced to abdicate his throne in March 1917, and the provisional government ordered the release of all political prisoners. Prisoner 5794206, Semyon Mandelkern, Jew, was among them, having survived almost four years in the Fortress of Peter and Paul.

When the gates of the Trubetskoy Bastion swung open for the last time, to permit thirty-four emaciated, sunken-eyed men to emerge into daylight, the crowd waiting on the snowy square cheered. "Hurrah for the heroes of the revolution! Death to the two-headed eagle!"

Years of isolation and silence made the roar of human voices harsh frightening the prisoners, some of whom took a backward step toward the shelter of the prison walls. A few held their hands before their faces, but whether to protect their eyes from the bright sunlight or to hide the weakness of tears was not clear.

The swift pace of events was all very bewildering to Simcha. Early in the year he had sensed a change in his jailors. Sometimes when the guard brought his food, he broke the rule of silence by speaking to him, and during a spell of hard cold, one of them had brought him a thicker blanket. Simcha had reasoned that there must be serious setbacks for the tsarist government. Then ten days ago there had been the unmistakable sounds of artillery fire from the direction of the city. He had sat on the edge of his cot, his head cocked, listening and trying to make out what was happening.

"Have the Germans come?" he asked the man who brought his soup.

Once this same guard would have knocked his head against the stones for asking, but now he merely shook his head glumly. "No, not them, not the Germans. That's the Russian people letting the government know they don't like not having enough to eat."

Simcha jerked as a cannon from the fortress fired a ball across the river.

The guard dropped his voice. "They say the army's joined the demonstrators." Then, having said too much, he hurriedly shuffled out, his felt boots as silent as always against the stones.

More startling yet, a week before the chimes from the bell tower of the Peter and Paul Church had ceased. No more "Have Mercy, O Lord" on the quarter hour, no "How Glorious Is Our Lord in Zion" on the hour, no "God Save the Tsar" at midnight. Oddly, it was lonely without the bells, and the days seemed to lose all form. "What's happening?" Simcha had asked the young jailor, the one whose job it was to take him outdoors for exercise. "The bells?"

"You don't know, do you? The tsar has been forced to step down."

Too much was happening too quickly. It was disorienting.

The previous day the doors to the cells had been left unlocked. A barber had come to shave the prisoners and to cut their hair, basins of washing water had been provided and clothing had been brought. The prisoners had been nervous and mistrustful, afraid to leave the shelter of their cells. Gradually the most courageous among them had ventured into the corridor. When nothing untoward happened, others followed, sidling along the walls, afraid to look into the faces of others. For some, it had been too emotional an experience, and after a short time they had gone back to their cells and pulled the doors shut behind them.

Simcha stood now on the threshold of the prison, looking out at the throng come, out of curiosity or respect, to greet those who were today released from their imprisonment. Some of them were embracing individual prisoners. For himself, he expected no one; his family in Polotsk were unlikely to know of his release, and his closest friends, Vera and Vassily—well, four years is a long time.

A gaunt woman, soberly dressed except for a bright red and yellow shawl drawn over her head and shoulders, tentatively stepped out of the crowd toward him. The winter sunlight glanced off the lenses of her spectacles and made her gray eyes appear almost translucent. "Semyon?" she asked uncertainly.

Vera? Had he then changed so much? His hand went up to his face, to the heavy beard that covered its lower half. He had been clean-shaven four years ago, he had stood straight and tall, and his body had been solid with flesh and muscle. Now he limped from pain that had taken up permanent residence in his left hip and leg, and he was thin to the point of emaciation.

But Vera had changed too. The years could not have been easy, for she looked thin, and there were fine lines around her eyes and mouth, too many for a woman so young.

They stood close together in the midst of the crowd, taking each other's measure. When she reached out a trembling hand, he was too overcome to take it.

"Semyon, it's Vera," she said unnecessarily. "I've come to take you home."

"Yes," he said. "Vera." He cleared his throat.

Gently she put an arm about him and led him toward the bridge that linked the island to the city. "You're free now," she said.

*V*era had an even smaller and dingier flat than before, in an area of the city where poor people lived in tenements as crazily jumbled as rabbit warrens. Feeling strange and shy with each other, they gradually settled into the routines of living under one roof. Vera had set up a cot for Simcha in the main room while she slept in the tiny bedroom alcove. She apologized for the food she put on the table, the bread hard and heavy with unidentifiable fiber, the tea hardly more than hot water with a couple of tea leaves floating in it, and only an occasional egg or piece of dried fish to eke out their diet; he assured her it was more than he had had in prison. Food was scarce everywhere, she told him, and he nodded, remembering how his guard had said that the people were rioting for bread.

An overwhelming lassitude had overcome Simcha. He knew he should not presume on his earlier relationship with Vera; afterall, she had little enough for herself. But, sick with recurrent fevers, digestive problems, and painful rheumatism from years spent in damp cells, he could not seem to make the decision to move out. Worse by far, the years of punishing isolation had made him so fearful of other people that he was terrified of leaving the flat, let alone fending for himself. He wanted desperately to see his parents, but he could not face the journey home. So he stayed, letting Vera forage for food and wash his clothes, rub his back when he was in an agony of pain, and sit by his side when he awoke frightened, thinking he was back in the fortress. Slowly, supported by Vera, a semblance of confidence returned to him.

With Vera at his side, Simcha ventured into the streets of the city. He was shocked at conditions in St. Petersburg—Petrograd—it was hard for him to remember to call it that. The streets and canals were littered with filth—there was no one to collect the garbage—and many of the houses had broken windows and slogans scrawled on the walls. "Bread, land, and peace!" was a favorite along with "All land to the people!" Few stores were open for business, and those that were had boarded up their windows to discourage looters. Thievery was brazen, carried out in broad daylight among dozens of witnesses; policemen seemed to be nonexistent. Simcha was shocked to see a peasant in a soldier's overcoat stagger down the steps of a vacated house, carrying a valuable oil painting. On Liteinyi Prospekt a group of the homeless built a bonfire of priceless dining room chairs. Then if anyone needed a reminder that the old days were dead, in place of the double-headed eagle that had always flown over the Winter Palace a huge blood red banner now fluttered. For two days after his first walk into the heart of the city, Simcha had turned his face to the wall and retreated into himself.

Vera was quiet around Simcha. He was grateful that she did not try to fill in the happenings of four years all at once; there was so much! She answered questions as he asked them, feeding him information in small doses; they were like a nurse and an invalid, he thought, or a mother and a child.

Over a period of weeks, by bits and pieces, he filled in the gaps of history. He learned from Vera that the war with Germany had been a series of catastrophic defeats ending with the soldiers throwing down their arms and running away to return to their families. Conditions at home were terrible, the economy overstrained, inflation out of control, transportation nonexistent, and everywhere people starving.

On International Women's Day, women factory workers and housewives had staged a mass demonstration to protest the shortage of food. By evening of that day, a hundred thousand workers had walked off the job in a sympathy strike. The government called their crack infantry regiments to put down the demonstrators but instead the soldiers had joined the people. Simcha had heard the gunfire from his cell.

The tsar had gone to army headquarters in Mogilev on the eve of the general strike. When he tried to return to Petrograd, his train was intercepted at Pskov, where he was forced to sign a declaration of abdication, and he was now under house arrest. A provisional government had been formed, sharing its authority with the "Petrograd Soviet of Workers and Soldiers' Deputies." It hadn't the power to hold the country together, thus setting the stage for the triumphant return of Vladimir Lenin from exile in Switzerland.

Simcha could not assimilate this dizzying progression of events. He could cope only by reducing it to the personal. "But how are you managing, Vera?"

She answered him with that careless toss of her frizzy head that he had once found enchantingly childlike. "Oh, like before, I do a little of this and a little of that to help out the party, and they pay me what they can." She laughed a little wryly. "It's not enough to buy caviar and vodka, but it's enough to live."

While Vera was at work one day, Simcha gathered up the threads of his courage to leave the flat alone. That first day he walked unsteadily to the end of the street. The next day he ventured a little farther, and since nothing unfortunate befell him, he continued. Looking for his old haunt, the Blue Lantern, he became confused and soon realized that he was hopelessly lost. Plunged into a panic state, all the streets began to look alike, and he could discern no landmarks from which to get his bearings. He hurried as fast as his limp permitted along winding streets that merged and blurred. Although a cold wind was blowing, he was sweating and his shirt clung wetly to his back. Nauseated, he threw up in a doorway and slumped, weeping helplessly, on a curb.

A *drozhki* stopped nearby. The driver, an old man, called down to him. "Too much to drink, brother? I'll take you home for a ruble!"

Simcha shook his head. "Sick. Not drunk."

"I'll still take you home for a ruble."

"I have no money, see?" He turned out his pockets. He had begun to shake with the chills of a fever. "Just tell me, please, how to get back to the Nevsky Prospekt."

"All right," said the *drozhki* driver. "But you look too sick to walk." The old man sat in his tall seat, indecisive, turning things over in his mind. Finally, resigned, he heaved a great sigh. "Get in. I'll take you home."

"I have no money."

"It's all right. My contribution to the revolution!"

*A*lthough Simcha never completely regained his health, a degree of strength returned to him. He ate whatever Vera put in front of him, and the hollows in his face and body began to fill in. As other appetites returned, so did his need to hold a woman in his arms. Vera was willing but more tense than he remembered.

"What is it?" he asked.

"Nothing. You've been gone a long time."

He thought of her old wildness that had made of their lovemaking a battleground from which he would emerge with bites on his neck and long scratches on his back. He had called her his Gypsy and his tigress lover. There had always been a passionate sexuality in her that had sparked the intense fire between them. But not now. He thought perhaps she held back, worried by his fragility. Or was it that they had both grown older with suffering? They were more like friends of an older time than like lovers. In any case, the cot in the front room was folded up and Simcha returned to Vera's bed.

*K*nowing how Vera felt about Vassily, Simcha did not tell her when he left the flat one day to seek out his old friend.

When he'd asked after him, Vera's voice had taken on a nasty edge.

"Ah, yes, your *dear* and *very good* old friend, Vassily Chernov," she had said. "He's made a real success of the revolution. A deputy in the Petrograd Soviet! And grown rich in the bargain!"

A woman at the office of the Soviet gave Simcha Vassily's address. At first he thought she had made a mistake. The building, overlooking the Moika Canal, was so grand that it might once have been an aristocrat's palace. He stood looking up at it for several minutes before he roused himself to go inside. The building had been divided into four apartments; Simcha found Vassily's name on the uppermost.

Vassily himself answered Simcha's knock at the door. "Semyon! My dear fellow! How wonderful to see you!" The two men embraced and then stood back, surveying each other. Simcha saw that Vassily had put on weight, rather an unhealthy amount, and he looked bloated and sallow, his flat black eyes almost disappearing in the pouches beneath them. He wore a spade-shaped beard now, both the beard and his hair streaked with gray. "But how long have you been in Petrograd? I thought you were in prison somewhere!"

"I was set free." Surely, Simcha thought, if Vassily were a deputy in the government, he would know that political prisoners had been released!

"Come in, come in, my boy! I want to hear everything!"

Drawn into a large, open room, Simcha looked about him at the rich Oriental carpets on polished floors, the tall, draped windows, the graceful furnishings which included even a grand piano.

Vassily, following the line of Simcha's vision, laughed. "A change for the better, eh, Semyon? Sit, sit, my friend. I shall bring tea, and we shall talk."

While Vassily was in the kitchen, Simcha leaned back in the chair and closed his eyes. He inhaled the smell of floor wax and lemon oil. Remembering Vassily's shabby room in the boardinghouse where he had lived, he found the change in Vassily's circumstances extraordinary. Everywhere he had been in this city, he had observed hardship and poverty. Vera was living from hand to mouth. And Vassily—?

His old friend returned, bearing a tray of thickly sliced white bread, a saucer of jam, a dish of sweet butter, canned peaches, and a pot of steaming tea. An abundance of treasures! Simcha's forehead wrinkled in thought. But how could it be when there were shortages of flour, sugar, tea, every kind of foodstuff! Nowhere in the city had he seen food like this at any price!

"You are wondering if I am a wartime profiteer! Of course not!" Vassily added sanctimoniously, "Not that there aren't plenty who got rich serving in the Soviet! A shame, too, when we are at war!"

"But this apartment—the food—"

"I inherited this place from one of the Duma members who went back to the country after the Duma was dissolved."

Simcha gestured toward the trayful of food. "And all this?"

"The scoundrel had a pantry full of this stuff. Vassily frowned. "What is this? Are you interrogating me to see if my heart's still pure?"

"How does a revolutionary rate a palace, Vassily?"

"You *are* interrogating me, aren't you? If you must know, I was rewarded for a favor I did the party."

"Oh? What favor did you do?"

"Not that it's any of your business, but I turned in the chief of the S.R. combat unit. The bastard was working for the tsarist police all the time he was plotting assassinations and blowing up buildings! Can you imagine? Unfortunately, he got out of the country alive." Vassily put a glass of strong tea at Simcha's elbow and carefully buttered a slice of bread for him. "Jam, Semyon?"

"I seem not to have much appetite."

A silence fell. Simcha's mind was busy, and he didn't like what he was thinking. Vera had warned him that prison had made him distrustful and suspicious. To calm himself, he consciously called up the memory of his old friend spooning soup into his mouth after the Bloody Sunday fiasco. He thought about the hours they had spent talking in coffeehouses, the chess games— His problem was that the remembered Vassily bore no resemblance to this pale and flabby man!

After a while Vassily broke the silence to ask, "Have you thought about what you will do now?"

Simcha shrugged. "I have a couple things in mind. I want to go home to Polotsk to see my parents—that first. I've been waiting until I had the strength to make the trip."

"And then?"

"I thought maybe I'd get married."

Vassily said thoughtfully, "I had a woman I loved once, only she turned out to be a lying bitch. Let me give you some advice, Semyon—find yourself a woman you can buy, if you like, but don't let yourself get personally involved!"

Simcha stared curiously at him but said nothing.

There was a short silence before Vassily recalled himself. Politely he asked, "Who were you thinking of marrying?"

"Do you remember Vera Stepanovna?"

Vassily looked at him cruelly. "Ah, Vera!" he said, grinning broadly. "Indeed I do! Vera is what you might call a true socialist. Once you were gone, Vera was glad to share whatever she had with all the comrades in turn."

Simcha was on the road to Polotsk at the end of October when Lenin seized command of the government, surrounded the Winter Palace where the provisional cabinet had taken refuge, and arrested its leader, Alexander Kerensky. It was of passing interest to Simcha, just one more of the changes of government that seemed now to occur daily. He was much more preoccupied with his efforts to reach home.

After a bitter quarrel with Vera, Simcha had had no one to turn to except Vassily Chernov. Refusing Vassily's offer to let him move into the apartment with him, Simcha asked him to lend him the railroad fare to Polotsk.

Vassily had removed a wad of ruble notes from his pocket, and, ever generous, had tossed the whole bundle to Simcha. If Vassily had not profited from the war, as he insisted, the Soviet must pay very high wages, Simcha thought, returning all but a few to him.

"I must warn you, though," Vassily said, "you may not be able to get on a train. And if you do, it may not go through to Polotsk."

"I'll make it," Simcha said grimly.

Train schedules did not exist. He had waited for four days and three nights for the train to arrive from Finland, sleeping on a bench in the station. When finally it pulled in, he was among the first on the platform to push and shove his way into one of the cars. He counted himself lucky to find a seat; many more were forced to stand in the aisles, clinging to whatever handholds they could find as the train bumped its way along its southeasterly course.

Three hours later, the train, its brakes screeching, came to such an abrupt halt that many of the passengers fell sprawling in the aisles.

"What's happening? What's going on?" Passengers peered out the windows but could see nothing except a crowd of milling men surrounding the train.

Someone was shouting. "Get off! Everyone off the train! This is as far as we go!"

Simcha collared the conductor. "I have a ticket all the way through to Polotsk!"

"Sorry. The track's been pulled up. And these—thieves"—he gestured at the rough lot of peasants clambering into the vacated cars and even onto the train roof—"want to go to Petrograd."

"But how will I get to Polotsk?"

The conductor shrugged. "You'll walk, like everyone else."

Trudging along the road, Simcha had plenty to occupy his mind. For mile after mile he observed fields burned to the ground, trees uprooted from orchards, and gardens destroyed. Here and there were scorched foundation bricks, all that remained of ancient manor houses that had been leveled by fire. Where cattle and sheep had previously pastured, there was no sign of livestock. Had the Germans, then, advanced so far into Russia, he wondered, or was it that the enmity of the peasants ran so deep that they would destroy out of revenge what they needed to sustain their own lives? The reality of revolution was becoming ever more clear to him. Ignorant people with no food to eat burned the grain. Those with no shelter destroyed the houses, with no clothing looted oil paintings. The tyranny of autocrats had been replaced by the tyranny of the underdogs, who were unfit to govern. Fearless leaders of the revolution had succumbed to the same cruelty and cupidity as their predecessors. Was it for this that he had squandered an education, disappointed those who cared for him, and suffered four years in the fortress?

Sick in heart and spirit, Simcha limped on. Sometimes a farmer came along who gave him a lift in a cart. Some nights he crept into a barn, if he could find one that still stood, to sleep; some nights he slept under the stars. He ate berries from roadside bushes and occasionally found a householder willing to sell him a bit of cheese, a dipper of milk, or a crust of bread for an exorbitant amount of cash.

He had plenty of time to reflect on his last quarrel with Vera. He had been determined to ignore what Vassily had implied about her. As far as he knew, Vera had been perfectly faithful to him during the two years they had lived together before his arrest. And no one could ask for a better friend than she since his release. Nonetheless, doubts had begun to nag at him, making a misery of his life. He had begun watching her for signs that she didn't want him with her. When she went out to work or to look for food, even though she came back with money or bread, he was sure that she had had a tryst with another man. He dwelt obsessively on how she had changed toward him sexually, become compliant rather than passionate, often too tired to make love at all. In the sick recesses of his soul he reasoned that if that was not a sign that there was someone else, what was?

The end came on a night of the full moon in October. He had rolled over in bed and awakened when he brushed against her. She was lying on her back, her mouth slightly open, her face naked and vulnerable without her spectacles. With a lurch of his heart he noticed how thin her face was, the bones prominent beneath the skin and hollows where there should be none. The coldness that had been like a lump within him seemed to melt, and he wanted to care for her, to ease the cares that even in sleep lay heavily upon her. Tenderly he reached to take her in his arms.

She snorted slightly in her sleep and turned away.

"Vera—" he whispered.

She turned back to him, coming awake abruptly as she always did. "What is it? What is it? Is something wrong? Are you ill?"

He put his hand on the mound of her belly. "Let's make love, Vera."

"Are you crazy! It's the middle of the night, and I have to go to work in the morning!" Angrily she pulled away from him, turning on her side.

"You used not to care if it were the middle of the night!" he said petulantly.

"I used not to be hungry all the time. I used not to be exhausted! I used to be younger!"

"Yes? Well, maybe you weren't getting it from other men then too!"

Vera pulled herself upright in the bed. "What do you mean by that?"

"Admit it, Vera, tell the truth for once! I'm only one of the men you sleep with, isn't that right?"

"Oh, sure," she said sarcastically. "I have sex with the next one in line while I'm waiting my turn at the baker's. Sometimes I have sex at the butcher's in exchange for a soup bone. Or queuing up at the dairy. Those are the only times you're not with me!"

Simcha was furious. "It must be in those places, then, because I'm sure as hell not getting much from you at home!"

"Is that what this is all about, Semyon? I'm not satisfying you? Has it occurred to you that I may be too damned tired to do anything in bed but sleep? *You* are not out there scrounging to find a store with something to sell for our meal. *You* are not standing in line for two hours to find they've run out of eggs just as you get to the head of the line! *You* are not worrying yourself sick that the money won't last till the end of the week! No, you're here in the flat, brooding about whether I'm making love with somebody else!"

"If you want me out, why don't you stop beating around the bush and say it directly!"

Vera's voice was worn. "I don't want you out, Semyon. I thought you knew how I feel about you."

"I thought I knew too. And then I found out that all the while I've been gone, you were sleeping around—with anyone and everybody!"

"Who told you that?" Her voice was dangerously quiet.

"Vassily."

"Did he tell you he wanted to crawl into my bed too?" Simcha did not respond. "I bet he didn't!"

"Can you deny it?"

"You want to know, Semyon? Sure, I had other men while you were away. After you were arrested, I had no place to go. The landlord put me out on the street. I was cold. I was hungry. The police were after anyone who worked for the party, and there were no other jobs to be had. What should I have done? I moved in with Konstantin Markoff, and I slept with him. And when he left to go to Zhitomir a year later, I lived with Kolya for ten months. And then with Sasha Mosolov! What would you have had me do, Semyon? You served your time, I served mine."

He slapped her. "How dare you compare what you did with how I suffered! I can't believe that I was going to ask you to marry me! You're no better than a whore!"

Vera picked up the lamp that stood at the bedside and threatened him with it. He easily knocked it from her hand, and it fell with a crash on the floor. "Get out!" she screamed. "Get out! Get out! I never want to see you again!"

There was quiet rejoicing in Polotsk and at Spokoinaya Zemlya, for not only had Pyotr Voronov returned from the war, but Simcha Mandelkern had survived the fortress to make his way home.

For the time being, grizzled Igor Karpovitch of the peasant soviet—the old *zemstvo* was no more—had been able to keep the local peasants in check. The hotheads, home from the war and mouthing Lenin's promise of "All land to the peasants!" had been avid to wreak their vengeance on the Voronovs and to seize the land. When, out of long habit, they had come to discuss their grievances with Karpovitch, he had been plain-spoken. "Don't be foolish. If you set fire to the house and cut down the crops, what will be left for you? Spokoinaya Zemlya will be yours soon enough, I promise you, so keep it safe!"

"Is the bastard steward to go free, then?" growled one of the men.

"Everything in its time," said Karpovitch.

They had grumbled, but there was sense in what Karpovitch said about preserving the estate; they could wait for their revenge on Fedotov.

Thus it was that when Simcha, on his way home from Petrograd, made his way up the road past the estate, he found hay piled in the fields as usual, winter rye almost ripe for harvesting, and men peaceably digging up potatoes. He caught a glimpse of the house, standing intact, behind pear and apple orchards. It was as if the revolution had not reached this far. Fedotov was always a lucky devil, he thought, and yet his heart thrilled to see all safe and as it had always been.

Malkeh and Yoysef were stricken when they saw how changed Simcha was. It was apparent at once that he was ill, his skin jaundiced and his body bent double in frequent spasms of pain. But it was not only the body that had suffered. The spirit that had been like a clear flame had been extinguished. At twenty-seven Simcha seemed an old man.

"Simcha, my son, you should perhaps see a doctor?" Malkeh asked hesitantly.

"You worry too much, Mammeh. I'm all right."

"But you are so thin. You eat nothing, and then I hear you vomiting outside."

Simcha laughed. "Ah, Mammeh, will you have my belly fat while the workers starve? What kind of revolution do you think this is anyway?"

Malkeh's face was sober, her eyes sad. "A bad one."

Simcha's eyebrows arched upward. "I am surprised to hear you say that."

"I never wanted revolution."

"Didn't you, Mammeh?"

"What are you talking about?"

Simcha shrugged. "I've had plenty of time to think about it, Mammeh. You and Yevgeny Fedotov were the first radicals I ever met. I am what I am because of you two."

Malkeh's blue eyes blazed fiercely. "What do you mean by that?"

Yoysef said uncomfortably, "This is no way to talk to your mother—"

Simcha addressed Malkeh alone. His tone was reflective but his expression severe. "You spared me nothing! I grew up knowing all about the pogrom when Uncle Dovid was killed and how a drunken peasant attacked you in the market square. I heard you cursing the recruiters who took Herschel away and the *Okhrana* that burned your schoolbooks. You rightly hated the tsar and his government, and you taught me that to be weak is to be abused. Your mistake was in thinking that education would make me strong."

"And so it would have if you hadn't dropped out of the university!" Malkeh cried.

Simcha shook his head. "No, Mammeh. Education just made me different. As for Fedotov, in his own way he was as wrong as you were."

"What do you mean?"

"He really seemed to believe it possible to have a society where all men have equal opportunities. What he gave me was a philosophical rationale for hating those with power and distrusting those without. And he gave me Plato, Locke, Rousseau, Thoreau to bolster his own unrealizable ideals!"

"You blame us, then, for your years in prison?" Malkeh asked bitterly.

"No, no," Simcha said wearily. "You meant me no harm."

"Have you lost your faith in the future, then?" Yoysef asked.

Simcha averted his eyes. When he looked up again, his face was troubled. "I don't know, Papa. I don't know what I feel anymore. It's not the way I thought it would be."

It was the only time in the weeks he spent in Polotsk that Simcha talked about what he felt. Afterward he retreated more into his protective shell. He spent hours every day sleeping and reading in his bed, and when he was up, he seemed to prefer the company of poor, addled Aunt Golda to that of his parents. There was a certain kinship, he thought, between two such lost souls as him and his aunt.

He took pleasure in working beside Golda in thoughtless chores like washing and combing the wool that Malkeh would knit into sweaters and shawls for the winter. In his aunt's company, the physicality of being together was enough in itself; there was never a need to explain oneself. The two of them, bundled against the cold, took leisurely walks in the woods, making frequent stops to rest. And sometimes in the evening Simcha would read aloud to Golda from a book of Aesop's fables.

Looking at them, Malkeh felt like weeping. Had Simcha gained his freedom from the fortress only to be locked inside the prison of his tormented self?

When it was almost time for Simcha to return to Petrograd and he had made no move to visit Spokoinaya Zemlya, Malkeh suggested that she drive him in the cart to the estate to visit Yevgeny Fedotov and the count.

"I do not plan to go, Mammeh," he said. "I have nothing to say to either of them."

Malkeh looked at him, astonished. "But Simcha, they have always been so good to you—to us as a family! When you were arrested, I don't know what we'd have done without Fedotov!"

"I guess he had his own reasons for patronizing us." He shrugged. "Courtiers used to have their pet monkeys. Maybe we were his pet Jews."

Yoysef, thin-lipped, asked, "When did you become so cynical? Is disloyalty to friends what they taught you in Petrograd?"

Simcha shook his head. "I'm sorry. I don't know what I believe anymore." He chewed thoughtfully at his underlip. "I guess Yevgeny Fedotov is himself a victim."

"A victim?" Malkeh was puzzled. "I don't think he would like being called that."

"Just because he was born a bastard, he had no inheritance rights, no name, no honor—"

Malkeh frowned. Finally she said slowly, "True, Yevgeny Fedotov does not bear the Voronov name, but everything he has ever done has brought honor to it. He was more father to young Pyotr than Count Andrei ever thought of being, he was the keeper of the land, and he tried to give the peasants a better life, though God knows they didn't love him for it."

"Born too soon," Simcha said with an edge of sarcasm.

Malkeh shook her head. "No. The Bolsheviki wouldn't have understood him any better than the peasants have."

It was late November when Simcha felt ready to return to Petrograd. There was precious little for him to go back for, yet he could not in good conscience stay longer in Polotsk. He would have to find some way of supporting himself. Undoubtedly a job would be found in the bureaucracy of the new government for someone like him, a martyr of the revolution. All he wanted was a quiet niche somewhere and a dull routine job that would do no harm to anyone.

Perhaps Vera would take him back.

Snow lay thick upon the ground. Yoysef was to take Simcha back to Petrograd in the sleigh. From their small cache of stores, Malkeh took food to send with him. There was also the suit of clothes Yoysef had made for him, and underclothing, stockings, shirts, and a warm sweater knit from the very yarn that he had carded with Golda. There was a box of books—in Yiddish, Russian, and German—that the children in America had sent just before the war; they might perhaps distract Simcha from his unhappy thoughts. On impulse, Malkeh slipped into the box a packet of letters that had arrived over past years from Chaim, Chaya Leya, and Dvoreh. Malkeh hoped that, as Simcha's mental and physical condition improved, he would become more interested in the other children and their lives in America.

On the last morning, the family joined hands at the kitchen table. "Go in peace. Return in peace," Malkeh said.

Golda thrust an ill-knit scarf into Simcha's hands. "I made it myself!"

Simcha kissed the two women and climbed into the sleigh beside his father. Yoysef flicked the reins, and without further delay the horse took off at a steady trot.

Malkeh, her arm about Golda's shoulders, watched until it became nothing more than a small dot in the roadway.

"Will Simcha be back in time for supper, Malkeh?" Golda asked. "I have saved a piece of bread for him."

"No, Golda. It will be a long time until Simcha is back in this house. If ever. Come, it is cold! Let's go inside now, and I'll give you a glass of tea with the last of our raspberry preserves in it."

Chapter 61

Month by month Chaim watched Manya's body swell with the shape of the child that would be born in early September. He knew he should take steps to give the baby his name. A dozen times a day he decided that he must ask Rosalie for a divorce in order to marry Manya, but there never seemed to be a good time to talk. Always there was a business decision to be made, a manufacturing crisis, a meeting with officials from the War Department. The indecisive days drifted by.

How ironic, Chaim thought, that at the same time his personal life was falling apart, his business was thriving as never before. Rosalie was a marvel at management. When other war contractors were meeting production schedules by turning out sloppy products, the Mandel Company consistently met its deadlines, staying within cost, and giving the government good value for its money. Chaim had installed a quality control system in the factory, but it was Rosalie who had instituted bonus incentives and competitions among teams of workers. Mandel's was the first factory in the area to open its own cafeteria and to hire a nurse to treat minor illnesses and injuries. It was not a matter of benevolence but rather the means for curtailing tardiness and absenteeism.

The factory was doing so remarkably well after only two years that Chaim wanted to sell the retail stores. Rosalie demurred. "The war and the government contracts won't last forever, Hy, and we need some diversity. Of course, we can always convert to the manufacture of civilian clothing, but when we do, it will help to have an outlet for it. Besides, the stores are turning a nice profit, and with Sam Taylor to manage them, we don't have to spend time worrying over them."

As always where business decisions were concerned, Chaim conceded that Rosalie was right, and there was no further discussion of selling Hy's Workingmen's Stores.

The Mandel marriage was indistinguishable from Mandel Enterprises. Rosalie's and Chaim's day started early in the morning. On the way to the plant Rosalie reviewed the morning news in two newspapers, bringing up items that might have an impact on the business; afterward she reviewed the day's schedule for Chaim. For his part, he enjoyed the twenty-five-minute drive to the plant behind the wheel of a Ford touring car purchased from the profits of their first government contract. At the factory before eight o'clock, they would not leave again until six-thirty or seven in the evening. During the day they would probably meet several times for brief conferences, either in Rosalie's office in the administrative suite or in Chaim's cubbyhole on the factory floor. They might or might not have lunch together, depending on the schedule, but they always ate supper after work at the same indifferent but convenient restaurant. When they went home, it was to the same small rented house where they had lived for some time. In the evenings, while Chaim was in the garage, polishing the chrome on the car or whisking away dirt that might have accumulated on the engine, Rosalie was behind her desk for another hour or two of work. At ten o'clock they bent close to the radio to hear the news, after which they retired to twin beds.

Although Rosalie spoke now and again of finding a more adequate place to live, it was no longer important to her. They had little home life to speak of, entertaining confined to business meals at restaurants. If Rosalie thought at all of her old mah-jongg acquaintances, it was with a small sense of satisfaction. They might have patronized the Mandels once, but see who was important now!

The reality of the marriage was such that it permitted Chaim to block out thoughts of his personal dilemma for whole hours at a time.

"*W*hat have you brought me this time, Chaim?" Manya teased as Chaim put a velvet box into her hands. "The tsaritsa's crown jewels?"

He shook his head wordlessly, watching while she opened his gift. He was aware that Manya was not pleased.

"A betrothal ring, my lover?" Manya mocked, lifting the gaudy diamond from its nest. "I'll soon have to grow another hand to wear all the jewels you bring me!"

Chaim flushed. The ring had been a mistake. All the propitiatory offerings he carried to her were mistakes. He knew what they were, and Manya knew too. She was right to reject them, he thought despairingly. Why should she want the gifts of his uneasy conscience?

Chaim had grown gaunt under the pressure of conflicting demands. Rosalie. Manya. The baby. The business. From moment to moment he blamed Manya for destroying the good thing that had been between them for so many years, and in the next instant he melted at the prospect of holding in his arms a child of his seed. He tortured himself imagining how he would tell Rosalie about Manya and the baby, and at the same time he knew that he never could.

Stopping to see Chaya Leya and Herschel on Harriet Street after leaving Manya, his mind was filled with gloomy thoughts. The baby might die in the womb. Rosalie might find out about his second life and leave him. There might be a scandal that would destroy the business. His family might disown him. Manya might die. Rosalie might kill herself over his betrayal.

"Chaim," Chaya Leya said, concerned for him, "you look terrible these days. Are you sick?"

"No," he said shortly.

"Worried? The business?"

"No."

"Rosalie?"

"I'm not worried!" he snapped. If only he *could* tell someone, what a relief it would be! But as much as he wished for it, he could not bring himself to confess his shame to his sister.

"There's something on your mind."

"Chaya Leya, you sound more like Mammeh every day! Let me be!"

That night after Chaim had gone home to Sacramento and Chaya Leya and Herschel were in bed, Chaya Leya moved close to her husband, laying her head on his chest. After a while she said, "I think something's wrong between Chaim and Rosalie."

"I thought they were getting along all right," Herschel yawned.

"No, it's something serious. I'm worried about Chaim. I think they might separate."

"Never," Herschel said.

"Because she needs him so much, you mean?"

"No. Rosalie'd get along if she had to, I imagine. I was thinking of how much Chaim needs *her*."

Chaya Leya raised herself on an elbow. "You mean that, don't you?" she asked curiously.

"I do. Actually, no matter how it looks from the outside, the two of them are a perfect fit. She needs him to assure her she's a woman. He needs her to take charge. Marriages don't just happen by accident. There'll be no separation."

"I hope you're right."

On Passover that year, there was a full table: Chaya Leya and Herschel with their daughters Hannah, Becky, and Jenny; Dvoreh and Lev with Saul and Ruthie; Rosalie, who had driven up from Sacramento with Sam Taylor, Chaim having pleaded a mysterious emergency; and Berel and Soreh Levy with their boy Isaac. Herschel led the service, and everyone except the smallest children took turns reading from the Haggadah.

Herschel said a special prayer that night for those still in exile, concluding: "We were slaves to Pharaoh in Egypt, and the Lord freed us. Had not the Holy One delivered our people, then we, our children, and our children's children would still be enslaved. Let us, then, ask God to remember those who are still in bondage in far-off lands and to free them even as He freed the rest of the House of Israel." Sadly he bowed his head. Several minutes passed in silence. Even the children remained quiet, sensing the gravity of their parents' meditations.

Chaya Leya and Dvoreh, Herschel and Berel, thought of the family in Polotsk and of Simcha, wherever he might be; there had been no word from any of them during three years of war. Lev, who did his best to block out the circumstances of his leaving Riga, wondered fleetingly how his mother was faring, about whether Reuben had shouldered his responsibilities, and whether his sisters were contributing to her care. For Soreh it was the painful memory of a pretty, well-cared-for house on Yekaterinovskaya Street that occupied her.

Clearing his throat, Sam Taylor continued the service. "In every generation, each person should feel as though he himself had gone forth from Egypt. It was we who were slaves, we who were strangers. And therefore you shall not oppress a stranger, for you know the feelings of the stranger, having yourselves been strangers in the land of Egypt."

They drank wine as directed by the service, even the children. The adults in turn read aloud the story of plagues visited on Egypt, the flight into the desert when there was no time to leaven the bread, the Red Sea parted and manna supplied by God for the sustenance of His people.

Before the reading was quite finished, Chaya Leya excused herself to finish preparations for dinner. And what a feast it was, from the sheer perfection of creamy gefilte fish garnished with the reddest of horseradish to the feathery-light sponge cake!

It was late when all the food was eaten, the traditional songs sung, the hidden matzo found by the children and redeemed with chocolates, and the Cup of Elijah mysteriously drained (only Ruthie, Saul, and Jenny were young enough to believe that their table had been visited in fact by the Prophet; Becky, Hannah, and Isaac were in on the joke of Herschel himself draining the wine cup when he went to the door to open it for Elijah who, it was said, visited every Jewish household during the seder). By the time it was all over, everyone was pleasantly tired and a little drunk.

Herschel left to drive the Levys home in his motor car; Lev, with Ruthie trailing behind, carried little Saul upstairs on his back; and Hannah was delegated by her mother to see that Jenny and Becky brushed their teeth before bed.

Chaya Leya, tired now that she could relax, sank into a comfortable chair and put a cushion behind her back. For once she did not demur when Dvoreh offered to wash the dishes. Sam Taylor, whom the family had grown to know and like this past year, said he would gladly help. As they went off to the kitchen, their good-natured raillery drifted back into the front room, and Chaya Leya smiled to hear Dvoreh so happy.

Rosalie and Chaya Leya remained alone in the front room. "Will you and Sam be driving back to Sacramento tonight, Rosalie?"

"Sam has a room at a hotel. I hoped I might stay here tonight."

Chaya Leya looked up, surprised. "Of course. There's a daybed on the sleeping porch. I'll just go and get some linens and a quilt—" She made a movement to get out of her chair.

Rosalie put a hand on her arm. "Please. I can do that later. I thought I might talk to you for a little while in private."

Chaya Leya, alert now, sat back.

Rosalie was nervous, twisting her rings and biting her lips. Finally she said, "I didn't know who else to go to. I need to talk to someone or I'll lose my mind!"

Chaya Leya waited for her to go on. Her eyes never left Rosalie's face, but she was very much aware of everything about her from the simple suit of cream silk to the pink-polished fingernails. Everything declared Rosalie to be a woman whose person was well cared for, yet the rouge did not disguise the pallor of her skin, nor the powder the deep shadows beneath her eyes. Surprised, Chaya Leya thought that this was a woman who knew trouble firsthand.

Rosalie was not someone who had grown up talking to a mother, sisters, girlfriends. She didn't even have a vocabulary for feelings. She sat, therefore, stricken dumb and staring at the wall behind Chaya Leya's head until her sister-in-law wondered if she had changed her mind about telling her what was on her mind. At last, her voice so soft that Chaya Leya had to lean forward and strain to hear, Rosalie said, "It's Hy—Chaim. I thought you probably understand him better than anyone—"

"What's the matter with Chaim?"

Rosalie struggled for control. There were tears very near the surface, but Rosalie was a woman who did not cry. "I don't know. I simply don't know. He's been acting so strange for the last two or three months! He's lost interest in the business, and he doesn't eat, and I hear him pacing the floor at night. And he's so irritable—whatever I say makes him mad! When I ask what's bothering him, he just says 'nothing' and slams out of the house."

Chaya Leya frowned. "Is he sick?"

Rosalie shook her head. "I don't know. I don't think so. I don't know what to think."

Chaya Leya asked carefully, "Are you getting along with each other?"

Rosalie looked away. "In business we are—we have been, until lately."

"At home?"

Rosalie took a handkerchief from her alligator bag and dabbed at her reddening eyes.

Chaya Leya said gently, "There's more to a marriage than being business partners, I think."

Rosalie stood up. "I know. But you see, that—side of our life together—love, I mean—hasn't ever been important, not since at first. Why should it be now?"

Chaya Leya rocked slowly in her chair, weighing what Rosalie had said. Not important? To whom? She doubted that Chaim would say so, unless—? Abruptly she asked, "Where *is* Chaim tonight?"

Rosalie said, "I don't know. I couldn't ask." Chaya Leya flinched from the pain in her sister-in-law's voice. "Oh, tell me what to do, Chaya Leya! He's all I have in the world! It's not as though I had a family, children! If we had ever had a baby, maybe things would have been different, but—"

Chaya Leya reached out and touched her arm ever so softly. "What do you *think* is going on?"

Rosalie looked directly into Chaya Leya's eyes. "I think he has another woman."

Chaya Leya closed her eyes. There was another time when Chaim had been obligated to one woman and loved another.

"What shall I do, Chaya Leya?"

"Do? Sometimes it's best just to let things work themselves out. Be patient, Raizel."

"Rosalie!" the other woman responded from habit, then laughed shakily at her foolishness. "Chaya Leya, Hy and I haven't always gotten along so well, but I don't want to lose him!"

Chaya Leya took Rosalie's hands into her own. There was the barest trace of a smile on her lips as she thought of her father's bearing gifts to Dagda after a long separation from her mother, as she remembered Herschel standing on a train platform telling her that no matter what had happened, she was his woman. "I've noticed over the years that the men in our family are not so easily lost as all that. I think you can count on Chaim."

"Manya, who will go to the hospital with you if I'm not here?" Chaim was worried, looking at her grossly swollen belly and wondering how one tiny baby could make her look like there was a watermelon in there!

"Oh," she said offhand, "I'll just call a taxi, I guess."

"Maybe I should hire someone to stay with you until—after, you know."

Manya threw back her head and laughed. Looking only at her face, he could ignore her distended body and see his familiar, playful Manya. Chaim put his hand out and stroked her gleaming head. Her hair was long and soft, a dark auburn, like autumn leaves just before winter drops them on the ground.

"You are very beautiful," he said, moving closer and nuzzling her neck.

"I am fat!" she said. "But in a week or two, my Chaim, I will be as you like me. And then won't we make love all day and all night!" She patted her middle. "This one's going to have to learn that he can't come between his papa and me."

"You think it's a boy?"

"I don't know. I don't care. Do you?"

"No. Have you thought about a name?"

"Have you?"

Chaim shook his head. "I think you should name the child."

"All right, then, if it's a girl I'll call her Natalya, and if, God willing, it is a boy, Mikhail."

As her time drew even closer, Chaim spent more of his time in San Francisco. It hurt him to think of her bearing their child alone in some impersonal hospital, no one waiting outside the delivery room to care whether she was all right, whether the baby was fine and perfect.

On the other hand, it hurt Rosalie when he disappeared for days on end. He knew he had not been fair to her. In the last few months he had cut her out of his life, and she did not even know why. Poor Raizel! Poor Manya! He had really made a mess of things, hadn't he?

On an afternoon early in September, Manya had a sudden urge to go to the Church of Our Lady of Kazan. It was not her usual church, but she had heard there was a wondrous icon there that wept real tears. Maybe if she lit a candle before the Virgin Mother, She would send her an easy birth. She begged Chaim to come with her.

"You know I won't go into a Christian church, Manya!" He was irritated. Weeping images! Damn-fool old country superstition!

"I know my time is near, and I want to talk to Our Lady," Manya said in a tearful voice. "If you won't come with me, I will walk to the church by myself!"

"Come on, Manya! It's a long way! I'll drive you and wait for you in the car."

"No!"

Chaim sighed. Manya had displayed a streak of stubbornness and irrationality during her pregnancy that threatened to drive him out of his mind. He could name many instances of erratic behavior, the worst of them her insistence last April that he come stay with her because a fortune-teller in the park had foretold an imminent disaster. She had been so hysterical when she telephoned his office that he had feared she would miscarry. It being Passover, her timing could not have been more inconvenient. How could he explain his absence at the seder to Rosalie or to Chaya Leya? Since no explanation was possible, he didn't even try.

Now her lower lip protruded in a pout. "If you won't come into the church with me, I don't want you to drive me!"

"Oh, come on, Manya, that's silly!"

"No, I said!"

Chaim knew it was better to humor her when she was like this. He telephoned for a taxi, and while they waited, he bundled Manya's coat around the bulk of her body and tied her head scarf securely under her chin. "You look like a fat bear!" he told her, kissing her on the end of her nose. "Now, you tell the taxi not to go away, to wait for you outside the church, Manya.

Tell him you'll pay for his time, understand?" he stuffed some bills into her coat pocket.

Manya scowled. "You're very extravagant!"

While Manya was gone, Chaim sat at the kitchen table reading the newspaper. On the front page was a firsthand account of the exploits of the American Expeditionary Force that had finally gone into action at Château-Thierry. By God, he wished he had been there with General Pershing! Producing uniforms and making money from it seemed tawdry somehow, definitely cowardly though he had, after all, done his darnedest to enlist.

He skimmed through the rest of the news. The Germans were using aircraft to bombard England, and there was an interesting story about the first use of armored tanks. He thought that he and Rosalie might do well to buy stock in companies that produced airplanes and tanks, especially the former, which might have a future after the war. He made a mental note to discuss this with Rosalie.

He turned the page. An editorial about the situation in Russia caught his eye. The writer deplored the "coup" against the tsar that had destroyed the only real competence in the country. It spoke of revolutionary groups as "riffraff" and predicted a coming dark age for Russian power, culture, and technology. Chaim shrugged. Simplistic thinking. Westerners were not willing to invest the time to understand Russian history, and consequently most trivialized what was happening.

Chaim lit a cigar and then quickly put it out again. Since Manya's pregnancy, the smell of cigar smoke bothered her. He glanced at the clock. She had been gone almost two hours. She could have lit a hundred candles to the Virgin in the time she had been gone. He shrugged. Probably she was punishing him for not going with her and had stopped to see a friend or to have a cup of coffee in the little Russian bakery she liked. He would be glad when all this was behind them and Manya returned to her normal, easygoing self.

Restless, Chaim walked from one room to another, stopping for a time in the baby's room. Manya had put up a white wallpaper with circus animals on it and had painted the woodwork white. He opened a drawer in the chest and fingered the contents, little handknit sweaters in pink and blue and yellow, woolly sleepers and soft cotton diapers. He leaned over the crib, trying to imagine how an infant would look tucked under the pretty blanket. Would the baby look like Manya or like him, he wondered. He hoped if it was a girl that she would be just like Manya.

After a while he went back to the living room and stood looking out the front window. Fog was already settling on the street. He wished Manya would get home. He moved to the kitchen and turned on the stove under the kettle so that a nice glass of hot tea would be waiting when she walked in the door. He put the glass into its enameled holder and set it on the kitchen table next to a little dish of sliced lemon, the sugar bowl, and a pretty cotton napkin. That done, he did not know what else to do with himself. He could not seem to settle down to anything. When there was still no sign of her, he shut off the gas ring under the bubbling kettle and went into the front room to watch out the window. Where was she?

A yellow taxicab pulled into the curb. What was the matter with that fool cab driver anyway! He was on the wrong side of the street! Manya should have insisted that he deposit her directly in front of her door. She was just too soft, careless. Probably paid the driver too much too.

Because of the fog, he could not clearly make her out. She was just a large, lumbering shape in a dark coat squeezing out of the taxi. He thought he saw her look up and wave at the lighted window but could not be sure. Then the cab was pulling away and Manya stepped off the curb. She should have gone to the corner where there was a crosswalk, but she never paid attention to things like crosswalks.

She was in the street when a black sedan materialized out of the fog. Chaim could see it from the window, though not all that clearly. When Manya sensed the automobile moving toward her, she stopped suddenly, either confused by the headlights or paralyzed by the danger.

"Manya! Look out!" Chaim shouted, rapping frantically on the window.

At the last moment Manya tried to run back to the curb, but she was too heavy to move quickly enough. Horrified, Chaim watched the black car trying but failing to stop in time. It struck Manya, thrusting her body up so that it came to rest with arms outstretched across the hood before rolling off to lie without moving in the street.

Chaim was down the stairs and kneeling beside Manya's body before he was even aware of leaving the flat. Blood matted her red hair and stained her forehead. As he gathered her in his arms, her eyes fluttered open for an instant. There was shock and terror in them but no sign of recognition. He sat there in the middle of the street, holding her across his lap until the ambulance came and took her away.

Chaim telephoned Chaya Leya from the hospital, and she came at once. As soon as he saw his sister enter the waiting room in her plain neat coat and matron's hat, her kind face creased with anxiety, Chaim lost his composure and began to sob, the tears running down his face and soaking into his shirt collar.

Chaya Leya held him to her breast, stroking his head and making soothing noises. She had held him just like this when she was eight and he five, and the twins, Channah and Yaakov, had died of diphtheria.

"If I had gone to church with her like she wanted—"

"Shh," Chaya Leya said.

"Did you know—about her?"

"I guessed."

"There was a head injury. She's in a coma. Oh, God, Chaya Leya, she's going to die!"

Chaya Leya drew him down on a bench and rocked him in her arms. She said nothing. What was there to say?

"Her name is Manya, Manya Aksakova. I am all she has in the world."

"Yes, yes," Chaya Leya said.

After a while the convulsive sobbing began to taper off. Chaim was ashamed. "I'm sorry. I must look like a fool!"

"No."

Chaim blew his nose and dried his eyes on a handkerchief his sister handed him. They sat quietly side by side in the cold, impersonal hospital waiting room, waiting for Manya Aksakova to die.

In little bursts the story of Chaim's relationship with the Russian woman was told. If there were surprises in it for Chaya Leya, her face did not register them, even when Chaim told her about the baby.

"The doctor said they will try to take the baby from her," he said.

Chaya Leya nodded.

"But I don't care about the baby! I just care about her, about Manya! Why did I refuse to go to church with her? It was such a little thing she wanted! She never asked for much."

"God decided her time on earth was finished. It didn't matter whether you went with her or not."

They lapsed into silence. Sometime later Chaim said, "I know what you must think of her, Chaya Leya, but she wasn't a loose person, you know—she is—was—a good woman."

"I'm the last person to judge anyone else," Chaya Leya said. "Things happen. People come together without anyone's planning it."

It grew dark outside the windows. The lights in the ceiling came on but did nothing to warm the room. A nurse brought coffee in paper cups but had no news of Manya. The doctors were performing a cesarean section.

"And Manya, my—wife?" Chaim asked.

The nurse shook her head.

It seemed a long while before a doctor came out, moving rapidly toward them through the swinging doors from the surgical suite.

"Mr.—is it Mr. Aksakova?"

"Mandel."

"You have a fine pair of children, Mr. Mandel, twins, a boy and a girl. You can see them in a few minutes."

"My wife—?"

"There's no hope for her." The doctor was gentle. "She died in the accident, really, only her heart doesn't seem to know it."

Chaya Leya's soft voice said, "She had to live to give the babies life."

The doctor scratched his jaw. "Well, yes, you might say that. Luckily she was almost at term, and the infants are big and lusty. They came into the world bawling their heads off!"

"They must know they've already lost their mother," Chaim said, beginning to cry again himself.

The doctor went away, and a nurse led Chaim and Chaya Leya to the nursery window, where they could see the two babies. As the doctor had said, they were big and healthy-looking, not at all red and wrinkled like infants in nearby baskets. There was a crown of red fuzz on the girl's head, and the boy was dark. They looked nothing alike.

Chaim stared. His babies. His son and his daughter. His heart constricted with pain and with something else—pride, love. Seed of his seed. *His!*

"What names shall we put on the birth certificates?" the nurse asked.

He had asked Manya that same question, years ago, it seemed. What had she said? Chaim tried to focus his mind on the problem, remembering how they had sat across from each other in the living room, the autumn sun making patterns on the rug while they talked casually about a name for the baby. "Mikhail, if it's a boy, I think, and Natalya if it's a girl," she had said.

"Mikhail and Natalya," he said, spelling the unfamiliar Russian names for the nurse.

*T*hey stayed at the hospital into the night. Chaim telephoned Manya's church on Geary Street, and the priest came to the hospital to administer the last rites. It was as though Manya had been waiting for that. A few minutes after Father Basil left, her breathing slowed and stopped. Heartbroken, Chaim made all the arrangements for her burial before he and Chaya Leya went from the hospital.

It was almost dawn. Chaim wasn't sure at first where he had left his automobile. This whole day—yesterday—had the quality of mist and nightmare.

"What will you do about the babies, Chaim?" Chaya Leya asked when they were driving home to Harriet Street.

"Do?" He looked up, surprised. "Why—I don't know—they're my responsibility—I don't know—" He leaned his forehead for a moment on the steering wheel. "I'll support them, take care of everything they'll ever need—"

"But who will raise them?" Chaya Leya prodded gently.

Chaim looked blank. "I just can't think now—"

"Did Manya have family—a mother, sisters?"

"No, no one."

Chaya Leya was quiet for a while. The sun was beginning to come up. It would be a clear, fine day. "I have been thinking about it, Chaim."

"Yes?"

"Take them home to Rosalie."

"It would kill Rosalie!"

"You underestimate her."

"What would I tell her? You don't understand, Chaya Leya! It would destroy her."

"She would be hurt, of course. But destroyed . . . she's not that destructible."

"No, no! I can't do it to her! She must never guess!"

"I see." Chaya Leya lapsed into silence. After a while she said, "Well, maybe you needn't tell her they're yours. Tell her that a friend of yours died suddenly, and since there are no relatives, you'd like to adopt the children."

"But she'll know! Rosalie's smart!"

"She'll know but she won't know. Listen to me, Chaim, telephone your wife and ask her to come take the babies home with you. She's always wanted children."

"I don't know."

"She won't question. She's proud, and besides, she cares for you."

"I can't think now. I just want to lie down and forget everything!"

"Yes." Chaya Leya said, patting his knee. "I'll make up a bed for you as soon as we get home, and when you're rested, we can talk some more."

Chaim slept heavily, and when he awoke, the flat was quiet, Herschel gone to the store, the older children in school, Dvoreh's Saul at a neighbor's. Although it was afternoon, Chaya Leya made breakfast and sat quietly across the kitchen table while Chaim tried to eat.

"I can't believe she's dead," Chaim said forlornly, pushing the plate of eggs away from him. "There was something so big, so grand about her. When she laughed, everyone had to laugh with her. It was like the whole world was in on the joke. She was not just a woman I slept with, you know; she was my friend. When I lost the store in '07 and again when things were bad in '13, without a moment's hesitation Manya handed me all her savings. She didn't ask a single question. That's what you do for a friend."

"Those are wonderful qualities. Your children are lucky to have been born to such a mother."

Chaim groaned. "Oh, the children! What am I going to do about them?"

Chaya Leya said quietly, "Do you want to place them for adoption?"

Chaim glared at her. "Give my children away! Of course not!"

"Do you want to hire someone to take care of them for you?"

"I can't do that! Children need to have a home, a family, parents—"

Chaya Leya was silent. She had made her point.

"Do you really think it might work out—with Rosalie, I mean?"

"I am confident."

For the first time since the accident, a small ray of hope lightened Chaim's spirits. Maybe it could work. Maybe Raizel and he could raise the children together. He trusted Chaya Leya's judgment on matters of the heart. Slowly he said, "Well, I'll have to take the chance. I'll telephone her."

Chapter 62

Two armistices were celebrated on Harriet Street in 1918: the Russian one first on March 3, and on November 11, the American thanksgiving for Germany's defeat. The family breathed a collective sigh of relief when, shortly thereafter, a brief reassuring letter arrived from Polotsk.

The Rosens, Levys, and Goldenburgs were among the throngs of San Franciscans who streamed toward Market Street for the big parade marking the end of the war. People were in a euphoric holiday mood, friends hugging each other on the street, strangers, even, exchanging greetings and wartime experiences. The war had been kind to the family. It was not like Harbin with the Japanese practically on the outskirts of the city or like France with fighting in hedgerows. None of them had died in the war, and even the Spanish influenza that had swept the country in late October had passed them by. The general prosperity of the times had brought a measure of stability to Herschel and Berel's secondhand furniture store. Perhaps the only casualty of the times was Lev's job, which he had lost when Mr. Kurilov was an early victim of the flu.

The parade was a huge success. Veterans of the Great War, some crippled and riding in open automobiles, moved along the broad open boulevard in military formation, the army and navy bands playing stirring Sousa marches. The crowds on the sidewalk, hysterical with pride, waved flags and wept for joy. Lev hoisted four-year-old Saul to his shoulder so that he could see the heroes marching by while Herschel did the same for five-year-old Ruthie. Berel had purchased flags for everyone from a vendor in the crowd, and the children waved and cheered until they were hoarse. Following the uniformed men came the fraternal orders: the Sons of Italy, the Lions Club and the Shriners, the Masons and the Oddfellows, the YMCA and the Salvation Army, the Red Cross and the B'nai B'rith, and many more. Sandwiched between various union groups carrying the banners of their trade, and the elaborate floats of local businesses came the schoolchildren, the Boy Scouts, Campfire Girls, and Girl Scouts accompanied by school bands, musically uncertain but strong in enthusiasm. Bringing up the rear were representatives from the firehouses and police stations. A long parade, which everyone agreed was the best they had ever seen.

Walking home afterwards, the children were giddy from excitement and the adults pleasantly tired. Teenagers Hannah and Isaac walked ahead of the family group, pretending to be independent, but Jenny, Becky, and Ruthie had constantly to be chided for lagging behind. Saul, between his parents, held tightly to their hands. Conversation was desultory, and swung between the parade, the recent epidemic, and "home."

"I wonder why Mammeh wrote so little," Dvorch mused.

"My guess is they're worried about censorship," Herschel offered.

"Well, anyway, we know the important thing, that they're all right." Dvoreh turned to check on the girls. "Hurry up, slowpokes!" she called back to them.

"Mama, I'm cold!" Saul complained.

"When we get home, I'll fix some nice hot cocoa. Will you like that?"

He nodded. "Papa, will you carry me?"

"What! A great big boy like you!" Lev exclaimed, swinging him up in his arms.

"I'm sorry Chaim wasn't here for the parade," Berel said wistfully. "He used to come to the city all the time, but we've hardly seen him this past year!"

Chaya Leya smiled. "Between the twins and the business, Rosalie and Chaim have their hands full at home."

Dvoreh laughed. "Can you believe the luck of those two? They didn't find just one baby to adopt, but a whole family! And what a manager that Rosalie turned out to be! She works and mothers those babies without blinking an eye!"

"The nurse and the housekeeper must be a help to her too," Chaya Leya said dryly.

At home, while Chaya Leya heated milk for the children's cocoa, Herschel poured small glasses of brandy for the grown-ups. "I give you peace!" he said.

"Family and friendship!" added Berel.

"Prosperity!" said Soreh.

"Health," whispered Dvoreh, averting her eyes, which had been resting on Lev. Although she would not have admitted it to anyone, she was increasingly worried about him.

After the Widow Kurilov had pulled the shades over the windows and padlocked the door of the bookstore for the last time, Lev had remained at home with the children while Dvoreh went each day to her work at the department store. He spent his days staring from the windows and reading from the Zohar, a central kabbalistic text which had been given him by Mrs. Kurilov as a parting gift. In the midst of the virulent influenza epidemic, the mystic teachings seemed to speak to Lev with greater weight and meaning than ever before. Book in lap, brooding, he sat near the front window of the flat, watching people pass on the street below. Which would still be well by nightfall? Which of those who sickened would die?

Dvoreh never gave a thought to her own health, but in the afternoons she flew home from work, and the strained look did not leave her face until she had felt Ruth's forehead and checked to be sure there was no telltale flush on Saul's plump cheeks.

"You worry too much about them," Lev told her. "The fingers of the angel of death haven't come anywhere near them. They are under divine protection."

"I hope you're right. There are so many sick," Dvoreh said heavily.

Lev's voice was bleak. "Dvoreh, I know you don't like me to talk about this, but I could tell when I looked into her face that Dora Katz was going to die. I could see it, like a sign burned on her forehead, and that was three days before she took sick! I tell you, Dvoreh, I see things no one else sees. I can sense death."

It was a strange remark, but then, Dvoreh thought, Lev often said odd things. He had been upset lately. Perhaps she should not leave him to care for the children. He doted on Saul and Ruthie, but sometimes his mind wandered and he forgot about them too.

On the evening of Armistice Day Dvoreh repeated her toast firmly: "To health!" she said, and reached out to take Lev's hand.

*P*leasantly fatigued from an afternoon spent outdoors at the parade, at peace as the world itself was at last at peace, Chaya Leya fell into a sound and restful sleep almost at once.

Dawn had not yet broken when there was a pounding on the door of the flat. When Chaya Leya, still struggling with her wrapper, opened the door, skinny twelve-year-old Isaac stood shivering on the doorstep. "Papa sent me in a taxi to get you," Isaac gasped, hoarse with terror. "Mammeh's terribly sick. She's crying from the pain in her back and legs, and she has a terrible headache."

Chaya Leya dressed swiftly and woke Hannah, giving her instructions for getting the younger children off to school.

"When will you be back?" Herschel asked.

She shook her head. "I'll get word to you later."

She lifted her coat from the hook by the kitchen door and went swiftly down the stairs to the waiting cab, the frantic boy babbling at her heels.

"Be quiet, Isaac," she said softly, "your mammeh is strong. She'll be all right."

For two days Chaya Leya did not come home, and when finally she did, it was only to inspect her children and to change her clothes. Dvoreh spelled her at Soreh's bedside but was so terrified of bringing home the disease that Chaya Leya finally told her to stay away. When Berel came down with it, too, Lev was pressed into nursing duty.

For several days Soreh tossed and turned in the grip of a high fever. The nights were the worst. In her delirium Soreh raved about a monster with white hair, and about fire, destruction, and blood. Her eyes glazed with terror and fever, she tried to jump from the bedroom window, and Chaya Leya had to wrestle her back to bed.

"No! No!" she moaned, turning her head from side to side on her pillow. "Don't hurt me anymore! I won't fight you! Do what you want, only don't hurt me!" Soreh's teeth were clenched, her face twisted in some terrible private anguish.

There was more, but Chaya Leya chose not to listen. Everyone knew, by word of mouth if not by experience, what happens during a pogrom; Chaya Leya did not have to hear it.

Soreh's fever was very high. Chaya Leya dampened cloths and wrapped them about her friend's body. A crisis was fast approaching. Either Soreh's fever would break this night, or her heart would give out. Her weakened constitution could not sustain another twenty-four hours of such high temperature.

Exhausted, Chaya Leya sat down in a chair beside the bed to watch and wait. She leaned her head back in the chair but dared not close her eyes lest she fall asleep. She thought about Soreh's ravings. In the old country Jews lived in the midst of a people who, at a nod from the government, were transformed into rapists, thieves, and murderers. Jewish women were fair prey to rapacious neighbors, their menfolk helpless to protect them. Nine months after a pogrom, one could expect babies to be born who were fair and coarse-featured; the community of Jews circumcised the males, taught the girls the ways of pious women, and pretended not to notice if they looked somewhat different. Berel and Soreh's only child, Isaac, was such a one. Never mentioned, Chaya Leya had always known it.

A good boy, Isaac, and a loving child, for a long time now talking of going to a yeshiva to study for the rabbinate. Was there perhaps in him an awareness of difference and a need to repudiate the biological father who had made him?

Just before daybreak Chaya Leya was still keeping vigil at the bedside. From time to time she leaned over to feel Soreh's skin. She thought that the forehead seemed somewhat cooler—or was it imagination? The restlessness had greatly diminished, too, and Soreh seemed to have drifted into normal sleep. Had the crisis passed, then? Again and again in the next hour Chaya Leya checked. The body temperature was definitely lower. Thank God! During the next hour it continued in its downward course.

Chaya Leya allowed her eyes to close. She could scarcely remember when she had last spent a night between sheets. She slept. A faint noise from the bed sometime later was enough to bring her fully awake.

"What is it?" she asked. "Do you want something, Soreh? A little water?" She thought that the sick woman looked better.

Soreh was struggling to sit up, and Chaya Leya helped raise her against her pillows. "Chaya Leya," she whispered.

"Yes, I'm here." Chaya Leya bent close to hear.

"Did I—say anything? I had such—dreams—"

"You've been raving for a couple of days."

Soreh gripped Chaya Leya's hands and pulled her closer. Her forehead was beaded with sweat. "Doesn't mean—anything, what people say—when they're sick—"

"Of course not."

Soreh struggled still. "Berel—? Isaac? Were they here?"

Chaya Leya shook her head. "No one was here but me, Soreh."

The sick woman sank back into her pillows. "Just—nightmares—"

Soreh began to cough, and Chaya Leya held a glass of water to her lips. "Yes," Chaya Leya said to reassure her. "I understand that."

Soreh sighed deeply and closed her eyes. Chaya Leya took the glass into the kitchen. When she returned, Soreh was soundly asleep.

S oreh was weak, and it would be a long time before she could rise from her bed. The deep, painful cough was slow to disappear. But her temperature was normal, and her thready pulse had steadied. The doctor shook his head in disbelief. Soreh's case had gone into pneumonia and still she had recovered. She had a strong constitution; he wished he could say as much for her husband.

While Chaya Leya was tending Soreh, Lev sat beside Berel's bed, sponging him with washcloths dipped in vinegar and water, changing the sweat-soaked sheets, and holding him in his arms when the sick man thrashed in an agony of pain and dark visions.

Lev grew thin and sunken-eyed himself but refused to leave Berel's side even when Chaim arrived from Sacramento. "I can't leave him," he said, tormented. Berel was going to die. He had seen the sign upon his forehead as clear as could be.

Over and over Lev whispered in Berel's ear, "Don't be afraid. The earth where we'll lay you is warm and soft, the most peaceful bed you've ever known. Don't struggle to stay. Go in peace. There is no happiness greater than the perfect peace of death."

"What are you saying?" Chaim cried fiercely. "Tell him Soreh and Isaac need him, we all need him! Tell him he must live for us, for himself!"

When the end came, both Chaim and Lev were with Berel. He opened his eyes wide and gazed directly at Chaim. For the first time in three days he spoke clearly, as if continuing a conversation. "I have known nothing but joy since I first met Soreh Glanzer. I don't want to leave her and Isaac so soon! Pray for me, Chaim, Lev! You have been good to me!"

Even as he spoke, he was becoming cyanotic.

Chaim cradled Berel in his arms, but Berel was already dead. Soreh, still so ill herself, did not know for almost a week that her husband had died, and by that time, he was in his grave.

By the end of November the "Spanish Lady," as the newspapers had fancifully named the influenza strain, had packed her deadly bags and moved on. Chaya Leya and Herschel looked at their healthy children and gave thanks to God that their loss, while great indeed, had not been more.

For a time only Dvoreh knew that there was still one uncounted victim of the epidemic. Lev had finally become quite mad.

*I*n the private sanitarium, which Chaim insisted on paying for, Lev's agitation gradually lessened, and after a few months he was well enough to come home. He seemed himself again, a little thin, a little more quiet, but to all appearances quite sane. The family agreed with Dvoreh that it had been a transient spell, brought on by the stress of the influenza epidemic and Berel's death.

Lev had never been more tender and loving toward Dvoreh and the children, and for an hour or two a day he was even able to work in Herschel's furniture store, answering the telephone and performing routine menial tasks. Even so, in the unacknowledged recesses of her mind, Dvoreh registered small signs of illness, the sudden withdrawal of attention, the recurrent insomnia, the unprovoked outbursts of irritability. As the weather became dark and cold with winter, the fog that settled over the city seemed also to settle over Lev's mind.

"You must take him back to the hospital," Chaya Leya told Dvoreh.

Dvoreh swallowed hard. "I hate to see him locked up. Besides, the cost is terrible."

"You have a family to help with that."

"I can't keep taking from you and Chaim." Dvoreh's face crumpled, and she hid it in her hands. "Oh, God, Chaya Leya, I don't know what to do!"

"What does his doctor say?"

"That he can't predict what will happen. He says that sometimes this kind of sickness can go away as suddenly as it comes."

Eventually Dvoreh decided that she must get Lev away from the city—a quiet country place, she thought, preferably one without the depressing fog that hid the sun for days at a time. Hadn't things grown worse only when the sky turned dark with winter? She was sadly torn. There was Lev, and there were the children. To whom did she owe her primary concern? With Lev's condition deteriorating every day that she hesitated, she changed her mind a dozen times a day. If she rehospitalized Lev, she could maintain her job and be with the children. On the other hand, since Saul and Ruthie had always spent more time in Chaya Leya's household than in their own, they could handle separation better than Lev could. If only she could be sure of the right thing to do! Lev had no one but her, while Saul and Ruth had a whole family of aunts and uncles and cousins. Finally only half convinced that she was doing the right thing, Dvoreh gave up her job and rented a cottage in Los Gatos, a sleepy little town sixty miles south of San Francisco. She would leave the children with Chaya Leya and give Lev her full-time attention.

On a Sunday in March, Herschel drove away from Harriet Street with Dvoreh and Lev. Ruthie waved bravely from the living room window, but Saul had locked himself in the bathroom and refused to come out to say good-bye to his parents. When the automobile turned the corner, Ruth threw herself into her aunt's lap and gave way to tears. For once Chaya Leya had no comforting words to offer the little girl.

For Dvoreh, living isolated from her children and the family was exile, but for a time Lev seemed to thrive. She might cry herself to sleep at night, but during Lev's waking hours she was determinedly cheerful. Spring merged with summer, increasing Dvoreh's longing to be with her children. She posted daily letters, and once a week, on Sunday, went to the hotel where there was a telephone from which to call home.

Herschel and Chaya Leya brought the children to see their parents every fourth Sunday, but the visits only aggravated their mutual wounds. Lev was distracted by the children's presence and often slept straight through the day, growing angry when their noise disturbed him.

One day without warning Lev disappeared from the cottage. The man who delivered milk recognized him and brought him home to Dvoreh.

"Found him on the railroad tracks. Seemed not to know where he wanted to go," the milkman said.

"Thank you for bringing him home." Dvoreh pressed a quarter into his palm.

The man returned it. "No thank you, lady. You got troubles enough."

After she had fed Lev a bowl of warm soup, she put his chair in a sunny place on the screened porch and tucked a light blanket around his knees. "If you want to go someplace, dearest, we can go together," she told him. He did not seem to hear.

The next day he walked into the traffic on the road, causing a touring car to swerve into a fence. The sheriff recognized Lev and accompanied him home.

It was the beginning of the end. Lev was wily in the ways he devised to escape from Dvoreh. In utter desperation one day she stood with her back to the screen door to prevent his leaving. In a frustrated rage, he struck her. Shocked and frightened, Dvoreh dropped her guard and Lev ran outside.

The police finally found him. He had lost himself in the wooded hills behind town and tumbled into a shallow ravine. He was bruised and scratched, and, worse, he was incoherent.

Afraid to leave him alone for a moment, Dvoreh asked the policeman to telephone Chaya Leya. That evening Herschel arrived and drove them back to San Francisco, Lev in the backseat mumbling, Dvoreh in the front, weeping.

He was no better in San Francisco, but, at least, help was near at hand. For the whole of one dreadful day he paced the flat, answering voices that only he could hear. At dinnertime, Dvoreh took him gently by the arm and guided him to the table. She filled his plate with brisket and peas and tied his napkin around his neck gently, as if he were one of the children. He seemed not to recognize her and continued his conversation with unseen apparitions. The children sat frozen and white-faced in their chairs.

"Please eat, Lev. You love pot roast," Dvoreh said quietly.

"Excuse me," he said, as if to unseen presences beside him, and turned burning eyes on his wife. "You're always at me. 'Do this. Do that. Eat, Lev. Go to bed'! I don't know who you are!"

"I'm Dvoreh, your wife." Dvoreh's voice was mild but her eyes were watchful. "I want to take care of you."

"Oh, I know what you love!" Lev raged. "You want my money for hats and dresses. You don't care about me! Don't pretend! I've seen how you look at my brother Reuben with loving eyes while for me you have nothing!"

A look of pure hatred stared out of Lev's eyes. Bread knife in hand, he lunged across the table. Dvoreh put her hands up to protect herself, and the blade made a long deep gash across her left wrist.

Saul jumped up from his chair and grabbed his father's arm while Ruthie ran screaming down the stairs.

Dvoreh, trembling violently, wrapped her napkin around her wrist to staunch the blood. "Give me the knife, Lev," she said in a voice that was deceptively calm.

The knife clattered to the floor. "Did I hurt you? Who are you? Did I hurt you?" Lev asked, pale with shocked disbelief.

"No, dearest, I'm all right. Come rest a little."

Herschel burst into the kitchen with Chaya Leya a step behind. Herschel helped Lev into bed while Chaya Leya took the children downstairs and Dvoreh went to call the doctor.

There was no longer a choice. It was clear that Dvoreh could not care for her husband at home. Chaim, who arrived in the morning, said that cost should not be a consideration; Lev could return to Woodland Greens or to another sanitarium, whatever was best. Dvoreh shook her head and explained what she'd been told at the hospital the night before. The psychiatrist had led her into a small office. His voice had been kind but firm. "Mrs. Goldenburg, your husband has an incurable illness."

"What do you mean?" Dvoreh had faltered. "He's just very mixed up sometimes."

Dr. Kantor nodded. "That's true. But what causes it *is* a disease, and unfortunately it's the kind that can only become worse over time."

"If it's a disease, why don't you have medicines for it? Why are you telling me this?" Dvoreh was frightened.

"I'm trying to prepare you for the future. My recommendation is that you commit him to the state hospital."

"But that's—isn't that a place for people who are—who won't get better?"

"Not necessarily. However, I must tell you that in my opinion Mr. Goldenburg's periods of sanity will become less and less frequent as time goes on. The state asylum has a lot of experience taking care of people with this kind of illness."

"Suppose I decide to take care of him myself?"

Dr. Kantor shook his head pityingly. "You've already tried that. Next time it might not be your wrist."

"So you see, Chaim," Dvoreh explained to her brother, "it makes no sense at all to spend your money on private hospitals. The doctor told me there is quite a good state asylum not far from here. They have workshops there and classes, even a farm where the patients can work."

"Are you sure, Dvorehleh?" Chaim asked, reverting to the diminutive of childhood.

"I'm sure."

*C*haya Leya talked it over with Herschel. "It is a tragedy for everyone. The asylum is two hours from here by bus. Dvoreh talks about moving closer, but how will she support herself? At least here, the Emporium was willing to give her back her job. Even if she *could* find work closer to the hospital, who would watch the children while she's away from home?"

Herschel was thoughtful. "Between us and Chaim, I guess we could support her—"

"Dvoreh will not allow that! And anyway, that's not fair to you and our girls."

"It hasn't been fair that you've raised Dvoreh's children for six years either."

"Have you resented it, then?"

"You know I love Ruth and Saul. If I've resented it, it's been for you. Our own girls are pretty well grown now, but you haven't had any freedom in years!"

Chaya Leya sighed. "Sometimes I hate it myself. I'm not a saint, Herschel."

The next morning Chaya Leya sat down and composed a letter to her parents in Polotsk. She didn't know if it would reach them. If it did, she didn't know whether what she asked was possible. Still, it was necessary to do something.

My dearest Mammeh and Papa,

I plead with you to come to us as soon as possible. It hurts me to tell you of Dvoreh's trouble. Lev is incurably ill. If Dvoreh is to raise her children and make any kind of life for herself and them, she must have help. Chaim and I are mindful of what Mammeh said about helping each other, and we have done so over the years, but now Dvoreh's situation is beyond what either of us can do by ourselves. I don't know how difficult it is to leave Russia. The steamship tickets for you and Simcha—and Aunt Golda too—we can manage with no problem. Dvoreh needs you desperately. Please come.

Chapter 63

*P*yotr Voronov and his uncle sat in the latter's little office behind the kitchen, talking far into the night. There was none of the usual lighthearted give-and-take, and the bottle of cognac that stood on the desk between them had been left untouched. On this last night together, there was both much and nothing to say, but neither could bear to part just yet.

There was a heaviness in Pyotr's voice, when at the end he concluded, "There is nothing else to do. Ekaterina and the children must go now while there's still a chance to get across the border. Thank God *Maman* and the prince are already in Paris and can take care of them!"

Fedotov sighed. "I know you're right, Petya, and yet—"

"There's no 'and yet,' Uncle. I've known it since I got home from the war, but I thought there would be more time. When I got the message last week from my old colonel that Lenin is about to issue an edict abolishing private land ownership, it was clear that the end is very near. I shouldn't have waited so long! Pray God I can still get my family away."

"And yourself, Petya."

Pyotr shook his head. "I don't care about myself as long as Ekaterina and the boys get across the Finnish border. I hate that I can't take them myself!"

"We've gone all over that, Pyotr. You are already a wanted man, a fugitive—everyone with a title is! It is much safer to entrust your family to Yoysef. If they are challenged along the way, they will look to be a proper Jewish family going to Karelia to safely wait out the war with relatives."

The younger man sighed. "But how will I know they are safely across?"

"Nothing is sure anymore. But I know that Yoysef Mandelkern will protect them as if they were his own. With his life if need be!"

The two men fell silent, each occupied with his own thoughts. Is it to end like this, then, Fedotov wondered, an entire lifetime spent in the service of the Voronovs come to nothing? What would happen to Spokoinaya Zemlya when it passed from Voronov hands? He could imagine no greater disaster than turning the estate over to Karpovitch and his gang of peasants.

"You must go tonight also," he told Petya.

"I am ready." Pyotr thought of the waggish wartime saying that Russians seemed always able to snatch defeat from the jaws of victory. Theirs was indeed a nation under a curse. "I will ride south to join Denikin's White Army. They won't be particular about accepting a one-eyed veteran as long as I'm willing to die fighting the Bolsheviks!"

Yevgeny Fedotov shuddered. "I'd rather you were willing to live to get to France!"

"God grant it! I would ask you to come with me, but I know already what you would say."

"I will never leave Spokoinaya Zemlya."

"I know."

The two men sat together yet awhile in silence.

Pyotr said, "It is my fate to fight against the evil overtaking Russia; it is yours to try to preserve the land for some future Voronov. I'm afraid both are hopeless causes."

Fedotov turned to look out the window at the night. Already the moon was on its downward course. "I don't know how I could have been so wrong! I sat back comfortably, thinking that the revolution would come about gradually, without violence. The Jewess said once that that wasn't in the Russian character. Now I see she is right about that. The Reds are not fit to rule this land."

"Neither was the tsar."

"Our country's tragedy is that there is never a middle ground for us."

The two men embraced soberly.

"No one could ask for a better father than you have been to me, Uncle," Petya said quietly.

The amber of Yevgeny Fedotov's eyes glazed over with a suspicion of withheld tears. He managed a shaky smile. "Let's not be premature with the eulogies! I've got a few good years left!"

"God grant it. And yet, Uncle, I fear that we will never meet again."

Fedotov nodded. There was nothing left to say.

Petya went to awaken the countess and to complete his own preparations to leave Spokoinaya Zemlya for the last time.

Yevgeny Sergeivitch sat on in the dark, staring from the window, watching for Yoysef Mandelkern to come in his wagon to take his family away.

*J*t was dangerous for Pyotr Voronov to accompany them for more than a short distance on the road toward Finland. The sky had scarcely lightened when Yoysef pulled his wagon to the side of the road, and the young count reigned in his horse beside it.

"You must come no further, *Gospodin*," Yoysef cautioned Pyotr. "Peasants will be going to the fields soon, and they may remember seeing us together."

"I know, I know." Pyotr was torn by anguish at the prospect of parting from his wife and sons.

"I will walk into the woods," Yoysef said, climbing down, "so you can say good-bye in private. But don't be long."

"Thank you," the young count said.

For each of the boys—Igor, aged fourteen, Pavel, ten, Boris, eight—their father had a special message of love, a blessing, and an embrace. Then Pyotr turned to his wife, pushing back the white *tichl* she wore in imitation of a pious Jewish wife. The gesture reminded him of how his hands had trembled when he had lifted her veil for the bridal kiss fifteen years before. Ekaterina's face was strained and white, but he thought her more beautiful than she had been as a young girl, and his heart overflowed with love.

"Be brave, beloved! I give into your care my most precious possessions, these children we made together in love. Teach them always to honor their inheritance, the name Voronov—it is all I have to give them."

"You don't have to stay in Russia!"

"But I do. I was raised to honor my name and my Motherland. I can't change that." He bent to kiss her, and she clung to him.

The countess was sobbing and the boys frightened when Yoysef returned. He sighed. So much trouble in this world, he thought. He clucked to the horses, and the wagon started off with a lurch. God willing, he would find places to change horses on the way, and, pushing the animals to their limit, they could perhaps reach the border crossing within six or seven days. Fedotov had given him gold for fresh horses and bribes, and together they had bent over maps to study the route. Yoysef had traveled through this northerly region in his youth, and now he called from his memory the names of towns and shtetls where they might be given safe shelter. They were headed for Viipuri, on Vyborg Bay. Fedotov had heard that it was a safe crossing place.

*P*yotr Voronov strained his eyes after the wagon until it disappeared. Then he turned south. There was no way he would ever know whether they found the Finnish border.

His own grueling journey consumed many weeks of traveling by night and sleeping in lonely places by day—in burned-out barns, in open, overgrown fields, and occasionally, when he was lucky enough to happen upon one, in a cave. Not sure exactly where he would find the "White" forces of General Denikin, he took his bearings from the position of the sun, heading always south toward the Don River. Denikin's stronghold was amid the Cossacks in the region of Rostov-on-Don.

*B*ack in Petrograd after his visit to Polotsk, Simcha had to find a way of supporting himself. But first he must find Vera and throw himself at her feet, begging forgiveness. What a fool he had been to give way to jealousy and recriminations! What had he expected her to do while his life was ebbing away in the fortress? Join a convent? She had done what she needed to do to survive. And he had every reason to believe that in her heart she had never ceased to belong to him. Why else would she have been at the prison to meet him when the gates swung open for the last time? Could she otherwise have tended him so tenderly? Put up with his irrationality? He knew now that his behavior was the result of four years of isolation and hardship that had eroded his sanity. He would make Vera see that that jealous, erratic bundle of nerves was not the real man!

Simcha made his way to Vera's flat through the streets of the city, grown even dirtier and more chaotic than before. There was no answer to his rap on the door, and he sat down on the step to wait for her return. An hour passed. He stood up to stretch his game leg and the hip that ached unconscionably when the weather was cold. He paced up and down in front of the house, to ease the pain.

A rough man in an old gray army uniform, a red armband around the sleeve, marched over to him. Simcha hadn't noticed him before, but he must have been watching from the shadow of the building across the street.

"Hey, there! What are you doing?" the newcomer asked. His accent was as coarse as his appearance.

"What does it look like I'm doing? I'm walking on the street here in front of this house."

"Don't give me any smart answers or I'll give you a fat lip!"

"And who the hell are you?"

"Politzeeya!"

"Oh? Since when are there police these days in Petrograd?"

"Comrade Lenin's orders! Now I ask you again: What are you doing here?"

"I'm locked out of my flat, and I'm waiting for my friend to come home and let me in."

"Then just go sit nice and quiet over there on the steps. And from now on, watch your dirty mouth—comrade!"

Simcha sank down on the step once more, but it was growing colder by the minute. Finally he chanced knocking on the door of the adjoining flat. He could hear people talking inside, but at his knock the voices fell silent. No one came to the door. He tried two more flats with no better result. Since the revolution, people were afraid of unexpected knocks at their doors. Come to think of it, how was that different from before? *Plus ça change, plus c'est la même chose!* Simcha crossed his arms across his chest, slapping himself for warmth. When would Vera be back?

It was growing dark, and he could see a dark bundled shape turning into the street. Ah, Vera, at last! He hurried down the steps toward the woman, only to hesitate, overcome by uncertainty. Shorter than Vera. Fatter, too, though that could be the padded clothing she wore against the cold. He walked slowly toward the woman, and passing her, nodded. Not Vera. He went back to the building and huddled in the doorway, waiting. He had lost all track of time and it had grown dark when finally someone climbed the rickety steps toward him.

"Vera!" he called. "It's Semyon!"

The woman on the stair loosened her head scarf so that it dropped back, and he could see that this woman's hair was gray and her face wrinkled.

"Vera Politsovskaya?" he asked.

The woman shook her head.

"But she used to live here!"

"No one by that name here now," the woman said wearily. "I've been here almost two months."

"Are you sure?"

"This is my flat." She fished the key from her pocket as though to prove it.

"Did you happen to hear where she went?"

The woman barely bothered to shake her head. It was a silly question that deserved no answer.

Simcha turned away. There was nothing to do but go back to the cheap room where he was staying. In the morning he would go to the printing office where she had sometimes found odd jobs. But now that the Bolsheviks *were* the government, there would no longer be a clandestine press, would there?

In the next two days Simcha tried the Housing Bureau, the Government Printing Office, and the Petrograd Soviet, all without tangible results. He wished now that he had paid more attention to the names of friends she had sometimes mentioned. He had been so self-involved he had barely listened to any details of *her* life; his was the only important one. How could he have been such a fool!

Discouraged and not knowing where else to turn, Simcha found himself on Vassily Chernov's doorstep.

Vassily seemed to be in the midst of packing, the gorgeous apartment strewn with boxes, barrels, and straw. Since Simcha had last been there, Vassily seemed to have accumulated many more possessions.

"Ah, come in, come in, my young friend!" Vassily said. "I'd offer you a glass of tea, but as you can see, I'm busy preparing for my move! How about some vodka, though? No? Cognac perhaps?"

"Where are you moving?" Simcha asked, bewildered by the welter of materials on the polished floor.

Vassily was wrapping an exquisite set of Italian demitasse cups in paper before fitting them into a rapidly filling barrel. "Moscow. Didn't you hear anything when you were in the provinces? Lenin is moving the capital to Moscow!"

"No, I didn't know." Simcha freed a chair from a pile of shirts, putting them on the piano before he sat down. He watched Vassily stow away one richly ornamented object after another—a china tea service, crystal, a pair of Dresden shepherds and shepherdesses, an ormolu clock. From what palace, he wondered, had these been stolen? He was no longer surprised, as he had been at first, that the leaders of the revolution had come to this point. It reminded him of those trick pictures that contain two complete faces; you see one or the other depending on whether you focus your eyes on the dark or the light—now this one is uppermost, now that, the color different but the faces complementary.

After a while he said, "Vera's moved. Do you have any idea where she is or how I might find her?"

Vassily lifted his shoulders in an expressive shrug. "I thought you were through with her, Semyon."

"Do you know where she is?"

"No idea. Good riddance, if you ask me."

"I didn't. Who might know?"

Vassily shook his head. "People come and go all the time."

"Her friends—you seemed to remember before whom she was living with while I was away?"

"Did I?" Vassily scratched his head, his expression casual but his opaque black eyes watchful. "Sorry. I can't think of a soul right now. I've got a lot on my mind!"

Simcha drew on his coat and wrapped his scarf about his neck. "Well, if you should remember anything, I'd appreciate your help." He coughed a little, embarrassed that he was again on the asking end of things. "Good luck with your move."

Vassily slipped an arm through Simcha's to walk him to the door. Seemingly on impulse, the older man suddenly said, "Why don't you come to Moscow with me? You've got nothing to do here, do you?"

"I need to find Vera. And a job," he added. The money, given him by Yoysef at parting, was almost gone now.

"A job's no problem. I've got connections in the government."

"So I see," Simcha said dryly.

"As for Vera, your chances of finding her are practically nil. At least in Moscow there may be some central party records."

"I can't give up just like that, Vassily. If she is in Petrograd, I'll find her. I'm not going to leave until I've tried!"

"Up to you!" Vassily leaned forward to kiss Simcha on both cheeks. "Well then, good-bye, my friend. If you change your mind you'll find me at the central offices of the *Cheka*!"

Simcha was honestly puzzled. *"Cheka?* What is that, Vassily?"

Vassily gave him an incredulous look. "You really have been out of touch, haven't you! The whole name is the All-Russian Extraordinary Committee to Combat Counterrevolution. But you can call it"—he paused for dramatic effect—"the Bolshevik secret police!"

Chapter 64

*V*assily prepared carefully for his mission in Byelorussia, ordering reinforcements from the local soviet, handpicking the men to accompany him, even himself meticulously arranging train schedules. Nothing must go wrong. It was to be for him not only the culmination of his career, but also an exquisite exacting of long-overdue payment. With Yevgeny Fedotov dead, the Voronovs dispossessed, and Spokoinaya Zemlya transformed into a state-run *kolkhoz*, there would be vindication for everything that he had been and done, perhaps then he could finally rest. He told the troubling, demanding visions—no longer just Marta Pirumova, but now also his parents and his sister Olga, that their time was fast approaching.

The men assembled on a bright fall morning at Moscow's Central Railroad Station—Archille Mishkin and Karp Mosolov, known as "strong arms" at the *Cheka*, Arkady Runich, and Semyon Mandelkern. He could have managed well with only Archille and Karp to support him, but it amused him to include Arkady, once his superior in the S.R. and now reduced to dependence on him, and Semyon who, as reluctant witness, would now pay the penalty for earlier ties to Fedotov and Spokoinaya Zemlya. Vassily rubbed his hands in satisfaction.

The train was two hours late in leaving. Vassily was annoyed. Somehow the new regime could not seem to manage to make anything run on time! When the passengers were finally allowed to board, the train was filthy, the samovar was cold, and a family of dirty peasants was occupying the best compartment, which Vassily had intended for his party.

"Out! Out!" Vassily ordered the interlopers.

"You can't order us around no more!" the father said in a truculent tone.

"I can't?" Vassily blustered. "I am on official business for the state!"

"I got here first," the peasant said with an unpleasant thrust of his jaw. "You heard there's been a revolution? You're no better than us—"

"Get out at once or I'll have you put off the train entirely," Vassily said coldly.

The burly *mujik*, having assessed his chances of being physically displaced, refused to budge. He had not seen Karp and Archille, who had been on the platform overseeing baggage, until they were on either side of him.

Vassily waved his bodyguards aside. Savoring the moment, he took his *Cheka* card from his pocket and waved it under the peasant's nose. "Do you know what this is? Of course not! You can't read, can you? This is my identification. I'll read it to you. 'Be advised that Vassily Yulevitch Chernov, member of the duly instituted Communist Party, is an officer of the *Cheka*. Citizens are advised to cooperate fully.' I'm sure you know what that means!"

Even the peasant understood the powers of the secret police. Paling, he rose at once and, trailed by his wife and three snot-nosed children, left the compartment without a word. The woman made a slight obeisance as she passed Vassily, which pleased him greatly.

Simcha, fascinated, had watched this exchange from Vassily's side. The dramatic upturn in Vassily's fortunes had uncovered an autocratic bent in his character. Where now, Simcha thought, was yesterday's champion of the dispossessed peasant?

With distaste Vassily used his handkerchief to dust off the plush banquettes vacated by the *mujik*'s family and waved the four others to their seats, the giant Karp sharing one with Vassily, and Archille, Arkady, and Simcha sitting across from them. After a few false starts the train began its westward run. Vassily consulted the timetable. The trip should take no more than five and a half hours, but one had to adjust for breaks in the track, engine problems, and inexperienced train crews; it was safe to count on twelve hours.

Simcha closed his eyes, pretending to sleep. This whole assignment made him feel ill; it was exactly the kind of thing he had hoped to avoid when he took a clerical position in the Agricultural Bureau. Having decided to avoid Vassily when he moved to Moscow, it was a job he had found on his own. In fact, Vassily had found *him*, even tucked away as he was in the basement of a government building far from the Kremlin. What was it that Vassily wanted from him? Why had he commandeered him for a temporary *Cheka* assignment? He said he required an impeccable witness, a man who had always known the estate (and a hero of the revolution besides!) to assure the proper execution of the transfer of ownership of Spokoinaya Zemlya. That, of course, was nonsense! Since when did the new government ever worry about proprieties! Beyond his comprehension as it was, Simcha turned his thoughts elsewhere. There were other mysteries to worry about; for instance, the nagging worry of where Vera had disappeared to.

In Petrograd he had followed a series of disheartening dead ends. He had spent three fruitless months combing the city, before heeding Vassily's advice to check party files in Moscow. But the records office was in no better shape than anything else in the new order. Unable to think of what else to do, Simcha had at last admitted failure and settled into the dull life of a low-level civil servant. He didn't much care where or how he lived. What difference—Moscow or Petrograd? His only goal was to get through his days unnoticed and with as little pain as possible. Idealism had once given his life purpose, but the revolutionary vision had proved a chimera and his faith in man's morality unjustified. He was an empty shell now, mistrusting relationships and unable to connect with his past. Vera might have saved some part of his humanity, but she was irretrievably lost to him.

Against his will, he had been drawn into this crazy expedition of Vassily's to claim Spokoinaya Zemlya for the state. Long ago he had deduced that Vassily's interest in the Voronov family was not casual. It was obvious that Vassily was embarked on a mission of revenge, the claiming of aristocratic lands not usually within the purview of the *Cheka*. But why involve him?

Vassily's voice broke into Simcha's thoughts. "You'll soon be home, eh, Semyon?" he said. Eliciting no response, he turned to inform the others in the compartment: "Semyon Mandelkern here was raised at the knee of the steward of Spokoinaya Zemlya."

Simcha closed his eyes.

"Why don't you tell our fellows here what the house was like, Semyon—the ballroom with the mirrored walls and the crystal chandeliers, the two parlors and the library, the bedrooms with brocaded walls—"

"Why don't *you*?"

Vassily merely laughed.

Simcha's memories were different. If he so wished, he could have told them about Maria Feodorovna's busy kitchen with the smell of good things simmering on the stove; he could even yet describe the rich taste of milk still frothy and warm from the cow, the way buttery cookies melt in the mouth and preserves retain the fragrance of ripe apricots and strawberries.

For whatever it was worth, he could have called up Fedotov's austere office, its big desk, the bookcases crammed willy-nilly with heavy volumes, foreign journals, jars of soil samples, folders overflowing with correspondence from all over the world. He could have told them further about the verdant coolness of the deep woods where once he had walked, could have described how one came suddenly upon the house, rising magically from behind silvery birch trees. If necessary, he could even yet have detailed the arrangement of the stables, the poultry yards and the flower conservatory. The storerooms themselves were worthy of an hour's remembrance, for who of them had ever seen so much food: the sides of bacon, homemade sausages and wheels of cheese; buckets of butter and sacks of cereals; the barrels filled with apples, pears, and plums; the cones of sugar and jars of jams; the pickled beets, mushrooms, carrots, cauliflower, sauerkraut! But the ballroom and the great dining hall, the bedrooms and the library? He had never been in that part of the house.

Lulled by his visions of Spokoinaya Zemlya, the motion of the train, and the murmur of his companions' voices, Simcha slept.

*V*assily was remembering his family's hut with its dirt-packed floor where five of them had lived in one room, his mother's pinched face, the swollen bellies of his sisters, the cruelty of the priests in the village school. He grunted. Against all odds he had risen to a position of power, as Yevgeny Fedotov would shortly find out for himself. It was not as high as he aspired, but high enough to wangle this assignment. When he returned to Moscow, successful from having seized a major landholding, it would be to greater status. His star had been on the ascendant ever since that lucky day when he had stumbled upon Azev's treachery and turned him in.

Vassily glanced over at Semyon, who appeared to be sound asleep. Once he had been able to sleep like that. He remembered the boy Semyon who had marched with Father Gapon on Bloody Sunday. They had both been in love then, with Lenin and the Social Democratic Party, with the noble peasant and the worthy factory worker. For Vassily, the end of faith had come when he discovered that Marta was betraying him with a party leader and Yevno Azev was working for the tsarist police. Ah, well, he had learned something from those experiences: It is always better to be on the winning side, an exploiter rather than a victim. Since he had discovered that, all manner of good things had fallen to him, the most special, the power to punish.

*W*hat Yevgeny Fedotov noticed first was how silent the house was. He remembered that old Katya, the last of the house servants, had not appeared that morning to prepare his tea. The pleasant bustle of housekeeping activity had formed a background to his entire life in this house, and he had never noticed, until now when it was gone. In the unusual stillness he could hear the sharp crack of a birch twig splintering, the soughing of the wind at the windows, and even the subtle shift of the roof tiles. It was cold. Old Katya's husband, Slava, had not come from the stables to start the fire in the stove.

There was still a little pile of logs and kindling near the porcelain oven, enough to heat the small room. Fedotov arranged the fuel awkwardly, trying to remember how Slava usually laid the fire. He put a match to it. It flickered and went out. He tried another, wedging it under the kindling; it went out also. He crumpled an agricultural article he had been reading and lit it, stuffing it into the firebox. Thank heavens the wood caught before the entire box of matches was gone! He closed the oven door and sat down behind the desk to wait for the warmth to ease the pain in his arthritic joints.

Gradually they had all gone off, the household staff, the stable hands, the gardeners—God alone knew where they had all disappeared to. There wasn't work for them in Polotsk or Vitebsk, or Petrograd for that matter. At least if they had remained at Spokoinaya Zemlya, he would have seen that they had enough to eat. More fools, they! And now Katya and Slava had gone too. He felt a quite ridiculous sense of hurt. They had not even told him they were going, not said good-bye.

The desktop looked unfamiliar cleared of its usual clutter of papers, pens, and ledgers. The work of the estate had long since ceased, and he had nothing to occupy himself. He opened a drawer and took out an account book, riffling idly through the pages. The figures were neatly written in long, straight columns, with notations in his strong hand detailing expenditures. He thought proudly that he could account for every ruble that had ever passed through his hands, every kopeck! No landlord ever had a better estate manager than Yevgeny Fedotov!

He smiled grimly. As if it mattered! No Voronov would hold this land again. It was just a matter of time until the Reds came for it. Maybe today. Perhaps that's why Katya and Slava, those two faithful ancients, had not come to work this morning; servants were always the first to know. Fedotov's heart was heavy in his chest. He had spent his lifetime building, nurturing, preserving the land, and for what? Well, let the Bolsheviks come. He was tired of waiting.

When Karpovitch met them at the train station, he had a small cadre of men with him. "We have guns, just in case there is opposition. We will ride in with you and take Spokoinaya Zemlya in the name of the Peasant Soviet."

Karpovitch had aged to a grizzled grayness, yet he still exuded strength and shrewdness.

"Just keep the peasants in line," Vassily said coldly. "I don't want the estate destroyed. It belongs to the government now, not them."

Karpovitch's shaggy eyebrows rode up. "The government? What happened to Lenin's promise of 'all land to the people'?"

"The government *is* the people." Vassily did not want to debate issues with Karpovitch just then. He changed the subject. "Will there be resistance, do you think?"

Simcha said nervously, "You said there would be no violence, Vassily!"

Karpovitch was sullen. "Fedotov is alone. Count Pyotr and his family disappeared months ago—in the spring—and the servants have been gone a long time."

"You won't harm him?" Simcha asked, his voice rising.

Karpovitch shrugged. He didn't recognize this pale, anxious man as someone he had once known as the youngest of Fedotov's pet Jews.

Vassily was testy. "Let's get going!"

Karpovitch had horses for the five men from Moscow. A poor horseman, Simcha would have preferred a *drozhki*, or better still to remain in Polotsk, but he was resigned. Vassily had been clear that he was to keep away from his parents' house until afterward; there must be no alarms. Shrugging off Karpovitch's contemptuous offer of assistance, he mounted unaided and followed the others onto the main road.

In a short while the dozen or so armed men were clattering into the courtyard of the manor house. The dogs that had once guarded the house were long since gone, the gateman dead, and the broken iron gates swung lazily on their posts. The paint was peeling on the front of the house and the paths had not been cleared of leaves. Simcha's heart lurched to see how run-down it had become.

The windows were dark. The house appeared deserted.

Vassily leapt down from the horse. "Goddamn it!" he snarled. "The house is empty! Fedotov's escaped!"

Simcha slid off his mount and stood beside Vassily, blowing on his hands.

"What do you care? It's the estate we came to claim," Arkady said reasonably.

Karpovitch pointed to where a thin plume of smoke rose from a chimney in the kitchen wing. "He's here," he said shortly.

Vassily barked orders to the peasants to secure the stables and the outbuildings. To Karpovitch he said, "You take Archille and Karp here and search the front of the house and the bedrooms; make sure no one's hiding there. I'll take the back."

"But that's where Fedotov will be!" Karpovitch grumbled. "You don't make sense!"

"What? Do you think I can't manage one old man?"

Old man? Simcha was confused. He never thought of Fedotov except as the vigorous man of his middle years, but, indeed, he must be seventy or more!

"Arkady, you and Semyon secure the granary."

Simcha resisted. "No. If Yevgeny Sergeivitch is in the house, I go with you—"

"Do what you're told!" Vassily growled. "I can take care of him by myself."

Stubbornly Simcha stood his ground. "You insisted that I come with you to support the government's claim—that's what you said. I don't mean to be sent away now."

Vassily's look was freezing but his voice was placatory. "Look, Semyon. The granary's important. It may be all that stands between the peasants and starvation next year. I need someone I can trust to see that it's padlocked. If I send one of Karpovitch's thugs, God knows how much he'll steal for himself! You go along now to show Arkady the way."

Simcha hesitated. In truth he did not want to face the man whom he had once wished were his father. He believed with all his heart that wealth should be shared and not belong to a handful of people, and yet the feeling persisted that what they were doing was wrong. He had an uncomfortable sense of shame. "You won't hurt him—?"

"I promised, didn't I?" Vassily clapped Simcha on the shoulder, one comrade to another. "Now go! We need to save the grain."

"But what *will* you do with him, Vassily?"

Vassily's patience was wearing thin. "I'll appoint him a commissar!" He turned curtly to Arkady. "Take this man with you and get out of here!"

When Arkady and Simcha were gone, Vassily drew an old-fashioned revolver from his holster, checked the chambers, and released the safety catch. It was big and ugly, designed to blast huge holes at long range. At close range, it would mutilate its target.

He knew exactly what he wanted to do to Yevgeny Fedotov.

*Y*oysef, troubled, hurried into the house from the garden where he and Golda had been digging up the last of the potatoes. "Malkeh! Just now I saw armed men riding past, on the road toward Spokoinaya Zemlya. They were too far away for me to see clearly, but I think that troublemaker Karpovitch was with them."

Malkeh dropped the spoon with which she had been stirring a pot of soup. Her eyes were wide and dark with alarm. "Has it come at last, then?"

Yoysef said, "It may be nothing, but maybe I should go see if *Gospodin* Fedotov is all right."

Malkeh grasped his sleeve. "Yoysef, no! You said the men were armed!"

"I'm not foolish, Malkeh. I certainly don't plan to start a fight with a dozen men with guns. I'll just take a little look around; they won't even know I'm there."

"They have gone to take Spokoinaya Zemlya away from him," Malkeh said with grim certainty.

"Well, then, there'll be no reason for them to harm him. One man alone can't do anything to stop them."

"I am going with you."

"No, you aren't."

Malkeh used both hands to lift the heavy kettle from the fire.

"Yes, I am."

*W*hen the door to the office sprang open, the steward rose to his feet and came forward slowly, his hands upturned to show that he was unarmed. The man who entered was dressed in the uniform recently adopted by the Red Army, a large revolver in his hand. He kicked the door shut behind him.

"Yevgeny Sergeivitch Fedotov, enemy of the people, I claim the lands and all the belongings of Count Pyotr Andreivitch Voronov in the name of Vladimir Ilyich Lenin and the Supreme Soviet Government."

The steward shrugged slightly. "All right," he said calmly. "I've been expecting you. The books and ledgers are in order. You will find them in the desk there."

The man did not lower his gun. It was pointed directly at Fedotov's head.

The steward said wearily, "You can put down that revolver. I am offering no resistance."

A cold smile played around the intruder's mouth, but the gun did not waver. "You don't recognize me, do you, Fedotov?"

"Should I?" Yevgeny looked at the man curiously. He shook his head. There was nothing familiar about this bloated middle-aged man with graying hair and beard—except, perhaps, for the odd eyes. They reminded him of someone. So many people cross one's path in a lifetime you can't remember them all. What did this thug want of him?

"No, you wouldn't remember. To you, we were all like peas in a pod. Just a bunch of dirty, illiterate peasants. When you destroyed my father with your whip, you didn't even recognize him as a human being! To you, I guess, he wasn't a man."

"I whipped your father? Nonsense! I never beat the men. Never!"

"You did that day. You rode into the market square where my father was having an argument with a Jewish bitch who was trying to cheat him. Without asking him what was wrong, you attacked him and left him for dead in the snow."

Fedotov leaned back against the desk. He said slowly, "I remember that day—"

Vassily smiled. "I thought you might."

"It wasn't that way, you know."

"Don't lie, Fedotov! It's too late. I was a little boy when the men carried my father home. You ruined my family and killed my mother and sisters—and all for a Jewish whore!"

Yevgeny felt a flush of anger. "The woman was trying to make a living, and she was far along in her pregnancy, did you know that? The man—your father, was it?—was drunk and he was kicking her in the abdomen! He deserved to be whipped! In fact, I should have hanged him!" There was more that he could say, but he stopped himself. There was no point in trying to reason away unreasoning hatred. He stiffened as the other man sighted along the barrel of the gun, but the time was not yet. His assailant still had things to say.

"Look at me, Yevgeny Sergeivitch! See if you can remember my face!"

Fedotov stared at him, puzzled. The clue had to be in those flat black eyes. He had known only one person with eyes like that. This man was older, of course—in his mid-forties perhaps, and flabby from dissipation. And there were other changes. Somewhere over the course of the years he had shed his diffidence and picked up the habit of authority, and yet, it must be he—the thieving scoundrel! "Vassily Ossipovitch?"

"You never connected your clerk Vassily to that family, did you? But, of course, you were never interested in knowing anything about me. I worked hard—long hours too—and you never once said 'Vassily, you are doing a good job' or 'Vassily, thank you for your work.' It was only when your friends came that you trotted me out to show off to them. 'Look, this is my trained monkey who thinks he's a man because I taught him to read and write in my wonderful peasant school'!"

"You could have had a career, you were smart," Fedotov said, "but instead you stole from us. And you tried to get us killed in the pogrom!"

"Yes, I'm sorry I miscalculated that! The men were too drunk by the time they got here. I wanted you all dead. But peasants are patient—isn't that what you always said, Steward? I could wait for my revenge."

"You think you'll get that by killing me, I suppose?" Fedotov laughed mirthlessly.

"That's part of it. But first I want you to know that it was I who turned Semyon against you, I who encouraged him to drop out of the university, I who helped put him in prison! Where do you think he is now, your devoted pupil? Outside with the peasants, taking Spokoinaya Zemlya away from you but too gutless to face you directly. That's *my* work, Fedotov."

Yevgeny's chest felt as though a steel band were tightening around it and a fire had invaded his arm and shoulder. He gasped, trying to take in enough air to breathe. The pain of loss had become more than he wished to bear.

Vassily took his enemy's pallor and the beads of sweat on his forehead as fear. Ah, it was sweet indeed to bring his childhood nemesis down. Like a lover, he needed to prolong the pleasure as long as possible. "How will you like it, Steward, when Spokoinaya Zemlya becomes a palace of culture for the people? Maybe we'll turn the ballroom into a gymnasium and make some retarded clerk the manager of the place—someone who doesn't know one end of a hoe from the other! Too bad, eh?"

Fedotov's thoughts came in short bursts between the waves of pain. So much hate, he thought, so much poison in this man! Vassily had destroyed lives because of it, not the least his own.

He wanted to lie down, he was tired, nauseated. It would be good to close his eyes. He said wearily, "Get on with it, kill me if you're going to."

"I will, don't worry. But I will not make it quick and easy for you. I want you to suffer a long time like my family and I suffered a long time. I've thought about this for years. I am going to shoot you in the gut, carefully so as not to kill you outright, and then I'll leave you to die slowly, alone here on the floor, where no one will find you for a while."

The steward cried out, but not from fear. There was a crushing weight upon his chest.

Vassily almost laughed to see Fedotov suffer. He raised his gun and took aim.

But before the first shot Fedotov had slumped, dead, to the floor.

Enraged, Vassily emptied the gun into the lifeless body.

*Y*oysef left Malkeh with the little horse-drawn cart in a covering copse while he investigated. Gingerly he entered the courtyard. There was evidence that many horses had been tethered there, but he saw no one about. A crudely lettered sign nailed to the door read: KEEP OUT! PROPERTY OF THE SUPREME SOVIET GOVERNMENT. TRESPASSERS WILL BE SHOT!

Cautiously Yoysef crept around the house, peering in the windows. Two men sat in the large parlor at the front of the house. A decanter of Voronov port and a bottle of vodka were open on the table between them, and they were most certainly drunk. He saw no one else. He went back to Malkeh. "It looks like everyone's gone except for a couple of peasants who are too drunk to notice anything! I'm going in by the kitchen door. If I'm not back in ten minutes, I want you to leave!"

"I'm going in with you."

"No!"

"I'm more afraid sitting here alone than I'll be in the house with you."

Yoysef knew when it was fruitless to argue with Malkeh.

They found Yevgeny Fedotov lying on the floor in the little office near the kitchen.

Kneeling beside him, Yoysef saw the holes blasted in the body. He turned white. "Go back to the cart!" he said shortly to Malkeh.

She fell to her knees on the other side of Fedotov's body. After a while she took off her shawl and spread it gently. "Who would do such a thing? They must have shot him a half dozen times!"

Yoysef sighed. "Someone full of hate."

*B*efore Simcha left to return to Moscow, he came to his parents' house. He found the mirrors turned to the wall, a candle burning on the windowsill, and his mother, clad in deepest black, the sleeve of her dress rent, sitting on the floor.

"Dearest Mammeh, who has died? Aunt Golda—? Who?"

"What are you doing here, Simcha?" Malkeh asked sharply. "Why are you in Polotsk?"

"I came on business for the government, Mammeh."

"What do you have to do with the government?" With some difficulty, but refusing his help, she got to her feet. Her eyes, the same color blue as his, peered into his face.

Simcha was patient. "Mammeh, you know that Vladimir Ilyich has declared all land belongs to the state. I was sent here to witness the government's claim to Spokoinaya Zemlya. I don't choose what I do!"

Malkeh raised her arm and struck Simcha across the face. It made a sharp sound in the tense, silent room. "And killed Yevgeny Sergeivitch in the bargain!"

Simcha took a step backward. "No one said anything about any killing! I was at the granary. You must be mistaken! Why would anyone kill an old man like Fedotov?"

"You tell me!"

A look of confusion crossed Simcha's face. "There is no point in it—it must have been Karpovitch's peasants—but why didn't anyone speak of it? You are sure?"

Malkeh's look was full of contempt. "You were with them. How is it that you came to rob our dearest friends? How is it that you didn't keep a madman from shooting him, who was a second father to you?"

Simcha could see that there was no answer that would ever be acceptable to his mother. Nor, for that matter would he ever be able to explain his passive acquiescence to himself. Fedotov dead! But neither Vassily nor Karpovitch had spoken of it! He and Arkady had returned from the granary just as the men were mounting to ride back to town.

"How did Fedotov take it?" he had asked Vassily as they rode toward Polotsk.

"How should the bastard take it!" Vassily had snapped. He was in a foul mood.

Simcha had held his peace.

But he shouldn't have. And knowing how vulnerable Fedotov was, he should have insisted on being there when the government order was presented to him. He had never doubted that Vassily's mission was personal and vengeful.

Simcha stood before his mother, his head bowed so that his scrawny neck showed, his hands dangling from the too-large sleeves of his coat. His body was as frail and thin as a child's, but his face was ancient.

"Get out of my house," Malkeh said in a deadly quiet voice. "I don't need your kind of child! I disown you. I never want to see you again!"

She turned a rigid back to him.

"Mammeh—" Simcha reached out a hand, touched her shoulder. Coldly she shrugged him off. "Listen, Mammeh, let me explain—I didn't know—"

She was ice. She would not turn. She would not look at him.

"Please, Mammeh—" He knelt at her feet, clinging to her skirt, but she was implacable.

There was nothing that he could say. Sick with grief and despair, Simcha went slowly from the house, closing the door quietly behind him.

Chapter 65

*F*or Pyotr Voronov it had seemed an endless journey until finally he reached the main body of General Denikin's advancing "White" forces near Tambov. Travel-worn and begrimed from the road, his beard and hair overgrown, he was mistaken for a peasant and handled roughly by the band of horsemen to whom he surrendered himself.

"Take your hands off me! I'm Major Pyotr Andreivitch Voronov, you fools! Let go so I can show you my discharge papers!"

The Cossack outriders eyed him with suspicion. It was known that foolhardy Reds had tried on occasion to infiltrate Denikin's volunteer army. The last one—ha! What fun they had had with him before he died!

Pyotr's papers were creased and dirty from the journey, but the leader of the band, though he could not read, recognized the imperial double eagle of the seal.

"You could have stolen these!" he snarled, and twenty rifle muzzles pointed at a place between Pyotr's eyes.

"But I didn't." When needed, Pyotr could summon the arrogant authority of a long line of Voronovs. Uneasily, the men backed off a step or two.

"All right," the speaker conceded. "We'll take you into camp and let the general himself decide what to do with you. But I warn you, if you're a spy, we'll cut off your balls and stuff them up your arse!"

Surrounded by Cossacks, Pyotr, more captive than guest, was escorted into a military enclave half concealed in a wooded ravine. Looking about him with an eye experienced in war, Pyotr guessed that this was the command center of Denikin's forward forces. There were perhaps a hundred fifty tents scattered about and at least that number of makeshift shelters; he calculated a thousand men and fifteen hundred horses. Riding into camp, he had counted forty large field artillery pieces—more than they had had at Lodz during the war—and there might be additional weapons elsewhere. A well-equipped army, then, he thought with relief. He had heard that the Allies, principally England and the United States, were supplying the Whites but had discounted the story.

An early darkness was falling, and a myriad of small cooking fires gave off mouth-watering smells. Pyotr's stomach recalled that it had received nothing for two days save for a crust of bread and a handful of millet, chewed raw. They actually had meat here!

While the leader of the patrol went to make his report, one of the men who had ridden in with him took Pyotr's horse and another led him to one of the tents to wait. Pyotr could see the man's shadow against the tent wall, his rifle, bayonet fixed, in hand. While resenting it, he also approved of this evidence of military discipline. After a while, an orderly brought him a pail of cold water, a slab of yellow soap, and a rough towel. Pyotr stripped to the skin to scrub his face and body, thankful that his saddlebag still held one fairly respectable shirt. It was too bad that he couldn't say the same for trousers and boots, but he brushed off the former and used his discarded shirt to rub the dust off the latter. It would do. He had trod a long road since the St. Petersburg Cadet School!

After a wait so long that he had begun to wonder whether he had been forgotten, a young, neatly pressed officer arrived to lead Pyotr to the well-appointed tent of the general. He saluted the older man smartly.

General Anton Ivanovitch Denikin, chief of the volunteer army, was every inch the professional soldier. His tenacity, drive, and native intelligence had overcome the circumstances of a humble birth and marked him early as a man to be reckoned with. Commanding the Iron Brigade during the World War, he was a hero of the Carpathian campaign, having held off the German army for eleven days with more guts than ammunition. He was an imposing man, solidly built, with an abundance of graying hair and beard. Tonight he was dressed in an immaculate uniform, formal except for sword and boots, his feet incongruous in slippers. He held Pyotr's papers in his hand, and his piercing gray eyes coolly appraised the visitor. Pyotr held himself tall and proud, despite his worn clothes and shaggy appearance.

Voronov was a name well known to Denikin. During his cadet days at the General Staff Academy in St. Petersburg he had served alongside Andrei Petrovitch, then Count Voronov, probably this young man's father. In truth they hadn't much cared for each other, Voronov even then a wastrel and a roué, Denikin known as a grind and a prude.

"I remember your father," the general said without inflection. "Whatever happened to him?"

"He died in a hunting accident when I was a child," Pyotr said.

"These papers say you served with distinction and were retired as a major. Where did you lose your eye, Major?"

"At Molodechno, sir."

"Hard days, eh?"

"Yes, sir."

"And what have you been doing since?"

"I went home to my family in Byelorussia for a while, but—" He didn't have to complete the sentence; everyone knew what had happened to the great estates. "I sent my wife and sons away. I pray God they made it across the border and are in France by now."

There was a little silence. Denikin had a family of his own. When he spoke, his voice was warmer than before. "Sad, sad, that you should return home to lands you defended from the Germans, only to find that the 'Communists' had confiscated them!" He sighed. "Better that we had lost to the Germans! At least *they* are civilized, whereas these riffraff are not! 'Communists' they are calling themselves these days, as though to convince us that their government is based on a *community* of interests! But don't let me get started on that! Sit down, sit down. You will have supper with me and we will talk."

Later General Denikin said, "This upstart Lenin has unleashed a 'Red Terror' on the land. And we Whites reply in kind with a terror of our own." His voice fell and his face looked drawn and sad. "No one is untouched by civil war. I trust that we will win—because we *must*!—but for those of us who live through it, the experience will not only have crippled the body, it may very well have deformed the soul!"

"I am perhaps presumptuous, General, but I cannot help wondering what will happen when we *do* win. Will we put the same dishonest officials back in power to perpetrate the same crimes against the people all over again?"

"Oh," General Denikin said carelessly, "I suppose we will restore the

Romanovs to the throne. As for the rest, I haven't thought that far ahead. If you press me, I would have to say that it doesn't matter to me whether you stand on the left or the right as long as you love the Motherland."

They ate, a good warm meal of roast pork with white beans, and drank a robust red wine so good that it could have come from the cellars of Spokoinaya Zemlya. At the end of the evening, the general wrung Pyotr's hand. "You are most welcome to join us, my young friend. There is plenty of work for an experienced campaigner!"

Riding as commandant of one of the White companies all through the rest of that spring, Pyotr was happy. At Tsaritsyn, where the elite Eighth and Ninth Red Armies had mounted a massive attack against Denikin's main force, he distinguished himself for fearlessness in the field and was promoted to a colonelcy. Like Denikin himself, Pyotr felt committed to the cause of God and Motherland.

During the warm months, Denikin's men thrust northward to within two hundred versts of Moscow, planning to join forces with General Yudenitch's volunteer army making its sweep South from the Baltic. Meanwhile, the third White leader, Admiral Kolchak, was consolidating his hold on lands in the Urals and Siberia. But success was not to last. Inexorably, in fierce and savage fighting, the Red forces pushed the Whites back until even Denikin's stronghold in the Don basin was threatened.

Pyotr Voronov's company was all but decimated in the heavy action. The remnants were reassigned to the cavalry of Cossack General Mamontov.

Mamontov was not Denikin. The bulk of his troops were wild and undisciplined, as interested in plundering the countryside as in freeing it from the Reds. The Cossacks made little distinction between the property of the Bolsheviks and that of the indigenous population. Their brutality was legend, causing many who would otherwise have supported the Whites to turn against them. Horror stories began to drift back from the lands held by Mamontov's men. When a detachment of Whites trapped a handful of Bolshevik factory workers in a sleepy little town on their route, they blinded and mutilated them before burying them alive. The Reds repaid in kind, adding their own heinous refinements. A White soldier who was captured could count on a slow death by torture; a Red the same. Sadism became an end in itself, one side no better than the other.

While Pyotr did not believe every detail of the reported cruelties, he could not ignore what he witnessed himself. As the men grew bored and restless, frustration found an outlet in the indiscriminate slaughter of civilian populations—for their property, their women, or merely for entertainment. Condoned, or at least ignored, by the generals, a colonel had as little hope of holding his men in check as in restraining a flood. One attempt had already been made on Pyotr's life by an unseen assailant. The bullet had merely grazed his shoulder;

given the crack marksmanship of the Cossacks, perhaps it was meant to warn him off, not kill him. He began to distrust his own men.

As Cossack excesses in the Ukraine eroded support for the Whites, the leadership resorted to old ways to unite the populace. A virulent anti-Semitic propaganda campaign was mounted, making the usual scurrilous allegations of ritual murder and linking the Jews to the Bolsheviks. Wasn't the notorious Trotsky's name really Lev Davidovitch Bronstein, after all? The pogroms of 1919 began in the northwestern corner of the Ukraine and moved in a steadily broadening stream throughout the region. Pyotr heard the mutterings of his men and knew, with sickening certainty, that he would be helpless to contain the violence that was coming. From earliest childhood Pyotr Voronov had accepted Jew-baiting as a fact of life—deplorable perhaps but an integral part of the peasant character and not important enough to confront directly. Now a Jewish tailor named Yoysef Mandelkern had risked his life to take his wife and sons across the Finnish border, and his feelings had changed.

As the Reds began to pile one success on another, the campaign against the Jews picked up momentum: "Kill the Jews and save Russia" was an ancient cry but effective still. Pyotr's company was in Fastov at the end of September when a five-day orgy of butchery took place.

At the beginning, Pyotr had tried to stem the killing. Riding his horse into the midst of the rampaging men, he had ordered them to stop and had threatened them with his saber. When that had no effect, he had fired his revolver into the air. A thrown stone knocked him from his horse. He would have been set upon and beaten to death had not a fellow officer pulled him from the clutches of his own command.

"Are you crazy, Voronov!" the other colonel had screamed at him.

"They're killing civilians, for God's sakes!" Pyotr shouted, leaking blood from a gash in his cheek and struggling to get loose from the arms of his rescuer.

"Just *Zhidy*! Why do you care?"

"They're innocent, that's why!"

His companion gave him a strange sidelong look. "You've not got some of that Jew blood in you, have you?"

Pyotr wrenched himself away. "Maybe I have! Better Jew than Cossack scum!"

"Look, you may not be saved next time! Keep away from the men till this is finished! If you can't stand the sight of blood, get out of town until it's over! It's been a tough war. The men need some release. And we need a way to rally the peasants to the White cause!"

It might have been good advice but Pyotr not could bear either to witness the carnage nor could he close his eyes to it. Having lost his horse, he wandered on foot through the city. That's how he happened to see men preparing to torch a three-story apartment building, its occupants still inside.

Desperate, he grabbed the sleeve of a nearby man. "Stop it!" he shouted. "Can't you see those people will burn to death?"

The man turned a wolfish grin on him. "Why do you think we nailed beams across the doors!"

"I'm Colonel Voronov, and I order you to stop before it's too late!"

The man threw back his head and laughed. When Pyotr grasped his shirtfront, the soldier knocked him to the ground.

Pyotr was helpless. The fire had taken hold now, and the whole structure rang with one long shrill scream. He could not stand it and ran away.

But there was no place to hide from the horror. Here were a group of stalwart soldiers, handsome, strong, the pride of the army of the Don, and they had surrounded five frail old men who had been praying in their synagogue. He stood watching while the Cossacks stripped the old men naked. When they stood shivering with fear and cold in the midst of their tormentors, they were made to dance—bullets sprayed at their feet hurrying their steps—while chanting from the liturgy of their religion. It was a scene out of hell!

He moved on. The gang rape of a very young girl was in progress, but already in this civil war the sight of rapes had become commonplace. He noticed as he passed that the child's eyes were glazed over, and she was, mercifully, already dead. The soldiers may or may not have known that as they took their turns on top of the body.

He came to the edge of Fastov and sat down under a tree to wait until the rage had died and he could reclaim his company and leave this shameful place. The town smelled of fire and blood and dead bodies, but here it was a pleasant fall day. Pyotr reached up to pick an apple from the tree overhead, but its round fullness reminded him of a woman's breast, and he was sick.

*P*yotr knew for a fact that General Denikin was a brave man who believed he was saving his country, but something terrible had been unleashed, and it could no longer be contained. For two years the armies of the Whites and the Reds had surged back and forth across Russia. Where the Reds won, they looted, pillaged, and raped. Where the Whites won, they looted, pillaged, and raped. Mass executions of the populace followed in the wake of both armies. No one dared go into the fields to work. What little *was* grown was commandeered by one army or the other. Pyotr was sickened by the smell of blood, the sight of weeping women, starving children, burning villages. What difference did it make in the end who torched a building, bayoneted a child, ravaged a widow?

Until he actually rode out of camp, Pyotr Voronov did not recognize that he had been planning his escape for months. He went alone, taking nothing with him except a revolver for defense and a saddlebag filled with what little food he could scavenge. He went out in the early hours before dawn, when sentries are cold and bored and not as alert as they might be.

He headed west with a vague notion of crossing the border into Rumania. As he rode, he imagined himself arriving in Paris. It should not be difficult to locate the house of the refugee Prince and Princess Trubetskoy. At whatever hour it was, he would rap gently on the door, once, twice. Perhaps it would be the middle of the night and a sleepy servant would summon Ekaterina from her bed. There, in the great hall of his mother's house, he and Ekaterina would stand, devouring each other with their eyes.

Pyotr did not see the group of ragged men until they leapt out from the bushes and grabbed his terrified horse by the bridle.

It was a ridiculous way for a life to end. There was no ideology involved. These people cared little whether he was White or Red, Russian or German or Jew. They killed him for the bread in his saddlebags and for the horse that they would later butcher for meat. He did not even have a chance to use his revolver. If he had had time to reflect on it, the very foolishness of his fate would have made Pyotr cry.

Chapter 66

$\mathcal{F}$edotov's death had cheated Vassily of the revenge he had savored in anticipation for almost forty years. Like so much else in his life, at the very peak of exquisite fulfillment, fate had taken a quixotic twist and denied him his moment of victory. It had been thus during the Polotsk pogrom when the steward and his Jews should have died but didn't; again when the beautiful Marta Pirumova had seemed completely his while betraying him with another; still again when foolproof plans to assassinate the traitor Sipyagin had gone wrong. Why, he asked himself, why was he frustrated at every turn! Had God Himself turned His back on him? Peasants liked to say: "Fear not gods or devils, fear people." Yes, that was it. He was surrounded by enemies who worked against him and thwarted him at every turn.

He had done well in the *Cheka*, of course, but that was no thanks to anyone but himself! Some of the most ingenious tortures yet devised had come from his fertile brain. It was he who had recommended crucifixion in Ekaterinoslav and Kiev, he who had had Chekist executioners strap White officers to planks in Odessa and push them slowly into roaring furnaces or vats of boiling water, he who had suggested a return to the biblical punishment of stoning. "To us," he wrote in a *Cheka* newspaper, "all is permitted, for we are the first in the world to raise the sword in the name of freeing all from bondage. Only the complete and final death of the old world will save us from the return of the old jackals."

He might be denied retribution in more personal ways, but in the wholesale killing of his class enemies, there was a kind of settlement of accounts, and for a while, after one of these orgies, he rested easier.

Always he had to be watchful against those who would do him harm. They were everywhere. He had noticed lately that one of the security officers on Bolshaya Lubyanka Street gave him odd glances when he entered the prison where he had his office. He had ordered the man to produce his documents. "Can you prove that your name is really Viktor Alexandrovitch Ivanov?" he had asked him.

"Why, n-n-no, sir," the man had stuttered. "I have only my papers. Would you like to see my discharge from the army?"

"Ha! Those could be forged too!" Vassily stormed into his office, where he wrote the man's name in a notebook. He would make sure to watch him in the future!

There were others who were more potent enemies than Ivanov. It could not have been accidental this morning, for instance, to find Semyon Mandelkern at the Agricultural Department warehouse from where government officials of a certain level drew their food supplies. He had never seen *him* there before, which only served to prove his point!

"Ah, my young friend Semyon!" he had greeted him with an affability he didn't feel. "And what are you doing here?"

"Not shopping," Simcha had said shortly. "People like me take their chances on the street with everyone else."

"Do I detect a note of envy? It doesn't suit you, Semyon! Is there anything here you would like me to buy for you? A little treat from an old friend?"

"I would choke on it."

Semyon had been cold toward him ever since he'd moved to Moscow, and had avoided him since the trip to Byelorussia. It had been a favor to take him away from his dreary little clerical job and give him a trip home to claim Spokoinaya Zemlya! And what had he done with it? He had bolted from the official party to come back to Moscow without leave or permission before the work was finished! He could have had him severely punished for that. But, out of his former regard, he had done nothing.

"I am on duty here this morning," Simcha had said coldly. "Can I help you find anything?"

"Have the chocolates come in from Switzerland?"

"Why, yes. This way—sir!"

Vassily, escorted by an unwilling Simcha, filled a basket with Westphalian ham, Swiss chocolates, a half dozen oranges from Egypt, a dozen eggs. It gave him pleasure to see the look of envy, disguised as contempt, on Semyon's white face, and he added to his basket French-milled soap, powdered milk (from a Red Cross shipment from the United States), bread, and a round of Swiss cheese. He knew as well as Simcha did that almost nothing was available on the outside for ration tickets, and on the black market flour cost seven thousand rubles a sack, ten eggs a thousand rubles, four pounds of soap five hundred, with prices still rising. On the streets of Moscow and Petrograd young women sold their bodies for a loaf of bread or a small piece of meat. It was said that only Red Army soldiers, who received extra rations, could afford their price. Government officials, of course, seldom paid anything for sex.

Simcha packed up Vassily's order, filling out the requisite forms—always there were forms, worse now than in tsarist times!—and waiting while Vassily signed them in his bold, arrogant handwriting.

"We must see each other again," Vassily said, smiling like *Babushka*'s wolf.

Simcha did not respond. Vassily felt certain a little investigation would reveal evidence that the boy was involved in counterrevolutionary activity.

*A*t first Simcha had been hurt and angry at his mother's irrationality. She had misunderstood events at Spokoinaya Zemlya if she thought for a moment that he was responsible for Yevgeny Fedotov's death. He had known nothing of it until she had told him. He, too, felt grief and an unexpectedly poignant sense of loss, but in a war—and that was what was happening here, wasn't it?—people on both sides got killed.

Mammeh expected him to have stood with Fedotov no matter the odds or the consequences. But how could he, a lone man, in poor health at that, have protected his old teacher? On the other hand, in allowing himself to be sent to the granary that day, had he not passively participated in Fedotov's murder?

Gradually Simcha's anger with Mammeh was replaced with a feeling of acute loss. He thought of her all the time. He remembered the silky feel of her hair between his fingers when, as a child, she had allowed him to braid her long tresses. He thought of mornings when she had bent, holding out to him a sugared slice of bread, still hot from the oven. He remembered evenings when the aura of lamplight about her head gave her the holy look of the Virgin in an icon.

"Let me read you this verse, my son," she would say. "Hear how the words flow like water in a stream—" And she would read aloud, her voice dark as velvet, with an indescribably sweet edge of huskiness.

He recalled how, leaning close to him to ponder some difficult problem

Fedotov had set for him, she smelled of soap, and the herbs she hung in her clothes.

He remembered that the eyes she had rested upon him were starry with pride, because he was at the university, and there was an eagerness to know about his life in the city at the same time she was concerned that he was drifting away from home and family.

She loved him, and he her. And now this bitterness had come between them. She had sent him from her house. She had not responded to his letters.

In the final analysis, who had killed Yevgeny Fedotov—was it Karpovitch's peasants? Vassily? Or was it his own passivity?

There was no food to be had even in the country. In the three-year course of the civil war, between 1918 and 1921, crops had been burned and livestock destroyed. The waste was senseless. Hundreds of thousands of people, most without political beliefs of any kind, had been killed or made homeless in the fighting. Two million more, perhaps the ablest of all but labeled "class enemies" by the regime, had fled Russia for the west. Currency was worthless, transportation a shambles, industry almost at a standstill.

In Polotsk it was the famine of 1890 all over again except that Malkeh and Yoysef were no longer young and strong, and there was no Yevgeny Fedotov to take charge. The Communist authorities requisitioned whatever little yet grew in the fields. The peasants were enraged. So this was the government that had promised "bread, peace, and land to the people"? Even the tsar himself had not taken *all* the grain! Yet, for all that, the rural population, able to grow and squirrel away some food for this own use, was better off than the city dwellers.

Yoysef's tailor shop had been virtually idle since 1915, when the men had gone off to war against the Germans and Austrians. Through the years Yoysef had lovingly oiled the sewing machines and polished the metal to a soft shine. The tailor's dummies stood wrapped in clean cloths against the walls, looking like ancient mummies. Large spools of black, gray, and white thread, and shiny scissors in several sizes, were impaled on spindles above the cutting table, but the table itself was bare, and there were no bolts of cloth on the shelves.

Since the government ration was inadequate to sustain life, days were now spent in the relentless quest for food. Malkeh and Golda grubbed in the earth for potatoes and carrots, often eating these half frozen and either unripe or rotten. Turnips, beans, and radishes had been planted where Malkeh's dahlias had once grown, the tiny plot guarded—Malkeh and Yoysef took turns at night—lest someone steal the vegetables as they poked through the earth. They had lost two hens to thieves a few months before and were no longer taking chances. They missed having eggs, and had seen no meat in months. Fish could be caught in the river, but after Malkeh saw the bloated corpses floating downstream from God knows what disaster of war, she ruled against eating fish. Other people swallowed their squeamishness, and some died as a result.

Every day now, Yoysef walked—the horse and cart were long since gone—along the roads outside the city, searching for whatever would keep them for another week, or another day. Sometimes he was successful in bartering his skill with a needle for a little flour, a container of milk, a rind of cheese. Then there was cause for celebration. The only other things left to trade were Malkeh's books and the sewing machines, which no one wanted. Soon Yoysef would make his way to Vitebsk or Petrograd to sell Malkeh's and Golda's wedding rings and earrings. He hoped someone would still want such things.

𝓜alkeh was sitting in her customary chair in the kitchen, her hands lying idle in her lap, when Yoysef came home without so much as an onion for a whole day's heartbreaking excursion. Yoysef's heart turned over to see how the hardships of the past five years had streaked her beautiful golden hair with white. Her cheekbones, covered with too little flesh, stood out sharply; indeed all roundness had left her body. When she smiled, a rare occurrence these days, a flicker of brightness might momentarily warm her lovely eyes, but the light within had dimmed when Fedotov was killed and Simcha banished. She had become a hollow person, a husk.

"Where's Golda?" he asked.

"Lying in bed. I don't think she has the strength to get up. We must find some better food for her soon. Take my jewelry. Maybe you can trade it for a chicken. A little soup would do wonders."

"Yes, all right. I'll go tomorrow." He massaged his tight forehead with his fingers.

Physically Yoysef had fared better than the women. Burned brown from the sun, his lean body hardened by his daily excursions in search of substance, he seemed little changed. Even his hair and beard had remained thick and mostly dark. The difference, he thought sometimes, was in the way each confronted deprivation. Malkeh hugged her losses to her and Golda was eager for death to claim her, but Yoysef counted as blessings his health and the hope that he would someday be reunited with his children.

"Nothing today, Malkeh. I guess it's boiled potatoes for supper again." His voice was bright with forced cheerfulness.

"I'm glad that the children are in America." She picked at a loose thread in her skirt. "Do you know that it is *shabbes* tonight? Do you suppose that they are eating brisket and *kugel*?"

Yoysef sank down in a chair opposite her. He took her hand in his.

The skin felt like paper. "The children write to us all the time, asking when we will come to them. Let me ask Chaim to send tickets, and we will go to San Francisco, the three of us. And then we shall eat all the brisket and *challah* and honey cake that our hearts desire!"

"We have waited too long, I'm afraid. The government may not allow us to go. Besides, I am too weak, and Golda—"

Yoysef took her hand. "We will find a way."

"Now that Mammeh is dead, we have nothing to keep us here anymore." Malkeh's tone was bitter.

"I guess not." Yoysef shook his head sadly.

"At least Mammeh didn't suffer. Better to go instantly from a stroke than to die from hunger."

"Yes."

"When Golda dies, there is no one to stay for."

When she refused to have his name spoken aloud in the house, it was fruitless for Yoysef to argue with Malkeh that Simcha was still their child. Yoysef had thought about his son a great deal in his long solitary walks in the countryside. How Simcha could have been trapped into participating in the confiscation of Spokoinaya Zemlya was not difficult to see, but that he had had anything to do with Fedotov's death was not credible. He had tried to tell this to Malkeh, but she had refused to listen. Yoysef's heart ached when he thought of the suffering of those two—Malkeh no less than Simcha. He himself had been wrong to allow himself to be influenced by how Malkeh had hardened her heart toward their son. Her weakness was her implacable nature, his was his protectiveness of her even when Malkeh was wrong.

Restless, Yoysef stood and wandered over to the shelf where he kept his whittling knife and odds and ends of soft wood. He picked up his knife and tried it gently against his thumb. "I heard something interesting today."

"What?"

"You know the man Moscow sent to nationalize Spokoinaya Zemlya? You will never guess who that was—"

Malkeh frowned. "What are you talking about?"

"That Bolshevik official turned out to have been born right here in Voronov village! I think I remember him—the one whom *Gospodin* Fedotov trained to work in the estate office?"

"Who stole the countess's jewels!"

Yoysef scratched his beard. "Yes, I'd forgotten that. The police never caught up with him."

"Nor Yevgeny Sergeivitch either." Malkeh closed her eyes, the better to visualize him. "He was a surly boy. I could never remember his name."

"Valery? Viktor. Something like that?" offered Yoysef.

Malkeh's heart turned over in her breast, and a coldness like death descended upon her as she remembered a cold and dreary peasant hut on the edge of the forest, and a child with implacable hate in his eyes.

*Y*oysef had prepared a cushioned chair at the table and carried Golda in so that she could celebrate the Sabbath with them. Their meal was a couple of half-rotting potatoes with neither bread nor wine to bless. Malkeh lit one stubby *shabbes* candle (a regular candle cut into thirds), and for a short while it spread a sputtering light over the tattered white cloth. They ate slowly, chewing each mouthful a long time to make it last. Golda was fretful, lacking understanding of why there was so little food. "But we always used to have chicken soup on the Sabbath!" she complained.

Malkeh laid her hand over Golda's, and her voice was comforting. "And we will again, dearest, just as soon as I can find a nice fat chicken!"

The rapping at the kitchen door was so furtive that none of the three was sure at first that they had heard anything.

Malkeh looked frightened. It was not unknown for hungry peasants to break into households for whatever little they might steal there. "Don't go to the door," she whispered, reaching her hand out to Yoysef.

He pushed back his chair. "Malkeh," he chided gently, "it is the Sabbath."

"So what if it is? Who do you think is there, the prophet Elijah?" she called after him when he went to unbar the door.

When he saw the two rough-looking men standing in the doorway, Yoysef thought that Malkeh's worst fears had come to pass. He took a step backward. "Yes?"

"Mandelkern?"

"Yes."

"Come out here. We have something for you."

Malkeh was at Yoysef's elbow. "Don't go with them, Yoysef! They mean to kill you!"

"Stay here, Malkeh. I will just see what they want."

Before she could protest further, he stepped outside where the two men were waiting. There was a covered cart pulled into the sheltering darkness of the stable.

"What is it?" he asked softly.

"A gift for you. From Moscow."

Malkeh had ignored Yoysef's command and followed him outside. "We know no one in Moscow!" she exclaimed. "Get away from here!"

Yoysef lifted the tarpaulin from the cart bed. His eyes widened. It was filled with sacks of flour and sugar, jars of honey, a keg of herring, dried meats. Quickly he lowered the flap. Black market obviously. He calculated whether these men would take Malkeh's jewelry in exchange for some part of the food. If caught, speculators and their customers were shot on the spot, but Golda was surely dying and Malkeh was wasting away almost as fast as she. Furtively he peered around to see if any suspicious lights had come on in neighboring houses. None. He must take a chance, for Malkeh and his sister.

"Come in, and we will talk," he said, leading the way. Only the leader of the two followed, the other staying to guard the treasure in the cart.

Inside the kitchen, Yoysef said, "We have no money, Comrade, but—"

The man shrugged. "Am I asking?"

Golda peered around her at the sound of a strange voice. Agitated, she clutched at Malkeh. "What is it? What is it?"

Malkeh said eagerly, "My books—"

"The stuff's been paid for."

"Paid for!"

"Who paid for it?" Malkeh sensed a trap. The Communists were no better than the tsar's secret police!

"It's all right. The man who signed for it is a high government official. There won't be any trouble."

Simcha! It could only be Simcha who had arranged this! Yoysef flashed a quick look at Malkeh. "Our son Simcha is sending us food."

Malkeh said coldly, "I have no son by that name."

"Where shall I unload it?" the man asked.

Malkeh's voice rose, became shrill. "Take it back! I want no charity from strangers!"

"Malkeh, please—"

"Take it back! Take it back!"

Yoysef recognized the beginnings of hysteria. She would begin screaming in a minute, and then the neighbors would come, and then—who knew? Maybe the police would be called, and they would all be executed.

"We don't want it," Yoysef said painfully. Sugar! Flour! Meat and herring! Carefully parceled out, the food would sustain the three of them for months! Golda would live, and Malkeh might become more like her old self. How could he send it away? He took hold of Malkeh's hands. "If not for yourself, Malkeh, think of Golda!" he whispered fiercely.

"What? What did you say?" Golda's querulous voice asked.

Malkeh looked from Golda to Yoysef and back again. Fear clutched her heart when she saw how frail her sister-in-law had become, her body scarcely the size of a child's. "All right. Just enough for Golda. I will not touch it!" She turned to the stranger. "Tell the Mr. Bigshot in Moscow how little we took—to save a life!—but tell him that his parents don't want anything from murderers!"

The man was incredulous. "Are you sure?" he asked when he walked outside with Yoysef. "It's all meant for you."

Yoysef was tempted. From the cart he chose some dried fish and meat. The rest he could hide in the cellar for later; he would make up a story that he had traded for it. But she would know—

"Yes, I'm sure. If you see the man who asked you to bring this, tell him that his mother will accept nothing from him." The men began tying the tarpaulin over the wagon bed once more. "But that his father is grateful."

*V*assily let himself into the flat with a passkey. It was scarcely more than one room with an alcove for a cot and a small brazier for cooking and heat. He had plenty of time to search the place for incriminating evidence; it would be hours before Semyon would return from work in the Agricultural Bureau, and, anyway, how long could it take to sift through everything contained in such a small space?

He started in the "bedroom." One pair of ragged trousers, a frayed shirt, and a winter coat, sheepskin-lined but old and full of holes, hung on hooks on the wall. Two sets of underclothes were on a self-made shelf suspended over the bed. The cot had no sheets and only one thin army-style blanket drawn over a skimpy mattress. The man lived like a monk! Not that his wages as a clerk at Agriculture would provide anything very elaborate! Too bad about Semyon. There was a time when Vassily had offered to help him find a job in line with his talents, but he had turned down that help.

Vassily lifted the mattress, searching for anything hidden beneath it. It was amazing how many people secreted away letters, money, books, things that could get them in trouble, in the most obvious of places! There was nothing beneath the mattress except some gray dust curls. With distaste, Vassily pushed it back in place.

The rest of the room was almost as bare as the alcove. There was a cupboard with a couple of cracked plates, a glass, a bowl, a few utensils. There was little food, only part of a loaf of unspeakable state-made bread, and one egg. You would think that someone who took his turn clerking in the state warehouse would have the imagination to put away a little something for himself. But not Semyon! He had always suffered from the pride of self-righteousness!

Still it was strange that there was so little here, Vassily thought. Surely a counterrevolutionary spy would be paid something, especially when his target was as important to the *Cheka* as Vassily. His lip curled in scorn. It would be like the little bugger to do it for nothing!

On one dirty wall hung an avant-garde Cubist painting. It was in a style that the state would soon ban as without artistic merit. He stood peering into it as though it might give him a clue to Semyon's character, but it meant nothing to him. It was merely a series of slashes of color, orange and scarlet and purple, against a black-painted canvas. A stark white female torso, distorted with three globelike breasts, was somewhat off center, an unwinking eye placed where the navel might be.

In a corner of the room was one straight chair, a box next to it serving as a table. Vassily picked up a copy of Pushkin's poems that was lying on top and riffled through it. People often hid letters and papers in books. Nothing. Knowing Semyon as a reader, he was surprised that there were not more books.

So far he had turned up nothing. Was it possible that he had been mistaken about Semyon's spying on him? Unless he had hidden something under the floorboards or in the walls—and to check that would require tools for tearing out partitions—there was nothing here. Nevertheless, he took down the painting and passed his hands over the walls and then removed his boots to see if he could feel a loose floorboard. Nothing. In an excess of frustration, Vassily kicked the box-table, and, flimsy as it was, it toppled over.

Bonanza! The box, which he had carelessly assumed to be empty, was filled with books! Some of them were in that strange abomination of a language, Yiddish, which he could not read. A few were in Russian—*The Brothers Karamazov*, for instance, *Crime and Punishment*—Dostoyevsky's work was politically all right, but a philosophical treatise by the Jew-loving philosopher Vladimir Solovev was not. Many books were in German which Vassily read fluently: Theodor Herzl's *Der Judenstaat* and *Altneuland*. Vassily looked through those, laughing to himself at the very idea of a Jewish state! Still, Zionism was a matter that the *Cheka* kept under surveillance. He laid the Herzl books on a pile to carry away with him. In English, which he read haltingly, was *A Journey to Eretz Israel* by Elhanan Levensky and *Looking Ahead* by someone named Henry Mendes. More subversive materials, no doubt. Most of the books carried the stamp, in English: "Kurilov's Jewish Bookstore, 2834 Geary Street, San Francisco, California." On the very bottom of the box was a packet of letters tied with a string. Again these were in Hebrew script so that he could not read them himself. Some were yellow with age. After noting postmarks in the United States, damning enough, he laid these aside. There was enough here to take Semyon Mandelkern into custody. If needed, they could manufacture additional evidence to convict him.

"You see, Marta," Vassily said aloud as he carried the books and letters into his own apartment a little later, "if you search long enough, there is always something! And when Semyon is in the cellars of the Lubyanka, then I will find out who set him to spy on me!"

hen the letter from Polotsk reached the Agriculture Bureau and was directed to him, Simcha was almost afraid to open it. Mammeh! Had the food that he'd sent softened her heart just a little? Whatever she might have thought, his intention had not been self-serving. He was desperately worried for them.

When he thought about how he had used Vassily Chernov to feed Mammeh, Papa, and Aunt Golda, Simcha was happier than he had been in a long time. The arrangements had been simple enough. He had merely waited until he was assigned once more to the party warehouse. There, he had gathered together a selection of long-lasting and nourishing foodstuffs. Listing these on one of the required bureaucratic forms, which Vassily had unwittingly signed (and Simcha had kept) from the last time he was there, he submitted it to Vassily's account. After that it was merely a matter of hiring someone willing to transport the stuff to Polotsk. Grisha Glinkoff had been at Peter and Paul Fortress at the same time as Simcha and was happy to do him a favor, particularly when Simcha told him he could keep ten percent of everything for his own use.

Simcha tore open the envelope with shaking fingers. His father's hand. He was overcome with disappointment, and he had to lay the sheet of paper on the desk for a bit until he could take it up to read.

My dearest son Simcha,

I send you loving greetings and many thanks for the gift. What we took was only enough for Aunt Golda, who is failing fast. I am strong and can do without, and your mammeh is stubborn, as you know. I am deeply warmed by your care, my son. It tells me what I already knew, that you are a good man who never intended ill to anyone, most especially not to old friends at Spokoinaya Zemlya. Mammeh will realize that someday when her hurt is not so new. Our grief for Fedotov has been great, and so I beg you to be patient with your mother. I do not know what will befall us. We are no longer young, and times are very hard. We consider going to America. Chaim has written to say that he has a friend in the American government who may be able to get us the permission we need to leave Russia. I don't know. There are so many obstacles. And I hesitate to leave you behind.

Your mammeh's mother had a stroke and died recently. A shock to everyone, and yet at age ninety she had outlived her allotted span of days. Uncle Zalman remains hale. But Aunt Golda may not last until this letter finds you.

This estrangement from your mother will not last forever, my son, I ask you to believe that. And whether in joy or in need, remember that you are of our blood and beloved in our eyes.

May God watch over your days and your nights and bring you his most precious gift, peace. Your father, Yoysef Mandelkern.

Vassily was right about one thing. He had enemies. Maybe that was inevitable for one who had risen in the *Cheka*. Julius Ehrenthal, for instance, once Marta's lover and still close to Lenin. Posted to New York shortly after Marta's tragic death, he had lost track of Vassily for a time; Chernov wasn't exactly a rising star in the party, and for a long time he had virtually disappeared from view. Surfacing later within Dzerzhinsky's special organization, however, he had attained notoriety for his cruelty and corruption. As long as Lenin needed the *Cheka* to consolidate his hold on the country, there was no way that Julius could challenge any part of Dzerzhinsky's operation. Therefore, he settled back to wait until Vassily should make the inevitable misstep that would ruin him. When the time came, he would have something to say about the murder of Marta Braun, one of Lenin's earliest field agents.

Wily Arkady Runich, who had recruited Vassily for the S.R. combat team but later made a smooth transition to the Bolsheviks, was another who waited for Vassily to make a mistake that would put an end to his heretofore charmed life. Forced to toady to Chernov under threat of exposure as Yevno Azev's lieutenant, he bore him no love. There would come a time, though, Runich thought, when he might confess his earlier connection with Azev with impunity and tell what he knew about Chernov's working with the S.R. to give false information to the Bolsheviks. Dzerzhinsky should be interested in knowing, too, how the action at the Panovsky Weapons Plant had been betrayed by Chernov to the *Okhrana*, leading to the arrest of five brave young Bolsheviks.

Semyon Mandelkern, a hero of the revolution, was also biding his time for the appropriate moment to share information about an unauthorized murder at an estate in Byelorussia—not of a White Guard, not of a member of the nobility, but of an unarmed and nonresisting *employee*, the steward of the place they had been sent to liberate.

Viktor Ivanov, a security officer on Bolshaya Lubyanka Street, also waited for the right time to come forward. Since Vassily Chernov had inexplicably begun to harass him, Ivanov had taken certain measures to protect himself, the most important being the collection of a dossier on his enemy. He could name names and give dates when young women brought in for questioning were raped, when bribes were accepted, and large gifts were solicited under threat of blackmail.

*I*t was Ivanov who took the anonymous telephone call which reported that subversive literature had been seen in the apartment of one Vassily Yulevitch Chernov.

Chapter 67

*A*s usually happened when he could clearly see a successful end to a problem, Vassily was relaxed and cheerful. He had carried the books and letters taken from Simcha's flat to a safe, discreet place in his own lodgings. He would sift through them carefully in the next few days, putting together a tight case against young Semyon. He needed to prepare well in case Semyon was protected by someone high up (as Vassily was convinced was the case). Also there must be no public outcry when a hero of four years in the Peter and Paul Fortress was executed.

Vassily quite looked forward to spending that evening going through the letters from America. Not that he could read them, but at least he could study the postmarks and see if there were obvious clues. The letters would be the clinching argument, he could see that, and it was all to the good that they were written in Yiddish script, adding that much more credence to evidence of a Zionist plot!

Two of Vassily's old enemies would be gone then, Semyon and Fedotov. While he had not actually killed Fedotov, it was almost the same. And he had already instructed Karpovitch to have some peasants set fire to the tailor Mandelkern's house.

Vassily was humming as he went about his afternoon's work. He had spent a peaceful morning observing interrogations in progress in the sub-basement of the prison. Now, after a luncheon of blini with beluga caviar and sour cream, he had settled down in the quiet luxury of his office to review some dossiers on old S.R. comrades.

A discreet tapping on his office door announced a visitor.

"Come," he called absently.

The door opened on Ivanov. "Well? What is it now?" These people bothered him for decisions about every little thing! He would have to speak to Dzerzhinsky about their irresponsibility.

Ivanov edged daintily into the room. Vassily could see that three other men formed a phalanx behind him. He was perplexed at this.

Ivanov stuttered a little on the first word—"C-C-Citizen," he said. Then the voice grew stronger. "You are under arrest."

Vassily thought it some kind of joke. *He* was the one who placed people under arrest. Was this a game?

Two security men approached the desk and grabbed him by the arms, raising him from his chair.

"Get your hands off me!"

The faces of the men who held him showed no emotion, nor did their grasp loosen. Only Ivanov seemed affected by the prisoner's anger. He wiped perspiring hands on his trousers.

"You fools!" Vassily shouted, "I am your superior! I shall tell Comrade Dzherzhinsky of this outrage!"

"You'll have your chance to tell plenty," Ivanov muttered.

"I'll see you hanged! I'll make certain that they torture you first!" Vassily threatened.

"Yes, C-Citizen," Ivanov said, "you just do that."

Vassily was dragged toward the door. He was strong, but they were stronger. When he resisted, the third man punched him in the gut, knocking the wind out of him momentarily. He bent double, but the guards pulled him upright.

He was taken to one of the cellars, a place so deep underground that noises could not be heard in the offices on the street level.

When he had recovered his breath he asked coldly, "What am I charged with?" He was still arrogant.

"We don't have to tell you," one of the guards growled.

The other commanded, "Keep quiet until you're ordered to speak!"

"I demand to know—it's my right—" Vassily had begun to sweat.

The same one who had punched him in the belly raised his fist and crashed it into his jaw. The pain was blinding. He wondered if his jaw had been dislocated. They still held him so that he could not raise his hand to feel his face.

Ivanov smiled. Chernov had always been a bastard, holding himself above the rest of them. He remembered how his friend Grizik had been shipped off to a posting in northernmost Siberia when one of the prisoners escaped. And he remembered his own humiliations at the hands of this man. Well, the time for settling accounts had come. One of the toughest *Cheka* men, the one they called "Mischka the Dwarf," had been called to soften Chernov up before the interrogation got truly under way.

Ivanov consulted the paper in his hand. It wouldn't hurt to give this son of a bitch something to worry about while he was waiting for the party to begin. "You want me to tell you the ch-ch-charges? Not much. Just working with the Mensheviki and the S.R. to undermine the government. Intercourse with hostile foreign persons. Promoting a Hebrew-Zionist plot. And a long history of treacherous double-dealing to undermine the r-r-revolution." Ivanov consulted the paper in his hand. "Oh, yes—and stealing from the state warehouse."

Vassily's eyes widened. He tried to slow his racing pulse. He had to stay calm. Think. What did they have on him? Who had informed? What had been said? "Who told these lies about me?" His voice sounded funny; probably his jaw was broken, not merely dislocated.

"You will know who did his duty when we want you to know, Jew!"

"What did you call me? I am not a Jew!"

"Lie all you want, you will soon be singing your heart out!"

He wanted to ask more, but just then a giant of a man pushed open the heavy metal door into the interrogation room. Mischka. The joke about the "Dwarf" wasn't amusing anymore.

Vassily confessed to everything. There was no point in trying to sort out what was true from what was not. In the end, it did not really matter.

On the morning they took Vassily to the courtyard to be hanged, he was strangely calm.

"Do you have anything to say for yourself, prisoner?" the captain of the guard asked.

Vassily shook his head. The noose was put around his neck.

"A last cigarette?"

Vassily nodded, and because his hands were bound behind him, the captain held it to his lips so he could draw in a lungful of smoke.

The prisoner did not seem as nervous as the guards. He had a concentrated look upon his face, as if he were trying to put something together. Gradually a look of pure delight and astonishment, quite mad really, crossed his face.

"Are you ready?"

The prisoner nodded, smiling.

Later, when the captain of the guard told his comrades in the wardroom about the last moments of Vassily Chernov, he pursed his lips, frowning at the effort to understand what had occurred. He had presided over many executions, but he had never before seen anyone laugh the moment before the trap was sprung open and the rope jerked tight to break the neck. "It was strange. I wonder what Chernov was thinking."

If Vassily could have said what was on his mind at that last moment, it was that it had occurred to him that they would bury him in the Jewish cemetery, perhaps the very one where Marta had been laid to rest. That certainly *was* a joke, was it not?

*C*haim said, "Well, it's all arranged. All the paperwork is approved, and the steamship company has the money for the tickets. If they leave Cherbourg on the twenty-fourth of March, they should be here toward the end of April."

Dvoreh was breathless with emotion. "I can't believe Mammeh and Papa are really coming! It's taken forever!"

Rosalie bristled. "We had to use all our influence in Washington to work it out!" Her voice took on an accusatory note. "After all, your brother Simcha *is* a Communist!"

Chaya Leya laughed. "Well, that's more respectable in Russia than it is here, Rosalie. Anyway, you and Chaim did a grand job, however long it took." She began to stack the dinner plates and silverware in front of her.

Chaim was practical. "Now we should look for a house, maybe near the state hospital, so that Dvoreh can be closer to Lev, and Mammeh and Papa can have a big garden!"

Dvoreh sat up very straight in her chair. "No! We are going to wait until Mammeh and Papa are actually here to see what *they* want to do, where *they* want to live! I won't have them think that you brought them to America only for my sake!" Overcome with embarrassment, her pale face was mottled with patches of color.

"Oh, for heaven's sakes!" Rosalie exclaimed.

Chaya Leya clasped Dvoreh's hand in hers. "No, Dvoreh's right. Let's wait and ask them."

After Chaim and Rosalie had gone, and the children and Herschel were in bed, Dvoreh and Chaya Leya sat on at the dining room table, picking at the crumbs of an apple torte and talking idly.

Slowly Dvoreh said, "You know, I don't think Mammeh ever wanted me to marry Lev, though she didn't exactly say so. She told me once she thought the Goldenburgs were odd—different—"

"So? What difference does that make now?"

"Oh, I don't know! Maybe she'll feel I got what I deserve!"

"What nonsense! Mammeh would never be so cruel."

Dvoreh looked at her sister curiously. "You never used to feel that way about Mammeh, Chaya Leya."

The older sister flushed. "You're right. For a lot of years I thought she didn't care about me."

"And now?"

"After I grew up I tried to imagine what it was like for Mammeh to lose two children in a day's time. And I realized that if, God forbid, Jenny and Becky should catch something bad and be gone between one day and the next, I would go crazy with grief, just the way she did!"

"Even though you had another child?"

"Especially! Because from then on I would always be afraid to put too much of my love in her lest she be taken from me too."

The women sat for a time without speaking. At last Chaya Leya said, "I think you are right about waiting to see what Mammeh and Papa would like to do. I think I know, but the choice should be theirs."

Dvoreh rose, yawning. "Well, I have to go to work in the morning. I'd better go upstairs to bed."

Chaya Leya nodded.

Dvoreh put her arms around her. "I hope you know how much I love you, Chaya Leya."

*M*alkeh and Yoysef had come through a very bad time. First had been the sadness of Golda's dying. She had not been herself for years, but nevertheless it had been hard to say good-bye. At the end she had had the shiny, expectant look that Malkeh remembered from their earliest days as young women. They buried her next to Dovid in the cemetery on the edge of the city.

Then one night, inexplicably, their house caught fire. Luckily Yoysef was not yet asleep, and he was able to control the flames before any real damage was done.

At about the same time, the letters from America began to arrive, heavy with a freight of sad news, much of it already old—Berel dead, Lev incurably ill, and Dvoreh struggling desperately to raise her children alone. Chaya Leya begged them not to delay coming.

The decision did not come easily. While they remained in Polotsk there was always the chance that Malkeh and her younger son would be reconciled. It had been almost three years since she had driven Simcha from the house, and there had been no communication between them since his gift of food had been rejected. Malkeh pretended ignorance of the regular exchange of letters between Simcha and Yoysef, but Yoysef always left Simcha's letters where Malkeh could find and read them. It was how Malkeh knew that Simcha had left Moscow to work on a *kolkhoz* that raised hogs in the Ukraine. How perfectly fitting, Malkeh had thought with irony, so communistic! Take a young man learned in Greek and Latin, political science and economics, and put him to work feeding pigs in the Ukraine!

Only once had Yoysef broken the unspoken code of silence. A year ago he had said abruptly that Vassily Chernov, the malignant ex-clerk at Spokoinaya Zemlya, was dead. Malkeh had been flooded with relief. No longer would he be a threat to her son.

They had a long time to get used to the idea of leaving. Months passed while passports were issued, steamship tickets arranged, and a myriad of official details settled. Still uncertain that it was the right thing to do, Malkeh had commenced packing.

On a January afternoon, Yoysef carried into the house an innocuous white envelope with his name on the front, typewritten.

"I wonder who's writing to us?" he said to Malkeh, sitting down beside her at the table where she was peeling potatoes for the evening meal. He turned the unopened letter over in his hands, looking thoughtfully at the address.

"Where's it from?" Malkeh asked anxiously. They received few letters. Official correspondence had to be bad news. The authorities weren't going to let them leave! Hadn't she known it all along?

"I don't know. It was posted from Lutsk."

"Where is that?"

Yoysef did not answer. He slit open the envelope with a strong thumbnail and drew out a single sheet of paper. His eyes ran down the typed paragraphs.

"Well, what is it?"

Yoysef's hand had begun to tremble, and then with a cry he dropped the letter on the table.

"What is it? What's the matter?"

Yoysef's eyes turned flat in his ashen face. For a long moment he could not speak. At last, his voice choking, he said, "He's dead! Simcha's dead. Typhus."

The only sound in the kitchen was the clatter of the bowl hitting the floor and shattering. Malkeh slumped from her chair unconscious among potatoes and shards of broken glass.

In the days that followed the letter was read and reread. Brief and to the point, it was from the general secretary of Simcha's *kolkhoz* near Lutsk.

Dear Comrades Mandelkern:

It is my official duty to notify you that your son, Semyon Mandelkern, expired on Saturday, the twenty-third of November, 1922, at Soviet Collective Farm Number 26 at Lutsk, region of the Ukraine. Official cause of death was typhus.

When sickness struck the kolkhoz *early in December (there having been an outbreak of an epidemic throughout the Ukraine), Comrade Mandelkern proved himself an exemplar of the Communist ideal, selflessly remaining on duty night and day to nurse those stricken. Regrettably Comrade Mandelkern's own constitution was not as strong as his courage, and there was no way to save him when he himself contracted the illness.*

On the behest of the Lutsk Soviet and as General Secretary of Kolkhoz Number 26, I have written to the Commissar for Agriculture in Moscow, recommending Semyon Mandelkern for a posthumous Order of Lenin. As his parents, you should be proud that your son died as he lived, a true hero of the Soviet Nation!

Since your son possessed nothing that was not owned by the state, there are no personal effects to send on to you. Because of the danger of contamination, the bodies of all who died of typhus were cremated at once.

Sincerely, Valery Zenzinov, General Secretary

When Malkeh would have sunk into a despondency like that which had followed the deaths of Yaakov and Channah those many years before, Yoysef was like iron, insisting that they continue with preparations for going to America. They must leave Polotsk no later than the tenth of March to be sure of arriving in Cherbourg in time to board the steamship for New York. It was already mid-January.

As long as Yoysef was beside her, his stronger will prevailed. Malkeh would kneel beside the trunk to put in a tablecloth, an embroidered dresser scarf, a towel with a crocheted edge, before sinking to the floor, overcome by fatigue, her head resting against the edge of the old trunk. If Yoysef left her for a moment, she forgot what she was doing, and time stopped while she stared into space. Why was she here on the floor? She would look at the tablecloth as if she did not recognize it, take it out, smooth it, lay it on a chair. Yoysef would find her like that, sunk in the lethargy of despair. Angrily he would ball up the tablecloth and throw it back into the trunk.

Once in a while it would all come back to her with a searing vividness of painful detail.

"Yoysef—"

"Yes?"

"I must go to this place, this Lutsk, and say kaddish at Simcha's grave."

"Nonsense!" Yoysef said gruffly. "There's typhus there—it's probably quarantined. Besides, he was cremated, there is no grave."

"I still want to go—"

"There's no time."

"I *need* to do this, Yoysef!"

"No."

"But—"

"There's only *one* thing you need to do. Pack up what you want to take to America."

The years of sustained loss had not been kind to Malkeh. Now Simcha's death had deepened the lines around her mouth and drained the color from her eyes. Yoysef had to harden himself lest he give in to pity and be sucked into Malkeh's despair.

The tears ran down Malkeh's furrowed cheeks. "You don't understand! I never had a chance to say good-bye to him!"

"Whose fault was that?"

Malkeh had never known him to be so cruel. "I wanted to hurt him, to teach him a lesson, but I never meant it to go on so long! I couldn't stop! I kept thinking of Yevgeny lying there in a pool of blood with all those bullet holes in him and all the while Simcha was at Spokoinaya Zemlya with the murderers!" A new freshet of tears choked her. "If only I had known I would never see him again!"

"Rabbi Eliezer said to repent one day before our death."

"But one doesn't know when that will be!"

"Exactly."

Malkeh turned her face from him. "I wish I were dead!"

Yoysef glared at her. "Oh, that's very good, Malkeh! That really helps everybody!" He began to pace back and forth, the planks of the kitchen floor creaking under his boots. His face was pale with fury when he turned on her. "I've had enough, Malkeh! I'm sick of hearing about *your* guilt, *your* needs, *your* unhappiness! You are not the only one in this house! I mourn

Simcha as much as you do, but I'm not ready to trade a life in America for a grave in Russia." He stamped out, slamming the door behind him.

Now Yoysef seemed to be angry all the time. While Malkeh sat in her rocking chair, he threw things haphazardly into the trunk. He seldom spoke. Malkeh scarcely recognized this grim stranger for the Yoysef she had known for almost forty-five years of married life. "Why can't you understand what I'm going through?" she demanded in a pitiful voice.

"Simcha is dead, the others live," Yoysef said impatiently. "Dvoreh needs you. If you abandon those who live, you will spend your last years alone. Not only will the children never forgive you, I won't either."

"How can you talk to me that way!"

"And what's more, Malkeh, even if I have to leave you here alone, I intend to be on that ship when it leaves France."

Her eyes widened in alarm. "You wouldn't do that—?"

"I would! Just maybe I've had all the self-pity I can take." Giving her one last black look, he closed himself into the tailor shop next door. She could hear the blows of his fist against the wall. She had never known him like this. She was aware for the first time that she could lose him.

Her legs trembling from the effort, Malkeh rose from her chair. How exhausted she was! Still, by late afternoon, she had taken things out of the trunk and refolded them neatly before replacing them.

Yoysef knelt beside her to help.

They worked in silence for a few minutes.

"Nothing turned out the way I wanted," she said at last.

Yoysef was grim. "Are you talking about the children? They were not given us to fill our needs, not even to please us!"

She was quiet for a long time. "I loved him most, you know."

*I*n the end Yoysef decided that they must leave the trunk, with its accumulation of household articles, behind. Everything must fit into two bundles they could carry with them aboard ship. After years of hardship, there was not much left anyway. A few worn and shabby pieces of clothing mostly. Malkeh mourned a few special things she must leave behind, like the silver samovar Uncle Zalman from Vitebsk had given them for their wedding and the copper pot in which she always made gefilte fish. She had given these over to the care of the *rebbetsen*, the elderly rabbi's wife. Malkeh did find room in her bundle for the candlesticks she had used every Sabbath eve of her marriage.

Malkeh's eyes grew bright with emotion when she picked up a lacquer box, the fairy-tale figures still bright on its lid. Yevgeny Sergeivitch had brought it to her filled with chocolates when she was ill after the assault in the market square before Boruch was born. Dear Yevgeny! How she missed him! She could not imagine what her life might have been without his energizing presence. Her existence owed a certain richness and depth to him. He had taken her out of her own narrow past and given her a window to the world outside. She laid the box aside to take.

Books she could leave behind, except for a special few. Lovingly she touched a book of collected stories by Isaac Meyer Dik given to her by Mammeh Frumma when her first child was born; its paper had yellowed, and the pages made a dry, crackling sound when they were turned, but the red leather binding was still soft and rich. *Anna Karenina* had been the first book given her by Yevgeny Sergeivitch, and the volume of Chaim Bialik's poetry was from the girls of her school's first graduating class—she smiled remembering how Peshka Rubin had wept with nerves when she made the flowery presentation! Last of all there was a translation of H. G. Wells's *The War of the Worlds*, brought her from St. Petersburg by Simcha on one of his rare visits home from the university. These four she would take to America, and she would invite Hodl Nachman to help herself to whatever remained.

Much would be left for scavengers. Friends and family had mostly disappeared, dead or gone to other places in Europe or to America. It was useless to try to sell anything, because no one these days had money. One morning she and Yoysef would simply dress themselves and carry their bundles into the street, closing the door behind them and leaving the key in the lock. When they were gone, the strangers who now occupied the houses on either side of them would help themselves. Some other housewife would knead bread in Malkeh's brown bowl, and maybe someday another tailor would use Yoysef's machines to make a caftan or a silk dress to be worn to shul on the High Holy Days.

Yoysef carefully wrapped a collection of small wooden farm animals in cotton rags. When he noticed Malkeh watching him, he explained shyly that the grandchildren might like to have them.

She nodded. Grandchildren—seven of them in California whom they had never seen. Would it be difficult, she wondered, for the children to get used to their old country *bobbeh* and *zeydeh*? She bit her lip, a little frightened at the thought. American children would expect American ways.

"What are you thinking, Malkeh?"

"I was wondering whether we'll be able to talk to the grandchildren. Suppose they only know English?"

"Then we'll learn English."

"At our age?"

Yoysef put an arm around her. "Don't worry! In America, they say, they have discovered the Fountain of Youth."

It did Yoysef good to see Malkeh laugh.

After a while she said, "Our children have grown apart from us, and *their* children will not understand either our language or our ways. They don't know our history."

Yoysef turned back to the cupboard where he was sorting odds and ends that had been accumulating for years. There was a certain amount of truth in what Malkeh said. It had been over twenty years since they had seen Chaya Leya and Chaim, almost that long since Dvoreh had left. In the intervening years marriages had taken place, children had been born, there had been disasters—earthquakes, epidemics, war, and financial depressions in America, and revolution, civil war, famine, and death in Russia. All that had happened while they were apart would create a gulf between them. As for their grandchildren, there would not even be a common starting point between them.

Yoysef thought of his mother and father who had remained at the center of the family until the very day that death overtook them. There was a time when he had thought that someday he and Malkeh would hold the same central place in the generational chain. How could he have guessed that the children would scatter, and certainty and stability would go out of the world?

Yoysef pulled an old copybook of Simcha's out of the back of the cupboard where it had become wedged between two shelves. Judging from the laborious handwriting, Simcha must have been ten or so when he wrote in it. He glanced at Malkeh, debating whether to show it to her. He slipped the copybook into his coat pocket.

*A*lmost everything was finished at last. With some of the money that Chaim had sent, Yoysef paid the *shammes* at the cemetery to take care of the graves of the children—Boruch, Channah, and Yaakov— and those of Mammeh Frumma, Papa Avrom, Golda, Dovid, and Auntie Lifsa. A handsome present was given to the ancient priest of the Voronov village church to see that the graves of Yevgeny Fedotov and Maria Feodorovna were tended. They journeyed to Dagda to make the same arrangements for Malkeh's parents. The visit to the graves seemed to calm Malkeh. The spirits of these who were close to her heart had gone before her to the unknown of *Olam Habo*, and their dust had already returned to the soil. The memory of who they had been would be borne with her and Yoysef to the new land.

Now that departure was almost upon them, the hours of the last few days were difficult to fill. Malkeh had walked slowly through Polotsk, marveling at how much the city had grown since she had come here as a bride. Clearing off the snow, she had sat for a few minutes on a bench at Napoleon's Wall, imprinting the beloved and familiar view forever on her memory. When she returned home it was late afternoon and Malkeh was tired. She unloosened her shoes and sat down in the rocker with a glass of tea. She might have dozed for a bit, for it was almost dusk when she opened her eyes. It was the approach of a visitor that had awakened her. Actually, two visitors, a man and a child. Probably hungry and looking for something to eat. She could give them part of the Sabbath loaf at least. She went to the door but opened it only a crack. She had learned caution during the civil war.

"Yes?"

She could see them better now. The child was a girl of four or five, a kerchief tied under her chin, yellow plaits hanging below it on either side. Enormous blue eyes stared out of a face that was much too pinched. Her lips were blue with cold, and her hands were jammed into the pockets of a worn overcoat that was too big for her and too thin for such weather. She could scarcely hobble in floppy boots; through holes in the toes, Malkeh could see they were stuffed with newspaper. The man, her father, Malkeh assumed, was roughly dressed and looked at first glance to be a peasant. Malkeh took in his unshaven jaw and untidy hair, the rope knotted around his coat for a belt. He held the child with one hand while the other carried a small bundle. Malkeh wondered what they were doing here. Not many strangers found their way to the Jewish quarter. Maybe they were Jews. Touched by the child, she decided she would give them what food she had in the house. She could buy more with the money that Chaim had sent.

"Comrade Mandelkern?" the man asked.

Malkeh's heart began to beat fast with fright. What did it mean that this man knew her name?

"Yes."

"May I—we—come in?"

"My husband will be home in a minute—" Malkeh said nervously, holding the door against them. The little girl was shivering from cold and drooping with fatigue. They must have walked a long way today. On sudden impulse Malkeh threw open the door. "Come in."

The man made a half bow. *"Spaseba."*

"Will you sit?" she asked.

He shook his head. "I am only passing through on my way north."

"Then—?"

"For her mother's sake I agreed to bring this child to you."

"I don't understand."

"The letter explains everything."

The little girl slowly unbuttoned her coat. Pinned to her dark pinafore was an envelope. Malkeh, her hands trembling so badly that she could scarcely force open the pin, finally got the envelope loose.

"Pardon me for asking, Citizen, but if you have a piece of bread to spare, I shall be on my way. I promised to deliver the child, and I have done so. Now I must go—it's better for me to travel at night—"

This was no peasant. He was well-spoken, his accents that of an educated man. Malkeh was stunned. He actually planned to leave the child and go away! She couldn't think what to do. Why wasn't Yoysef home yet? "Yes, yes, of course." She went to the kitchen and wrapped the loaf, a piece of cheese, and some apples in a cloth. Slowly she returned, handing the man the parcel but watching the child all the while.

The child's eyes widened at the sight of food.

"Thank you." He bent over the child and pressed his lips to her forehead. "Be a good girl now." He turned toward the door.

Malkeh was energized by his imminent departure. "Wait! You can't just bring me a child like this! We are leaving for America in a few days!"

"The letter explains everything," he said again. "I must go."

He was so quickly out the door that Malkeh could scarcely catch him. "Wait!" Malkeh demanded.

He shook off the hand she had laid on his arm and broke into a half run.

Malkeh stood uncertainly in the road, looking after his retreating figure. What was this new trouble that had come upon them! Slowly she returned to the house. The child was still standing in the middle of the room in her thin coat and clumsy boots.

Malkeh looked at her, tight-lipped with consternation. What in God's name were they going to do with her? In a few days they would be on their way to Cherbourg!

The little girl looked back, her gaze curious, patient, and direct.

"You are hungry, I am sure," Malkeh said finally, helping the child with her coat before leading her into the kitchen. "I will find you something to eat, and then I will read the letter and find out what this is all about."

Sitting at the table, the little girl wolfed down a plate of sliced cucumbers and cheese. She appeared to be half starved, but who wasn't these days? Malkeh sliced more cheese and poured the last of the milk into the child's cup.

Malkeh could scarcely take her eyes from the small face, with its high cheekbones and tilted, long-lashed eyes of purest blue; the bright hair was as golden as her own had been at that age. The unopened letter was still in her pocket, not forgotten, for she already guessed what it would say.

"What is your name, little one?" Malkeh asked when the child's chewing had finally slowed.

"Lenina."

"Your family name?"

The little girl was puzzled.

"Your mother's name?"

"Ah! Vera Stepanovna."

So! "I knew her," Malkeh said slowly. "And your father?"

"I don't know. He was a hero of the revolution, but I didn't know him."

The child was clearly exhausted. She could ask questions later. Malkeh led her to her own bed and covered her with the goosedown quilt. As soon as the child closed her eyes, she slept.

Malkeh sat down then to await Yoysef's return. She took the letter from its envelope, unfolding it clumsily.

My dear Madame Mandelkern,

Perhaps you will remember me? We met in St. Petersburg after Semyon was arrested. I recall that you were kind to me.

By the time you hold this letter in your hands, you will have acquainted yourself with Lenina, the daughter of myself and your son, born the year following Semyon's release from the fortress. Her Name Day is April 20, and she was born in 1918. I am sending her to you by a friend who risks much to bring her. I can no longer keep her, and I pray that you and your good husband will remember me kindly and provide for her. Semyon never knew that he fathered a child. He had turned from me long before she was born, because of lies told him by a "friend." Now I am informed that he is dead.

Do not think that I give my child up lightly. There is no other way. The times are such that I must send her away to protect her. I dare not write you in any detail what is happening. I can only say that I expect momentarily to be arrested. You must believe that my only crime is loyalty to Trotsky. Stalin stops at nothing to eliminate opposition!

Let Lenina forget me, her mother, for I will never hold her in my arms again.

I kiss you from the heart.

Vera Stepanovna Politsovskaya
For your own safety and the child's, I give you no address by which to trace me.

The letter fluttered to the floor. Simcha's child! Malkeh's eyes glowed with blue fire. Who says that God no longer performs miracles!

Chapter 68

On a bright morning in late April, all the family, dressed in their best, were gathered at the ferry building in San Francisco.

The previous week Aunt Yenta and Uncle Yaynkel, along with Cousins Moishe and Lily, had met Malkeh and Yoysef at the boat when it docked in

New York. No Ellis Island for them, when Chaim had purchased first-class tickets (in Cherbourg Yoysef had cheerfully exchanged two first-class tickets for cabin-class accommodations for three). It had been a reunion of great emotion for them all, and four days later Moishe saw them aboard a train bound for San Francisco.

Moishe, reached by telephone, had told Chaim that they had brought a surprise with them from Russia.

"What surprise?" Chaim was testy. "There's not one thing from Russia that we want!"

"This one you'll want," Moishe assured him jovially, and although Chaim pressed him, Moishe refused to explain. That Moishe! Always he had some joke or trick up his sleeve!

Chaim consulted his pocket watch. Rosalie said, "Watching it isn't going to make the time go faster, Hy. It's at least ten minutes yet!"

Guiltily Chaim put the watch back in his pocket. He wondered what Mammeh would think of this American wife of his, so cool and elegant, her hair bobbed like a boy's, dressed in a black wool suit she called a "Chanel," chains of real gold around her neck. His eyes swung to the five-year-old twins, whom Rosalie persisted in calling "Nat and Mike" until even he had dropped "Natalya" and "Mikhail." Awed at the prospect of meeting grandparents from far-off Russia, those two scamps stood quietly for a change at their mother's elbow. He saw how Raizel smoothed Mike's thick dark hair with her fingertips and retied the sash on Nat's frilly dress. She was a good mother, he thought, and she loved the children with her whole heart. Chaya Leya had been right when she had told him to take the children home to her. Having them had made a happy difference in their lives, although Rosalie would never be the kind of wife he had once imagined he wanted.

She said now, "This really is silly! They could have gotten off the train in Sacramento!"

"I wanted us to be all together when they arrived," Chaim answered. They had had this discussion before. Rosalie would never understand what it meant to be a family, together.

He glanced toward Chaya Leya, who was leaning slightly against Herschel. Now, *that* was a love affair, he thought. The three girls were gathered around their parents, Hannah so pretty and grown up at nineteen, and her younger sisters, Becky and Jenny, so alike in their dark good looks that they might be twins. Looking into Chaya Leya's good plain face was like seeing Mammeh standing there, Chaim thought, but, of course, Mammeh would have changed in twenty years. She and Papa must be well past sixty now. One never thought of one's parents growing older.

He started to take out his pocket watch again but, remembering Rosalie's reproof, he stayed his hand.

"What could they be bringing with them?" Dvoreh asked for at least the tenth time.

"Who knows!" Chaim shrugged. "That Moishe and his games!" he muttered darkly. "Anyway, we'll know in a few minutes."

Chaim was irritated to see that Dvoreh was biting her fingernails. He wanted to tell her to stop this minute, but, of course, she wasn't a child to be scolded. All of them were tense with the waiting, but she most of all; her face was pale and positively clammy. Did she think that Mammeh and Papa would judge her because Lev Goldenburg had become ill? It didn't matter how many times she was told otherwise, she still felt that if somehow she had been a better wife, Lev would be among them instead of living out his sad days in an institution!

Chaya Leya had also noticed Dvoreh's agitation and moved closer to give her a little hug. "Just wait until Mammeh and Papa meet Saul and Ruth! They're going to be so happy to see what a good job you've done!"

Dvoreh began to cry. Seeing how upset their mother was, Saul looked down, sullenly scraping the toe of his new oxford on the floor, but Ruthie came quietly to Dvoreh's side and put a reassuring hand in hers. At nine Ruth was too mature for her age. Chaya Leya handed Dvoreh a clean handkerchief. "None of that, now!"

"This will be the first time we have all been together in twenty-three years!" Chaim said suddenly.

"Not all," Chaya Leya corrected him sadly. "We have lost Simcha."

*T*he ferry ride was not long, a matter of twenty minutes or so. They stood on the deck under the overhang of the pilot house so that they could see the city as it came into view. It was a morning of sun and light, the caplets dancing beneath the bow of the boat.

"Are you warm enough, child?" Malkeh asked the little girl.

She nodded shyly. "We will see my aunties and the uncles soon?" she asked. There was something endlessly fascinating to Nina in the idea of having relatives.

Malkeh squeezed her hand. "Yes, and cousins too. You have a whole big family now, little one."

"They are my mother's family too, *Babushka?*"

"Of course."

"Then she will have aunties and uncles and cousins, and come here too?"

"Maybe someday."

The view over the water was magnificent, but Malkeh closed her eyes against it. She needed a few minutes without distraction to compose herself.

That promise she had made long ago, that someday they would be all together in a peaceful land, had been kept, even if not by her doing. With one
exception. For Simcha, the promised land had never been America, but rather
a better, happier Russia. He had lost his dream in bitter disillusion.

She thought of her other children, each in turn. She would tell Chaya
Leya someday soon that she had been wrong about Herschel. And Chaim,
who had struggled so in childhood to meet her expectations—he should know
how proud she was of his success. And Dvoreh. Malkeh's heart overflowed
with love and pity for this daughter whom life had treated so harshly.

She had always hoped the children would love one another and draw
on one another's strength. And they had. Except for Simcha, whose difference had driven him from the fold too soon. She hoped that in the little
time they had had together, Vera Stepanovna had given him someone to
cleave to. It was not good to be alone.

The trip was almost over, the commuters massed at the end of the
deck, waiting to pour into the ferry building and from there to the streets.
The boat edged into its pier, its nose bumping gently against the pilings.
Malkeh and Yoysef stood a little off to one side so as not to be caught in
the jostling crowd. They had waited so long already, there was no reason to
hurry now. The child was hanging on to Yoysef's hand, her face shyly hidden in his coat.

Now that the moment had arrived, Malkeh and Yoysef hesitated, excited but a little frightened by the changes they must confront.

"I must look like a peasant!" Malkeh whispered fiercely to Yoysef.
"Why didn't I let Yenta lend me a hat and a proper dress when we were in
New York!"

Yoysef looked down at her. She had taken the plain scarf from her
head, and the breeze had loosened her hair. Perhaps it was only a trick of
the light, but her hair looked as splendidly golden as when he had first laid
eyes on her. A faint pink had touched her cheeks, and her eyes were warm
and bright, like the perfect spring sky. "You look beautiful," he said. So
what if her coat was shapeless and rusty, like an old-country woman's? She
was still the most elegant woman he had ever seen.

"Ready?" Yoysef asked.

Malkeh nodded.

Glossary of Foreign Terms

Alevai (Aramaic): I hope, I wish

Amah (in the Orient): a children's nurse

Aveyreh (Hebrew): transgression, sin

Babka (Russian): a yeast-dough cake, made with fruit, nuts, and butter

Babushka (Russian): grandmother

Balabosteh (Hebrew-Yiddish): housewife, matron, mistress of the house

Banya (Russian): Russian bath

Bar mitzvah (Hebrew): religious ceremony by which a male Jew becomes a formal member of the community at age thirteen

Bashlyk (Russian): hood

Beshert (Yiddish): inevitable, predestined

Bimah (Hebrew): elevated platform in the synagogue from where the Torah is read

Bobbeh (Yiddish): grandmother

Boizamoi (Russian): dear God; my God!

Bris (Yiddish): the act and ceremony of circumcision; in Hebrew "b'rith mila"

Bromfen (Yiddish): liquor, whiskey

Bublitchki (Russian): thick, ring-shaped rolls; bagels

Chai (Russian): tea

Challah (Hebrew): a braided loaf of bread made with white flour, sugar, and eggs traditional for the Sabbath

Chaver (Hebrew): comrade, friend

Chevrah kaddisha (Hebrew): burial society

Cheyder (Hebrew): school where Hebrew is taught to boys, often in the synagogue itself; plural *cheyderim*

Cholent (Yiddish): Sabbath dish, usually of meat, potatoes, groats, and fat prepared the day before and slowly cooked from Friday afternoon for the Saturday evening meal

Chometz (Yiddish): food that is forbidden to be eaten during Passover

Chornyi khleb (Russian): black bread, sometimes called "soldiers bread"

Chupa (Hebrew): wedding canopy

Chutzpah (Yiddish): gall, brazen nerve, effrontery

Davening (Yiddish): praying

Do svidanya (Russian): Good-bye; until we meet again; variation: *Do skorova svidanya*: may we meet soon again

Dreck (Yiddish): trash, garbage, excrement

Drozhki (Russian): a light four-wheeled open vehicle

Dybbuk (Hebrew): evil spirit, incubus, usually the soul of a dead person that enters a living person

Feigel/ feigeleh (Yiddish): an endearing term that literally means bird or dear little bird

Funt (Russian): measure of weight, somewhat less than a pound

Gabai (Hebrew): synagogue trustee or manager

Goluptchik (Russian): term of endearment, dear little pigeon

Gospodin (Russian): gentleman, mister, sir (term of respect)

Gostinny dvor (Russian): literally "merchants inn" but colloquially refers to the central marketplace of a city

Grechnevaya kasha (Russian): buckwheat porridge

Gymnasium (Russian): secondary school, high school

Haggadah (Hebrew): story of the Passover read on the first two nights of the holiday

Halacha (Hebrew): the basic body of Jewish oral law

Hamal (Turkish): porter

Hamam (Turkish): Turkish steam bath

Hamantaschen (Yiddish): three-cornered cakes, thickly filled with poppy seeds, raisins, or prunes, traditionally eaten on Purim.

Iconostasis (Greek): a partition or screen on which icons are placed, used to separate the sanctuary from the main part of the church (Eastern Orthodox)

Ivrai (Russian): Jew

Izba (Russian): cottage, hut, peasant house

Kaddish (Aramaic): mourner's prayer

Kashruth (Hebrew): religious dietary laws

Khossen (Hebrew): bridegroom

Kiddush (Hebrew): blessing over the wine consecrating the Sabbath or a religious holiday

Kokoshniki (Russian): an elaborate holiday headdress

Kolkhoz (Russian): collective farm

Kvass (Russian): a sour-sweet beverage made by fermenting mixed cereals and adding flavoring such as fruit or peppermint.

Landsleit (Yiddish): countrymen; singular: *landsman*

Lapti (Russian): common summer footwear made of the woven fibers of elder, linden, or basswood trees

Lokshen (Yiddish): noodles

Lokshen kugel (Yiddish): a pudding made with noodles, eggs, and fat

Lubymii (Russian): beloved (masculine form); feminine: *lubymaya*

Magen David (Hebrew): the six-pointed shield of David

Malenkaya (Russian): little one (feminine form); masculine: *malenkii*

Mandelbrodt (Yiddish): a twice-baked cookie made with almonds

Marozhenoye (Russian): ice cream

Maven (Hebrew): expert, connoisseur

Mazeltov (Hebrew): good luck!

Melamed (Hebrew): teacher, usually of small children

Mikva (Hebrew): ritual bath used for purification

Mincha (Hebrew): religious service in the late afternoon

Minyan (Hebrew): the ten male Jews required for religious services

Mishigass (Hebrew): insanity, madness

Mitzvah (Hebrew): divine commandment, good deed; plural: *mitzvoth*

Mujik (Russian): peasant

Nafka (Aramaic): prostitute

Nagaika (Russian): whip, often with metal ends

Nyet (Russian): no

Oblavy (Russian): roundup, usually by police or army

Oisvarf (Yiddish): a dissolute person, a scoundrel, a bum

Okhrana (Russian): the tsar's Security Police

Olam Habo (Hebrew): the world to come

Oobloudok (Russian): bastard

Papirosi (Russian): cigarettes

Payos (Hebrew): earlock worn by some orthodox Jewish males

Pesach (Hebrew): spring holiday commemorating the exodus of the Israelites from Egypt; in English, Passover.

Piroshki (Russian): small pies filled with meat or vegetables

Plita (Russian): kitchen range

Pochemu (Russian): why?

Poshtalon (Russian): postman

Purim (Hebrew): Jewish festival commemorating the rescue of the Jews of Persia from extermination

Reb (Hebrew): teacher; title given to a learned and respected man; used also as an equivalent of mister

Rebbetsen (Hebrew): wife of a teacher or rabbi

Rosh Hashanah (Hebrew): fall holiday celebrating the beginning of the Jewish New Year

Rubashka (Russian): man's shirt

Sarafan (Russian): a long, pyramid-shaped jumper worn with a billowy-sleeved blouse

Seder (Hebrew): the festive meal on the first two nights of the Passover holiday

Shabbes (Yiddish): the Sabbath

Shadken (Yiddish): marriage broker

Shaharit (Hebrew): morning prayer, one of the three prayers required of Jewish men

Shammes (Hebrew): sexton or beadle of a synagogue

Shandeh (Hebrew): shame

Shchi (Russian): cabbage soup

Shifskarte (Yiddish): ship ticket

Shiksa (Yiddish): a non-Jewish woman, especially a young one

Shiva (Hebrew): seven days of intensive mourning after the death of a close relative

Shlimazel (Yiddish): a born loser

Sh'ma (Hebrew): prayer of affirmation of the Jewish faith

Shofar (Hebrew): ram's horn blown on Rosh Hashanah as part of the ritual

Shokhet (Hebrew): person authorized to slaughter animals for food according to the requirements of kashruth

Shtetl (Yiddish): small town, village, occupied by Jews in eastern Europe

Shul (Yiddish): synagogue

Siddur (Hebrew): the daily and Sabbath prayer book

Simchas Torah (Hebrew): a Jewish holiday in celebration of the completion of the annual reading of the Torah

Spaseba (Russian): thank you; *spaseba bolshoi*: thank you very much

Speculanti (Russian): speculator, black marketeer

Spokony nochee (Russian): good night; have a peaceful night

Ssylno kutorzhniki (Russian): convicts sentenced to prison, as differentiated from *ssylno poselentsy*, who were men sentenced to forced labor

Taiglach (Yiddish): a Jewish confection made of dough cooked in honey with nuts, raisins, and spices

Tallis (Yiddish), *tallith* (Hebrew): a shawl with fringed corners traditionally worn over the head or shoulders by Jewish men during prayers

Tarantass (Russian): a large four-wheeled carriage without springs

Tchervonitz (Russian): a former Russian gold coin

Tefillin (Hebrew): ritual leather boxes containing pertinent passages from the Torah

Tichl (Yiddish): headscarf; shawl

Tzaddik (Hebrew): a man of surpassing virtue and righteousness

Tzedokeh (Hebrew): righteousness; justice; helping one's fellow man

Tzimmes (Yiddish): a sweetened combination of dried fruit, vegetables, and meat

Ukha (Russian): a clear fish soup

Verst (Russian): a measure of distance, roughly two-thirds of a mile

Yeshiva (Hebrew): rabbinical academy
Yiddishkeit (Yiddish): Jewish way of life
Yom Kippur (Hebrew): Day of Atonement
Yontef (Hebrew): holiday; *Erev yontef*: pre-holiday
Zakuski (Russian): appetizers, snacks, refreshments
Zdrahstvoyteh (Russian): hello
Zemstvo (Russian): elective district council in prerevolutionary Russia
Zeydeh (Yiddish): grandfather
Zmiros (Hebrew): joyous melodies sung after the Sabbath meal
Zuneleh (Yiddish): dear little son

About the Author

Marjorie Edelson, born in San Francisco and raised in Sacramento, California, is a first generation American. With degrees from the University of California, Berkeley, and Smith College, she is a licensed clinical social worker. *Malkeh and Her Children* is her first published work of fiction.

Ms. Edelson lives in Palo Alto, California, with her husband, Eric, and an aging German shepherd named "Dido." The Edelsons are the parents of three grown children.